East Comes West

8.95

EAST COMES WEST

Asian Religions and Cultures in North America

E. Allen Richardson

The Pilgrim Press
New York

Photographs are by the author except where otherwise indicated.
Illustrations are by William Condron.

Library of Congress Cataloging in Publication Data

Richardson, E. Allen, 1947–
   East comes West.

   Bibliography: p. 195.
   Includes index.
   Summary: Examines four Asian religions—Hinduism, Buddhism, Sikhism, and Islam—as they are manifest in the United States and Canada.
   1. North America—Religion.   2. Hinduism—North America.   3. Buddhism—North America.   4. Sikhism—North America.   5. Islam—North America.   [1. Hinduism—North America.   2. Buddhism—North America.   3. Sikhism——North America.   4. Islam—North America.   5. North America—Religion]   I. Title.
BL2520.R5   1985   291'.097   82-13247
ISBN 0-8298-0480-3

The Pilgrim Press, 132 West 31 Street, New York, New York 10001

To Betty

Contents

Illustrations and Maps

ix

Acknowledgments

A text on Asian religions and cultures in North America was first proposed to Pilgrim Press in 1978. During the years of research and development that followed, practicing Hindus, Sikhs, Buddhists, and Muslims were interviewed across the United States. As the writing progressed, religious leaders from each faith and scholars in the field gave advice and counsel. I am indebted to a number of persons who in the following capacities at the time of the research read drafts of the chapters and provided suggestions for further amplification of the text: Rev. Toshio Murakami, Director of the Bureau of Education, Buddhist Churches of America; Dr. David S. Steward of the Pacific School of Religion; Rabinder Singh Bhamra, General Secretary of the New York Gurdwara (The Sikh Cultural Society of New York, Inc.); Dr. Emily C. Brown and Dr. J. Michael Mahar, both of the Department of Oriental Studies, University of Arizona; Dr. K.C. Patel, President of the Bochasanwasi Swaminarayan Sanstha, Flushing, New York; Dr. Alagappa Alagappan, a United Nations career official and Founder Secretary of the Hindu Temple Society of North America; Dr. Muhammad Abdul-Rauf, Director of the Islamic Center, Washington, D.C.

I am especially grateful to Dr. Paul R. Sherry, formerly publisher of Pilgrim Press, who accepted a proposal for a text in a new, undeveloped area of study. His enthusiasm and constant support throughout the research and development were a great asset to the completion of this book.

All four chapters were critiqued by Dr. Alfreda E. Meyers, who spent numerous hours reviewing drafts of the text and making suggestions for their amplification based on her years in the field. The book was carefully edited and revised under the watchful eyes of Dr. Robert E. Koenig, Editor-in-Chief, Russell G. Claussen, and Susan Converse Winslow. Photographs were processed by J. L. "Woody" Wooden, who brought out the fullest potential from each print. The text was illustrated by William Condron, who gave considerable attention to accuracy and detail.

I am also indebted to Rev. T. Thomas Boates, Jr., (formerly, Area Minister, Metro/Suffolk Area, New York Conference, United Church of Christ), who suggested the need for curricula on Asian religions in North

America, and to Rev. Lois Sundeen (Associate Conference Minister, Central Atlantic Conference, United Church of Christ), who gave advice as the work progressed.

Finally, a group of friends helped this book to reach fruition. My special thanks to Claire Beslow, who skillfully prepared the index; Mona Bannerji, who provided many insights into Indian communities in North America; Kathy Moore, who assisted with the glossary; John Skillin, who helped in locating data on the images of Indians and Arabs in film; Linda Wilkens, who aided in the documentation of immigration statutes; Donald and Eunice Stuart, who extended the hospitality of their home during research visits to San Francisco; and Larry O'Connell, who helped an idea become a reality and who, with his sister, Moira, provided hope and encouragement throughout the writing. To these persons, to my parents, and especially to my wife, Betty, who typed several drafts of the text and whose belief in me was a constant source of support, my deepest affection and gratitude.

E. Allen Richardson

Spelling and Transliteration

Terms used in this text are in more than seven different languages. For the convenience of the reader, diacritical marks have been omitted; each word is spelled according to its most accepted usage. Where possible, spelling corresponds to sounds normally made in English. For example, the aspirated s in Sanskrit and Sanskrit-derived languages is transliterated sh, as in *Shakti, Vaishnava, Shabad*. Readers are urged to consult accepted grammars and dictionaries of each language for additional data on pronunciation.

Introduction

The idea for a text on Asian[1] religions and cultures in North America was prompted by the observation of several neighborhoods in Queens, New York, in 1977. The communities were experiencing dramatic change with the influx of large numbers of Indians, Chinese, Japanese, and Koreans. Signs of revitalization and renewal were apparent among four great faiths: Hinduism, Buddhism, Sikhism, and Islam.[2]

Indigenous forms of each of the four religions have in the past attracted much attention both in scholarly works and in the media. However, the ongoing transplantation of classical Asian religions to North America by immigrants who by virtue of birth are practicing Hindus, Buddhists, Sikhs, or Muslims has rarely been studied. Because their worshiping communities are supported by common bonds of diet, ethnicity, and national origin, these devotees, the subject of this text, have rarely sought converts from outside the faith. Some groups, fearing any direct association with the "secular West," have even chosen isolated locations to build temples or retreat centers. In other cases, places of worship are confined to ethnic neighborhoods where persons outside the faith rarely visit.

This rapid evolution of mainstream Asian religions in the United States is illustrated by the continuing development of each of the four faiths since data for this text were originally gathered in 1980. In many parts of the country both the concentration of Asian peoples and the religious institutions they support have visibly increased. The sustained growth of Asian-American neighborhoods is demonstrated by changes in sections of Flushing, New York. Parts of this densely populated area show strong Chinese and Korean influence. Still other areas are predominantly Indian. Spice and sari shops, and a variety of other businesses all serve the immigrant community. Coincidentally, two Hindu temples built in the 1970s (which are described in detail in the first chapter) are located on the same street where the house of the seventeenth-century Quaker John Bowne has become a shrine for religious freedom.

In other less heavily populated areas, Hindu temple traditions also continue to be initiated. In Allentown, Pennsylvania, for example, the

Hindu Temple Society of the Lehigh Valley has regular gatherings. In 1984, the Society received permission from a local zoning board to begin construction on the valley's first Hindu temple and Indian cultural center.

The growth of Buddhist temple traditions is equally significant. For example, in 1981, Yehan Numata, the head of a Buddhist foundation in Japan, established a new temple in Springfield, Virginia. Called Ekoji, or the "Buddhist Temple of the Gift of Light," the facility is temporarily housed in an office building where it serves members of the faith in the vicinity of the nation's capital. A foundation located at the temple will help support an ambitious new project—the translation of the complete Buddhist canon.

The Buddhist Churches of America has established the only professional institution of higher education ever created by a Buddhist organization in the United States. Called The Institute for Buddhist Studies, this unique school established an affiliate relationship with the Graduate Theological Union in Berkeley, California, early in 1985. Such a significant example of interfaith cooperation and Christian-Buddhist dialogue is part of the dynamic afforded by the lasting presence of mainstream Asian religions in North America.

Both in response to global events and because of continuing patterns of Asian immigration, Sikhism and Islam have also developed rapidly in a variety of U.S. and Canadian cities. Unrest in the Punjab in India in the summer of 1984 and the subsequent military occupation of the tradition's holiest of shrines, the Golden Temple, have had a significant impact on Sikhs the world over. In the United States, the reaction to the events in India was swift. In July 1984, 2,500 Sikhs gathered in Madison Square Garden in New York to outline their response to the situation and to form an international Sikh organization with temporary headquarters in New York.[3] The assassination of Indian Prime Minister Indira Gandhi four months later and the attacks on Sikhs in India that followed gave additional support for a representative organization for devotees no longer in India. For Sikhs, who understand the current turmoil in the historical perspective of their faith, the unrest has theological as well as political ramifications.

The global resurgence of Islam has similarly had an important impact on Muslims living in North America. Here, the resurgence has taken several forms. The foremost of these are the changes that have taken place in the organizational development of the faith. In 1982, the Islamic Society of North America (I.S.N.A.) was formed addressing a variety of needs. Located in Plainfield, Indiana, the body was founded as an umbrella organization for five groups including the Muslim Students' Association of the United States and Canada, the Muslim Communities Association (also formed in 1982), the Association of Muslim Social

Scientists, the Islamic Medical Association, and the Association of Muslim Scientists and Engineers.

The growth of this new organization and its member groups has given Muslims an even greater opportunity for the consolidation of leadership and resources. An older body, the Federation of Islamic Associations in the United States and Canada, whose history is described in chapter four, was founded as a pioneering effort to give Muslims a national voice. However, the formation of I.S.N.A., which has rapidly achieved a position of authority among Muslims in the United States, was made possible by organizations such as the Federation of Islamic Associations, which helped Muslims work together at a critical period in their history in North America.

As Muslims have consolidated their organizational structures, so they have also continued to increase the number of Islamic associations and mosques. One estimate from the Muslim Students' Association suggests that thirty mosques have been opened near college campuses since 1979 along with sixty new chapters of the organization.[4] The geographical diversity of the new institutions is staggering, ranging all the way from a center established at I.S.N.A. headquarters in Plainfield, Indiana, to a rural mosque in Abiquiu, New Mexico, to a Muslim community center opened in South Brunswick, New Jersey, in 1983.

The evolution of Asian religions in North America is a complex, rapidly unfolding phenomenon, supported by dramatic trends in immigration. The liberalization of immigration laws in 1965 precipitated the movement of large numbers of Chinese, Japanese, Indians, and other Asian peoples to the United States. The legislation established a ceiling of annual immigration of 290,000 and permitted entry of no more than 20,000 persons from each country per year.

According to 1980 census figures[5] the growth of Asian communities has accelerated rapidly since the 1970 census was taken. Chinese, the largest Asian-American population, increased by 85.3 percent. However, Koreans showed the most dynamic growth. Since 1970 their numbers have swelled to a remarkable 412.8 percent. Other Asian populations including Japanese, Vietnamese, and Indians are sizable minorities. The largest of these, the Japanese, has been estimated at over 700,000 persons.

The expansion of these minority communities has also been aided by patterns of migration in which, over a period of years, entire families may be brought to the United States. This is often facilitated by relatives in the United States, who sponsor parents, siblings, and even cousins who wish to emigrate.

In keeping with these trends the four religions described in the text have developed both in terms of grass roots organizations and national structures. Readers are cautioned that because this process of growth is ongoing, each faith requires careful study so that its further expansion can be accurately understood.

The text will show how the evolution of Asian religions in North America has occurred not only in metropolitan areas but also in less densely populated regions. Chinese Buddhists, for example, have erected a large temple complex near South Cairo, New York. There, against a serene wooded backdrop, the community worked to preserve its religious heritage and Chinese culture. In a like manner, Sikhs in Yuba City, California, have erected a *gurdwara* (temple) in an agricultural area. This temple, like its predecessor in nearby Stockton, California, is a symbol of Sikh unity and pride.

East Comes West

Main gateway *(rajagopuram)*, The Hindu Temple, Flushing, New York.

CHAPTER ONE

Hindus in North America

An Overview

As one of the most ancient religions, Hinduism is uniquely linked to the history and culture of India where its roots began almost five thousand years ago. Hindu believers share a philosophical, ritualistic, and cultural heritage that reflects this long history of sustained development and enrichment.

Hinduism provides a path for every devotee. Most worship a personal deity chosen from the pantheon of thousands of gods. The pantheon is dominated by three gods: Vishnu, Siva (pronounced Shiva), and Brahma, although Brahma is rarely worshiped today.

This triad of gods appears in a variety of incarnations, or lesser forms. Through many different incarnations, each god is part of a hierarchy extending to the most isolated village deity. In this way, lesser gods, often associated with specific villages, share in the authority and transcendence of the greater deities, who are in the Vedas, or sacred scripture. For Hindus, the authority of the gods is communicated through scripture and culture and affects even the most remote corner of India.

The Vedas are written in Sanskrit, a classical language related to modern European tongues. There are four Vedas: the Rig, Atharva, Yajur, and Sama. Containing collections of hymns, formulae, and prose commentary, these four books reflect the religious traditions of a nomadic Aryan people who had settled the upper reaches of the Indian subcontinent by 1500 B.C.

While the majority of Hindus orient their devotional life around the worship of iconographic forms of the gods, the tradition offers another path. Through the rigors of exhaustive study and training, the Hindu holy man[1] seeks *moksha*. *Moksha*, the fruit of meditation, is the spiritual release of the soul from the endless process of rebirth, or reincarnation— the belief that the soul of a person does not die with the body, but is reborn in another animate body.

The holy man renounces the material world and contemplates Brahman. Brahman, the first principle of the universe, is understood to exist behind all life and matter, knowing no point of creation or time of death. This one spirit transcends all the gods. For the average devotee,

3

Brahman is often too ethereal to be worshiped. Yet, it is actively sought by those who follow the way of the ascetic.

The ascetic practices *yoga*, a word derived from the Sanskrit root *yuj* meaning to yoke or join together. The rigorous discipline of *yoga* includes precise methods of breath control and is designed to yoke the individual consciousness with Brahman. The holy man who engages in this spiritual quest pursues a difficult path of mental and physical discipline that only a few are able to complete.

The image of the holy man is a powerful cultural influence, associated with miracles and superhuman feats. One North Indian devotional sect, the Vallabha Sampradaya, thus acknowledges the miraculous birth of its founder. According to the sect's scriptures, Vallabhacharya was born in a grove of Champa trees in central India. The infant was stillborn and left for dead. However, Vallabha's mother urged her companions to return to the scene the next day, having had a premonition that something important had happened. There, in the forest, the parents found the child very much alive, surrounded by a protective fire. As a holy man, the baby was protected by deity.

In North America, the model of the holy man, rooted in scripture and mythology, is constantly revitalized by traveling ascetics. Dressed in ochre robes, the garb of the Hindu ascetic tradition, Hindu holy men honor their followers by coming to their homes when in the United States. Unlike priests, who are hired to celebrate specific rituals, holy men perform a broad range of duties. Through installation ceremonies and other special rites, they reaffirm the faith of their supporters. Charismatic, much like the sectarian founder figures whose doctrine they represent, these contemporary spiritual leaders hold an important place in the lives of their followers.

Often the presence of these religious specialists has been highly dramatic. For example, in 1912 a Hindu ascetic crossed the southwestern deserts of the United States on foot. He was one of a group of teachers representing a philosophical tradition and popular nineteenth-century movement called Vedanta, which first brought the image of the holy man to North America. To a casual observer of this seemingly unique event, the holy man might have appeared out of his element. As a Hindu holy man and Vedanta lecturer he was not.

In North America, holy men may inspire the organization of temples, regular worship, or expressions of intense devotion called *bhakti*. Most devotees integrate these diverse aspects of the tradition to suit their individual needs and their inherited way of life.

Yet, no matter what path one follows, the tradition teaches a basic world view. Hindus understand time to be cyclical, having no beginning or end. Hence, there can be no moment of creation or an apocalypse when history comes to a halt. Within this cosmological order, each soul journeys on a continuing process of birth and rebirth governed by the universal law of *karma.*

Karma is a system in which the individual soul, or *atman,* is reborn in a position determined by its actions during the previous life. Each deed affects *karma* and shapes the form of future reincarnations. The system is built on the acquisition of merit. Merit is accrued from good works, demerit from immoral acts. The total system is completely impartial and affects every form of life including the gods. *Karma* is also affected by *dharma,* or moral law. Hence, to follow your *dharma,* to acquire merit, to worship a personal god, and to continue a station in life based on birth, helps to define individual Hindu identity.

Hindus in the United States share this same world view. They are part of a developing minority from South Asia,[2] which also includes Sikhs, Muslims, Jains,[3] and Christians. Most are well educated professional people who make North America their permanent home; many have been exposed to Western culture previously in large Indian cities.

Despite their familiarity with urban areas, Indian immigrants frequently have been misunderstood in North American cities. A holy man, clad in traditional garb, recently startled a neighborhood boy in New York City[4] who had no idea that such persons existed. While such differences in dress are the most visible evidence of the clash that sometimes occurs when East so abruptly meets West, the majority of immigrants experience deeper conflicts. Indians, much like their European predecessors who came to the United States earlier, have had difficulty in retaining their cultural identity in a new land. This has resulted in departures from orthodoxy. Perhaps the clearest example of this loss of tradition is found in the caste system.

According to Hindu scripture, there are four ideal classes (*varna*): Brahmins (priests), Kshatriyas (soldiers), Vaishyas (merchants), and Shudras (laborers). These classes historically have been confused with caste, which is far more complex.

In India, several thousand caste groups called *jatis* maintain complex patterns of social interaction. Each *jati* is perpetuated by the intermarriage of its members, who, by virtue of their birth, share in the same occupation, and often reside in the same geographical area.

Each *jati* is also associated with a particular level of purity or pollution. The most pure are the gods, and the priests who serve them. The least pure are persons such as leatherworkers, who by virtue of their inherited profession come into contact with dead tissue. Since pollution can be transmitted by touch or food, *jati* is supported by strict rules governing relationships as well as food preparation and consumption. Such a complex system has often broken down outside India where traditional patterns of social relationships and food preparation are not easily maintained.[5]

Traditional *jati* occupations are difficult to preserve in North America. Most Hindu immigrants exercise a choice in selecting a job or career and are not restricted to the form of work practiced by their fathers or grandfathers. Further, in India, *jatis* are economically and socially interdependent, exchanging goods and services. In the United States, where ethnic neighborhoods may include persons speaking different languages from distant parts of the Indian subcontinent, there is little chance to support such traditional patterns. The breakdown of the system in these areas is complicated by the difficulty of perpetuating *jati* endogamy—intracaste marriage. Although many Hindu families in the United States go to great lengths to arrange such marriages, suitable mates cannot always be found.

Other parts of Hinduism have thrived in North America, showing the adaptability and resilience of the tradition. Hindus on this continent have gone to great lengths to maximize their heritage and retain a distinct "Indianness." They have created urban microcosms of their culture where important Hindu festivals are celebrated and temples are constructed much as they would be at home.

One such festival is Diwali, or the festival of lights, during which Hindus celebrate the victory of the god Rama over the demon Ravana. As a time of tremendous joy, firecrackers are exploded to mark Ravana's defeat. Candles are burned to honor the triumphal return of Rama and his queen, Sita. Diwali is also a new year's festival and the appropriate time to commemorate the victory of the forces of light over those of darkness. In North America, Diwali recreates a uniquely Indian atmosphere in which ritual, food, and dress appear much as they would in South Asia.

Hindu temples in the United States are centers of pilgrimage and fulfill artistic and cultural functions. They unite and integrate different sects and ways of life. Temple priests, chanting ancient formulae and modern scripture, perform their tasks much as would be expected in India. Devotees take *prasad* (sweets offered to the gods and distributed among worshipers as blessed) in the way their parents taught them.

Temples in India often provide the motivating force behind the new North American movements. The transplantation of these institutions has required adaptation and ingenuity in which ancient rituals may be performed with the help of modern conveniences. The contrast can be startling. For example, in the photograph on page 38, a priest dedicates the archway of a temple in Pennsylvania by pouring water on top of the structure in a special rite. A utility truck belonging to a power company assists the priest by supplying a ladder for his climb.

Similarly, in New York, in order to continue the ancient tradition of the temple chariot where deities are paraded through village streets atop a huge lumbering cart, a sect rents a truck. In cities across North America, large festivals are adapted to churches, universities, or private auditoriums. Monks in the United States and Canada may opt to travel by car instead of the more traditional manner of walking. Pilgrimages, where devotees return to a temple or shrine from all over North America, may be facilitated by jet plane.

Yet, the struggle between the retention of orthodoxy and adaptation is not always as easy as these examples might indicate. The prevalent image of India in the West as backward and dirty is often transmitted in school. Since Hinduism is so closely tied to India, the image of the religion itself suffers from these stereotypes. Parents must educate their children in the knowledge of the India and Hinduism they know and love, while at the same time they promote a new self-image in the United States.

Despite such persistent obstacles, Hindus have worked hard to transplant their tradition. Priests, trained in India, have been sent to North America at great expense and trouble. Bronze figures have been crafted 12,000 miles away and carefully brought here. Temples have been carved block by block and shipped to the United States where they have been reassembled. North American Hindus have published newsletters, held cultural events, and dedicated shrines as their sects grow. The Indian residents of the United States and Canada have contributed money and work to the completion of these tasks. They have sought, with great difficulty, to make their ancient faith live in a new land.

The Hindu Tradition

Hinduism has a diverse religious and cultural tradition that varies from village to village in South Asia. But its fundamental beliefs, attitudes, and practices continue in India and North America. There are three constant elements of the tradition:

- Scripture as a source of authority
- Devotion, or *bhakti*
- Ritual

Hindus depend on the daily integration of these components in their lives regardless of which particular god or goddess they worship.

Scripture as a Source of Authority

For Hindus in North America or in India, scripture is an important link with a 3,000-year-old Vedic tradition. The Vedas are collections of sacred texts that comprise the Hindu canon. Family priests brought from India for festivals and celebrations are traditionally specialists in Vedic formula and ritual. They help translate the authority of the canon and other pieces of scripture into personal acts of devotion.

The priest relies on the authority of the Vedas—collections of poetry and prose, hymns and incantations. Written in Sanskrit, they are a primary part of a rich scriptural and sacramental tradition. A wider body of post-Vedic scriptures that includes the Epics (sources of mythology), the Puranas (treatises), the Sutras (discourses on ritual and religious law), and sectarian texts has had a greater appeal for many Hindus in the United States. The total body of Hindu scripture is voluminous, providing multiple sources of authority.

The Vedas were originally oral accounts handed down verbally from generation to generation until about the eighth century B.C. when the first of the four "books" was written. The Rig Veda consists largely of hymns and sacred poetry. The remaining three Vedas, the Yajur, the Atharva, and the Sama, were written to interpret and supplement the Rig Veda. The Vedas were sacred scripture to members of a ritual sacrificial cult, the Aryans. The Vedas reflect the ritualistic practices of this nomadic people, who first appeared about 1500 B.C. in the upper reaches of the Gangetic plain—in what is now the Punjab.

The Aryans acknowledged the primal forces of nature and gave them personality and intelligence. The gods they worshiped were not just experienced by priests and seers, but were seen by everyone in placid as well as defiant acts of nature. They were conceived as powerful and intimate. The lightning and the storm were Indra, known for his violent temper and strength. The wind was Vayu, seen in July and August when the monsoon ravaged the countryside. Fire—often uncontrollable—was Agni. These deities were the recipients of intense devotion and sacrifice by members of the sacrificial cult. The Vedas, as sacred scripture, reflect the cult's concern for the indwelling spirit in all natural forces.

While some Vedic hymns are written in praise of gods who are spirits within nature, others extol deities who later became important members of the Hindu pantheon. In one hymn, for example, the god Vishnu measures the earth's circumference in three great strides, denoting his power and greatness:

> Three steps he made, the herdsman sure,
> Vishnu, and stepped across (the world).

> The mighty deeds I will proclaim of Vishnu,
> Who measured out the earth's extremest spaces,
> And fastened firm the highest habitation
> Thrice stepping out with step all-powerful.[6]

Each of the four Vedas is made up of four types of literature in a gradual evolution of philosophy and ritualism. As the basis of the tradition, the hymns (Samhitas) are poetic texts that inspired prose commentaries (Brahmanas), treatises (Aranyakas), and philosophical tracts (Upanishads).

The Upanishads were composed about 600 B.C. and are known as the "Seal of the Vedas" since they conclude the canon. They contain a variety of approaches to the basic issues of the nature of being and the reality of the universe. They develop the important concepts of Brahman and *atman*, which for subsequent Hinduism became basic elements of the tradition.

In the Upanishads, Brahman (not to be confused with the god Brahma or the priestly class Brahmin), is understood to be the underlying reality behind the universe. Brahman is seen as one, indivisible and all pervasive. The Upanishads declare that Brahman *is* the individual soul (*atman*). Thus, the way to Brahman is inward. Those seeking to experience this deepest level of reality, the Upanishads teach, need not look beyond themselves.

While the Upanishads are the philosophical cornerstone of Hinduism, the Epics and Puranas contain much of the tradition's mythology. The Puranas are stories of the gods containing descriptions of individual deities and their incarnations. The word *purana* means ancient and is indicative of the important place in Hindu mythology that these texts occupy. The tradition recognizes eighteen Puranas as canonical, although their total number is larger. Together the Puranas reflect the character and structure of Hindu society in the first millennium and are a component part in the early development of Hindu theism.

The Epics, Ramayana and Mahabharata, are sweeping narratives, filled with romantic legends of gods and their consorts engaged in heroic adventure and great battles. Both texts have inspired dance and drama. Dancers use stereotyped gestures (*mudras*) to trace the narrative of such deities as Rama and Sita, whose heroic adventures are an important part of Hindu mythology.

This literature emphasizes ideal patterns of life that are models for proper behavior and ethics. For example, in Diwali festivals celebrated by Hindus in the United States, the victory of Rama over the forces of the demon Ravana inspires values of heroic adventure and devotion to a just cause and praises Rama as a cultural model of a son, husband, and leader. Indian films continue these themes, often blending the identity of their heroes and heroines with those of Rama and Sita.

A popular Purana, the Bhagavata, is often used as an inspiration for drama. The miracle play, or *Ras Lila*, in North India brings the Purana to life. Actors, treating their work as a form of devotion, portray the deity Krishna in numerous exploits as a divine lover sporting with milkmaidens in the forest near Mathura in north central India. Devotees come from miles around to see the religious drama and to make their pilgrimage. While the *Ras Lila* is a source of entertainment, its popularity is due to its religious significance. The miracle play is an intense outpouring of emotion and love, which are present in devotional Hinduism, or *bhakti.* The gods who come to life on the outdoor stage have inspired painting, dance, and drama for hundreds of years.

Similar dramas are enacted in the United States. In Flushing, New York, for example, a Hindu temple has established a center for Indian culture where dance and drama are performed in order to integrate the authority of Hindu mythology into the life of the temple.

Similarly, India clubs and voluntary associations across the United States sponsor films and dance that emphasize the importance of these cultural models. A dancer may act out parts of the Ramayana. A film may portray a hero who is a holy man. Even in secular films—where stars wear Western dress, live in high-rise apartments, and dispense with ritual—evidence of the influence of scripture can often be found. In one movie, for example, a newlywed couple is shown in a brief interlude, dressed as Radha and Krishna, flirting in a wooded park. Like the divine pair whose love is dramatized in the Bhagavata Purana, they demonstrate their affection in keeping with scripture and tradition. Further, Hindu children are fond of reading stories of the gods in comic book form. These magazines, printed in regional tongues, dramatize the exploits of major deities taken from scripture. The heroic exploits of the gods are easily adapted to this medium, which reaches the homes of Hindus the world over. Krishna may be seen in any of his numerous incarnations. Rama may be portrayed in battle as the stories of the Ramayana come to life. This medium is a popular and enjoyable way to learn mythology. For Hindu children in the United States and Canada, it is a significant link with cultural heroes and holy places 12,000 miles away.

Devotional tracts inspired by sectarian founder figures are also considered sacred scripture by Hindus. For example, the Bochasanwasi Swaminarayan Sanstha, a western Indian sect active in the United States, has two sources of scripture written in the vernacular and accessible to any devotee. The first, the Vachanamritam,[7] is a collection of discourses that provide a model for correct thought and action. The other, Shikshapatri,[8] is a code of ethics, which followers use daily.

Obviously, the question of what is sacred scripture is quite complex. Most Hindus regard the four Vedas as the canon and accept each part, culminating in the Upanishads, as revelatory. However, the post-Vedic scriptures, although technically outside this canon, are so deeply engrained in Hindu culture that they also are understood as authoritative and among devotees in the United States are often more popular. They emphasize common values and elevate patterns of life based on a close association with deity.

The god Krishna.

For example, stories surrounding the birth of Kabir, a sixteenth-century devotional saint, contain elements of the divine. The infant miraculously appeared in a lotus flower in a village pool. His mother, recently wed, came to drink and saw the boy. Adopting the child, she raised him as her own. Kabir later taught:

I was not born of a woman, but manifested as a boy. My dwelling was in a lonely spot nigh to Kasi (Benares) and there the weaver found me. I contain neither heaven (air) nor earth, but wisdom only. I have come to this earth in spiritual form and of spiritual significance is my name. I have neither bones nor blood nor skin. I reveal to men the Shabda (word). My body is eternal. I am the highest being. These are the words of Kabir who is indestructible.[9]

Such birth stories are illustrative of links between the founder figures of sectarian traditions and the god(s) they serve. The stories emphasize the authority of the leader by virtue of this close, personal association with a god and establish his authority as a teacher and a holy man.

Devotion, or *Bhakti*

The city of Mathura is characterized by temples, pilgrims, and legends of the god Krishna, who, according to tradition, spent his youth in the forests outside the city. Mathura is a holy place where *bhakti* is a way of life. The streets are narrow, twisting paths filled with throngs of pil-

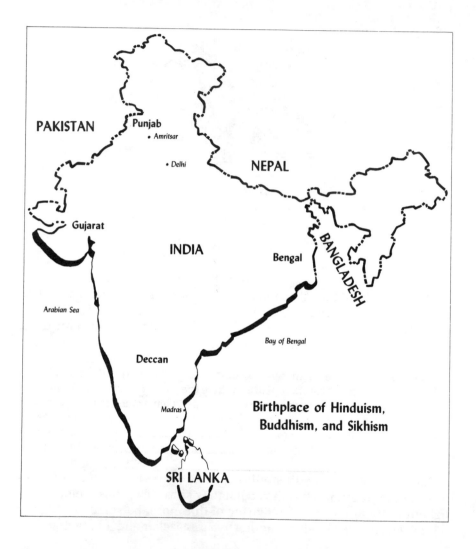

PAKISTAN

Punjab

• Amritsar

• Delhi

NEPAL

Gujarat

INDIA

Bengal

BANGLADESH

Arabian Sea

Bay of Bengal

Deccan

Madras •

Birthplace of Hinduism,
Buddhism, and Sikhism

SRI LANKA

grims, merchants, horse-drawn carts, bicycle rickshaws, and travelers. The pilgrims, who have come to see the city where Krishna was born, are served by a specialized group of shops, guest houses, and priests.

In a temple dedicated to a form of Krishna, a crowd gathers shortly before noon. There a figure of the god will be revealed from behind closed curtains to a waiting group of devotees. Priests prepare the temple grounds. Police are stationed at the edges of the shrine to keep the crowds back. The figure itself, surrounded by accoutrements of gold and silver, is garlanded and dressed for the occasion. One devotee, watching the preparations, has "Ram" tatooed over his body. Like most Hindus, he sees no contradiction in worshiping two or more gods. In this case, both are incarnations of the deity Vishnu.

All these actions are expressions of *bhakti*. The chanting, the emotional fervor, the singing, the ritual itself, are part of a devotional tradition whose origins are lost in Indian history. *Bhakti* is not any one rite, any single chant, or even a series of acts. It is an attitude that permeates these activities.

Bhakti also was a historical movement in North India that became popular in the fifteenth through seventeenth centuries. It was characterized by intense devotion to a personal god and the use of vernacular languages instead of Sanskrit, which only priests and the well-educated could understand. The *bhakti* movement was a renaissance of Hindu piety that enabled the masses to gain greater access to the great tradition of Hinduism.

Leaders of the *bhakti* movement promulgated their religion among the common people and royalty alike. For each, the movement had economic as well as spiritual advantages. Sects built new temples with land grants provided by nobility. By patronizing *bhakti* sects, regents hoped to foster support from segments of the population they often could not reach.[10]

Bhakti sects were known as *sampradayas*. *Sampradayas* were confederations of devotees who found meaning in the search for God through the release of intense emotion. Each *sampradaya* was an established tradition with a history, a lineage of religious leaders often descended from a founder figure, and a body of scripture.

The appeal of these devotional sects often was a result of the mystery and divinity that surrounded such figures. Vallabhacharya, whose birth stories were cited earlier in the chapter, was a charismatic leader associated with an incarnation of Krishna.

The myths surrounding Vallabha's discovery of a bronze icon contain elements of the miraculous. The icon, a large figure of Krishna, was buried beneath the surface of a small mountain near Mathura. Only an arm of the deity protruded. Assuming that the casting was an icon, a local farmer had worshiped it for years, not realizing that the rest of the god remained hidden beneath.

According to sectarian sources, Vallabha heard the deity calling out for milk and recognized the voice as Krishna's. He immediately began to worship the god, which was subsequently unearthed and enshrined in a temple.

After the *sampradaya* had been organized, and seven figures of Krishna installed in its temples, the god continued to influence Vallabha's descendents. This enhanced their authority in the eyes of devotees and helped them further the interests of the *sampradaya*, which eventually spread across northwest India.

In A.D. 1669, when the sect moved several hundred miles to the north, the figure of Krishna was placed in a small cart for the journey. Although the move may have been prompted by the possibility of patronage from a Rajput prince, it was explained as an attempt to flee from the onslaughts of the Muslim Emperor Aurangzeb, who sought to destroy Hindu icons.

Accompanied by priests and Vallabha's son, the cart was taken from one city to another for sanctuary. After several unsuccessful attempts to find a suitable home for the deity, the cart miraculously became stuck in the mud and could not be moved. This was interpreted by Vallabha's son to be an expression of the god's will, which now had claimed the spot as his new home. Enshrined in a magnificent temple, this deity has remained there for more than 300 years, continuing to be worshiped by Vallabha's heirs.

Through such dramatic narratives and the art and literature that they inspired, *bhakti* became a popular religion of its day. Royalty and the poor alike found meaning in the worship of gods who could be experienced on a personal level.

To Hindus in North America, *bhakti* is equally important. For many non-Indians who have adopted part of the Hindu tradition, it is a strong influence. Members of the International Society for Krishna Consciousness (Hare Krishna),[11] for example, teach basic *bhakti* doctrines first propounded more than 400 years ago in North India.

Further evidence of *bhakti* can be found in Indian shops that, besides selling *saris* and spices, may offer devotional art for sale. Paintings of Krishna, Rama, Siva, and other deities are rendered in a highly stylized way to inspire devotion. In India, such paintings and prints are usually found in shops outside of temples and shrines where they are purchased by pilgrims. Once in the home they are frequently placed near an altar.

Ritual

The most ancient, constant, and readily observable part of Hinduism are rituals through which the figure of god is treated as a king. Festivals, temple worship, and the private acts of devotion practiced in the home all honor the deity as a visiting emperor, worthy of the finest care.

Puja, the care of a bronze icon through bathing, dressing, feeding, and entertaining on a regular basis, constitutes the fundamental act of Hindu ritual in the temple or home. The figure, a dwelling which the deity has through his or her grace consented to inhabit, goes beyond symbolism. It contains the very power of the god. Deities are often understood as sources of superhuman energy with the power to break the physical laws of nature.

In order for the god to reside in the figure, it must be cast without flaw. After a casting is made, the god's eyes are opened ritualistically by a priest *(pujari)*, who bids the deity to enter the figure. Reciting Sanskrit incantations called *mantras*, the priest invokes the power of the god in the bronze.

Hindus in the United States worship figures that are crafted in India. These icons are cast in the traditional manner by families who for generations have performed this highly skilled task. Often, the process takes several years before the finished bronze is ready for dedication and installation. Most U.S. temples bring craftsmen from India to secure the figure in its abode. In the orthodox manner, priests are transported from India to dedicate the figure and invoke the power of the god in the casting.

Only the finest materials are used to complete the sanctum sanctorum, or inner sanctuary. The deity is enthroned and receives his devotees as a king greets his subjects.

The daily temple routine continues the regal imagery. The priest awakens in the early morning, and bathes the god with milk, clarified butter *(ghee)*, and perhaps the juice of a coconut. All of these substances are highly valued and suitable for a god or king.

These elaborate preparations and the daily cycle of *pujas* offer the average devotee an opportunity to experience a transcendent world. Nothing in the temple is reminiscent of the mundane environment outside. The bronze figures, the incense, the Sanskrit incantations, the sculpture and valuable marble are all a part of a divine realm. The temple is a palace where each god rules with total authority. By participating in a *puja*, the worshiper secures merit and builts a loftier foundation for his next reincarnation.

A visitor to any temple can witness the use of these elements and other religious symbols. For example, during the *pujas* conducted every day, a bell marks the start of the ritual. It is a reminder to the devotee that the rite has begun and is a signal to the god that his subjects have now come to honor him. As the priest *(pujari)* begins the *puja*, a helper breaks a coconut with a wooden stick. The sound echoes throughout the sanctuary as the coconut milk is made ready for the god's bath. The deity will be dressed in the finest clothes. Incense is burned to sweeten the air. Everything is done for the god's benefit and care, maximizing the effect of a transcendent world.

The priests who conduct *puja* are considered the personal servants of the deity and may reside in the temple they serve. Their daily schedule is determined by the regimen of the god rather than by the convenience of the worshipers. Washing, dressing, and feeding are done on the same basis as for an honored guest. Thus, whether performed by a male householder or temple priest, *puja* treats the deity as a personal god who blesses his subjects.

The Integration of Ritual, Devotion, and Scripture in the Life Cycle

Hindu tradition posits a model of behavior and devotion. In this model, there are four stages of life: those of student, householder, retiree, and ascetic. The model is the foundation for the integration of religion with all other aspects of life in a strongly patriarchal society. In this sequence, a student learns the ways of the Vedas, and becomes proficient in Sanskrit and the teachings of the major schools of Hindu philosophy. He adopts a profession and marries. He raises a family and instructs a son in the duties expected of the eldest male member, including rituals conducted at funerals and in honor of ancestors. Then, leaving his vocation, he begins a gradual withdrawal from society, eventually leading to full renunciation. Becoming an ascetic, he devotes his full time to the worship of a tutelary deity.

The pattern is ideal; few complete all four stages. However, there is no requirement that the model be followed in its entirety. Rather, each devotee meets whatever part of it is possible. The concern is for the integrated life in which a variety of approaches are combined to suit individual needs.

For devotees in the United States and Canada, the opportunities for leading a traditional life in keeping with this scriptural model are rare. The significance of the model for them, as for most middle-class educated Hindus, lies in its emphasis on an integrated life in which worship, religious instruction, and meditation are interwoven with vocation and family responsibilities. For example, a chemical engineer sets aside part of each morning for meditation and worship. He also educates his son in the proper way to perform *puja*. In a nearby temple a young man is studying to become a priest. Each day after work the novice travels to the temple. There, after worshiping, he teaches classes in *yoga* to the children of Hindu families in the area. For both men in this strongly patriarchal tradition, Hinduism is a total way of life.

A Brief History of Hinduism in North America

Hinduism was encountered rarely in North America before 1893. The number of East Indians immigrating to the United States and Canada in the eighteenth and early nineteenth centuries was minute. During this period, however, Hindu influence attracted the interest of intellectuals through the works of Emerson, Thoreau, and others.

In 1893, a Parliament of Religions convention was held at the Columbian Exposition of the Chicago World's Fair. The Parliament assembled devotees, priests, and theologians representing the world's religions. Buddhists from Japan, Sri Lanka (Ceylon), and Indochina; Muslims from the Middle East; Jews and Christians from the United States all participated in the gathering.

The Parliament is often remembered for the charisma of Swami Vivekananda,[12] the first Hindu priest to be acclaimed widely in North America. Vivekananda was a disciple of the nineteenth-century Hindu Renaissance leader, Ramakrishna, who worshiped the goddess Kali. The renaissance of which he was a part was a popular resurgence of Hindu mythology, scripture, and practice that swept across India. Vivekananda, by virtue of his presence at the Parliament, became its international spokesperson and was widely sought as a lecturer and teacher.[13]

Early Arrivals

By 1912, a burgeoning Indian population had settled in many U.S. cities, particularly in San Francisco. Most were middle-class citizens who sought to further their education and establish their careers.

For this Hindu and Sikh minority, life in the United States often was filled with bewilderment as cultural traditions entirely different from those in South Asia were learned. One Hindu writer claimed that whenever he stopped in small Midwestern towns, crowds gathered about him. He responded to these incidents by concluding that farmers in rural areas of the United States were quite unusual:

> Well, they are amazingly "nervy," these country people. They are so inquisitive. True it is not very annoying when you get used to their ways; but yet, at the same time you cannot help noticing that it is just in their bones to make other people's affairs their own at the shortest possible notice. They are frankly and openly interested in the brightness of your teeth, the colour of your hair and the price of your wearing apparel. They will think nothing of pulling out your watch chain, weighing it and measuring it and confidently asking "What you gave for that?"[14]

What the author experienced were differences in cultural understandings of privacy. To the farmers, the writer was a foreigner. The Hindu was educated and acculturated in India to conform to the values of privacy of the British middle class and reacted accordingly.

Problems of cultural differences often were more brutal. Between 1907 and 1914 the Canadian government passed a series of continuous-journey clauses that greatly hampered the ability of families to join their husbands in Canada.[15] Under the authority of the Immigration Act, 9 and 10, Edward VII, immigrants were prohibited from entering any Canadian port except by direct passage, which no ship sailing from India did. This meant that Hindu and Sikh men who had moved to British Columbia could not bring their wives or children to their new homes.

The Indian population of the United States and Canada was stereotyped. Anyone who wore a turban was judged to be a Hindu, even when many were Sikh. Both religious groups were falsely called uneducated. This was ironical, since many Indians who could afford the expensive steamship passage to North America were urbanized, educated, and successful.

In North America a growing anti-Asian movement demanded the expulsion of all "Orientals"—Chinese, Japanese, and Indian. By 1907 the number of Indian immigrants to the United States had increased almost four times over the previous year. Leaders of organizations such as the Asiatic Exclusion League sought to terminate the rapid increase. Articles in popular magazines of the day nurtured a fear of persons who did not look, dress, or speak like Caucasians in the Western world. Brahmins, who by virtue of their caste could not eat with non-Brahmins, were not understood. On crowded ships where dietary restrictions were hard to maintain, those Indians who refused to eat with the masses were looked upon as uncooperative. An article in *Collier's National Weekly* entitled "Hindu Invasion" stated, "It has happened for instance, that it was not convenient to allow them their own way in the matter of preparing food. They have simply starved until it was convenient."[16] What the magazine called "convenience" were cultural traditions thousands of years old. Breaking dietary restrictions often meant rejection at home and the loss of ritualistic status. Instead of attempting to understand such important parts of Hindu religion and culture, the press seized on what it deemed unnatural examples of behavior and called for additional governmental regulations on immigration. The Indian population was dismissed as a menace and encouraged to return home.

In spite of such attacks, Hindus who brought their religion to North America were determined to establish roots. They rarely were given the chance. Many were forced to return to India following outbursts of public opinion and restrictive immigration laws passed between 1917 and 1924. Those who did stay were often men, separated from their families for years at a time. Indians who were unmarried could rarely afford a steamship ticket home to find a wife. Instead, many Hindus and Sikhs in California married Mexican-Americans.[17]

Between 1912 and 1915 several Hindu organizations were formed to unify the voice of the new minority community. The Hindu National Association in Chicago and the Hindu Association of the United States in California became important cultural influences. The latter published a newspaper called *Ghadr* (mutiny). *Ghadr* became a voice of revolution. Calling for an end to the mistreatment of Indians and the termination of British imperialism in India, it sparked repeated concern in the Indian community. Directed by the revolutionary Har Dayal,[18] the newspaper led a movement that became a reformist tradition in India and in the United States. Har Dayal, a prolific writer, published numerous articles in this newspaper and in periodicals printed in India such as *Modern Review*. He achieved an international reputation as a commentator on Hinduism in North America.

However, Har Dayal and others like him could not stop the momentum that had begun in the press. The cry of exclusionists for stringent restrictions on immigration from Asia aroused public attention. The Congress reacted to these sentiments by enacting a series of laws, culminating with the Immigration Act of 1924 (the "Johnson-Reed" Act).

The 1924 law extended the concept of a national origins quota system, which, had been initiated three years earlier through the Immigration Act of 1921. It also upheld the declaration of the Immigration Act of 1917 that as inhabitants of a barred zone, Indians could not be admitted to the United States.

These laws were bolstered by state alien land acts and by a Supreme Court decision on February 19, 1923, that affirmed the use of racial restrictions on Indian naturalization. In "United States v. Bhagat Singh Thind," Justice Sutherland declared that Indians were neither "white persons" nor Caucasians. Hindu and Sikh immigrants had often claimed to be Aryan, citing their descent from the nomadic Aryan hordes who settled parts of North India around 1500 B.C. The court denied the contention that Aryan represented a racial type and that Indians could therefore be identified as Caucasians, or white people. This decision firmly supported the Immigration Act of 1917, 1921, and 1924 and gave legal backing to the demands of the exclusionists. Thereafter, Indian immigration to the United States was forced to a standstill. By 1926 most of the Hindus and Sikhs who had become naturalized citizens had been forced to leave the country.

Several years earlier, in 1919, the Ghadr party in North America had been crushed. Support for the movement had come from German consular officials in San Francisco.[19] When the United States became involved in World War I and declared war on Germany, the party and its supporters were seen as conspirators and brought to trial. Although the movement was revived in 1924, it never regained its former status as a symbol of Indian identity in the United States and resistance to British domination in India.

With the flow of immigrants from India cut off, the Indian population in the United States rapidly declined. However, the vision of life in the United States that had originally brought so many Indians to U.S. shores, remained attractive even though further immigration was not possible. Indian authors writing for *Modern Review* and other periodicals wrote home about colleges and universities in the United States. Others talked about the cultural differences between India and North America. Their readers, like themselves, were middle-class Indians who had already made the transition from village to urban life in South Asia. For these Indians, and for their friends and relatives who had lived in North America, the vision of the United States as a land of opportunity persisted.

Over the course of the next two decades interest in India was gradually renewed. The 1939 Golden Gate International Exposition in San Francisco paid considerable attention to South Asia. At the 1933 Chicago World's Fair, an international group met to continue the theme of the 1893 Parliament of Religions. Out of the 250 speakers present 30 were from India. Further, the increased popularity of Mahatma Gandhi in the United States helped to improve the image of Hindus. Knowledge of Gandhi's non-violence coincided with a growing interest in the United States in pacifism. In addition, he was perceived as a holy man who, with sacrifice and devotion, remained obedient to his faith even in the face of extreme hardship. The Mahatma awakened feelings of deep admiration for the simple, virtuous life, for his insistence on non-violence, and his resolute determination to promote societal change without force.

Gandhi utilized the Hindu teaching of *ahimsa* (non-violence) in shaping his message. This doctrine emphasized the avoidance of injury to any living thing and is an important part of Hindu, Buddhist, and Jain religious traditions. By emphasizing the role of *ahimsa* as a disciplined method of resistance and change, Gandhi offered Hindus the opportunity to use their religious heritage as a way of overcoming oppression.

Even with the growing popularity of Gandhi, however, Hindus in North America still were subjected to discrimination, harassment, and frequent injustice. Often they were erroneously identified as a racial rather than religious group. An Arizona statute in 1939,[20] for example, forbade the marriage of Caucasians with Negroes, Chinese, or "Hindus." This law is particularly curious since the number of East Indians in the southwest was extremely low. It indicates that "Hindus" were not only misunderstood, but were subject to great mistrust and suspicion.

The stereotypes of India and Indians had long-standing roots in the history of Christian missions and literature. As early as 1911, one incensed author writing for an Indian periodical voiced his concern: "Indeed, with missionaries on the one hand portraying India as a land where 'every prospect pleases' but where 'man is vile,' and portraying the people as 'heathen' who 'in their blindness bow down to wood and stone,' and with writers like Kipling on the other hand, representing the Indian people as 'half devil and half child,' it surely would be a wonder if the impression generally prevailing in America, . . . as to what the Indian people really are, were not more or less one-sided and untrue."[21] Popular texts such as Katherine Mayo's *Mother India*[22] continued to fuel these images.

Films depicted the "Hindu" as a mysterious, often sinister member of esoteric cults. *Gunga Din,* the most provocative of these films, led the American public to an even greater suspicion of Hindus,[23] who were portrayed as either wise and treacherous, or totally subservient devotees. Gunga Din, who, at the loss of his own life, saved the regiment from complete destruction, was nevertheless portrayed as sullen. He was the good Indian who sought to please his superiors. Conversely, the guru who led hordes of followers into battle against the British was characterized as sinister and conniving. He instilled blind devotion and fanaticism among a native population the film portrayed as ignorant and corrupt.

Hindus continued to be depicted in later films, and in popular humor, as backward members of a "third world" country influenced by superstition and idolatry. For those Hindu professors, doctors, and engineers who, educated in the best North American tradition, lived and worked in the United States and Canada, the injustice of this attitude was often painful.

Even in such difficult circumstances, Hindu organizations continued to serve the Indian community at a time when it was not being renewed with infusions of immigrants from India. Hindu lecturers spoke on college campuses and at Indian cultural organizations. Small groups of devotees met in retreat centers in California. Priests preserved the orthodoxy of rituals and festivals. Frequent performances of Indian classical dance enabled Hindus to retain strong cultural and religious links with their homeland.

Slowly, strong Indian cultural associations were formed. In 1937, the India League of America was formed (in New York) to revitalize the community on the East Coast. The group, which hoped to promote interchange between Indians, was also dedicated to improving the image of India in the United States. In April, 1940, the India League began publication of *India Today*, a periodical voicing concern for the accurate dissemination of information relating to South Asia. The League also sponsored recitals of Indian music and dance. Annual meetings were

Major Languages of India

held on the birthday of Gandhi and the celebrated poet Rabindranath Tagore. Meetings in major cities were sponsored by the League in cooperation with other organizations.

New Opportunities

In 1946, Indians were given the legal right (through the Luce-Cellar Bill) to seek U.S. citizenship. This landmark bill reversed earlier legislation that had barred Indians from seeking naturalization. India was allotted a fixed number of persons who could become U.S. citizens. However, the quota was small. Only 100 Indians were given the right each year to undergo the naturalization process. This came at a time when the Indian population in the United States had been reduced to a mere 1,500 persons.[24] Thus the revitalization of the community was gradual.

Real change did not come until 1965 when the national origins quota system was eliminated through the passage of a new immigration act signed into law by President Lyndon Johnson.[25] Thereafter, the number of Indians in the United States increased dramatically. India clubs and voluntary associations, which had expanded in the 1950s, grew rapidly. Linguistic and cultural associations of Bengalis, Telugus, Gujaratis, and other regional populations (see map, page 22) were formed. Many of the new arrivals settled in large cities. In the New York metropolitan area, where clusters of Indians opened shops, theaters, and restaurants, the Indian population was reported to have reached over 100,000 by 1978.[26] As a result of this growth, the Hindu temple tradition became rooted in North America.

Conflicts

Hinduism is not just a series of doctrines, books of scripture, or beliefs. It is part and parcel of Indian culture. To be a Hindu in the orthodox sense is to be born into the faith and into the caste system. Hindus in the United States cannot separate their Hindu identity from the way that they have been brought up as Indians. Their Hinduism is part of their caste affiliation, the way that they perceive themselves, and the beliefs that they may hold. In North America, Hindus often face considerable struggle in understanding and coping with a vastly different culture that frequently challenges these basic perceptions.

The rapid growth of Indian populations in the United States since 1965 has not been without hardship. For many, there has been great difficulty in adjusting to Western culture. For those with no relatives here, the difficulties have been harder to overcome. In India, the problems of adjusting from village life to that of larger cities, for example, are tempered by constant support from those at home. Even distant cousins may forge important connections to aid the difficult transition. In the United States, where the extended family is 12,000 miles away, Indians often experience loneliness and feelings of alienation. In larger metropolitan areas, Indian cultural associations help to solve these problems, but most smaller cities do not have such groups. Separation from parents can be a source of great anxiety. One Indian writes:

> There is a sense of pervading guilt among Indians who feel that they have abandoned emotionally if not financially their parents to their own fate in order to enjoy the fruits of materially prosperous life in this country. The parents' frequent communications from India detailing their physical ailments and economic hardships (real or imagined) compounds this sense of guilt.[28]

Adjustment to the West is particularly difficult for women, who are expected to remain in the home and retain traditional values. Many Indian women have come to the United States with husbands who entered the country as students or professionals. These wives may have had little preparation for living in a Western culture. Often they come directly from a village and understand little or no English.

Such women may be unable to function outside the microcosm of Indian culture usually found in a large city. For these persons, the home and a cluster of Indian shops are the nucleus of their world. Frequently there is little need to learn English, and interaction with non-Indians is discouraged.

The problems for these women and their families are manifold. Many put large amounts of energy into rearing their children in the same manner as would be expected in India. When social contact with non-Indian youth is discouraged, many Hindu children rebel. Since the mother is most often responsible for raising children in South Asia, she receives the brunt of the rebellion, which is directed at the way of life she so proudly embodies. She is placed in the difficult position of rearing offspring she cannot fully understand. In a nuclear family, she usually is the one with least exposure to the West.

In order to help alleviate such rebellion, some parents encourage visits to India and may even enroll their children in schools there. Yet, resentment may be increased and any attempt to nurture an appreciation of India thwarted.

One Indian family, for example, was concerned that their son was adapting to his environment more than they really wanted. As he drew near the age for the thread investiture ceremony (marking his entrance into the adult world), his parents decided to send him to India. Previously, he had only visited South Asia on trips that necessitated continuous travel. After the boy was sent to India to live with his grandparents for the summer months, it was decided that he should complete his next school year in Delhi. Now, separated from his friends in New York and alone in a culture that seemed alien, he began to resent what his parents had done.

The difficulties for Indian women in the United States are further increased when children move out on their own or go off to college. The life of these women now centers completely around their husbands. While the husband is at work during the day there is little to do. Language barriers prohibit contact with non-Indians and many husbands are not eager to have their wives venture out in a manner not befitting tradition. Many Indian men rigidly expect their wives to behave as they would in India. The wife is not only discouraged from working but also from developing the necessary skills to move freely in a Western society.

Indian women outside of urban microcosms of India have been forced to adapt. Those who live in the suburbs must interact with non-Indians. Neighbors are usually not Asian-Americans and have little knowledge of India. Grocery stores, spice and *sari* shops, and cinemas are all at a distance. English is necessary for day-to-day shopping or conversing with a neighbor.

Women who have been highly educated and trained as doctors, writers, nurses, and in other skilled professions are able to move freely in both India and the United States. Many of these women have changed their traditional lifestyle so that they can become a more active part of North American society. One of the most noticeable changes has been the adoption of Western dress in place of the *sari* except for special occasions and dinners.

Indian children, of course, bridge cultural gaps between East and West every day. Values often collide when parents and peers voice different expectations. One of the strongest emotional conflicts for Hindu children is dating. Teenagers of Indian parents grow up in two worlds. One, in the home, is a uniquely Indian atmosphere where conservative values governing marriage are upheld. There, dating is rarely encouraged. Indian children, however, also experience the world of peer pressure to conform to standards of dress and behavior of the West.

The result of the clash of value systems between the two worlds is often utter confusion. One Hindu teenager commented, for example, that while she longed to be like other youth who dated, she did not want to offend her parents. For her, as for many others, the choice of a suitable lifestyle was affected by conflicting loyalties.

In addition, most parents are anxious to assure their own parents and grandparents in India that orthodox values are being upheld. In India, children are a source of great pride and their education in matters of tradition is of tremendous importance. Even though separated by great distance, families in India keep close watch on their family in North

America and especially children. Periodic visits often center around the birth of a child or the performance of life cycle rites.

As the most Westernized part of the extended family abroad, children live in two cultures that each expect conformity. Often U.S. citizens by birth, they are also uniquely Indian. They want to do everything that their non-Indian friends can do but do not want to alienate their parents.

In conclusion, the problems posed by alienation, the changing role of women, and the clash of value systems between cultures have been especially noticeable since 1965 when the growth of Indian communities accelerated. However, these problems have been part of the Hindu experience in North America for over sixty-five years.

The Hindu Temple

It is a weekend in August. The place is the Shree Akshar Purushottam temple in Flushing, New York.[29] On this particular Saturday and Sunday the temple is busy with activity. The parking lot is filled with cars. People can be seen arriving from different parts of the United States and Canada. Members of this Vaishnava devotional sect (the Bochasanwasi Swaminarayan Sanstha) return to celebrate the anniversary of the temple's dedication. They greet one another by saying "Jai Swaminarayan"—"Praise to the Lord Swaminarayan." As greetings are exchanged, devotees enter the temple, leaving their shoes outside. In this and most forms of Hinduism, all footwear must be removed so that the interior of the shrine will not be polluted in any way. Leather or any substance associated with dead animals is considered impure.

The atmosphere inside the temple is formal but joyful. There is rhythmic chanting—"Swaminarayan, Swaminarayan"—accompanied by the sounds of bells and clapping as the intensity of devotion grows stronger. The chanting is occasionally broken by the recitation of scripture. Prayers are repeated. There is *arati*, the ceremonial waving of a lighted wick in front of the icon. *Arati*, a common practice in many forms of Hinduism, honors the deity and purifies the devotee.

To the members of this sect who have traveled hundreds of miles, the temple is a focal point of their religious tradition. It is a holy place where lasting expressions of Hinduism are able to transcend barriers of great distance.

The Hindu temple also is an institution with great strength and adaptability. It has survived the ravages of countless invasions of the Indian sub-continent by Persians, Greeks, and barbaric and nomadic tribes. It has outlasted periods of economic decline. It has persisted because it is part of the religious, cultural, and economic fiber of Indian society. In some villages it is a source of livelihood for numerous persons who serve

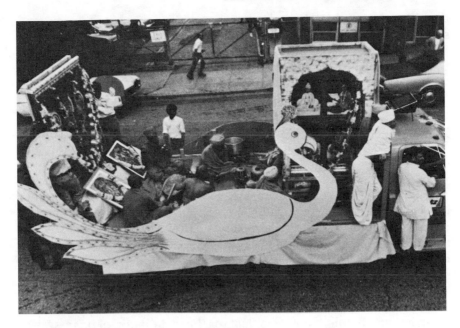

Float prepared by the Shree Akshar Purushottam Temple, Flushing, New York.
Courtesy: Dr. K.C. Patel, President, Bochasanwasi Swaminarayan Sanstha.

the central icon and reside on temple lands. The cooking of food offered to the deity, the care of attendant shrines, and the maintenance of shops selling religious goods call for specialized personnel. Usually these positions are defined by heredity and caste. Historically the temple has retained a vital autonomy that has helped to insulate it from change. Supported by rent from lands leased to tenant farmers, by the donations of the faithful, and often by the patronage of princes and kings, it has had no single allegiance except to the god or gods it serves.

The temple integrates the Great and Little Traditions of Hinduism. The Great Traditions are the theological and literary traditions of the Vedas and the triad, Siva, Vishnu, and Brahma. Little Traditions are "lesser" patterns of worship and ritualistic behavior, which may take the form of the adoration of village gods, snakes, and animals. The temple acknowledges the larger Vedic pantheon, but in a blend of mythology and ritual it incorporates local patterns of devotion. Its uniqueness lies in the ability to venerate simultaneously the large and the small under a common umbrella of Sanskrit doctrine and authority.

In North America, the temple is in a totally new environment. It is removed from traditional sources of income and support, isolated from the village labor which is vital to the complex functions it performs, and separated from the indigenous Great Traditions of India. Thus, the temple is forced to import what it needs at great cost of time and money. Stone workers, priests and attendants, architects, and other functionaries are brought from India.

The dramatic growth of the Hindu temple in the United States is a recent phenomenon. Removed from its origins and the ways of life that have nourished it for thousands of years, the temple continues to thrive. It adapts and changes, but at the same time it protects its rich history and culture.

An example of the temple's adaptability is the tradition of the *ratha*, or chariot. In India a deity is customarily paraded around the community prior to an installation or during a festival. Huge wooden carts, pulled by devotees, rumble through village streets carrying the god, who surveys the temporal realm. The carts are so tall that power lines may be removed to make way. Crowds cheer and flowers are laid in the path of the oncoming procession as village after village witnesses a god who is treated as king.

In an extension of the same tradition, the members of the Shree Akshar Purushottam temple prepared a float for the installation of its images in 1977. Shri Pramukh Swami and a retinue of priests had arrived from India for the occasion. A large collection of decorations, flowers, and accoutrements for worship were assembled to make the float suitable so that there would be no conflict with tradition. In New York City, the wooden chariot used in India gave way to a flat-bed truck. The group of icons accompanied by priests and the visiting spiritual leader were paraded through the city streets atop a float propelled by a gasoline engine instead of the labor of hundreds of devotees.

In a rural setting, where the use of a temple cart was more feasible, the Sri Venkateswara temple in a wooded tract outside Pittsburgh imported a wooden *ratha*. Crafted of teak in South India, the cart was decorated with intricate designs. The *ratha* was visible evidence that links with the orthodox temple tradition in India were being maintained. Both the float used in New York and the teak cart in Pittsburgh were functional symbols of the royalty and divinity of the icon. Decorated with the finest of art and the best of materials, they became portable thrones, bearing their sacred host through his temporal realm, and illustrating the persistence of tradition.

Hindu temples in India are part of Vaishnava, Saiva (pronounced Shaiva), or Shakti sectarian traditions. Vaishnava temples house different forms of the deity Vishnu and his incarnations or consorts. Saiva temples venerate the god Siva and frequently house the symbol of the god's procreative energy, the *lingam*, or phallus. Shakti, a term that

Temple cart (ratha), Sri Venkateswara Temple, Pittsburgh, Pennsylvania.

Courtesy: Dr. Raj Gopal, Secretary, Sri Venkateswara Temple.

connotes the energy and protective qualities of the mother goddess, incorporates elements of sacrifice.

These three divisions are not denominations as commonly understood in North America. They do not have ecclesiastical hierarchies or denominational structures. Their identity is found on a local level and in the larger schools of theology and doctrine that each tradition represents.

Whatever their sectarian affiliation—Vaishnava, Saiva, or Shakti—temples in the United States are supported by devotees from a wide geographical area. Donors to the Sri Meenakshi (Shakti) temple in Texas in a two-month period in 1979, for example, included persons from Maryland, Georgia, Kansas, Quebec, Florida, Illinois, California, New Jersey, and Washington state.

The tremendous support for U.S. temples has many reasons. Each institution is an important link with the Indian subcontinent. For many Hindus who have become U.S. citizens, the temples are also symbols of the perpetuation of their unique way of life in a foreign land. Art, music, and culture are strong parts of the temple's activities. In addition, the temple is a holy place where merit can be achieved by eating the sanctified food called *prasad* that has been offered to the gods.

Hindu temples in North America help devotees to protect their unique way of life in an environment that, whether in India or the United States, is totally removed from the secular world. They are sources of religious and cultural identity that re-establish several basic ingredients of Hindu culture—the continuum of purity and pollution, the transcendence of the gods, and the possibility of achieving merit in this life to better the next.

Temple Architecture

In India there are two distinctive styles of temple architecture, that of the North and that of the South. The former is characterized by spires peaking high above a central sanctuary. The inner sanctuary is located beneath the highest spire and at the very heart of the temple. The latter is typified by large gateways, or *gopurams*, at each of the cardinal directions. These sculpted entrances are carved with scenes from Hindu mythology and the lore of the individual temple. Inside the grounds are a variety of shrines. A temple pool (usually referred to as a "tank") for ablutions, dormitories for the staff of resident priests, and the sanctum sanctorum itself comprise the temple complex. The larger temples in South India are magnificent structures, combining the best of Hindu art and architecture with the functional needs of the deity. Those in North India are often newer because of the destruction of many large temples by invaders. In the Deccan, a plateau region influenced by North and South, temples exhibit a unique synthesis of both forms of architecture.

In North America, the same artistic and architectural conventions are followed. Temples built by North Indian sects often show spires. South Indian temples include large *gopurams*. Many temples are designed to follow construction patterns of particular periods in the history of Hindu art and architecture. The Hindu Temple in Flushing, New York, for example, has recreated a black granite *vimana*, or towering structure, above the central icon. Constructed in the style practiced by the southern Indian kings from the tenth through the twelfth centuries, the *vimana* is a visible link with tradition.

The following pages show the similarity of temples in the United States and in South Asia. Page 32 shows the *gopuram* (gateway) of the renowned temple of Kanchipuram near Madras, South India. Page 33 shows a frontal view of The Hindu Temple in Flushing. The structure of the *gopurams* is the same from the large entrance to the gold finials atop the tower.

Temples in North America are different from those in India because they are constructed for community worship and as cultural centers. In India, temples remain open for devotees to pray when they wish. In North America, supplicants often travel great distances to worship and so congregational gatherings are at appointed times. This is especially true in those temples that have begun to use the services of Brahmin priests in the community. These men, who by virtue of their birth may perform priestly functions, hold full-time positions in the secular world and are available to the temple for limited periods of time.

In the majority of Hindu temples in India there is no room for community worship. Rather, each supplicant walks around the central shrine, which is understood to be a symbolic gesture of the utmost respect.

Temple Worship

Puja, the ritualistic bathing, dressing, and feeding of icons, continues much the same in North America as it has in India for several thousand years. The figure is often cast of bronze or a combination of five metals (gold, silver, copper, lead, and iron) called *panchaloha*. Usually the figure is cast in India where craftsmen shape every detail with great precision. Every aspect of the figure must be exact, and every facial feature in perfect accordance with the Shilpa Shastras, treatises describing the process of construction, dedication, and installation of icons.

Temples in North America as in India often house a major deity and several subordinate gods. The gods are frequently accompanied by animal forms called *vahanas* on which they ride. If the sect is Saivite, the

Gateway (*gopuram*), Kanchipuram, South India.

The Hindu Temple, Flushing, New York.
Courtesy: Dr. Alagappa Alagappan, Founder-Secretary, The Hindu Temple Society of
North America.

vahana is often Nandi the bull. If the sect is Vaishnavite, the carrier may
be the bird Garuda, which in Hindu mythology carries his divine master
Vishnu into battle.

A connection is drawn between the symbol of U.S. national identity,
the bald eagle, and the Garuda, which often appears to be an eagle-like
creature, by leaders of The Hindu Temple Society of North America.
Since the deity Vishnu is traditionally understood as a preserver with no
specific geographical identity, this is a significant adaptation of the
tradition.

Such an adaptation exemplifies the desire of Hindus in the United
States to establish permanent roots here, to make important theological
transitions so that the great gods of Hinduism are no longer confined to
the countries of South Asia where the myths about them originated.
Most important, such correlations give devotees so far from home a new
identity that helps to bridge ancient traditions and the modern world.

Pujas at most temples are conducted at appointed times, often in the
early morning and evening. Since most devotees work from nine to five,
some temples have made special arrangements so that commuters can

Interior, The Hindu Temple, Flushing, New York, showing the black granite *vimana* (towering structure) over a deity.

Courtesy: Dr. Alagappa Alagappan, Founder-Secretary, The Hindu Temple Society of North America.

worship on their way home from work. Unlike most temple traditions in India, the regular gathering of the religious community is a highly valued part of this tradition.

Whether or not worshipers are present, the care and feeding of the deity continues. In some *pujas*, incantations are repeated to the god as a Brahmin priest walks around the central shrine. This is known as *pradakshina*.

In the early morning, the priest awakens the god and may give the bronze figure a showerbath, or *abhisheka*. The priest is understood to be the god's personal attendant and servant. He performs the showerbath as if attending a king. The act emphasizes the god's transcendence by virtue of the rich substances that are poured on him. It also shows the common ground he shares with those who worship him. The showerbath symbolizes this commonality and allows the devotee to look on his god in a personal way.

The showerbath, dressing, and feeding of the icon are all parts of *puja* performed on an assigned schedule. Special *abhishekas* are celebrated on selected occasions. A schedule for the Sri Venkateswara temple, for example, lists *abhishekas* to the temple's major deities on Saturday and Sunday mornings. These rites supplement the daily *pujas* (9:00 to 10:00 a.m. and 5:00 to 6:00 p.m.) and other rituals that are conducted throughout each day.

Most temples in North America continue the Indian tradition of celebrating a special *puja*, sponsored by devotees. Temples offer a variety of *pujas* that can be performed on advance notice. A suggested donation for one *puja* is twenty-five dollars.

Temples also supply forms whereby devotees can sponsor *pujas* by mail. This convenience allows worshipers who may not be able to attend the temple personally, to earn merit and experience the deity's grace. *Prasad*, the visible symbol of the god's love, is mailed to these persons.

Three U.S. Temples

One of the first temple associations organized since 1965 is The Hindu Temple Society of North America, which was established in 1970. The Society's first temple was erected on the site of a former Russian Orthodox church, in Flushing, New York. It offers its clientele a place for regular worship as well as for festivals and cultural events. While the temple primarily serves the diversified Indian population in the New York metropolitan area, it also has attracted some devotees indigenous to the United States.

The god Ganesh.

The Flushing temple (designated The Hindu Temple) was erected to honor the god Ganesh and other major deities. Ganesh, an elephant-headed deity, is understood to be the lord of auspicious occasions and is often associated with the beginnings of special events. Although the inner sanctuary of the temple houses a figure of Ganesh, the institution provides additional shrines for Vaishnavite and Saivite bronzes including a Siva *lingam*, or phallus. The temple thus recognizes the authority of different Hindu traditions. Leaders stress, for example, their affection for Master Subramuniya, founder and guru of the Saiva Siddhanta Church. The church, started in 1957, maintains shrines in Hawaii, California, and Nevada.

Leaders often speak of the ecumenical nature of the temple. Its medallion includes symbols from five major religions. This important adaptation of tradition shows the interest of the sect in relating to an existing American inter-faith movement in the United States.

The Hindu Temple was made possible by contributions from the government of Andra Pradesh in India and the Tirumala Tirupathi Devasthanam. The Tirupathi temple is one of the most revered centers of pilgrimage in India and has developed an international reputation for its architectural, ritualistic, and theological importance.

In a work camp in Andra Pradesh, 150 craftsmen sculpted huge granite blocks for the towering *vimana* above the sanctum sanctorum of the U.S. temple. After two years of work, each block was crated and shipped to the United States on the liner *Vishwa Apurva* ("Lord of the Universe"). Groups of *shilpis*, skilled in the manufacture of icons, soon followed.

Yantras, sacred designs carrying great power, were placed in each shrine, and were prayed to for five years in order to assure the potency of the New York and Pittsburgh temples in which they would be installed. Later, they were installed by the spiritual leader His Holiness Sri La Sri Pandrimalai Swamigal, who came from India for the occasion. This took place on July 4, 1977, as a symbol of The Hindu Temple Society's intention of establishing permanent roots in the United States.

The task of erecting a Hindu temple in the United States was formidable. Plans for the temple were begun in India, but had to be redesigned to meet local requirements in New York. Once stones for the temple had been shipped from India, the cost of transporting them from the harbor was an additional $17,000. Further, artisans sent to the United States from India had difficulty adjusting to the hard winters. Often, they were skilled only in the use of the traditional implements of their craft and had not worked with modern machinery. The resolution of these and other hardships shows the persistence of the Hindu leaders in linking holy sites and orthodox tradition in India with developing temples in the United States.

Since 1970, the Bochasanwasi Swaminarayan Sanstha, a North Indian devotional sect, has been active in the United States, notably at the Shree Akshar Purushottam Temple in Flushing. A comparatively recent movement, the Sanstha follows the teachings of Shri Saha-

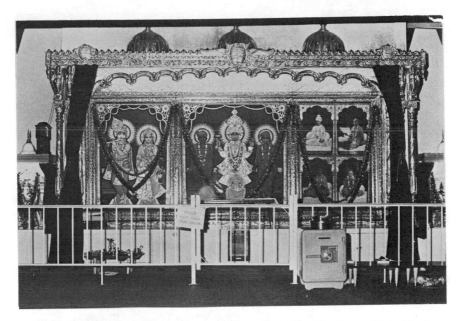

Icons in the Shree Akshar Purushottam Temple, Flushing, New York.

janand Swami (1781–1830). The sect recognizes Shri Sahajanand Swami as an incarnation of Krishna. Members of the Swaminarayan Sanstha are almost exclusively Gujarati[30] and share a common language and cultural identity. However, admission to the sect is open to anyone regardless of nationality, religion, or sex. Many members of the fellowship come from East Africa and Great Britain where the Sanstha has flourished.

The Swaminarayan temple tradition is extremely orthodox in doctrine and ritual. The glass icon shown above was originally shipped to Uganda. After political unrest, however, it was moved to the sect's headquarters in the United States where adherents of the movement have recently settled. Before the icon could be installed in the Flushing temple, artisans were brought from India to make sure that the setting was prepared in an orthodox, accepted fashion.

On August 28, 1977, a permanent temple was dedicated by Shri Pramukh Swami, the spiritual head of the Sanstha. Accompanied by a retinue of priests and devotees, he toured North America before his return to India.

The Swaminarayan Sanstha plans additional temples in North America. The presence of the Sanstha's spiritual leader in the United States and Canada is evidence of the sect's desire to develop a perma-

Annakut festival, Shree Akshar Purushottam Temple, Flushing, New York.

Courtesy: Dr. K.C. Patel, President, Bochasanwasi Swaminarayan Sanstha.

Sri Venkateswara Temple, Pittsburgh, Pennsylvania.

Courtesy: Dr. Raj Gopal, Secretary, Sri Venkateswara Temple.

nent, lasting tradition here. The sect receives visitors from outside the faith in an open, generous manner. *Prasad*—food offered to and consecrated by the deity—is often given as a sign of respect and friendship.

On June 8, 1977, the Sri Venkateswara temple (page 39) was dedicated in Pittsburgh, Pennsylvania. The temple is crafted in an architectural style unique to South India. Boasting a fifty-foot *gopuram*, the temple appears much like its parent institution, the Tirupathi Devasthanam.

The Sri Venkateswara temple was dedicated by priests performing a

Erecting the main gateway *(rajagopuram)* and Maha Kumbhabhishekam ceremony, Sri Venkateswara Temple, Pittsburgh, Pennsylvania.

Courtesy: Dr. Raj Gopal, Secretary, Sri Venkateswara Temple.

Maha Kumbhabhishekam ceremony (page 39). In this ancient rite, holy water is poured over the top of the *gopuram* to bless and sanctify it.

Since its completion, the temple has drawn thousands of pilgrims, who look upon it as a center of pilgrimage and an extension of a prestigious temple in India. The Sri Venkateswara temple offers a wide range of traditional religious services including special *pujas*, festivals, and wedding ceremonies. It serves a clientele made up of different regional groups speaking several languages. Accordingly, the resident priest at Sri Venkateswara is trained in Hindu, Telugu, Tamil, and Kannada— four major Indian tongues. Unlike his counterparts in village temples throughout India, he must meet the needs of a diversified population with linguistic, regional, and cultural differences.

The temple shares the concern of other Hindu religious institutions for cultural events. It promotes concerts and sponsors Indian classical dance.

A guide to the Sri Venkateswara temple pinpoints vegetarian restaurants in the area, assuring visitors that orthodox dietary restrictions can be maintained. Several motels offer supplicants special rates, much like a *dharmshala*, or retreat house, in India. To complete the pilgrimage, the temple offers a selection of devotional articles for sale including *puja* implements, such as coconut, incense sticks, and devotional pictures.

The Sri Venkateswara temple continues the established pattern of Hinduism in North America by cultivating strong links with orthodoxy. It is a center of Indian culture and religion, and of multiple sources of authority. Scripture, iconography, art, dance, and drama are all found in its midst.

Hinduism in the Home

The most meaningful part of Hinduism is frequently the ritual, prayer, and devotion that are conducted at home. The home is the center of Hindu culture—a place where customs of worship, marriage, and traditions affecting caste, diet, and language are maintained. In India many marriages are conducted in the home, where the family priest leads the couple through rites that stem from Vedic ceremonies.

Home Worship

In India, icons are often kept in a specially constructed niche in the home. There, the male householder—in a patriarchal tradition—bathes, feeds, and entertains his personal and family god as his father and

An altar in a home.

Courtesy: Dr. Alagappa Alagappan, Founder-Secretary, The Hindu Temple Society of North America.

grandfather did before him. He performs *puja* much as a priest in a temple does. In North America, an altar may be placed in a bedroom or den. The family's guardian deity is situated on a table, often in the company of other figures, pieces of scripture, or devotional pictures. There, a personal, family, and even village god may receive *puja*.

Hindus usually expect the eldest male to take the responsibilities of honoring the family god and of fulfilling tradition. If there is a son, he may assist in rites that he will eventually perform in his own family unit. These rituals include forms of ancestor worship wherein adult male devotees assure the safe passage of parents and grandparents to distant heavens or future rebirths.

Before worship can begin, the male participants are cleansed. They approach the altar without shoes so that there will be no pollution or impurity present. Often, the men are bare-chested, wearing the sacred thread, a mark of their "twice born" status as members of the upper three classes of the Hindu caste system. Candles are lit, incense is burned, and the deity is presented with flowers and other offerings. A small brass vessel to the side of the altar contains water so that the god can be given a daily showerbath. The figure is dressed in clean garments as prayers are chanted in a low, reverent voice. Sweets are offered for the deity's pleasure. All is made harmonious and pure for the god, who out of grace has consented to reside in the home. Thus, *puja* is conducted each day at home much as it is in the temple.

Diet

Most Hindu families prepare meals in the same fashion as in India. Curries, combinations of fresh spices, are ground for each meal. Many Hindus are strict vegetarians. Meat, eggs, or any animal by-product are considered defiling and are not eaten by orthodox practitioners since such foods are all associated with dead tissue.

Hindus have found it difficult in North America to find food that conforms to their dietary restrictions. One university student, for example, could not find processed foods made without polluting ingredients. As a chemist, he knew that enzymes, drawn from animal tissue, are found in many foods. As a result of this he lost weight and could not maintain a regular diet. Arriving in the United States before the popularity of health food stores, he had few alternatives for preserving the strict dietary traditions that he had held since a child. Even when invited to the home of a sympathetic friend who had prepared a dinner of macaroni and cheese, the problems were not resolved. The cheese contained an enzyme produced from the tissue of a dead calf, the worst possible source of pollution.

The ubiquitous Indian restaurant has become a way of meeting difficulties such as these. Cooks of high ritualistic status prepare vegetarian dishes in different pots from those that contain meat. The orthodox can find suitable meals prepared without any animal by-products. Spice shops and Indian grocery stores now import many of the necessary ingredients for traditional foods.

Many Hindus, however, compromise to varying degrees in maintaining dietary traditions. For children, there is great temptation to eat meat outside the home. In school lunches or in socializing with friends, the pressure to conform is intense. While strict patterns of vegetarianism break down in these instances, some children are careful to continue dietary laws, and abstain from eating meat.

The *Samskaras*

The Hindu *samskaras* mark the transitional phases of life. These rites of passage, which differ in number according to variant traditions, are the basis for a regulated, defined life in which each stage of maturation is integrated into an ideal pattern of behavior drawn from the Vedas. Among the twelve more popular *samskaras*, ceremonies of birth, first

feeding, adolescence, marriage, and death are the most commonly celebrated.

The *samskaras* are times of great family pride. Relatives send gifts and
close friends are invited as a priest guides his charges through the most
important transitional periods of their lives. In return for these services,
as in all rites conducted by a priest, the Brahmin is given gifts as well as
money. In India such gifts may include food or even livestock.

Hindus in North America often celebrate the *samskaras* with their
parents in India. There, the family priest establishes continuity with
orthodox tradition for family members who may be separated by
thousands of miles. Hindu children born in North America may be taken
to India to receive the ritualistic services of the family priest.

At times the *samskaras* may be celebrated in North America. Some
Hindu families in the United States have flown their priest from South
Asia for such special celebrations. In one marriage conducted in the
U.S., the groom's mother brought the necessary articles for the proper
completion of the rite: a red *sari* from Benares (Hindu brides traditionally wear something red), a banana leaf, and a *dhoti* (a loose-fitting
cotton garment worn by men). As the bearer of orthodox Hindu tradition,
it is the mother's responsibility to assure that the rites are done properly.

One of the most significant *samskaras* is Upanayana, or the rite of
investiture. A boy entering adolescence, if a member of the upper three
classes of the caste system (and hence considered "twice born"), is
presented with a sacred cord, worn from shoulder to waist, to mark his
new status. The celebration shows his coming of age as a man and his
assumption of adult responsibility. The boy may now perform *puja* and
begin to think of his future duties as a householder.

Upanayana is not only a sign of maturation; it marks the child's entry
into the system of purity and pollution. The acquisition of the sacred
thread is a sign of ritualistic cleanliness. The rite recognizes the coming
of age of a son and emphasizes the patriarchal tradition of which he is a
part. In Hindu culture, a male child is essential to the family's well-
being. The son, instructed by his father, prepares not only to conduct
family *puja* but to officiate at the death of a parent and in the observance
of ancestral rites.

However, for many Hindu women in the United States the emphasis
on patriarchal traditions such as Upanayana poses enormous difficulties since it stresses orthodox models of behavior. These intensify
pressures for women to conform to a traditional role at home.

Like the rest of the *samskaras*, Upanayana is most often conducted by
a priest who recites incantations and assures the child's continued well-
being. Upanayana is a time of great celebration and joy. All members of
the extended family are invited to be present, special food is prepared,

the finest *saris* are brought out, and the child is instructed as to what is expected of him.

With the construction of more Hindu temples and with the increased availability of priests, rites such as *Upanayana* can be conducted in North America much as they would be in India. While most families still prefer to celebrate important ceremonies such as this in South Asia, the temple presents the possibility of expanding the tradition on North American soil.

Marriage-Ties with the Home in India

For the Hindu, selecting a wife or husband requires great effort and the consultation of a variety of persons. For this reason, marriage contracts are most often negotiated in India, where the proper functionaries are found.

Most Hindu marriages are arranged in consultation with a family priest and astrologer. Astrologers provide necessary advice on the most auspicious times for enacting the rite and the compatibility of the astrological signs of an intended couple.

Primary considerations for a marriage include the economic well-being of the family, the dowry, the corporate family contract (in which the birth of children is of considerable importance), and the fulfillment of caste obligations. The father and brothers of marriage partners do the negotiating. Often, the couple do not see one another before the contract is agreed upon. Everything is conducted according to tradition in order to assure that the match will be a harmonious association in which each branch of the new family will be satisfied.

When the time comes for the actual ceremony, the prospective husband or wife often returns to India. When a male journeys to India and comes back with a bride, he may appear in many North American circles to have suddenly and quite miraculously fallen in love. On the contrary, the usual process requires not weeks but rather a lifetime of preparation.

In some cases returning to India to marry is not feasible. Students, caught in such situations, may choose their brides in the United States. They may advertise in the matrimonial section of Indian newspapers to locate persons of compatible status. This is a common occurrence in India. Indian newspapers published in the United States make the continuation of this practice possible.[31] They cater to a readership that utilizes a variety of services—from advertisements of Indian-owned businesses to matrimonial listings. Matrimonial requests are often placed by families looking for a suitable match for their son or daughter. Once the request is answered, only the priest, astrologer, and heads of the two households can determine if the couple is compatible.

In Hindu marriages, the strength of the family network usually dictates the degree of orthodoxy with which the marriage contract is completed and honored. A strong extended family in India is assurance that family traditions will be respected. Once the marriage has taken place, the family network maintains firm links with bride and groom. The husband's mother is a dominant force in Indian family life and exerts tremendous influence on the continuation of tradition. Even though she may not live in the United States, the mother-in-law still retains a large degree of control, seeing that the family conforms to expected standards and values. Indian women are raised to assume that they will accept the authority of the mother-in-law. In the United States or India, the responsibility of accommodating to the marriage is placed on the woman.

Hindus in North America, however, are frequently not able to marry exactly as they would in India. Caste endogamy—the practice of marrying within one's *jati*—is difficult to maintain in the United States. Not all families can afford the cost of returning to India to marry. Since considerations in establishing a marriage also include questions of identity relating to clan (*gotra*) and village, a suitable match for these persons thus becomes the closest approximate choice. Indian newspapers and cultural associations may help in the process, but as the relative number of Indians in the United States is small, considerations of caste are difficult to preserve. The caste system is a precisely controlled social order that is perpetuated by patterns of *jati* intramarriage. Any variation in marriage patterns weakens the system considerably so that its actual function may be negligible.

In North America, other customs affecting marriage remain intact. In the majority of cases the family continues to arrange marital alliances. The extended family remains an important ideal and serves a significant function in patterns of migration to the United States.

The family network thus not only determines marriages, it works to integrate relatives into suitable economic positions. Even distant relatives are highly valued. Far-removed members of the family often are established in their respective professions in the United States through the influence of the family in India. For example, a shopkeeper in New York may send for his cousins in Bombay. When they arrive in the United States, he will assure their comfort and well-being, and often will employ them to help run the business. On a larger scale, Hindus have utilized family ties to operate small industries over a wide geographical area. In California, a large percentage of the motel industry is managed by Gujaratis who have utilized their family connections to further their business interests.[32]

Lapses from the tradition of arranged marriages, which has contributed to the continuity of Hinduism, are rare. Most Hindus marry according to the combined wishes of both families, who arrange the match. Marriage to non-Hindus usually makes any subsequent return to India difficult. Such marriages are defiled in the eyes of orthodox practitioners, since non-Hindus are outside the system of purity and pollution.

Thus, the home reinforces the authority of the extended family in India. It functions as an extension of the family network, often helping cousins and other relatives to emigrate. Religious, cultural, and economic links persist despite pressures to conform to Western society.

Orthodoxy and Tradition Among Hindus in North America

This chapter has emphasized the desire of born Hindus to maintain orthodox religious traditions and practices (in the temple and the home) in North America. Members of different Hindu sects have created institutions in the United States that provide educational, cultural, and ritualistic ties with India. Children who have never seen Indian soil are nurtured through India clubs, temples, language classes, and the authority of the extended family in South Asia.

The desire for orthodoxy has been shown in art and architecture. Temples constructed in the United States copy existing patterns of architecture in India, often reproducing styles of well-known, distinctive periods. Carving inside temples follows similar conventions. Bronze figures are crafted in keeping with the Shilpa Shastras so that every detail or gesture conforms to tradition. Since most figures are cast in India by families who have specialized in the art for generations, there is little chance of significant variation.

The regular visit of holy men and sectarian leaders provides an additional check on orthodoxy. In some instances these visits are marked with much pomp and ceremony as the priests are introduced to officials of local government and given the opportunity to tour the area. The leaders assure devotees that their *pujas* and festivals are in keeping with the established norm. Their presence—and the blessing of a new shrine or temple—assures believers that the tradition continues without interruption. Such visits often are financed by temples in North America and reflect the desire of the religious community to conform to standards set by parent institutions in India.

Classical Hinduism has no ministers or ecclesiastical officials who draw large numbers of worshipers by virtue of their rhetoric. Instead, the god is the focus. Through the ritualistic gift of *prasad*, which can be mailed to distant supplicants, the deity grants merit. Pilgrims, often at great personal expense, earn merit through visits to the temple.

In the United States these important functions of Indian temple traditions are magnified. The fact that the Hindu temple can be found only in selected areas of the country makes pilgrimage more difficult—and by the same token more rewarding. When, for example, members of the Swaminarayan sect travel from throughout the United States or Canada to attend annual festivals at their North American headquarters in New York, there is evidence that pilgrimage is an important tradition.

In India the temple, depending on its size and popularity, may serve a clientele who speak but a few languages. In North America, however, temple leaders play an integrating role and additional languages become more important.

Differences in life-style between Hindus in North America and in India can be a source of frustration and tension. Older family members remaining in South Asia find customs and practices of a westernized environment difficult to comprehend. The rapid pace of life, the difficulty in finding vegetarian food, and other cultural differences are often subjects of discussion. Hindu visitors find life in the United States difficult when they cannot take an accustomed walk to the temple each day. Also, some Hindus in North America have adopted different views of ritual and worship from those in India. While parents remain believers in the power of icons and in the real presence of the god in the bronze, in the United States Hindus frequently see the icon as a symbolic representation of deity. Also, they are accustomed to honoring several forms of scripture from other religions in their daily devotions. These points of view are often irreconcilable and in each case reinforced by the demands of the culture in which they are held. Such differences are far less important than the links with orthodoxy that keep constant checks on Hinduism in North America. If a son or daughter in the United States changes his or her beliefs, there will be discussion of the matter with parents in India. The periodic return of North American Hindus to South Asia not only reaffirms cultural identity, but also serves to re-establish standards of orthodoxy and tradition.

Hindus in North America are middle-class, upwardly mobile persons. They tend to be well educated and are often skilled, contributing members of society. Some have been here for decades while others have only recently arrived. Centers of Hindu culture, including Indian restaurants, spice shops, theaters, temples, and shrines, facilitate the adjustment of new arrivals. They also help preserve important traditions that can be threatened by the rapid assimilation of the Indian minority into the mainstream of professional life in the United States.

Fashion show.
Courtesy: Sitalaprasad Misra and India Club, University of Arizona.

In some cities Indian films can be found on television as well as in local theaters, and Indian classical music is played on the radio. Dance and drama are performed frequently by artists living in the area and by visiting professionals. Indian clubs and cultural associations periodically sponsor such events, often drawing large audiences of persons from different parts of the country.

Gatherings in temples may provide the opportunity for worship of different deities. A fashion show (page 48) may give children an opportunity to wear a regional dress and to re-affirm their Indian heritage. Yet despite the fact that most Hindus in North America are highly educated, well paid, professional people, they have frequently been discriminated against. One journalist writes, for example, of the eggs that have been thrown at a temple in Flushing, New York, and the gangs of men who harass Indian residents near-by.[33] Another temple, in Elmhurst, New York (since moved), experienced similar problems. In these communities, as in so many other urban microcosms of Hindu culture in the United States, there is often a sharp demarcation between neighborhoods. The Indian communities, dotted with restaurants, shops, or temples, are a world apart from other segments of American society only a few streets away.

At times the two worlds clash. In one such instance a holy man was mugged, causing great distress among his followers.[34] While such violent attacks are rare, they point to the clash of cultures often within a few blocks of each other. Hindus are frequently feared by older people in the neighborhood, who stereotype them as aggressive and dominant. Such images are ironical since members of Hindu communities usually keep to themselves and shun any attempt to proselytize non-Hindus.

While Hinduism in North America is regulated by the concerns of the parent tradition in India, a strong desire exists to establish a permanent presence. Most temple traditions currently active in North America have extensive campaigns of construction and development. In those cities where there currently are no temples, small groups of devotees often meet in private homes. In a hierarchical system these home shrines are strengthened by the activities of larger temples in the United States, which in turn regard the parent institutions in India as legitimating sources of authority. This is similar to practices in Indian villages, where a hierarchical ranking exists between personal and family gods, village deities, and the more powerful icons in large temples. Each god serves a specific function to a particular body of worshipers. In like fashion, each deity is subject to the greater voice of tradition.

By recognizing this hierarchical system of authority, Hindus in North America continue a rich tradition that crosses religious and cultural lines. Hinduism is a vast network of rituals and festivals reinforced by scripture and established patterns of behavior. In North America, this network continues, strengthened by the growth of temples of various sects. The energy, commitment, and dedication that has accompanied the construction of Hindu temples in North America is evidence of a developing tradition renewing itself in a new environment.

The god Siva dancing.

CHAPTER TWO

Buddhists in North America

An Overview

Twenty-five hundred years ago, a young prince of India named Siddhartha Gautama (563–483 B.C.) renounced all ties to his noble birth. He left wife and child and a future free from economic hardship, and sought release from suffering, which he understood to be an inescapable part of life. The path to this release, or enlightenment, was arduous. Gautama studied the great systems of yoga, practiced physical austerities that brought him to the point of death, and followed the teachings of different gurus. None of these ways brought him any closer to a release from the cycle of birth and rebirth and suffering. Only after a period of prolonged meditation did he finally achieve release (or nirvana). From then on, Gautama became the Buddha, the Enlightened One.

He gathered a small band of disciples and formulated what he had learned into a systematic series of doctrines and practices that became known as the Middle Way. This path, midway between the comforts of a worldly existence and the extreme physical austerities practiced by religious teachers of Gautama's day, has since become a way of life for thousands of Buddhists throughout much of Asia and in the West. They follow two major traditions, called Mahayana and Theravada.

The older doctrine is termed Theravada, "the way of the elders." Also called the southern school, Theravada practice is close to the original form of Buddhism taught in India by Siddhartha Gautama, the Buddha.

The Theravada tradition is the only survivor of eighteen schools of early Buddhism. Theravada doctrine presents the arhant as an ideal—the monk who, having gained superhuman powers, is able to control his mind in the same manner as a Hindu ascetic. The historical Buddha is venerated as the greatest of teachers, but he is not deified.

Mahayana Buddhism (literally, "the Great Vehicle," also called the northern school) developed from a reformist tradition in India that sought to democratize the Theravada school, which was disdainfully called Hinayana, "the Lesser Vehicle." Mahayana Buddhists proclaimed, in numerous sects, that the Middle Way was open to everyone. The Buddha was conceived as a divine being. Siddhartha Gautama was recognized as one of many Buddhas, each fulfilling a different function.

51

Statue of Shinran Shonin in front of the New York Buddhist Church. This cast bronze figure was retrieved from Hiroshima after World War II. Undamaged by the atomic bomb, it was brought to the United States at great expense. It remains a symbol of the persistence of a major Mahayana tradition in North America and the theological dominance of its founder.

Mahayana Buddhists emphasize the role of *bodhisattvas*, divine beings who out of compassion aid all devotees who wish to achieve enlightenment. They are recipients of prayer, ritual, and intense devotion, and are often looked upon as saviors who liberate their worshipers from all suffering.

Today the Mahayana and Theravada schools co-exist throughout Southeast Asia. Dominant Mahayana traditions are found in China, Japan, and Korea. Theravada Buddhism flourishes in Sri Lanka, Laos, Burma, and Thailand. Each tradition reflects doctrinal differences that affect the character of the order of monks (*sangha*) as well as the role of the laity.

Despite their doctrinal differences, both schools hold similar views on the basic tenets of the faith. They follow the Buddha, who, born a Hindu, accepted the processes of *karma* and rebirth, as well as the virtues of compassion and non-violence as necessary parts of life. Thus, *ahimsa* (non-violence) is a way of life for Buddhists from different backgrounds. It is applied uniformly to animal and human life. For example, a Theravada monk in Washington, D.C., takes extreme care to sweep insects from his body rather than to kill them. Similarly, a lay Buddhist in San José, California, spends time each week caring for fish in a pond next to a temple. The pond and adjacent Japanese garden are important symbols of the Buddhist values of harmony and tranquility.

In each case, the avoidance of injury to any living thing is coupled with compassion. Laity and monk alike emulate the historical Buddha who preached reverence for all life and gentleness. Following this principle, devout Buddhists take great care never to inflict harm.

The doctrine of *ahimsa* is so strong that it was a dominant influence in the conversion of the Indian ruler Asoka (pronounced Ashoka), who first spread the teachings of the Buddha outside of India. According to legend, Asoka (274–232 B.C.) had waged several wars in an effort to subdue as much of the subcontinent as possible. But when he realized that his conquests had produced suffering among innocent villagers, he renounced violence and adopted the Middle Way. Under Asoka's guidance, Buddhism became a state religion and quickly spread to Sri Lanka and Southeast Asia.

Like Asoka, most Buddhists continue to abhor war. In Burma, Thailand, and other countries, the monastery traditionally is a refuge through which supplicants are not subject to conscription. Lay devotees may enter the order of monks for several months or a period of years. During that time the monastic rule and the teachings of the Buddha govern their lives. The *sangha* demands strict obedience to an ordered life in which the community of monks governs the behavior and attitude of its members. Finally, it encourages the practice of non-violence and the values of gentleness and compassion.

Buddhists in the United States often face conflicts when their heritage of non-violence is not understood. Unlike countries in Southeast Asia where Buddhism is a state religion and where monasteries are wealthy institutions, there are few such refuges in the United States. Moreover, immigrant communities often lack solidarity and are not able to speak with one voice against acts of war or violence. Thus, for most, conflicts between life in North America and the Middle Way of the Buddha are personal matters, tested by allegiance to family ties and tradition.

While attitudes of non-violence and beliefs in *karma* and rebirth are common to both Hindus and Buddhists, the traditions have important differences. The foremost of these differences is the Buddhist doctrine of no-soul, first propounded by Gautama. As a reformer who was not satisfied with the popular Hindu religion of his day, Gautama rejected the idea of soul, which he saw as illusory. He reasoned that since the world is constantly changing, nothing can be permanent. Hence, there can be neither soul nor, by the same token, a God.

The Buddha also rejected caste. Stressing the equality of all believers, Gautama offered the Middle Way to the lowest and the highest, the pure and the unclean, the elite and the despised. Women, who rarely were given the opportunity to practice asceticism in Indian society, were welcomed into the order of monks. In spite of these egalitarian roots, however, the *sangha* has remained a male-dominated institution.

As a foundation for his teachings, Gautama set forth several basic truths. Borrowing the Hindu concept of *dharma* (moral law or truth), the Buddha taught the *dhamma* (the Pali equivalent of *dharma*). Pali, an Indo-European language, became the classical language of the Buddhist scriptures.

The core of the *dhamma* included four basic assumptions about the human condition, which became known as the Four Noble Truths. The first Noble Truth was the conviction that life inherently involves suffering. Second, the cause of suffering was understood to be craving or desire. In Buddhist vocabulary this became "thirst," the insatiable desire for love, material goods, or power. Thirst, or desire, was seen as unending and inescapable to all but the enlightened. Third, Gautama acknowledged that there was a method to find salvation, liberation from the cycle of birth and rebirth. Finally, the fourth Noble Truth pointed to the Eightfold Path as the way to enlightenment.

In teaching his disciples the Eightfold Path, the Buddha preached a total system of morality. He taught that the search for enlightenment must start with the purification of the mind and the adoption of standards of behavior. The Eightfold Path, which was a basic system of discipline derived from *yoga*, proclaimed Right Views, Right Intention, Right Speech, Right Action, Right Livelihood, Right Effort, Right Mindfulness, and Right Concentration. Right Views acknowledged the Four Noble Truths. Right Intention, Right Speech, and Right Action contributed to the preparation for enlightenment by regulating actions affecting others. Through Right Livelihood and Right Effort, the devotee lives a contemplative life, avoiding injury to any living being. Strict non-violence becomes a rigid doctrine for the Buddhist pursuing enlightenment, or *nirvana*, which is spiritual freedom and detachment from desire. Finally, Right Mindfulness and Right Concentration help the disciple of the Buddha to still the mind through breath control, posture, and sustained meditation.

The Eightfold Path incorporated basic elements of the great systems of *yoga* that were part of the cultural milieu in which the Buddha lived. Following these teachings, Buddhists practice methods of intense concentration, which vary in different countries and sects. The object of the concentration remains the same, however. By disciplining the mind and detaching it from either anxiety or pleasure, devotees learn to still their thoughts. They learn to act gently and compassionately without seeking satisfaction or esteem from what they do. By so doing, they extinguish desire and gradually are disengaged from the cycle of birth, rebirth, and suffering.

These basic tenets are held by the many Buddhist groups throughout the world. Major forms of Buddhism in North America defined by country of origin include Japanese (Nichiren, Zen, Jodo Shinshu), Thai, Cambodian, Laotian, Vietnamese, Burmese, Sri Lankan, Korean, Tibetan, and Chinese (T'ien T'ai and Pure Land).[1] This chapter examines these basic tenets and the way of life they represent as practiced by persons born into three Buddhist traditions now active in North America: Theravada, Chinese Mahayana, and Jodo Shinshu (a Japanese Pure Land sect). Each of the three traditions has undergone revitalization in the last twenty years.

A monk from Sri Lanka, after a career as an educator and administrator in Buddhist colleges and universities in South Asia, was sent to Washington, D.C., by his order to establish and maintain a *vihara*, or temple.[2] This member of the *sangha*, or Buddhist clergy, participated in a dynamic rebirth of his tradition. Entering the United States for the first time, unsure of his ability to function in a Western culture, he adapted quickly. With the help of officials of the governments of Sri Lanka and Thailand, he organized a monastic community. As a traveling monk and classical Buddhist scholar, he helped revitalize his religious tradition in a new environment.

The Buddhist Churches of America, a Jodo Shinshu (Pure Land) denomination, recently celebrated its seventy-fifth anniversary in the United States. The celebration served as a period of revitalization and reaffirmation of important religious and cultural traditions.[3] Members recognized both their Buddhist orientation and their identity as United States' citizens. As an expression of this unique heritage, the denomination published a two-volume work, giving the history of each member church.[4] New programs were instituted and elements of Japanese culture emphasized. Programs of music, dance, cooking, and theater marked the occasion.

Chinese Buddhist leaders have sought to revitalize their tradition by building new temples and religious centers. Often these institutions are constructed away from ethnic communities in order to extend their religious traditions into new areas. Larger facilities are built to supplement the small temples and shrines usually found behind shops in Chinatowns. A temple in the Catskill Mountains of New York State, for example, offers the benefit of a large wooded tract that can be managed and landscaped in traditional Chinese fashion. A lake on the property is tranquil and calm, reflecting Buddhist values of inner peace. Several small temples honor different *bodhisattvas* in the Mahayana, or northern Buddhist, tradition. Chinese-American workers maintain an apartment for monks, who frequently come to the temple. The complex, much like smaller temples in the New York City's Chinatown, is a self-contained, self-sufficient environment in which the Chinese Buddhist way of life predominates, albeit in a rural American setting in the United States.

This chapter stresses the ethnic pride of each Buddhist group, showing the importance of rituals, festivals, and other expressions of Buddhist culture. It emphasizes the desire of Buddhists from three different parts of the globe to maintain their heritage despite great difficulties.

For these devotees, Buddhism is far more than a series of logical deductions about suffering or voluminous tracts of scripture that comprise different versions of the canon. It is a complete world view in which they have been immersed from infancy.

The spirit of the tradition is not easily broken. When the Chinese Communists forced the exile in 1959 of the Dalai Lama, the spiritual head of Tibet, for example, they assumed that they had broken the back of the religion. But the tradition continued to thrive, despite the imposition of a secular state that took the place of the indigenous Buddhist theocracy. The laity continued to spin prayer wheels, sending prayer after prayer aloft to the heavens. The heart of this unique Buddhist culture could not be splintered.

This same spirit exists in each Buddhist community in the United States and Canada. Buddhism in North America or Asia is a way of life that for over 2,000 years has withstood changes of government, patterns of exile, and the trauma of immigration. For those devotees who have come to the United States from Southeast Asia, China, or Japan, the tradition continues to shape their identity and heritage.

The Buddha and Buddhism

The Buddha

Siddhartha Gautama, founder of one of the world's great religions, was born in 563 B.C., a prince of the Sakya clan most probably in Nepal.

Details of his birth, childhood, renunciation, and enlightenment are enveloped in myths and symbols of a prince, a holy man, and a teacher that reflect the culture. He was raised in royal surroundings and—as expected in a patriarchal society—married and produced a son. His future was secure in the knowledge that he would become king. As a prince, father, and student of the scriptures, Gautama's life fulfilled the Hindu traditions. But in mid-life, Gautama renounced his royal status and entered on a spiritual quest that culminated in his enlightenment, earning him the title of *Buddha*. The term Buddha means "Enlightened One" and is derived from the Sanskrit word *bodhi*, or knowledge.

The Buddha's birth is often described in epic, sweeping terms suitable for a member of the Hindu pantheon or a king. In one account, the infant was conceived in the Tushita heaven as Gautama's mother, Queen Mahamaya, was magically impregnated by the future Buddha. In other accounts the child was conceived after a white elephant—a symbol of royalty in Hindu culture—entered the Queen's side. The child was delivered in a sacred grove of Lumbini trees. Gautama was dropped into a golden net, surrounded by gods and kings. Two streams of water fell from the sky, miraculously cleansing his mother. The earth shook in acknowledgment of the event.

Siddhartha's childhood also is described in a manner suiting a prince or a holy man. Receiving the attention of kings and sages, he was revered for his authority. The gods granted him protection and guarded his palace. He grew up studying the Hindu scriptures.

The story of Gautama's renunciation presents the image of an ascetic. His renunciation of a life of royalty was preceded by a conversion experience during which the prince saw four signs. In swift succession, he met an old man, frail and bent with age; he looked upon the torment and unpredictability of disease; and he viewed a corpse. In each event he realized the inevitability of suffering and the impermanence of life. Suddenly he was jolted to the realization that neither the riches of the palace nor the security of his position as heir apparent would protect

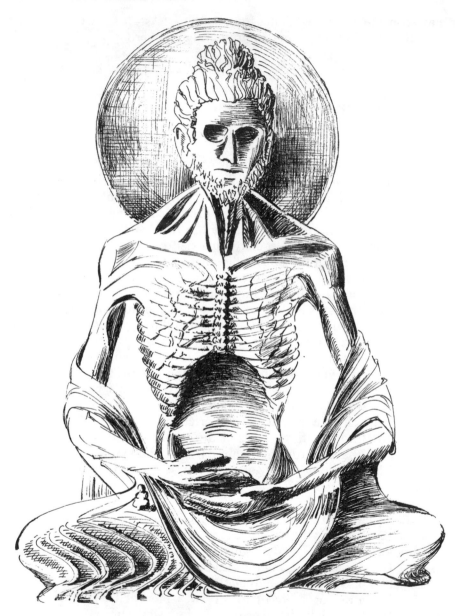

GAUTAMA

Gautama Buddha practising austerity.

him from eventual suffering and torment. The fourth sign, a mendicant who had renounced the world, convinced Gautama to renounce his life of privilege and begin a quest for spiritual enlightenment.

Gautama's renunciation took place at night when, with the help of the gods, the palace and the city of Kapilavatthu had been placed in a deep sleep. Gautama looked upon his wife and child for the last time. Deities positioned themselves under the hooves of his horse, Kanthaka, to muffle the sounds of his flight. Off he rode, abandoning his position, wealth, and the comfort of a close family life. The efforts of the Hindu gods to help him reach enlightenment reflected the cultural setting of the Buddha's career.

As a prince in a Hindu society, Gautama followed the accepted paths of asceticism and renunciation. As a holy man, he expected the gods to play an important part in his life, just as other Hindu ascetics understood themselves to be under the watchful eyes of the gods. Heads of devotional sects, for example, have been described as the personal servants of their gods and are often associated with the direct intervention of the holy in human affairs.

In his search for enlightenment, Gautama studied with the great teachers of his day. For a period of six years he wandered from guru to guru. He practiced austerity, fasting for days and weeks to purify his mind and body. He concentrated for great lengths of time, becoming frail to the point of death (see illustration on page 58). He practiced different methods of meditation and breath control, becoming proficient in each. Like other great reformers, he made pilgrimages to recognized centers of authority and tradition.

Gautama prepared for his enlightenment under a Banyan tree. Assuming the lotus position (a cross-legged posture derived from *yoga*,) he resolved not to arise until he had achieved *nirvana*—the state of ultimate freedom and enlightenment. During the course of this prolonged meditation he was tempted by the demon Mara, who symbolized both the love of the temporal world and the suffering that was produced by craving it. Mara had followed him during the six years of his preparation and now sought to dissuade the prince from reaching his goal.

As a Hindu ascetic, Gautama's concentration was so developed that he was able to remember former lives. He came to be an enlightened being who, fully aware of all his previous incarnations, was victorious over life and death. In passing through this stage of meditation, Gautama established his authority over all who sought release from the cycle of birth and rebirth.

When enlightenment finally came, the gods who had assembled before the sage were elated. The earth shook as a symbol of his undisputed authority and divinity. Some texts suggest that as a sign of his new powers, Gautama rose in the air. He had conquered suffering by eliminating all desire. He had outlined a new path, the Middle Way.

The Buddha's Life as a Pattern

In winning enlightenment, Gautama established a pattern of a perfect life. The example of his renunciation, prolonged meditation, and eventual liberation was so powerful that it established a ceremonial sequence for coming-of-age rituals in different cultures, regardless of which form of Buddhism was practiced.

For the lay Buddhist in North America, the tradition of the Buddha's enlightenment continues to be a formative influence. Children are taught to emulate the Buddha as a gentle and compassionate being. Devotees are urged to adopt the Middle Way and the mental and physical discipline of meditation.

An article in a Korean-American newspaper[5] published in Los Angeles describes the rigors of life in the *sangha*, where monks replicate the Buddha's search for enlightenment. During their novitiate, young men learn the rules and customs of the order. They are taught to memorize and study scripture. The work is so intense that the novice rises at 3:00 a.m. and may not fall asleep until 7:00 the following night.

Once the novice learns to meditate, the intensity of the discipline increases. As a monk he will often meditate facing the wall and may be allowed only five minutes of exercise during each fifty-minute period. Food will be brought in and placed behind him so that he may eat and return to his concentration with little loss of energy or unnecessary movement.

On becoming a monk, the novice drops the name of his parents and adopts a Buddhist title. This name change, part of the process of entering the *sangha* in most Buddhist countries, symbolizes his complete renunciation of all ties to the world, following the example of Gautama when he left his family home.

The monk looks to the Buddha as a pattern for the perfect life, which is highly disciplined and free from suffering. By sitting for hours at a time and by isolating himself from any emotional attachment to family or friends, he conditions both body and mind. At times he pushes his body to the limits of endurance. Korean monks, for instance, have meditated for an entire week once a month without any sleep. The process is not regarded as an ordeal but as a total discipline in which a pattern of life initiated over 2,000 years ago is experienced.

Meditation often gives those who practice it startling benefits. Students discover that their Buddhist training helps them to eliminate peripheral thoughts and worries and to focus their minds. As a measure of his power of concentration, one student often amazed his friends by balancing an egg on end on a hard surface. The trick could only be performed by focusing his mind on the egg and eliminating all other thoughts or concerns that unconsciously might cause him to move. While Buddhists and Hindu *yogis* frequently refrain from exhibiting their powers, such demonstrations are evidence of the way in which these disciplines enable their practitioners to direct their minds with remarkable intensity.

The Middle Way and the Tipitaka

Before his final enlightenment and death, Gautama preached doctrines known for their inherent logic and rational observation of the human condition. In propounding the Four Noble Truths and the Eightfold Noble Path, the Buddha suggested that, while life was rooted in suffering, there was a way to liberation. That path, interpreted by Buddhists in different cultures, has been called the Middle Way. The Middle Way can be seen as analogous to a lotus. As the lotus petal does not touch the water on either side, so the practitioner of the Middle Way avoids both extremes of meditation through physical austerity and of worldliness.

The teachings of the Middle Way were an alternative to self-mortifying practices of asceticism. The Buddha had fasted to excess. He had assumed the lotus position for prolonged periods of time, and had

Lotus, symbol of the Middle Way.

meditated almost to the point of death. These pursuits, based on the doctrines of Hindu ascetics of his day, had failed to further his grasp of enlightenment.

The Middle Way inspired the creation of scripture known as the Tipitaka ("three baskets"), which is a source of authority for all Buddhists. As its name suggests, this canon is divided into three collections, or baskets (pitaka) including: Sutta (discourses), Vinaya (rules of conduct), and Abhidhamma (doctrine). This threefold division is used by Theravada and Mahayana traditions alike. There are many versions of each Tipitaka in the various Buddhist countries. Collections are voluminous and often include thousands of texts.

Specific texts in each Tipitaka canon differ. Scriptures in the Mahayana tradition, for example, emphasize the bodhisattva ideal. Texts in the Theravada canon, on the other hand, stress the role of the historical Buddha. Both collections frequently use the model of the Buddha addressing his disciples as a way of teaching doctrine and ethics.

The Theravada Tipitaka is a voluminous collection of historical and mythological texts. It is written in Pali, the sacred language of this early Buddhist school. Pali texts were preserved on palm leaves, bound together much like a book. As early as 247 B.C. this canon was complete.[6] The Washington Buddhist Vihara maintains a complete collection of the Tipitaka.

The Mahayana Tipitaka is often known by individual texts that have achieved widespread popularity. One such text, the Lotus Sutra, speaks of the multiplicity of Buddhas, which became a basic Mahayana tenet. In sharp opposition to the doctrines of the Theravada school, the Sutra proclaims that the hearing of one verse will secure enlightenment.[7]

The Tipitaka has inspired numerous art forms. Chinese and Japanese paintings reflect the beauty and tranquility of Buddhist heavens. Similarly, paintings of Buddhist hells show the torment of insatiable craving and are graphic illustrations of the need of a compassionate Buddha. Similarly, the Tipitaka incorporates a wide variety of myths and legends. Jataka tales, for example, are stories of the Buddha's previous incarnations. They are filled with superhuman accounts of mythical beings and are a source of entertainment for children and adults. The Jataka accounts were written by Theravada leaders as part of the canon to help strengthen the image of the historical Buddha, who was reborn for the last time after triumphing over all previous existences.

The Sangha

The sangha, as initiated by the Buddha, is the order of monks, the ascetic association through which doctrines are maintained. It is a patriarchal federation of male Buddhists in which Gautama's renunciation and enlightenment are guides for proper conduct. For a *bhikkhu* (monk) the *sangha* is the heart of Buddhist tradition. Whether it be the most solitary forms of Zen or the ritual of Theravada Buddhism, the way to enlightenment is through the *sangha*. The beginner is reminded of the importance of the monastic community in his vows, which confirm his absolute obedience to the Three Jewels of Buddhism: the Buddha, the *dhamma*, and the *sangha*.

The monk is required to live in complete purity. He takes a series of vows, the Five Precepts, in which he agrees not to harm any creature, nor to engage in stealing, lying, drinking alcoholic beverages, or sexual immorality. This rigorous code of conduct, which is especially detailed for monks in the Theravada tradition, is also found in the Hindu disciplines of yoga, which greatly influenced the Buddha. In both religions, the process of meditation is understood to be dependent on a state of ritual purity that can be achieved only through the acquisition of positive *karma*.

In acknowledging the Three Jewels and vowing to obey the Five Precepts, the monk is often reminded of the Buddha's foremost disciple, Ananda, who was a devoted follower of the Middle Way. Ananda is of such importance to the tradition that he is assigned the role of narrator of significant incidents in the life of Siddhartha. Theravada devotees, revering this close friend of the Buddha, have erected a statue of the disciple behind the Washington Buddhist Vihara.

For Theravada Buddhists, the *sangha* has been supported traditionally by the laity. In South Asia, monastic landlords often draw their income from temple lands. In North America, the monks' support comes from direct contributions of the laity, and they also may receive living allowances from the *sangha* at home.

Theravada monks are respected as the caretakers of tradition, and are often respected scholars. *Bhikkhus* may teach courses in the classical languages Sanskrit and Pali.

For the Buddhist Churches of America, the *sangha* has become the worshiping community. It includes both clergy and laity. Affirming a Buddhist "priesthood of all believers," B.C.A. doctrine defines the *sangha* as the Church.

By borrowing Christian terminology and structure, the B.C.A. functions much as a Protestant denomination. Since many second and third generation Japanese-Americans retain few ties with their heritage, the Church has been forced to use other than traditional Buddhist models of organization and education.

In order to reach Buddhists who have moved out of ethnic communities, the denomination has adapted a Protestant model of ecclesiastical organization. B.C.A. clergy are educated as ministers and worship services are held on Sunday mornings. Ministers travel into the suburbs

Ananda, disciple of Gautama Buddha.

beyond the older Japanese-American communities that at times are no longer sources of strength. While the process has been costly and has fostered problems of identity within the denomination, it has helped the Church to survive a difficult time in its history.

The Zen tradition as practiced in North America has made a different adaptation. The *sangha* is made up of students and teachers who maintain a strictly defined relationship. The teacher is a *guru par excellance* who leads the way, whether through the beauty of Japanese *haiku* poetry (usually associated with Zen) or in long hours of meditation.

Each monastic tradition relies on the same symbols of authority, but has cultural variations. For example, the robe is a dominant symbol of the Buddha's renunciation and enlightenment and is worn by *bhikkhus* in Mahayana and Theravada schools alike. However, the color of the robe may vary from country to country. In North America, the importance of color continues. Korean *bhikkhus* wear gray robes. Ceylonese Theravada and Chinese Mahayana monks wear ochre (yellow-orange, a sacred color). B.C.A. ministers, adapting to Western culture, have adopted the black robe, a symbol of authority and respect in both academic and ecclesiastical circles.

Theravada Buddhism in North America

In 1893 a group of Theravada monks and laity from Ceylon (now identified as Sri Lanka) addressed the Parliament of Religions in Chicago, a prestigious gathering of clergy and laity from the major religions. They spoke of the significance of the historical Buddha and represented the oldest continuous school of Buddhism in existence. This was the first time that Theravada Buddhists had been received popularly in North America.[8]

By 1893 in American and European intellectual circles, the Pali canon was already known. In 1844 a Frenchman, Eugene Burnouf, had translated part of the canon into French. Earlier, a Hungarian (Alexander Csoma de Koros) and two Englishmen (Brian Hodgson and George Turnour) had independently collected scripture in Nepal, Tibet, and Ceylon.[9] However, by far the most notable of all the Pali scholars were Hermann Oldenberg and T. W. Rhys Davids. Oldenberg published an edition of the Vinaya between 1879 and 1883.[10] Davids was the founder of the Pali Text Society, which was dedicated to the collection and publication of remaining Pali texts.

While these scholars labored on Buddhist scripture, a lay Theravada missionary, Anagarika Dharmapala, traveled in Europe, China, and the United States.[11] Dharmapala urged both the reform and the revitalization of the *sangha*. He organized the Maha Bodhi Society in 1891, one of the first international Buddhist societies.

Dharmapala sought the continuation of a monastic way of life integral to the Theravada tradition. He saw the Buddha as a source of authority and the way of the elder, or monk *(thera)*, as a model for a perfected life that could be brought to the West.

Dharmapala sought reforms in the *sangha* that increased the role of the laity. In so doing he departed from traditional Theravada practice in which the laity have only played supportive roles, leaving the pursuit of total renunciation, or leadership, to the *bhikkhus*. Assuming authority for precipitating change, he looked to the *sangha* as a co-partner in reform.

Lay Participation

While Dharmapala's programs were not as successful as he would have liked, they initiated a model of lay involvement that has been carried abroad. After 1965, when devotees from Theravada countries immigrated to the United States, many in the spirit of these reforms sought the establishment of *viharas*. Continuing the traditional support of the *sangha*, they have, in cooperation with their governments' embassies, helped fund the presence of monks in the West.

Lay Buddhists and members of the *sangha* frequently cooperate in maintaining Theravada values, adapting them to a Western society. In most Theravada countries, for example, begging is an important and expected function of the *bhikkhu*. In North America, most *bhikkhus* prefer not to beg, in order to avoid misunderstandings with persons who are not aware of the dignity of the tradition. Instead, a *thera* may receive food offerings from the laity. These offerings are usually left at the temple door. As in most Theravada countries, monks need not acknowledge the gift of food which lay devotees are expected to provide. Through the gift of food offerings, however, the laity acquire merit and assure their own reward.

The accrual of merit is a cross-cultural phenomenon that is part of Buddhist and Hindu traditions. The roots of the process are found in the theory of *karma*, which states that rewards in the form of more positive rebirths are directly related to the good works done now. Likewise, demerit results when the basic moral laws of the universe (including the virtues of compassion and non-violence) are broken. Thus, among Thai, Burmese, and Ceylonese supplicants, the laity vicariously participate in the renunciation of monks by supporting their daily regimen. Members of the *sangha* continue to be symbols of utmost purity and authority.

For this reason the presence of Theravada monks in North America is vital to the tradition. In wedding ceremonies and in the variety of ritualistic services that monks perform, the lay person is offered a chance to gain merit.

Continuing Reform

The close association of laity and clergy in North America has been influenced by reforms in each Theravada country. Among Ceylonese-Americans, for example, the tradition of the monk as an educator results from continuing reforms in Sri Lanka during the last eighty years. As *bhikkhus* founded numerous colleges and universities, monks became both teachers and administrators. This increased their visibility and influence in the society. While such reforms enhanced the developing role of the clergy, they also reflected a new interest in the laity. Lay devotees such as Dharmapala sought total reforms in the tradition and the expansion of Buddhist education. In North America, laity and clergy, continuing the efforts begun by Dharmapala and others, participate in a mutual process of education and revitalization.

For Thai devotees, a similar tradition of close association between the *sangha* and laity has existed for nearly 200 years. As a result of reforms in the Thai *sangha* during the eighteenth and nineteenth centuries, monks became active educators and developed their image as sectarian organizers in the United States.

The Thai Buddhist monks and laity share in the task of establishing temples (called *wats*) in different parts of the country. Temples have been built in North Hollywood, California, and Silver Spring, Maryland.[12] As evidence of the broad dimensions of this interaction, the Thai government has joined with the government of Sri Lanka to support a *vihara* in Washington, D.C.

Continuing Traditions

The establishment of temples and the securing of monks assures members of this developing community that important customs will continue. In the Thai Buddhist tradition, the *thera* is a symbol of authority. He represents a way of life so pervasive that for centuries Theravada Buddhism has been a national religion in Thailand. In the United States the *thera* holds the same respected role. He is an earthly representative of the model of devotion and discipline begun by the Buddha. He follows the Middle Way with great dignity and pride. Moreover, he is a symbol of the stability of Thai culture in a Western environment.

As a result of the redefinition of the *sangha* and the expansion of lay support in Burma, Thailand, and Sri Lanka, some *bhikkhus* have become international figures. Like Anagarika Dharmapala in 1893, they are highly educated, well-informed persons who spread Theravada doctrine throughout Europe and the United States.

In 1964, a Ceylonese monk and missionary, the Most Venerable Madihe Pannaseeha, visited the United States.[13] A year later the Sasana Sevaka Society, a large, prestigious monastic association in Sri Lanka, sent another monk to Washington, D.C., to develop the Buddhist Vihara Society. Since 1968, additional monks have entered North America. Theravada societies and temples have been organized in Toronto and Los Angeles.

The activities of these *viharas* and the *bhikkhus* who direct them are varied. Lectures are frequent. Often there are classes in Sanskrit and Pali. Festivals are celebrated as part of the temple's ritualistic life.

The Washington Buddhist Vihara

The Washington Buddhist Vihara (Washington, D.C.) is in a house once owned by the government of Thailand. Since 1968 the temple has become a center for meditation, study, and retreat for hundreds of Theravada Buddhists in the United States. Organized with the help of the governments of Sri Lanka (Ceylon), Thailand, and the Sasana Sevaka Society, the temple is the first of its kind in the United States.

Leadership of the Vihara has included the Venerable Dr. Dichwela Piyananda, a monk and teacher. Dr. Piyananda holds the title of *Mahathera* ("Great Elder") among Buddhist clergy in Sri Lanka. After a career as monk, college founder, administrator, and teacher, he came to the United States to begin a *vihara*. Mahathera Piyananda came to North America to repay a personal debt to Col. Henry Steale Olcott, who emigrated from the United States to Sri Lanka in the latter part of the nineteenth century in order to experience Theravada Buddhism first hand.

Mahathera Piyananda's parents were close friends of Col. Olcott, whom he knew as a child. With deep affection for his parents' close friend, Dr. Piyananda arrived in Washington in 1967, owning little more than his saffron robe, the traditional garb of the Theravada Buddhist monk, who has sworn vows of poverty. He had never been in North America and had seldom traveled outside South Asia where he had built a career as an educator and a school administrator. Though anxious about his unfamiliarity with the West and the difficulties of working in an English-speaking country, Dr. Piyananda quickly adapted to life in the United States. He describes the experience:

> By happy coincidence I discovered that my fears were totally unfounded. With the assistance from my admirable colleague, Ven. Gunaratna, I have

lived to see the Washington Buddhist Vihara grow by leaps and bounds. Not only was I given the means and encouragement to obtain the Doctor of Philosophy degree from the Catholic University of America, but I found that true friends consisting both of American supporters and followers of my own faith, were always at hand to inspire and direct my efforts. Today, the Vihara, with its emphasis on the precepts of Theravada Buddhism, is not only a haven for those who seek spiritual renewal, but for those who desire instruction in Pali, Sanskrit, meditation, the tenets of Buddhism, and the Buddhist history and culture. Now that I am nearing the seventy-year mark on life's yardstick, I can truly look back and say that my years of service on behalf of the Buddha's work and mission have brought deep joy, satisfaction and fulfillment. These experiences, added to those gained in Toronto, Canada, where I assisted in the establishment of still another Buddhist Vihara, has [sic] taught me that life can be truly blessed if one has fast friends, devoted colleagues, and firm faith in the goodness of man and in the power of the mind to transcend the trivial.

Therefore, even as the moon follows the path of the constellations one should follow the wise, the intelligent, the learned, the much enduring, the dutiful, the noble: such a good and wise man one should follow.[14]

For this monk, fulfillment is found in following the ideal of the *arhant*, the spiritually disciplined and academically trained ascetic, who is free from all attachment. The monk lives in poverty, wanting neither material possessions nor emotional ties. Taking great pride in teaching the great truths of his tradition, he educates the laity in matters of language, culture, and meditation. Fulfilling this role, this *bhikkhu* continued his graduate education in the United States and helped establish two *viharas*. As a follower of the ascetic tradition of Gautama, he practiced a life of renunciation in North America similar to that which he knew in Sri Lanka. With the help of lay Buddhists, his *viharas* have become centers of Ceylonese culture and the Theravada ecumenical spirit.

The Traveling *Bhikkhu*

The Theravada *bhikkhu* in North America has expanded a century-old tradition of Buddhist practice in the United States and Canada. With the resurgence of the *sangha* in Theravada countries, the scholastic and devotional tradition of the teacher-monk has become international. *Viharas* have been established in the West Indies, Greece, and Europe. The continuation of the tradition in the United States, where Buddhism has developed rapidly, is expected.

Links with orthodoxy and tradition are maintained through visits of traveling *bhikkhus* from Asia. Like the Chinese Buddhist monk who journeys from Taiwan to New York to revitalize the religious communities of his followers, so Theravada *bhikkhus* visit *viharas* in the United States and Canada. Their presence is a dramatic and authoritative link with the parent tradition.

At times, they are asked to participate in the ritualistic life of the community. One Burmese monk, for example, conducted a service of ordination at the Washington Buddhist Vihara.[15] The rite was performed in a traditional manner. In Burma the candidate would mount a horse and enter the monastery much as Gautama renounced the world by riding Kanthaka when he left his palace. In this case, a horse was impractical, but other symbols of the tradition were maintained. The candidate removed his clothes—symbolically abandoning material wealth and the secular world. He donned the robe of the *bhikkhu*. His head and eyebrows were shaven in a sign of complete humility and renunciation. He was given a new name. According to tradition, he no longer would be considered a member of his family. Instead, beginning a new life, he renounced everything he had loved or known. To his parents, who took great pride in such important occasions, their son had begun a new life.

The monks who perform such rites often conduct a daily routine similar to that of monks in Theravada countries.

> 4:30 a.m.—Food offerings.
> 8:00 a.m.—Reception of guests.
> 10:30 a.m.—Meal.
> 12:00 noon to 1:00 p.m.—Performance of ceremonial offices.
> 2:00 to 5:30 p.m.—Rest period.
> 7:30 p.m.—Sermon and meditation session.[16]

Significantly, this schedule is designed intentionally to benefit the laity. The food offerings provide the donor merit. The sermon and meditation session are instructive; they are designed to facilitate devotion and to enhance interest in the faith.

The Theravada *bhikkhu* links Buddhism in North America to a tradition and a way of life dating back to the original Indian forms of Buddhist piety. The monk is a symbol of the perseverance of tradition and the revitalization of an ideal that before 1893 was rarely encountered outside of Theravada countries. Skilled in the ancient tongues of Sanskrit and Pali, the *bhikkhu* is an advocate of Buddhist scholarship and education. His yellow robes and shaven head symbolize a complete withdrawal from the mundane world. His skills as an organizer and a teacher permit him to carry his ancient tradition 12,000 miles beyond his home, establishing new institutions similar to those in which he was educated and trained.

The Buddhist Churches of America

The Buddhist Churches of America (B.C.A.) is a denomination affiliated with the Jodo Shinshu school of Pure Land Buddhism.[17] This tradition, popular in China and Japan, is a major Mahayana sect. While Pure Land Buddhists acknowledge and revere the teachings of the historical Buddha, they worship Amida Buddha, the deified guardian of a Buddhist heaven known as the Western Paradise or the Pure Land. This concept of the Western Paradise was popularized in Japan by a twelfth-century reformer, Shinran Shonin.

Shinran spread the doctrine of the *nembutsu*, a prayer or incantation containing the words "Nama Amida Butsu" ("Praise to Amida Buddha"). By repeating the *nembutsu* devotees thus praise Amida Buddha and, according to Jodo Shinshu doctrine, are lifted into the Pure Land upon death. The Pure Land, often painted as a paradise, is understood as both a heaven and as the capacity for enlightenment, or *nirvana*, within every devotee.

In the twelfth century, Shinran began his quest for enlightenment by entering the Tendai monastery at Mount Hiei. Tendai was the prestigious Pure Land sect in Japan at that time. Studying the rigorous teachings

Shinran Shonin

Shinran Shonin, founder of
the Jodo Shinshu school
of Pure Land Buddhism.

of this monastic Buddhist tradition, he became dissatisfied, and instead sought out a master, Honen, who was an influential teacher in the Pure Land school. As Honen's popularity grew, both men were forced into exile by members of the *sangha* who feared them. In isolation from his master, Shinran synthesized his own theology and doctrine, which became the foundation of Jodo Shinshu beliefs. He became a master of his own school, writing treatises and training disciples. Eventually returning to Kyoto, where he had met Honen, Shinran was pardoned.

Shinran identified himself with a historical line of Pure Land teachers and patriarchs in India (Nagarjuna and Vasabandhu), China (T'an-luan and T'ao-ch'o), and Japan (Genshin and Honen). Each patriarch, from Nagarjuna in the second century to Honen in the fourteenth, was a dominant figure in his culture and religion. By linking their doctrines with his own, Shinran assured that his reforms would be accepted in the larger Mahayana tradition.

Shinran's Teachings in North America

Jodo Shinshu in the United States was started in 1898 when a branch of the Young Men's Buddhist Association was chartered in San Francisco. The Y.M.B.A., a strong Buddhist organization in many parts of Asia, propounded the teachings of the Buddha. The Y.M.B.A. in San Francisco brought isolated members of the Jodo Shinshu faith together. Later, in 1899, Abbot Myonyo Shonin in Kyoto sent two ministers to the United States.[18] This came at a time when large numbers of Japanese emigrated to the United States, many of whom were eager to farm.

By 1900 this Buddhist missionary effort had grown. The Y.M.B.A. established its headquarters in San Francisco, and started two satellite temples—one in Fresno and one near Sacramento. By 1910, a larger building was erected in San Francisco. This church (see page 73) remains the oldest Jodo Shinshu temple in North America.

The religion spread rapidly. In 1915 a group of Buddhist bishops met President Woodrow Wilson in Washington D.C. The Church now included centers in twenty-five cities from Los Angeles to Seattle. Jodo Shinshu ministers, trained in Japan, kept devotees aware of their cultural identity and background. The Church and the Y.M.B.A. played an important part in the cohesiveness of the Japanese-American community. At a time when the press spoke of the Asian "menace" and called for the expulsion of all Orientals, Jodo Shinshu temples became centers of tradition, refuge, and solidarity.

This was especially important as tensions heightened over Japanese immigrants on the West Coast. By 1907, these pressures had resulted in federal legislation (Immigration Act of February 20, 1907) that sought to exclude Japanese laborers from entering the United States through neighboring countries. In the same year the United States government quietly began talks with Japan to restrict passports issued to laborers. These negotiations became the basis for severe reductions in Japanese immigration.

In addition, in 1911 a treaty between the United States and Japan (Treaty of February 21, 1911) denied Japanese immigrants the right to own land for agricultural purposes. This restriction was strengthened by alien land acts in states with large populations of Japanese, including California and Washington. The land acts not only prohibited Japanese from owning farms, but prevented them from entering into contracts with U.S. citizens who did.[19]

In the next decade, demands for the exclusion of Japanese on the West Coast grew stronger. The Japanese Exclusion League of California, organized in 1919, called for even tighter controls on immigration.[20] This was coupled with the demands of other exclusionists for the expulsion of all Asiatics including Chinese, Japanese, and "Hindus," who were commonly perceived as a menace to labor and society in the United States. The Immigration Act of 1924 was a final decisive measure. The Act

San Francisco Buddhist Church, San Francisco, California.

established a national origins quota system. Excluded from the quotas, which were based on questions of race, were persons deemed ineligible for citizenship, including Japanese.

As these and other restrictions increased and immigration from Japan to the United States became more difficult, Japanese Buddhists were forced to depend more on themselves. By 1930, dependence on Jodo Shinshu ministers from Japan had decreased.

Japanese born in the United States, or *nisei*, were permitted to train for the clergy. These future ministers began their Buddhist education in the West and completed it in Japan, offering their congregations the benefits of both cultures, and a tie with language, belief, and doctrine centuries old. However, most Jodo Shinshu ministers were still sent from Japan for several years at a time. The clergy were often born into the faith and raised by families who expected the eldest son to continue an inherited position as priest of the local temple. For these persons the opportunity to come to the United States as missionaries presented a chance to extend religious and cultural traditions to devotees who had immigrated to North America.

In an attempt to link the U.S. Jodo Shinshu mission with the broader authority of Mahayana tradition, leaders undertook a pilgrimage to Kyoto in 1935. There they met with other Mahayana priests and ministers and with officials of the government of Thailand (Siam). This series of conferences produced a direct and internationally recognized link between Buddhist organizations in Asia and the West. As a result, a *stupa*—which by tradition houses ashes of the Buddha—was planned in San Francisco.[21] Built on top of the San Francisco Buddhist Church (see page 73), the *stupa* was a visible link with the larger Buddhist faith. For devotees, the event symbolized the permanence of the Jodo Shinshu tradition in the United States.

The feeling of growth did not last for long. In seven years the United States was at war with Japan, placing the fortunes of Japanese-Americans in jeopardy. For most Japanese-Americans the Second World War was a terrible experience. Herded into camps where only the barest minimum of belongings were allowed, many lost all their possessions and property. Community networks were dissolved or fragmented.

Difficulties began soon after the Japanese attack on Pearl Harbor. All persons of Japanese descent were carefully scrutinized. Buddhist ministers, as community leaders with great influence, frequently were viewed with suspicion. As fear increased and the American public cried for revenge, the Buddhist community reacted chaotically. Some Buddhists removed family shrines from their homes and discarded tracts of scripture; anything Japanese or Buddhist had the danger of being labeled un-American.[22]

Buddhist clergy made daily calls to the Federal Bureau of Investigation and other government agencies hoping to convince authorities that they were loyal citizens who posed no threat to national security.[23] Some talked of changing the name of the organization from the "Buddhist Mission of North America" to the current title "Buddhist Churches of America" to emphasize their loyalty.

The efforts of the clergy were unsuccessful. Beginning in February, 1942, and lasting through that spring, persons of Japanese descent living in the United States were directed (by Executive Order 9066) first to Assembly Centers and then to detention camps, which were identified as "Relocation Centers."

Life in the camps was arduous. Detainees were cut off from friends and the neighborhoods they had known. The camps were built in remote sections of the country, far from the large cities where most Japanese had settled. Some detention centers in the Southwest were erected in the desert where temperatures during the day reached well above 100°.

There were few ways of continuing patterns of daily worship in captivity. Many home altars, which are an important part of Jodo Shin-shu worship, had been destroyed or placed in storage. One detainee, forced to improvise, constructed a makeshift altar out of pieces of metal found in the desert.[24] Others did without.

These difficulties were compounded by the threat to sectarian identity when members of different Buddhist groups were forced to worship together.[25] Children who were educated into the tradition while in the camps found such patterns of joint worship confusing. Since Pure Land Buddhists venerate Amida Buddha, prayers to the historical Buddha, Gautama, were a source of frustration.

Out of this traumatic experience, however, a fresh awareness of the temple as a source of strength and solidarity arose. In the face of hostility, Jodo Shinshu institutions stood as vital, integrating, and supportive centers of tradition. Temples were transformed into storehouses where families could leave their possessions. However, with the worshiping community in detention, many temples were subsequently burglarized and their contents lost. In the camps themselves, Jodo Shinshu priests brought hope to many. The Western Paradise of Amida Buddha became a symbol of salvation to come, while meditation offered a way of coping with the harsh environment of the camps.

The recovery of the community after the war was quick. Within ten months after the declaration of peace, 110,000 Japanese-Americans had returned home. Most who came back were forced to start over again. Family fortunes had been depleted, property vandalized, and spirits reduced. However, the process of rebuilding took precedence over all other concerns. For the Jodo Shinshu temples, it meant a chance to revitalize and reaffirm a unique Buddhist history.

Buddhist leaders quickly took charge after the detention centers were

Buddhist Churches of America National Headquarters, San Francisco, California.

closed, opening their temples to aid the resettlement.[26] Temples were transformed into hostels where food, shelter, and companionship could be found. Upon release from the camps, most detainees had no place to go and few funds were available. Help from the government was minimal and in most cases amounted to a token sum (frequently twenty-five dollars) handed out upon release. The hostels were thus a welcome sight. By 1949 most of the temples were helping the Japanese re-assimilate into society. The clergy took an active role in the process, securing food and jobs for the laity.

After the war a remarkable change occurred in temple organization. Incorporating under a new name, the Buddhist Churches of America, temples now saw themselves as churches (although both designations continued to be used), and worked hard to become an accepted part of the communities around them. This change was precipitated by an intense desire to establish permanent roots. Even those persons who had suffered in the camps now looked on the United States as a home. One Jodo Shinshu bishop, for example, after a difficult experience in the Topaz detention center where his wife had died, wrote the following inscription which was later placed on his own tombstone a few years later:

> Bury my ashes
> In the soil of America
> And into Eternity
> May the Dharma prosper.[27]

He now felt the United States was to be his permanent home.

After the war, many members expressed similar sentiments. In 1948 the B.C.A. held a Golden Jubilee, celebrating its roots in the United States.

The Church sought stronger ties with U.S. companies. Realizing the dangers of financial collapse by many Japanese-American-owned businesses that were just recovering economic stability, the Church entered into agreement with large corporations. In 1949, the B.C.A. negotiated a contract with the Union Oil Company facilitating the purchase of gasoline, kerosene, cleaning solvents, and other necessary goods for the operation of its temples. This agreement helped to revitalize the churches.

For the lay devotee who lived through the camp experience and the changes that took place afterwards during the resettlement, such ties were important. They symbolized a new recognition of Japanese citizens who celebrated their Buddhist heritage and their loyalty to the United States. In keeping with this new image, the clergy stressed their role as ministers, while individual churches adopted educational programs similar to those in the denominational life of other traditions.

The new Church offered devotees a way of educating their children as Buddhists. Many had never seen Japan and as *nisei* were born in the United States. Through Sunday school programs and the development of curricula, the Church now offered its members the flavor of Protestantism and a way of participating in accepted patterns of denominational life.

Moreover, the denomination was assured of social acceptance. By giving its devotees all of the elements of the status quo including Sunday morning worship and community dinners, it downplayed the image of an esoteric Oriental religion. For the general public who understood little about Buddhism this reduced apprehension and helped nullify the popular image of suspicion and mistrust that Asian immigrants so frequently encountered.

By the early 1950s, attitudes in the United States towards Japanese and other Asian peoples had begun to soften. Legislators voiced concern for the removal of restrictions against Japanese immigration. In 1952, Congress passed the Immigration and Nationality Act. In the same spirit as earlier legislation directed at Chinese (1943) and Indians (1946), this act gave Japan (and other Asian countries) a token annual quota.[28] However, like the other acts, this was only a minor step toward the liberalization of immigration restrictions, which occurred in 1965 when the national origins quota system was eliminated.

Throughout the decade, the Buddhist Churches of America continued to rebuild and revitalize the denomination. In 1959, the Church built its present headquarters at 1710 Octavia Street in San Francisco.

Housing the administrative offices, the center replaced a two-room location that had been used since 1938. Like the *stupa* erected twenty-four years earlier, this building symbolized the permanent presence of the Jodo Shinshu tradition in the United States.

Jodo Shinshu Worship

Gassho, or prayer, is a familiar term to any member of the Buddhist Churches of America. When in the course of temple worship a B.C.A. minister declares that it is time for *gassho,* worshipers place their folded hands in a circle of beads known as the *juzu.*[29] Juzus are made of materials such as glass, jade, and sandalwood. A formal *juzu* has 108 beads, which in Hindu and Buddhist circles is a holy number. However, the number of beads used in most *juzus* in North America is either 54 (one-half) or—more often—27 (one-quarter). The *juzu* is similar to a rosary and aids the supplicant who recites the *nembutsu.*

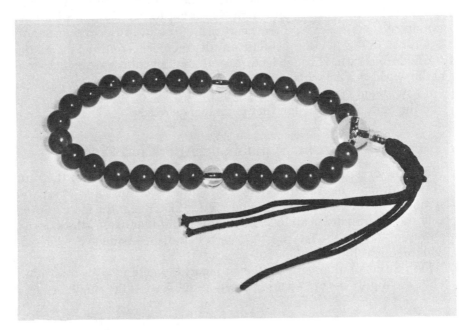

A juzu (devotional beads).
Photo: J.L. "Woody" Wooden, Tucson, Arizona.

Gassho is an important part of faith *(shinjin)* and salvation in the Pure Land.

The visitor to any of the B.C.A. churches and temples in the United States is often aware of the unique blend of Japanese culture and North American religious traditions in each Sunday morning service. The minister, for example, performs a function similar to that of Protestant clergy. He addresses the congregation in a homily. There are also creeds and hymns.

However, in the midst of the worship the minister calls for a period of meditation. Here, all similarities to Christian doctrine or ritual end. The congregation join "in *gassho*" as a gong reverberates throughout the temple. The pungent smell of incense and the altar crafted in Japan are striking elements of a uniquely Japanese tradition.

The synthesis of East and West, though a potential source of conflict, has given the Buddhist Churches of America flexibility. The external symbols of religion, the use of creeds, seminary-trained ministers, and services on Sunday mornings, have helped it appear as part of the mainstream of denominational life in the United States. This has enabled the Church to disseminate the teachings of the Buddha beyond ethnic neighborhoods to an extent that other forms of Buddhism have not always achieved. Yet, the heart of the tradition remains uniquely Buddhist. In B.C.A. churches and temples members continue to practice the Eightfold Path. Through lectures and seminars they are taught to look at the world in a detached way. Like the historical Buddha, their path to enlightenment is inward, away from the turmoil of suffering and greed and the pain of the illusion that permanence exists.

Jodo Shinshu Symbolism: Altars and Creeds

While the organizational structure and pattern of worship of the Buddhist Churches of America reflect a synthesis of East and West, the symbols within the faith are uniquely Buddhist. By far the most impressive and meaningful of all B.C.A. symbols is the altar itself—the external representation of the internal "Western Paradise" inside every devotee who practices the *nembutsu*.

Jodo Shinshu altars are crafted in Japan in keeping with tradition.[30] They are highly decorated and placed at the head of the sanctuary on a

Altar, Berkeley Buddhist Church, Berkeley, California.

platform. Usually a standing image of Amida Buddha occupies a central position on the altar, symbolically protecting the Pure Land. Candles symbolize the light of Amida, while incense conveys his regal nature. According to tradition, the candles contain no animal fat, in keeping with the Buddha's emphasis on strict non-violence, which forbids contact with any animal by-products. Members of this tradition enforce these prohibitions, assuring that the altar is not defiled. Flowers placed on the altar remind the supplicant of the impermanence of all life.

Creeds, much like the altar, interpret the function of the holy. They identify the nature of the sacred and the devotee's expectations from regular worship.

The Daily Creed of Jodo Shinshu, used in member churches of the B.C.A. denomination, fulfills several of these functions. First, it identifies Amida Buddha, who is experienced through the repetition of his name. Then, it reflects on the human condition and the need of a compassionate teacher. The Right Path and the True Teachings identify the method through which the devotee seeks enlightenment. The Creed ends with a statement of compassion, a basic tenet of all Mahayana traditions.

Printed in English, the Creed helps persons born outside Japan understand the significance of the tradition:

> I affirm my Faith in Amida's Infinite Wisdom
> and Compassion. Reciting his Sacred Name,
> I shall live with strength and joy.
>
> I shall look up to Amida's Guiding Light. As I
> reflect upon my imperfect self, I live with
> gratitude for His Perfect Compassion, which
> surrounds me at all times.
>
> I shall follow Amida's Teachings. I shall
> understand the Right Path and resolve to spread
> the true Teachings.
>
> I rejoice in Amida's Wisdom and Compassion. I
> shall respect and help my fellow men and work for
> the good of my community.[31]

Unity and Diversity in B.C.A. Temples and Churches

The uniformity of doctrine and ritual is apparent to any visitor to a B.C.A. temple or church. Each institution exhibits a common interpretation of important Mahayana doctrines and is part of a larger denominational structure.

However, each structure is also unique. Some exhibit strong Japanese influence. Others are more westernized in their architecture and organization. Three examples of the unity and diversity of B.C.A. temples and churches in California are those in San José, Palo Alto, and San Mateo.

The San José Buddhist Church Betsuin

The word *betsuin* is important to members of the San José Buddhist Church Betsuin. It designates the center of a district established by the Buddhist Churches of America to facilitate denominational organization. *Betsuin* temples frequently are strong institutions with important histories. The San José Buddhist Church Betsuin, for example, is one of the largest and oldest B.C.A. churches in the United States. Founded in 1902, it had grown by 1977 to include 1,250 families in fifteen communities.

The San José Buddhist Church Betsuin is uniquely Japanese. A traditional Japanese garden next to the temple symbolizes the value of cultural traditions. Stocked with Koi—fish bred and collected in Japan for their beauty and color—the garden and pond are carefully maintained. A prominent member of the Japanese-American community in San José attends the site each day. As he prunes the foliage to exacting standards and measures the water temperature, he symbolically serves Amida Buddha. The garden and the pond are kept in perfect balance and harmony. They represent the tranquility of Amida's Pure Land and are a lasting source of merit, which is accrued from their care. The garden also symbolizes the vitality of Japanese culture and the Buddhist values of harmony and tranquility. The pond is much like the analogy of the wandering ox, popular in Zen.[32] The ox, often uncontrollable, is rarely at rest. Like the conscious mind, it darts from one activity to another, refusing to be tethered. Yet, through the Middle Way, the ox can be stilled. In much the same manner the meticulously groomed garden and quiet pond tame elements of nature. Unlike fast noisy streams or rivers that often overflow their banks, water in the pond symbolizes the inner peace of the Pure Land.

The altar in the temple represents classical Japanese religious art. Decorative panels conceal the iconographic representation of the Pure Land.

The immediate area surrounding the San José temple reflects many elements of Japanese culture. A gallery next door sponsors exhibits of *bonzai*. Japanese dance and drama are frequently performed in the neighborhood. Restaurants serve Japanese food. While these elements of tradition are not always easy to maintain, the San José church attempts to protect and preserve its heritage.

San Jose Buddhist Church Betsuin, San Jose, California.

Traditional Japanese garden, San Jose Buddhist Church Betsuin, San Jose, California. The pond is stocked with valuable fish imported from Japan.

Interior, San Jose Buddhist Church Betsuin, San Jose, California, showing traditional carving and modern pews.

The Palo Alto Buddhist Church

In contrast to the San José Buddhist Church Betsuin, the Palo Alto Buddhist Church is a highly westernized temple. While still preserving Buddhist values and tradition, it has adopted a role similar to other religious institutions in the United States. The church is in a suburban neighborhood not far from Stanford University. Its membership consists of middle-class, white-collar professionals. Many are young married couples who are highly acculturated, mobile persons.

The church hosts a wide range of activities that resemble those of other religious institutions in similar settings. A youth group (Junior Young Buddhist Association) goes on ski trips. Youth workshops on drugs and other programs of social value are presented. Adult forums are often held.

The Palo Alto Buddhist Church draws members from a wide geographical area. The minister spends much time in adjacent communities where new members are frequently found. In these locations he conducts worship in devotees' homes.

The San Mateo Buddhist Church

The San Mateo Buddhist Church exhibits an equal blend of Western influence and Japanese tradition. The church is located in an ethnic neighborhood in this community south of San Francisco.

A minister, as the oldest son in his family, inherited the position of priest. Born into the tradition, his father was a Jodo Shinshu priest in Japan and a B.C.A. minister in the United States. He stressed the importance of linguistic traditions, remarking that it is difficult to preach in English when often the same concept in Japanese can be said in a single word.

The San Mateo Buddhist Church stresses Buddhist education. Each year the church hosts a lecture series for which scholars and sectarian officials are brought to San Mateo. These spiritual leaders are a source of orthodoxy and tradition, often clarifying theological and doctrinal perspectives.

In sum, each church combines important elements of the larger Mahayana tradition to meet local needs. The Palo Alto Church adopts the *dhamma* to a highly mobile middle-class population. The San José Buddhist Church Betsuin, as the headquarters of a B.C.A. district, preserves symbols of Japanese Buddhist culture. The altar, pond, and garden are visual reminders of Mahayana values of peace and inner harmony. For devotees, they also represent the Pure Land. The San Mateo church, stressing the value of education, helps its members understand their role in the *sangha*. The celebration of Sangha Day in this church enables children born in the United States to become familiar with elements of dress, language, and art integral to Japanese culture. Local churches such as that in San Mateo are aided in this work by organizations such as the Young Buddhist League, which holds conventions of as many as 1,000 persons. Similarly, scouting programs such as the Association of Japanese Boy Scouts organize tours of Japan where important temples and cultural centers may be visited. As evidence of this continuing concern for youth, the Buddhist Churches of America maintains a Department of Education, which provides curricula for local churches as well as speakers, films, and other resources. Through these efforts, each church maintains ties with a cross-cultural tradition and continues to acculturate children and adults into the faith.

The Revitalization of Chinese Buddhism

Chinese Buddhism (a Mahayana tradition), more than 125 years old in the United States, is a developing religion.[33] Since 1965 monks from

San Mateo Buddhist Church, San Mateo, California.

Taiwan and Hong Kong where the tradition has flourished have been sent to North America to revitalize and reorganize the *sangha*. Since the resumption of diplomatic relations with mainland China this trend will undoubtedly increase. Temples, once confined to rooms in tiny Chinatown shops, are being constructed outside ethnic communities. For example, in a section of New York's Catskill mountains dotted by abandoned farm houses and fields, three monks have established a small monastery. Converting a frame house into a retreat center where they live and meditate, the monks serve a large temple two miles away. None of the three *bhikkhus* speak English. The monk in charge of the monastic community has worked in Taiwan. Now middle-aged, he was responsible for training hundreds of monks before coming to the United States. The others are from Southeast Asia, showing the interdependence of the *sangha* in a new environment. From this base, monks travel to temples in New York City and in upstate New York.

Temple Mahayana, less than two miles from this monastic community, is one of the largest and newest Chinese Buddhist temples on the East Coast. Maintained by the Eastern States Buddhist Association in New York City, the temple represents efforts of Chinese Buddhists to revitalize their tradition. This temple, like many others, is a self-contained environment where religious and cultural traditions can be maintained without Western contact or interference. For example, cooks who serve a small apartment in the temple for visiting monks speak little or no English and prepare traditional Chinese dinners. A caretaker finds in the temple an environment where he can maintain the type of life he once knew in Asia. Temple grounds contain numerous shrines to different popular Chinese Buddhist *bodhisattvas.* Each shrine is constructed like a village temple in China with little Western architectural influence. A lake on the property is a tranquil reminder of the Buddhist value of serenity and inner peace.

Temple Mahayana is a T'ien-T'ai institution reflecting the doctrines of a major Chinese Buddhist sect. T'ien-T'ai Buddhism, named after the mountain in China where it first was adopted, is a highly structured, orthodox tradition that recognizes the Lotus Sutra as a source of authority. Supplicants often worship the *bodhisattva* Kwan-Yin, popularly conceived as a goddess of mercy in South and East Asia. In Indian Buddhism, Kwan-Yin was originally conceived as Avalokiteswara. In Japan, she was called Kannon.

Other Chinese temples in the United States belong to the Pure Land tradition. Originating in the fifth and sixth centuries B.C., Pure Land Buddhism was spread in China by a succession of patriarchs. Urging the recitation of Amitabha Buddha's name they offered salvation to their devotees. In the eleventh century, Shan Tao expanded and democratized Pure Land theology, insisting that access to the Western Paradise was available to everyone who repeated the phrase, "Namo Amito Fo," which in Japan under the reforms of Shinran Shonin became "Nama Amida Butsu." Like T'ien-T'ai temples, Pure Land shrines allow supplicants to worship individually and corporately, prostrating themselves before icons of important *bodhisattvas.* Monks lead meditation sessions and teach lay adherents cultural and religious traditions.

Before 1965, when Chinese immigration to the United States was changed radically by legislative reforms, large temples such as Temple Mahayana were virtually non-existent. Now, since more than 75,000 Chinese have entered the United States between 1966 and 1977, bhikkhus and lay leaders have begun a revitalization of their tradition.

Roots in the United States

The roots of Chinese Buddhism in North America go back to the mid-nineteenth century when thousands of Chinese came to the United States looking for employment after the discovery of gold in California in 1849. Many came from Kwangtung province in southeastern China. Although the Imperial Chinese government had discouraged emigra-

Pure Land altar, Buddhist Association of America, San Francisco, California, bearing images of three *bodhisattvas* (divine beings).

tion, officials in this province ignored the ban. In the wake of the T'ai P'ing rebellion, which had left lasting economic scars, emigration was an attractive alternative. In the United States, officials in the mining and railroad industries quickly recognized the potential of the Chinese as a fresh source of labor and employed many new arrivals. This movement was formally acknowledged by the Burlingame Treaty of 1868,[34] out of which came a removal of the Imperial ban on immigration to the United States.

The Chinese immigrant brought ancient religious traditions to North America including Buddhism and Taoism. Popular Taoism contained elements of magic, while the larger tradition had both patterns of meditation and a profound mysticism. The latter stressed the interdependent relationship between *yin* and *yang*, opposing forces in nature. The Taoist saw the basic process of the universe as one of change in which opposites, such as light and darkness, summer and winter, male and female, were part of the cosmological rhythm called the *tao*, or "way."

Many Chinese practiced both Buddhism and Taoism simultaneously. Temples that included elements of both religions were popular in China, and in some cases were built in the United States, where the dual

Che Kan Kok Temple, a Buddhist-Taoist foundation, San Francisco, California. The priest stands before the altar with icons from both traditions.

Courtesy: Marcelo M.K. Tse, Director, Che Kan Kok Temple.

Altar, Buddhist Association of America, San Francisco, California. Family names behind the altar stress the veneration of ancestors and the continuity of Chinese Buddhism in North America.

tradition is still practiced today. (See photo, page 89.) Syncretism was common in China, where popular religious practices were influenced by Buddhism, Taoism, Confucianism, and patterns of ancestor worship.

Although the Chinese did construct temples (see photo, page 91), religion for most people was decidedly more personal than institutional. The early immigrants were not so much concerned about building temples as they were about perpetuating the religious traditions practiced by the family for generations.

Many Chinese immigrants were contract laborers unable to afford the price of passage who agreed to work off the debt by making monthly payments to company representatives after they arrived. The Chinese laborers were popular with industry because they were willing to live in mining towns or railroad camps under frontier conditions. Most Chinese were hard workers who were used to laboring long hours at little pay. Further, much to the pleasure of the corporations, the Chinese were largely self-sufficient. Many spoke little English and preferred to interact only with their peers. Most prepared their own foods and were little trouble to company cooks, who had to please large numbers of men.

While the mines and the railroads were a source of steady income for the Chinese, they offered little financial or career advancement. Against these difficulties and the harsh frontier conditions, many Chinese immigrants went into business for themselves. They opened shops of many types and developed a lasting entrepreneurial tradition that gave them financial security and a growing independence from the larger society.

However, this dramatic change did not come easily. Those immigrants who arrived in the United States heavily in debt found few ways of making their fortunes—a goal that had caused many to leave their homeland. As their determination persisted, other areas of employment were soon found. In the Southwest, for example, immigrants worked for the military as civilian laborers.[35] Still others farmed while a fortunate few opened profitable businesses.

Chinese shopkeepers were frequently stereotyped as launderers or restaurateurs.[36] In reality, they worked in many small businesses. Their success was brought about by a combination of loyalties that included the family, clan, and numerous mercantile associations, which gave the minority an important element of cohesiveness. Through mutual cooperation the Chinese gained control over networks of small businesses from dry goods industries to grocery stores. Chinatowns on both coasts were marked by a new aura of prosperity as this change took place.

The growth of the Chinese minority and their religious traditions, however, was soon brought to a dramatic halt. In a backlash reaction a growing number of Caucasians feared the economic rise of Oriental populations, whom they often viewed as ignorant and divisive.

In 1882, President Chester Arthur signed the Chinese Exclusion Act

Weaverville Joss House (1869), Weaverville, California, one of the earliest examples of a Chinese Buddhist temple in North America.
Courtesy: California Historical Society.

(May 6, 1882). The Act was the first in a series of laws before 1900 that sought to prevent Chinese from immigrating to the United States. It was followed by the Scott Act (1888), which limited the ability of immigrants to return to China to visit family members, and the Geary Act (1892), which required all Chinese in the United States to hold valid certificates of residence.[37] These measures helped the government restrict immigration and at the same time keep an eye on those Chinese who remained. They came after intense public pressure in which labor organizations and the press, claiming that the Chinese made it difficult for Caucasian workers to find jobs, demanded tighter controls on immigration. Thus, in a brief ten-year period, the cries of exclusionists not only resulted in the limitation of Chinese immigration, but virtually prevented Chinese-Americans from revitalizing cultural and religious traditions by returning to visit their homeland. As a result of these measures, families were splintered and Chinese Buddhist communities in major cities were rarely revitalized.

Chinese temples in the United States continued to be maintained by lay devotees. Shopkeepers who had constructed small temples behind their stores found few *bhikkhus* to conduct worship or attract new devotees.

A quota system, instituted in 1943, did little to change the situation. The new law stipulated that incoming Chinese must be skilled workers, parents of Chinese-Americans, or spouses and children of resident aliens.[38] Little room was left for religious leaders.

Not until 1965, when U.S. immigration quotas based on race were eliminated, did noticeable revitalization of Chinese Buddhist temples begin. By 1970 the numbers of Chinese reaching the United States were more than three times larger than in 1960. New York, San Francisco, Los Angeles, and other major cities were the centers of this new influx.

The Role of the *Bhikkhus*

The *bhikkhus* who have come to North America in the last fifteen years are a highly mobile population who frequent Taiwan and Southeast Asia, in addition to temples in the United States. The *bhikkhu*, carrying the doctrinal and cultural authority of Chinese tradition to devotees in the West, reinforces a monastic ideal. He is also a strong proponent of the education of the laity.

Many U.S. Chinese temples now shun all contacts with the West, which is associated with secularism. Instead, the temple is carefully preserved as a microcosm of Chinese culture. It is enhanced with examples of art and architecture that help recreate an environment of harmony and purity where the Eightfold Path of the Buddha is a total way of life.

For Chinese-American children, the temple often represents ties with a culture that they have experienced only through their parents. One temple, for example, began a school to educate its children in a Buddhist environment. Another, in a rural area, maintains a cemetery for followers, assuring the faithful that in life and at the time of death their Chinese traditions continue.

Newer temples may be built in secluded tracts away from the influence of a Western, urban culture. Some temples on the East Coast protect their location by publicizing their activities only within the Chinese community. Chinese newspapers inform devotees of festivals, regular gatherings of the temple membership, and the construction of new institutions.

A Chinese Buddhist monk lives in a temple much as he might in Taiwan, shunning Westernization, and conducting his life in keeping with rules of the *Vinaya*. He continues the tradition of an ordered day, spending much of his time in meditation and study. Eating but twice a day he rises at five a.m. in keeping with scriptural traditions. His day begins and ends with scripture. In the morning he walks outside the temple to feed pigeons. As a *bhikkhu* he is sworn to lead a compassionate life and to show kindness and mercy for all living creatures. The birds flock around him for the handfuls of grain that he throws on the ground.

The gesture of feeding pigeons is highly symbolic. The *bhikkhu* practices *ahimsa*, or strict non-violence, much in the manner of the historical Buddha. The doctrine is maintained so strictly that adherents frown on the swatting of a fly or stepping on an ant.

Breakfast is eaten from six to seven a.m. The only other meal that will be eaten is at noon. After breakfast the *bhikkhu* writes. As the head of the temple he publishes tracts for devotees. This *bhikkhu* is also in charge of a Buddhist association in Hong Kong. Other monks in temples across North America write tracts that are distributed simultaneously in Taiwan and in the United States. Many such pieces of literature are printed in Chinese and English.

The *bhikkhu* greets visitors in the morning, who may range from devotees who worship at his shrine to dignitaries. Then, he naps.

Four o'clock is the time for meditation. Entering the temple he bows before the image of the Buddha. The meditation is followed by another period of scripture reading and by worship. He may prostrate himself as many as 500 times before the Buddha image, a feat that requires good physical condition.

The day ends at one or two a.m. He sleeps but three or four hours a day and conducts a total pattern of meditation, study, and worship that would be exhausting to any but a conditioned, trained person.

Significantly, this *bhikkhu's* routine includes no begging. Traditionally, members of the *sangha* beg for food offerings from devotees. The donation of food is a way for the giver to achieve merit and is regarded as a duty. In the United States, however, where begging is not understood as a religious act, the tradition is rarely practiced.

Because begging is not practical in the West, it is usually necessary for monastic leaders to maintain bank accounts for purchases of food and travel. The *bhikkhu* is often an international figure who is highly mobile. One teacher may be in charge of eight to ten monks on both East and West Coasts. He may also have responsibilities in Hong Kong or Taiwan. As a leader and organizer of a growing institution, he visits new temples and encourages their growth and expansion.[39]

The *bhikkhu* follows reforms begun in China. In 1928 the Chinese monk T'ai-Hsu achieved an international reputation as a lecturer in Europe and the United States.[40] Promoting the reform of the *sangha* actively, T'ai-Hsu worked with Mahayana and Theravada leaders alike, visiting Buddhist centers in South and Southeast Asia and in the West. While T'ai-Hsu's efforts did not achieve major reforms in China, they did initiate an image of the *bhikkhu* as politically and socially active—an international figure who sought to revitalize an ancient tradition. The

Communist victory in China halted reforms of the type that T'ai-Hsu had sought. The example of this world traveler is followed by monastic leaders from Taiwan and Hong Kong who are reshaping the Buddhist tradition wherever devotees are found.

In keeping with T'ai-Hsu's concerns for ecumenicity, Chinese bhikkhus frequently cooperate with other members of the sangha. Bhikkhus from Burma, Taiwan, Hong Kong, and other countries work together—at times living in the same ascetic community.

Similarly, bhikkhus have given aid to Vietnamese refugees even though they may practice different forms of Buddhism. In New York, for example, one Chinese temple has provided food, housing, and assistance in securing employment for needy refugees. In the company of monks who have traveled extensively throughout Southeast Asia, refugees find compassion and understanding. By serving the bhikkhu and working in his kitchen they help preserve the values that they have inherited.

U.S. temples also maintain an international function by publishing tracts in English and Chinese for adherents in Asia and North America. On the other hand, temples in the United States keep a library of Buddhist publications from different parts of Asia, assuring close association with leaders of the sangha and being a link in a continuing chain of Mahayana traditions around the world. The bhikkhu is frequently a reformer, promoter, and organizer. Through his efforts, the temple is not isolated from parent traditions in Asia and is a participant in change and revitalization.

Because this basic pattern of life is part of so many cultures, the regimens of a Chinese Pure Land monk and a Theravada bhikkhu are similar. Each monk, for example, plots each day carefully and lives it according to an established pattern of behavior regulated by the rules of conduct of the religious community. The Chinese master feeds pigeons in the early morning—a symbolic act that shows his concern for the sanctity of all life. He may also receive alms in a traditional manner. Similarly, the Theravada monk teaches his devotees the complexities of meditation out of concern for their well-being. His life is a model of ethical behavior and scholastic activity in its simplicity and purposefulness. The B.C.A. minister, expressing the same values, organizes classes for the lay community. He values gentleness and compassion and teaches these traits to his lay followers.

Likewise, whether it be a B.C.A. service on Sunday mornings, the water-pouring ceremony of a Theravada monk, or the solitary chanting of a Chinese Pure Land master, the Middle Way teaches detachment from the secular world. Most Buddhist clergy adhere to these values. While a Pure Land monk may retain a small savings account or a

Theravada *bhikkhu* own a few possessions, each remains detached from the material world.

Detachment does not mean that the *bhikkhu* or minister avoids life. Buddhists argue that because they have learned to live without desire and remain detached from ambition or material temptations, they are able to put more energy into tasks at hand. Meditation sharpens the mind so that powers of concentration can be directed as needed without the burden of unrestrained thoughts draining mental energy.

Perhaps the greatest commonality shared by the three forms of Buddhism surveyed in this chapter are the roots each tradition has established in North America. The Jodo Shinshu faith has an eighty-year history in the United States. Chinese Buddhism has been practiced here since the 1850s, when immigrants brought a mixture of Confucian and Buddhist ritualism to California. Theravada Buddhism, the most recent arrival, has developed *viharas* and societies intended to have a lasting presence.

Each transplanted tradition has been supported by temples and monastic organizations in Asia. Theravada monks from Sri Lanka, for example, often draw support from the *sangha* while living in the United States. Chinese Pure Land masters maintain strong ties with Buddhist universities and monastic associations in Taiwan.

In supporting U.S. temples, the *sangha* as a whole has become international and inter-cultural. Monks from Mahayana and Theravada countries visit the United States and Canada to experience the transplanted tradition firsthand. They revitalize the *sangha* in distant countries, bringing the voice of authority and orthodoxy. They assure parent temples that their efforts abroad are fruitful. These visits have important parallels in other Asian religions now active in North America. For example, the Hindu tradition of the holy man who travels from temple to temple—and, today, from South Asia to New York—is well documented. Similarly, Sikh teachers and religious leaders in the spirit of Guru Nanak (the first Guru, or prophetic leader, of the Sikh tradition) travel from Europe to East Africa, the United States, and wherever there are large populations of devotees in distant lands of their heritage and culture.

Most of the traveling *bhikkhus* are highly respected sectarian leaders or scholars who maintain active roles in Asia and the United States. One *bhikkhu*, for example, is president of a monastic association in Hong Kong and in New York. In the United States he helps to establish new temples, traveling from one city to another.

The *sangha* has become highly mobile and adaptable. Unlike the stereotype of Buddhist monasticism decades ago, which portrayed the *bhikkhu* as a static participant in tradition, the *sangha* is a dynamic federation. *Bhikkhus*, because of the international scope of the monastic tradition, do not worry about where they will sleep or what they will eat. Whether their trip is to New York's Chinatown, a farmhouse in the Catskills managed by the laity, or Taiwan, they are rarely beyond reach of their support community. These monks never stay in a hotel or motel. They always stay in Buddhist institutions, as required by the *Vinaya*, or code of conduct.

Most temples, depending on their size, are equipped to take care of the needs of any traveling *bhikkhu*. Novices cook, clean, and care for the Master's needs, earning merit by serving those in authority. Similarly, the Buddhist community in many B.C.A. churches provides a house on the temple grounds for its ministers. The temple is the guardian of tradition and the sustainer of a way of life that is centuries old. Providing goods and services for the monk or minister is an expected and widely practiced phenomenon that draws its scriptural authority from the acts of the Buddha's disciples and the laity that serves them.

The *sangha* is a close association. Frequently, Theravada and Mahayana *bhikkhus* become friends, participating in a mutual effort to transport tradition and authority to the United States. This interaction has historical roots. Prior to the Parliament of Religions in 1893, a Theravada lay devotee, Anagarika Dharmapala, visited Mahayana countries urging religious leaders to re-establish Indian Buddhist traditions. Founding the Maha Bodhi Society, which became an international Buddhist institution, Mahayana and Theravada devotees alike were urged to seek reform and renewal. Dharmapala's work was courageous and unique. It facilitated cooperation between two traditions that have often been at doctrinal odds with each other.

Similarly, Jodo Shinshu leaders in the United States met with Buddhists from Southeast Asia to secure ashes of the Buddha for a *stupa* atop the San Francisco Buddhist Church. These events and the periodic attempts to form world Buddhist federations and organizations in the last eighty years—for clergy and laity alike—illustrate the concern of Mahayanists and Theravadins for a continued close association.

In the United States, where Buddhism is a developing religion and where the *sangha* is relatively small, such close association often provides mutual support. For example, on Sixteenth Street in Washington, D.C., four different Buddhist temples are within a few miles of each other. Korean (Mahayana) and Theravada *bhikkhus* enjoy a warm relationship.

Conflicts

Despite such important ties, most Buddhist immigrants in North America have experienced difficulties in maintaining the way of life they inherited. Children drift away from the tradition and, in some cases, meet Christian groups who try to convert them.

While the threat to the preservation of tradition does not always come from proselytization, other sources are just as real. The turmoil within Chinese communities in New York and San Francisco, for example, is a persistent threat to those devotees who wish to maintain a traditional way of life. Increased instances of gang warfare and vandalism make it difficult to have programs at night. Youth are frequently more interested in secular matters than religion.

Concerned about the influence of secularism, leaders of the Buddhist Churches of America have put special emphasis on education in recent years. By adopting a Protestant model of weekend conferences, forums, seminars, and the continued use of audiovisual resources, the B.C.A. has attempted to offset decline. B.C.A. seminars offer devotees deeper and more academic discussions of important elements of the faith. Frequently, resources from the recently created Institute of Buddhist Studies, a seminary for B.C.A. clergy in Berkeley, California, are used. The Church has also developed extensive curricula about the life of the Buddha, the history of the denomination, and Buddhist doctrine. These materials are prepared in English but often incorporate elements of Japanese language and culture.

In some cases, concern for the maintenance of tradition has led to innovations such as the construction of monasteries and retreat houses by Chinese Buddhists. By offering their devotees a place of worship and relaxation away from traditional Chinatowns, leaders are more able to control the environment in which the faith is practiced. Once inside these compounds, traces of the Western world quickly vanish. English is rarely spoken. Food is prepared in traditional Chinese fashion in a total environment where architecture and landscape are reminiscent of Asia.

In some cases, any intrusion in these new centers by persons outside of the faith is discouraged. Temple locations, festivals, and celebrations are publicized only among members of the community. This attitude is a departure from normal practice where the occasional visitor is welcomed. It shows the increasing fear among persons born into the faith that their cultural and religious heritage is threatened by inroads from the "secular West." Thus, the Chinese temple tradition quietly expands unnoticed by persons outside of the ethnic community.

The mobility of the worshiping community has been a source of difficulty for members of all three Buddhist traditions. As their level of affluence and education has increased, second-, third-, and even fourth-generation families frequently move away from the Chinatowns, the Japanese communities, or other ethnic neighborhoods where they originally settled in order to improve their economic position.

Ways of meeting these problems vary. A B.C.A. minister in northern

California sought to meet the difficulty by regularly traveling to the homes of supplicants where he would conduct worship. In suburbs of Washington, D.C., Thai Buddhists have strengthened their communities by building several temples.

In each case, this diaspora is cause for concern as religious leaders strive to maintain orthodoxy and preserve tradition. A frequent remedy has been the importation of members of the *sangha* from Asia who help to revitalize the tradition. Yet even this solution has not always been successful. For third- and fourth-generation Japanese or Chinese-American devotees, few active ties remain with their homeland. The *bhikkhu* is a symbol of a way of life they never knew.

Despite these problems, the *sangha* continues to be the most important instrument of revitalization and reform for Buddhists in the United States. For Chinese Buddhists, the presence of monks from Asia inspires increased lay involvement and the construction of new temples and retreat houses. For B.C.A. leaders, the *sangha* is the corporate body of believers. In this tradition, revitalization is the responsibility of clergy and laity alike.

Finally, for Theravada monks, the *sangha* re-creates a religious and cultural environment that educates and trains laity and clergy. The *sangha* is defined as an extension of the monastic community abroad. Monks may receive living allowances and other missionary benefits from the branches of the *sangha* to which they belong.

In each of the three traditions, religion and culture are interdependent. Chinese temples may encourage language training and a continuation of Asian values. Temples become microcosms of an environment to which many lay devotees are unable to return. Similarly, B.C.A. temples frequently stress Japanese culture and tradition. Theravada *viharas* support the teaching of Sanskrit and Pali. In each instance, language, regional customs, and religion are joined together in a common matrix of tradition. For these Buddhists, temples in North America are extensions of those at home, providing a way in which persons born into the faith in Asia can continue to experience their religion and culture.

Thus, Buddhist immigrants in North America have a unique world view in which the cultural ideals of detachment and enlightenment are transmitted from one generation to the next. Because these ideals are so completely different from those of the larger U.S. culture, devotees frequently face inner turmoil. While, for example, the association of God and country might be meaningful to practitioners of the Judeo-Christian tradition, it is a non sequitur to Buddhists, who deny the existence of a life-creating God.

Even in those segments of the North American population who are not overly religious, Judeo-Christian values frequently persist. The Hindu-

Buddhist concepts of rebirth and the cyclical nature of time are completely foreign. Further, the Buddhist understanding of a direct relationship between desire and suffering is antithetical to ideals of progress and achievement common in the West.

Hence, Buddhists in North America struggle to retain a sense of belonging and purpose in an environment where their cultural ideals frequently are misunderstood. Second-, third-, and even fourth-generation devotees are forced to look beyond the United States for reinforcement of the Buddhist world view. By sponsoring Buddhist missions and visits for members of the *sangha*, who are symbols of purity and enlightenment, the tradition is maintained and rejuvenated. Children, learning the languages of their grandparents and great grandparents, are educated as Buddhists from infancy. In these and other areas many Buddhists have worked hard to maintain a rich cultural and religious heritage while at the same time looking to the United States as a new home.

Buddhism in Perspective

This chapter has traced the development of three Buddhist traditions in the United States, demonstrating their history, development, and recent growth. Each of these three forms of Buddhism has reaffirmed important symbols of the faith including the *bhikkhu* and the temple. The temple is significant because it re-creates a sacred world that is often identified with the realm of enlightenment and the *bodhisattvas*, or Buddhas, who achieve it. The *bhikkhus*, ministers, or other members of the *sangha*, are a link between this purified realm, the temporal world, and the Asian cultures of which they are a part.

Other Buddhist cultures in the United States have also relied on these symbols and have experienced simultaneous patterns of growth. For Indo-Chinese Buddhists, for instance, the authority of the *bhikkhu* and the temple are important links with their homeland. In Washington, D.C., 15,000 to 20,000 Indochinese live in ethnic neighborhoods.[41] Even though most are not affluent, devotees hope to build temples in Virginia and Maryland. Similarly, in Rye, New York, twenty Laotian families have sponsored a Buddhist monk, the first Laotian *bhikkhu* in the New York area.[42] For these refugees, the arrival of the monk, a former abbot of a temple in Laos, was a time of great celebration. The presence of a *bhikkhu* from their homeland is so important that these lay Buddhists have agreed to provide him with food and housing and are responsible for his support.

The *bhikkhu*, like others discussed in this chapter, observes the rigorous rules of the *sangha* even though in North America he may see other monks infrequently. His celibacy, patterns of diet, and reluctance to show emotions are part of an ancient tradition. The monk is perceived by his followers as a perfected being and a powerful cross-cultural symbol of the way of the Buddha.

Buddhist wheel of causation.

CHAPTER THREE

Sikhs in North America

An Overview

Sikhism, like Hinduism, is a religion of India. The Sikh faith has been linked historically with the culture of the Punjab, a region in northwest India and Pakistan with its own political, cultural, and linguistic identity.

Although Sikhs stress that their faith is distinct from Hinduism and Islam—the two major religions of India—the tradition shares a common cultural background with other religious movements in South Asia. Like Buddhism and Jainism, Sikhism developed through the reforms of one teacher who, although born a Hindu, sought a new way.

The first Sikh was a prophetic teacher named Nanak (A.D. 1469–1539). Capturing the spirit and energy of the Hindu *bhakti* movement (see page 13), which stressed the intense worship of a personal god, Nanak embarked on a career of service and discipleship.

He became identified as a guru, a figure of wisdom and authority in Hindu society.[1] Traditionally, the teacher-disciple (guru-chela) relationship has been an important part of Hinduism. Expanding this emphasis on the authority of a single teacher, Nanak associated the concept of guru with the power and insight to receive the direct revelation of God.

Guru Nanak posited the existence of one God and rejected the Hindu pantheon. He became the first founder figure of an indigenous monotheistic Indian religion. He taught his followers, whom he called Sikhs, or disciples, that God could be experienced by all persons, not just by priests or holy men. Thus, he rejected restrictions of caste, based on birth and family heritage.

As the Sikh tradition developed in the fifteenth, sixteenth, and seventeenth centuries, other Gurus succeeded Nanak. In all, ten spiritual leaders attained the position of Guru and became identified with the formative history of the faith. The ten Gurus gave the Sikh religion its scripture, organization, and a distinct sense of personal and corporate identity. The Gurus compiled poetry, hymns, and prose writings into the Guru Granth Sahib.

This sacred text is understood to be a Guru in its own right. In the

101

Sikh Temple, Stockton, California.

absence of any living teacher, it is a source of authority that governs the life of the Sikh community.

By 1699, when the tradition of the Sikh Gurus was well established, the tenth Guru, Gobind Singh, gave the community five identifying symbols. These symbols, called the five K's, are

> Kesh (uncut hair)
> Kangha (comb)
> Kara (steel bangle)
> Kirpan (short sword)
> Kach (undershorts)

Each symbol represents a discipline of the Sikh tradition. They also reflect important qualities of the faith. The undershorts symbolize purity; the long hair, the comb, and the bangle represent unity; and the short sword stands for the willingness to defend the faith.

In other religions, the clergy wear such outward signs of devotion. The Buddhist monk may shave his head and don a yellow robe. A Hindu holy man is identified in much the same way. Sikhs, however, reserve the symbols of their tradition for each male devotee. In lieu of clergy or ecclesiastical officials of any kind, each Sikh is responsible for maintaining the community of faith. The five K's reflect this responsibility. They also symbolize the evolution of a patriarchal tradition in which male devotees don the visible signs of leadership and spiritual well-being.

The five K's, however, were only presented after a unique demonstration of loyalty, which has become a mystical symbol of the authority of the Guru. According to legend, Guru Gobind Singh summoned his followers in Anandpur during a major North Indian festival, called Baisakhi, on April 13, 1699. He decreed that those who swore allegiance to him should demonstrate their loyalty by submission to death. One devotee, stepping forward out of the crowd, was taken into a tent that the Guru had prepared. The congregation heard the sound of a sword falling and assumed the man dead. Guru Gobind Singh emerged with blood dripping from his sword. Four other Sikhs in turn pledged allegiance to the Guru and went into the tent prepared to die. At the end of the fifth execution, Gobind Singh emerged from the tent, but to the crowd's surprise he was followed by the five Sikhs, alive and unharmed.

On Baisakhi Day in 1699, Guru Gobind Singh followed this dramatic test of loyalty by a discourse and celebration. Amrit, or nectar, was prepared by mixing water with sugar and was stirred with the Guru's sword. This nectar was, according to Sikh teachings, transformed from water by the blessings of the Guru. The amrit was given to the assembled masses to drink and was sprinkled on their heads and eyes by the Guru as an act of baptism (pahul).

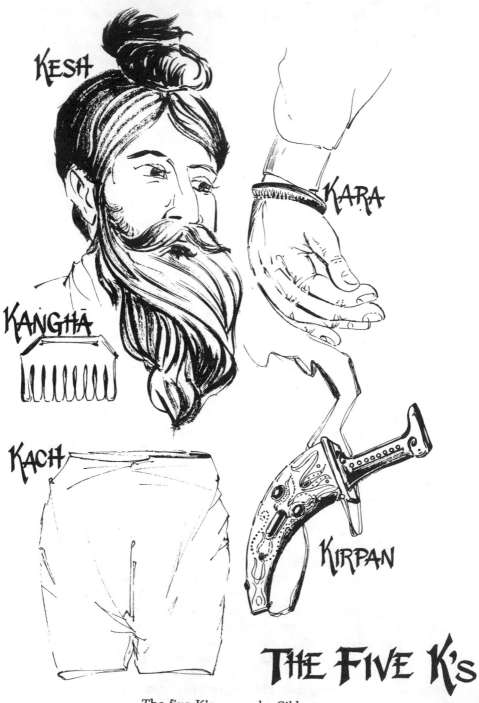

KESH

KARA

KANGHĀ

KACH

KIRPAN

THE FIVE K's

The five K's, worn by Sikh men.

This event has been recognized as the birth of a unified Sikh community, or *Khalsa*. The *Khalsa* is conceived in Sikh theology and tradition as a brotherhood whose members undergo formal initiation or baptism.[2] It is a utopian community that is guided by the teachings of the Sikh *Gurus* who are God's chosen representatives. The *Khalsa* is distinguished from the *panth*, which was also established by Guru Gobind Singh. The *panth* is the disciplined Sikh community, whose members work for the common good. Hence, the orientation of the *panth*, unlike the *Khalsa*, may be political.[3]

As a measure of commitment to the *Khalsa*, the Guru demanded that his disciples live in a distinct manner, observing a code of ethics that demanded abstinence from tobacco and prohibited eating meat not killed according to the rules of the Qur'an. It also forbade the use of intoxicants, adultery, or stealing. Further, Sikhs were enjoined not to participate in Hindu icon worship, to attend pilgrimages, or in any way to become identified with either Hinduism or Islam.

The significance of the *Khalsa* should not be underestimated. The followers of Nanak were a close-knit community, whose channels to God were the Guru and his teachings. Under the leadership of Guru Gobind Singh, however, the Sikh community was reorganized into the *Khalsa*, a brotherhood of devotees unified by a common allegiance to God and his Guru, Nanak.

The *Khalsa* provided for the common good of the brotherhood. For example, it provided food *(langar)* for the Sikh community and offered the temple, or *gurdwara*, as a temporary shelter for anyone in need. These provisions were available to all and reflected the social reforms of the ten *Gurus*.

The ideal of the *Khalsa* led to a reaction from Sikhs the world over when the Indian government used military force in the Golden Temple in Amritsar in June 1984. They not only expressed outrage over the presence of troops inside the temple and the ensuing violence but also reaffirmed the authority of the *Khalsa*.

The *Gurus* thus gave their followers a unique bond that rejected divisions of caste. This equality was symbolized by the adoption of the name Singh (lion) by male members of the faith, and Kaur (princess) by females. At the birth of a child these suffixes are given in a naming ceremony, which has become part of Sikh tradition. However, in common use, both Kaur and Singh can be taken as middle or last names.

This chapter stresses the continuation of the ideals of the *Khalsa* by Sikhs who have emigrated to North America. It is thus concerned with the classical form of the faith as practiced by Punjabis. Readers are also urged to explore a movement called 3HO that has adopted parts of Sikhism including the five K's in the United States. The two movements should not be equated, however, because there are significant doctrinal and cultural differences between them, which have been a source of conflict.

The chapter stresses how Punjabi Sikhs in North America have practiced their faith even in difficult circumstances. Between 1907 and 1914, for example, Sikhs endured great difficulties when the Canadian government passed a series of continuous-journey clauses that prohibited Indians from entering the country except by direct passage—which was not available at the time. As a result, many Sikh men were separated from their wives and children for months and even years at a time.

The chapter also demonstrates how Sikhs have adapted their religion to life in North America. For example, in New York, a *gurdwara* has been constructed from a church, an altar being converted into a dais upon which the Guru Granth Sahib rests. The transformation of the sanctuary is so complete that it appears uniquely Indian. Pews are removed and replaced by carpet so that devotees may sit in traditional Indian fashion. Arches are sculpted in a manner reminiscent of the Golden Temple at Amritsar, the holiest shrine of the Sikh religion, built by the fourth and fifth *Gurus*. Where a choir once stood, Sikh musicians now sit on the floor with harmonium (an accordion-like instrument), *tabla* (drums), and other instruments.

The ability of Sikh leaders to utilize Protestant churches to meet their needs shows how the faith has utilized facilities of a different culture. It demonstrates the vitality of the *Khalsa*, which has transcended barriers of great distance and culture.

The Sikh Religious Tradition

Guru Nanak

The Sikh religion, based on the teachings of a succession of *Gurus*, or spiritual teachers, is one of the newest Indian religions. Unlike Hinduism, which had no single founder figure, Sikhism grew out of the teachings of the prophetic leader Guru Nanak, who was born in A.D. 1469.

Nanak shaped his theology at a time when devotional Hinduism, or *bhakti*, was practiced throughout North India. *Bhakti* (see page 13) was both a historical movement and an intense emotional attitude toward a personal god. *Bhakti* stressed intimate relationships with major deities such as Krishna and Siva and their lesser incarnations, which were other forms of the same deity. Leaders of the *bhakti* movement stressed the use of vernacular languages instead of Sanskrit. This helped devotees from outside the priestly tradition to understand scripture. The *bhakti* movement became popular among the masses and, by the fifteenth and sixteenth centuries, had become the religion of both princes and peasants.

Guru Nanak lived at a time of revitalization, reform, and an emphasis on devotion. His own dynamic theology stressed obedience to a single God and the solidarity of the worshiping community. Rejecting ritualism as a restrictive system of regulations, he urged his supporters to turn their attention to God. He proclaimed that Sikhs—disciples—were neither Muslim nor Hindu, but followed an independent system of belief and practice.

Nanak, a charismatic leader, was successful in attracting converts from both Hinduism and Islam. Because he preached the equality of all persons, the early Sikh movement was especially attractive to Hindus who sought to better their social position. Finding his support among the commercial classes, Nanak denounced beliefs that stressed renouncing the world as a pathway to God.[4] Instead, he offered theological support for all vocations by boldly asserting that a Sikh must accept responsibility and live in the world.

Nanak's theology stressed the oneness of an omniscient God. It rejected both the Hindu pantheon and the underlying cosmic principle of Hindu philosophy, called Brahman. However, Guru Nanak accepted the ideas of *karma* and rebirth, which were important parts of the Hindu culture in which he had been born. *Karma*, an impartial, universal law, assumed a cause-and-effect relationship between moral acts and a beneficial rebirth.

Nanak elevated the cultural understanding of a *guru* from that of a religious teacher to one who is an instrument of the divine will. The Sikh Guru was understood to have the ability to receive God's revelation, and to transmit it among the faithful. Since gurus were already powerful and influential parts of Hindu society, the change was easily introduced. The Sikh Guru became one who discerned and interpreted God's acts. Nanak selected his successor, who inherited the title of Guru. In turn, each of the succeeding nine Gurus carried on the tradition, which culminated with the death of the last Sikh Guru, Gobind Singh, in 1708.

Nanak further taught his followers that the nature of God could be perceived and experienced. He rejected the idea of fatalism and instead preached free will—the ability to affect one's own destiny. Nanak rejected the way of the *yogi*, or Hindu ascetic, but he affirmed the mystery of God. Convinced that the way to the sacred was mystical rather than speculative, he described his own visions of the holy. He looked to God as creator of all, the source of good and evil alike.[5] For Nanak, God was both immanent and transcendent. Thus, God could be experienced in a deeply personal way and understood as a divine being. Further, Nanak taught that God's love could be experienced as grace, which is available to all persons.

The Guru developed the concept of *Shabad*, or word. He taught his disciples that the creative spirit of God is made manifest in the divine word. However, the word was also identified with the personality and teachings of the Guru. This equation increased the authority of the Guru who was directly associated with the will of God.

Nanak also taught that by meditating on God's name, the Sikh could experience *Shabad*. God's name was termed *Nam*. Unlike the Hindu discipline of *yoga*, Sikh meditation did not depend on either physical or mental exercises. Instead, Nanak preached that by meditating about God, the disciple could experience the holy. The technique of *Nam* depended on repetition. The disciple who meditated and repeated God's name thus moved closer to experiencing the Guru's vision of the sacred.

The process of meditation, however, was understood to be difficult. Sikhs were urged to think only about God. Disciples were instructed to so discipline their consciousness that the mind would not wander. God was understood to be within reach of the faithful, yet beyond absolute comprehension.

The concept of *Nam* was expressed in the Japji, a creed, or affirmation, that stresses the importance of *Nam*. One of the most sacred parts of the Guru Granth Sahib, the Japji is repeated by Sikhs at home and in the *gurdwara*. Part of the Japji concludes:

> By hearing the Name, man obtaineth a knowledge of the
>   continents, the worlds, and the nether region.
> By hearing the Name, death doth not affect one.
> Nanak, the saints are ever happy.
> By hearing the Name, sorrow and sin are no more.[6]

As an extension of the concept of *Nam*, Sikhs adopted the word *Wahguru* or "Wonderful Lord." Repetition of this holy term was seen as a way of obtaining access to the Lord. Thus for Nanak, God was revealed through different aspects of *Shabad*, rather than through icons or multiple incarnations as in Hinduism. *Shabad* was an expression of truth and sanctity, accessible to humankind through the teachings of the Guru. Both *Nam* and *Shabad* were understood as avenues of meditation and hence as ways of experiencing God. But they were differentiated clearly from the classical forms of Hindu asceticism in which the devotee renounced the world in totality through a succession of levels of concentration.

The Ten Gurus

By teaching that the Guru received revelation and transmitted divine will and truth, Nanak laid the foundation for the subsequent teachings of nine other Gurus, who established Sikhism as a way of life over the next two centuries. Each Guru embellished the faith with his own personality and theology, but retained the core doctrines of Nanak. Sikhism became an organized, expanding religion for the followers of this chain of leaders, who continued to look to the basic teachings of Nanak for inspiration and authority.

Each Guru contributed to an ongoing process of regeneration of the faith. For example, the second Guru, Angad (1504–1552), solidified the Sikh community after the death of Nanak and helped the religion develop a strong sense of history and identity. He compiled hymns that reflected Nanak's teachings and other devotional material into a book, the Guru Granth Sahib, which was the beginning of the Sikh scriptures.

In propagating the teachings of Nanak, Guru Angad utilized the institution of *langar*, a free kitchen that provided food for members of the community as well as for persons in need. Under his direction, *langar* became a way of promoting the equality of all believers.

Guru Angad was succeeded by Guru Amardas (1479–1574) who established twenty-two districts and trained missionaries to spread the religion among Hindus and Muslims throughout India.[7] Henceforward, the tradition became known for its efficient administration. Unlike classical Hinduism, Sikhism emphasized the assembly of devotees (*sangat*) and developed solidarity in the regular gathering of the worshiping community.

Under the leadership of Guru Ramdas (1534–1581), devotees were required to contribute tithes, often assessed at one-tenth of personal income. The continuation of this practice enables Sikhs around the world to mobilize large sums of money for the construction of *gurdwaras*.

Through the community kitchen, the tithing system, and the gurdwara (which temporarily housed any devotee in need of shelter), the Sikh community became remarkably self-sufficient. Because of this sustained independence, Sikhism also became highly transportable. Providing for the economic and spiritual needs of a close body of members, it evolved into a self-regulating and self-governing body of believers that could take root wherever the community was situated.

Guru Ramdas and his son Guru Arjan (1563–1606) directed the construction of Sikhism's holiest shrine, the Golden Temple (page 110). Located at Amritsar in the Punjab, the temple became important for Sikhs the world over. Although Sikh doctrine forbids pilgrimage, the Golden Temple has attracted large numbers of devotees throughout its history. Both Guru Ramdas and Guru Arjan envisioned the monument as a symbol of Nanak's concern for the equality of all believers. As a sign of this tenet, the Gurus designed four gateways, which lead into the sanctuary. These gates represent the four classes of the Hindu caste system: Brahmins (priests), Kshatriyas (soldiers), Vaishyas (traders), and Shudras (laborers). Although caste is in reality a complex pattern of interrelationships between endogamous groups or *jatis*, these four classes are

The Golden Temple, Amritsar, India, the holiest of Sikh temples.

understood to be the scriptural basis of the system. By erecting equal entrances for each class the Sikh Gurus nullified the hierarchical division of society first propounded in the Vedas.

Guru Arjan was martyred in 1606 when the Mughal emperor Jahangir accused him of sedition. The story of his arrest, torture, and subsequent death is central to the Sikh faith. According to tradition, Guru Arjan was accused of helping to support a revolt led by Jahangir's son, Khusrau, against his father. He was brought before the Mughal court to answer charges of treason, but the Guru refused to recant his position or compromise his faith, and was sentenced by decree of the Emperor to torture and death.

Guru Arjan was recognized quickly as a martyr whose life was an exemplary pattern of service and devotion. This tradition is so strong that many Sikh families even today name their male offspring Arjan.

Guru Arjan was the first Sikh leader to become a martyr. His death is used to support the development of the Sikh martial tradition, which continues to this day.[8] Guru Arjan's successor, Guru Hargobind (1595–1644) promoted the defense of the religion by force, when the Mughal Empire accelerated its attempt to destroy the Sikhs. Sikh dissension had become a threat to the stability of an already floundering state that was wracked by internal conflict and the armed resistance of religious and political factions. Hargobind became a symbol of Sikh resistance when, according to legend, he simultaneously brandished two swords. One sword represented the spiritual authority of the Guru and the other was the martial strength of the *Khalsa*. Hargobind's successor, Guru Har Rai (1630–1661) also supported the use of force. Though he did not actually participate in battle, he did help to organize a cadre of armed devotees who were prepared to fight.

The eighth and ninth Gurus both died in service to others. Guru Har Kishan (1656–1664)[9] became ill and eventually succumbed as a result of helping to care for cholera victims in Delhi. His successor, Guru Tegh Bahadur (1621–1675), contributed hymns to the ongoing development of Sikh sacred scripture, the Guru Granth Sahib. Tegh Bahadur attempted to establish a Sikh republic in Anandpur, North India, but his work was thwarted by the Emperor Aurangzeb, who executed him at Delhi in 1675.

The tenth Guru, Gobind Singh (1667–1708), completed the prophetic tradition of his predecessors. Like Tegh Bahadur, Gobind Singh attempted to build a Sikh state in the Punjab. During the course of bitter fighting, Aurangzeb died and hostilities ceased. The succeeding Emperor, Bahadur Shah, established cordial relations with the Sikhs.

Gobind Singh enjoined each Sikh to display the outward symbols of the five K's. He elevated the Granth to the level of Guru and proclaimed that the succession of living Gurus had ended. The *Khalsa* was thus solidified as the body of baptized believers who accepted a common allegiance in the Sikh brotherhood. Sikhism became a strongly patriarchal movement that emphasized the authority of the instruments of divine revelation, the ten Gurus.

The Guru Granth Sahib

The tradition of Nanak and the ten Gurus is preserved in a book (granth) of sacred writings, begun by Guru Angad (see page 109). It included hymns that reflected Guru Nanak's teachings and other devotional literature. In order to emphasize the sacredness of the book, Guru Angad popularized a special script (called Gurmukhi) to use in writing the Granth.[10] As a result, the Sikh scriptures were transmitted in a written form independent of Persian, Sanskrit, or the vernacular dialects.

Under succeeding Gurus, the Granth was gradually expanded to contain a variety of poetry and hymns, including the poetry of Hindu saints who wrote of close, personal relationships with God. The saints were often leaders of the Hindu bhakti movement. Like the Sikh Gurus, they de-emphasized restrictions on worship and prayer that had become so much a part of Hinduism. The Granth was not organized by topic or chronology but by raga. A raga is a sequence of notes in Indian classical music that denote a mood or emotion. Ragas are to be sung at particular times of day. By structuring the composition of the Granth according to raga, the Sikh scriptures suited the mood and emotion of worship at any particular time.

Eventually the text was titled Guru Granth Sahib by Guru Gobind Singh, the last of the ten Gurus. The term Guru gave the Guru Granth Sahib equal rank with the historical Gurus of the faith. Sahib is a term of respect used to address persons of authority. The combination of words Guru, Granth, and Sahib indicates the tremendous respect given the text, which reflects the tradition of the Gurus. The text is seen as knowing no limitations of birth and death. It is an eternal, living voice of authority for Sikhs. The Guru Granth Sahib thus magnifies the role of Nanak and the succeeding Gurus as founders of the tradition and as continuing sources of inspiration.

The dominance of the Guru Granth Sahib can be observed in any Sikh home. The book is placed in the highest possible position. Similarly, in the temple, it is always placed on a dais. It is covered by a canopy and given a position suitable to royalty. The Guru Granth Sahib is revered, but never worshiped. According to Sikh doctrine and the teachings of Guru Nanak, only God can be worshiped. But the book, in the absence of any living Guru, is a spiritual guide containing God's direct revelation.

The Guru Granth Sahib is the only authoritative scripture in the Sikh tradition. Its words in matters of doctrine and ritual are binding and are not questioned. The text may be supplemented, however, by devotional texts or interpretive literature such as the *Rehat Maryada* and the *Dasam Granth*.

The *Rehat Maryada* describes the singing of hymns (*kirtan*), the reading of the Granth, and the distribution of blessed food (*parsad*). The document also provides information on ethics and the performance of rites of passage such as birth, baptism, marriage, and death. This text was published in the Punjab in 1945 and later printed in English in Great Britain. Many Sikhs, however, attribute it to the period of the *Gurus*.

The *Dasam Granth* is a collection of poetry and prose attributed to Guru Gobind Singh and Hindu poets of the same period. It contains information about the Guru's life, Hindu mythology, and popular Hindi poetry. Like the *Rehat Maryada*, it is not considered canonical or on the same level as the Guru Granth Sahib.

While some Sikhs find great meaning in tracts such as the *Rehat Maryada*, it is never compared with the Granth, which holds absolute authority in the tradition. For the Sikh, there is one God and one source of revelation. These cannot be compromised.

A Sikh temple (*gurdwara*) is designed for the care and regular reading of the Guru Granth Sahib, which is supervised by a lay devotee, or *Granthi*. The *Granthi* is not a minister or a priest. Sikhism has no ecclesiastical officials or trained clergy. Rather, the *Granthi*, who reads the holy book and leads in community worship, is drawn from the Sikh community. A *Granthi* is employed by the *gurdwara* on the basis of his good character and his ability to keep outward symbols of the Sikh tradition. Many Sikh weddings in the United States are performed by *Granthis*, though any Sikh fulfilling the requirements of tradition and obtaining a license from the state can perform the same function. The willingness of *Granthis* to conduct weddings and funerals suggests a process of adaptation and assimilation to life in North America in which the clergy are expected to play a role of great influence.

Social Reform

The nine *Gurus*, relying on the theological foundations of Nanak, preached the existence of a monotheistic God, who was perceived as a creator. They reinforced the important concepts of *Shabad* (word) and *Nam*, through which the devotee could experience the holy. In addition, they reinforced Nanak's reforms, which disavowed the caste system and the Hindu social hierarchy.

The term caste is frequently misleading, and is often confused with the four-fold class system (*varna*) in the Vedas. As discussed in chapter one, there are hundreds of *jatis* in India whose members intermarry and share a common occupation, which is designated by birth. Each *jati* is ranked according to cultural perceptions of purity and pollution. Physical contact with persons of lesser *jati* status or eating in their company can be sources of pollution.

The *Gurus*, however, insisted on the equality of all believers, and introduced practices within the Sikh community to dissolve these distinctions. Such conventions as the free kitchen *(langar)*, in which devotees of high and low *jati* status ate together, ignored Hindu dietary restrictions. The free kitchen was in contrast to cooking areas in Hindu homes, which are highly restricted. As a further way of negating *jati*, the *Gurus* proclaimed that the *gurdwara* was open to all persons regardless of their *jati* status. This was in sharp contrast to Hindu temple, where admission to the inner sanctuary was highly regulated.

In the United States, Sikhs have continued faithfully the tradition established by the *Gurus* following the moral code based on the mutual responsibility of members of the *Khalsa*. All persons are admitted freely to the *gurdwara* or given *langar* regardless of their status at birth. For example, during the depression in the 1930s, food was distributed to the hungry at the Stockton *gurdwara* whether they were Sikhs or not. The basic theological conviction that such visible evidence of God's care could not be denied to anyone affirmed the theology of Guru Nanak.

The Cultural Dimension

Sikhism as a religious tradition includes a body of culturally defined beliefs and practices. As Punjabis, Sikhs share a common language, are members of distinct cultural groups, and are acculturated to a North Indian way of life that has been carried over to North America. The Punjab is a geographical area now incorporated in both India and Pakistan (see map, page 12). In 1947, the subcontinent was partitioned into what is now the Republic of India and the Islamic state of Pakistan, dividing this land in two. The Punjab means "land of five rivers." It is bordered in India by the Himalaya mountains on the north, the Rajasthani desert on the south, and Pakistan on the north and the northwest. It is a fertile land with a long agricultural history.

As a people, Punjabi Sikhs have exhibited strong adaptability. In British India, Sikhs frequently served in the army and were often cavalrymen. Many worked as grooms and were accustomed to work around horses. When the day of the horse ended, they easily adapted to alternate forms of transportation. In many North Indian cities today, for example, Sikhs are taxi drivers and mechanics. Other Sikhs have entered a variety of professions, such as medicine and law.

In Canada, Sikhs have worked in the lumbering industry and the mines. In the eastern United States, Sikhs have become doctors, scientists, or engineers. In California, Sikhs have worked in agriculture, as in parts of the Punjab.

In each of these overseas locations and in South Asia, Sikhs have historically been concerned about maintaining the distinct nature of their faith and identity. The leaders of the faith have rejected any attempt to assimilate the tradition back into Hinduism. In India, this issue is so important, that the Akali Dal, a Sikh political party, has sought repeatedly to establish a separate, Punjabi-speaking state[11] in order to be free from what they perceive as discrimination by the Hindu majority. While this position has frequently been voiced, it has been recently pursued through acts of violence by a faction of militant Sikhs.

Tensions between Hindus and Sikhs escalated, leading in June, 1984, to an attack by the Indian army on a band of Sikhs headquartered in the Golden Temple and, that November, to the assassination of Prime Minister Indira Gandhi by some Sikh bodyguards. These dramatic events have affected Hindu and Sikh communities throughout India and abroad and continue to be profound sources of division. In the United States, however, where members of both faiths are part of the same Indian minority, there is a greater tendency for long-term cohesiveness. This tendency is strengthened by the consideration that Hindus and Sikhs represent the same racial stock and may even be members of the same India clubs and cultural organizations.

Marriage and Family Structures

While the Guru Granth Sahib prohibits discrimination on the basis of caste, Sikhs—like other groups of people in South Asia—find a strong cultural identification with endogamous groups. Endogamy, the practice of marrying within a defined group, regulates patterns of marriage for most Sikhs in India and for those who have come to North America. Among Jat Sikhs in Yuba City, California, for example, the tendency to marry other Jats has been well documented.[12] Jats, an agricultural people who form a strong part of the *Khalsa*, have settled in California's fertile valleys. Besides continuing the tradition of marrying other Jats, they also have perpetuated the cultural pattern of village exogamy in which husbands and wives are selected from different villages. The practice of marrying outside the *gotra* also continues among the Yuba City Sikh population. *Gotras* are patrilineal groups that trace their origin to a common ancestor.

Sikhs in North America continue to support the traditional role of the extended family. The ideal of the extended family may be perpetuated by bringing aunts, uncles, brothers, and sisters to be relocated in the same community. This demonstrates the considerable economic power of the extended family, which is able to pool resources to aid its members.

For Punjabis, as for the majority of other East Indians, marriages frequently are arranged. Even in the United States, where romantic love is idealized, this cultural pattern prevails. Parents may rely on the authority of older family members in India to decide the most suitable match for their children.

An arranged marriage offers a variety of benefits to both spouses. It provides security for each partner, since the question of divorce is almost non-existent in traditional households. It helps the couple to establish a household and provides an opportunity to bring additional family members to the United States. It also assures the perpetuation of the faith and reduces the possibility of intermarriage among persons of differing religious backgrounds.

For Sikhs, as for Hindus in the United States, arranged marriages can be a source of conflict. Children who are taught at home to conform to traditional Indian values are motivated outside the home to act like other youth. Sometimes parents may impose conflicting values on their children based on their own desire to adapt to life in the United States and yet to retain their Punjabi heritage. One girl, for example, reported that her parents urged her to adopt values accepted as normative in the United States—to get good grades, to speak proper English, and to wear stylish clothes. However, it was expected that they would choose her husband.[13] Situations like this often become sources of rebellion and frustration that lead to breaks with tradition. Support for traditional ways can come from the extended family, who urge that such important customs as marriage continue according to accepted North Indian standards.

For Sikhs and Hindus, the parents and grandparents in India can exert enormous pressure to conform. In both traditions, the husband's mother is a source of authority who frequently strives to make her will known in all matters of marriage and religion. The family in India plays a continuing role among sons and daughters in North America. The family network is strong and exerts great pressure for its wishes to be carried out.

Whereas the husband and his mother are frequently dominant forces in the extended family, the wife's role is subordinate. In Sikh and Hindu families in North America, women are seen as secondary. The wife remains at home while her husband works outside. She may originate in a remote village in the Punjab and speak little English, following her husband to a new land where she is not prepared for the culture or the social climate of her new home. In North America, she is expected to assume her traditional role of maintaining her home and educating her children. Like her Hindu counterparts, she may have little opportunity to assimilate into North American life. Her home is often her world. She has little chance to interact with non-Indians and few ways of meeting persons outside of her tradition.

For Sikh women, these problems and frustrations may be tempered by regular contact with other Punjabis in the *gurdwara*. Sikhism in North America emphasizes the regular gathering of devotees, who worship together. These community gatherings provide mutual support and strength. The *gurdwara* also may provide an opportunity to find a suitable mate. If this is not successful, help may be obtained from several Indian newsletters published in the United States that offer matrimonial columns. A man or woman intent on marrying may advertise in these columns to find a spouse of suitable background. A Punjabi Sikh, for example, may cite his age, place of birth, degrees, and occupation as well as his expectations in a mate. His ad probably will provide information about a dowry and his family in the United States. In the case of a woman, her family often advertises for her. Again, questions of status and financial position are primary, since marriage in the Hindu and Sikh traditions is as much an economic as a religious concern.

Language

Punjabi is one of fifteen major languages in India. As a North Indian language it arises from Sanskrit and shares common conventions in writing and pronunciation with other related languages. Among overseas Sikhs, Punjabi holds a special place as a religious and cultural link with the homeland. Whenever possible, children are taught Punjabi at home or in the *gurdwara*. Some *gurdwaras* offer Punjabi classes so that children born outside of India may learn the language from native speakers. Hymns sung during worship are written in Punjabi and cannot be translated without detriment to the tradition. For the child who understands the language, hymns and discourses take on added significance. Moreover, the *tabla* (drum) and harmonium accompaniment to the vocalist reinforces traditions of Indian classical music that otherwise might be left behind.

Dress

Sikhs in the United States and Canada frequently maintain conventions of Punjabi dress. For men, the turban is worn as an outward and visible symbol of faith. It may contain five or six yards of muslin and differs from Hindu turbans, which are loose fitting. Traditionally, Sikhs have worn a miniature sword symbolic of the *kirpan*. The turban is frequently worn with an Indian *kurta* (a cotton shirt) and *pajama* (loose fitting pants). Many men wear Western dress, however.

Women wear the traditional *shalwar* and *kamiz*. Unlike a *sari*, which reaches to the floor, the *shalwar* is pants made of bright silks or other fine materials. The *kamiz*, like a *kurta*, is a long shirt, except that it frequently extends well beyond the waist and may be embroidered with gold thread. Punjabi women also may wear a *sari* and cover their heads with a scarf known as a *dupatta*.

The wearing of the *shalwar* and *kamiz* or *sari* reflects Indian concepts of modesty and propriety. Moreover, the *shalwar* is a highly practical garment that can be worn for housework or for social occasions.

Thus, Punjabi culture continues to hold an important place in the religious life of North American Sikhs. Language, dress, and common cultural values all affect the manner in which ceremonies are performed and belief systems adopted. Children born into the faith outside the Indian subcontinent are helped by these Punjabi traditions to develop their sense of identity. For them, to be Sikh is to be Punjabi and to accept a way of life that has been refined in North India for more than 400 years. By maintaining strong links with families in India, overseas Sikhs have demonstrated an ability to successfully carry a North Indian pattern of life to different parts of the world.

A Brief History of Sikhs in North America

In 1906, 6,000 immigrants from India were estimated to have settled in Canada.[14] In the United States in the following year, over 1,000 Indians entered the country.[15] This was almost four times the number that had arrived the year before.

The new immigrants were properly identified as East Indians, a term that went back to the days of the British East India Company. Many were Sikhs who saw North America as a land of opportunity where fortunes could be made. Moreover, political turmoil, riots, and unrest in the Punjab made the possibility of a fresh start in a new land attractive.[16]

Most of the Sikhs were loyal, dedicated members of the *Khalsa*. They were instilled with the spirit that had led to the Sikh revival in the 1870s in India. The revival, like its Hindu counterpart, which is often called the "Hindu Renaissance," was a popular resurgence of idealism and piety. For Sikhs, it symbolized the independence of their faith from either Hinduism or Islam.

This stance was important since throughout its history Sikhism has been interpreted by Hindus as a reformist tradition that eventually would be absorbed back into Hinduism. Sikhs have been particularly sensitive that their religion be understood as a distinct and independent religion of its own. The Sikh revival reaffirmed these feelings.

In Canada, leaders of the Indian minority dreamed of a new India where immigrants could work in a variety of occupations and trades. This was especially true in British Columbia where, in Vancouver, the first *gurdwara* in North America had been erected. As one Sikh author, Nand Singh Sihra, wrote:

> Moreover one would see them in each and every part of the town going hastily this way or that way carrying out all sorts of trades in real state [sic] and landed property, dairy farms and agriculture, mill industry and lumber works. In short, British Columbia is not only a new world for the older one, but it is a new India. . . .[17]

Whether or not Indians in British Columbia were as affluent as this writer seemed to think is debatable. What mattered was the strength of his vision, which looked to the Canadian northwest as a permanent home for the East Indian minority. As discrimination by the Caucasian majority in Vancouver and Victoria increased, however, the threat of official restrictions on immigration from India also heightened. Canadians became concerned about the loss of jobs in the lumbering and mining industries, which employed the greatest number of Sikhs.

Reacting to this threat, Sikh leaders sought to sway the popular stereotype of Asians as backward and poor. Sihra even concluded that his countrymen were predominantly enterprising capitalists who had already made their fortunes:

> Amongst our people in British Columbia, I am quite at a loss to point out even a single individual who does not own any landed property and is not a possessor of about seven or eight thousand rupees. In the city roads the best dressed man will be found to be an Indian.[18]

Such pleas for acceptance were rarely heard as pressure mounted for new legislation. Between 1907 and 1914, the Canadian government passed a series of continuous-journey clauses under the authority of The Immigration Act, 9 and 10, Edward VII. These clauses forbade immigrants from landing at any Canadian port unless they had traveled by direct passage. No ship company at the time sailed from India to Canada non-stop. The legislation thus restricted any further immigration from South Asia.

Other clauses in the same act specified that "Asiatics" could not land in Canada unless they possessed a sum of $200.[19] This provision was intended to prevent unskilled Indian laborers from entering Canada. But, it also directly affected patterns of migration in which family members sponsored relatives who wished to emigrate. For most Indians, the expense of steamship passage was enough; the additional burden of

$200 was an effective barrier to immigration. Further, for those Indians who had come from a village background, the problems of coping with international bank transfers were often insurmountable.

As a result of this legislation, and other restrictive measures that required payment of large sums for entry into the country, families were often kept apart. In many instances, wives and children were unable to join their husbands in Canada.

In one case, a Sikh resident of Vancouver who had lived in the city for four years returned to India to get his wife and child.[20] When the reunited family arrived at the port of Vancouver, immigration officials refused to let the mother and baby come ashore, and threatened to force them to return to India. The situation was eventually resolved when the family paid a cash bond of $1,000 to officials in order to enter Canada legally. To a former Indian soldier, however, who had helped to defend the British Empire, the events were humiliating.

In other cases there was so much red tape that families were delayed for months and subjected to great expense before being admitted to Canada. For example, the President of the Vancouver Khalsa Diwan Society (the first gurdwara in North America) returned to India with another Sikh in 1911.[21] Both men hoped to bring their families home with them to Canada. However, steamship passage for the women and children that would comply with the continuous-journey regulations could not be obtained. In desperation the Sikhs and their families traveled to Hong Kong and to San Francisco where they were refused entry. After three months of travel, they sailed for Vancouver, arriving on January 22, 1912, aboard the steamship Monteagle. There, the two Canadian residents were allowed to disembark but the families were informed that they would be sent back to India. The incident was settled eventually again by the payment of large cash bonds that permitted entry into Canada.

In 1914, a bizarre incident became widely publicized as a display of Sikh unity in Canada in the face of the restrictive legislation.[22] A band of militant Sikhs, determined to test the continuous-journey clause, chartered a ship of Japanese registry in Hong Kong. The Komagata Maru set sail to Canada with a band of over 350 men who hoped to land in Vancouver. By chartering a ship in Hong Kong, where direct passage to Canada could be obtained, the Sikhs hoped to meet the requirements of the law. Additional justification for the attempt was supported by the fact that the Sikhs were loyal British subjects and that Hong Kong was a British possession.

The Sikhs arrived at Vancouver, determined to disembark. They were met by a tug carrying 120 policemen and 40 immigration officials. However, when the small craft maneuvered within range of the

Komagata Maru, angry Sikhs poured a barrage of missiles fashioned from any piece of iron or coal loose on board at the authorities.

The resistance was short-lived and the Sikhs were prevented from disembarking. Despite this setback, the case was pleaded before the Canadian authorities. A Board of Inquiry met to hear the owners of the Komagata Maru, its passengers, charterers, and one Sikh, Munshi Singh, who appealed his personal case for entry into the port.[23]

Singh, like many other Sikhs in Canada, stressed that he was a farmer who had come to Canada to work the land and, in time, to purchase a farm. In denying the appeal, the Board refused to accept the defendant's intention of farming, even though he owned farm land in India, which he valued at the sizeable sum of 25,000 rupees. Ascertaining that Munshi Singh had on his person less than the $200 required by the Immigration Act, the Board summarily dismissed his appeal, even though the defendant reported he was able to wire home for additional funds. Thus, the Board reaffirmed the intentions of the Canadian government to bar Indians from entering the country, with little regard for their ambitions or interests in settling in Canada.

With all legal avenues of appeal exhausted, the *Komagata Maru* and its passengers sailed for India. Disembarking in Budge Budge, the Punjabis were met by British authorities. A riot broke out in which the Sikhs were fired upon and several were killed. The bold journey that had taken a band of devotees around the world, determined to dramatize an inequitable law, ended in bitter defeat. Yet, for Sikhs in the United States and Canada, the event instilled greater loyalty and solidarity. The misfortunes of the passengers of the *Komagata Maru* demonstrated the plight of Sikhs in North America, who often were forced to use desperate measures to assure the continuation of their way of life.

These incidents illustrate the importance of the family for Sikhs in North America. They also show the determination of prominent members of the *Khalsa* to remain in Vancouver, often resorting to desperate measures to have their wives and children with them. Rather than leaving North America in frustration and returning permanently to South Asia, these Sikh leaders now looked to Canada as their home.

In the United States, similar opposition to Indian immigration had arisen. The continued growth of the new minority evoked suspicion and fear, particularly in San Francisco where many Hindus and Sikhs had settled. Indian immigrants were perceived as a menace. They were commonly identified as a body of itinerant laborers who would work for low wages. One article in 1910 claimed:

They outnumber all other Asiatic passengers on transpacific liners bound this way, and in San Francisco and its suburbs "Hindu town" is now as familiar as Chinatown or any other distinctly foreign settlement. . . . Many of the Hindu immigrants are ex-soldiers. . . Few of them have been used to hard labor, and with the people of this land they have nothing in common unless it is the desire for money. A number of the latest arrivals were asked why they had come to America, and the answer in each case was: "Money."[24]

Such portrayals of the Sikh and Hindu community fueled an impression of hordes of uneducated laborers who threatened the job market and contributed little to U.S. society. The term "Hindu" became a stereotype and was applied to any Indian wearing a turban. Members of both religions were labeled "ragheads," who, backward and uneducated, were a threat to the national interest.

As pressure increased for an end to the large influx of Indians, members of the Khalsa Diwan Society in Stockton, California, became concerned. The Society, which maintained the oldest *gurdwara* in the United States, had become an important symbol of Sikh unity. In 1914 it dispatched a representative to Washington to meet with a Congressional committee and with two leaders of the Hindu Association of America. The Sikhs and the Hindus feared restrictions on further immigration.

Interior, Sikh Temple, Stockton, California, showing the dais and the canopy that covers the Guru Granth Sahib during worship.

Both groups sought to prevent the passage of an Asiatic Exclusion Law, which was supported by a powerful lobby—the Asiatic Exclusion League.

The League earlier had lobbied for governmental restrictions on Chinese and Japanese immigration. By 1908, when over 1,700 Indian immigrants entered the United States,[25] the League again sought limitations on what it perceived as a new Asian threat.

The possibility of restrictive legislation was dangerous to the Sikhs for several reasons. Foremost, it threatened to break cultural patterns within the Punjabi community. Since most Sikhs and Hindus in the United States were men, limitations on further immigration meant that many wives and children would be unable to rejoin their families. As women were the main channel through which the tradition was passed on to children, any cutoff would threaten the further development of the faith in the United States.

The League's activities brought the Indian minority into the political process. More important, it brought the Hindus and the Sikhs together. This was a considerable achievement since the two populations came from different backgrounds. Most Sikhs in California were farmers; Hindus had entered a variety of professions. The two groups now rallied, however, in an unprecedented show of Indian unity in the United States. Leaders of the Khalsa Diwan Society and the Hindusthan Association met together and, between 1913 and 1924, carried out a movement called Ghadr, or "mutiny."[26]

Ghadr was a response both to restrictions on immigration in the United States, and to British imperialism in India, which the leaders of the revolutionary movement linked together. As chapter one indicated, the leader of the Ghadr movement was Har Dayal, the editor of a newsletter that pleaded the movement's cause. The Ghadrites hoped to free India from the yoke of British rule and by so doing to precipitate a revolution. They were nationalists who were fully convinced that British rule was responsible for their problems in North America as well as at home in India.

In 1914 and 1915, the movement had swelled into an active political force. As the United States prepared to enter World War I, several thousand Sikhs left California to return to India to initiate the revolution and overthrow the British. But the mission was a failure. Most of the revolutionaries were killed, captured, or never returned.

Later, by 1919, when Ghadr leaders in the United States had been arrested and tried, the movement came to an end. Ghadr leaders had eagerly sought the collaboration of German officials both in Great Britain and in the United States, hoping to take full advantage of the political unrest.

When the United States declared war on Germany, the German consular officials who had supported the movement and the Ghadr leaders were arrested. The association of Sikhs and Hindus fell apart. To make matters worse, the Hindu editor of the Ghadr newspaper, Ram Chandra, was shot to death in the courtroom by a Sikh. The coalition of Sikhs and Hindus had always been fragile and had been characterized by mutual mistrust and suspicion. In particular, the Sikhs felt that funds supplied to the movement by the Germans had been misappropriated by Ram Chandra.

As the Ghadr movement disintegrated, the future of the Indian minority was dealt a severe blow by federal legislation and by a Supreme Court decision. As noted in chapter one (page 19), the United States Supreme Court ruled in 1923 that the claim of a Sikh to be Caucasian by virtue of his Aryan descent was invalid and hence was not grounds for naturalization. The case, United States v. Bhagat Singh Thind, reinforced existing restrictions on immigration from India. It supported race as a primary consideration in determining which aliens could not enter the country. This was similar to what had already taken place in Canada and was in keeping with earlier immigration statues in the United States. The Immigration Act of 1917 had declared that no aliens from within specified limits of latitude and longitude (including India) could be admitted to the United States. The Immigration Act of 1921 had initiated a national origins quota system, which was finalized in the Immigration Act of 1924. India was not assigned a quota. These measures virtually eliminated the ability of Indians to immigrate to the United States. They created a policy that remained in effect until 1946, when India was assigned a token quota after the passage of the Luce-Cellar bill.

The subsequent decline of the Sikh community in the United States was the direct result of this legislation, which suspended all further immigration from India. The restrictions left the Sikh and Hindu communities fragmented. Members of the extended family, an important part of both communities, were barred from entering the United States. The cost of sea passage prohibited all but the most important visits home. Under these difficult conditions, departures from orthodoxy were common as devotees were isolated from important sources of authority overseas.

One result of this cultural isolation was the relaxation of many Indian religious conventions. In the Stockton gurdwara, devotees were not always required to cover their heads or take off their shoes on entering the gurdwara, nor were the five K's stressed.

Further, chairs were eventually installed in the temple. While at first these changes may appear immaterial, they reflect the increased assimilation of Sikhs into the mainstream of life in the United States. In traditional Indian gurdwaras, Sikhs sit on the floor. The custom is a cultural convention common to Hinduism, Sikhism, and Islam. This practice permits the holy book (or icon) to be placed well above the heads of the worshiping public. This symbol of respect was threatened by the changeover to chairs. In the Stockton *gurdwara*, chairs were an offensive symbol to traditionalists of accommodation to Western values. In the 1960s they became a major point of controversy during a period of reform and revitalization.[27] When leaders of the *gurdwara* stressed a return to orthodox ways, the chairs were perfunctorily removed.

The reduction of immigrants also meant that the *Khalsa* was revitalized rarely. With few Sikh women in the United States, men were forced to marry outside their culture and religion. Since women were counted on to teach children the faith and to reinforce the ideals of the tradition, the marrying of non-Sikh women meant that a necessary segment of the tradition was missing, and the religion was severely diluted. Many adopted the now dominant life-style of their in-laws. Children grew up in ignorance of their East Indian heritage, learning the faith of their mothers who knew little of Sikhism.

The absence of new arrivals from India meant that *Granthis* (who are symbols of Sikh values and tradition) were selected from persons already acculturated in the United States. With few *sants* (Sikh scholars) able to address *gurdwaras* and with the limited access of the North American population to news from home from visiting friends or relatives, the Sikh community was isolated.

By the end of World War II, however, the image of India and Indians had improved. Perhaps the greatest force for this change was Mahatma Gandhi, who dramatically equated the popular conception of the poverty-stricken Indian masses with the virtues of dignity and devotion. The frail figure of the Mahatma spinning cotton captured the heart of the nation. Gandhi was recognized as an exponent of nationalism and freedom, which was part of the "American dream." Through repeated exposure in the press, consciousness about India gradually was raised. Gandhi's impact, coupled with the support of India as an ally in World War II, helped prepare the country for the eventual relaxation of immigration restrictions.

The change came in 1946, when the United States Congress adopted the Luce-Cellar bill, which had been sponsored by Clare Booth Luce and Emanuel Cellar. The bill was passed as an amendment to the Nationality Act of 1940. The legislation was a victory for Indians, who, for the first time since the introduction of a national origins quota system, were assigned a quota. One hundred Indians a year were now permitted to enter the country.

Although the Luce-Cellar bill was the subject of considerable debate in the Congress, its passage was aided by the lobbying efforts of Sikhs in California. A Sikh, D. S. Saund, who later became the first Asian Congressman in the United States, led a campaign among Punjabis on the

West Coast.[28] By circulating flyers in the Punjabi language, he appealed to supporters of the tradition and dramatized the cohesiveness of the minority group.

The Reaffirmation of Sikhism in the United States

Although the Luce-Cellar bill was a legislative victory for Indians living in the United States, it was only a small step in reviving a religious tradition that had been static for years. The arrival of a limited number of Indians in the United States each year had little effect on the rejuvenation of Sikh religious and cultural traditions, which had been weakened and diluted since 1924. Not until 1965, when the national origins quota system was eliminated, did immigration patterns change significantly. Sikhs and Hindus from Uganda, Great Britain, Fiji, and other nations poured into the United States. Immigration statistics show that the number of Indians entering the country in 1966 was more than four times that of the previous year.[29] By 1970, over 8,700 Indians immigrated to the United States.

New arrivals from these countries and from India often practiced the orthodox form of the faith, maintaining the five K's and shunning accommodation to Western values. Since 1965, a variety of cultural societies have attracted a core of dedicated followers, due in large measure, to the influence of these Sikhs.

This revival was made possible also by the general climate of reform and renewal in the United States, which encouraged new forms of religious expression. As Christians debated the theological implications of the liberalizing Second Vatican Council (Vatican II), a large number of cults reflecting Asian influence were born. Although not as widely publicized, the classical faiths of Hinduism, Buddhism, Sikhism, and Islam all experienced a similar time of growth and expansion.

Unlike previous waves of Sikhs entering the United States, who settled for the most part in California, the new arrivals spread across the country. In 1971, Sikhs in the Gulf Coast area held their first meeting. Property was purchased in 1973 near Houston, Texas, and subsequently a gurdwara was built. In October, 1973, the mayor of Houston proclaimed Sikh Day. Later, Guru Nanak's birthday was celebrated in the new temple.

In July, 1974, however, the new gurdwara was destroyed by fire. Construction was begun on a new building. By April, 1977, a two-story temple had been erected and a year later a fund-raising drive begun for the installation of a dome. The swift reconstruction of the temple is dramatic evidence of the importance of this gurdwara and the strength of the revitalization effort.

On the East Coast in New York City the organization of a Sikh center in Flushing and a gurdwara in Richmond Hill (The Sikh Cultural Society of

New York) was visible evidence of the new arrivals. Many Sikhs came from Great Britain bringing rich religious and cultural traditions. In Paramus, New Jersey, Sikhs organized the Guru Singh Sabha in 1975. The society brought together Sikh families for monthly meetings during which hymns, discourses, and lectures were held. Another society, the Garden State Sikh Association, was formed in 1972.

On the West Coast, Sikhs in California discussed the construction of a new *gurdwara* in Yuba City. By 1969, land had been secured and plans made for the erection of a building. The *gurdwara* that eventually was built cost $250,000 and opened in 1970. From 1974 to 1976 the temple hosted a variety of major festivals including Baisakhi and birthday rites of Guru Gobind Singh and Guru Nanak.

Similarly, in San Francisco, devotees planned a Bay area *gurdwara*. In Los Angeles a small temple was opened in 1969.

These, and other *gurdwaras* and Khalsa Diwan Societies in different parts of the United States and Canada, show the strength of the movement since 1965. Thus, established Sikh communities were revitalized by newcomers from India. Each congregation rediscovered important religious and cultural traditions that reaffirmed its identity and individuality.

Library, Sikh Temple, Stockton, California.

A *Gurdwara* in New York City—An Example of the Revitalization of a Sikh Community

Sikhs recognize the gurdwara as a center of authority and tradition. The temple is holy space by virtue of the presence of the Guru Granth Sahib. It is a symbol of the solidarity of members of the *Khalsa*. Very often, its construction becomes a way of renewing the religious community and of reinstituting essential values. In New York City, where a gurdwara was constructed in 1972, Sikhs have reaffirmed their spiritual heritage and cultural identity.[30]

In the last twenty years, there has been a rapid increase of East Indians in New York. Three Hindu temples and more than a dozen linguistic and cultural associations meet a variety of needs of this developing Asian-American minority. Since 1965, when the numbers of Indians in New York increased dramatically, Sikhs have achieved a visible presence in the area. The arrival of Sikhs from Europe and India has re-established *keshadari* values and stimulated a resurgence of tradition. *Keshadari* Sikhs maintain all outward symbols of the faith (the five K's) as opposed to *sahajdhari*, who do not.

As a result of this sustained growth, Sikhs in New York City acquired a former Methodist church in Richmond Hill, Queens. Conducting extensive renovation as well as modification of the interior of the sanctuary, leaders established the largest gurdwara on the East Coast. This temple, often referred to as the New York Gurdwara, was organized and incorporated under the name The Sikh Cultural Society of New York.

After the purchase of the church, pews were removed from the sanctuary, together with all symbols of the original use of the building. Carpet was installed throughout, so that members might sit facing the dais in traditional Sikh fashion.

In making these changes, leaders secured the assistance of prominent members of the *Khalsa*, who often served the community as *Granthis*, reading the Guru Granth Sahib during worship. The first *Granthi* was a respected Sikh scholar from the Punjab. The second had been the head *Granthi* of a Delhi gurdwara and had also worked in London. These men were an important link with Sikh traditions in India. Their presence emphasized the authority of the new gurdwara and evidenced the interest of leaders in preserving doctrinal and ritualistic ties with South Asia. The gurdwara links Sikhs in Europe and the United States and establishes a chain of communication among devotees in the West.

Sikhs in Great Britain already had begun a practice of locating gurdwaras in renovated church buildings. Richmond Hill has many older Protestant churches, some of which are in their last stages of institutional life, and purchasing a building offered many advantages. The most obvious of these was to use the space in a similar way.

The church building is suited to large gatherings of people. It contains classrooms, community kitchens, and large halls for dinners. The sanctuary of the New York Gurdwara accommodates 500 regular worshipers as well as larger gatherings of several thousand on festival days. The classrooms were suitable for Punjabi classes, and large rooms in the basement were ideal for serving *langar*. Additional space was easily found and converted into an apartment for the *Granthi*, who normally resides in the *gurdwara* he serves.

Sikh communities in Great Britain, Canada, and the United States frequently have adopted a congregational form of worship, in which the community assembles for prayer at designated times. This pattern is especially useful to a community such as the membership of the New York Gurdwara, which is scattered throughout the New York metropolitan area. Large congregations help to sustain enthusiasm for the tradition and help to promote the *gurdwara* as an established center of Sikh culture and education.

Further, the practice of worshiping on Sunday strengthened the cohesion of members of the *Khalsa*, who now saw one another at regular intervals. The Sunday service permitted devotees to meet afterwards for a common meal, or *langar*.

The adaptation of the custom of Sunday worship in the United States also helped the Sikh community assimilate into a Protestant and Catholic neighborhood that was not familiar with Indian religions. The appearance of several hundred persons outside the converted church building on Sunday mornings was an expected event that, aside from differences in dress, drew little attention.

Leaders quickly established the orthodoxy of the Gurdwara. Devotees entering the church removed their shoes and placed them in a room to the side of the main entrance. For children, or guests who did not wear turbans, cloth was provided to cover the head. No chairs were permitted in the sanctuary. Supplicants sat on a carpeted floor, as in India. Facing the Guru Granth Sahib, men remained on the left, with women and children on the right.

The Guru Granth Sahib is the focus of the temple. Men and women entering the sanctuary walk to the dais and prostrate themselves before the holy book. Usually, an offering of money or flowers is placed on a low table directly beneath the Granth. The *Granthi* behind the dais retains the traditional function of protecting the text in his role as its personal servant. Holding a silver-handled fan, he wafts the air above the text (page 130). In this instance, and in many others, the Granth is treated as a Guru in its own right, and is carefully protected. The fan symbolizes the honor afforded the text, which is shown the same respect as an emperor or a great teacher.

The fan, the dais, and the act of prostration stress the sanctity of the

Sanctuary, New York Gurdwara, Richmond Hill, New York. The *Granthi* fans the Guru Granth Sahib during worship.

book, its royalty, and its authority. They are a pervasive part of Hindu, Sikh, Buddhist, and Jain religious traditions, which see the holy as a source of regal authority in Indian culture. This emphasis is extended with the use of the term *diwan* for the assembled congregation. Originally referring to the court of a Mughal emperor, the word suggests the obeisance of a large group of subjects before a source of unlimited authority.

The tradition of placing the text above the heads of the worshiping congregation is a universal symbol of sacred authority. Protestant Christians, for example, observe much the same symbolism in church when the minister ascends the pulpit to read the Bible. In other traditions, the same elevation of the holy is commonplace, suggesting the natural tendency to symbolize divinity by the visible affirmation of its dominance.

In the Sikh tradition the Guru Granth Sahib is a source of revelation and a spiritual guide—a living *Guru*—for devotees. It equips Sikhs, as disciples, to surrender their will to God, in keeping with the heritage of the *Khalsa*.

During the *diwan* at the New York Gurdwara, which usually begins at

11:00 o'clock on Sunday mornings, a variety of activities take place. These activities are similar in most gurdwaras in India or North America and stress the homogeneity of Sikh ceremonial traditions. Included are prayers (ardas), devotional hymns (kirtan), discourses by learned and scholarly devotees (katha), and readings from the Guru Granth Sahib. Musicians, often including harmonium and drum players, sit on the right side of the dais. After the diwan, which may last two hours or more, the community gathers for a common meal (langar). A typical schedule for worship in the Gurdwara includes:

- hymns (kirtan)
- discourses (katha)
- prayer (ardas)
- community dinner (langar)

The diwan is highly structured. Each hymn, sung in Punjabi, stresses the longing of the devotee for the companionship of God. The discourse interprets the meaning of the tradition for the present day. Ardas is a specific prayer that has a strong creedal function. Langar is visible evidence of the deity's grace. Parsad, sweet balls of food distributed directly after worship and before langar, impart the blessing of God to each participant.

Links with India

The New York Gurdwara frequently hosts Sikh scholars and visiting lecturers, as do other Sikh temples in the United States. These teachers (sants) are often charismatic leaders who—much in the tradition of Guru Nanak—are missionaries to the Sikh community.[31] They may receive financial support for their lectures, enabling them to travel to centers of Sikhism in the United States, Canada, Great Britain, Fiji, and Africa, where they teach and lecture among other Punjabi Sikhs born into the faith. These teachers are a link to Sikhism in India and, like the leaders of each of the classical traditions discussed in this text, make no attempts to proselytize persons outside of the faith. Their appearance in North America gives the religious community the benefit of the scholastic discipline and a strong devotional tradition.

Not all Sikh communities, however, are enthusiastic about the sant tradition. Some devotees argue that the role of sants has been overemphasized. Such disagreements within the Sikh community are evidence of the diversity of expression in the faith, which frequently has been stereotyped as homogeneous.

Many Sikhs stress that their faith is uncluttered with excesses of ritual or elaborate doctrine because of the reforms of Guru Nanak, who was repelled by the complicated rituals of Hinduism. In reality, however, Sikhism is highly complex. Sikh theology, for instance, is extremely mystical. While the basic concepts of *Shabad* and *Nam* can be quickly introduced, they contain subtle nuances of doctrine that only the well-trained can understand fully.

Festivals

The New York Gurdwara celebrates major Sikh festivals. One such celebration, Baisakhi Day, marks the anniversary of the founding of the *Khalsa* in 1969 (see page 103) and is a time of great pageantry. In the three-day celebration, which is usually held in April, participants celebrate a variety of ceremonies associated with Baisakhi Day. During one such rite called Akhad Path, the Guru Ganth Sahib is read for forty-eight continuous hours. The reading emphasizes the dominant role of the Guru Granth Sahib in Sikh ceremonies. The day itself is an important time when the assembled community reaffirms common values and traditions.

In 1977, in connection with the Baisakhi Day observations, members of the New York Gurdwara performed Amrit Parchar for the first time in the sanctuary. This rite is the formal induction of Sikhs into the *Khalsa*. While it is usually conferred on adolescents, it can also be celebrated by adults. However, regardless of age, each Sikh who has accepted the *Guru's* nectar, affirms the dominance of the brotherhood. Although most who are initiated in this manner are Punjabis, the tradition places no restriction on its membership. During the rite in the New York Gurdwara, celebrants re-enacted a core drama from the Sikh tradition. The ceremony was administered by Panch Piyares (Five Followers) in a repetition of the 1699 event, when five devotees, offering their lives to the *Guru*, formed the nucleus of the *Khalsa*.

Another annual festival in the New York Gurdwara (and in most U.S. and Canadian Sikh temples) is the celebration of Guru Nanak's birthday in late November. The rituals connected with this celebration usually last for three days. *Langar* is served, and hymns are sung. Dignitaries, including well-known Sikh historians and officials from the Punjab, are invited to speak in order to reinforce ties with India.

The New York Gurdwara puts special emphasis on the education of children. Temple leaders teach classes in the history of the faith and Sikh doctrine, as well as Punjabi. Further, the Gurdwara has helped support a Sikh youth camp in a state park near Pittsburgh. The camp has been utilized as a retreat, much as Christian groups send their children to retreat centers for religious instruction. By borrowing this concept, Sikh leaders helped their children achieve a greater knowledge of their own tradition in an environment that has few distractions. Further, by emphasizing such common U.S. activities as hiking and swimming, they help reach children who have been born as Sikhs and United States citizens.

In these ways, leaders of the New York Gurdwara have striven to maintain the orthodoxy of Sikhism on the East Coast by forging links with theological, cultural, and ritualistic traditions in India. The use of a *Granthi* with a prestigious reputation in India helps to establish the temple's orthodoxy. The continuation of the values of Sikhism—the maintenance of the five K's, the covering of heads in the sanctuary, and the removal of chairs from the worship area—assures the integrity of the faith in a North American environment. The frequent appearance of men and women in the *gurdwara* in full Punjabi dress reinforces the function of the temple as a source of authority. Children born in North America are immersed in this Indian environment each Sunday morning as they participate in worship, attend language classes, and eat Punjabi food.

Finally, the New York Gurdwara, like many other temples in North America, maintains strong ties with other U.S., Canadian, and European Sikh societies. The *Khalsa* is an international Sikh community which actively sustains its member institutions and promotes common values among them.

Authority and Tradition Among Sikhs in North America

Sikhism in North America reflects the historical struggle of members of the tradition to retain vital sources of authority. These sources include the Guru Granth Sahib, lecturers from India, the Punjabi family, and the solidarity of the *Khalsa*.

The authority of the Guru Granth Sahib on this continent, much as in India, is never questioned. For example, when the text is moved from one location to another, it is held aloft as a sign of respect. In the *gurdwara* itself, it is always covered by a protective canopy. Sikh congregations go to great lengths to insure the protection and care of this text, which carries the authority of a living *Guru*. The *gurdwara* is defined by the presence of the Guru Granth Sahib. For those communities that have been unable to build *gurdwaras*, the use of a hall, church, or other building often suffices. The key is the Guru Granth Sahib, which defines what is and what is not sacred space, and which sets the boundaries of the faith. It reminds the devotee, for example, that family obligations must always be kept as a priority. There is no room for the ascetic who renounces the traditional structures of society for purposes of study, penance, or worship:

> He who forsaketh his parents to listen to the
> Vedas, shall never know their secret.

He who forsaketh his parents to perform penance
in the forest shall go astray in the wilderness.

He who forsaketh his parents to worship gods and
goddesses, shall lose the reward of his devotion.[32]

For the Sikh, the reward of devotion is nothing less than the experience of God, which is attained through hearing the divine word (*Shabad*) and by repeating God's name (*Nam*).

Many Sikhs in North America resolutely maintain both obedience to the tradition and a strong supportive family role. The organization of the *Khalsa*—in which the patriarchal structures of Punjabi society are reinforced by devotion and participation in the regular activities of the community—makes this possible. The *gurdwara* as the locus of the *Khalsa* actively integrates family members. Each has a defined role according to culture and tradition. For example, women may prepare *langar* in the *gurdwara*'s kitchen. This food, in addition to providing an occasion for community gathering, has immense theological significance. *Langar* affirms the equality of all who partake of it and bestows on them the blessings of God. *Langar* cannot be refused to anyone. It is distributed as a sign of God's compassion and blessing. Children participate in the communal meal as well as in classes. They may also accompany their parents in the sanctuary. Sikh men participate in the organizational life of the *gurdwara* and fulfill a variety of roles.

For Punjabis, the home in India and in the United States or Canada continues to be a source of cultural authority. Marriages, for example, are frequently arranged in cooperation with parents in India. Hence, a Sikh in North America often will return to India for the marriage, thus strengthening ties with the extended family. The home is also a place where children are nurtured into the faith. The values of *keshadhari* Sikhism are instilled at an early age and are important in the child's development. Language, diet, and the traditional roles of both parents are maintained as part of this ongoing process of nurture.

The *Khalsa* is a continuing source of authority for Sikhs in North America. In study circles and in *gurdwaras*, community consensus is an important support for tradition. It sets standards for the education of children. Punjabi schools and classes in Sikh doctrine help acquaint children with the faith who may have never been to India. Likewise, the community worships together and joins for *langar*. The common meal reinforces the solidarity of the Sikh congregation and provides an opportunity for persons with like backgrounds to converse.

In times of crisis, the *Khalsa* has been historically a source of strength. For members of the Khalsa Diwan Society of California in 1914, for example, the *Khalsa* became an active political force as Sikhs utilized the religious community's appointed representatives to speak in Washington on its behalf. Later, in 1946, when Congressman Dalip Singh Saund sought passage of legislation that would allow Indians to become U.S. citizens, the Khalsa was able to lobby effectively. Sikhs all over California sent circulars written in Punjabi that urged support of the reforms.

Because Sikhs find such meaning in the fellowship of believers, members of the community rarely distinguish between the sacred and the secular. To be a Sikh is to display the outward symbols of the tradition at all times. There is no stipulation anywhere in the faith that the five K's be worn only inside the gurdwara, or that other identifying marks of the faith be restricted. Sikhs in the Indian army—and recently in Vancouver, British Columbia—objected when authorities required them to change the turban for military headdress or hard hat.[33] In refusing to obey these regulations, Sikh leaders defended the wearing of turbans in the gurdwara or at work as a mark of their obedience to God. Although not one of the five K's, the turban is an outward symbol of Sikh unity and pride.

The gurdwara as the nucleus of the Khalsa often serves educational, cultural, and religious functions. Gurdwaras in India and the United States place great emphasis on the study of doctrine and theology. In Stockton, California, Sikhs have built a library near the temple as evidence of this concern (see page 127). The New York Gurdwara also maintains a library and supplements educational programs with classes in Punjabi and Sikh history.

In Ottawa, where devotees meet regularly for study and worship, Sikhs have established two educational organizations. The Sikh Study Circle and the Canada Sociological Research Centre cooperate on projects for the continuing education of Sikhs in North America.

These and other Sikh groups frequently publish tracts and books in English. While this reflects a certain degree of assimilation, it also shows the concern of devotees that their faith not be misunderstood or misrepresented. The editor of one such periodical commented, for example, that such publications were written with non-Sikhs in mind.

Sikhs thus look to the same sources of authority in North America as in India. The Khalsa reinforces standards of behavior and determines how the orthodox tradition is to be followed. The Guru Granth Sahib continues theological and doctrinal authority. It is a spiritual guide that includes the essence of the teachings of the ten Gurus. As the locus of spiritual, cultural, and economic traditions, the family continues in the West to preserve important customs. Marriage, life cycle rites, dietary traditions, and language are all maintained in the family unit. Children who speak English at school frequently are taught by their parents to speak Punjabi at home. Each of these mutually supportive traditions helps bolster a sense of community that Punjabi Sikhs have successfully transported around the world. The gurdwara, which enhances and integrates the component parts of this support system, is the center of scriptural, doctrinal, ritualistic, and cultural authority for Sikhs in the West.

Further, some *Granthis* have become accustomed to conducting marriages and funerals. By virtue of the tradition, the *Granthi* is the caretaker of the Guru Granth Sahib and conducts his activities in keeping with this primary obligation. In North America, however, his role may be extended. By conducting important life cycle rites, like other religious specialists in the Judeo-Christian environment of which he is a part, the *Granthi* can relate to the cross-cultural needs of the Sikh community.

The adoption of the eleven o'clock Sunday morning hour and the extension of the function of the *Granthi* demonstrate the remarkable ability of Sikhism to adjust without jeopardizing essential elements of doctrine. The Sikh faith—a highly organized, efficient tradition—has been able to adapt easily to different cultures in Africa, Fiji, Great Britain, and North America.

The faith is particularly well suited to a Judeo-Christian, North American culture, whose roots are firmly planted in a history of self-governance. The *gurdwara*, much like a New England town meeting, is administered in a democratic fashion, allowing the expression of different points of view. As a monotheistic religion with a strong sense of the activity of the holy in history, Sikhism places great value on the corporate will of the community. The tradition of the *Guru* is highly prophetic, stressing the cohesiveness and self-reliance of the *Khalsa*. In North America, this self-reliance is demonstrated by the continuing ability of Sikhs to pledge their time, money, and differing skills for the common good of the faithful.

Sikh symbol incorporating a sword.

CHAPTER FOUR

Islamic Cultures
In North America

An Overview

In the mid-seventh century a revolutionary religious movement swept across the Hijaz, a western portion of what is now Saudi Arabia. The charismatic leader of this faith was Muhammad, who was perceived as a prophet and the messenger of God.

Muhammad was an extraordinary leader who achieved a reputation as a statesman, orator, and brilliant strategist. In the face of persecution and open hostility to his religious movement, he is credited with unifying the Arabian people under the banner of Islam. Yet, in spite of these accomplishments, Muhammad could neither read nor write and had little formal education. Orphaned while still a child, he had been raised by an uncle and a grandfather.

After he had married and established a family, Muhammad received the first of a series of revelations that were to continue throughout his lifetime. The record of these revelations later became the Qur'an.[1] Citing Allah (the Arabic word for God) as the source of his visions, Muhammad attracted a small band of followers in Mecca, where he had been born. As the revelations grew in intensity and frequency, his circle of supporters expanded.

As the Prophet's popularity increased, opposition also developed. Muhammad had preached a vision of reform in which human affairs were made subordinate to the will of one God, Allah. This was a radical change from the indigenous religion of Arabia, which was a combination of idol worship and animism, in which natural objects were given spiritual or supernatural powers. Muhammad condemned these practices and insisted that, instead of seeking to placate false gods, his followers must submit themselves totally to Allah, the one God. Thus, the faith became known as Islam, which means "submission." Those persons who submitted to Allah were called Muslims.[2]

137

The Islamic Center, Washington, D.C., with a minaret, from which the call to prayer was traditionally given.

By A.D. 622, tensions had increased in Mecca, forcing the Prophet to flee. In the company of his supporters, he emigrated to a neighboring city, Medina. This event marks the beginning of the Islamic calendar and is called the *Hijrah*.

In Medina, Muhammad established a model for a society in which Allah was seen as the foundation for a just social order. Each Muslim was required to lead a disciplined life in which five duties were considered authoritative and obligatory. These duties were designated as the Five Pillars of Islam. They included a statement of belief (*shahadah*), pilgrimage (*Hajj*), regular prayer (*salat*), fasting (*sawm*), and a tithe (*zakat*), which was distributed among the poor.

The first *Hajj* took place several months before the Prophet's death in 632. Muhammad led a group of Muslims from Medina back to Mecca, which by this time had been recaptured in the name of Islam. The Hajj drew its authority from a sacred shrine, a black stone cubicle known as the Ka'bah, which according to Muslim tradition had been established by the prophet Abraham. In the course of time, the original purpose of the Ka'bah had been forgotten. Instead, it had become a sanctuary for the indigenous religions of Mecca and a center for the worship of idols. Reaffirming the prophetic monotheism of Abraham and Moses, Muhammad revitalized the worship of Allah and restored the Ka'bah to its original use.

The *shahadah*, or profession of faith, is a creedal statement that defines the identity of a Muslim. It declares: "There is no God but Allah and Muhammad is his messenger." By the sincere repetition of this statement, any person can become a Muslim.

The simplicity of the *shahadah* is an example of the importance of conversion in the Muslim faith. However, the emphasis of the *shahadah* is on the voluntary acceptance of Islam. To accept Islam is to acknowledge the dominant will of Allah and his continuing role of judgment, punishment, and mercy.

Salat, or regular prayer, is conceived as a precisely controlled act of devotion. It is repeated five times a day at fixed periods of time determined by the position of the sun. The five periods of prayer are: sunset (*maghrib*), night (*isha*), dawn (*fajr*—the time between the dark of night and the actual rising of the sun), noon (*zuhr*), and afternoon (*asr*). Before prayer begins, the supplicants wash ritualistically, taking care to cleanse face, hands, and feet. The prayers themselves, like the purification beforehand, are precise. Each prostration or body movement is an act of obeisance. This remarkable homogeneity, with some very minor variation among different schools of Islam, came to symbolize the theological equality of all Muslims. The repeated prostration suggests dramatically that the devotees surrender themselves completely to God. Prayer, the essential act of devotion, affirms the dominance of the divine will and at the same time celebrates the mercy of Allah.

Much like prayer, *zakat*, or almsgiving, is highly regulated. As a fixed percentage, *zakat* is assessed at one fortieth of each Muslim's annual income. Theologically, it is defined as a loan to God to be distributed among the poor and needy.

Sawm, or fasting, like *zakat*, is a dramatic symbol of obedience to God. Muslims fast in order to purify their bodies, to become more aware of the holy, and to show humility and abstinence. In the month of Ramadan (the ninth month of the Muslim calendar year), fasting from dawn to sunset is an expected duty of all able adult believers.

Each of the Five Pillars symbolizes the surrender of the Muslim to God and the commitment of the faithful to live in a ordered society in which the will of Allah rules every aspect of human affairs. Although Islam was later to develop its own strain of mysticism called *sufism* (which has often been perceived as heterodox), the orthodox tradition denied both asceticism and monasticism. Instead of fleeing from the world to find God, the Muslim was disciplined to live in it, continually acknowledging the sovereignty of Allah.

Preaching this revolutionary vision, Muhammad won over most of Arabia by the time of his death. He had fulfilled two roles. Foremost, he was understood to be the culmination or seal of the prophetic tradition that had begun with Abraham. Second, as the very messenger of Allah, he was the source of authority for questions of law and government.

At the time of his death, Muhammad had not designated a successor to continue this second important function. Soon a schism arose over the governance of the faithful. One group of Muslims appointed Abu Bakr, a member of the Quraysh tribe of Muhammad, as Caliph ("successor"). However, a rival faction opposed Abu Bakr and disputed his claim to the office since he was not a blood relative of the Prophet. They supported Ali, Muhammad's son-in-law and cousin. The schism later resulted in the creation of two opposing parties that continue to this day. The majority who selected Abu Bakr as Caliph were known as Sunnis. The party that supported Ali was called collectively Shi'a.[3]

As the rivalry between the two opposing factions increased, violence erupted. Ali was assassinated and his son Hasan poisoned. In 680 under the leadership of Abu Bakr's armies, who tried to crush the dissidents, Ali's second son, Husayn, was killed in battle.

Today, Shi'i Muslims view the killing of Husayn as a decisive event in the history of their faith. Husayn is perceived as a martyr and the day of his death is seen as a holy day.

Because of the important position that Ali holds in the Shi'i faith, certain individuals have been designated as his spiritual descendants. These persons, called *Imams*, have been perceived as possessing the power of revelation. Distinctions between Shi'i sects have been based on succession to the historical role of *Imam.* Some Shi'a (Zaidis) have recognized five *Imams* while others (Ismailis) have acknowledged seven. Still others have distinguished twelve. The tradition of the Twelvers has been the official religion of Iran since the sixteenth century.

Shi'i Muslims, however, are a minority in the Islamic world. They are found in Yemen, Lebanon, Iran, Iraq, and Zanzibar as well as parts of India and Pakistan. While Shi'a in these and other countries differ with the orthodox Sunnis over the question of the *Imam,* the two schools are much alike in other ways. In matters of prayer and theology, distinctions between the traditions are often insignificant.

This chapter describes the perpetuation of both Shi'i and Sunni forms of the faith among Muslim immigrants in North America. Although the adoption of Islam among converts in the United States is beyond the designated purpose of the text, readers are urged to explore it through other sources. Devotees previously identified as Black Muslims (and later as Bilalians) are the subject of numerous works that examine the history and growth of the movement now designated as the American Muslim Mission.[4] The authority of this tradition has recently been formidably challenged by a leader, Louis Farrakhan, whose organization, The Nation of Islam, seeks to return to the tenets of Elijah Muhammad, who developed the faith after it was established in the United States by W. D. Fard.

Several levels of Muslim tradition in North America are described, including ethnic identity, sectarian affiliation, and a general adherence to the universal brotherhood of Islam. For example, Pakistani Muslims in the United States often maintain their own mosques and encourage the marriage of devotees within their communities. Similarly, for many U.S. and Canadian Muslims, sectarian affiliation helps instill an important level of personal and corporate identity. Yet, beyond these components of a diversified religious tradition, Islam is also an integrative force that forges common bonds of loyalty to God among different peoples. The chapter illustrates this cohesive quality of the faith. It shows, for example, how fourteen governments of Muslim countries cooperated to build a multimillion-dollar mosque in Washington, D.C. Such a dramatic level of cooperation between representatives of diverse cultures shows the strength and appeal of the message of the Prophet across thousands of miles.

Islam is a total way of life that affects numerous aspects of belief, daily regimen, and culture. In keeping with this level of commitment, Muslim families maintain strong ties with the Islamic culture of which they are a part. Children are brought up in the faith from infancy.

The reader is introduced to one Islamic culture, the Arab Muslims, who maintain strong ties with their homeland. Muslims of Arab extraction have lived and worked in North America for several generations. In some cities, such as Dearborn, Michigan, large communities of Lebanese live in an environment similar to that of their parents and grandparents who first came to this country. Restaurants, coffee houses, grocery stores, and other shops enable members of the community to continue important dietary traditions and elements of their culture.

While the history of such communities demonstrates the growth and revitalization of Islam in North America, devotees often admit that the practice of their faith here has been difficult. In a non-Muslim environment where many persons are not familiar with Islam, stereotypes and prejudices about the tradition have been a source of hardship for many. For example, during the Iranian revolution in 1979, fear and misunderstanding about Islam were prevalent in the United States. Islamic organizations and mosques became suspect even though in many cases there were few, if any, links with Iran. Some places of worship were desecrated. Distinctions between Shi'i and Sunni Muslims were frequently distorted or not made clear.

False generalizations about Muslims abound. Islam is often perceived as monolithic and uniform. Such a view not only ignores the cultural differences between Muslims, but dangerously oversimplifies the faith. Whenever isolated groups of Muslim fundamentalists have waged war in the name of the faith, the tradition has been stereotyped as violent. The attack of militants on the Ka'bah in November, 1979, caused reaction throughout the West. The Islamic world was perceived as violent and fanatical even though the vast majority of Muslims were outraged by the attack. While the terrorism was in reality the result of a band of extremists, it became quickly associated with the general character of Islam.

This chapter introduces the student to Islamic cultures in North America with the hope that it will help prevent such misunderstanding in the future. Accordingly, it prepares the reader to encounter the faith with the hope that it will be observed and appreciated, both as an important movement among North Americans who have converted to the faith and in those forms described here.

The Prophet

The most recent major Semitic religious tradition, Islam is a monotheistic religion with a strong doctrine of divine activity in human affairs. It is seen as a human response to God that is guided by a chain of prophetic teachers who are instruments of God's revelation. Accordingly, the tradition includes a succession of many prophets, including

Adam, Noah, and Abraham. Jesus is also understood to be a prophet. However, Muslims reject the idea of a son of God (Qur'an-Surah IX. 30) and the crucifixion itself (Surah IV. 157). Since, according to the Islamic view, the unity of God cannot in any way be compromised, there can be no deified Christ and no resurection. These concepts are looked upon as distortions of the original teachings of Jesus. Further, Muhammad is never seen as divine. Rather, he is the seal of the prophets, the messenger of Allah who, in vision after vision, transmitted divine revelation in the form of the Qur'an.

The teachings of Islam continue the Judaic understanding of a prophet as a social reformer and a teacher of morality. The prophet is understood to act on the authority of God, but not above nor independent of the law of God.

Prophets usually appear in a time of social unrest when the traditional structures of society are breaking down. Muhammad thus began to experience visions when the fabric of Meccan culture was disintegrating. Like much of the Middle East, the nomadic culture surrounding Mecca depended on the existence of clans who upheld the importance of the family and the religious community. But the clan structure in Mecca was deteriorating, while the interests of the dominant mercantile segment of the population prospered.

The popular religion of Mecca was a tradition in which natural objects were given spiritual or supernatural powers. Muhammad's earliest preaching condemned this image worship as being idolatrous. To replace it, he proclaimed obedience to the one God, Allah.

Muhammad followed the usual path of a prophet. He preached the existence of a single God, he condemned popular religious practices that deified objects, and he sought reforms in the social fabric of his day. As his prophetic visions increased in intensity and duration, it became apparent to his supporters that Muhammad spoke with the authority of God. The substance of these visions, which became the Qur'an, were recognized by his followers as of divine origin transmitted to him by the angel Gabriel. Since Muhammad was illiterate, the record of the Qur'an became written evidence of the deity's miraculous intervention in human affairs. Accordingly, Islam has preserved the original language of the revelations, which are understood to be the very words of Allah.

Like the prophets before him, Muhammad's life was filled with dreams and visions that he perceived as emanating from God. These experiences were so powerful that he is reported to have sought solitude away from the bustling commercial city of Mecca. By the time of his Call, Muhammad was a respected businessperson who had achieved a good reputation as a trader and commercial agent. He had married a wealthy widow and had raised a family. Yet, those who knew him well must have seen the dramatic evidence of his continuing struggle to understand the visions that often left him exhausted. The effect of these experiences on Muhammad's life was undoubtedly traumatic. At the very point in his career when he had achieved a position of respect and accomplishment secure from economic worry, Muhammad was challenged to accept a new and potential dangerous role. As the visions increased and Muhammad became even more convinced of his encounter with God, his anxieties accelerated. At the same time he became aware that he had been selected by God as a prophet.

Three incidents in Muhammad's life show how he fulfilled the role of a prophet. The first was a conversion experience on Mount Hira, which is deemed to be his Call. According to Muslim tradition, the setting of Muhammad's visions was often the mountains. In Semitic religions, high places usually have symbolized the power and sovereignty of a monotheistic God. Moses, for example, sought God atop Mount Sinai. Muhammad, in a similar manner, sought the solitude of Mount Hira outside Mecca to escape the moral decay of the city below and to seek a place where God could best be approached. It was here that Muhammad first became aware of the deity's direct intervention in his life. The Qur'an records the first verses revealed to Muhammad:

> Recite!
> In the name
> Of the Lord and Cherisher
>   who created—
>
> Created man, out of
> A [mere] clot
> Of congealed blood:
>
> Proclaim! And thy Lord
> Is Most Bountiful—
>
> He Who taught
> [with] the Pen—
>
> Taught man that
> Which he knew not.[5]

The experience of revelation was intense. Muhammad felt compelled to share what he had learned. Though he continued to experience revelations through most of his life, the initial theophany atop Mount Hira remained one of the most powerful of his encounters with the holy. Moreover, his conversion experience was a graphic example of revelation that was in keeping with existing patterns of prophetic tradition. God had spoken, as he had numerous times before in history, through an intermediary who became charged with the transmission of revealed knowledge. In accepting this first revelation, Muhammad assumed the role of prophet who would again and again voice the judgment of Allah. As a reformer, Muhammad acknowledged the unquestioned authority of God. In pronouncing God's decree, he became the instrument of salvation—often at great personal danger.

The second incident that established Muhammad's authority as a prophet was the Hijrah in A.D. 622. This emigration was a highly dramatic journey in which the Prophet fled from Mecca to Medina. There, he solidified his support. The event is so important that it marks the beginning of the Muslim calendar.

Though the move to Medina was prompted by the increased hostility of residents of Mecca to Islam, the emigration came to symbolize the acceptance of Muhammad by a growing band of supporters as a messenger of God. Muhammad entered Medina as a victor. Commanding enough support to proclaim the city a center of the faith, he sought to bring Islam to the agricultural peoples of a distant town. The move marked a transition in the manner by which the faith was propagated. Up to this time Muhammad had preached only to members of his own tribe, the Quraysh. Now he broadened his appeal. Uprooting his followers from what had become a hostile environment, the Prophet led his supporters to the oasis of Yathrib. By transforming the oasis into the holy city Medina, Muhammad secured a political and economic base among an economically and socially stable community.

The most visible result of this transformation was the creation of a lasting model of the Islamic state. In Medina, Muhammad created a totally Muslim environment in which all aspects of life were to be governed by God. The city was transformed carefully to bring this about. Even Muhammad's house, set outside the perimeter of Medina, was constructed with a courtyard that could be used for worship. Medina enacted the concept of the Islamic state: there was no division between sacred and secular. The influence of Medina as a model for Islamic society retains its symbolic importance today.

For example, the same model has motivated many of the reforms in the Iranian revolution of 1979. After the fall of the Shah and the establishment of a new government by the Ayatollah Khomeini, elements of Western influence in Iran were purged. While reasons for many of these changes are political, they also are religious. The Shah was symbolically identified with the murderers of Ali and his sons, from whom the Shi'a movement is descended. This identification had been noticeable especially on the tenth day of Muharram when Husayn, the son of Ali and grandson of the Prophet, was killed in battle in Karbala in Iraq. Shi'i demonstrators used this day during the revolution to show their hatred for the Shah, and, by virtue of the close association of the Pahlavi government with the United States, their animosity toward that country. Such outpourings of emotion were also influenced by the association of the image of the United States with secularism in a country where the Islamic model of no separation between sacred and secular is an ever-present ideal.

For Shi'i Muslims in Iran, it is logical for an Ayatollah to guide the creation of an Islamic state. The title Ayatollah means "sign of God"[6] and is given to Muslim leaders of high repute and spiritual authority. Each Ayatollah is deemed to be a representative of the *Imam*. Some Shi'a in Iran identify Ayatollah Khomeini with the word of the *Imam* so closely that he is seen as the just authority for all questions of law and government.

The values propagated in Medina continue to be normative for Muslims in North America. They reflect the cohesion of the Islamic community and the authority of the *Imam*, or religious specialist (which should not be confused with the Shi'i *Imamate*, the spiritual lineage of Ali). The *Imam* guides and develops the practical application of the Qur'an to Muslim society. He does not exercise the same function as do Judeo-Christian clergy. Educated in exegesis and theology, he is primarily an interpreter of the Qur'an. In North America, where pressures to conform to the cultural model of a priest or minister can be a source of conflict, the *Imam* is a unique symbol of the authority of Qur'anic tradition. By his words, he helps devotees to interpret the will of Allah as contained in the Qur'an. His actions are to demonstrate a mode of behavior rooted in submission to God.

Most *Imams* are highly respected teachers. Frequently, they write tracts on points of doctrine, thus enhancing their traditional role. Some *Imams* have produced entire courses that help devotees far from mosques or Islamic centers to benefit from their teachings. The *Imam* also regulates worship. By announcing the call to prayer from a minaret, if the mosque is built in traditional fashion, he reinforces the times and manner of prayer prescribed in the Qur'an.

The third incident in Muhammad's life that dramatized his authority as a prophet was the *Hajj*, or pilgrimage, in 632. By 632 the use of the Ka'bah had been fully restored. When Muhammad led supplicants on the *Hajj*, he dramatized the importance of pilgrimage and affirmed his own role as the spiritual heir of Abraham whose sanctuary he had purified. The *Hajj* became a duty expected of all Muslims. By praying at the Ka'bah, they reaffirmed their own obedience to Allah and the authority of the one God throughout their lives.

For Muslims in North America or elsewhere, the *Hajj* remains a most important duty. A devout Muslim plans to make the journey at least once in a lifetime. After making the pilgrimage, supplicants assume the respected title of *Hajji*, which may be prefixed to their names.

The *Hajj* is a powerful experience that is at the very heart of Islam. For Muslims in North America it is a return to the spiritual homeland of their forebears. Once they have boarded a plane chartered for the *Hajj*, devotees enter a sacred world in which religion affects every action. As a mark of the equality of pilgrims and as a symbol of their purified status, each devotee wears a white, seamless, two-piece garment. During the *Hajj* this garment and the sanctified food that is consumed during the journey symbolize a continued state of purity. The pilgrim lives in a state of *ihram*, or restriction, in which all aspects of behavior are regulated precisely.

Most pilgrims arrive in Jidda, forty-five miles from Mecca (see page 148). Once entering Mecca, the supplicant is plunged into a world open only to Muslims. Members of other religious traditions are forbidden to enter the holy ground.

In Mecca, the pilgrim is surrounded by thousands of other devotees from all over the world. Muslims from Africa, the Philippines, Spain, Saudi Arabia, and the United States converge on this sacred place to take part in a series of rituals. Most perform *tawaf*: walking around the Ka'bah seven times. Many yearn to kiss the black stone set in the corner of the Ka'bah. The stone is ascribed to Abraham, who is believed to have built the first shrine on the ground where the Ka'bah now stands. By performing these ancient rites, the pilgrim reaffirms the authority of Allah in his or her own life and atones for past misdeeds. The *Hajj* is an act of submission before God. While rooted in the prophetic reforms of Muhammad, it is centered on God's will.

The *Hajj* crystallizes the links between the revelation of Allah contained in the Qur'an, his messenger Muhammad, and each pilgrim. By walking around the Ka'bah, by touching the stone laid by Abraham, and by other acts, the pilgrim forges personal ties with tradition. He or she receives support for the only pattern for a devotional life that can exist in Islam—the total submission and commitment to God.

Sources of Authority in Islam

Because of its divine origin, the Qur'an is a source of absolute authority in the Muslim tradition. Its significance for the present is determined through a process of exegesis in which the original meaning of the text is explained. The Qur'an is also a model for questions of law, ethics and social organization.

In addition to the Qur'an, Muslims recognize *hadiths* as a source of authority. A *hadith* is a story about the Prophet. It stresses the dominance of Muhammad's actions, judgments, and opinions in hundreds of different matters. These examples drawn from the Prophet's life are regarded as *Sunna*, or direct avenues of authority that have become custom.

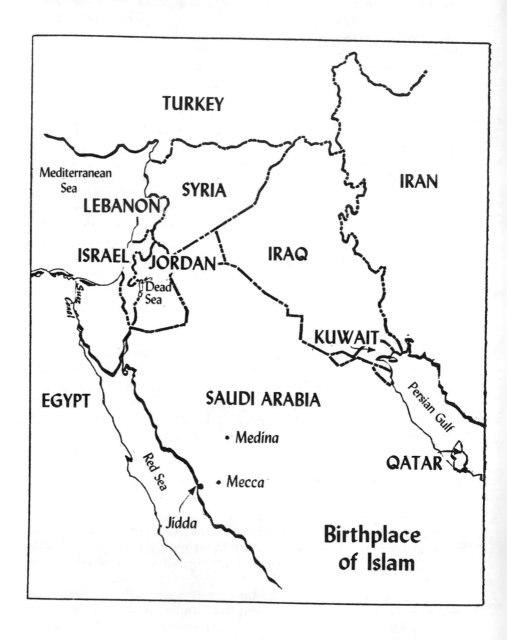

Birthplace of Islam

The number of *hadiths* is enormous and greatly varied. *Hadiths* can be found for almost every ethical concern or individual act. Each *hadith* is tested for authenticity by a detailed examination of the chain of transmission reaching back to Muhammad. This chain of transmission may be even more important than the content of the *hadith*, since it establishes a dramatic link with the actual words and deeds of Muhammad. Without such verification, the *hadith* loses its authority and becomes subject to speculation.

Islamic jurisprudence, or sacred law, is interpreted in traditional ways. Muslim jurists recognize several sources of authority—the Qur'an, custom based on an example of the Prophet's life *(sunna)*, consensus *(ijma)*, and deductive logic through the use of analogy *(qiyas)*. The last category applies accepted principles of Islamic jurisprudence to new areas of inquiry. There are six major schools of law *(Shari'a)* in Islam, each of which recognizes these sources with differences in emphasis. The six schools are Hanafi, Maliki, Shafi'i, Hanbali, Ja'fari, and Zaidi. Each school establishes standards of conduct that affects all aspects of behavior.

In Islamic states, the law is administered by the *ulama*, a prestigious class of conservative scholars. The *ulama* historically have exercised an important check on the state, upholding the rule of *Shari'a*.

Because different schools of Islamic law may recognize different *hadiths*, the obligations and restrictions for individual devotees can vary. This variety has allowed Islam to become strongly adaptable. As a result, the Muslim faith can be practiced in vastly different cultures and has developed different sectarian traditions.

Muslims in North America may belong to any of the six schools of law depending on their country of origin and belief system. For example, the Maliki school often predominates among immigrants from parts of Africa and Egypt, while the Hanafi school is accepted by many Turkish, Indian, and Pakistani Muslims. Each school directly influences the Islamic culture of which it is a part in matters such as marriage, divorce, and patterns of social interaction.

In the United States, as in other non-Muslim countries where the basic institutions of Islamic jurisprudence are absent, there is no *ulama* to administer law or correct actions of the state. In addition, *Shari'a* regulations may conflict with United States civil law. For instance, *Shari'a* law regulates questions of inheritance, prescribing how estates are to be divided among family members. The extended family is often a primary concern in such matters. In countries such as the United States or Canada where civil law predominates over religious concerns, many devotees are caught between the expectations of the family overseas and the legal requirements of the country in which they live.

A Brief History of Muslim Immigrants in North America

In 1933 a New York newspaper reported that a trial had been postponed in order to allow the complainant, an Indian Muslim, to return home so that he might engage in purificatory rites before being sworn in.[7] As a Muslim, the complainant would not take an oath on the Qur'an without first completing a series of rituals, which in his tradition were obligatory.

This brief incident undoubtedly surprised the court officials who witnessed it as well as the public who read of the account. It was unusual because a court of law had temporarily halted its proceedings to allow a Muslim to purify himself before being sworn in with the Qur'an. The court thus sanctioned the substitution of the Qur'an for the Bible and in so doing recognized the complainant's freedom of religion. This was significant since Islam was now formally being recognized as a legitimate religion of a minority group in the United States. Moreover, the sanctity of the Qur'an was acknowledged for those who swore on it.

The optimism that this incident sparked was in sharp contrast to the frustration experienced by first-generation Muslims who had emigrated from Syria and Lebanon in late nineteenth and early twentieth centuries. These early settlers had little opportunity to nurture or practice their faith. Many were isolated from other Muslims. Most spoke little English and had few personal ties in North America. One early Syrian Muslim, for example, came to the United States in 1902—alone and unsure of where he eventually would settle.[8] He had booked passage on an impulse after seeing many of his friends do the same thing. Coming from an agricultural background, he had few skills that could be used in urban areas. He had no choice but to earn his livelihood as a peddler, like many of his countrymen in the same situation. He had no relatives in the United States and had little idea of how to reach other persons from a similar background. He was alone and unprepared. Arriving in the United States, he traveled from New York to Detroit, affiliating in both places with Syrian Christian communities. He found few other Muslims and no community to bolster the traditions he had learned as a child. His plight illustrated the trauma of many other early immigrants who came from the Middle East to North America hoping to further their position at a time of economic distress at home. Some Muslims came to the United States at the invitation of sponsors who were a success in business and had come from the same region.[9] These influential patrons helped new arrivals adjust to their surroundings, and often aided them in finding employment and housing. Frequently they became mediators with civic officials. In short, they provided a bridge between the two cultures.

Many immigrants in this early period lost their Islamic identity and were quickly assimilated. Most found few ways of supporting their religious tradition. The majority of Lebanese and Syrians in the United States were Christian. Thus, Muslim immigrants had little option but to join their compatriots if they wanted the fellowship of persons speaking the same language and understanding the same culture.

By 1914 this early period of assimilation and fragmentation had ended. More Muslims had entered the United States. Islamic organizations in New York and in the Midwest had attracted a growing number of devotees. Muslims in Cedar Rapids, Iowa, for example, had established the beginnings of an Islamic community.[10] Many immigrants were peddlers who later became small shopkeepers, supplying farmers in the area with needed goods. By 1920 the community had established its first mosque by converting a rented hall. In 1929, plans were made for the construction of a formal mosque. An *Imam* was hired to help oversee the effort.

During this early period, Muslims frequently met in small groups for worship and the celebration of major holidays. In Brooklyn, New York, in 1925, Muslims met in a room above a Syrian cafe to celebrate the feast that ends the month of Ramadan, a period of fasting. This festival, called Id al-Fitr (one of two major festivals abbreviated as Id), is a time of great rejoicing in which Muslims may offer special prayers, don new clothes, and exchange gifts. A local paper reported that the gathering included persons of different nationalities from the metropolitan area.[11] Such gatherings were significant, since they marked the end of earlier patterns of fragmentation and the establishment of a new unity, which transcended ethnic or national identity.

During this time, Arab merchants had settled in different parts of the Midwest and had established communities in Ohio and Indiana. In 1914 an Islamic Center was incorporated as a non-profit organization in Michigan City, Indiana.[12] Members of this community were mostly Syrian and Lebanese who continued the Arab mercantile tradition. Soon the community erected a mosque, which attracted Muslims from three states since no other Islamic centers were nearby.

The Michigan City mosque became a supportive, integrating institution that helped its members express their Muslim identity. The mosque revitalized ethnic and religious traditions, reviving for its members the values and ways of life that they had learned as children. Reflecting its expanding role, the mosque reorganized in 1924 under the name "Asser El Jadeed Arabian Islamic Society." "Asser El Jadeed" meant "The Modern Age." The name affirmed both the Arabic and Islamic heritage of its supporters.

Both the Cedar Rapids and Michigan City mosques began important services to devotees, which continue today. For example, land was obtained for cemeteries. This was highly significant since Muslim funerals require burial in a distinctive manner. The corpse is interred without embalming. In most Muslim countries, the body is cleansed, wrapped in a shroud, and interred in a plot that faces Mecca. The eldest sons share the responsibility of the burial.

Muslim cemeteries are usually maintained without elaborate headstones. Theological support for this practice comes from the Islamic injunction that all believers are equal. The only judge of the merit of any individual is Allah, who is both merciful and just. Thus, most Muslims reject the use of expensive monuments or mausoleums at the time of death. While this practice has been violated by powerful heads of state and members of the aristocracy in different Muslim cultures, it remains a standard that is often followed today.

The cemetery in Cedar Rapids, Iowa, opened in 1948. The six and one-half-acre tract met the needs of devotees across the wide geographical area of Iowa, South Dakota, and Indiana. Each plot was carefully surveyed to face Mecca precisely.[13]

The establishment of Islamic cemeteries in the United States was highly significant. It offered Muslims the opportunity to bury their dead in a manner prescribed by their religion rather than the customs of cemeteries run for the use of Jews and Christians. Previously, most Muslims had little choice but to inter their loved ones in plots that rarely faced Mecca in cemeteries that were not designed to meet their needs.

By making possible the continuation of these customs, leaders of the Cedar Rapids and Michigan City mosques were insuring that in life and at the time of death, pervasive elements of Islamic culture would be maintained. This was important since Islam is a total way of life. Earlier Muslim immigrants had experienced a fragmented existence in which dislocated elements of Islamic culture were maintained sporadically. By 1924, with two established mosques providing services to devotees, the beginnings of a more inclusive tradition had taken place.

The traditions begun in Michigan City and Cedar Rapids soon spread to other parts of the country. Gradually, a movement arose to disseminate information about Islam and to organize Muslim communities. By the late twenties, many large cities in the United States and Canada had active Muslim organizations. In New York an *Imam* disseminated tracts on Muslim doctrine to devotees on the East Coast. A group of Palestinians and Syrians formed the Young Men's Moslem [*sic.*] Association. An Arabic newsletter, *El-Bayan*, kept members of the faith informed of Muslim events and practices. Other Islamic populations in the Midwest and the East followed similar practices.

Where feasible, Muslim societies brought *Imams* from the Middle East to serve congregations in the United States. The *Imam* was an important link with the authority of tradition. For instance, the Cedar Rapids mosque hired a prominent Saudi as its *Imam*, who remained there until 1938. Succeeding other religious leaders from different parts of the

Middle East, the *Imam* was an attractive symbol of the vitality of the Cedar Rapids Islamic community. He became a motivating force behind the construction of a new mosque and the perpetuation of lasting traditions.

By the mid-1940s, two events had symbolized dramatically the ability of Muslims in North America to establish needed links with Islamic countries and to develop an increasing sense of cooperation and unity. The planning of the Islamic Center in Washington, D.C., and eight years later in 1952, the birth of the Federation of Islamic Associations in Cedar Rapids, Iowa, marked a major transition for Muslims in the United States. Muslims had striven to re-establish links with authority and tradition. Now, Islamic communities sought lasting symbols of their identity as fresh arrivals strengthened the tradition in North America.

The birth of the Islamic Center in Washington, D.C.,[14] was a highly significant symbol of cooperation between Islamic governments and Muslims in the United States. As the largest, most elaborate project of its kind in North America, the construction of the Center had tremendous significance. It marked the formal acknowledgment of North America as a foreign mission field to which Islamic countries proudly sent their highly trained and skilled personnel.

The construction of the mosque was a symbol of Islamic unity for the fourteen Muslim nations that contributed to the project. Their cooperation upheld the image, so often voiced in the tradition, of the universal brotherhood of Islam. This was significant since the Islamic world historically has been divided by differences in culture, national identity, and doctrinal affiliation.

For example, the war between Iraq and Iran in the early 1980s had roots in the history of Islam.[15] As Islam spread across the fertile crescent in the mid-seventh century, it encountered different cultures. While the inhabitants of present-day Iraq (formerly Mesopotamia) were largely Arab, the population of Iran (formerly Persia) was Indo-European. Islam had been brought to Persia in 637 when Arab forces from Mesopotamia were victorious at the battle of Qadisiyah. The battle is still a source of great emotion and has been cited as a reason for revenge in Iran.

The divisions between the two countries were increased by the murder of Husayn, the son of Ali in 680. As the Islamic world separated into Shi'i and Sunni, so the populations of these bordering states adopted different allegiances. Today, Iran is predominantly Shi'i while Iraq includes both Sunni and Shi'i.

Hence, the early history of the Islamic world, much as that of the Christian church in Europe, has been characterized by idealogical, political, and cultural differences. Yet, the utopian ideal of the brotherhood of Islam has always been a persistent goal that has sought to overcome these divisions. The construction of an Islamic Center in the United

The Islamic Center, Washington, D.C., with a devotional inscription in Arabic over the arches of the facade.

States with the full cooperation of Muslim governments that have not always been in accord was a powerful symbol of this vision.

The idea for the construction of an Islamic Center in Washington was conceived by a U.S. Muslim businessperson and the Egyptian ambassador in 1944. By 1945 the initiative of these two leaders had led to the creation of a Washington Mosque Foundation to secure contributions from Muslims and friends across the United States. After the laying of the cornerstone for the mosque in 1949, the Foundation's executive committee began to assign quotas to the governments of major Muslim countries for underwriting the Center's estimated cost. The effort proved successful. Fourteen governments had contributed funds and gifts in kind to the project by the time it was completed in 1957. In the process, leaders had established avenues of continuing support from the Middle East. The Director's salary, for example, was to be provided on a continuing basis by Egypt. *Imams* were to be supplied by Al-Azhar University in Cairo, one of the most respected Islamic educational institutions and a source of orthodoxy and theological authority.

Located on a 30,000-square foot tract of land, every detail of the Islamic Center was planned strictly according to tradition. The minaret, the marble columns, and the archways of the mosque conform to precise standards of Islamic architecture, replicating the finest patterns of construction.

The Islamic Center was an unprecedented venture that marked an increased level of religious cooperation among Muslim countries in support of a U.S. mission. The Center became a symbol of Muslim unity and identity in the United States. It continues to support an Islamic consciousness among the various Muslim communities across the nation.

The formation of the Federation of Islamic Associations (F.I.A.) in 1952 continued the efforts of the Washington Mosque Foundation to broaden the image of the United States as the home of a significant Muslim population. It also marked a heightened level of cooperation among U.S. Muslims, who now supported a truly North American federation.

The F.I.A. was conceived by an American soldier in World War II. Abdallah Igram had been incensed when he discovered that the armed forces did not recognize the designation "Muslim."[16] Further, no reference to Islam could be inscribed on dog-tags. After his discharge in 1945, Igram returned to his home in Cedar Rapids, Iowa, determined to help end such examples of discrimination. He began working toward the realization of a new dream—the establishment of a society for Muslims that would unify the voice of Islam in North America. The response to Igram's dream was overwhelming. More than 400 Muslims met in Cedar Rapids in 1952 and formed the International Muslim Society. A year later in Toledo, Ohio, a second convention attracted more than 1,000 persons. In 1954 in Chicago the organization adopted a constitution and a new name, "Federation of Islamic Associations in the United States and Canada." Abdallah Igram had served as the president of the International Muslim Society and its successor, the F.I.A., until 1955. His dream had become a reality. The F.I.A. emerged as a coordinating body that sought to promote a greater cohesiveness between U.S. and Canadian Muslims.

The F.I.A. interested the government of Egypt in its efforts when, soon after the organization's formation, two F.I.A. officials met with the head of state, Gamal Abdel Nasser. He contributed $50,000 toward a new mosque in Detroit. They also secured the pledge of the services of four Imams who would come to the United States.

This event was highly significant for several reasons. First, it firmly established the ability of Muslim immigrants to transcend regionalism and to look beyond their individual mosques and communities. Second, it demonstrated the ability of Muslims in North America to perpetuate the authority of the foremost Muslim University, Al-Azhar, strengthening the formal ties with orthodox Islamic tradition. Through these efforts, the Muslim community in the United States secured an avenue for the regular revitalization and enrichment of its practices.

The formation of the F.I.A. with its ability to gather Muslims from all over the United States and Canada into cooperative ventures, helped pave the way for other North American Islamic organizations, which are continuing to evolve rapidly both in structure and number. One of the most significant of such recent organizations is the Muslim Students' Association. With headquarters outside Indianapolis, Indiana, the M.S.A. is a coordinating agency for graduate and undergraduate Muslim students on campuses across the United States and Canada. With the sharp increase in immigrants from Arab countries, South Asia, and other parts of the Muslim world, the M.S.A. serves a large body of students, many of whom remain in the United States after the completion of their education. The increase of these persons in the United States was dramatically aided by the reforms in immigration laws in 1965 and the elimination of the national origins quota system. Some have married U.S. citizens and entered a wide range of professions and occupations. This new population is highly skilled and well educated. The Muslim Students' Association, drawing on these resources, has established numerous programs that often reach beyond the campus. For example, the M.S.A. supports an Islamic Press, which distributes publications among its member associations. Many of the publications help the M.S.A.'s members—the majority of whom have been in North America less than six years—to continue their religious traditions. The M.S.A. helps fresh arrivals to practice their faith in a non-Muslim environment and, if they wish, to prepare for a lasting residence in the United States and Canada.

In order to realize these goals, the M.S.A. has developed a highly refined and efficient organizational structure. The agency is divided into zones that include the western, central, and eastern parts of the United States, and two zones in Canada. Each zone is divided into regions under the administrative supervision of regional representatives. Zones hold regular council meetings and often sponsor conferences on varying points of Muslim doctrine and practice.

The Muslim Students' Association was formed in response to the need for Islamic organizations directed at specific Muslim populations. Today the Islamic Medical Association, the Association of Muslim Social Scientists, and the Association of Muslim Scientists and Engineers are examples of this type of federation. They are professional groups that are concerned with a theological correlation between occupation and religious beliefs. Such professional groups are able to lobby vigorously on behalf of their Muslim members and to help counteract misconceptions and prejudices about Islam.

In 1982, the Muslim Students' Association formed a parent organization, known as the Islamic Society of North America. The new body included the professional associations already formed, the M.S.A. itself, and the Muslim Communities Association. The total organization has gathered substantial authority and support among Muslims in North America and is often viewed as being in a position of leadership.

Another coordinating agency, the Council of Muslim Communities of Canada, was formed in 1972, succeeding a smaller, more regional organization, the Ontario Council of Muslim Communities. In 1977 the body included forty Islamic associations and mosques. The Council encourages Islamic education in Canada.

At a time of the global resurgency of Islam, these organizations maintain supportive relationships with centers of Islamic orthodoxy and authority in the Middle East and with such international bodies as the Muslim World League. They may also interact with important domestic organizations such as the Council of Imams, which is an association of Muslim spiritual leaders.

Thus, in little more than sixty-five years, Muslims in North America have generated a strong community identity. Islamic associations and mosques exist in almost every state. Maintaining strong support relationships with the seats of Islamic learning and government in the Middle East, the community takes pride in its diversified ethnic and cultural heritage, but at the same time acknowledges a common monotheistic tradition. Although both Shi'i and Sunni forms of Islam are practiced in North America, doctrinal identification is usually not a source of conflict or division since all Muslims are members of a minority. Recent studies have demonstrated that in communities where Shi'i and Sunni mosques exist, the affirmation of one's identity as a Muslim is a unifying thread. For example, in Dearborn, Michigan, where members of the Zaidi Shi'i sect and Sunni Muslims have emigrated from different parts of Yemen, sectarian differences are recognized, but they do not disrupt the community.[17] Both Shi'i and Sunni Yemenese participate in a Yemeni Benevolent Association, they have intermarried, and marriage partners frequently stress the fact that both are Muslim rather than emphasize doctrinal differences. This attitude reflects a change from Muslim countries, where such patterns of intermarriage are infrequent.

Membership in religious groups may also be a source of great pride.[18] Near Edmonton, Alberta, for example, a Druze community replicates customs and patterns of social relationships found in a Lebanese village. The reconstruction of these important traditions is so complete that according to one researcher there were few real differences between this Canadian community and the one in Lebanon, except for a change in dress.[19] These Druze, like those in the Middle East, acknowledge the messianic leadership of an eleventh-century Caliph, al-Hakim, who is recognized as an *Imam* in the Shi'a tradition. The Druze faith draws its name from al-Danazi, who spread early doctrines of the faith. Like other Shi'i movements, it is based on hidden revelation and the strong cohesion of the worshiping community. The Druze tradition, however, is regarded by many to be outside the orbit of Islam.

In conclusion, Muslim sects and reformist movements depend on the re-establishment of traditions transported from great distances. The Druze community in Edmonton, Alberta, achieves this end by reconstituting social relationships and important customs in Canada exactly as they were done in Lebanon. In much the same way, Ahmadiyya groups in major U.S. and Canadian cities forge links between leaders of the movement in Pakistan and devotees in North America. In each case, Islamic movements offer the devotee a chance to continue customs of belief, law, ritual, and patterns of social relationships begun overseas.

The Mosque in North America

In a large two-story building in a residential section of San Francisco, members of a Muslim community worship together every Friday. Downstairs, there are classes in Qur'anic exegesis, while the upstairs loft has been converted into a room for prayer. There, sheets have been placed on the floor so that the sanctuary will remain pure. Devotees enter the prayer room without shoes, having washed in the kitchen below. They pray facing a large window in the direction of Mecca, while a leader of the community begins the call to prayer.

This scenario is repeated in mosques across the United States and Canada. Each mosque varies in manner of construction and appearance. Some, such as the Islamic Center and Mosque in Cedar Rapids, are modern while incorporating distinctive architectural conventions from the Middle East, such as the dome. Others, as in a Tucson, Arizona, mosque, are entirely functional and are built in part of a home. Still others, such as Masjid Al-Arkam in Worcester, Massachusetts, have been erected in converted churches. A few, however, fully replicate distinctive patterns of architecture and decoration found in Muslim countries. The Islamic Center in Washington, D.C., for instance, combines elements of Muslim art from many different nations.

Decorations in mosques such as the Islamic Center are confined to calligraphy and geometric and floral designs. Islam forbids any religious art that depicts the human figure including that of the Prophet Muhammad. Any art that risks establishing idols or ascribing substitutes for God (a sin called shirk) is intolerable to all schools of Islam. Passages from the Qur'an may be inscribed inside as a reminder for the faithful that the mosque is the house of God. The photograph on page 160 shows an

The Islamic Center, Cedar Rapids, Iowa, with a modern mosque building that retains the traditional dome.

example of the intricacy of design and detail as incorporated inside the Islamic Center in Washington, D.C.

The sanctuary of a mosque is covered by carpets. There can be no chairs, pews, or other obstructions that might hinder the movements and acts of prostration that are part of prayer. Instead, the emptiness contributes to a strong sense of tranquility. Thus, even in the midst of a worshiping community, the devotee can be alone with God. Moreover, in the carpeted interior of the mosque, all devotees are completely equal and on the same level.

Unlike most churches, mosques are not built for lengthy processions or for the display of choirs or large organs. Except for the *minbar*, or pulpit used by the *Imam* to address the assembled community, the sanctuary gives the feeling both of open space and of intimacy. A large open chamber may be interspersed with ornate pillars that permit devotees to seek Allah corporately, yet privately, in a defined space.

Symbolic of their role in the Islamic community, many U.S. and Canadian mosques are constructed to facilitate large assemblies of devotees. Muslim holidays such as New Year's Day (the first day of the lunar month of Muharram), the Prophet's birthday, and the beginning and end of the fast period of Ramadan are festive occasions that draw

Interior, The Islamic Center, Washington, D.C., detail of pointed
arches, devotional calligraphic inscriptions, and floral motifs.

Sanctuary, Albanian Islamic Center, Harperwoods, Michigan, where an *Imam* reads to the faithful.

Courtesy: Imam Vehbi Ismail, Albanian Islamic Center.

large crowds. At these times, the community may gather in anterooms of the mosque to celebrate the event.

Regardless of their appearance, mosques in North America fulfill several important functions. Foremost, they are houses of prayer, with prayer rooms, or sanctuaries, that face Mecca as directly as possible. When the sanctuary is in a building designed originally for another purpose, the prayer room is arranged so that devotees face Mecca. By facing Mecca, supplicants are reminded regularly of the origins of their faith. Whenever regular prayer is observed on Friday the worshiper acknowledges the prophetic traditions of Abraham and Muhammad and the importance of Mecca.

The mosque is also a center of Muslim education. In some cases, Islamic leaders have arranged Sunday school programs at a time convenient for a Western, urbanized society. In many Muslim Sunday schools, language studies and theological issues are of prime importance. The mosque is a place where Arabic is taught. Second-, third-, and even fourth-generation Arab-Americans, Pakistanis, Indonesians, and other

Islamic peoples gain the opportunity to learn the language of the tradition.

Many mosques have installed Islamic libraries to encourage the theological education of their supporters. One of the primary purposes of the Islamic Center in Washington, D.C., for example, was the construction of a place where regular Islamic research could be conducted. Smaller mosques throughout the United States and Canada offer similar services. For example, a mosque in Tucson, Arizona, maintains a collection of Islamic newsletters and publications, offering supplicants a chance to maintain essential ties with other U.S. Muslim communities.

Mosques and Islamic centers frequently publish newsletters to attract new members and promote activities of the center and inform devotees of programs in other centers. Whether a newsletter promotes the construction of a new mosque or the study of the Qur'an, Muslims have found it an effective way to maintain contact.

The educational function of the mosque is perhaps best dramatized by a feat that was recorded in the Cedar Rapids Gazette in 1936.[20] Two boys, seven and twelve years old, had achieved a reading knowledge of the Qur'an. For Muslims throughout the Midwest, the event held great significance. It demonstrated that in the United States the mosque could continue to function as the predominant means of educating children in the tradition. A reading knowledge of the Qur'an is a highly valued part of the faith, because it enables devotees to explain the text in its original language. No translation of the Qur'an can be authoritative. A knowledge of Arabic is essential if the text is to be read in the same form as that revealed to Muhammad.

Muslim education is influenced by da'wah, the preaching of the Prophet's message. Da'wah is considered by many U.S. and Canadian Muslims as an integral part of all religious instruction, and essential for the success of adult education programs.

Some mosques have been able to maintain their educational programs without the services of an Imam. Under such conditions, members share regular duties and leadership. For example, a mosque in Toledo, Ohio, in 1960 was administered by a board of trustees. Six or seven lay preachers shared the responsibility of the Friday homily. Even without the benefit of a full time Imam, the mosque maintained a strong educational program that included classes for children.

Mosques in North America may include large numbers of particular ethnic segments of the Muslim community, such as Lebanese in Dearborn, Michigan, Pakistanis in New Jersey, or members of the American Muslim Mission in Brooklyn, New York. The worshiping community is a source of solidarity for each ethnic group. For instance, a group of Syrian and Lebanese immigrants erected a mosque in Cedar Rapids, Iowa, in 1934. Except for its dome, the building had little in common with the elaborate mosques in the immigrants' homeland. The walls were made of wood instead of stone. Instead of graceful lines the features of the sanctuary were plain. However, the significance of the mosque was not its method of construction or appearance. Rather, for that small group of Muslims, it was a powerful, physical symbol of the perpetuation of their faith and way of life in the United States.

Because mosques are such important symbols of the continuity of Islam in North America Muslim groups have worked hard to erect them. Frequently they have found opposition from persons outside of the tradition. For example, when a band of twenty families sought to erect a school and religious center in New Jersey's Hunterdon County, they encountered hostility from local residents. The Pakistanis requested a zoning variance that would allow the structure to be built. The community reacted out of fear and clearly did not understand Islam. A meeting of the local board of adjustment to decide the matter was the largest ever held in the area. As emotions surged, the issue became linked to questions of patriotism. A newspaper account reported, "The crowd was so large . . . that the engines in the firehouse had to be moved outside to accommodate the turnout. Many of those attending had been attracted by anonymous flyers, embossed with an American flag, that were distributed earlier and which urged that the township's zoning laws be upheld."[21]

Regardless of their ethnic heritage, all Muslims in the United States are members of a minority by virtue of their faith. While most have experienced misunderstandings about their religion, they usually find support in the regular gatherings of the worshiping community. For instance, a second-generation Arab-American living in the Midwest commented that throughout his life he had been forced to explain and defend his faith to peers and associates. Some had little idea who Muhammad was and few realized that Muslims, like Christians or Jews, share a Semitic heritage in which the worship of a single God is paramount. In the mosque this man was able to talk with persons of similar backgrounds who also had experienced these frustrations.

Similarly, Muslim communities foster the continuation of traditional values. The importance of keeping the traditions is stressed to teenagers. They are urged to abstain from alcohol, avoid dating, unlike non-Muslim peers, and marry according to the wishes of parents, who will secure a suitable mate. In the interim, to offset what otherwise would be a very isolated life among persons who do not understand Islam, the mosque offers the companionship of other devotees who share a common world view.

The mosque is thus the heart of the Islamic community in North America. It is a symbol of Muslim identity in an environment that often has not understood Islam and has been hostile to it. Whether it is

Islamic Center, Michigan City, Indiana, with arches and a dome.

constructed in the best architectural traditions of the Middle East or in the home of a resident *Imam,* a mosque is an extension of the spirit and devotion of each unique Muslim community.

Arab Muslim Culture

The Muslim world is culturally diverse. Islam is widely practiced in parts of South, Southeast, and East Asia as well as Europe, Africa, and the Middle East. In each Muslim society, Islam directly affects patterns of diet, dress, and interpersonal relations.

The history of Islamic peoples in North America reflects this diversity. Muslims in the United States and Canada include devotees from such distant places as India, the Philippines, Iran, and Arab countries as well as indigenous persons who have converted to the faith. This section is focused on one of the largest populations of immigrant Islamic peoples, Arab Muslims, who have actively practiced their faith here for over seventy years.

As members of a religious minority in the United States and an ethnic minority, Muslims from Arab countries living in North America have been subjected to misrepresentations about their culture and religion.

Many people have little understanding of what an Arab is and often accept popular images of nomadic bedouin as the norm. In reality, the Arab world consists of a variety of Christian and Muslim peoples in: Saudi Arabia, Yemen, Democratic Yemen, Oman, the United Arab Emirates, Qatar, Bahrain, Kuwait, Iraq, Jordan, Syria, Egypt, Libya, Morocco, Tunisia, Algeria, southwest Iran, and parts of southern Turkey. There is no single "Arab" identity or way of life. Rather, the term correctly refers to a diverse group of people who share a regional identification and linguistic, political, and historical bonds. By far the greatest unifying force in the Arab world has been Islam. Under the banner of Islam the Arab civilization achieved its greatest triumph and formed distinctive patterns of science, art, architecture, law, and government.

In the United States, Arab peoples have been subjected to persistent stereotypes that ignore both the diversity and depth of this civilization. In film, newspapers, and other media, Arabs have been described in romantic terms based on popular perceptions of bedouin.

For over half a century, the motion picture industry has had a love affair with adventure films set in the Arabian desert. Since the days of Rudolph Valentino in *The Sheik* (1921) and Douglas Fairbanks in *The Thief of Bhagdad* (1924), the allure of swashbuckling romance and battle in the desert sands has stirred the imagination of moviegoers.

However, this genre of films has been marked by pervasive stereotypes about Arabs and Islam. Arab peoples have consistently been portrayed as the warlike inhabitants of a barren wasteland whose only occupants are bedouin and camels. Films such as *Beau Geste* (Ronald Coleman, 1927) portrayed an Arab horde of 4,000 who without mercy attacked 40 legionnaires.[22] The movie was an epic of its day, but sacrificed accuracy in the interest of drama. Like other films in the genre, it was made thousands of miles from any Arab country, in this case, in Arizona. Other films used romantic images of Arabs to evoke fantasy. The Middle East was seen as a land of mythical beasts, magic carpets, and an ever-present medievalism.

It is this last association of Islam and the Arab world with medieval imagery that continues to this day. Many Americans view Islamic society as primitive and opposed to all forms of progress. It is still dominated by such stereotypes as the "law of the desert" in which water is seen as more precious than human life. In the movie *Lawrence of Arabia* (Peter O'Toole, 1962), this was the underlying motive behind the murder of a tribesman who sought to steal water from a well. Such characterizations continue to portray Arab peoples as barbarian. A group of Canadian Muslims protesting this symbolism recently spoke out against a cartoon that depicted the early Arab Muslims as a plundering horde. Similarly, Arab Muslims voiced objections to the designation ABSCAM, asserting that it defamed their image.[23]

Rudolph Valentino and Agnes Ayres in *The Sheik* (1921). The film
catapulted Valentino into stardom and simultaneously popularized the
stereotype of Arabs as barbarian adventurers who lived by the same
moral code as pirates or outlaws. In the film a young English woman
(Ayers) plans a trip into the Arabian desert against the will of her
family. She is capured by a sheik (Valentino), who carries her off to
his desert lair, where they eventually fall in love.

In addition, since rising gasoline prices became a source of public
frustration and anger, persons from the Middle East have been stereotyped as wealthy. The perception of the ruthless bedouin hordes
popularized in film has been augmented with an image of affluence. For
the majority of Arab-Americans who come from modest backgrounds,
this understanding is a source of great uneasiness. On college campuses
with large international student bodies, it has often resulted in prejudice
and discrimination.

The Middle East has remained an enigma to many persons in the
United States. Textbooks rarely provide an accurate understanding of
either the relevance of the Middle East in world history or the presence
of Arab peoples in the United States. In *Scratches on Our Minds: American Images of China and India*,[24] Harold Isaacs suggests that many
people remain uncertain about the term "Asia" or such regional designa-

tions as "Far East" or "Middle East." He concludes that this confusion among schoolchildren, in particular, has been increased by the use of maps that have as geographical center the longitude of Peoria, Illinois.[25] These charts, which have replaced the older Mercator projection, divide Asia into distorted masses. On such maps designations of the "Far" or "Middle" East have little relevance to the actual location of countries.

These misunderstandings about the Arab world persist even though some Arab neighborhoods have existed in North America for over sixty years. In Michigan, for instance, a third-generation Arab-American community is stitll dominated by the ever-present coffee house, Syrian restaurant, and grocery stores, suggesting continuity in dietary laws and social relationships among immigrants.[26] Such neighborhoods, showing varying degrees of traditionalism, are found across the United States and Canada. In New York, for instance, grocery stores specializing in Middle Eastern foods are a common sight along Brooklyn's Atlantic Avenue. The small shops are often dramatic evidence of the extended family in the United States. They may be managed by family members who employ nieces, nephews, and even distant cousins, who are all treated as important members of the household.

For thousands of Arab Muslims, Islam is a unifying thread that reinforces a strong sense of identity. Islamic concepts of marriage and the extended family, the community, and such basic traditions as diet have helped many Saudi Arabian, Lebanese, Syrian, Palestinian, and Yemenese groups retain their cohesiveness.

A particularly cohesive city is Dearborn, Michigan, where there is the greatest concentration of Arab-Americans in the United States, 95 percent of which are Muslim.[27] There a Lebanese village has been reconstituted in the midst of an urbanized, industrial area. As many as 600 members from the same village live within five blocks of one another.[28] In this tightly knit community, many persons are related, and live together much as their parents and grandparents did in Lebanon.

For this highly traditional Muslim society in the United States as for others, marriage is an important institution. Most members prefer to marry within their culture and religion. Many children grow up expecting to live in the same neighborhood and practice a life-style similar to that of their parents.

Qur'anic tradition suggests that Muslim men may marry members of other Semitic religions, including Jews and Christians. But, since Arab culture perpetuates a strong patriarchal tradition, the assumption is made in such marriages that any children will be brought up in the faith of their father.

Marriage rites in the United States are often performed by an *Imam.* According to *Shari'a* law this is not necessary, however. Any qualified

Muslim who is familiar with the tradition can perform a marriage. In many Islamic countries a village registrar is responsible for conducting the rite.

However, since clergy in North America usually perform marriages, many *Imams* follow the Western convention and do likewise. Some Sikh *Granthis* in the United States have accepted the same role. However, neither *Granthis* nor *Imams* are perceived as clergy within their respective traditions. Instead, they are religious specialists with specific tasks that frequently differ from those of ministers or priests. For example, *Imams* are respected Muslims and scholars who are responsible for leading the faithful in prayer. They are symbols of Islamic values and provide a model for other Muslims to follow. *Imams* do not exercise a pastoral role as a minister is expected to do. Indeed, there is no office of pastor in Islam and the symbolism of a shepherd is not applied to leaders of the faith.

In North Amemrica, when *Imams* have been stereotyped as clergy, they have experienced difficulty in maintaining their traditional roles. They may be expected to perform some of the duties of a pastor and at the same time uphold the orthodox Islamic values of the faith they represent. Most *Imams* are particularly sensitive about this issue, which can be a source of tension and frustration.

Islamic associations and mosques play an important part in sustaining the marriage. Large gatherings of Muslim families reinforce the dominant values of the tradition, bringing persons of similar backgrounds together. Through the association of different families, bonds are forged that frequently culminate in marriage. Moreover, as in Muslim countries, these ties have economic as well as religious and social importance.

Among orthodox Muslims, the tradition of the dowry is usually continued in North America. The dowry is an example of how the extended family takes part in the marriage process. Frequently, the husband gives his wife *mahr*. This is a gift that symbolizes the marriage contract. The marriage may be formalized in a document known as the *nikkahnama*, in which the arrangements for the dowry and *mahr* are made. The *nikkahnama* is a cross-cultural concept of great significance. It can determine the division of the estate after a divorce, (which in Islamic law is considered binding if declared by the man three separate times). Frequently, after a divorce, the *mahr* (often including jewelry) is the property of the bride. It establishes a form of security for the woman while at the same time regulating the separate but independent worlds of husband and wife.

In the *Purdah* system, common in Muslim countries, men and women move in different worlds. The role of the female is inside. She is the guardian of the home and the family. By tradition, she is prohibited from entering the outside world of her husband. By the same token, she may wear the *burka*, a cloak that shrouds the body and covers the head. The *burka* allows the inside world of which she is an integral part to be transported intact. It also reinforces cultural standards of modesty and propriety.

In North America, the use of garments such as the *burka* is impractical. Vestiges of the *Purdah* system, however, do survive among the more traditional families. In Dearborn, Michigan, for example, Lebanese women often continue the same pattern of life as in the Middle East. They safeguard the home and important family traditions. They do not frequent coffee houses, which are the traditional domain of the men. Yet they maintain a dominant role in the education of their children into the tradition and the perpetuation of the faith in the family. The use of large sunglasses or clothes that cover the wrists and ankles may serve a function similar to the *burka*. As Muslim women keep traditions of modesty and propriety and maintain their accustomed role in the home, *Purdah* survives, though in a less visible form.

The role of the Muslim woman is powerful in her own realm. She is responsible for the continuation of dietary laws, for education, and for a variety of social networks that are integral to the culture of which she is a part. In many Muslim societies she may be a cousin of her husband. This helps to assure that the extended family will function as an economic unit.

However, the role of Muslim women in North America can also be filled with frustration and confusion. While many second- and third-generation Muslim families have assimilated into life in the United States and Canada, newer arrivals often have not. Wives may be expected to conform to customary standards of dress and behavior that are difficult to maintain in a non-Muslim society. They may know few other Muslim women and feel alone and alienated from the North American culture of which they are now a part. Similarly, they may be discouraged from holding a job or planning a career and instead be expected to remain in the home.

For single women additional conflicts may arise. Muslim women frequently do not date. Because of Islamic prohibitions on music and dancing they may be unable to accompany their friends to school functions. The rejection of these common elements of life in the West causes many to be misunderstood and to face enormous conflicts.

The problem is compounded for Western women who marry Muslim immigrants. They are often expected to conform to the world of their husband and to adopt his way of life. For those wives who are unfamiliar with Islam or Muslim culture, the resultant problems are enormous when the freedom they have always expected is threatened by the values of their husbands. However, despite these hardships and conflicts, many couples have been able to work out a satisfactory accord.

However, the wife in these instances may also be an important factor in helping her family to assimilate into life in the United States. A study among Syrian and Lebanese Muslims in Chicago showed that in such cases a large percentage of women work and, in fact, are a primary means through which traditional patterns of family life in the Middle East are broken.[29] In such instances, the customary patriarchal role of the male is weakened as the family adapts to a new economic situation in which both spouses contribute to the combined income.

The matter of diet presents other complications in North America. Traditionally, Muslims may not consume liquor or pork or eat meat that is not slaughtered in keeping with Islamic law. These dietary obligations are kept in obedience to Allah and as a way of supporting a high level of ritualistic purity. Unless a Muslim is pure, he cannot engage in regular prayer or read from the Qur'an. Hence, great care is taken to avoid sources of contamination.

In Arab Muslim communities, dietary restrictions are maintained carefully. Problems may arise, however, for school children or for those in any institution unfamiliar with Islamic traditions. One Dearborn school solved these problems by providing an alternative protein diet for Muslim children whenever pork was served in a school lunch.[30] In other communities with large populations of Muslims, butchers sell meat slaughtered in the proper fashion.

For Arab Muslims in North America, language is another important element of culture and religion. Children born in the West often are bilingual. Many families speak Arabic at home and want to raise children in the language of their parents or grandparents.

Recently, there has been a strong movement among Islamic communities to provide formal language instruction. A private school in Philadelphia, for example, specializes in Arabic education for children. Some Islamic associations also offer courses in Arabic, and a variety of Islamic presses in the United States provide correspondence courses.

The proliferation of Islamic publishers shows the evolving strength of the Muslim community to provide for the continuing education of its members. Contrary to the popular impression of Islam, such organizations rarely proselytize and usually seek their market among persons already within the faith. The presses also reflect the economic strength of the Arab Muslim community in North America. Many professional persons have invested their time and savings in such ventures.

The ability to understand written Arabic has immense theological importance. As noted earlier, it enables the believer to read the Qur'an in its original language and to interact with a source of scriptural authority that cannot be understood through translation. Further, knowledge of the spoken language helps children to absorb the traditions of their parents. It is a link with both religion and culture and a continuing source of pride.

Maintaining traditions of marriage and the extended family, diet, and language is crucial to this diversified population of Muslims. They are aided by increasing numbers who have entered the United States since 1965 when immigration laws were changed radically. A growing number of students from Arab countries have been educated at colleges and universities in North America. Many marry and remain. Becoming leaders of Islamic societies and mosques, these devotees help nurture patterns of prayer and diet, and encourage the retention of Arabic. These new immigrants often assist others in understanding difficult verses or patterns of language in Qur'anic study. They are important sources for renewing the religion and culture of their predecessors.

Also, the generations of Arab Muslims have made significant contributions to the total life of the United States and Canada. Many have excelled as engineers, scientists, and doctors.[31] They have retained pride in their Middle Eastern heritage while at the same time they have been productive citizens of the communities of which they are a part.

Renewal and Adaptation in Muslim Communities in North America

In 1978, a New York newspaper reported that a coalition of Islamic countries had agreed to help finance a proposed $20,000,000 mosque on the city's upper east side.[32] The plans for the complex included a school, an exhibit hall, and a library, which were part of a sweeping modern structure that incorporated distinctive elements of Islamic architecture. A minaret in the futuristic design complimented the vertical thrust of the New York skyline. The article suggested that the idea for the mosque had been supported for ten years by three Arab states—Saudi Arabia, Kuwait, and Libya—which had put up seed money for the project. By 1985, however, no further steps had been taken.

This strategy of international Muslim cooperation is part of an evolving tradition in North America in which links with Muslim leaders and heads of state or religious leaders in the Middle East have been forged repeatedly. Following a pattern begun in the 1930s, when *Imams* were brought to Iowa from the Middle East, the undertaking reflects the same motivations that led to the building of the Islamic Center in Washington in 1957.

Established mosques with long histories of activity in North America continue much the same tradition, inviting important religious leaders from the Middle East to visit their communities. They accept the invitations because of a continuing concern of Muslim countries for followers in the United States and Canada. These leaders are important symbols of renewal. Their presence helps reaffirm basic values and re-establishes ties with the Semitic origins of the faith. Such visits also help to perpetuate the Islamic community in North America.

Often among recent immigrants, links are maintained faithfully with family members who remain in Muslim countries. The continued nurturing of Muslim children in the faith is a matter of deep concern for relatives abroad. Parents maintain an active role in the perpetuation of cultural traditions that are important links with Islam. The extended family is often a primary concern. Even distant cousins are highly valued. Such close ties with family members overseas provide a support system for relatives who come to North America.

Further, since the mosque is the most visible symbol of the community's identity, devotees go to great lengths to establish mosques that can perform several functions. The mosque is a place where entire families meet for regular worship and for major festivals. It may be a multipurpose structure constructed so that devotees can congregate for Qur'anic exegesis. Often, it includes a place for common meals and gatherings.

Mosques in North America may resemble their Middle Eastern counterparts, as, for example, the Islamic Center of Toledo in Perrysburg, Ohio, which includes the domed sanctuary and minarets characteristic of traditional Islamic architecture. Or they may be entirely functional, adapting a home or church for purposes of worship and study. Such adaptations show the ability of Muslims to practice their faith, using available resources to the best possible advantage. The theological requirements of a mosque, however, are met once the site has been purified and the proper direction for prayer established.

The erection of mosques also is a way of spreading the prophet's message (da'wah). In an effort to overcome prevalent stereotypes about Islam, groups like the Council of Muslim Communities in Canada have established public relations divisions to provide accurate representation of the tradition.

Da'wah may also include the distribution of informative literature and the establishment of Islamic presses. Devotees in Cedar Rapids, Iowa, for instance, help support a press that publishes information about the faith in English. This service is particularly important for third- or fourth-generation Muslims who may have little knowledge of Arabic.

Similarly, some Muslim associations have developed their own curricula supplemented with linguistic aids for persons not fluent in Arabic, courses in the language itself, and texts on Islamic theology and doctrine. These materials, written by leaders of the tradition and hence considered authoritative, are part of an ongoing process of Muslim revitalization. Moreover, their sheer abundance demonstrates the economic solidarity of the Muslim community and its willingness to invest time and resources.

As educational institutions, mosques adapt traditional functions of the *madrasa*, or Islamic school. In the Ottoman Empire, the *madrasa* was an important component of the mosque where *Shari'a* law was learned, jurists trained, and teachers educated. Often subsidized by the state, the *madrasa* provided for the continued assimilation of children into the tradition.

In the United States or Canada, the functions of the *madrasa* may be met in a variety of ways. The community may establish a library or an Islamic school. The sketch on page174demonstrates the practical applications of this concept used to plan a Muslim Community Center in Silver Spring, Maryland. A mosque, two classroom buildings, a library, and administration building are included.

Muslims in North America frequently experience conflict when Islamic teachings are contrary to the basic institutions of life in the West. For instance, the concept of paying or receiving interest is against Islamic law. In North America where interest payments or credit cards affect every sphere of economic activity, the devout Muslim who seeks to live in accordance with *Shari'a* law faces major conflicts.

Almsgiving (*zakat*) can also be problematical for Muslims in North America. In Islamic countries *zakat* may be collected by the state or community. In North America, similar arrangements are clearly impossible. Yet, for all Muslims, the payment of *zakat* is an expected duty. In order to help alleviate this dilemma, some Islamic groups have adapted the tradition in innovative ways. Leaders of the M.C.C. project in Silver Spring, Maryland, urge their benefactors to consider donations to the center as *zakat*. The construction of this large complex that will meet the needs of large numbers of Muslims is looked upon as charity.

There also are conflicts experienced when differences of opinion become issues between generations. For example, one of the most emotional issues in Islam is music, which has been a source of scholarly debate since the first Muslim century.[33] The debate centers on the propriety of music and dance in an Islamic society. Since in Muslim theology there can be no distinction between sacred and secular, the question of the legitimacy of musical expression is not a matter of its association with religion. Rather, any type of music can be a source of dissension. However, most Muslims agree that musical forms associated with sensuality are forbidden.

In the United States, the dissension on this issue is frequently intergenerational. Muslim children feel enormous peer pressure to join their friends at dances, rock concerts, or social gatherings of which music is a part. For high school students in particular, family restrictions that forbid going to the senior prom or a school dance can be a source of immense frustration. Further, the popularity of music throughout youth

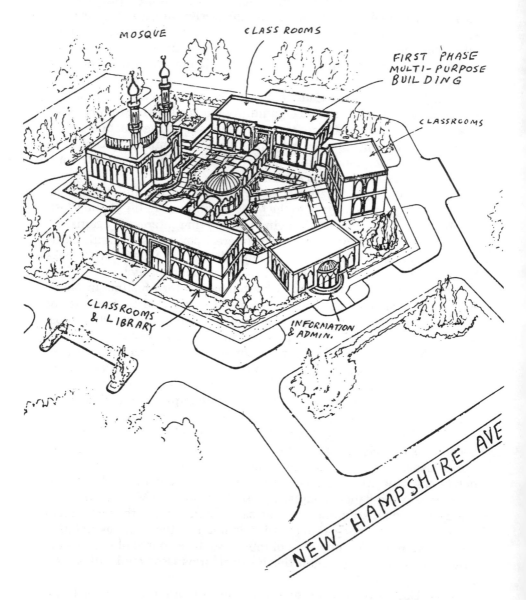

Drawing for planned Muslim Community Center, Silver Spring, Maryland. The complex includes a mosque, library, classrooms, and other buildings.

Courtesy: Abdul Rauf, M.D., Editor,M.C.C. Bulletin, and Member of the Board.

culture makes the conflict difficult to ignore. For parents, however, who still have family members in Muslim countries where *Shari'a* is predominant, the assimilation of their children can be quite threatening. In addition, the periodic visit of Muslim dignitaries to Islamic societies in the United States increases the pressures to conform to accepted standards of behavior.

The issue is compounded by the fact that many non-Muslims have been exposed to Islamic culture and have little sympathy with restrictions they do not understand. Accounts of Islam in the newspaper or radio may be distorted or taken out of context. For example, during the Iranian revolution (1979–1980), the media reported that music had been banned. On popular television programs, this became a matter of ridicule. By implication, the humor reinforced existing stereotypes of Islam as antithetical to the modern world and virtually medieval. The long-standing debate on the subject within the Islamic world was ignored.

Thus, we have seen how, for almost three quarters of a century, Muslims have nurtured their faith in North America. At first fragmented and with few methods maintaining basic traditions, many Muslims were unable to find ways of sustaining their culture or beliefs. In less than fifty years, however, community leaders have re-created a dynamic base. Constructing mosques, opening Islamic schools, and establishing links with sources of authority in the Middle east, they call the faithful back to God:

> And He is God: there is
> No God but He. To Him
> Be praise, at the first
> And at the last:
> For Him is the Command,
> And to Him shall ye
> (All) be brought back.
> Qur'an,[34]
> *Surah xxviii:70*

Islamic star and crescent.

Notes

Introduction

1. The word *Asia* is often a source of confusion. In this text it includes the wider civilizations of India, the Middle East, China, and Japan and the nations that these civilizations have historically influenced. See also John M. Steadman in *The Myth of Asia: A Refutation of Western Stereotypes of Asian Religion, Philosophy, Art and Politics.* A Clarion Book (New York: Simon and Schuster, 1969).
2. Other Asian religions practiced in the continental United States include the Jain and Parsi traditions.
3. Marvine Howe, "Sikh Parley: 'We are United, We are Angry'," *New York Times,* July 29, 1984, p. 9.
4. Colin Campbell, "Moslem Students in U.S. Rediscovering Islam," *New York Times,* May 13, 1984, p. 44.
5. John Hebers, "Surge in Immigration Now Means Chinese are Largest Asian Group in U.S., *New York Times,* July 30, 1981, p. A12.

Chapter One: Hindus in North America

1. The concept of the Hindu holy man is explored by Mira Reym Binford et al. in *Four Holy Men: Renunciation in Hindu Society,* Contemporary South Asian Films (Madison: University of Wisconsin, 1976).
2. South Asia includes India, Pakistan, Sri Lanka, Sikkim, Bhutan, and Bangladesh, whose populations exhibit distinctive patterns of social organization and structure, language, and religion. Some sources also include the nations of Nepal and Afghanistan.
3. Like Hinduism and Sikhism, the Jain tradition originated in India. Jains follow the teachings of Mahavira, a contemporary of the Buddha. The model for salvation in the Jain tradition is the ascetic, who strictly adheres to the law of *ahimsa* (nonviolence) and practices extended periods of meditation.
4. Edward Langley, "The Indians of Queens," *New York Daily News* (Sunday News Magazine), June 1, 1980, p. 6 ff.
5. For further information on caste among immigrant Indian communities, see Barton M. Schwartz, ed., *Caste in Overseas Indian Communities* (San Francisco: Chandler Publishing Company, 1967).
6. Rig Veda 1.22.18, in Eric Washburn Hopkins, *The Religions of India* (Boston: Ginn and Company, 1895), p. 57.
7. H. T. Dave, trans., *Shree Swaminarayan's Vachanamritam* (Bombay: Bharatiya Vidya Bhavan, 1977).
8. Shree Sahajanand Swami, *Shikshapatri: A Compendium of the Code of Conduct* (Ahmedabad: Bochasanwasi Shree Aksharpurushottam Sanstha, 1977).
9. G. H. Wescott, *Kabir and the Kabir Panth* (Cawnpore: Christ Church Mission Press, 1907), pp. 7–8.
10. E. Allen Richardson, "Mughal and Rajput Patronage of the Bhakti Sect of the Mahara-

jas, the Vallabha Sampradaya, 1640–1760 A.D." (Ph.D. dissertation, University of Arizona, 1979).

11. While this work is concerned with the social customs and religious practices of persons born into the faith, readers are also urged to explore the adaptation of Hindu doctrines in North American movements that serve predominantly non-Indian clientele. This phenomenon, which incorporates elements of classical Hindu worship and devotion, exists in numerous groups and societies. Organizations such as the International Society for Krishna Consciousness publish informative tracts and guides to the faith.

12. Swami is an honorific title used to designate a Hindu ascetic.

13. The Vedanta movement, of which Vivekananda was a part, was the first of several Hindu Renaissance traditions that hoped to attract devotees in the United States. The Theosophical Society and other groups found devotees among intellectuals of the day.

14. Suhindra Bose, "Travelling Through the Country in America," *Modern Review* 9 (January to June 1911): 251.

15. For more information on the effect of this legislation, see "Indians in Canada: A Pitiable Account of their Hardships by One Who Comes from the Place and Knows Them," *Modern Review* 14 (August 1913): 140–149.

16. "Hindu Invasion," *Colliers National Weekly* 45 (March 26, 1910): 15.

17. Bruce LaBrack, "Occupational Specialization Among California Sikhs: The Interplay of Culture and Economics" (Syracuse, New York, 1975). Dr. LaBrack has done extensive research on Sikhs in California.

18. Emily C. Brown, *Har Dayal: Hindu Revolutionary and Rationalist* (Tucson: University of Arizona Press, 1975).

19. Emily C. Brown, "Historical Background of the Sikh Movement in the United States" (Tucson, Arizona, October, 1978).

20. The law was entitled, "An act to amend section 2166, revised Code of 1928, relating to prohibited and void marriages (63–107 Arizona Code 1939)." The law continued similar prohibitions enacted in 1931.

21. J. T. Sunderland, "Principal Horamba Chandra Maitra in America," *Modern Review* 9 (January to June 1911): 151–152.

22. Katherine Mayo, *Mother India* (New York: Harcourt, Brace, 1927).

23. See Harold I. Issacs, *Scratches on Our Minds: American Images of China and India* (New York: John Day Co., 1958), pp. 241–242.

24. Bruce LaBrack, "The East Indian Experience in America" (Syracuse, New York, 1975).

25. The law (HR2580), was signed by President Lyndon Johnson at the base of the Statue of Liberty on October 3, 1965.

26. "Indians in Flushing Blend 2 Cultures," *New York Times*, December 18, 1983, Sec. 1, p. 64.

27. In some texts Hindi may be designated "Hindi-Urdu." Urdu, spoken in Pakistan and in parts of India, uses the same grammar, but employs Persian script.

28. Prakash N. Desai and Dhawal Mehta, "Indians in America: The Lonely Crowd" *Asian/Pacific American Heritage Week* (Potomac, Maryland: Asian-Pacific American Heritage Council, Inc., 1980), p. 9.

29. The names of temples and persons are spelled as cited in sectarian literature. *Shri* or *Shree* (most often transcribed *Sri* but pronounced *shree*) is used to indicate respect. The publications of temple organizations, in addition to personal visits and interviews, have been valuable resources in preparing this chapter. For example, see "The Hindu Temple Society of North America" (New York: The Hindu Temple Society of North America, 1978).

30. The Gujarat is a region in western India with a political and cultural identity.

31. One such newspaper, *India West*, is published weekly in El Sobrante, California. Others are published on the East Coast.

32. An article in the *San Francisco Examiner and Chronicle* (April 29, 1979) suggests that one out of every six motels and hotels in California is owned by Gujaratis, who have utilized the family network to perpetuate business interests.

33. Edward Langley, "The Indians of Queens," *New York Daily News* (Sunday News Magazine) June 1, 1980, p. 6 ff.

34. *Ibid.*

Chapter Two: Buddhists in North America

1. A small number of Japanese Shingon Buddhists are also reported to practice their tradition in the United States. See Emma McCloy Layman, *Buddhism in America* (Chicago: Nelson Hall, 1976), pp. 110–111. Readers are also urged to explore Buddhist movements among indigenous Caucasian devotees. While such groups are outside of the scope of this text, which examines the religion of persons born into the faith, they represent a complex and evolving tradition.
2. Theravada *viharas* in the United States and Canada were first established to meet the needs of devotees born into the faith, but they subsequently have attracted non-Asian converts as well.
3. Links with tradition are suggested by the Buddhist wheel of causation used later in this chapter. The wheel is a Mahayana and Theravada symbol suggesting the unending process of suffering and rebirth and the opportunities for liberation found in the Middle Way. The symbol is so much a part of Buddhism that the Buddhist Churches of America has adopted it as a denominational symbol.
4. *Buddhist Churches of America*, 2 vols. (San Francisco: Buddhist Churches of America, 1974).
5. See Ahn Jung-Hyo, "Buddhist Monk's Life Lonely, Rewarding" in *Koreatown: The English Language Voice of the Korean-American Community* 1 (January 28, 1980): 4.
6. Edward J. Thomas, *The Life of the Buddha as Legend and History* (London: Routledge and Kegan Paul Ltd., 1927), p. 251. Thomas' work provides a detailed study of the accretions of tradition that surround the narrative of the life of the Buddha. It has been an important resource in the preparation of this chapter.
7. *Ibid.*, p. 183.
8. The Parliament of Religions created interest in some Theravada countries and brought new avenues of missionary endeavor to the West. This interest, however, was short-lived. By the mid-1920s, exclusionists had won a victory with the passage of the Immigration Act of 1924, which made immigration from Asia extremely difficult. Significant changes in U.S. immigration laws did not occur until 1965, when the national origins quota system was eliminated. Since 1965, monks and laity from Southeast Asian countries, such as Burma, Thailand, and Vietnam, have come to the United States.
9. Edward J. Thomas, *The Life of the Buddha*, p. xvi. See also John Henry Barrows, ed., *The World's Parliament of Religions: An Illustrated and Popular Story of the World's First Parliament of Religions, Held in Chicago in Connection with the Columbian Exposition of 1893* 2 (Chicago: The Parliament Publishing Company, 1893), p. 863.
10. Thomas, *The Life of the Buddha*, p. xvii.
11. Emma McCloy Layman, *Buddhism in America* (Chicago: Nelson-Hall 1976), p. 174. A transcript of Dharmapala's address to the Parliament of Religions is contained in Barrows, ed., *The World's First Parliament of Religions* 2, pp. 862–880.
12. Layman, *Buddhism n America*, p. 184.
13. *Ibid.*, p. 181.
14. Dhammapada, XV.12.
15. *Washington Buddhist*, Quarterly Newsletter of the Washington Buddhist Vihara 9, No. 3 (July–September 1978).
16. *Ibid.*
17. The Buddhist Churches of America is related to a larger Japanese Pure Land tradition, the Hompa Hongwanji, located in Kyoto, Japan. This tradition is described in detail in *Buddhist Churches of America*, 1, pp. 32–35. Historical data in this section are taken from the same volume.
18. *Ibid.*, p. 47. A discussion of Japanese Buddhism in the United States before 1924 is found in Tetsuden Kashima, *Buddhism in America: The Social Organization of an Ethnic Religious Institution* (Westport, Connecticut: Greenwood Press, 1977), pp. 3–28.
19. The alien land laws were challenged in cases that ultimately were decided by the United States Supreme Court. In Webb v. O'Brien (263 U.S., decided November 19, 1923), Porterfield v. Webb (263 U.S., decided November 12, 1923), and Terrace v.

Thompson (263 U.S., decided November 12, 1923), the court reaffirmed the right of states to prohibit Japanese aliens from owning or leasing farmland or from entering into contracts who did.

20. H. Brett Melendy, *The Oriental Americans* (New York: Twayne Publishers, 1972), p. 124.

21. The *stupa* is one of the oldest forms of Buddhist architecture and is venerated by Buddhists from different schools. *Stupas*, which housed fragments of the ashes of the Buddha, were first built during the reign of the Indian king Asoka. In the third century B.C., Asoka decreed that the Buddha's remains would be distributed for all to venerate. Gautama's ashes eventually were divided into hundreds of parts and distributed to Buddhist leaders, who, by constructing *stupas*, brought physical evidence of the enlightened one to their native lands. *Stupas* were marks of honor and prestige as well as monuments of great pride and veneration. They assured rulers that their lands were watched over by the *Tathagata*, who had forever shattered the wheel of suffering and illusion.

The Jodo Shinshu churches in the United States obtained a lot behind the Pine Street headquarters in San Francisco in preparation for the construction of its *stupa*. By 1937, the monument had been erected.

22. *Buddhist Churches of America* 1, p. 61.

23. *Ibid.*, p. 62.

24. *Ibid.*, p. 64.

25. *Ibid.*

26. Jane Imamura, "Half a Century" in Buddhist Churches of America, *Wheel of Dharma* 6 (April 1979): 2.

27. *Buddhist Churches of America* 1, p. 63.

28. The Immigration and Nationality Act—also known as the McCarran-Walter Immigration Act—was approved June 27, 1952. *U.S. Statutes at Large* 66 (1952): 163.

29. See Shinsho Hanayama, *The Story of the Juzu* (San Francisco: Buddhist Churches of America, 1976).

30. See Masao Kodani, *The Buddhist Shrine* (San Francisco: Buddhist Churches of America, 1976).

31. *Buddhist Churches of America* 1, p. 27.

32. Zenkei Jhiboyama, *The Six Oxherding Pictures* (Japan: privately published, 1965).

33. The illustration depicts the lotus, which often blooms in swamps or desolate areas. As a traditional symbol of the Middle Way, the lotus also represents the Buddhist *dhamma* and is an appropriate symbol of the revitalization of Chinese Buddhism in North America.

34. Foster Rhea Dulles, *China and America: The Story of Their Relations since 1784* (Princeton: Princeton University Press, 1946), pp. 72–73.

35. The Arizona Historical Society, "The Chinese Experience in Arizona and Northern Mexico 1870–1940" (Tucson, Arizona: 1979). Brochure.

36. *Ibid.*

37. The Scott Act was properly referred to as "An act to prohibit the coming of Chinese laborers to the United States"—*U.S. Statutes at Large* 25 (1888): 476. Like other Chinese exclusion laws (as late as 1904) and treaties with China, it addressed a single, specific racial question. See also Melendy, *The Oriental Americans*, pp. 58–60.

38. These regulations remained the same under the Immigration and Nationality Act of 1952 (the McCarran-Walter Immigration Act). Melendy, *The Oriental Americans*, p. 66.

39. In California, Chinese bhikkhus have started a Buddhist university (Dharma Realm University), attracting a substantial number of non-Asian converts born in the United States. Located in a unique city of devotees (City of Ten Thousand Buddhas—Talmage, California), the institution is the result of the work of one bhikkhu,the Venerable Master Hsuan Hua, who founded the Sino-American Buddhist Association in San Francisco.

40. Holmes Welch, *The Buddhist Revival in China* (Cambridge, Massachusetts: Harvard University Press, 1968), pp. 15–16, 51–71.

41. Robert Rice, "Indochinatown," *Across the Board* 17, No. 6 (June 1980): 12–24.

42. Charlotte Evans, "Laotian Buddhist Monk Finds a 'Heaven' in Rye," *New York Times*, December 1, 1980, Sec. B, p. 2.

Chapter Three: Sikhs in North America

1. Throughout this text, references to the Sikh *Gurus* are capitalized. However, in general usage, the term is not.
2. Bruce LaBrack, "Peaches and Punjabis: The Reconstitution of Sikh Society in Rural California" (Stockton, California, 1977), p. 3.
3. Baldev Raj Nayar, "Sikh Separatism in the Punjab" in Donald Eugene Smith, ed., *South Asian Politics and Religion* (Princeton: Princeton University Press, 1966), p. 162.
4. Fauja Singh, "Development of Sikhism Under the Gurus," *Sikhism* (Patiala, India: Punjabi University, 1969), p. 9.
5. Gobind Singh Mansokhani, *The Quintessence of Sikhism* (Amritsar, India: Shiromani Gurdwara Parbandhuk Committee, 1965), p. 86.
6. Max Arthur Macauliffe, *The Sikh Religion, Its Gurus, Sacred Writings and Authors* 1 (Oxford: Clarendon Press, 1909), p. 200. Macauliffe translates section eight of the *Japji* in the quote.
7. Mansokhani, *The Quintessence of Sikhism*, p. 17.
8. The symbol used in this chapter is a common Sikh insignia that reflects this martial tradition.
9. Scholars differ as to the spelling and dates of some of the Gurus. Guru Har Kishan may be identified, for example, as Har Krishen.
10. The formulation of Gurmukhi is a matter of scholarly debate. See Khushwant Singh, *A History of the Sikhs* 1 (Princeton: Princeton University Press, 1963), p. 52, n. 6.
11. Baldev Raj Nayar, "Sikh Separatism in the Punjab," Donald Eugene Smith, *South Asian Politics and Religion*, pp. 150–175.
12. I am grateful to Dr. Bruce LaBrack of Raymond-Callison College, University of the Pacific, for data provided in this section. Dr. LaBrack, who graciously shared his research with me, has done primary work on Sikhs in California.
13. See Bruce LaBrack, "Sikhs of California: A Study of Differential Cultural Change" (Ph.D. dissertation, Syracuse University, 1979).
14. Nand Singh Sihra, "Indians in Canada: A Pitiable Account of their Hardships by One Who Comes from the Place and Knows Them," *Modern Review* 14 (August 1913): 141.
15. Rajani Kanta Das, *Hindusthani Workers on the Pacific Coast* (Berlin: Walter de Gruyter & Co., 1923), Table VIII. Quoted in Emily C. Brown "Historical Background of the Sikh Movement in the United States" (Tucson, Arizona: October, 1978).
16. Mark Juergensmeyer, "The Ghadr Syndrome: Nationalism in an Immigrant Community," *Punjab Journal of Politics* 1, No. 1 (October 1977).
17. Sihra, "Indians in Canada," p. 143.
18. *Ibid.*
19. *The British Columbia Reports* 20 (Victoria, British Columbia: Colonists Printing and Publishing Company Limited, 1915), pp. 243–292.
20. Sihra "Indians in Canada," p. 147.
21. *Ibid.*
22. I am grateful to Dr. Emily C. Brown for sharing her data about this incident. See Emily C. Brown, *Har Dayal: Hindu Revolutionary and Rationalist* (Tucson: University of Arizona Press, 1975).
23. *British Columbia Reports* 20, pp. 243–292.
24. "Hindu Invasion," *Colliers National Weekly*, March 26, 1910, p. 15.
25. Das, *Hindusthani Workers*, Table VIII. Quoted in Brown, "Historical Background," p. 2.
26. Details about Ghadr cited here appear in, Brown, "Historical Background," pp. 4–5.
27. The chair controversy and the history of the Stockton and Yuba City *gurdwaras* have been explored by Dr. Bruce LaBrack. See LaBrack, "Sikhs of California."
28. Saund's autobiography is entitled, *Congressman from India* (New York: E. P. Dutton, 1960), p. 74.
29. U.S. Department of Commerce, *Historical Statistics of the United States, Colonial Times to 1970*, Part 1, Series C 89–119, p. c 102–114.
30. I am indebted to the leaders of The Sikh Cultural Society (95–30, 118th Street,

Richmond Hill, N.Y.) for much of the information provided in this section. See also, *The American Sikh Review* 1 (April 1977 ff.).
31. Some Sikhs emphasize that the term *sant* is not understood as a formal title or office.
32. Max A. Macauliffe, *The Sikh Religion, Its Gurus, Sacred Writings and Authors* 2 (Oxford: Clarendon Press, 1909), p. 126.
33. *The American Sikh Review* 1 (September–October 1977): 22.

Chapter Four: Muslims in North America

1. The spelling "Qur'an" is preferred over the more Anglicized "Koran" by the majority of Muslims.
2. The designation "Muslim" is preferred over "Moslem." The term "Mohammaden" is offensive and should not be used.
3. The singular form of the collective noun "Shi'a" is "Shi'i." "Shi'i" can also be used as an adjective.
4. See, for example, Charles Eric Lincoln, *The Black Muslims in America*, Revised Edition (Boston: Beacon Press, 1973) and Malcolm Little, *The Autobiography of Malcolm X* (New York: Grove Press, 1965).
5. The passage has been adapted from: *The Holy Qur'an, Text, Translation and Commentary*. Abdullah Yusuf Ali (Washington, D.C.: The Islamic Center, 1978), Surah 96: 1–5, pp. 1761–1762.
6. *Newsletter of the Task Force on Christian-Muslim Relations. A Project of the Commission on Faith and Order of the National Council of the Churches of Christ in the U.S.A.*, in cooperation with the Duncan Black Macdonald Center for the Study of Islam and Christian-Muslim Relations, The Hartford Seminary Foundation, No. 8, April, 1980. The *Newsletter* frequently reports on the continued development of Islamic centers and mosques in the United States and has been a significant resource in the preparation of this chapter.
7. This incident was originally reported in the *New York Tribune* and later received attention in *The Moslem World*.
8. Abdo A. Elkholy. *The Arab Moslems in the United States* (New Haven, Connecticut: College and University Press, 1966), p. 121.
9. Nasseer H. Aruri, "The Arab-American Community of Springfield, Massachusetts" in Elaine C. Hagopian and Ann Paden, ed., *The Arab-Americans: Studies in Assimilation* (Wilmette, Illinois: The Medina University Press International, 1969), p. 51.
10. Philip Harsham, "Islam in Iowa." *Aramco World Magazine*, November–December, 1978, p. 34.
11. H. I. Katibah, "Moslems of City Celebrating Pious Feast of Ramazan," [sic.] *Brooklyn Eagle*, April 18, 1925. Quoted in Beverlee Turner Mehdi, ed., *The Arabs in America, 1492–1977: A Chronology and Fact Book* (Dobbs Ferry, New York: Oceana Publications, Inc., 1978), p. 81.
12. "Islam in Michigan City, Past and Present" (Michigan City, Indiana: Islamic Center, n.d.).
13. Yahya Aossey, Jr., "Fifty Years of Islam in Iowa 1925–1975" (Cedar Rapids, Iowa: Unity Publishing Co., n.d.).
14. See Muhammad Abdul-Rauf, *History of the Islamic Center* (Washington, D.C.: Islamic Center, 1978).
15. A. O. Sulzberger, Jr. "Roots of War in the Gulf," *New York Times*, September 24, 1980, sec. A, p. 10.
16. Umhau Wolf "The Islamic Federation, 1952: 'Muslims in the American Mid-West,'" in *The Muslim World*, L (January 1960): 42–43. Quoted in Beverlee Turner Mehdi, ed., *The Arabs in America, 1492–1977: A Chronology and Fact Book*, p. 103. See also in the same volume (p. 111), Jay Walz, "Nasser Donates to U.S. Moslems: Two Midwesterners Fulfill Mission in Cairo—Imams Will Be Sent to Teach," *New York Times*, September 20, 1959, p. 21.

17. Barbara C. Aswad, "The Southeast Dearborn Arab Community Struggles for Survival Against Urban 'Renewal,'" in Barbara C. Aswad, ed., *Arabic Speaking Communities in American Cities* (New York: Center for Migration Studies, 1974), pp. 53–83.
18. For members of the Pakistani Ahmadiyya movement, often regarded by Sunnis as outside the theological boundaries of orthodox Islam, the community is a source of great strength. Ahmadiyya devotees recognize a succession of teachers who are direct descendants of the founder, Hazrat Ahmad, a nineteenth-century religious leader known as the *Mahdi*, or Messiah. Supplicants regard these men as successors to the *Mahdi* and as continuous sources of divine revelation. For this reason the movement is considered heretical by Sunni devotees, who see Muhammad as the seal of the prophetic tradition.

    Ahmadiyya missions were opened in the United States in the 1920s. They are still active. Others have been established in Canada. Each chapter is responsible to the Director General of the Ahmadiyya Muslim Foreign Missions office in Pakistan.
19. Louise E. Sweet, "Reconstituting a Lebanese Village Society in a Canadian City," in Aswad, ed., *Arabic Speaking Communities*, p. 50.
20. "Boys Master the Koran in Arabic," *Cedar Rapids Gazette*, January 12, 1936. Quoted in Mehdi, ed., *The Arabs in America*, p. 93.
21. Ronald Sullivan, "A Moslem School Upsets Hunterdon," *New York Times*, May 21, 1978, sec. xi, p. 20.
22. James Robert Parish and Don E. Stanke, *The Swashbucklers* (New Rochelle, New York: Arlington House, 1976), p. 118.
23. Accounts of correspondence between the F.B.I. and Muslim community and religious leaders regarding the ABSCAM designation appear in spring 1980 editions of the *Muslim Star* (Detroit, Michigan: The Federation of Islamic Associations).
24. Harold R. Isaacs, *Scratches on Our Minds: American Images of China and India* (New York: John Day Company, 1958).
25. *Ibid.*, p. 40.
26. Laurel D. Wigle, "An Arab Muslim Community in Michigan," Aswad, ed., *Arabic Speaking Communities*, pp. 155–167.
27. *Newsletter of the Task Force on Christian-Muslim Relations*, April, 1980.
28. Aswad, "The Southeast Dearborn Arab Community," p. 62.
29. Safia F. Haddad, "The Women's Role in Socialization of Syrian-Americans in Chicago," in Hagopian and Paden, eds., *The Arab Americans: Studies in Assimilation*, pp. 84–101.
30. Aswad, "The Southeast Dearborn Arab Community," p. 64.
31. One of the best-known Arab-Americans is Dr. Michael A. Shadid, who organized the first cooperative hospital in the United States in 1929. Dr. Shadid is recognized as a pioneer in the field of cooperative medicine.
32. Youssef M. Ibrahim, "'Showplace' Mosque Planned on East Side," *New York Times*, July 26, 1978, sec. B., p. 1.
33. For a summary of this debate see A. Shiloah, "The Dimension of Sound; Islamic Music—Philosophy, Theory and Practice" in Bernard Lewis, ed., *Islam and the Arab World; Faith, People, Culture* (New York: Alfred A. Knopf in association with American Heritage Publishing Co., Inc., 1976), pp. 161–180.
34. *The Holy Qur'an, Text, Translation and Commentary*, Abdullah Yusuf Ali, p. 1021.

Glossary

Hinduism

Agni—The Vedic god identified as fire.

abhisheka—A showerbath given the deity during *puja*.

Annakut—A festival celebrated in several North Indian *bhakti*, or devotional, traditions. *Annakut* commemorates the incarnation of Krishna as Mount Govardhan.

Aranyakas—Vedic treatises, often referred to as forest treatises, denoting their composition by hermits.

arati—The ritualistic waving of a lighted wick in front of a deity during *puja*.

Aryan—Nomadic invaders and immigrants who swept into parts of North India and the Punjab between 2000 and 1500 B.C.

Atharva—One of the four Vedas, containing numerous spells and incantations for a variety of purposes.

atman—The individual soul.

Bhagavad Gita—Literally, "The Song of God." The Gita, part of the Mahabharata, is the revelation of Krishna. It is one of the most popular Hindu scriptures. See MAHABHARATA.

Bhagavata Purana—A popular piece of Hindu mythology that has inspired poetry, art, and drama about the deity Krishna. See PURANA.

bhajan—A form of popular Hindu worship in which devotion, or *bhakti*, is expressed through hymns and songs.

bhakti—Devotional Hinduism, which became popular in the fifteenth through the seventeenth centuries in North India. *Bhakti* was both an attitude and a historical movement that fostered numerous *sampradayas*, or sects.

Brahma—Associated with the act of creation, Brahma is one of the Hindu *Trimurti*, or trinity, of Vishnu, Siva, and Brahma.

Brahman—The essence of the universe. The concept of Brahman represents ultimate reality in the Hindu tradition and is understood to be pervasive and all-knowing. Brahman is neuter and often identified as a cosmic principle.

Brahmanas—Prose commentaries containing discourses on ritual. A division of Vedic literature.

Brahmin—A priest. The upper *varna*, or class, of Vedic society.

dharma—Moral law, which in Hindu society is understood to uphold the social order.

dharmshala—A retreat house for Hindu pilgrims.

dhoti—A loose-fitting cotton cloth worn by men from waist to feet.

Diwali—The Festival of Lights. It recognizes the victory of Rama over the demon

185

Ravana. Diwali, a major festival, marks the new year on the traditional Hindu lunar calendar and is usually celebrated in October.

Dravidian—The indigenous inhabitants of the Indian subcontinent.

Epics—Post-Vedic scriptures including the Mahabharata and Ramayana, which are important sources of Hindu mythology.

Ganesh—An elephant-headed deity associated with good fortune and removing obstacles. In Hindu mythology, Ganesh is the son of Siva.

Garuda—The *vahana*, or animal carrier, of Vishnu, in the form of a bird.

Ghadr—"Mutiny." Ghadr was a movement developed in the United States opposing British rule in India. The Ghadr movement originated in California in 1912 and was championed by the revolutionary Har Dayal.

ghee—Clarified butter used in many Hindu rituals.

gopuram—Gateway. *Gopurams* are ornate, highly carved entrances to South Indian temples.

gotra—A patrilineal clan whose members are descended from a common ancestor. A component part of the *jati* system.

Great Tradition—The Vedic literary and ritualistic tradition.

homa—A fire sacrifice practiced by the Aryans. *Homa* is an important Hindu tradition often performed at marriage ceremonies.

Indra—The Vedic god often associated with lightning and the power of the storm.

Jainism—A religious tradition founded by Mahavira (599–527 B.C.). Jainism, like Buddhism, rejected the teachings and the authority of the Vedas.

jati—An endogamous social unit that is the basis of the caste system. Each of the hundreds of *jatis* has a particular level of purity and pollution, and a common occupation. *Jati* members may share patterns of social relationships and participate in common rituals.

Kabir—A *bhakti* saint in sixteenth-century North India. Kabir is known for his integration of Hindu and Islamic beliefs.

kalasham—Gold finals atop a *gopuram*, or temple gateway.

Kali—A Shakti goddess, the consort of Siva.

karma—The basic law of the universe through which one accures merit or demerit, shaping the character of future lives.

Krishna—An incarnation of Vishnu, who first became popular as a folk hero. Krishna is the subject of schools of miniature painting and iconography. He is often associated with the sectarian *bhakti*, or devotional movement, and is frequently depicted with his consort, Radha.

Kshatriyas—In the four-fold *varna* system, a class of soldiers.

lingam—A phallic symbol worshiped by Saivite Hindus as a sign of procreation and cosmic energy.

Little Tradition—Indigenous village traditions of the Indian subcontinent.

Mahabharata—A voluminous Epic set in the context of strife between two opposing armies, the Kauravas and the Pandavas. It contains the Bhagavad Gita, a poetic dialogue between Krishna and his charioteer, Arjuna.

mantra—An incantation.

moksha—Spiritual liberation, the end pursuit of the practice of *yoga*.

mudras—Symbolic hand gestures used in Hindu iconography and in Indian classical dance.

Nandi—The *vahana*, or animal carrier, of Siva in the form of a bull.

panchaloha—Five metals blended and used to cast images.

pradakshina—The circumambulation of a temple or the deity within, done as part of *puja*.

prasad—The consecrated food offered to a deity and distributed to celebrants.

puja—The worship of a Hindu deity, often in bronze form. *Puja* is the ceremonial bathing, feeding, and entertaining of icons on a regular basis.

pujari—A temple priest who performs *puja*.

Puranas—A body of texts that encompass a wide range of Hindu mythology and cosmology. The word *purana* means "ancient." As religious texts, the Puranas include ancient narratives concerning the deities Brahma, Vishnu, and Siva.

Rama—The seventh incarnation of Vishnu. Rama is the celebrated hero of the epic Ramayana.

Ramakrishna—A nineteenth-century leader of the Hindu Renaissance in India and devotee of the mother goddess, Kali. Through his disciple Swami Vivekananda, Ramakrishna influenced holy men and teachers who came to the United States.

Ramayana—An important Epic attributed to the sage Valmiki. It contains mythology surrounding the deity Rama, his wife, Sita, and the demon Ravana.

Ras Lila—A religious play or drama used to emphasize *bhakti*. The Ras Lila is often associated with the deity Krishna.

ratha—A temple chariot.

Rig—The oldest of the four Vedas, containing sacred hymns and poetry.

Rudra—The Vedic god identified with the power of the storm. Rudra is often understood to be the precursor of the Hindu deity Siva.

sadhu—A holy man or ascetic.

Sama—One of the four Vedas, containing hymns drawn from the Rig Veda for use during sacrificial acts of worship.

Samhitas—Vedic hymns.

sampradaya—A Hindu sect.

samskara—A rite of passage celebrating the transition periods of birth, adolescence, marriage, and death. There are twelve *samskaras* in all, though some sects recognize more.

Sanskrit—Literally "polished." The classical tongue of the Vedas and the sacred language of Hinduism. As a highly refined speech, Sanskrit was originally distinguished from the *prakrits,* or common tongues.

sari—A single piece of silk, often embroidered with gold or silver thread, worn by Indian women.

Saivite—(pronounced Shaivite)—Devotees of Siva.

Shakti—Procreative energy of the mother goddess, Durga, or Kali. Vaishnavism, Saivism, and Shaktism are three forms of Hinduism in current practice.

Shiksapatri—A code of ethics used in the Swaminarayan movement.

Shilpa Shastras—Treatises dealing with the crafting and installation of icons.

Shudras—In the four-fold *varna* system, a class of laborers.

Sita—The wife of the deity Rama.

Siva (pronounced Shiva)—Often associated with destruction. Siva is properly the deity who ends the recurrent cycle of the existence to make way for the subsequent recreation. He is one of the *trimurti:* Vishnu, Siva, and Brahma.

smitri—Literally, "that which is learned." *Smitri* refers to those Hindu scriptures outside the Vedic canon.

Sutras—Discourses on ritual and religious law.

Swaminarayan—A *bhakti* saint who organized a sect in western India in the late eighteenth century. The Swaminarayan movement now flourishes in the Gujarat and in the United States.

Upanayana—The investiture rite when a member of the upper three *varnas* is given a sacred thread signifying a "twice-born" status.

Upanishads—Philosophical tracts that are the last part of Vedic literature. The four-fold division of the Vedas includes Samhitas (hymns), Brahmanas (texts on ritual), Aranyakas (forest treatises), and Upanishads.

Vachanamritam—The major scriptural text of the Swaminarayan Sanstha.

Vahana—An animal carrier, or vehicle, popular in Vedic mythology. *Vahanas* often bore their divine riders into battle.

Vaishnavite—Devotee of Vishnu or of one of his incarnations.

Vaishyas—In the four-fold *varna* system, a class of merchants.

Varna—Class. *Varna* refers to the four class divisions of Hindu society—Brahmin, Kshatriya, Vaishya, Shudra—which are the scriptural basis of caste. The caste system, however, is composed of thousands of endogamous groups, or *jatis*.

Vayu—The Vedic god associated with the force of the wind.

Veda—The sacred texts of Hinduism that are considered canonical and authoritative. There are four Vedas: Rig, Yajur, Atharva, and Sama.

Vedanta—A major school of Hindu philosophy and a popular nineteenth-century movement that was carried to North America.

vimana—The towering structure above the *sanctum sanctorum* in a Hindu temple.

Vishnu—The preserver. The deity Vishnu is one of the *trimurti*: Vishnu, Siva, and Brahma.

Yajur—One of the four Vedas, containing ritualistic formulae that were part of the Vedic sacrificial tradition.

yantras—Sacred designs often used to decorate the area around an icon.

yoga—A disciplined system of meditation codified by Patanjali in the Yoga Sutras.

Buddhism

Abhidhamma[*Sanskrit: Abhidharma*]—One of the three *pitakas*, or baskets, of the Mahayana and Theravada canons. The Abhidhamma *pitaka* contains a body of highly refined doctrine.

ahimsa—Non-violence. *Ahimsa* is a basic tenet of all forms of Mahayana and Theravada Buddhism.

Amitabha or **Amida**—The Mahayana Buddha of the Pure Land, or Western Paradise.

anatta [*Pali*]—The doctrine of no soul, negating the concept of *atman*.

arhant—A monk who obtains extraordinary powers while seeking enlightenment. The ideal of the Theravada school.

Asoka—(pronounced Ashoka)—An Indian emperor (274–232 B.C.) who established Buddhism as a state religion. Asoka is credited with spreading Buddhism throughout most of the Indian subcontinent and instilling a spirit in his people that carried it beyond.

atman—Soul.

betsuin—A large temple, often the senior temple of a B.C.A. (Buddhist Churches of America) administrative district.

bhikkhu [Sanskrit: *bhikshu*]—A Buddhist monk and a member of the *sangha*.

bodhi—Knowledge. The word *Buddha*— The Enlightened One— is derived from this Sanskrit word.

bodhisattva [Pali: *bodhisatta*, also in common use]—A divine being who, approaching enlightenment, aids others to find spiritual release. In the Mahayana tradition, the *bodhisattva* replaced the Theravada *arhant* as an ideal.

bonzai—A Japanese style of decorative gardening, utilizing dwarf trees.

Buddha—An enlightened being, referring either to the historical Buddha, Siddhartha Gautama, or to the diverse Buddha figures of the Mahayana tradition. See also BODHI.

dhamma [Sanskrit: *dharma*]—A term of Hindu origin used by Buddhists to refer to doctrine.

Eightfold Path—A system of morality and mental discipline based on patterns of Hindu *yoga*. The Eightfold Path was taught by the historical Buddha as a means of achieving enlightenment.

Four Noble Truths—Four basic assumptions about the human condition taught by the historical Buddha. The Four Noble Truths include the fundamental perceptions that life inherently involves suffering, that desire is the cause of suffering, that desire can be extinguished, and that the way to achieve this end is contained in the Eightfold Path.

gassho—A term denoting prayer in the Buddhist Churches of America.

Gautama—The family name of the historical Buddha.

guru—In the Hindu tradition, a teacher who imparts religious knowledge to a disciple, or *chela*.

haiku—A form of Japanese poetry frequently associated with Zen.

Honen—A monk and teacher (A.D. 1133–1212) who propagated the *nembutsu* as a path to salvation in Japan. Honen was for a time a teacher of Shinran Shonin, whom the Jodo Shinshu Buddhist tradition recognizes as a founder figure.

issei—The first generation of Japanese immigrants in North America.

Jataka—Narratives of the former births of the Buddha that are popular forms of scripture.

Jodo Shinshu—"True Pure Land Teaching." A school of Pure Land Buddhism in Japan founded in the thirteenth century by Shinran Shonin.

juzu—A form of the rosary used by members of the Jodo Shinshu tradition as an aid for meditation.

karma—The system of merit and demerit common to Hindu and Buddhist cosmology.

Kwan-Yin—A popular Mahayana *bodhisattva* frequently associated with Chinese Buddhism. Kwan-Yin stems from the Indian *bodhisattva* Avalokitesvara.

Lotus Sutra—(Saddharmapundarika)—A highly popular Mahayana scripture that propounds the *bodhisattva* ideal and other teachings.

Maha Bodhi Society—An international society of Buddhists founded by Anagarika Dharmapala in 1891.

Mahamaya—In Buddhist mythology, the mother of the historical Buddha.

mahathera—A great elder in the Ceylonese Buddhist tradition.

Mahayana—The northern school of Buddhism. Literally, "the great vehicle."

mantra—In Hinduism a sacred word or sound. The *nembutsu* in Pure Land Buddhism is analogous to a *mantra*.

Mara—A Buddhist demon associated with the pain caused by suffering and desire.

Middle Way—The teachings of the historical Buddha, which were mid-way between the extremes of meditation through physical austerities practiced by others seeking enlightenment and worldliness.

nembutsu—*Nama Amida Butsu* ("Praise to Amida Buddha"). A sacral formula in the Jodo Shinshu Pure Land tradition.

nirvana—Enlightenment.

nisei—The second generation of Japanese-Americans, whose parents are *issei*.

Pali—The sacred language of the Theravada school.

pitaka [Sanskrit and Pali]—Basket. One of the three baskets (Tipitaka) of Buddhist scripture.

Pure Land—the Western Paradise. A Mahayana school popular in China and Japan.

samsara—The stream of birth and rebirth in Hindu and Buddhist cosmology.

sangha—The monastic orders of Buddhist clergy. For the Buddhist Churches of America, the *sangha* becomes the Church and includes laity as well as clergy.

Shinjin—"Faith," in the Buddhist Churches of America.

Shinran Shonin—(A.D. 1173–1262), the founder of the Jodo Shinshu school of Pure Land Buddhism.

Siddhartha—The given name of the historical Buddha.

stupa—A sacred place in Mahayana and Theravada traditions for the interment of the ashes of the historical Buddha. *Stupas* are frequently constructed with a dome and spire.

Sutta [Sanskrit: Sutra]—A sacred text. One of the Three Baskets (Tipitaka) of Buddhist scripture.

Taoism—An ancient Chinese religion associated with the teachings of the philosopher Lao-Tzu.

Tathagata—A title applied to the historical Buddha. The Tathagata is one who has achieved truth.

thera—Elder. A Theravada *bhikkhu*, or monk.

Theravada—The Tradition of the Elders, the southern school of Buddhism.

T'ien T'ai—A highly organized, orthodox form of Chinese Buddhism that recognizes the Lotus Sutra as a source of authority.

Tipitaka [Sanskrit: Tripitaka]—The three baskets, referring to the Sutta, Abhidhamma, and Vinaya. Three collections of scripture. The Tipitaka collections form the Mahayana and Theravada canons.

Three Jewels—The Buddha, the Dhamma, and the Sangha.

vihara—A Theravada temple.

Vinaya—The part of the Tipitaka composed of rules governing the *sangha*.

wat—A Thai *vihara*, or temple.

Yin-yang—Polar opposites occurring in nature, such as winter-summer, night-day, male-female. According to Taoist beliefs, the ebb and flow of these opposing principles is the basic process of the universe and part of the *Tao* (way).

Sikhism

A number of terms used in this chapter (*gotra, jati, karma, varna*, for example) are basic to an understanding of Indian society and the reforms that the Sikh *Gurus* sought to bring about. The reader is urged to consult the Hinduism section of the glossary for these words.

Akhad Path—A rite during which the Guru Granth Sahib is read continuously for forty-eight hours.

amrit—Nectar given Sikhs baptized into the *Khalsa* during the rite Amrit Parchar.

ardas—A short prayer recited after the *diwan*.

Baisakhi—A festival that marks the founding of the *Khalsa* in 1699. Baisakhi Day is usually celebrated in April.

bhakti—Devotion. The historical *bhakti* movement in North India was part of the theological and cultural milieu in which Sikhism was fostered.

chela—Disciple. The *guru-chela* relationship is an important part of Indian society.

Dasam Granth—A non-canonical collection of poetry and prose attributed to Guru Gobind Singh and others.

diwan—A regular service of worship. In Mughal India, the *diwan* was a royal court.

dupatta—A scarf worn by Punjabi women with *shalwar* and *kamiz*.

Ghadr—"Mutiny." A revolutionary movement of Hindus and Sikhs in the United States that between 1914 and 1919 actively opposed British rule in India.

Golden Temple—A *gurdwara* in Amritsar constructed under the direction of Guru Ramdas and Guru Arjan. Sikhism's holiest shrine.

Granthi—A highly respected Sikh who reads the Guru Granth Sahib during worship. *Granthis* are symbols of Sikh piety and exemplify the highest values of the faith.

Gurmukhi—A script popularized by Guru Angad for transcribing the Guru Granth Sahib.

gurdwara—A Sikh temple.

guru—A religious teacher. Gurus are an important part of Indian society. In the Sikh tradition, where the concept of the guru has been magnified, the term, capitalized, refers to ten historical figures who shaped the faith. It is also applied to the Guru Granth Sahib, which is regarded as a living Guru.

Guru Granth Sahib—The only text recognized by Sikhs as authoritative and canonical.

harmonium—An accordion-like instrument often used in Sikh worship.

Japji—A section of the Guru Granth Sahib adopted as a central prayer in the Sikh tradition.

Jat—An agricultural people who have formed an important part of the *Khalsa*.

kach—Undershorts. One of the five K's.

kamiz—A long shirt worn by women that frequently extends beyond the waist.

kangha—A comb. One of the five K's.

kara—A steel bangle. One of the five K's.

katha—A discourse during the *diwan*.

Kaur—"Princess." A name given to female members of the *Khalsa*.

kesh—Unshaven hair. One of the five K's.

keshadari—Sikhs who uphold ethical and moral requirements of the faith and the five K's.

Khalsa—The brotherhood of baptized Sikhs.

kirpan—A short sword. One of the five K's.

kirtan—Hymns sung by vocalists during the *diwan*.

kurta—A shirt often worn over loose-fitting pants *(pajama)* by men.

langar—A communal meal eaten after the *diwan*. *Langar* is also food distributed to persons in need.

Nam—A theological concept developed by Guru Nanak that stresses the repetition of the name of God.

pajama—Loose-fitting pants worn by men.

Panch Piyares—The five beloved. These men first formed the nucleus of the *Khalsa*.

panth—The total Sikh community. This is distinguished from the *Khalsa*, the brotherhood of baptized members.

pahul—A Sikh baptism during which *amrit* is sprinkled on the hair and eyes of devotees.

patit—A Sikh who has cut his hair and shaved. An apostate.

parsad—Sweet balls of food distributed among worshipers after the *diwan*.

Punjab—A geographical area now incorporated in both India and Pakistan. The history of Sikhism is linked with this land.

Punjabi—An Indo-Aryan language spoken in the Punjab. Punjabi, like other Indo-Aryan languages, is related to the parent tongue, Sanskrit.

raga—A sequence of notes in Indian classical music often associated with a mood or time of day. The Guru Granth Sahib is organized by *raga*.

Rehat Maryada—A tract of literature that describes the singing of hymns, the reading of the Granth, and the distribution of blessed food.

Shabad—Word. By concentrating on God's word (*Shabad*) as contained in the Guru Granth Sahib, Sikhs nurture a personal relationship with the holy.

sahajdhari—Sikhs who do not maintain the five K's.

sangat—Assembly of devotees.

sant—A Sikh lecturer or scholar of high repute.

shalwar—Pants made of bright silks or other fine materials, worn by women.

Sikh—Disciple. Member of a religious tradition founded by Guru Nanak.

Singh—Lion. A name given to male members of the *Khalsa*. Singh may be taken as a middle or last name.

tabla—A drum used in the performance of classical Indian music. The *tabla* is an important part of Sikh worship, and is often used with the harmonium to accompany vocalists.

Wahguru—Wonderful Lord. An incantation repeated as an integral part of Sikh meditation and worship.

Islam

Ahmadiyya—A Shi'i sect founded by a nineteenth-century reformer, Sir Sayeed

Ahmad. Sunni devotees regard the Ahmadiyya movement as heretical, while members of the sect claim to be Muslims.

Ali—Muhammad's son-in-law and cousin. Upon the death of Muhammad, when a Caliph, or successor, was chosen, the majority of Muslims followed Abu Bakr while a minority, the Shi'a, chose to follow Ali.

Allah—The Arabic word for God. Related to the Hebrew *El, Elohim*.

American Muslim Mission—The correct name for an indigenous Muslim movement in the United States, whose adherents were formerly known in popular usage as Black Muslims.

asr—A period of prayer in the afternoon.

Ayatollah—Sign of God. Iranian Shi'i Muslim leaders of high repute and spiritual authority. *Ayatollahs* are deemed to be representatives of the *Imam*.

burka—A shroud worn by some women in India and Pakistan as a mark of *Purdah*.

da'wah—The preaching of the Prophet's message. The educational function of the mosque is often seen as an expression of *da'wah*.

Druze—A Shi'i sect popular in Lebanon. Orthodox Muslims frequently regard the Druze movement as outside the boundaries of the faith. Druze acknowledge the messianic leadership of an eleventh-century Caliph, al-Hakim.

fajr—A period of prayer at dawn.

Five Pillars of Islam—Five basic duties required of every Muslim, including: regular prayer *(salat)*, tithing *(zakat)*, fasting *(sawm)*, profession of faith *(shahadah)*, and pilgrimage *(Hajj)*.

hadith—A narrative about the Prophet, stressing the dominance of Muhammad's actions, judgments, and opinions in any of hundreds of different matters.

Hajj—Pilgrimage. A devotee who makes the sacred journey to Mecca is termed *Hajji*.

Hijrah—The journey of Muhammad in 622 from Mecca to Medina, marking the formal establishment of the faith.

Husayn—The second son of Ali. Husayn was killed in battle in A.D. 680 as Abu Bakr's armies attempted to crush the Shi'a movement. Shi'i Muslims today see the death of Husayn as a decisive moment in the history of their faith and remember the anniversary of his death as a holy day.

Id—Id al-fitr is a major Muslim festival that marks the end of Ramadan, a period of fasting.

ihram—Restrictions placed on devotees during the Hajj, or pilgrimage.

ijma—In Shari'a law, the principle of consensus.

Imam—In the Sunni tradition, a religious leader who conducts prayer. In North America, *Imams* continue a role as educators and are recognized as highly respected persons. In the Shi'i tradition, *Imams* are spiritual leaders who transmit the revelation of God.

isha—A period of prayer at night.

Ismailis—Members of a Shi'i sect that recognizes seven *Imams*.

jamaat—A chapter in the organizational structure of the Ahmadiyya movement in the United States.

Ka'bah—A sacred shrine in Mecca that is the holiest place in the Muslim tradition. During the *Hajj*, Muslims walk around the Ka'bah, often touching a foundation stone that, according to tradition, was laid by Abraham.

madrasa—A school of Islamic instruction.

maghrib—A period of prayer at sunset.

Mahdi—Messiah. In the Ahmadiyya tradition, the reformer Hazrat Ahmad is seen as the *Mahdi*.

mahr—Money, jewelry, or other tangible symbol of the marriage contract, given by a husband to his wife at the time of marriage in many Muslim countries.

minbar—A pulpit in a mosque.

mosque—A place of Muslim worship.

nikkahnama—A formal contract in many Muslim countries in which the dowry and *mahr* are finalized.

Purdah—A complex cultural system in which Muslim women live in a separate domain from men. The woman is the guardian of the family and the home, while the man's domain is the place of business. Frequently, *Purdah* systems enforce strict standards of propriety and dress.

qiyas—In *Shari'a* law, the principle of analogy.

Qur'an—The revealed word of Allah dictated by the angel Gabriel to the Prophet Muhammad.

Qurayash—The tribe of Muhammad.

Ramadan—The ninth month of the Muslim calendar and a time of fasting.

salat—Prayer. One of the five pillars of Islam. The periods of prayer are: sunset *(maghrib)*, night *(isha)*, dawn *(fajr)*, noon *(zuhr)*, and afternoon *(asr)*.

sawm—Fasting. One of the five pillars of Islam.

shahadah—A creedal statement repeated by all Muslims, professing belief in Allah and His messenger, Muhammad. One of the five pillars of Islam.

Shari'a—Islamic law. The schools of Muslim jurisprudence include Hanafi, Maliki, Shafi'i, Ja'fari, and Zaidi.

Shi'a—The body of believers who hold allegiance to Muhammad's son-in-law and cousin, Ali. Shi'i Muslims are the numerical minority. The term *Shi'a* is a collective noun. *Shi'i* is a singular noun or adjective.

shirk—The sin of elevating persons or things to divine status.

sufism—Islamic mysticism. Sufis have always been considered heterodox by orthodox Sunni practitioners. However, the tradition has been a constant and important part of Islam.

sunna—Orthodox teachings of Islam, based on the Prophet's life, that are direct sources of authority.

Sunni—The body of believers who are the numerical majority of Muslims. The Sunni tradition is recognized as orthodox.

surah—A verse of the Qur'an.

tawaf—Walking around the Ka'bah during pilgrimage *(Hajj)*.

Twelvers—A Shi'i sect that recognizes twelve *Imams*.

ulama—The collective body of Muslim scholars and teachers.

Zaidis—Members of a Shi'i sect that recognizes five *Imams*.

zakat—Almsgiving. One of the Five Pillars of Islam.

zuhr—A period of prayer at noon.

Select Bibliography

This bibliography includes several types of materials designed to help readers who have had no prior knowledge of each religion or the culture(s) it represents. The listing also includes some advanced works that guide the student into each faith. The kinds of literature cited include:
- Surveys of each religious tradition, translations of scripture.
- Ethnic studies; studies of change and adaptation in immigrant communities.
- Historical overviews; stereotypes in newspapers and periodicals of immigrant groups.
- Sectarian publications and ethnic newspapers.
- Immigration legislation.

Hinduism

Archer, W. G. *The Loves of Krishna in Indian Paintings and Poetry*. New York: Grove Press, n.d.

Babb, Lawrence A. *The Divine Hierarchy: Popular Hinduism in Central India*. New York: Columbia University Press, 1975.

Banerjea, Jitendranath. *The Development of Hindu Iconography*. Calcutta: The University of Calcutta, 1956.

Binford, Mira Reym; Camerini, Michael; and Elder, Joseph. *Four Holy Men: Renunciation in Hindu Society*. Contemporary South Asian Films. Madison, University of Wisconsin, 1976.

Bloomfield, Maurice. trans. *The Atharvaveda*. Strassburg: Trubner, 1899.

Bose, Suhindra. "Travelling Through the Country in America." *Modern Review* 9 (January to June 1911): 251.

Bullard, Betty M. *Asia in New York: A Guide*. New York: The Asia Society, Inc., 1981.

Coomaraswamy, Ananda K. *The Dance of Shiva*. New York: Noonday Press, 1957.

——————and Sister Nivedita. *Myths of the Hindus and Buddhists*. New York: Dover Publications, Inc., 1967.

Das, Rajani Kanta. *Hindustani Workers on the Pacific Coast*. Berlin: Walter de Gruyter, 1923.

Dasgupta, Surendranath. *A History of Indian Philosophy*. Vols. 1–5. Cambridge: Cambridge University Press, 1952–1955.

Dave, H. T. *Life and Philosophy of Shree Swaminarayan*. London: George Allen and Unwin Ltd., 1974.

——————trans. *Shree Swaminarayan's Vachanamritam*. Bombay: Bharatiya Vidya Bhavan, 1977.

Dell, David; Knipe, David M.; McDermott, Robert A.; Morgan, Kenneth W.; and

Smith, H. Daniel. *Focus on Hinduism: Audio-Visual Resources for Teaching Religion.* New York: Foreign Area Materials Center, State Education Department, University of the State of New York and Council for Intercultural Studies and Programs, 1977.

Dimock, Edward C. Jr., and Levertov, Denise, trans. *In Praise of Krishna: Songs from the Bengali,* New York: Archer Books, 1967.

Dotson, Floyd, and Dotson, Lillian O. *The Indian Minority of Zambia, Rhodesia and Malawi.* New Haven, Connecticut: Yale University Press, 1968.

Embree, Ainslee T., ed. *The Hindu Tradition.* New York: Modern Library, 1966.

Farquhar, J. N. *An Outline of the Religious Literature of India.* Delhi: Motilal Banarsidass, 1967.

Frazier, Allei M., ed. *Hinduism: Readings in Eastern Religious Thought.* Vol. 1. Philadelphia: The Westminster Press, 1959.

Gupte, Pranay. "Hindu Temple, 'Just Like India,' Opens in Queens." *New York Times,* June 4, 1977, p. 23.

————. "Stamp of India Heavier in City." *New York Times,* June 4, 1978, p. 1.

Hill, W. Douglas P. *The Bhagavadgita: An English Translation and Commentary.* Oxford: Oxford University Press, 1966.

"The Hindu Temple of Society of North America." New York: Hindu Temple Society of North America, 1978.

Hollis, Robert. "Patel: A Big Name in Hotels—The Mysterious Innkeepers from India." *San Francisco Examiner and Chronicle,* April 29, 1979, Sec. A, p. 8.

Hopkins, Thomas J. *The Hindu Religious Tradition.* Encino, California: Dickenson Publishing Company (Religious Life of Man Series), 1971.

"Indians in Flushing Blend 2 Cultures." *New York Times,* December 18, 1983, Sec. 1, p. 64.

Isherwood, Christopher. *Ramakrishna and His Disciples.* New York: Simon and Schuster, 1965.

Issacs, Harold I. *Scratches on Our Minds: American Images of China and India.* New York: John Day Company, 1958; reprint ed., White Plains, New York: M. E. Sharpe, 1980.

Klass, Morton. *East Indians in Trinidad: A Study of Cultural Persistence.* New York: Columbia University Press, 1961.

Kondapi, C. *Indians Overseas: 1839–1949.* London: Oxford University Press, 1951.

Langley, Edward. "The Indians of Queens." *New York Daily News* (Sunday News Magazine), June 1, 1980, p. 6 ff.

Mayo, Katherine. *Mother India.* New York: Harcourt, Brace, 1927.

Michell, George. *The Hindu Temple: An Introduction to Its Meaning and Forms.* London: Paul Elek, 1977.

Miller, David M., and Wertz, Dorothy C. *Hindu Monastic Life: The Monks and Monasteries of Bhubaneswar.* Montreal: McGill-Queens University Press, 1976.

Morgan, K. W. *The Religion of the Hindus.* New York: Ronald Press, 1953.

Morris, H. S. *The Indians in Uganda: A Study of Caste and Sect in a Plural Society.* Chicago: University of Chicago Press, 1967.

Muller, F. Max, trans. *The Upanishads.* 2 Vols. New York: Dover Publications, 1962; reprint ed., Sacred Books of the East. Vols. 1 and 15. Oxford: Clarendon Press, 1979 and 1884.

Noss, John B. *Man's Religions.* New York: Macmillan Company, 1966.

O'Flaherty, Wendy Doniger. *Hindu Myths: A Sourcebook, Translated from the Sanskrit.* Baltimore: Penguin Books, 1975.

Radhakrishnan, Sarvepalli, and Moore, Charles A., eds. *A Source Book in Indian Philosophy.* Princeton: Princeton University Press, 1970.

Renou, Louis. *Hinduism.* New York: George Braziller, Inc., 1961.

——————*Religions of Ancient India.* New York: DeGraff, 1953.

Richardson, E. Allen. "Mughal and Rajput Patronage of the Bhakti Sect of the Maharajas, the Vallabha Sampradaya, 1640–1760 A.D." Ph.D. dissertation. University of Arizona, 1979.

Ross, Nancy Wilson. *Three Ways of Asian Wisdom: Hinduism, Buddhism and Zen and Their Significance for the West.* New York: Simon and Schuster (A Clarion Book), 1966.

Schwartz, Barton M., ed. *Caste in Overseas Indian Communities.* San Francisco: Chandler Publishing Company, 1967.

Shree Sahajanand Swami. *Shikshapatri: A Compendium of the Code of Conduct.* Ahmedabad, India: Bochasanwasi Shree Aksharpurushottam Sanstha, 1977.

Shridharani, Krishnalal. *My India, My America.* New York: Duell, Sloan and Pearce, 1941.

Sunderland, J. T. "Principal Horamba Chandra Maitra in America." *Modern Review* 9 (January to June 1911): 151–152.

Thapar, Romila. *A History of India.* Vol. 1. Baltimore: Penguin Books, 1966.

Wescott, G. H. *Kabir and the Kabir Panth.* Cawnpore, India: Christ Church Mission Press, 1907.

Zaehner, R. C. *The Bhagavad-Gita.* Oxford: Clarendon Press, 1969.

——————*Hinduism.* Oxford: Oxford University Press, 1962.

——————*Hindu Scriptures.* New York: Dutton (Everyman's Library), 1966.

Zimmer, Heinrich. *Myths and Symbols in Indian Art and Civilization.* New York: Harper, 1946.

The following citations are relevant to Hinduism and Sikhism. These texts include basic information about South Asian culture and civilization, Hindus and Sikhs in North America, and stereotypes of Indians in the West.

Bagai, Leona B. *The East Indians and the Pakistanis in America.* Minneapolis: Lerner Publications, 1967.

Basham, Arthur. *The Wonder That Was India.* London: Sidgwick Jackson, 1954. New York: Grove Press ed., 1959.

Brown, Emily C. *Har Dayal: Hindu Revolutionary and Rationalist.* Tucson: University of Arizona Press, 1975.

——————"Historical Background of the Sikh Movement in the United States." Tucson, Arizona: October 1978.

Desai, Prakash, and Mehta, Dhawal. "Indians in the America: The Lonely Crowd." *Asian-Pacific American Heritage Week.* Potomac, Maryland: Asian-Pacific Heritage Council, Inc., 1980, p. 9.

Guthikonda, Ravindranath, ed. *Indian Community Reference Guide and Directory of Indian Associations in North America.* New York: Federation of Indian Associations, 1979.

"Hindu Invasion." *Colliers National Weekly* 45 (March 26, 1910): 15.

Hopkins, Eric Washburn. *The Religions of India.* Boston: Ginn and Company, 1895.

India West. Published weekly in El Sobrante, California.

Juergensmeyer, Mark. "The Ghadr Syndrome: Nationalism in an Immigrant Community." *Punjab Journal of Politics.* Vol. 1, No. 1 (October 1977);

reprint ed., Amritsar, India: Department of Political Science, Guru Nanak Dev University, 22 pages.

LaBrack, Bruce. "Occupational Specialization Among California Sikhs: The Interplay of Culture and Economics." Syracuse, New York: 1975.

——————"The East Indian Experience in America." Syracuse, New York: 1975.

Lannoy, Richard. *The Speaking Tree: A Study of Indian Culture and Society.* London: Oxford University Press, 1971.

Lockley, Fred. "The Hindu Invasion: A New Immigration Problem." *The Pacific Monthly,* May 1907, pp. 584–595.

Mandelbaum, David G. *Society in India—Change and Continuity.* Vol. 2. Berkeley: University of California Press, 1970.

Nand Singh Sihra. "Indians in Canada: A Pitiable Account of their Hardships by One Who Comes from the Place and Knows Them," *Modern Review* 14 (August 1913): 140–149.

News India. Published weekly by Hiba Publishing, Inc., New York.

"The Position of Indians in Canada." *Modern Review* 12 (July to December 1912): 57–61.

Scheffauer, Herman. "Tide of Turbans." *Forum* 43 (June 1910): 616–618.

Spear, Percival. *A History of India.* Vol. 2. Baltimore: Penguin Books, 1965.

Steadman, John M. *The Myth of Asia: A Refutation of Western Stereotypes of Asian Religion, Philosophy, Art, and Politics.* New York: Simon and Schuster (A Clarion Book), 1969.

Thomas, Wendell Marshall. *Hinduism Invades America.* New York: Beacon Press, 1930.

Buddhism

Ahn Jung-Hyo. "Buddhist Monk's Life Lonely, Rewarding." *Koreatown: The English Language Voice of the Korean American Community* 1 (January 28, 1980): 4.

Arizona Historical Society. "The Chinese Experience In Arizona and Northern Mexico 1870–1940." Tucson, Arizona: 1979.

Barrows, John Henry. *The World's Parliament of Religions: An Illustrated and Popular Story of the World's First Parliament of Religions Held in Chicago in Connection with the Columbian Exposition of 1893.* 2 Vols. Chicago: The Parliament Publishing Co., 1893.

Bloom, Alfred. *Shinran's Gospel of Pure Grace.* Tucson: University of Arizona Press (Association of Asian Studies Monograph), 1965.

Buddhist Churches of America. 2 Vols. San Francisco: Buddhist Churches of America, 1974.

Buddhist Churches of America. *Death and Dying: Buddhist Reflections.* San Francisco: 1978.

——————*Celebration of Life of Buddha.* San Francisco: 1977.

——————*Wheel of Dharma.* Monthly Newsletter of the Buddhist Churches of America. San Francisco, California.

Bullard, Betty M. *Asia in New York City: A Guide.* New York: The Asia Society, Inc., 1981.

Ch'en, Kenneth. *Buddhism in China: A Historical Survey.* Princeton: Princeton University Press, 1964.

Conze, Edward. *Buddhist Texts Through the Ages.* Oxford: Bruno Cassirer, 1954.

——————Buddhism, *Its Essence and Development*. New York: Harper and Row, 1951.

——————*Buddhist Thought in India: Three Phases of Buddhist Philosophy*. Ann Arbor: University of Michigan Press, 1967.

Coomaraswamy, Ananda K. *Buddha and the Gospel of Buddhism*. New York: Harper Torchbooks reprint, 1964.

Crossette, Barbara. "Japanese Buddhists Hold a Summer Festival." *New York Times*, July 21, 1978, p. C18.

de Bary, William Theodore, ed. *The Buddhist Tradition in India, China and Japan*. New York: Random House, Vintage Books, 1972.

Dulles, Foster Rhea. *China and America: The Story of Their Relations Since 1784*. Princeton: Princeton University Press, 1946.

Earhart, H. Byron. *Japanese Religion: Unity and Diversity*. Belmont, California: Dickenson Publishing Company, 1967.

Goddard, Dwight, ed. *A Buddhist Bible*. Boston: Beacon Press, 1970.

Hanayama, Shinsho. *The Story of the Juzu*. San Francisco: Buddhist Churches of America, 1962.

Hebers, John. "Surge in Immigration Now Means Chinese Are Largest Asian Group in U.S.," *New York Times*, July 30, 1981, p. A12.

Horinovchi, Isao. "Americanized Buddhism: A Sociological Analysis of a Protestantized Japanese Religion." Ph.D. dissertation, University of California, Davis, 1973.

Hosokawa, William. *The Nisei: The Quiet Americans*. New York: William Morrow and Company, 1969.

Hotchkin, Susan. "Buddhists Hold Celebration in Warren Co.," *Daily Record* (Morristown, New Jersey), August 27, 1978, p. B10.

Imamura, Jane. "Half a Century." *Wheel of Dharma* 6 (April 1979): 2.

Jhiboyama, Zenkei. *The Six Oxherding Pictures*. Japan: privately published, 1965.

Kashima, Tetsuden. *Buddhism in America: The Social Organization of an Ethnic Religious Institution*. Westport, Connecticut: Greenwood Press, 1977.

King, Winston L. *In the Hope of Nibbana: An Essay on Theravada Buddhist Ethics*. La Salle, Illinois: Open Court Publishing Company, 1964.

Kitano, Harry. *Japanese Americans: Evolution of a Subculture*. Englewood Cliffs, New Jersey: Prentice-Hall, 1969.

Kodani, Masao. *The Buddhist Shrine*. San Francisco: Buddhist Churches of America, 1976.

Laymnan, Emma McCloy. *Buddhism in America*. Chicago: Nelson-Hall, 1976.

Marshall, George N. *Buddha: The Quest for Serenity—A Biography*. Boston: Beacon Press, 1978.

Mascaro, Juan, ed. *The Dhammapada*. Baltimore: Penguin Classics, 1973.

Maske, Monica. "Jersey Buddhists Gather for Lama's Arrival." *Sunday Star Ledger* (Newark, New Jersey), September 9, 1979, p. 1, Sec. 2.

McFarland, H. Neill. *Rush Hour of the Gods*. New York: Macmillan and Company, 1967.

Melendy, H. Brett. *The Oriental Americans*. New York: Twayne Publishers, 1972.

Needleman, Jacob. *The New Religions*. Garden City, New York: Doubleday, 1970.

Reichelt, Karl Ludvig. *Truth and Tradition in Chinese Buddhism: A Study of Chinese Mahayana Buddhism*. New York: Paragon Book Reprint Corporation, 1968.

Rice, Robert. "Indochinatown." *Across the Board* 17, No. 6 (June 1980): 12–24.
Robinson, Richard H. *The Buddhist Religion.* Dickenson Religious Life of Man Series. Belmont, California: Dickenson Publishing Company, 1970.
Ross, Nancy Wilson. *Buddhism: A Way of Life and Thought.* New York: Alfred Knopf, 1980.
Seki, Hozen. *The Great Natural Way.* New York: American Buddhist Academy, 1976.
Shibata, George E. *The Buddhist Holidays.* San Francisco: Buddhist Churches of America, 1974.
Spiro, Melford E. *Buddhism and Society: A Great Tradition and Its Burmese Vicissitudes.* New York: Harper and Row, 1970.
Suzuki, Beatrice Lane. *Mahayana Buddhism: A Brief Outline.* New York: Macmillan and Company, 1969.
Suzuki, Daisetz Teitaro. *Outlines of Mahayana Buddhism.* New York: Schocken Books, 1967.
Swearer, Donald K. *Buddhism in Transition.* Philadelphia: Westminster Press, 1970.
——————*Toward the Truth by Buddhadasa.* Philadelphia: Westminster Press, 1971.
Thomas, Edward J. *The History of Buddhist Thought.* New York: Barnes and Noble, 1967.
——————*The Life of Buddha as Legend and History.* London: Routledge and Kegan Paul, Ltd., 1960.
Thompson, Laurence G. *Chinese Religion: An Introduction.* Belmont, California: Dickenson Publishing Company, 1969.
Washington Buddhist. Quarterly Newsletter of the Washington Buddhist Vihara 9, No. 3 (July–September): 1978.
Woodward, F. L., trans. *Some Sayings of the Buddha.* New York: Oxford University Press, 1973.
Welch, Homes. *The Practice of Chinese Buddhism 1900–1950.* Cambridge, Massachusetts: Harvard University Press, 1967.
——————*The Buddhist Revival in China.* Cambridge, Massachusetts: Harvard University Press, 1968.
Wells, Mariann K. "Chinese Temples in California." Master's Thesis, University of California, Berkeley, 1962.
Wilson, Robert A., and Hosokawa, William. *East to America: A History of the Japanese in the United States.* New York: William Morrow and Co., 1980.
Yamaoka, Haruo. "New View of Buddhist Education." Doctor of Ministry dissertation, Pacific School of Religion, 1979.
Yoshifumi, Meda. *Letters of Shinran: A Translation of Mattosho.* Vol. 1. Kyoto: Hongwanji International Center, Shin Buddhism Translation Series 1, 1978.

Sikhism

The American Sikh Review 1, No. 4–5 (September–October 1977).
Butler, William. "Sikhs Here Wind Up Religious Celebration." *Daily News* (Queens), April 24, 1978, p. 1.
Barrier, N. Gerald. *The Sikhs and Their Literature; A Guide to Tracts, Books and Periodicals, 1849–1919.* Columbia, Missouri: Manohar Book Service for South Asia Books.

Cole, William Owen. *The Sikhs*. London: Routledge and Kegan Paul, Ltd., 1978.
─────────A *Sikh Family in Britain*. Exeter, England: The Religious Education
        Press (Man and Religion Services), 1973.
Cunningham, Joseph D. A. *A History of the Sikhs*. H. L. O. Garrett and R. R. Sethi,
        ed. Delhi: S. Chand, 1955.
DeBary, William T. et al. *Sources of Indian Tradition*. New York: Columbia
        University Press, 1958.
Desai, Rashmi. *Indian Immigrants in Britain*. London: Oxford University Press,
        1963.
Gardner, Ray. "When Vancouver Turned Back the Sikhs." *MacLeans Magazine*,
        November 8, 1958, p. 31.
LaBrack, Bruce. "Sikhs of California: A Study of Differential Culture Change."
        Ph.D. dissertation. Syracuse University, 1979.
─────────"Peaches and Punjabis: The Reconstitution of Sikh Society in Rural
        California." Stockton, California, 1977.
Lambert, Richard D., and Bressler, Marvin. *Indian Students on an American
        Campus*. Minneapolis: University of Minnesota Press, 1956.
Mansokhani, Gobind Singh. *The Quintessence of Sikhism*. Amritsar, India:
        Shiromani Gurdwara Parbandhuk Committee, 1965.
Macauliffe, Max Arthur. *The Sikh Religion, Its Gurus, Sacred Writings and
        Authors*. 6 Vols. Oxford: Clarendon Press, 1909.
McLeod, W. H. *Guru Nanak and the Sikh Religion*, Oxford: Clarendon Press,
        1968.
─────────*The Evolution of the Sikh Community: Five Essays*. Delhi: Oxford
        University Press, 1975.
Nayar, Baldev Raj. "Sikh Separatism in the Punjab." In Donald Eugene Smith, ed.
        South Asian Politics and Religion. Princeton: Princeton University
        Press, 1966, pp. 150–175.
Rawlinson, Hugh G. *India: A Short Cultural History*. New York: F. A. Praeger,
        1952.
Saund, D. S. *Congressman from India*. New York: E. P. Dutton, 1960.
Sethi, A. S., ed. *Journal of Comparative Sociology* (Interfaith Dialogue: Sikhism).
        Nos. 4 and 5 (1977 and 1978). Ottawa, Canada: Sociological Research
        Centre in Collaboration with Sikh Study Circle.
The Sikh Cultural Society of New York, Inc. *Constitution*. Richmond Hill, New
        York: 1973.
The Sikh Cultural Society. *Rehat Maryada: A Guide to the Sikh Way of Life*.
        London: 1971.
Singh, Fauja; Singh, Trilochan; Singh, Gurbachan Talib; Singh, J. P. Uberoi; and
        Singh, Sohan. *Sikhism*. Patiala, India: Punjabi University, 1969.
Singh, Gopal. *Translation of Sri Guru Granth Sahib*. Delhi: Gur Das Kapur and
        Sons, 1961.
Singh, Khushwant. *The Sikhs*. London: G. Allen and Unwin, 1953.
─────────A *History of the Sikhs, 1839–1964*. 2 Vols. Princeton: Princeton
        University Press, 1966.
Singh, T. et al. *Selections from the Sacred Writings of the Sikhs*. London:
        G. Allen and Unwin, 1960.
Smith, Donald E. *South Asian Politics and Religion*. Princeton: Princeton Uni-
        versity Press, 1966.

U.S. Department of Commerce. *Historical Statistics of the United States, Colo-
        nial Timesto 1970*, Part 1, Series C 89–119, 1975.
Wylam, P. M. *The Sikh Marriage Ceremony*. Kent, England: The Sikh Missionary
        Society U.K. (Publication No. 15), n.d.

Islam

Abdul-Rauf, Muhammad. *History of the Islamic Center.* Washington, D.C.: Islamic Center, 1978.

——————*The Life and Teachings of the Prophet Muhammad.* London: Longmans. 1965.

——————"Pilgrimage to Mecca." *National Geographic* 153, No. 11 (November 1978): 581–207.

Aossey, Yahya Jr. *Fifty Years of Islam in Iowa 1925–1975.* Cedar Rapids, Iowa: Unity Publishing Company, 1975.

"Arabs: A Clash of Cultures" (three articles). *Arizona Daily Star* (Tucson), May 27, 1979, Sec. B, p. 1.

Aramco World Magazine. Published bi-monthly by the Arabian American Oil Company, New York, New York.

Aruri, Nasseer H. "The Arab-American Community of Springfield Massachusetts." In *The Arab-Americans: Studies in Assimilation,* pp. 50–66. Edited by Elaine C. Hagopian and Ann Paden. Wilmette, Illinois: The Medina University Press International, 1969.

Aswad, Barbara C., ed. *Arabic Speaking Communities in American Cities.* New York: Center for Migration Studies, 1974.

——————"The Southeast Dearborn Arab Community Struggles for Survival Against Urban 'Renewal'." In *Arabic Speaking Communities in American Cities,* pp. 53–79. Edited by Barbara C. Aswad. New York: Center for Migration Studies, 1974.

Atiyeh, George N., ed. *Arab and American Cultures.* Washington, D.C.: American Enterprise Institute for Public Policy Research, 1977.

Berger, Monroe. "Americans from the Arab World." In *The World of Islam,* pp. 351–372. Edited by James Kritzeck and R. Bayly Winder. New York: St. Martin's Press, 1959.

"Boys Master the Koran in Arabic." *Cedar Rapids Gazette,* January 12, 1936. In *The Arabs in America, 1492–1977 A Chronology and Fact Book,* p. 93. Edited by Beverlee Turner Mehdi. Dobbs Ferry, New York: Oceana Publications, Inc., 1978.

Brockelmann, Carl. *History of the Islamic Peoples.* New York: Capricorn Books, 1960.

Chirri, Jswad Imam Mohammad. "The Five Daily Prayers." Detroit: Islamic Center of Detroit, n.d.

Cragg, Kenneth. *The House of Islam.* Encino, California: Dickenson Publishing Company (Religious Life of Man Series), 1975.

Elkholy, Abdo A. *The Arab Moslems in the United States Religion and Assimilation.* New Haven, Connecticut. College and University Press, 1966.

Gibb, H.A.R. *Mohamedanism.* New York: Oxford University Press, 1971.

Gotje, Helmut. *The Qur'an and Its Exegesis; Selected Texts With Classical and Modern Muslim Interpretations.* London: Routledge and Kegan Paul, Ltd. 1971.

Guillaume, Alfred. *Islam.* Revised Edition. Baltimore: Penguin Books, 1956.

Haddad, Safia F. "The Women's Role in Socialization of Syrian-Americans in Chicago." In *The Arab Americans: Studies in Assimilation,* pp. 84–101. Edited by Elaine C. Hagopian and Ann Paden. Wilmette, Illinois: The Medina University Press, 1969.

Hagopian, Elaine C., and Paden, Ann, eds. *The Arab-Americans: Studies in Assimilation,* Wilmette, Illinois: The Medina University Press International, 1969.

Haiek, Joseph R., ed. and publisher. *The American-Arabic Speaking Community Almanac*. Published annually by The News Circle, Los Angeles, California.

Hardy, P. *The Muslims of British India*. Cambridge: Cambridge University Press, 1972.

Harsham, Philip. "Islam in Iowa." *Aramco World Magazine* 26, No. 6 (November–December 1978): 30–36.

Hitti, Philip Khuri. *Islam, A Way of Life*. Minneapolis: University of Minnesota Press, 1970.

——————*The Syrians in America*. New York: George H. Doran Company, 1924.

The Holy Qur'an, Text, Translation and Commentary. Abdullah Yusuf Ali. Washington, D.C.: The Islamic Center, 1978.

Ibrahim, Youssef M. "'Showplace' Mosque Planned on East Side." *New York Times*, July 26, 1978, Sec. B, p. 1.

Isaacs, Harold R. *Scratches on Our Minds: American Images of China and India*. New York: John Day Company, 1958. Revised edition, M. E. Sharpe, Inc., 1980.

The Islamic Center. *Essentials of Muslim Prayer*. Washington, D.C., n.d.

——————"Islam and Muslims in North America." Washington, D.C., n.d.

Islamic Center (Michigan City). *Islam in Michigan City, Past and Present*. Michigan City, Indiana, n.d.

Katibah, H. I. "Moslems of City Celebrating Pious Feast of Ramazan (sic.)." *Brooklyn Eagle*, April 18, 1925. In *The Arabs in America, 1492–1977: A Chronology and Fact Book*, p. 81. Edited by Beverlee Turner Mehdi. Dobbs Ferry. New York: Oceana Publications Inc., 1978.

Khan, Muhammad Zafrulla. *Ahmadiyyat: The Renaissance of Islam*. London: Tabshir Publications, 1978.

Kritzeck, James, and Winder, R. Bayly, eds. *The World of Islam*. New York: St. Martins Press, 1959.

LeBon, Gustave. *The World of Islamic Civilization*. Geneva: Tudor Publishing Company, 1974.

Levy, Ruben. *The Social Structure of Islam*. Cambridge: Cambridge University Press, 1957.

Lewis, Bernard, ed. *Islam and the Arab World: Faith, People, Culture*. New York: Alfred A. Knopf in association with American Heritage Publishing Company, Inc., 1976.

——————*Islam from the Prophet Muhammad to the Capture of Constantinople* 2 Vols. New York: Harper Torchbooks, 1974.

Lincoln, Charles Eric. *The Black Muslims in America*. Revised Edition. Boston: Beacon Press, 1973.

Little, Malcolm. *The Autobiography of Malcolm X*. New York: Grove Press, 1973.

MCC Bulletin. Published six times a year by the Muslim Community Center, Inc., Bethesda, Maryland.

Mehdi, Beverlee Turner, ed. *The Arabs in America, 1492–1977: A Chronology and Fact Book*. Dobbs Ferry, New York: Oceana Publications, Inc., 1978.

The Muslim Star. Published monthly by the Federation of Islamic Associations, Detroit, Michigan.

The Muslim World: A Quarterly Journal of Islamic Study and of Christian Interpretation Among Muslims. Published by the Hartford Seminary Foundation in Hartford, Connecticut.

Newsletter of the Task Force on Christian-Muslim Relations. A Project of the

Commission on Faith and Order of the National Council of the Churches of Christ in the U.S.A. in Cooperation with the Duncan Black Macdonald Center for the Study of Islam and Christian-Muslim relations. *The Hartford Seminary Foundation.* No. 8, April 1980.

Parish, James Robert, and Stanke, Don D. *The Swashbucklers.* New Rochelle, New York: Arlington House, 1976.

Pear, Robert. "Capital Mosque Reflects Islam Turmoil." *New York Times,* August 24, 1980, p. 65.

Savory, R. M., ed. *Introduction to Islamic Civilization.* Cambridge: Cambridge University Press, 1976.

Shadid, Michael A. *Crusading Doctor.* Boston: Meador Publishing Company, 1956.

Shiloah, A. "The Dimension of Sound, Islamic Music—Philosophy, Theory and Practice." In *Islam and the Arab World: Faith, People, Culture,* pp. 161–180. Edited by Bernard Lewis. New York: Alfred A. Knopf in Association with American Heritage Publishing Company Inc., 1976.

Smith, Wilfred Cantwell. *Islam in Modern History.* Princeton: Princeton University Press. 1957.

Speight, R. Marston. *Christian-Muslim Relations: An Introduction for Christians in the United States of America.* Hartford, Connecticut: Task Force on Christian-Muslim Relations, The National Council of the Churches of Christ in the U.S.A., 1983.

Sullivan, Ronald. "A Moslem School Upsets Hunterdon." *New York Times,* May 21, 1978. Sec. xi p. 20.

Sulzberger, A. O. Jr., "Roots of War in the Gulf." *New York Times,* September 24, 1980, Sec. A, p. 10.

Sweet, Louise E. "Reconstituting a Lebanese Village Society in a Canadian City." In *Arabic Speaking Communities in American Cities.* Edited by Beverlee Turner Mehdi. New York: Oceana Publications, Inc., 1974, pp. 39–51.

Watt, W. Montgomery. *The Formative Period of Islamic Thought.* Edinburgh: Edinburgh University Press, 1973.

Wigle, Laurel D. "An Arab Muslim Community in Michigan." In *Arabic Speaking Communities in American Cities,* pp. 155–167. Edited by Barbara C. Aswad. New York: Center for Migration Studies, 1974.

Williams, John Alden, ed. *Islam.* New York: George Braziller, 1952.

Wolf, C. Umhau. "The Islamic Federation, 1952: 'Muslims in the American Mid-West'," in *The Muslim World* L(January 1960): 42–43. Quoted in *The Arabs in America 1492–1977: A Chronology and Fact Book,* p. 103. Edited by Beverlee Turner Mehdi. Dobbs Ferry, New York: Oceana Publications Inc. 1978.

"The World of Islam." *Time,* April 16, 1979, p. 40 ff.

Younis, Adele. "The Coming of the Arabic-Speaking People to the United States." Ph.D. dissertation. Boston University, 1961.

Legislation

United States—Federal Immigration Statutes

"An act to execute certain treaty stipulations relating to Chinese." *Statutes at Large* 22 (1882): 58–61.

"An act to prohibit the coming of Chinese laborers to the United States." *Statutes at Large* 25 (1888): 476–479.

"An act to prohibit the coming of Chinese persons into the United States." *Statutes at Large* 27 (1892): 25–26.

"An act to regulate the immigration of aliens to, and the residence of aliens in, the United States." *Statutes at Large* 39 (1917): 874–898.

"An act to limit the immigration of aliens into the United States," *Statutes at Large* 42 (1921): 5–7.

"An act to limit the immigration of aliens into the United States, and for other purposes," *Statutes at Large* 43 (1924): 153–169.

"An act to repeal the Chinese Exclusion Acts, to establish quotas, and for other purposes." *Statutes at Large* 57 (1943): 600–601.

"An act to authorize the admission into the United States of persons of races indigenous to India, and persons of races indigenous to the Philippine Islands, to make them racially eligible for naturalization, and for other purposes." *Statutes at Large* 60 (1946): 416–417.

"An act to reverse the laws relating to immigration, naturalization, and nationality; and for other purposes." *Statutes at Large* 66 (1952): 163–282.

"An act to amend the Immigration and Nationality Act, and for other Purposes." *Statutes at Large* 79 (1965): 911–922.

Supreme Court Decisions

Porterfield v. Webb. *U.S. Reports* 263 (1923): 225–233.
Terrace v. Thompson. *U.S. Reports* 263 (1923): 197–224.
United States v. Bhagat Singh Thind. *U.S. Reports* 261 (1922): 204–215.
Webb v. O'Brien. *U.S. Reports* 263 (1923): 313–326.

State Laws

"An act to amend section 2166, Revised Code of 1928, relating to prohibited and void marriages." *Arizona Code* 5 (1939): 4.

Canadian Legislation

The British Columbia Reports 20. Victoria, British Columbia: Colonist Printing and Publishing Company Ltd., 1915. pp. 243–292.

Index

1-2-88

BIOLOGICAL SCIENCES

DIRECTIONS. Most questions in the Biological Sciences test are organized into groups, each preceded by a descriptive passage. After studying the passage, select the one best answer to each question in the group. Some questions are not based on a descriptive passage and are also independent of each other. You must also select the one best answer to these questions. If you are not certain of an answer, eliminate the alternatives that you know to be incorrect and then select an answer from the remaining alternatives. Indicate your selection by blackening the corresponding oval on your answer document. A periodic table is provided for your use. You may consult it whenever you wish.

PERIODIC TABLE OF THE ELEMENTS

1 H 1.0																	2 He 4.0
3 Li 6.9	4 Be 9.0											5 B 10.8	6 C 12.0	7 N 14.0	8 O 16.0	9 F 19.0	10 Ne 20.2
11 Na 23.0	12 Mg 24.3											13 Al 27.0	14 Si 28.1	15 P 31.0	16 S 32.1	17 Cl 35.5	18 Ar 39.9
19 K 39.1	20 Ca 40.1	21 Sc 45.0	22 Ti 47.9	23 V 50.9	24 Cr 52.0	25 Mn 54.9	26 Fe 55.8	27 Co 58.9	28 Ni 58.7	29 Cu 63.5	30 Zn 65.4	31 Ga 69.7	32 Ge 72.6	33 As 74.9	34 Se 79.0	35 Br 79.9	36 Kr 83.8
37 Rb 85.5	38 Sr 87.6	39 Y 88.9	40 Zr 91.2	41 Nb 92.9	42 Mo 95.9	43 Tc (98)	44 Ru 101.1	45 Rh 102.9	46 Pd 106.4	47 Ag 107.9	48 Cd 112.4	49 In 114.8	50 Sn 118.7	51 Sb 121.8	52 Te 127.6	53 I 126.9	54 Xe 131.3
55 Cs 132.9	56 Ba 137.3	57 La* 138.9	72 Hf 178.5	73 Ta 180.9	74 W 183.9	75 Re 186.2	76 Os 190.2	77 Ir 192.2	78 Pt 195.1	79 Au 197.0	80 Hg 200.6	81 Tl 204.4	82 Pb 207.2	83 Bi 209.0	84 Po (209)	85 At (210)	86 Rn (222)
87 Fr (223)	88 Ra 226.0	89 Ac† 227.0	104 Unq (261)	105 Unp (262)	106 Unh (263)	107 Uns (262)	108 Uno (265)	109 Une (267)									

	58 Ce 140.1	59 Pr 140.9	60 Nd 144.2	61 Pm (145)	62 Sm 150.4	63 Eu 152.0	64 Gd 157.3	65 Tb 158.9	66 Dy 162.5	67 Ho 164.9	68 Er 167.3	69 Tm 168.9	70 Yb 173.0	71 Lu 175.0
†	90 Th 232.0	91 Pa (231)	92 U 238.0	93 Np (237)	94 Pu (244)	95 Am (243)	96 Cm (247)	97 Bk (247)	98 Cf (251)	99 Es (252)	100 Fm (257)	101 Md (258)	102 No (259)	103 Lr (260)

Lecture ①

Molecular Structure

Organic chemistry is probably the most feared topic on the MCAT. Few MCAT test-takers feel confident about their organic chemistry skills. If you feel confident about organic chemistry, it is probably either because you have a PhD, or because you have only taken first-year organic chemistry and haven't yet learned that organic chemistry is far more complex than your first-year textbook led you to believe.

Attempting to master advanced organic chemistry concepts in order to improve your MCAT score is not *just* a futile waste of time; it is likely to lower your MCAT score. The writers of the MCAT neither test nor claim to test any organic chemistry beyond "content typically covered in undergraduate introductory science courses". In fact, they go to great lengths to ensure that the test does not require knowledge beyond "content typically covered in undergraduate introductory science courses". If you *think* that MCAT might test more, and you look for more in an MCAT organic chemistry question, you are likely to overlook the obvious answer, which is based upon "content typically covered in undergraduate introductory science courses". You are also likely to spend more time on each question because you are choosing the answer from a larger pool of knowledge; more answer choices will *seem* possible within your larger, but inaccurate, context.

Any and all organic chemistry required to answer any question on the MCAT will be covered in this book. For the reasons stated in the preceding paragraph, it is possible that using other organic chemistry MCAT prep books to supplement this book could alter your perception of what is tested by the MCAT thereby lowering your score. We suggest against it.

You should expect questions to look complex and to *appear* that they require in-depth knowledge of organic chemistry. When answering such questions, consider only the simplest organic chemistry concepts and answer the questions accordingly.

1-1
Introduction

Structural formulae are representations of molecules on paper. The MCAT may use any or all of the various formulae so you should be familiar with all of them. The most basic form of structural formula is the **Lewis dot structure**.

1-2
Structural Formula

1-3

Lewis Dot Structures

There are three rules for forming Lewis dot structures.

1. Find the total number of valence electrons for all atoms in the molecule.

2. Use one pair of electrons to form one bond between each atom.

3. Arrange the remaining electrons around the atoms to satisfy the duet rule for hydrogen and the octet rule for other atoms.

Exceptions: Sometimes atoms break the octet rule. Molecules with such atoms include molecules with an odd number of electrons, molecules with an atom having less than an octet, and molecules with an atom having more than an octet. Compounds containing boron and beryllium may contain less than an octet. Molecules with an atom containing more than an octet must contain an atom from the third period or greater in the periodic table because only these atoms have vacant *d* orbitals available for hybridization.

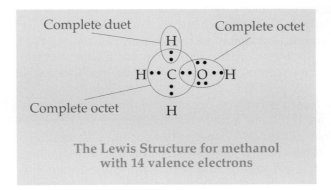

The Lewis Structure for methanol with 14 valence electrons

When writing Lewis structures, don't worry about which electrons come from which atoms. Simply count the number of total electrons and distribute them to complete the valence shells. It is useful to know the atom's **valence** (the number of bonds it forms). Some important valences for common atoms in organic chemistry are as follows: carbon is tetravalent; nitrogen is trivalent; oxygen is divalent; hydrogens and halogens are monovalent. (Halogens other than fluorine are capable of making more than one bond.)

It is also useful to know the **formal charge** of an atom. The formal charge is the number of electrons in the isolated atom, minus the number of electrons assigned to the atom in the Lewis structure. For instance, in the cyanide ion carbon has a pair of nonbonding electrons and one electron from each bond in the triple bond for a total of five electrons.

$$[:C \equiv N:]^-$$

cyanide ion

A neutral carbon atom has only four electrons, so the formal charge on carbon in the cyanide ion is minus one. It is important to know that, although the sum of the formal charges for each atom in a molecule or ion represents the total charge on that molecule or ion, the formal charge on a given atom does not represent a real charge on that atom. The actual charge distribution requires consideration of electronegativity differences among all the atoms in the molecule.

The **dash formula** shows the bonds between atoms, but does not show the three dimensional structure of the molecule.

1-4
Other Structures

The **condensed formula** does not show bonds. Central atoms are usually followed by the atoms that bond to them even though this is not the bonding order. For instance, the three hydrogens following the carbon in CH_3NH_2 do not bond to the nitrogen.

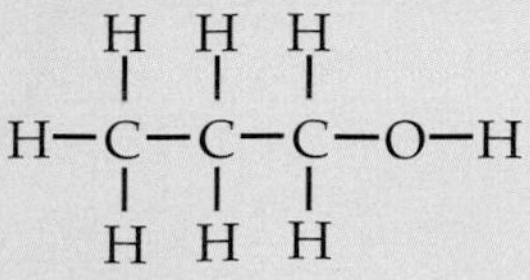

Dash formula   Condensed formula   Bond-line formula 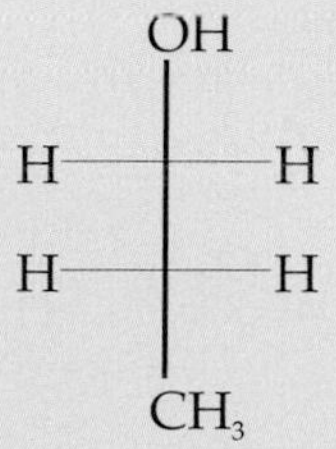   Fischer projection

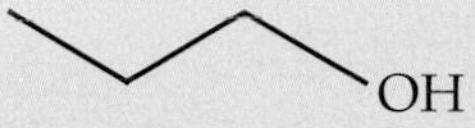

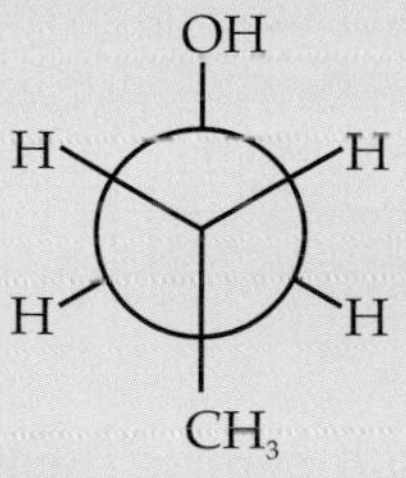

Newman projection 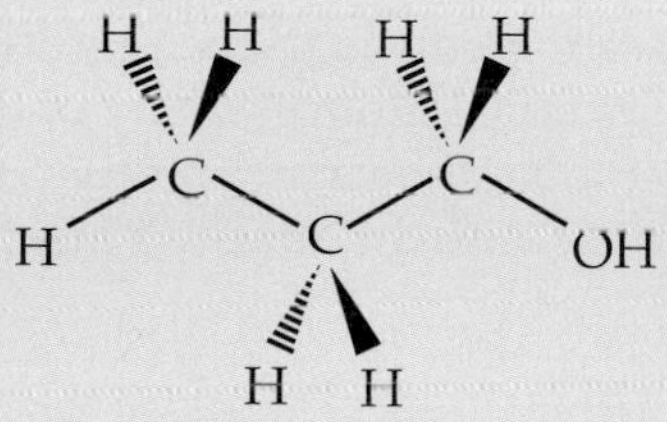   Dash-line-wedge formula 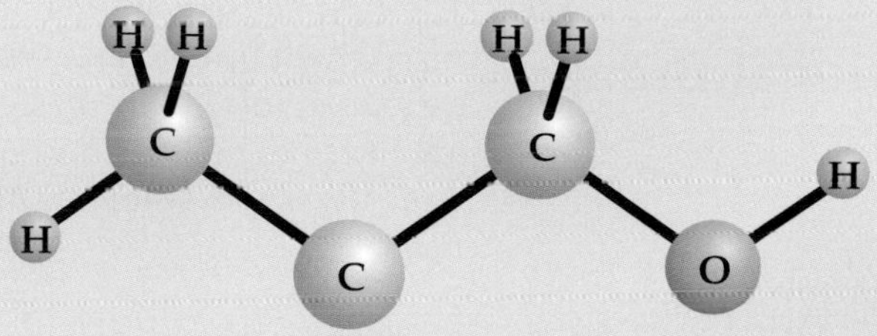   Ball and stick model

The **bond-line formula** is likely to be the most prevalent on the MCAT. In the bond-line formula, line intersections, corners, and endings represent a carbon atom unless some other atom is drawn in. The hydrogen atoms that are attached to the carbons are not usually drawn but are assumed to be present.

The **Fischer projection** is also important on the MCAT. In Fischer projections the vertical lines are assumed to be oriented into the page. The horizontal lines are assumed to be oriented out of the page.

The **Newman projection** is a view straight down the axis of one of the σ-bonds. Both the intersecting lines and the large circle are assumed to be carbon atoms.

In the **dash-line-wedge formula** the black wedge is assumed to be coming out of the page, the dashed wedge is assumed to be going into the page, and the lines are assumed to be in the plane of the page.

Unless otherwise indicated, in all **ball and stick models** in this manual covalently bonded atoms will be drawn to scale using comparisons of their atomic radii as single atoms. Although the sum of the atomic radii is a reasonable approximation of bond length, in the ball and stick models shown in this manual the bond length is drawn to approximately twice this length so that the atoms are clearly visible.

1-5
Index of Hydrogen Deficiency

The **index of hydrogen deficiency** indicates the number of pairs of hydrogens a compound requires in order to become a saturated alkane. Since a saturated alkane contains $2n + 2$ hydrogens (where n is the number of carbons), in order to find the index of deficiency of any compound, subtract the compound's total number of hydrogens from the number of hydrogens on a corresponding saturated alkane and divide by two. For this procedure count halogens as hydrogens. Of course, the index of hydrogen deficiency for any saturated alkane will be zero.

$$\text{Index of hydrogen deficiency} = \frac{(2n + 2) - x}{2}$$

n = number of carbons
x = number of hydrogens

1-6
Functional Groups

The first step in solving any organic chemistry problem on the MCAT is to recognize which functional groups are involved in the reaction. The MCAT tests only reactions involving the basic functional groups. Many of the molecules on the MCAT are likely to be large and unfamiliar; however, in order to solve an MCAT problem, it is only important to be familiar with the attached functional groups and how they react.

Functional groups are substituents with similar structure and similar chemical properties. The following two lists display functional groups. Memorization of List #1 is absolutely vital to success on the MCAT. List #2 is less important, but should still be memorized.

You must know these groups for MCAT Orgo! Stop now and memorize List #1.

List #1

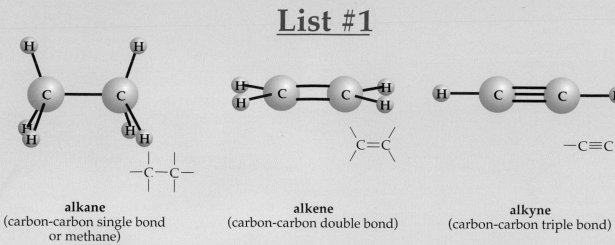

alkane
(carbon-carbon single bond
or methane)

alkene
(carbon-carbon double bond)

alkyne
(carbon-carbon triple bond)

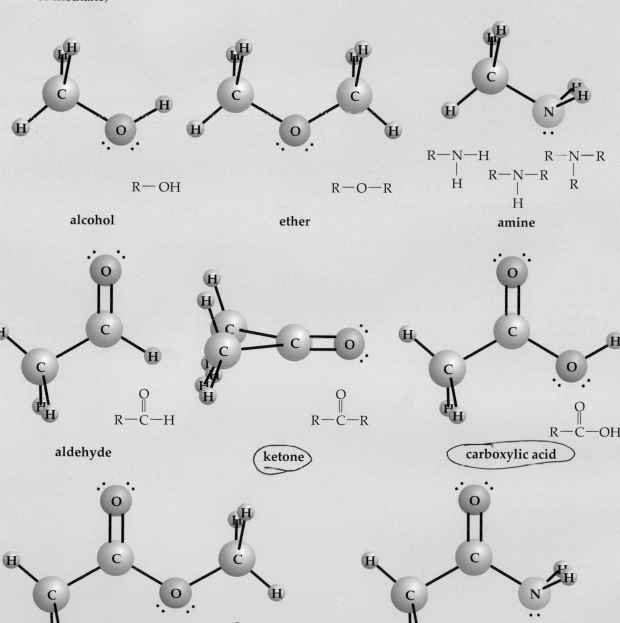

R—OH

alcohol

R—O—R

ether

R—N—H
    |
    H

R—N—R
    |
    H

R—N—R
    |
    R

amine

$$R-\overset{O}{\overset{\|}{C}}-H$$

aldehyde

$$R-\overset{O}{\overset{\|}{C}}-R$$

ketone

$$R-\overset{O}{\overset{\|}{C}}-OH$$

carboxylic acid

$$R-\overset{O}{\overset{\|}{C}}-O-R$$

ester

$$R-\overset{O}{\overset{\|}{C}}-NH_2$$

amide

List #2

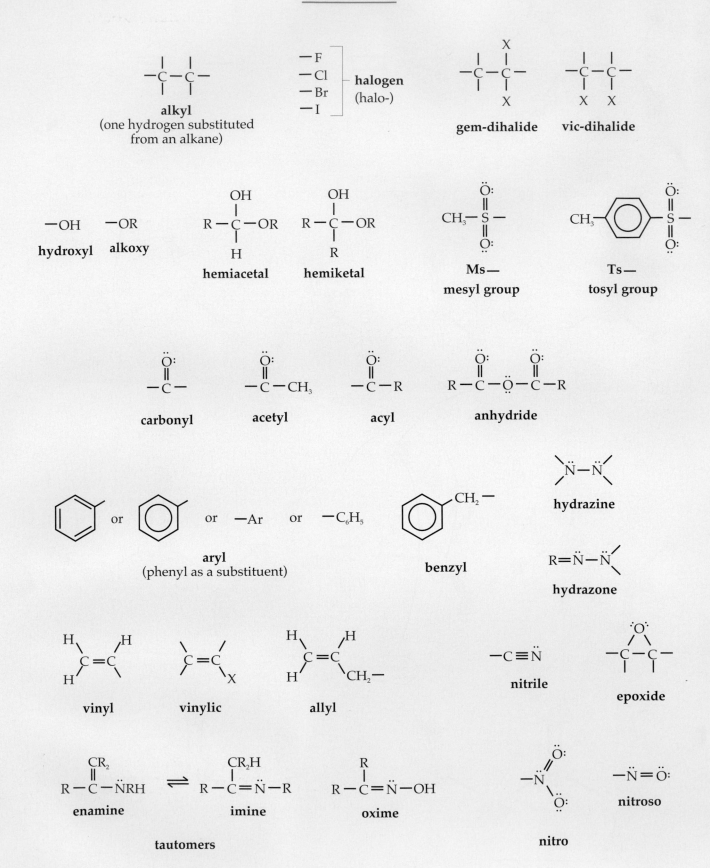

alkyl
(one hydrogen substituted
from an alkane)

halogen
(halo-)

gem-dihalide   vic-dihalide

hydroxyl   alkoxy

hemiacetal   hemiketal

Ms—
mesyl group

Ts—
tosyl group

carbonyl   acetyl   acyl   anhydride

aryl
(phenyl as a substituent)

benzyl

hydrazine

hydrazone

vinyl   vinylic   allyl   nitrile   epoxide

enamine   imine   oxime   nitro

tautomers

nitroso

The MCAT requires knowledge of basic organic chemistry nomenclature. For alkanes you must memorize the following:

prefix	number of carbons
meth-	1
eth-	2
prop-	3
but-	4
pent-	5
hex-	6
hept-	7
oct-	8
non-	9
dec-	10

In addition you should be able to recognize the following structures drawn in any orientation:

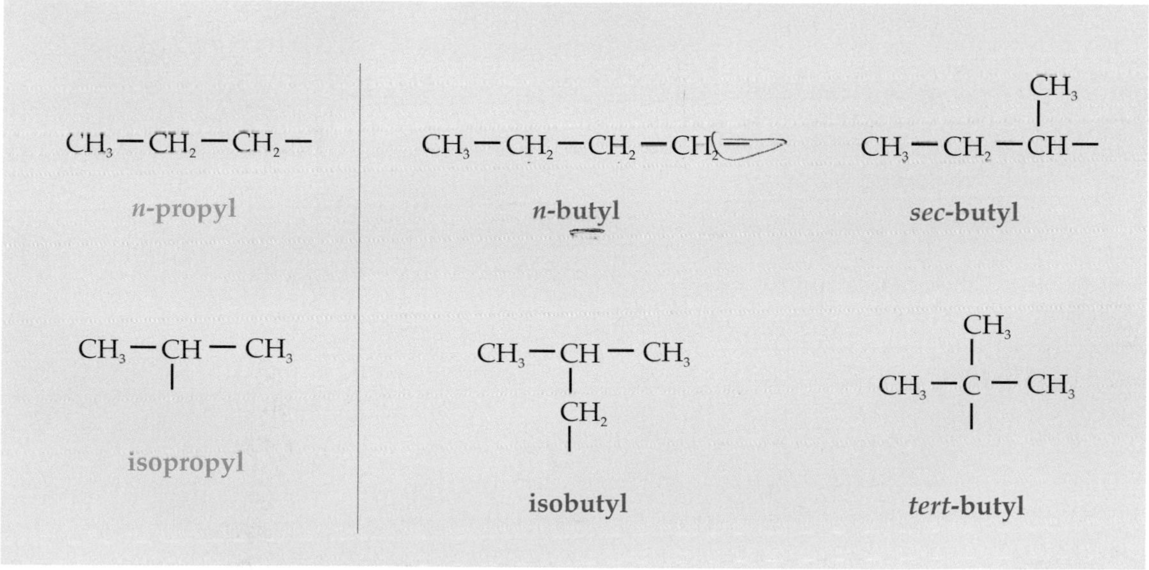

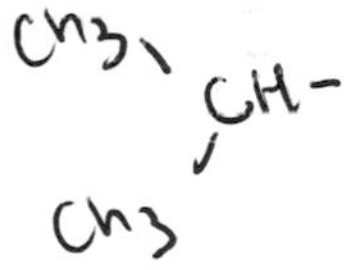

$CH_3-CH_2-CH_2-$

n-propyl

$CH_3-CH_2-CH_2-CH_2-$

n-butyl

$$CH_3-CH_2-\underset{\underset{CH_3}{|}}{CH}-$$

sec-butyl

$CH_3-CH-CH_3$

isopropyl

$$CH_3-\underset{\underset{CH_2}{|}}{CH}-CH_3$$

isobutyl

$$CH_3-\underset{\underset{CH_3}{|}}{\overset{\overset{CH_3}{|}}{C}}-CH_3$$

tert-butyl

$$\underset{CH_3}{\overset{CH_3}{\diagdown}}CH-$$

The following are the IUPAC rules for nomenclature:

- The longest carbon chain with the most substituents determines the base name.

- The end carbon closest to a carbon with a substituent is always the first carbon. In the case of a tie, look to the next substituent.

- Any substituent is given the same number as its carbon.

- If the same substituent is used more than once, use the prefixes di-, tri-, tetra, and so on.

- Order the substituents alphabetically.

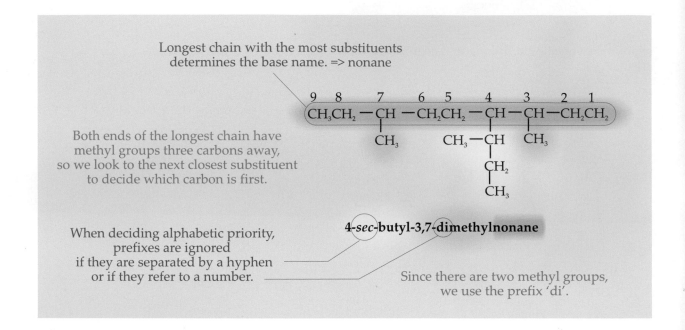

Longest chain with the most substituents determines the base name. => nonane

Both ends of the longest chain have methyl groups three carbons away, so we look to the next closest substituent to decide which carbon is first.

When deciding alphabetic priority, prefixes are ignored if they are separated by a hyphen or if they refer to a number.

4-*sec*-butyl-3,7-dimethylnonane

Since there are two methyl groups, we use the prefix 'di'.

1. β-D-(+)-glucose is reacted with methanol and dry hydrogen chloride. The product of this reaction is then treated with methyl sulfate and sodium hydroxide yielding methyl β-2,3,4,6-tetra-O-methyl-D-glucoside. Which of the following molecules is this product?

A.

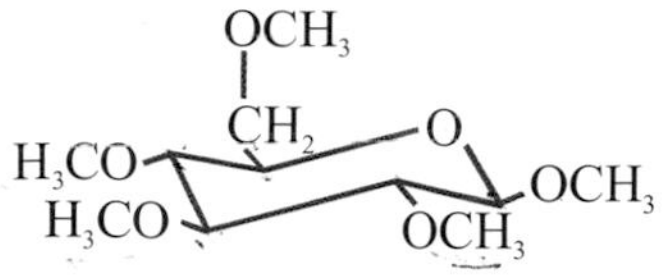

B.

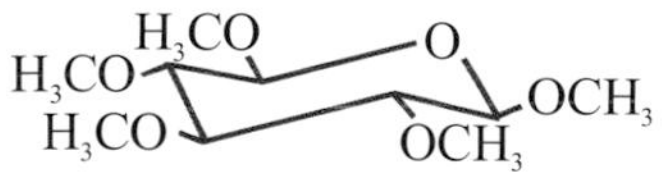

C.

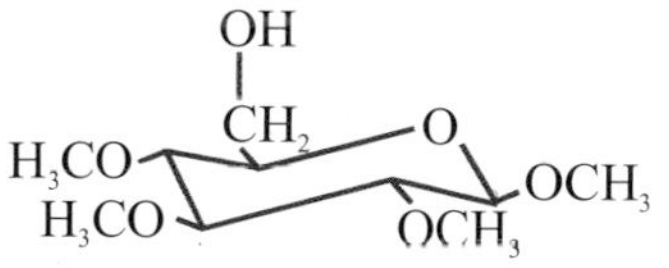

D.

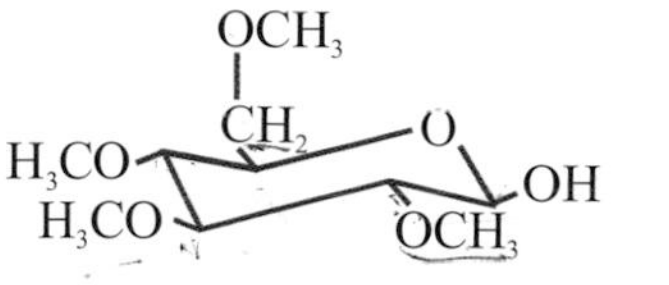

2. Benzoyl chloride reacts with ammonia to form benzamide. Which of the following molecules is the correct structure for benzamide?

A.   **C.**

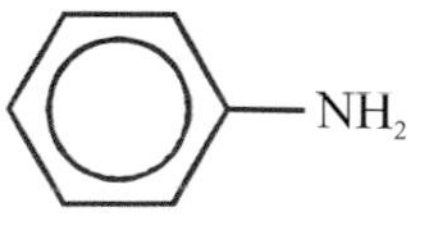

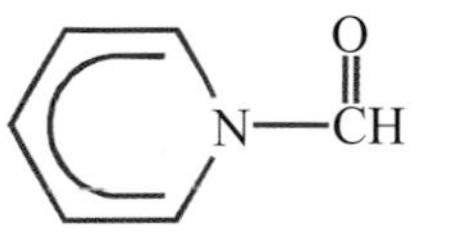

B. 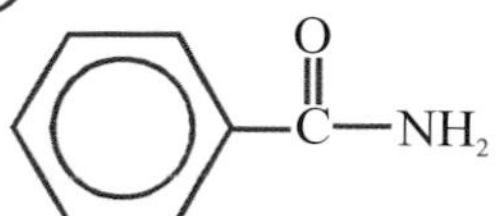   **D.**

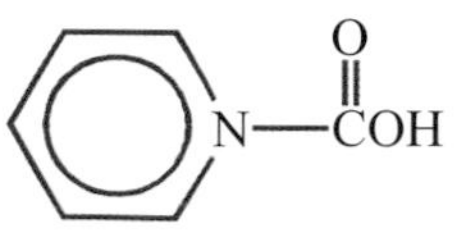

benzaomide

3. Of the bonds listed in the table below, the most stable bond is between:

Bond	Energy
$C_2H_5 - Cl$	339
$C_2H_5 - CH_3$	356
$H_2C = CH - Cl$	352
$H_2C = CH - CH_3$	385
$C_6H_5 - Cl$	360
$C_6H_5 - CH_3$	389

*bond energies given in kJ/mol

- **A.** a saturated alkyl group and a halogen.
- **B.** a saturated alkyl group and a methyl group.
- **C.** an unsaturated alkyl group and a halogen.
- **D.** an unsaturated alkyl group and a methyl group.

4. An α-hydroxy acid is heated to form the compound shown below. What functional group is created in this reaction?

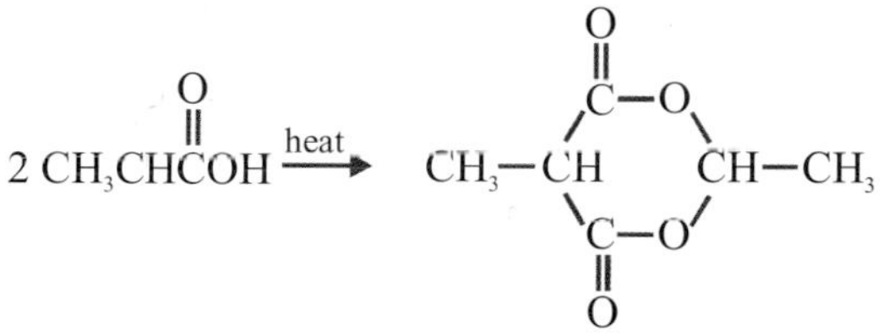

- **A.** ether
- **B.** aldehyde
- **C.** ester
- **D.** ketone

5. How many amide groups are there in the molecule of guanosine shown below?

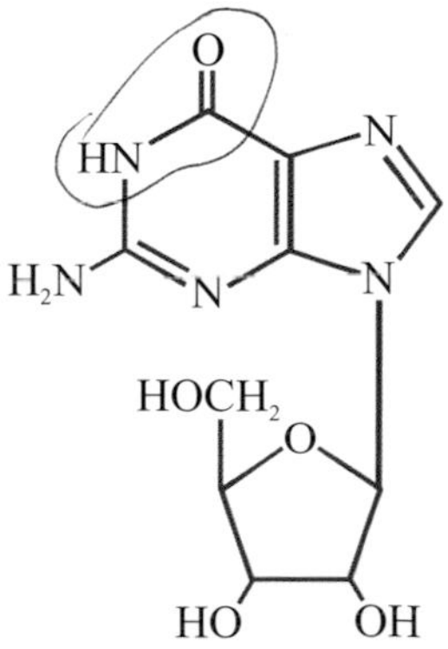

- **A.** 0
- **B.** 1
- **C.** 3
- **D.** 5

GO ON TO THE NEXT PAGE.

6. Just as ammonia, NH_3, is a weak Lewis base, there is a large group of nitrogen-containing organic compounds that behaves like weak bases and is known as:

A.   amides
B.   amines
C.   ethanol alcohols
D.   ethers

7. Which of the following functional groups are found in phenylalanine?

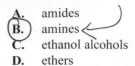

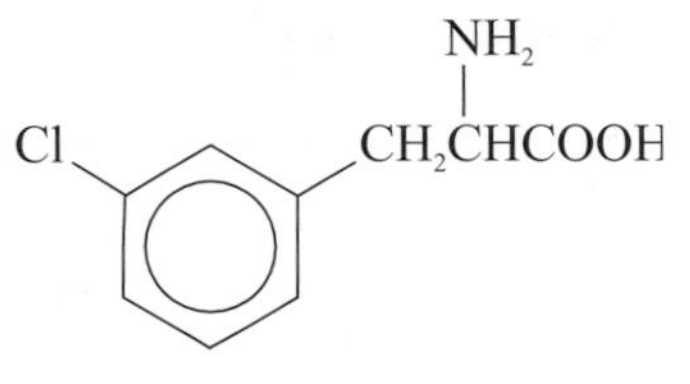

$$CH_2CHCOOH$$

$$NH_2$$

Cl

Phenylalanine

A.   alkyl, double bond and aromatic ring
B.   amine, carboxylic acid and aromatic ring
C.   double bond, amide, and alcohol
D.   aromatic ring, halide and ketone

8. Which of the following is the IUPAC name for this non-polar alkane?

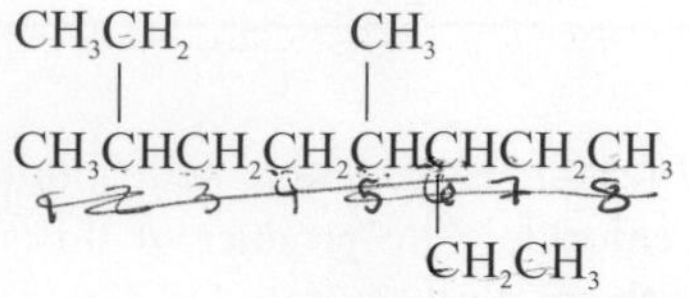

$$CH_3CH_2 \qquad CH_3$$
$$CH_3CHCH_2CH_2CHCHCH_2CH_3$$
$$CH_2CH_3$$

A.   3-Ethyl-4-methylheptane
B.   3-Ethyl-4, 7-dimethylnonane
C.   3-Methyl-7-ethyldecane
D.   3,4-Diethyl-5, 7-dimethylnonane

STOP.

MCAT organic chemistry is about tracking electrons through reactions of carbon compounds. If we can keep track of the electrons we can understand the reactions and we can master MCAT organic chemistry.

Electrons are negatively charged. They are attracted to positively charged nuclei. It is the **electrostatic force** between the electrons and the nuclei that creates all molecular bonds. Both nuclei tug on both electrons, and the result is a bond between the two nuclei.

Electrons are transitory passengers on their respective nuclei. They are in constant search of ways to unload some of their energy and will do so whenever possible. They are at their lowest energy state when they are nearest to a positive charge and farthest from a negative charge. Because negative charge in proximity to electrons raises their energy level, electrons will share an orbital with, at most, only one other electron. The only thing which prevents an electron from releasing all its energy and crashing into the positively charged nucleus is the quantization of energy. The electron must give up a minimum quantum of energy. This minimum amount is greater than the amount that would be released if the electron collided with the nucleus.

A bond is formed when a pair of electrons can lower their energy level by positioning themselves between two nuclei in such a way as to take advantage of the positive charge of both nuclei.

Two electrons are required to form a bond. Each of the bonded nuclei can donate a single electron to the bond, or, in a **coordinate covalent bond**, one nucleus can donate both electrons.

1-8
Bonding

You should know that it takes two electrons to form a bond. When the force between two objects is attractive and decreases with distance, the lowest potential energy level for those objects is when they are the closest to each other. Electrons are at their lowest energy level when they form a bond because they have minimized their distance from both nuclei.

A **σ-bond** (sigma-bond) forms when the bonding pair of electrons are *localized* directly between the two bonding atoms. Since the electrons in a σ-bond are as close as possible to the two sources of positive charge (the two nuclei), a σ-bond has the lowest energy and is the most stable form of covalent bond. Thus σ-bonds are strong. A σ-bond is always the first type of covalent bond to be formed between any two atoms; a single bond must be a σ-bond.

If additional bonds form between two σ-bonded atoms, the new bonds are called **π-bonds** (π-bonds). Because the σ-bond leaves no room for other electron orbitals directly between the atoms, the orbital of the first π-bond forms above and below the σ-bonding electrons. A double bond now exists between the two atoms. If still another π-bond is formed, the new orbital is formed on either side of the σ-bond. A triple bond now exists between the two atoms. Double and triple bonds are always made of one σ-bond and one or two π-bonds.

Although a π-bond is weaker than a σ-bond, π-bonds are always added to an existing σ-bond, and thus strengthen the overall bond between the atoms. Since bond strength is inversely related to bond length, the additional π-bonds shorten the overall bond. The bond energy of a double bond is greater than that of a single bond. Bond energy can be thought of as the energy necessary to break a bond.

The electrons in a π-bond are further from the nuclei than the electrons of a σ-bond, and therefore at a higher energy level, less stable, and form a weaker bond. This is important because less stability means π-bonds are more reactive. Third row elements form weaker π-bonds than second row elements. Double and triple bonds are rare for all atoms except carbon, nitrogen, oxygen, and sulfur.

1-9
σ and π Bonds

Any single bond is a sigma bond, and any double or triple bond contains one sigma bond.

Double and triple bonds are made by adding π-bonds to a sigma bond. Each additional bond shortens the distance between the bonding atoms.

Pi bonds are more reactive than sigma bonds. Carbon, nitrogen, oxygen and sulfur are the only atoms that commonly form π-bonds. Phosphorous forms π-bonds with oxygen in nucleotide phosphates such as ATP.

Pi bonds prevent rotation.

Another important point about π-bonds is their effect on spatial arrangement. The atoms bonded by a single σ-bond are free to rotate about the bonding axis but a π-bond locks its atoms into one spatial orientation preventing rotation.

1-10 Hybridization

If we examine the electrons of a lone carbon atom in its ground state we would see that its four valence electrons are in their expected **atomic orbitals**, two in the orbital of the *s* subshell and two in orbitals of the *p* subshell. The *p* electrons are at a higher energy state than the *s* electrons.

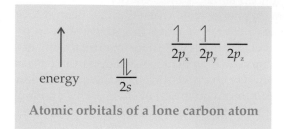

Atomic orbitals of a lone carbon atom

However, if we examine a carbon with four σ-bonds, we find that the four bonds are indistinguishable. Since the bonds are indistinguishable, the orbitals which form them must be equivalent. In order to form four σ-bonds, the electrons form four new orbitals. The new orbitals are hybrids of the old *s* and *p* orbitals and are equivalent to each other in shape and energy.

Atomic orbitals of a carbon atom with four σ-bonds

When one of these **hybrid orbitals** overlaps an orbital of another atom, a σ-bond is formed in the area where the orbitals coincide. π-bonds are formed by the overlap of pure *p* orbitals.

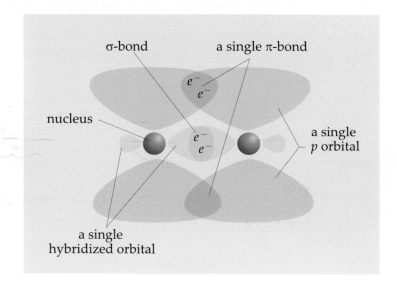

There are several types of hybrid orbitals: *__sp; sp²;__* *__sp³__*; *dsp³*; *d²sp³*; etc. In order to figure out the type of hybrid orbital formed by an atom on the MCAT, simply count the number of sigma bonds and lone pairs of electrons on that atom. Match this number to the sum of the superscripts in a hybrid name (letters without superscripts are assumed to have the superscript '1'). Remember, there are one orbital in the *s* subshell that must be formed first, three orbitals in the *p* subshell that must be formed next, and five orbitals in the *d* subshell to be formed only after the *s* and *p* orbitals are formed. For example, water makes two sigma bonds and has two lone pairs of electrons. Thus the sum of the superscripts in the name of the hybrid must add up to four. The oxygen in water must be sp³ hybridized.

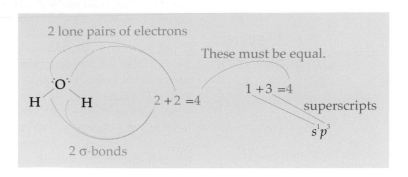

A hybrid orbital resembles in shape and energy the *s* and *p* orbitals from which it is formed to the same extent that *s* or *p* orbitals are used to form it. This extent is referred to as **character**. The superscripts indicate the character as follows: an *sp²* orbital is formed from one *s* and two *p* orbitals and thus has 33.3% *s* character and 66.7% *p* character; an *sp* orbital is formed from one *s* and one *p* orbital and has a 50% *s* character and 50% *p* character; and so on. The more *s* character a bond has, the more stable, the stronger, and the shorter it becomes.

When molecules are formed, s and p atomic orbitals hybridize to form new shapes and energy levels.

The electrons in an orbital seek to minimize their energy by moving as far away from other electron pairs as possible, thus lessening repulsive forces. This leads to specific bond angles and molecular shape for different numbers and combinations of σ-bonds and lone pair electrons.

HYBRIDIZATION	BOND ANGLES	SHAPE
sp	180°	Linear
sp²	120°	Trigonal planar
sp³	109.5°	Tetrahedral, Pyramidal, or Bent
dsp³	90°, 120	Trigonal-bypyramidal, Seesaw, T-shaped, Linear
d²sp³	90°	Octahedral, Square pyramidal, Square planar

Where more than one possible shape exists, the shape depends upon the number and position of lone pairs. Lone pairs, π electrons, and ring strain can distort the predicted bond angles. Lone pairs and π electrons require more room than bonding pairs. For example, the lone pairs on water make the bond angle 104.5°.

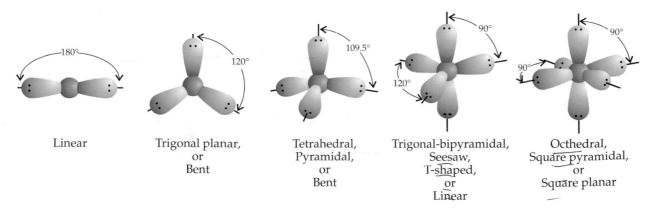

1-11
Electron
Delocalization

Sometimes bonding electrons are spread out over three or more atoms. These electrons are called *delocalized electrons*. For MCAT purposes delocalized electrons only result from π-bonds. Molecules containing delocalized electrons can be represented by a combination of two or more Lewis structures called **resonance structures**. The weighted average of these Lewis structures most accurately represents the real molecule. The real molecule must be at a lower energy than any single Lewis structure representing it since otherwise it would simply retain that structure. The difference between the energy of the real molecule and the energy of the most stable Lewis structure is called the *resonance energy*. Remember, the real molecule does not resonate between these structures but is a stable weighted average of all contributing structures.

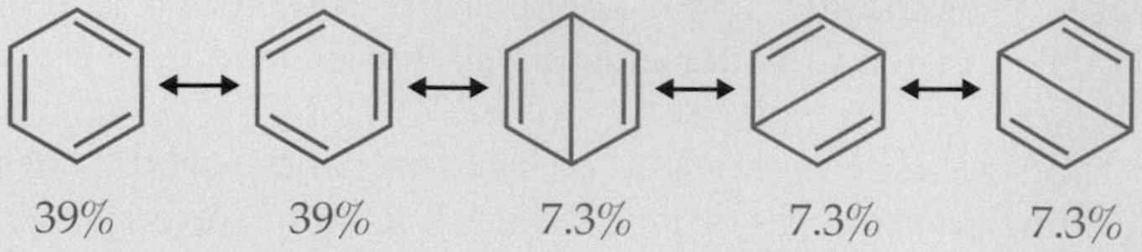

| 39% | 39% | 7.3% | 7.3% | 7.3% |

**Benzene resonance structures
and their weighted averages**

The following are **four rules for writing resonance structures**:

For all resonance structures:

- **Atoms must not be moved.** Move electrons not atoms.

- **Number of unpaired electrons must remain constant.**

- **Resonance atoms must lie in the same plane.**

- **Only proper Lewis structures allowed.**

The contribution made to the actual molecule by any given structure is roughly proportional to that structure's stability; the most stable structures make the greatest contribution and equivalent structures make equal contributions. In general, the more covalent the bonds, the more stable the structure. Separation of charges within a molecule decreases stability.

For MCAT purposes, two conditions must exist for resonance to occur: 1) a species must contain an atom either with a *p* orbital or an unshared pair of electrons; 2) that atom must be single bonded to an atom that possesses a double or triple bond. Such species are called *conjugated unsaturated systems.* The adjacent *p* orbital in a conjugated system may contain zero, one, or two electrons (as in another π-bond). The *p* orbital allows the adjacent π-bond to extend and encompass more than two nuclei.

The above two conditions are required but not always sufficient for resonance. Ring structures must also satisfy *Huckel's rule*, which states: planar monocyclic rings with $4n + 2$ π-electrons (where *n* is any integer, including zero) should be **aromatic** (display resonance).

A **dipole moment** occurs when the center of positive charge on a molecule or bond does not coincide with the center of negative charge. A dipole moment can occur in a bond or a molecule. The concept of center of charge is analogous to the concept of the center of mass. All the positive charge in a molecule comes from the protons of the nuclei. All the negative charge comes from the electrons. In chemistry the dipole moment is represented by an arrow pointing from the center of positive charge to the center of negative charge. The arrow is crossed at the center of positive charge. The dipole moment is measured in units of the *debye*, D, and given by the equation:

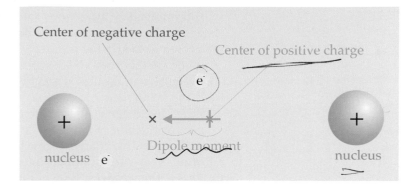

Center of negative charge

Center of positive charge

Dipole moment

nucleus   e⁻   nucleus

$$\mu = qd$$

where q is the magnitude of charge of either end of the dipole, and d is the distance between the centers of charge.

A molecule or bond which has a dipole moment is referred to as polar; a molecule or bond without a dipole moment is referred to as nonpolar.

A polar bond results from the difference in electronegativity of its atoms. Atoms with greater electronegativities attract the electrons in a bond more strongly, pulling the center of negative charge toward themselves, and thus creating a dipole moment.

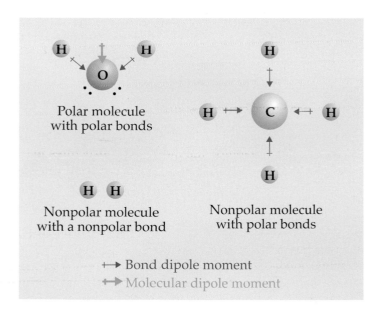

Polar molecule
with polar bonds

Nonpolar molecule
with a nonpolar bond

Nonpolar molecule
with polar bonds

⊢→ Bond dipole moment
⊢→ Molecular dipole moment

A molecule with polar bonds may or may not have a dipole moment. Since a dipole moment is a vector, it is possible for the sum of the dipole moments in the polar bonds of a molecule to equal zero, leaving the molecule without a dipole moment.

A dipole moment can be momentarily induced in an otherwise nonpolar molecule or bond by a polar molecule, ion, or electric field. The polar molecule or ion creates an electric field, which pushes the electrons and nuclei in opposite directions, separating the centers of positive and negative charge. Such dipole moments are called **induced dipoles**. Induced dipoles are common in nature and are generally weaker than permanent dipoles.

An **instantaneous dipole moment** can exist in an otherwise nonpolar molecule. Instantaneous dipoles arise because the electrons in a bond move about the orbital, and at any given moment may not be distributed exactly between the two bonding atoms even when the atoms are identical. Although instantaneous dipoles are generally very short lived and weaker than induced dipoles, they can act to induce a dipole in a neighboring atom.

Intermolecular attractions (attractions between separate molecules) occur solely due to dipole moments. The partial negatively charged side of one molecule is attracted to the partial positively charged side of another molecule. Dipole forces are much weaker than covalent forces, generally about 1% as strong. The attraction between two molecules is roughly proportional to their dipole moments.

When hydrogen is attached to a highly electronegative atom, such as nitrogen, oxygen, or fluorine, a large dipole moment is formed leaving hydrogen with a strong partial positive charge. When the hydrogen approaches a nitrogen, oxygen, or fluorine on another atom, the intermolecular bond formed is called a **hydrogen bond**. This is the strongest type of dipole-dipole interaction. It is hydrogen bonding that is responsible for the high boiling point of water.

The weakest dipole-dipole force is between two instantaneous dipoles. These dipole-dipole bonds are called **London Dispersion Forces**. Although London Dispersion Forces are very weak, they are responsible for the phase changes of nonpolar molecules.

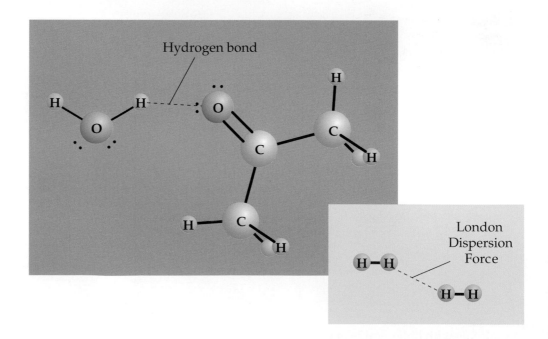

For this section, you should understand what hybridization is, and be able to identify *sp*, *sp*², and *sp*³ orbitals. Also, you must be able to recognize resonance structures. Learn the rules for resonance. Most of the bonding stuff is review from inorganic, but it is important. Understand that intermolecular and intramolecular forces are electrostatic. Make the connection between energy level of electrons and position relative to positive charge. In other words, as electrons move closer to positive charge they lower their energy level. Remember this by realizing that it would require energy input to separate opposite charges. Nature likes to spread the energy around. A system with low energy is a stable system. Thus, a bond is formed when electron energy level is the lowest.

Just a reminder: bond energy is closely related to bond dissociation energy and in many cases, it is the same thing. Bond energy is the average energy required to break a bond. Thus, high bond energy indicates a bond with electrons at very low energy, and is a stable bond. Recall from inorganic chemistry that this is because the high energy bond is really a high negative energy bond.

high bond energy — e⁻ at low energy

9. Pyrrole, shown below, exhibits resonance stabilization.

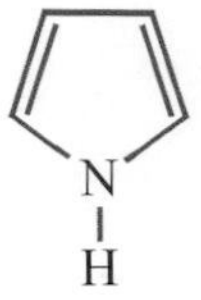

pyrrole

Which of the following is a valid resonance structure of pyrrole?

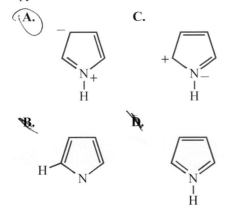

A.

B.

C.

D.

10. In the Wittig reaction a phosphorous ylide reacts with a ketone to yield an alkene.

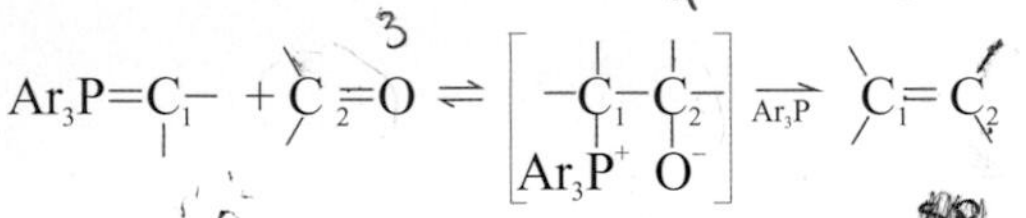

$$Ar_3P=C_1- \ +\overset{3}{\underset{}{C_2}}=O \rightleftharpoons \left[-\overset{|}{C_1}-\overset{|}{C_2}- \atop Ar_3P^+ \ O^- \right] \xrightarrow{Ar_3P} \ \overset{}{C_1}=\overset{}{C_2}$$

betaine intermediate

What is the hybridization of carbon 2 in the ketone, the betaine, and the alkene, respectively?

A. sp^3; sp^2; sp^3
B. sp^2; sp^2; sp^3
C. sp^2; sp^3; sp^2
D. sp^3; sp^4; sp^3

11. Benzene exhibits resonance. The carbon-carbon bonds of benzene are:

A. shorter and stronger than the double bond of an alkene.
B. longer and weaker than the double bond of an alkene.
C. longer and stronger than the carbon-carbon bond of an alkane.
D. longer and weaker than the carbon-carbon bond of an alkane.

12. The electron pair in the π-bond of an alkene have:

A. 33% p character and are at a lower energy level than the electron pair in the σ-bond.
B. 50% p character and are at a higher energy level than the electron pair in the σ-bond.
C. 100% p character and are at a lower energy level than the electron pair in the σ-bond.
D. 100% p character and are at a higher energy level than the electron pair in the σ-bond.

13. The structures below are 1,3,5-cyclohexatriene. Although double bonds are shorter than single bonds, the structures below could not qualify as proper resonance contributors for benzene because:

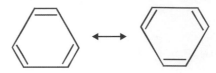

A. 1,3,5-cyclohexatriene is a higher energy molecule than benzene.
B. benzene is more stable than 1,3,5-cyclohexatriene.
C. benzene actually resonates between these two structures.
D. the positions of the atoms are different in the two structures.

14. When dealing with organic compound hybridization, which angle is associated with the strongest bond formation?

A. 109°
B. 120°
C. 180°
D. 360°

15. All of the following compounds have a dipole moment EXCEPT:

A. CH_3Cl
B. H_2O
C. Benzene
D. $H_2C=N=N$

16. Natural gas consists of chiefly methane, but also contains ethane, propane, butane and isobutene. Which of the following compounds is NOT found in natural gas?

A. sec-butane
B. 2-methylbutane
C. olefin (CH_2CH_2)
D. cyclopropane

18

STOP.

There is relatively little to know about stereochemistry on the MCAT. The concepts are not difficult to understand and can be easily memorized. The difficult aspect of stereochemistry on the MCAT is mentally manipulating three-dimensional molecular structures. The only way to become better at manipulating molecular structures is to practice. It is best to acquire a molecular model set and actually build some of the replica molecules with your own hands.

**1-13
Stereochemistry**

Isomers are unique molecules with the same molecular formula. "Iso" is a Greek prefix meaning "the same" or "equal". A lone molecule cannot be an isomer by itself. It must be an isomer to another molecule. Two molecules are isomers if they have the same molecular formula but are different compounds.

**1-14
Isomerism**

Conformational isomers or **conformers** are not true isomers. Conformers are different spatial orientations of the same molecule. At room temperature, atoms rotate rapidly about their σ-bonds resulting in a mix of conformers at any given moment. Because of the difference in energy levels between eclipsed and staggered conformers, staggered conformers can sometimes be isolated at low temperatures. The simplest way to distinguish between conformers is with **Newman projections**. The diagram below shows the Newman projections of the conformers of butane and their relative energy levels.

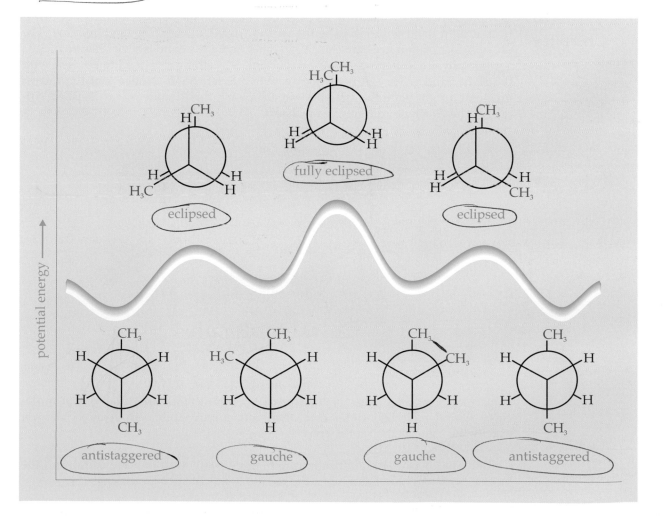

The simplest form of isomer is a **structural isomer**. Structural isomers have the same molecular formula but different bond-to-bond connectivity.

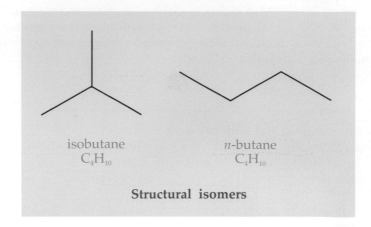

isobutane
C_4H_{10}

n-butane
C_4H_{10}

Structural isomers

If two unique molecules have the same molecular formula and the same bond-to-bond connectivity, they are stereoisomers. In order to distinguish stereoisomers we must first understand chirality.

1-15 Chirality

Try to describe a left hand by its physical characteristics alone, and distinguish it from a right hand without using the words "right" or "left". It can't be done. The only physical difference between a right hand and a left hand is their "handedness". Yet, the physical difference is very important. Something designed to be used with the right hand is very difficult to use with the left hand. Notice that the mirror image of a right hand is a left hand. In chemistry, this "handedness" is called **chirality**. The Greek word *chiros* means hand.

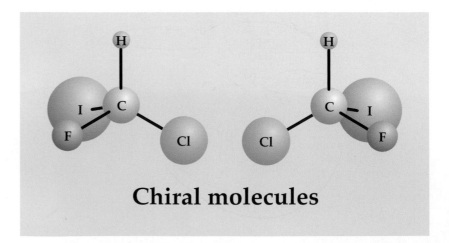

Chiral molecules

Some molecules also have "handedness". Such molecules are called **chiral molecules**. Chiral molecules differ from their reflections, while achiral molecules are exactly the same as their reflections.

Chirality has important ramifications in biology. Many nutrients are chiral, and the human body might not assimilate the mirror image of such a nutrient.

Chirality on the MCAT will mainly be concerned with carbon. Any carbon is chiral when it is bonded to **four different substituents**.

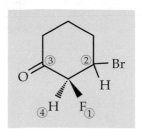

There is only one way to physically describe the orientation of atoms about a chiral center such as a chiral carbon. That is by **absolute configuration**. Since there are two possible configurations, the molecule and its mirror image, absolute configuration is given as **R** (*rectus*: the Latin word for *right*) or **S** (*sinister*: the Latin word for *left*). In order to determine the configuration of a given molecule, the atoms attached to the chiral center are numbered from highest to lowest *priority*. The largest atomic weights are given the highest priority. If two of the atoms are the same element, then their substituents are sequentially compared in order of decreasing priority until one of the substituents is found to have a greater priority than the corresponding substituent on the other atom. Substituents on double and triple bonds are counted two and three times respectively. In the molecule shown above, the carbon marked 2 has a higher priority than the carbon marked 3 because bromine has a higher priority than oxygen. The carbon marked 3 is considered to have two oxygens for priority purposes. Once priorities have been assigned, the chiral molecule is rotated about one of the σ-bonds as shown below so that the lowest priority group faces away. In this orientation a circle is drawn in the direction from highest to lowest priority for the remaining three substituents. The circle will point clockwise or counterclockwise. A clockwise circle indicates an absolute configuration of R and a counterclockwise circle indicates an absolute configuration of S. The mirror image of a chiral molecule always has the opposite absolute configuration.

1-16
Absolute
Configuration

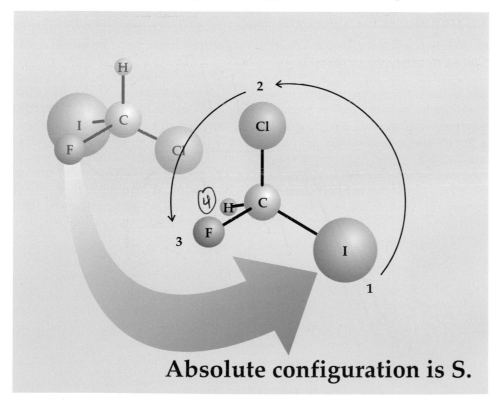

Absolute configuration is S.

The absolute configuration of a molecule does <u>not</u> give information concerning the direction in which a compound rotates plane-polarized light.

1-17
Relative
Configuration

<u>Relative configuration</u> is not related to absolute configuration. Two molecules have the same relative configuration about a carbon if they differ by only one substituent and the other substituents are oriented identically about the carbon. In an S_N2 reaction, it is the relative configuration that is inverted.

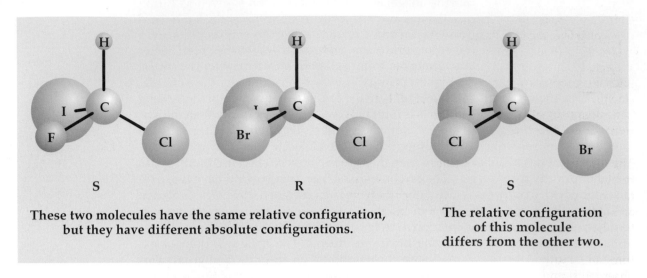

S   R   S

These two molecules have the same relative configuration, but they have different absolute configurations.

The relative configuration of this molecule differs from the other two.

1-18
Observed Rotation

The direction and the degree to which a compound rotates plane-polarized light is given by its **observed rotation**.

Light is made up of electromagnetic waves. A single photon can be described by a changing electric field and its corresponding changing magnetic field, both fields being perpendicular to each other and to the direction of propagation. For simplicity, the magnetic field is often ignored and only the direction of the electric field is considered. A typical light source releases millions of photons whose fields are oriented in random directions. A **polarimeter** screens out photons with all but one orientation of electric field. The resulting light consists of photons with their electric fields oriented in the same direction. This light is called **plane-polarized light**.

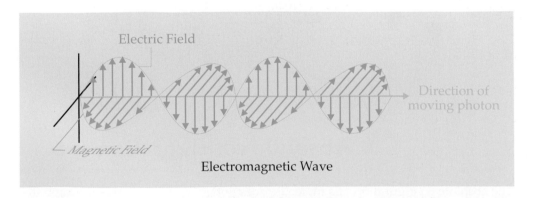

Electric Field

Direction of moving photon

Magnetic Field

Electromagnetic Wave

When a photon reflects off any molecule, the orientation of the electric field produced by that photon is rotated. The mirror image of that molecule will rotate the electric field to the same degree but in the opposite direction. In a typical compound where a photon is just as likely to collide with either mirror image, there are so many millions of molecules producing so many collisions that the photon is most likely to leave the compound with the same electric field orientation with which it entered the compound. No single molecular orientation is favored and so the net result is no rotation of the plane of the electric field. Such compounds are **optically inactive**. Optically inactive compounds may be compounds with no chiral centers, or they may be chiral compounds containing equal amounts of both stereoisomers. The latter is called a **racemic mixture**.

Chiral molecules can be separated from their mirror images by chemical, and in rare cases physical, means. The result of such a separation is a compound containing molecules with no mirror image existing in the compound. When plane-polarized light is projected through such a compound, the orientation of its electric field is rotated. Such a compound is **optically active**. If the compound rotates plane-polarized light clockwise it is designated with a **'+' or 'd'** for *dextrotary*. If it rotates plane-polarized light counterclockwise it is designated with a **'–' or 'l'** for *levorotary* (Latin: *dexter*; right: *laevus*; left).

The direction and number of degrees that the electric field in plane-polarized light rotates when it passes through a compound is called the compound's **observed rotation**. **Specific rotation** is simply a standardized form of observed rotation that is arrived at through calculations using observed rotation and experimental parameters. For instance, the degree of rotation to which polarized light is rotated depends upon the length of the polarimeter, the concentration of the solution, the temperature, and the type of wavelength of light used. Specific rotation is equal to the observed rotation after these adjustments have been made.

If you understand observed rotation, you won't have any trouble with specific rotation should it come up in a passage on the MCAT.

1-19
Stereoisomers

Two molecules with the same molecular formula and the same bond-to-bond connectivity that are not the same compound are called **stereoisomers**. Unless they are geometric isomers, stereoisomers must each contain at least one chiral center in the same location. There are two types of stereoisomers: enantiomers and diastereomers.

1-20
Enantiomers

Enantiomers have the same molecular formula, have the same bond-to-bond connectivity, are mirror images of each other, but are not the same molecule. Enantiomers must have opposite absolute configurations at each chiral carbon.

When placed separately into a polarimeter, enantiomers rotate plane-polarized light in opposite directions to an equal degree. For example, the specific rotation of (R)-2-Butanol is –13.52° while its enantiomer, (S)-2-Butanol, has a specific rotation of +13.52°.

Except for reactions with plane-polarized light and with other chiral compounds, enantiomers have the same physical and chemical properties.

When enantiomers are mixed together in equal concentrations, the resulting mixture is called a **racemic mixture**. Since the mirror image of all orientations of each molecule exist in a racemic mixture with equal probability, racemic mixtures do not rotate plane-polarized light. Unequal concentrations of enantiomers rotate plane-polarized light. In unequal concentrations, the light is rotated in the same direction as a pure sample of the excess enantiomer would rotate it but only to a fraction of the degree, the same fraction that exists as excess enantiomer. The ratio of actual

Enantiomers must have opposite absolute configurations at each and every chiral carbon.

What's this?
An-ant-in-a-mirror!

Enantiomers are mirror images of each other.

rotation to the rotation of pure sample is called *optical purity*; the ratio of pure enantiomer to racemic mixture is called *enantiomeric purity*. Optical purity equals enantiomeric purity for any mixture of enantiomers. The separation of enantiomers is called **resolution**.

For enantiomers, you must know that they have the same chemical and physical characteristics except for two cases: 1. reactions with other chiral compounds; 2. reactions with polarized light.

1-21
Diastereomers

Diastereomers have the same molecular formula, have the same bond-to-bond connectivity, are <u>not</u> mirror images to each other, and are not the same compound.

One special type of diastereomer is called a **geometric isomer**. Geometric isomers exist due to hindered rotation about a bond. Rotation may be hindered due to a ring structure or a double or triple bond. Since rotation is hindered, similar substituents on opposing carbons may exist on the same-side or opposite sides of the hindered bond. Molecules with same side substituents are called **cis-isomers**; those with opposite-side substituents are called **trans-isomers** (Latin: *cis*: on the same side; *trans*: on the other side).

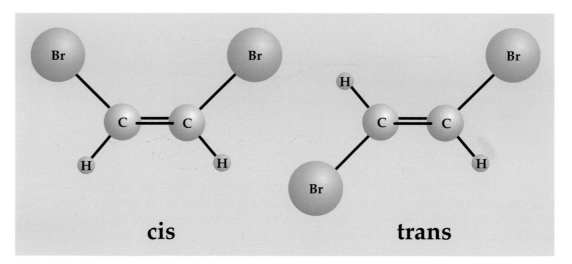

cis   **trans**

Geometric isomers have **different physical properties**. For the MCAT, it is important to know that cis molecules have a dipole moment while trans molecules do not. As a rule of thumb, the following predictions can be made concerning the melting and boiling points of geometric isomers: due to their dipole moment, cis molecules have stronger intermolecular forces leading to higher boiling points; due to their lower symmetry, however, cis molecules do not form crystals as readily, and thus have lower melting points.

The substituent groups in the cis position may crowd each other; a condition known as **steric hindrance**. Steric hindrance in cis molecules produces higher energy levels resulting in higher heats of combustion.

For tri and tetrasubstituted alkenes or ring structures, the terms cis and trans may be ambiguous or simply meaningless. The following system may be used to describe all geometric isomers unambiguously. First, the two substituents on each carbon are prioritized using atomic weight, similar to the system in absolute configuration. If the higher priority substituent for each carbon exists on the opposite sides, the molecule is labeled **E** for *entgegen;* if on the same side, then **Z** for *zusammen* (German: entgegen: opposite; zusammen: together).

Diastereomers have different physical properties (i.e. rotation of plane-polarized light, melting points, boiling points, solubilities, etc...). Their chemical properties also differ.

The maximum number of optically active isomers that a single compound can have is related to the number of its chiral centers by the following formula:

maximum number of optically active isomers = 2^n

where *n* is the number of chiral centers.

Two chiral centers in a single molecule may offset each other creating an optically inactive molecule. Such compounds are called **meso compounds**. Meso compounds have a plane of symmetry through their centers which divides them into two halves that are mirror images to each other. Meso compounds are achiral and therefore optically inactive.

Diastereomers that differ at only one chiral carbon are called **epimers**. If a ring closure occurs at the epimeric carbon, two possible diastereomers may be formed. These new diastereomers are called **anomers**. The chiral carbon of an anomer is called the **anomeric carbon**. Anomers are distinguished by the orientation of their substituents. Glucose forms anomers. When the hydroxyl group on the anomeric carbon on glucose is oriented in the opposite direction to the methyl group, the anomer is labeled α; when in the same direction, the anomer is β.

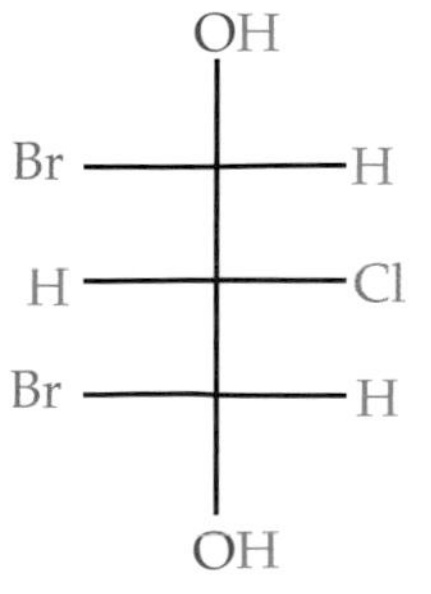

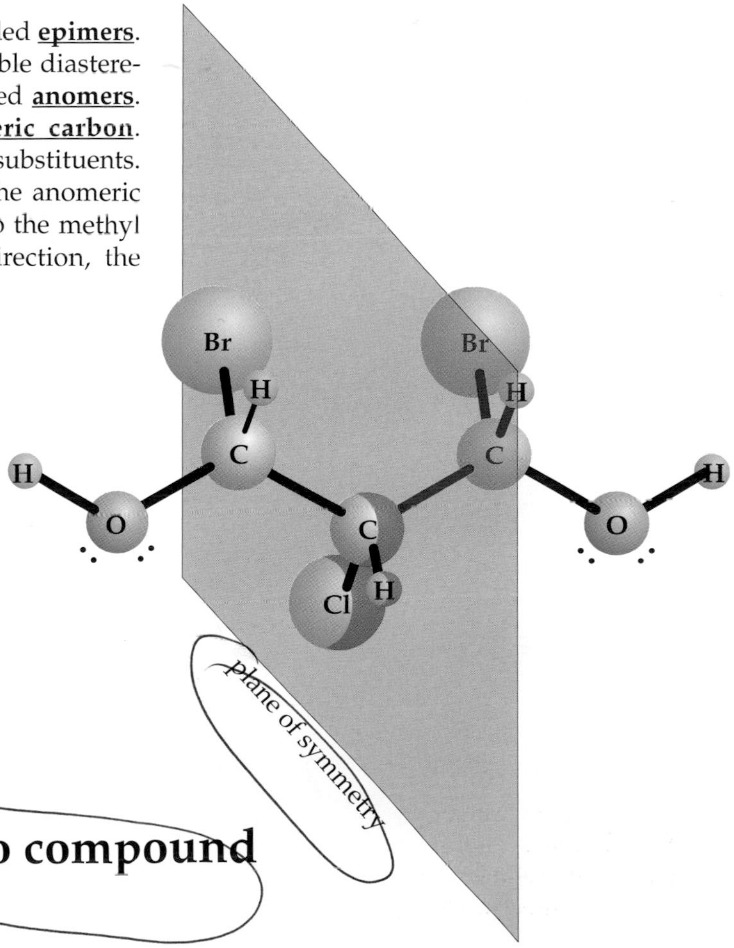

Meso compound

Questions 17 through 24 are **NOT** based on a descriptive passage.

17. Which of the following compounds can exist as either a cis or trans isomer?

A. $CH_3CH_2CCl=CClH$

B. 2-methyl-2-butene

C.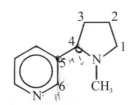

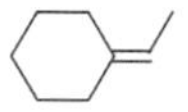

D.

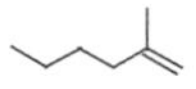

18. (−)-nicotine shown below is an alkaloid found in tobacco.

nicotine

At which of the following carbons does the structure of (+)-nicotine differ from (−)-nicotine?

A. carbons 1,4, and 6 only
B. carbons 4 and 5 only
C. carbon 4 only
D. carbon 5 only

19. All of the following compounds are optically active EXCEPT:

A. 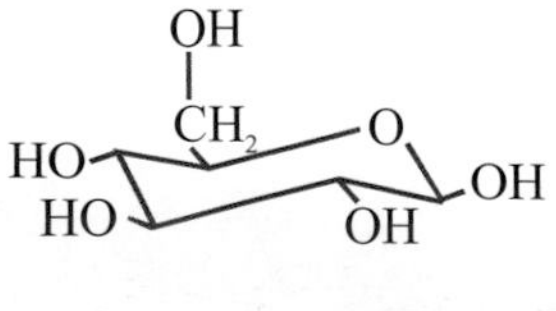
OH
CH₂
HO
HO
O
OH
OH

C. $CH_3CHClCH_2OH$

B. 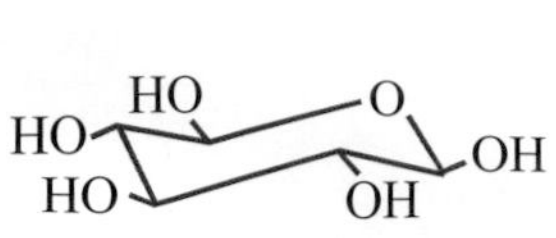
HO
HO
HO
O
OH
OH

D. 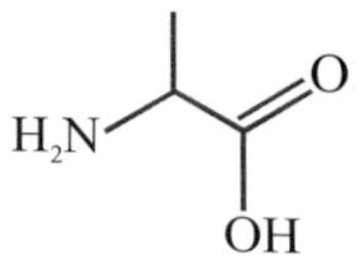
H_2N
O
OH

20. Which one of the following properly named compounds could exist in enantiomeric form?

A. 3-chloro-1-propene
B. 3-chloro-1,4-dichlorocyclohexane
C. *trans*-1,4-dichlorocyclohexane
D. 4-chloro-1-cyclohexene

21. Which of the following compounds is not optically active?

A.
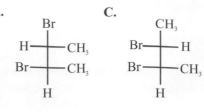

C.
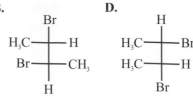

B.
Br
H₃C—H
Br—CH₃
H

D.
H
H₃C—Br
H₃C—H
Br

22. Which of the following characteristics correctly describe differences between structural (constitutional) isomers?

I. these compounds may have different carbon skeletons
II. chemical properties are altered due to differences in functional groups
III. functional groups may occupy different positions on the carbon skeleton

A. I only
B. II and III only
C. I and III only
D. I, II and III

23. When described using rectus or sinister, the spatial arrangement of substituents around a chiral atom is called:

A. achirality
B. absolute configuration
C. observed rotation
D. enantiomeric purity

24. Which of the following stereoisomers is a mirror image of itself?

A. anomer
B. epimer
C. meso compound
D. geometric isomer

26

STOP.

Hydrocarbons, Alcohols, and Substitutions

Methane and compounds whose major functional group contains only carbon-carbon single bonds are **alkanes**. Carbons in alkanes are referred to as **methyl, primary, secondary, and tertiary**, depending upon how many other alkyl groups are attached to them. Methyl carbons have no attached alkyl groups, primary carbons have one, secondary have two, and tertiary have three.

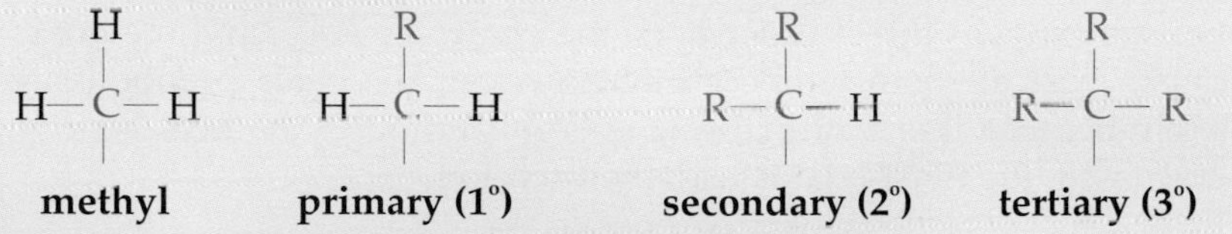

2-1
Alkanes

H	R	R	R
H—C—H	H—C—H	R—C—H	R—C—R
methyl	primary (1°)	secondary (2°)	tertiary (3°)

Carbon types
(R = alkyl group)

The **physical properties** of alkanes follow certain general trends. Boiling point is governed by intermolecular forces. As carbons are added in a single chain and molecular weight increases, the intermolecular forces increase and, thus, the boiling point of the alkane increases. Branching, however, significantly lowers the boiling point. Melting points of unbranched alkanes also tend to increase with increasing molecular weight, though not as smoothly. This is because intermolecular forces within a crystal depend upon shape as well as size.

Alkanes have the lowest density of all groups of organic compounds. Density increases with molecular weight.

Alkanes are almost totally insoluble in water. They are soluble in benzene, carbon tetrachloride, chloroform, and other hydrocarbons. If an alkane contains a polar functional group, the polarity of the entire molecule, and thus its solubility, decreases as the carbon chain is lengthened.

2-2
Physical Properties

To remember that alkanes have low density, think of an oil spill where alkanes float on water.

There is a lot to memorize with physical properties of alkanes. The most important things to remember are that molecular weight increases boiling point and melting point, and branching decreases boiling point but increases melting point. The first four alkanes are gases at room temperature.

↑M.W. => ↑B.P. => ↑M.P.

↑Branching => ↓B.P. => ↑M.P.

2-3 Cycloalkanes

Cycloalkanes are alkane rings. For the MCAT, remember that some ring structures put strain on the carbon-carbon bonds because they bend them away from the normal 109.5° angle of the sp^3 carbon and cause crowding. **Ring strain** is zero for cyclohexane and increases as rings become larger or smaller. The trend continues up to a nine-carbon ring structure, after which ring strain decreases to zero as more carbons are added to the ring. Less ring strain means lower energy and more stability.

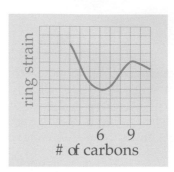

Cyclohexane exists as three conformers: the **chair**; the *twist*; and the **boat**. All three conformers exist at room temperature; however, the chair predominates almost completely because it is at the lowest energy. Although the boat configuration is often discussed, the twist-boat is usually intended.

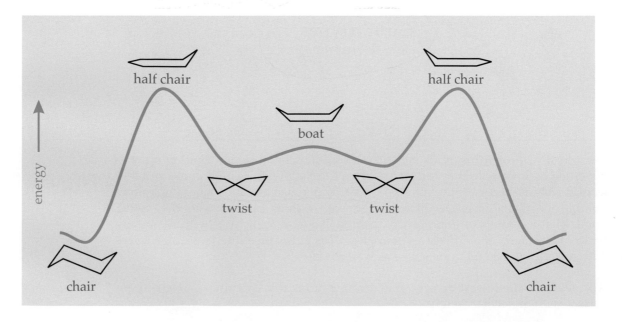

Each carbon on cyclohexane has two hydrogens. In the chair conformation, the two hydrogens are oriented in different directions. The hydrogens projecting outward from the center of the ring are called **equatorial hydrogens**; the hydrogens projecting upward or downward are called **axial hydrogens**. When the ring reverses its conformation, all the hydrogens reverse their conformation. Neither axial nor equatorial hydrogens are energetically favored. However, when the ring has substituent groups attached, crowding occurs most often between groups in the axial position. Crowding causes instability and raises the energy level of the ring. Thus most substituent groups are favored in the equatorial position.

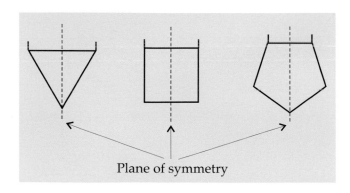

Hydrogens reverse orientation upon conformational change of cyclohexane.

Since the carbons in a ring cannot rotate about the σ-bonds, cis and trans isomerism is possible in a ring structure without a double bond. Ring structure cis and trans isomers have different physical properties, but the trends are not as predictable as alkene cis and trans isomers. However, like other cis molecules, ring structures with cis groups on adjacent carbons may experience steric hindrance resulting in a higher energy level for the entire molecule. Notice that for five-carbon rings and less, the cis isomers are meso compounds. The chair conformation of cis-1,2-dichlorocyclohexane (also for 1,3 and 1,4 isomers and higher carbon rings) exists in equilibrium with its own mirror image and thus is optically inactive as well.

The main things to know about ring structures are in terms of energy. For instance, for small rings, ring strain is lowest in cyclohexane, so it is the most stable ring structure. Also, large substituents in the axial position require more energy and create less stability.

Plane of symmetry

2-4
Combustion

Alkanes were originally called paraffins (Latin: *parum affinis*: low inclination) because they are not inclined to react with other molecules. They do not react with strong acids or bases or with most other reagents. However, with a sufficiently large energy of activation, they are capable of violent reactions with oxygen. This reaction is called **combustion**. Combustion takes place when alkanes are mixed with oxygen and energy is added. Combustion of alkanes only takes place at high temperatures, such as inside the flame of a match. Once begun, however, combustion generates its own heat and can be self-perpetuating.

For the MCAT you should know that combustion takes place when oxygen is added to an alkane at high temperatures. You should know that the products are CO_2, H_2O, and, especially, heat.

$$CH_4 + 2O_2 \xrightarrow{\text{flame}} CO_2 + 2H_2O + \text{Heat}$$

Combustion is a **radical reaction**. (Radical reactions are discussed in the halogenation section later.)

Heat of Combustion is the change in enthalpy of a combustion reaction. Combustion of isomeric hydrocarbons requires equal amounts of O_2 and produces equal amounts of CO_2 and H_2O. Therefore heats of combustion can be used to compare relative stabilities of isomers. The higher the heat of combustion, the higher the energy level of the molecule, the less stable the molecule. For cycloalkanes, comparisons can be made of different size rings on a "per CH_2" basis to reveal relative stabilities. Although the molar heat of combustion for cyclohexane is nearly twice that of cyclopropane, the "per CH_2" group heat of combustion is greater for cyclopropane due to ring strain.

Alkanes will react with halogens (F, Cl, and Br, but not I) in the presence of heat or light to form a free radical. Energy from light or heat homolytically cleaves the diatomic halogen. In homolytic cleavage each atom in the bond retains one electron from the broken bond. The result is two highly reactive species each with an unpaired electron and each called a free radical. This reaction is called halogenation.

Halogenation is a chain reaction with at least three steps. You must know all three steps for the MCAT.

1. **initiation:** The halogen starts as a diatomic molecule. The molecule is cleaved homolytically by heat or by UV light, resulting in a free radical.

2. **propagation:** The halogen radical removes a hydrogen from the alkane resulting in an alkyl radical. The alkyl radical may now react with a diatomic halogen molecule creating an alkyl halide and a new halogen radical. Propagation can continue indefinitely. Or:

3. **termination:** Either two radicals bond or a radical bonds to the wall of the container to end the chain reaction or propagation.

2-5
Halogenation

In halogenation, most of the product is formed during propagation, NOT during termination.

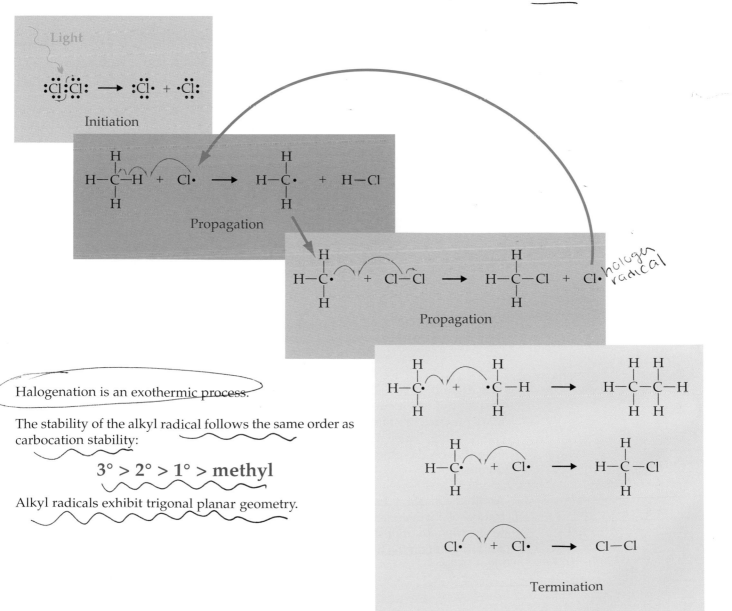

Halogenation is an exothermic process.

The stability of the alkyl radical follows the same order as carbocation stability:

$$3° > 2° > 1° > \text{methyl}$$

Alkyl radicals exhibit trigonal planar geometry.

The reactivity of halogens from most reactive to least is as follows: F, Cl, Br, I. Fluorine is so reactive that it can be explosive, whereas bromine requires heat to react and iodine won't react at all. *Selectivity* of the halogens follows exactly the opposite order. (Selectivity is how selective a halogen radical is when choosing a position on an alkane.) Even though we know the order of selectivity, we must be careful when predicting products. For instance, since chlorine is somewhat selective, we might suppose that the primary product of 2-methylbutane and chlorine reacting at 300°C would be 2-chloro-2-methyl butane, the tertiary alkyl halide. This would be wrong. Although chlorine is five times more likely to react with the single hydrogen on the tertiary carbon to produce the more stable tertiary radical, there are nine hydrogens attached to primary carbons and two hydrogens attached to the secondary carbon which can also react. Thus, on 2-methylbutane, a chlorine free radical will collide with a primary hydrogen nine times as often as it will collide with the tertiary. As a rough rule of thumb, assume the order of reactivity for chlorine with tertiary, secondary, and primary hydrogens will follow a 5:4:1 ratio. In other words, a primary hydrogen will require five times as many collisions to react as a tertiary and so on.

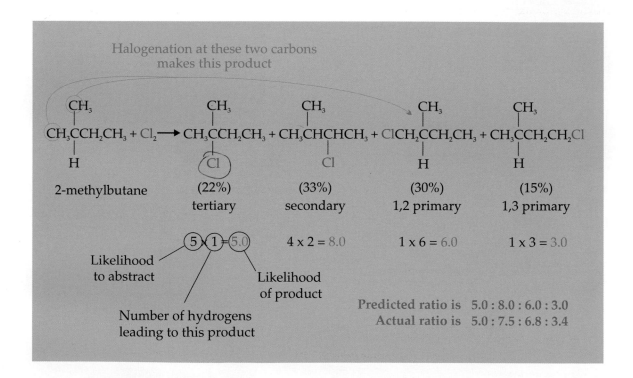

This example demonstrates that the rule of thumb is an estimate at best. Most importantly, it is a reminder that the tertiary product will not necessarily be the primary product. Bromine is more selective than chlorine and substituting bromine for chlorine in the same reaction will result in predominately 2-bromo-2-methylbutane. Fluorine, on the other hand, is so reactive that the primary product would predominate.

Another concern in halogenation is multi-halogenated products. Increased concentration of the halogen will result in the di-, tri-, and tetra-halogenated products, while dilute solutions will yield only monohalogenated products. This is because in a dilute solution the halogen radical is more likely to collide with an alkane than an alkyl halide.

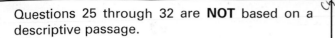

25. Which of the following compounds contains the fewest tertiary carbons?

A. $(CH_3)_3C(CH_2)_2CH_3$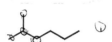
B. 4-isobutylheptane

C.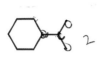

D.

26. Which of the following halogens will give the greatest percent yield of tertiary alkyl halide when reacted with isobutane in the presence of light?

A. I_2
B. Cl_2
C. Br_2 most selective
D. Isobutane will not yield a tertiary product.

27. Which of the following compounds produces the most heat per mole of compound when reacted with oxygen?

A. CH_4
B. C_2H_6
C. cyclohexane
D. cycloheptane

add in the notes

28. In a sample of *cis*-1,2-dichlorocyclohexane at room temperature, the chlorines will:

A. both be equatorial whenever the molecule is in the chair conformation.
B. both be axial whenever the molecule is in the chair conformation.
C. alternate between both equatorial and both axial whenever the molecule is in the chair conformation.
D. both alternate between equatorial and axial but will never exist both axial or both equatorial at the same time.

29. In an alkane halogenation reaction, which of the following steps will never produce a radical?

A. initiation
B. propagation
C. conjugation
D. termination

30. Cycloalkanes are a group of cyclic saturated hydrocarbons with a general formula of C_nH_{2n}. Which of the following compounds will display the LEAST amount of free rotation around a C—C single bond?

A. alkanes, which are relatively inert chemically
B. alkanes, which are able to form numerous types of isomers
C. cycloalkanes, which are limited by geometric constraints
D. cycloalkanes, which are polar and water soluble

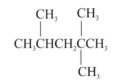

31.

$$CH_3CHCH_2CCH_3$$

with CH_3, CH_3, CH_3 substituents

In the above compound, how many hydrogen atoms can be identified as primary?

A. 3
B. 15
C. 17
D. 18

32. General reaction mechanism:

$$A—B + C—D \rightarrow A \quad C + B—D$$

What reaction type is being demonstrated by the equation above?

A. addition - adding
B. elimination - one reactant into 2 products
C. substitution
D. rearrangement

whole new product

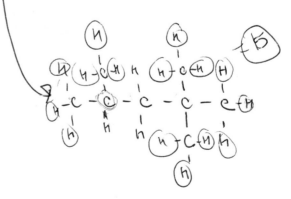

2-6 Alkenes

We are, of course, aware that the topic of alkenes has been removed from the list of topics tested by the MCAT. We suggest that this section will be helpful anyway.

If a carbon chain contains a carbon-carbon double bond, it is an **alkene**. Alkenes have π-bonds. π-bonds are less stable than σ-bonds; thus, alkenes are more reactive than alkanes. When dealing with alkenes, remember that π-bonds are electron-hungry. This explains why alkenes are more acidic than alkanes. When a proton is removed, the π-bond of the alkene absorbs some of the negative charge stabilizing the conjugate base. However, at the same time remember that the π-bond is a large area of negative charge and is thus attractive to electrophiles.

The more highly substituted the alkene, the more thermodynamically stable.

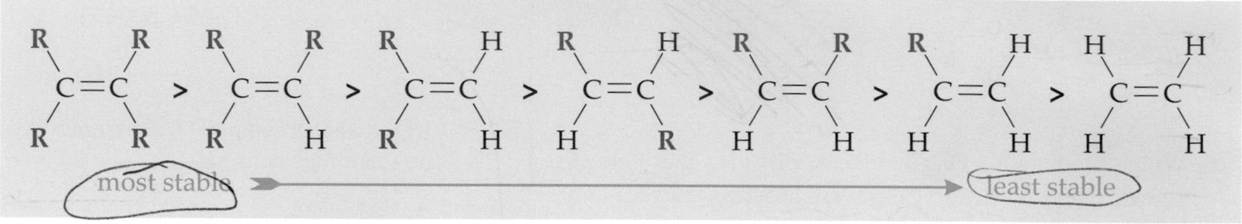

The diagram above refers to thermodynamic stability. When we discuss addition reactions you will see that the most stable alkene when mixed with an electrophile is the most reactive according to this diagram. This paradox is due to the intermediate, usually a carbocation. Since a tertiary carbocation is more stable, the energy of activation is lowered and a reaction with a tertiary intermediate proceeds more quickly. In general, to predict the alkene product, use the above diagram as a reference, but to predict the most reactive alkene to an electrophile, the order is based on cation formation and is nearly reversed.

2-7 Physical Properties

Alkenes follow the same trends as alkanes. An increase in molecular weight leads to an increase in boiling point. Branching decreases boiling point. Alkenes are very slightly soluble in water and have a lower density than water. They are more acidic than alkanes.

Alkynes, carbon chains containing a carbon-carbon triple bond, have similar physical property trends to alkanes and alkenes. They are only slightly more polar than alkenes and only slightly more soluble in water.

2-8 Synthesis of Alkenes

Synthesis of an alkene occurs via an **elimination** reaction. One or two functional groups are eliminated or removed to form a double bond. **Dehydration of an alcohol** is an E1 reaction where an alcohol forms an alkene in the presence of hot concentrated acid. E1 means that the rate depends upon the concentration of only one species. In this case, the rate depends upon the concentration of the alcohol. In the first step, the acid protonates the hydroxyl group producing the good leaving group, water. In the next and slowest step (the rate-determining step), the water drops off, forming a carbocation. As always, when a carbocation is formed, rearrangement may occur. **Carbocation stability** follows the same trend as radical stability. From most stable to least stable the order is: **$3°$, $2°$, $1°$, methyl**. Rearrangement will only occur if a more stable carbocation can be formed. In the final step, a water molecule deprotonates the carbocation and an alkene is formed. Notice that the major product is the most stable, most substituted alkene. The **Saytzeff rule** states that the major product of elimination will be the most substituted alkene.

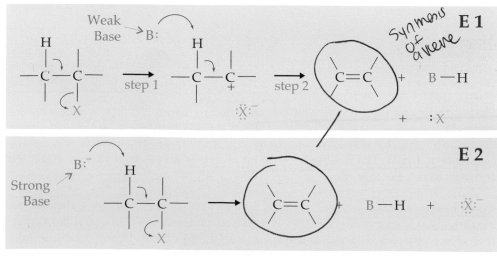

Dehydration of an Alcohol

Dehydrohalogenation may proceed either by an E1 mechanism (absence of a strong base) or by an E2 mechanism (a high concentration of a strong, bulky base). In the E1 reaction, the halogen drops off in the first step and a hydrogen is removed in the second step. In the E2 reaction, the base removes a proton from the carbon next to the halogen-containing carbon and the halogen drops off, leaving an alkene. The E2 reaction is one step. The bulky base prevents an S_N2 reaction, but, if the base is too bulky, the Saytzeff rule is violated, leaving the least substituted alkene.

Notice that in elimination, the base abstracts a hydrogen. This is a different behavior than that of a nucleophile in a substitution reaction. In a substitution reaction, the nucleophile attacks the carbon.

Dehydrohalogenation

2-9
Catalytic Hydrogenation

Hydrogenation is an example of an addition reaction. In order for hydrogenation to occur at an appreciable rate, a *heterogeneous* catalyst is employed. A heterogeneous catalyst is a catalyst that exists in a different phase (i.e. gas, liquid, solid, aqueous, etc.) than the reactants or products. Normally tiny shavings of metal act as the catalyst to form **syn-addition** (same side addition).

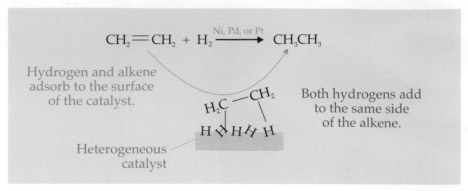

Syn Addition in catalytic hydrogenation

Hydrogenation is an exothermic reaction with a high energy of activation. Heats of hydrogenation can be used to measure relative stabilities of alkenes. The lower the heat of hydrogenation, the more stable the alkene.

Syn addition of alkynes creates a cis alkene.

2-10
Oxidation of Alkenes

Ozone is a radical, so it is very reactive, breaking right through alkenes and alkynes.

Oxidation of alkenes may produce glycols (hydroxyl groups on adjacent carbons) or oxidation may cleave the alkene at the double bond as in *ozonolysis*.

$$\underset{/}{\overset{\backslash}{C}} = \underset{\backslash}{\overset{/}{C}} \quad \xrightarrow[\text{2) Zn, H}_2\text{O}]{\text{1) O}_3} \quad \underset{/}{\overset{\backslash}{C}} = O \; + \; O = \underset{\backslash}{\overset{/}{C}}$$

Ozonolysis of an alkene

Alkynes produce carboxylic acids when undergoing ozonolysis.

2-11
Electrophilic Addition

Electrophilic addition is an important reaction for alkenes. When you see an alkene on the MCAT, check for electrophilic addition. An **electrophile** is an electron-loving species, so it will have at least a partially positive charge, even if it is only from a momentary dipole. The double bond of an alkene is an electron-rich environment and will attract electrophiles.

When hydrogen halides (HF, HCl, HBr, and HI) are added to alkenes, they follow **Markovnikov's rule** unless otherwise specified on the MCAT. Markovnikov's rule says "the hydrogen will add to the least substituted carbon of the double bond". The reaction takes place in two steps. First, the hydrogen halide, a Bronsted-Lowry acid, creates a positively charged proton, which acts as the electrophile. Second, the newly formed carbocation picks up the negatively charged halide ion. The first step is the slow step and determines the rate.

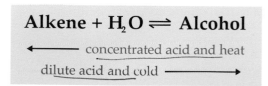

Electrophilic addition
via Markovnikov's rule
forming the most stable carbocation

The reaction follows Markovnikov's rule because the rule dictates the formation of the more stable carbocation. You should be aware that if peroxides (ROOR) are present, the *bromine*, not the hydrogen, will add to the least substituted carbon. This is called an **anti-Markovnikov addition**. The other halogens will still follow Markovnikov's rule even in the presence of peroxides.

The most reactive alkenes in electrophilic addition are the most thermodynamically stable. This is because they also have the lowest activation energy when forming carbocations. Hydrogen halides add to alkynes in nearly the same way they add to alkenes.

Alkene + H_2O ⇌ Alcohol
⟵ concentrated acid and heat
dilute acid and cold ⟶

Hydration of an alkene also follows Markovnikov's rule. Hydration takes place when water is added to an alkene in the presence of an acid. This reaction is the reverse of dehydration of an alcohol. Low temperatures and dilute acid drive this reaction toward alcohol formation; high temperatures and concentrated acid drive the reaction toward alkene formation.

Another reaction which creates an alcohol from an alkene is *oxymercuration/demercuration* (shown on the next page). This is a two-step process which also follows Markovnikov's rule but rarely results in rearrangement of the carbocation. A two-step theory has the mercury-containing reagent partially dissociate to ⁺Hg(OAc). The ⁺Hg(OAc) acts as an electrophile creating a *mercurinium ion*. Water attacks the mercurinium ion to form the *organomercurial alcohol* in an **anti-addition** (addition from opposite sides of the double bond). The second step is demercuration to form the alcohol by addition of a reducing agent and base.

What's important here is not to memorize the mechanism, but to realize that in organometallic compounds the metal likes to lose electrons and take on a full or partial positive charge.

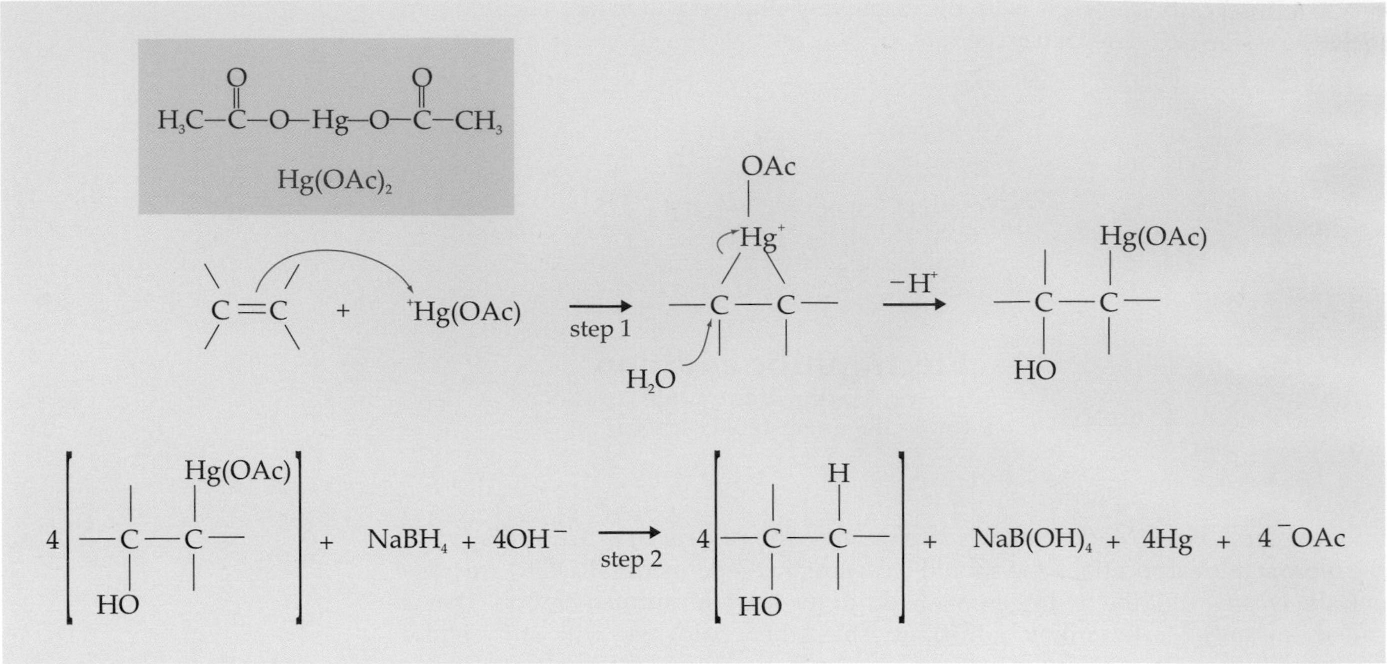

$$H_3C-\overset{\overset{\displaystyle O}{\|}}{C}-O-Hg-O-\overset{\overset{\displaystyle O}{\|}}{C}-CH_3$$

$$Hg(OAc)_2$$

Oxymercuration/Demercuration

If an alcohol is used instead of water, the corresponding ether is produced. This is called an *alkoxymercuration/demercuration* reaction.

Hydroboration provides yet another mechanism to produce an alcohol from an alkene. This is an anti-Markovnikov and a syn addition.

Notice that this reaction is in the presence of peroxide. This should help you remember that it is anti-Markovnikov. You may see hydroboration on the MCAT, but you probably won't have to know anything about it to answer the questions.

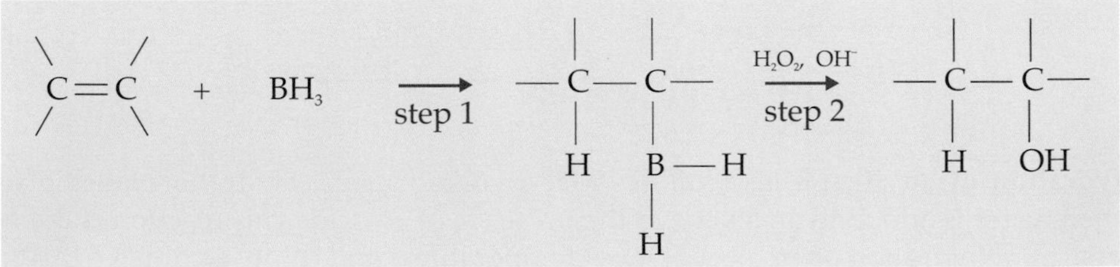

Hydroboration

Halogens are much more reactive toward alkenes than toward alkanes Br$_2$ and Cl$_2$ add to alkenes readily via anti-addition to form *vic-dihalides* (two halogens connected to adjacent carbons).

You should know halogenation of an alkene for the MCAT. Notice that alkanes will not react with halogens without light or heat, but alkenes will. Alkynes behave just like alkenes when exposed to halogens.

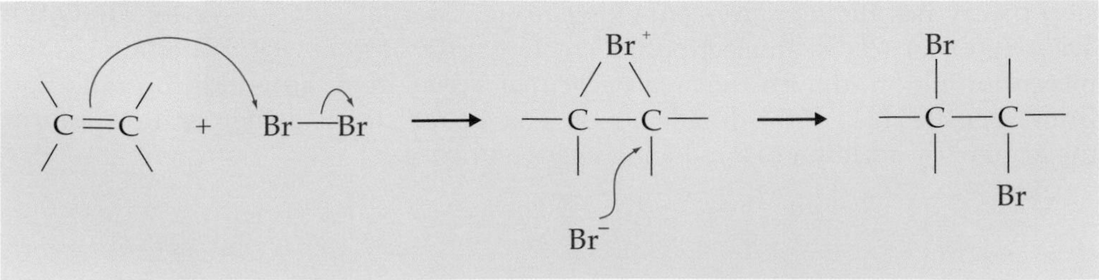

Halogenation of an Alkene

When this reaction takes place with water, a *halohydrin* is formed and Markovnikov's rule is followed where the electrophile adds to the least substituted carbon. Water acts as the nucleophile in the second step instead of the bromide ion. (A halohydrin is a hydroxyl group and a halogen attached to adjacent carbons.)

Benzene undergoes **substitution NOT addition**. If a functional group were added to benzene, it would disrupt the resonance and the compound would no longer be aromatic.

From stereochemistry, we know that resonance atoms must be in the same plane, so benzene is a **flat molecule**. Benzene is stabilized by **resonance** and its carbon-carbon bonds have partial double bond character. Although benzene is normally drawn without its six hydrogens, don't forget that they exist. If a benzene ring contains one substituent, the remaining 5 positions are labeled **ortho, meta, or para** as shown below.

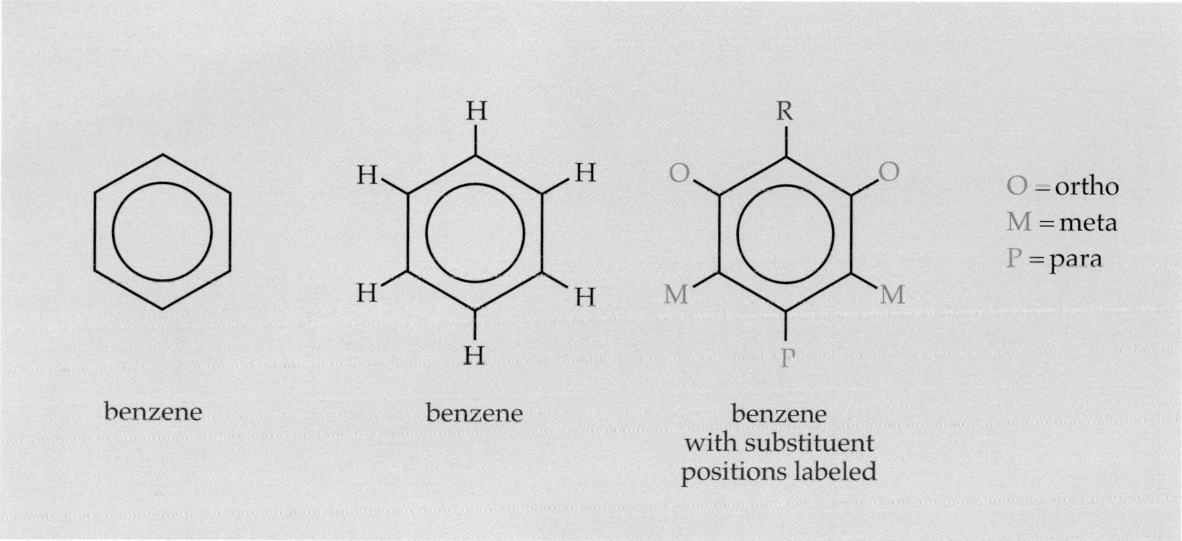

benzene   benzene   benzene
with substituent
positions labeled

O = ortho
M = meta
P = para

Don't let ring structures intimidate you. Since benzene only undergoes substitution, benzene presents little challenge on the MCAT. AAMC has announced that they will not ask questions on benzene starting in 2003. Nevertheless, it won't hurt to learn the names of the substituted positions: ortho, meta, para.

When an **electron withdrawing group** is in the R position, it deactivates the ring and directs any new substituents to the meta position. **Electron donating groups** activate the ring and direct any new substituents to ortho and para positions. **Halogens are an exception** to the rule. They are electron withdrawing and deactivate the ring as expected. However, they are ortho-para directors. (To deactivate the ring simply means to make it less reactive.) Knowing whether a functional group is electron withdrawing or donating can be very helpful in all of organic chemistry.

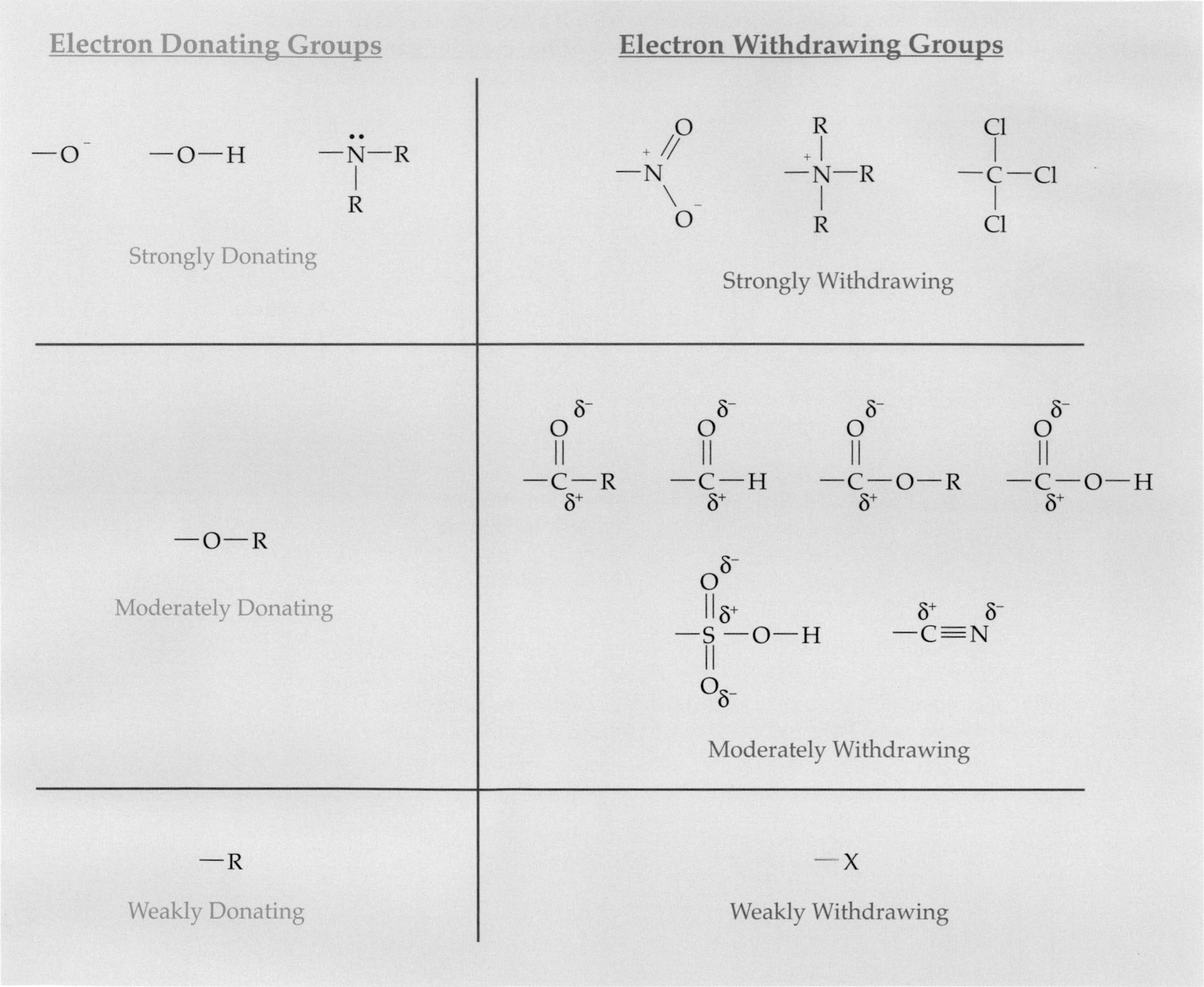

Electron Donating Groups	Electron Withdrawing Groups
Strongly Donating	Strongly Withdrawing
Moderately Donating	Moderately Withdrawing
—R Weakly Donating	—X Weakly Withdrawing

The groups are labeled in relation to the electron withdrawing-donating tendencies of a lone hydrogen atom. Hydrogen is considered neither electron withdrawing nor electron donating. Benzene, itself, is an ortho-para director and ring activator; however, for reasons that are well beyond the MCAT, it is best to consider benzene as electron withdrawing in most other situations.

It may help to familiarize yourself with the names of the following benzene compounds, but it is unlikely that a correct MCAT answer will require this knowledge.

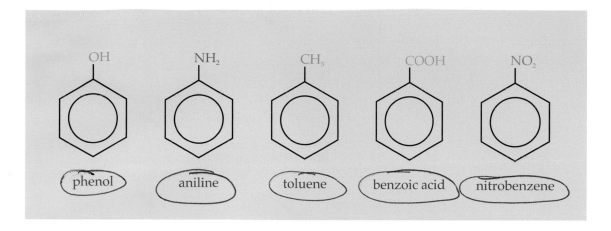

Don't memorize too many reactions. So far, you should thoroughly understand:

1. combustion;

2. halogenation of an alkane;

3. dehydration of an alcohol and the reverse reaction, hydration of an alkene;

4. electrophilic addition (via Comrade Markovnikov); and

5. halogenation of an alkene. Assume that alkynes behave like alkenes.

Rather than memorizing other reactions, be familiar with the behavior of functional groups. For instance, the double bond of alkenes makes a large electron cloud that is attractive to an electrophile, but alkenes withdraw electrons through their bonds, making them stabilized by electron donating groups, and making them more acidic than alkanes; benzene hates addition; etc. A strong start toward understanding functional groups is memorizing their electron withdrawing and donating natures. We will come back to electron withdrawing and donating properties time and again. Remember, the MCAT is not going to require that you have an obscure reaction committed to memory; much more likely, the MCAT will show you a reaction that you have never seen and ask you "why?" The answer will be because the functional group involved normally behaves that way. Know your functional groups.

33. Which of the following compounds is the most thermo-dynamically stable?

    A. $CH_3CH_2CH=CH_2$

    B. $CH_3CH=CH_2$

    C. ![structure: H3C and H on left carbon, H and CH3 on right carbon, C=C]

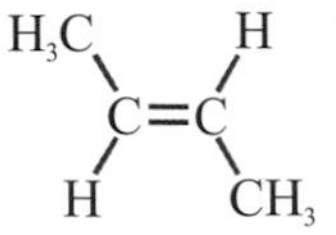

    D. ![structure: H and H on top, H3C and CH3 on bottom, C=C]

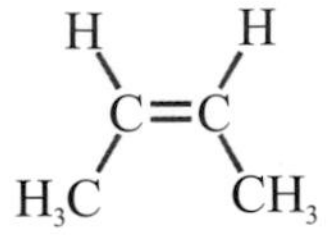

34. Which of the following compounds will be the most reactive with HBr?

    A. $CH_3CH_2CH=CH_2$

    B. $CH_3CH=CH_2$

    C. ![structure: H3C and H, H and CH3, C=C]

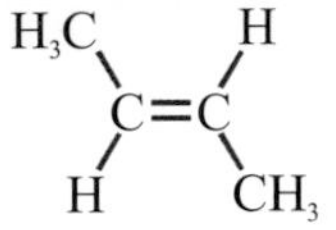

    D. ![structure: H3C and H, H3C and H, C=C]

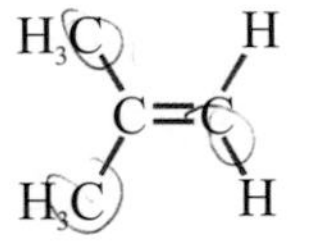

35. What is the product of the following oxidation reaction?

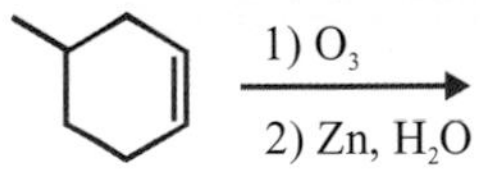

    ![cyclohexene structure] 1) O_3 / 2) Zn, H_2O

    A. OHC~~~CHO (branched with methyl)

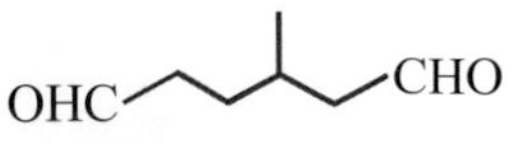

    B. ~~~COOH (branched with methyl)

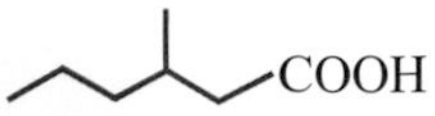

    C. CHO / CHO (two separate fragments)

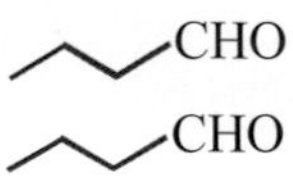

    D. OHC~~~CHO (branched)

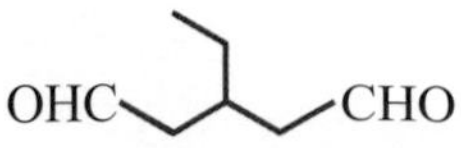

36. What is the major product of the following reaction?

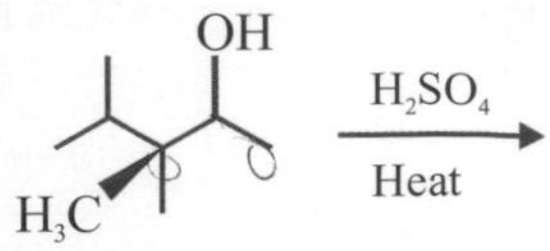

$\xrightarrow{H_2SO_4}$ Heat

    A. ![alkene structure]

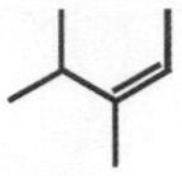

    B. ![alkene structure with H3C]

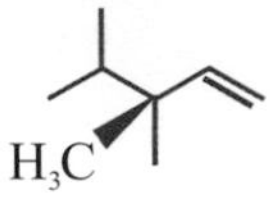

    C. ![alkene structure with H3C]

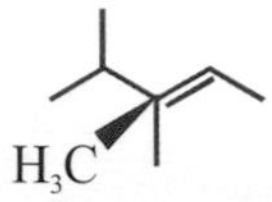

    D. ![structure with H3C]

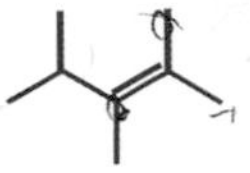

37. When 2,4-dimethyl-2-pentene is hydrated with cold dilute acid, the major product is:

    A. ![structure with OH]

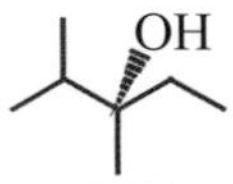

    B. ![structure with OH]

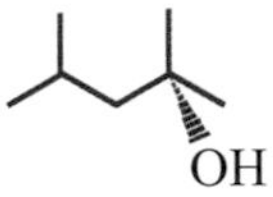

    C. ![structure with OH]

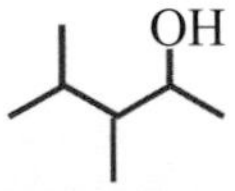

    D. ![structure with OH]

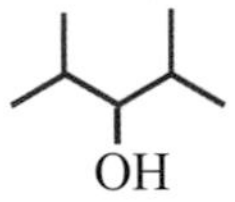

38. Anthracene is an aromatic compound described by which of the following characteristics?

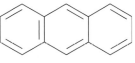

Anthracene

    I. cyclic
    II. planar
    III. satisfies Huckel's rule
    IV. has an even number of π electrons

    A. I and II only
    B. II, III and IV only
    C. I, III and IV only
    D. I, II, III and IV

39. Which of the following statements is true regarding the two reaction mechanisms and the deuterium (D) effect?

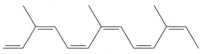

[1-Bromo-2-phenylethane]

[1-Bromo-2,2-dideuterio -2-phenylethane]

A. Deuterium (D) isotope is identical to hydrogen in every way.

B. C—H or C—D bond is broken in the reaction rate limiting step.

C. 1-Bromo 2 phenylethane reactant undergoes a one step substitution reaction.

D. Carbon hydrogen bond is stronger than the corresponding carbon deuterium bond.

40. Natural rubber is a diene polymer known as isoprene. What is the most likely explanation for isoprene's ability to stretch?

Isoprene (2 methyl-1,3-butadiene)

A. Isoprene undergoes vulcanization, which induces cross-linking between carbon atoms in nearby rubber chains.

B. Double bonds induce shape irregularities, which prevent neighboring chains from nestling together.

C. Alkane polymer chains orient along the direction of pull by sliding over each other.

D. Isoprene is able to undergo rapid hydration/dehydration reaction.

2-13
Substitutions

Substitution reactions occur when one functional group replaces another. Two important types of substitution reactions are **S_N1** and **S_N2**. These are substitution, nucleophilic, unimolecular and bimolecular. The numbers represent the order of the rate law and NOT the number of steps.

2-14
S_N1

An S_N1 reaction has 2 steps and has a rate that is dependent on only one of the reactants. The first step is the formation of the carbocation. This is the **slow step** and thus the **rate-determining step**. Since this step has nothing to do with the nucleophile, the rate is independent of the concentration of the nucleophile and is directly proportional to the concentration of the substrate. In an S_N1 reaction the **leaving group** (the group being replaced) simply breaks away on its own to leave a carbocation behind. The second step happens very quickly. The nucleophile attacks the carbocation.

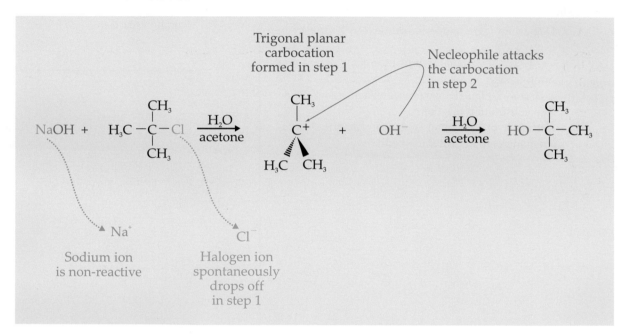

Substitution, Nucleophilic, Unimolecular

Notice that if the carbocation carbon began and ended an S_N1 reaction as a chiral carbon, both enantiomers would be produced. The intermediate carbocation is planar and the nucleophile is able to attack it from either side. Carbon skeleton rearrangement may occur if the carbocation can rearrange to a more stable form. Elimination (E1) often accompanies S_N1 reactions because the nucleophile may act as a base to abstract a proton from the carbocation, forming a carbon-carbon double bond.

Since the carbocation must be formed spontaneously in an S_N1 reaction, a tertiary substrate is more likely to undergo an S_N1 reaction than is a primary or secondary substrate. On the MCAT, probably only tertiary substrates will undergo S_N1. The rate of an S_N1 reaction is determined solely by the concentration of the substrate.

<u>S_N2</u> reactions occur in a single step. The rate is dependent on the concentration of the nucleophile and the **substrate**. (The substrate is the electrophile or the molecule being attacked by the nucleophile.) In an S_N2 reaction a nucleophile attacks the intact substrate from behind the leaving group and knocks the leaving group free while bonding to the substrate.

2-15

S_N2

inversion of configuration

Substitution, Nucleophilic, Bimolecular

Notice the **inversion of configuration** on the carbon being attacked by the nucleophile. If the carbon were chiral, the relative configuration would be changed but the absolute configuration might or might not be changed. Notice also that a tertiary carbon would **sterically hinder** the nucleophile in this reaction. The rate of S_N2 reactions decreases from methyl to secondary substrates. S_N2 reactions don't typically occur with tertiary substrates. If the nucleophile is a strong base and the substrate is too hindered, an elimination (E2) reaction may occur. In an E2 reaction, the nucleophile acts as a base abstracting a proton and, in the same step, the halogen leaves the substrate forming a carbon-carbon double bond. Bulky nucleophiles also hinder S_N2 reactions.

The strength of the nucleophile is unimportant for an S_N1 reaction but important for an S_N2 reaction. A base is always a stronger nucleophile than its conjugate acid, but basicity is not the same thing as nucleophilicity. If a nucleophile behaves as a base, elimination results. To avoid this, we use a less bulky nucleophile. A negative charge and polarizability add to nucleophilicity. Electronegativity reduces nucleophilicity. In general, nucleophilicity decreases going up and to the right on the periodic table.

2-16

Nucleophilicity

Polar protic solvents (polar solvents that can hydrogen bond) stabilize the nucleophile and any carbocation that may form. A stable nucleophile slows S_N2 reactions, while a stable carbocation increases the rate of S_N1 reactions. Thus polar protic solvents increase the rate of S_N1 and decrease the rate of S_N2. *Polar aprotic solvents* (polar solvents that can't form hydrogen bonds) do not form strong bonds with ions and thus increase the rate of S_N2 reactions while inhibiting S_N1 reactions. In S_N1 reactions, the solvent is often heated to reflux (boiled) in order to provide energy for the formation of the carbocation.

In *solvolysis* the solvent acts as the nucleophile.

2-17

Solvents

2-18
Leaving Groups

The best leaving groups are those that are stable when they leave. Generally speaking, the weaker the base, the better the leaving group. Electron withdrawing effects and polarizability also make for a good leaving group. The leaving group will always be more stable than the nucleophile.

2-19
S_N1 vs. S_N2

There are six things to remember about S_N1 vs. S_N2. Remember the six things as "The nucleophile and the five Ss": 1) Substrate; 2) Solvent; 3) Speed; 4) Stereochemistry; and 5) Skeleton rearrangement.

The nucleophile: S_N2 requires a strong nucleophile, while nucleophilic strength doesn't affect S_N1.

1st S: S_N2 reactions don't occur with a sterically hindered Substrate. S_N2 requires a methyl, primary, or secondary substrate, while S_N1 requires a secondary or tertiary substrate.

2nd S: A highly polar Solvent increases the reaction rate of S_N1 by stabilizing the carbocation, but slows down S_N2 reactions by stabilizing the nucleophile.

3rd S: The Speed of an S_N2 reaction depends upon the concentration of the substrate and the nucleophile, while the speed of an S_N1 depends only on the substrate.

4th S: S_N2 inverts Stereochemistry about the chiral center, while S_N1 creates a racemic mixture.

5th S: S_N1 may be accompanied by carbon Skeleton rearrangement, but S_N2 never rearranges the carbon skeleton.

Also remember that elimination reactions can accompany both S_N1 and S_N2 reactions. Elimination occurs when the nucleophile behaves as a base rather than a nucleophile; it abstracts a proton rather than attacking a carbon. Elimination reactions always result in a carbon-carbon double bond. E1 and E2 kinetics are similar to S_N1 and S_N2 respectively.

2-20
Physical Properties of Alcohols

Alcohols follow trends similar to hydrocarbons, but alcohols hydrogen bond, giving them considerably higher boiling points and water solubilities than similar-weight hydrocarbons.

Alcohols follow the same general trends as alkanes. The boiling point goes up with molecular weight and down with branching. The melting point trend is not as reliable but still exists. Melting point also goes up with molecular weight. Branching generally lowers boiling point and has a less clear effect on melting. Although alcohols follow the same trend as alkanes, their boiling and melting points are much higher than alkanes due to **hydrogen bonding**. The hydrogen bonding increases the intermolecular forces, which must be overcome to change phase.

Alcohols are more soluble in water than alkanes and alkenes. The hydroxyl group increases polarity and allows for hydrogen bonding with water. The longer the carbon chain, the less soluble the alcohol.

Alcohol   Water

Since an alcohol can lose a proton, it can act like an acid. However, alcohols are less acidic than water. The order of acidity for alcohols from strongest to weakest is: methyl; 1°; 2°; 3°. If we examine the conjugate base of each alcohol, the most stable conjugate base will be the conjugate of the strongest acid. Since excess charge is an instability, the most stable conjugate base will have the weakest negative charge. Methyl groups are electron donating compared to hydrogens, thus they act to prevent the carbon from absorbing some of the excess negative charge of the conjugate. Because a tertiary alcohol has the most methyl groups, a tertiary carbon can absorb the least amount of negative charge; the conjugate base of a tertiary alcohol is the least stable; and a tertiary alcohol is the least acidic.

2-21
Alcohols as Acids

Acid	pK_a
hydrochloric acid	−2.2
acetic acid	4.8
phenol	10
water	15.7
ethanol	15.9
t-butyl alcohol	18

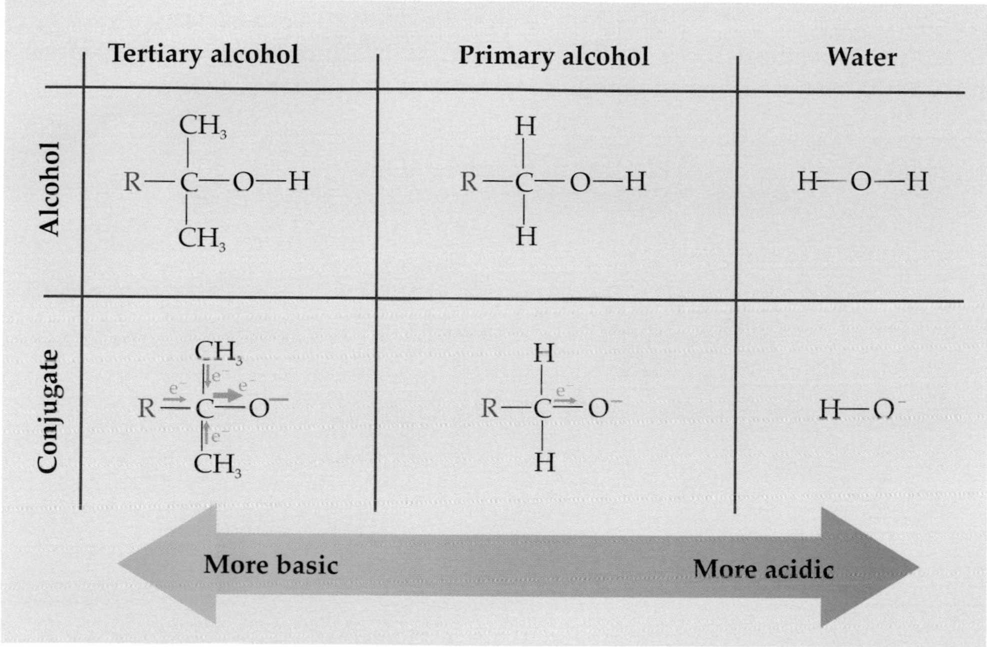

Electron donation and withdrawal helps to explain many of the reactions in MCAT organic chemistry. For instance, placing an electron withdrawing group on the alcohol increases its acidity by reducing the negative charge on the conjugate base.

We've already looked at several alcohol synthesis reactions: hydration of an alkene, oxymercuration/demercuration, hydroboration, and nucleophilic substitution. Another method of synthesizing an alcohol is with an organometallic compound. Organometallic reagents possess a highly polarized carbon-metal bond. The carbon is more electronegative than the metal, so the carbon takes on a strong partial negative charge. The organometallic reagent becomes a strong nucleophile and base. The most common reaction for organometallic compounds is nucleophilic attack on a carbonyl carbon, which, after an acid bath, produces an alcohol.

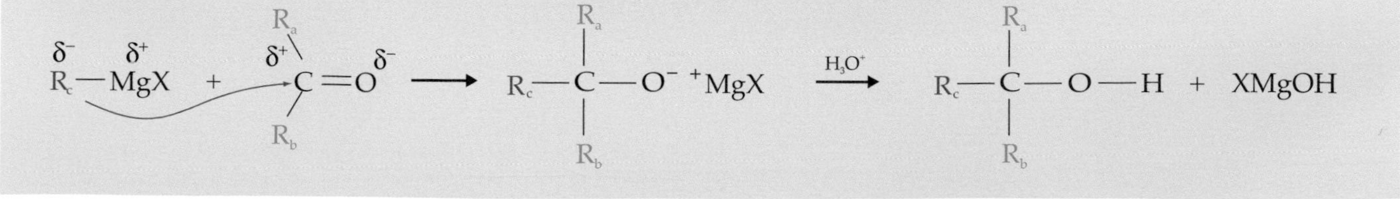

2-22
Synthesis of Alcohols

Grignard Synthesis of an Alcohol

Grignard reagents will react in a similar fashion with C=N, C≡N, S=O, N=O. The Grignard is a strong enough base to deprotonate the following species: O—H, N—H, S—H, —C≡C–H. Grignards will not form unless an ether is present.

In a nucleophilic attack mechanism similar to Grignard synthesis of an alcohol, hydrides (H⁻) will react with carbonyls to form alcohols.

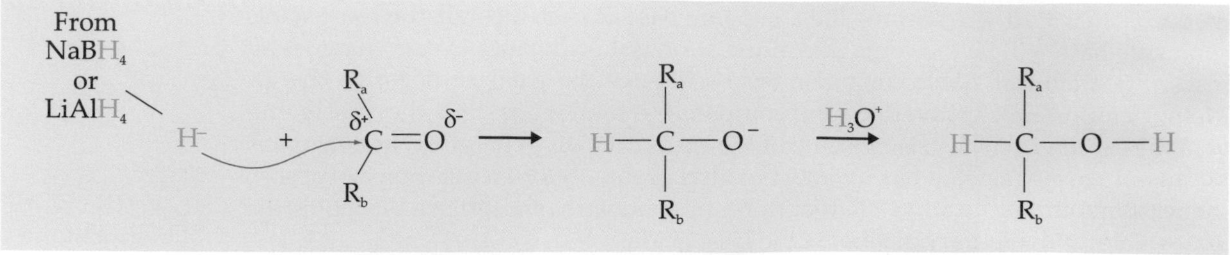

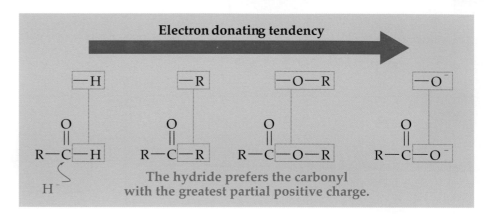

Reduction Synthesis of an Alcohol

Question: Why is it more difficult to reduce esters and acetates than ketones and aldehydes?

Answer: Because the group attached to the carbonyl of the ester or acetate is a stronger electron donor than an alkyl group or hydrogen. By donating electrons more strongly, it reduces the positive charge on the carbonyl carbon making it less attractive to the nucleophile.

In reduction synthesis, both $NaBH_4$ and $LiAlH_4$ will reduce aldehydes and ketones, but only $LiAlH_4$ is strong enough to reduce esters and acetates.

Electron donating tendency

The hydride prefers the carbonyl with the greatest partial positive charge.

2-23
Reactions with
Alcohols

We've already seen dehydration of an alcohol. Most of the time on the MCAT, if an alcohol is a reactant, it will be acting as a nucleophile. The two lone pairs of electrons on the oxygen are pushed out by the bent shape, and they search for a positive charge. The oxygen will find and connect to the substrate and the positively charged proton will drop off into solution.

Either...

nucleophile · substrate

Nucleophilic addition

Alcohols like to be nucleophiles.

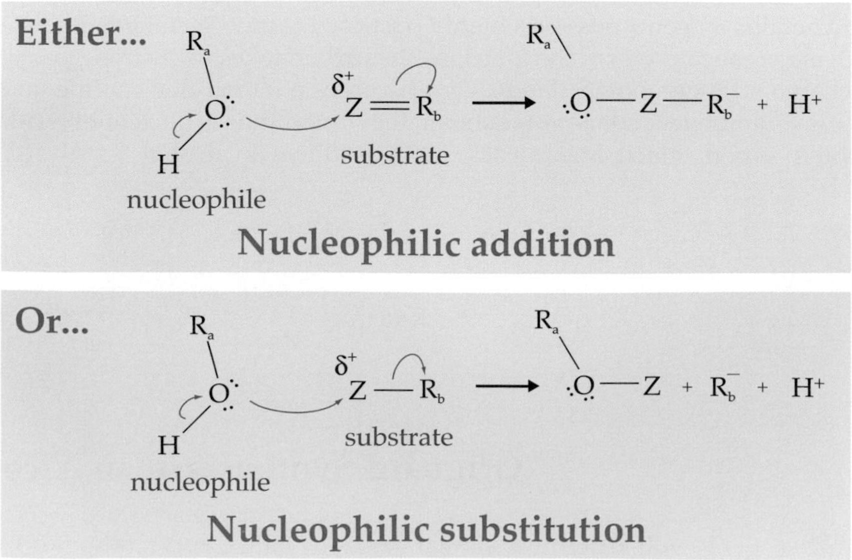

Or...

nucleophile · substrate

Nucleophilic substitution

Alcohols as nucleophiles

Primary and secondary alcohols can be oxidized. Tertiary alcohols cannot be oxidized on the MCAT. In organic chemistry, you can use the following rule to determine if a compound has been oxidized or reduced:

Oxidation: loss of H_2; addition of O or O_2; addition of X_2 (X = halogens)

Reduction: addition of H_2 (or H^-); loss of O or O_2; loss of X_2

Neither Oxidation nor reduction: addition or loss of H^+, H_2O, HX, etc.

Primary alcohols oxidize to aldehydes, which, in turn, oxidize to carboxylic acids. Secondary alcohols oxidize to ketones. In each case, the reverse process is called **reduction**.

2-24
Oxidation of Alcohols

A simple way to think of oxidation for any compound in organic chemistry is to consider the oxygen-to-hydrogen ratio of a molecule. If this ratio increases, then the molecule has been oxidized. If this ratio decreases, then the molecule has been reduced. This rule doesn't cover all situations, but it works well for many.

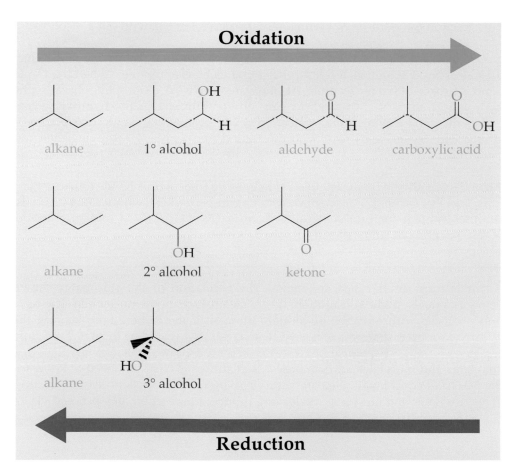

Generally speaking, *oxidizing agents* will have lots of oxygen and *reducing agents* will have lots of hydrogen. Below is a table of common oxidizing and reducing agents.

Oxidizing agents	Reducing agents
$K_2Cr_2O_7$	$LiAlH_4$
$KMnO_4$	$NaBH_4$
H_2CrO_4	H_2 + pressure
O_2	
Br_2	

2-25
Alkyl Halides from Alcohols

We saw in the S_N2 reaction that the halogen ion, as a weak base, is a good leaving group, and the hydroxyl group, as a strong base, is a good nucleophile. However, if the hydroxyl group is protonated by an acid, it becomes water, an excellent leaving group. The halide ion is an unusual nucleophile in that it is a very weak base and does not become protonated in acidic solution.

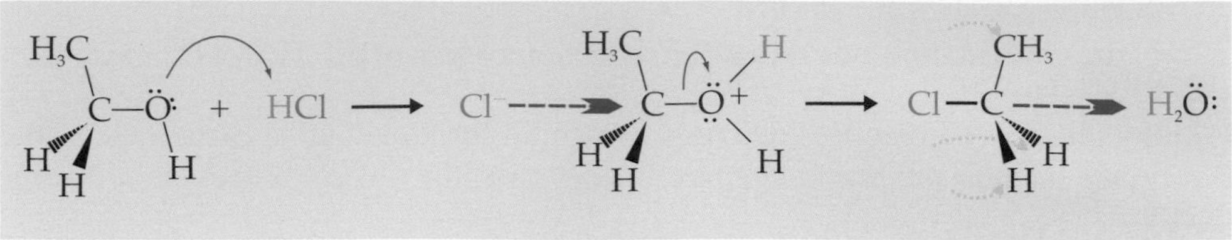

This reaction can occur as S_N1 with a tertiary alcohol or S_N2 with other alcohols.

Notice that this reaction breaks the C—O bond rather than the O—H bond. When the C—O bond is broken, alcohol is behaving as an electrophile. When the O—H bond is broken, it is a nucleophile. Alcohols are very weak electrophiles because the hydroxyl group is such a weak leaving group. Protonating the hydroxyl group makes the good leaving group water. However, protonating an alcohol requires a strong acid. Strong acids react with most good nucleophiles, destroying their nucleophilicity.

Alcohols can also be converted to alkyl halides by phosphorus halides such as PCl_3, PBr_3, and PI_3, via an S_N2 mechanism resulting in poor yields with tertiary alcohols. Another reagent for producing alkyl halides from alcohols is thionyl chloride, $SOCl_2$, resulting in sulfur dioxide and hydrochloric acid.

2-26
Preparation of Mesylates and Tosylates

Alcohols form esters called sulfonates. The **formation of the sulfonates** shown below is a nucleophilic substitution, where alcohol acts as the nucleohile. The reaction proceeds with retention of configuration, so if the carbon atom bearing the hydroxyl group is stereogenic, it is NOT inverted as it would be in an S_N2 reaction.

Tosylates and mesylates are commonly used sulfonates that you need to know for the MCAT. The sulfonate ions are very weak bases and excellent leaving groups. When tosylates and mesylates are leaving groups, the reaction may proceed via an S_N1 or S_N2 mechanism.

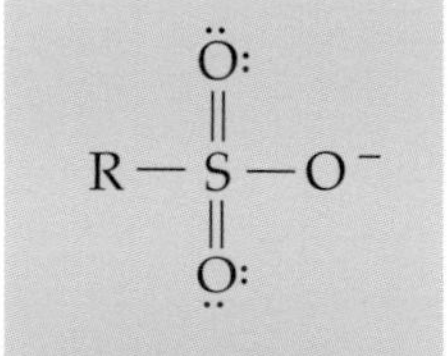

Sulfonate ion

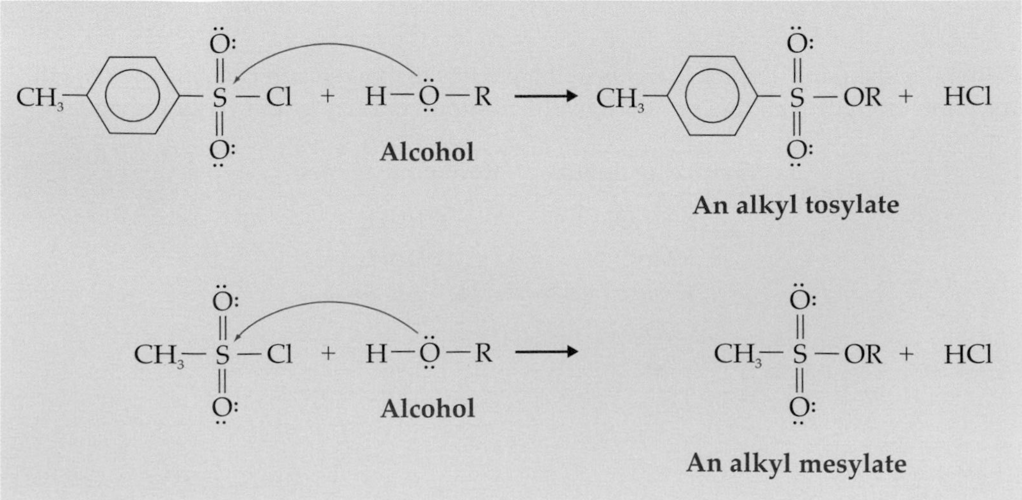

An alkyl tosylate

An alkyl mesylate

The **pinacol rearrangement** is a dehydration of an alcohol that results in an unexpected product. When hot sulfuric acid is added to an alcohol, the expected product of dehydration is an alkene. However, if the alcohol is a vicinal diol, it will form a ketone or aldehyde. The reaction follows the mechanism shown below. The first hydroxyl group is protonated and removed by the acid to form a carbocation in an expected dehydration step. Now, a methyl group may move to form an even more stable carbocation. This new carbocation exhibits resonance as shown. Resonance Structure 2 is favored because all the atoms have an octet of electrons. The water deprotonates Resonance Structure 2, forming pinacolone and regenerating the acid catalyst.

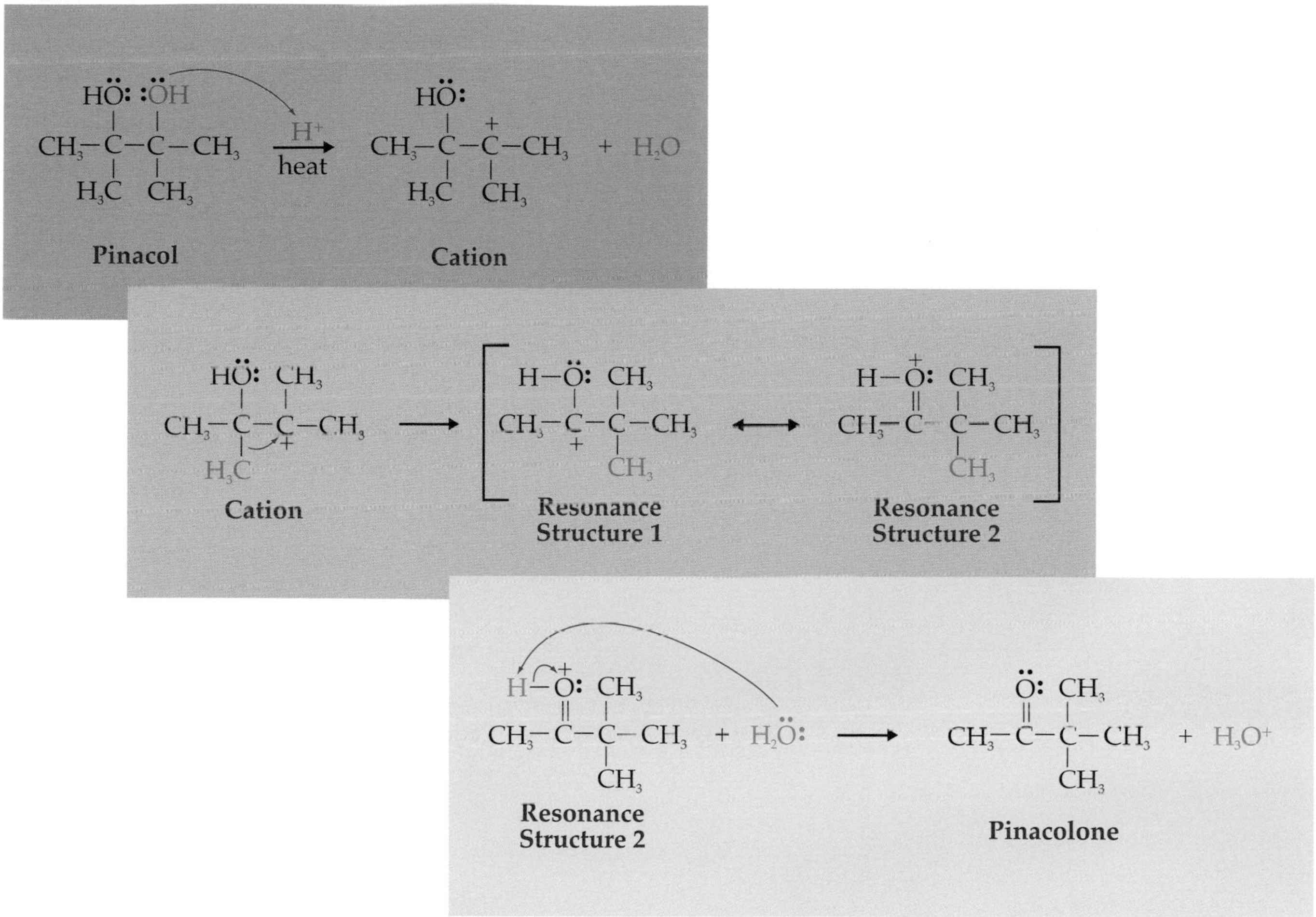

2-27
The Pinacol Rearrangement

Ethers (other than epoxides) are relatively non-reactive. They are polar. Although they cannot hydrogen bond with themselves, they can hydrogen bond with compounds that contain a hydrogen attached to a N, O, or F atom. Ethers are roughly as soluble in water as alcohols of similar molecular weight, yet organic compounds tend to be much more soluble in ethers than alcohols because no hydrogen bonds need to be broken. These properties make ethers useful solvents.

Since an ether cannot hydrogen bond with itself, it will have a boiling point roughly comparable to that of an alkane with a similar molecular weight. Their relatively low boiling points increase their usefulness as solvents.

2-28
Ethers

Ether is almost always the answer to solvent questions on the MCAT.

For the MCAT, ethers (other than epoxides) undergo one reaction. Ethers are cleaved by the halo-acids HI and HBr to form the corresponding alcohol and alkyl halide. If a large concentration of acid is used, the excess acid will react with the alcohol, as described above, to form another alkyl halide.

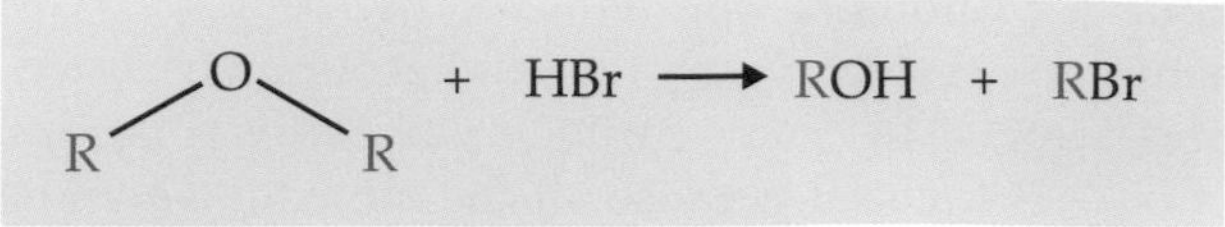

Ethers can also be oxidized to peroxides, but this is unlikely to be on the MCAT.

2-29 Epoxides

Epoxides (also called *oxiranes*) are three-membered cyclic ethers. They are more reactive than typical ethers due to the strain created by the small ring. Epoxides react with water in the presence of an acid catalyst to form diols, commonly called glycols. This is an anti-addition.

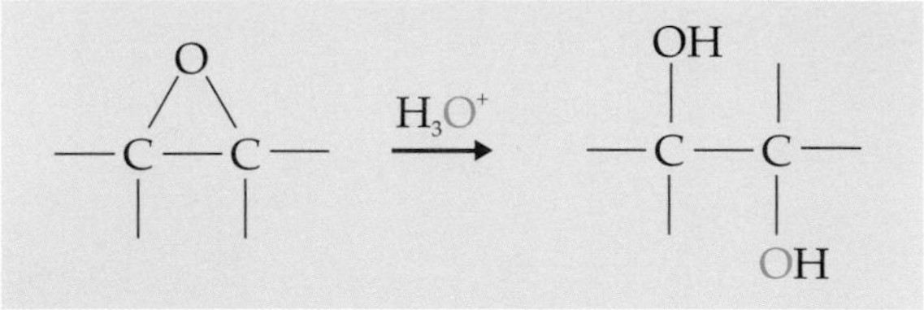

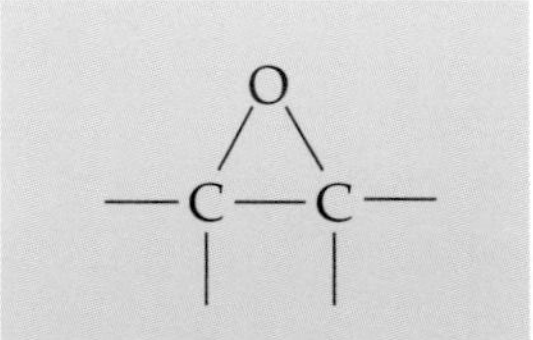

Epoxide

The epoxide oxygen is often protonated to form an alcohol when one of the carbons is attacked by a nucleophile.

An epoxide is an ether but is far more reactive. You don't have to memorize the reactions of epoxides for the MCAT.

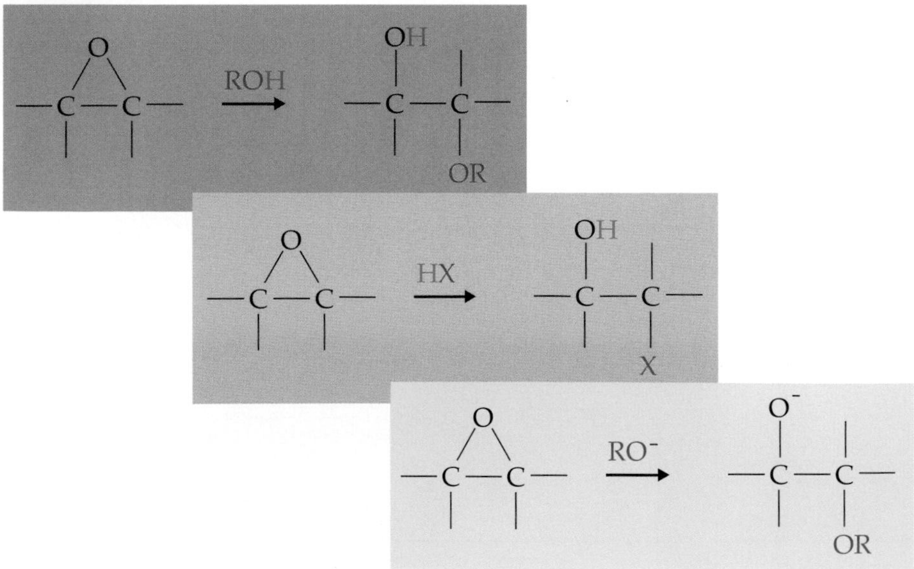

2-30 Acidities of the Functional Groups

Now that you know all about the important functional groups, it is a good idea to know their acidities. From weakest to strongest acids, they are as follows:

$$H_3C\text{-}CH_3 < H_2C\text{=}CH_2 < H_2 < NH_3 < HC\equiv CH < H_3C\text{-}\overset{O}{\overset{\|}{C}}\text{-}H$$
$$< H_3C\text{-}CH_2\text{-}OH < H_2O < H_3C\text{-}\overset{O}{\overset{\|}{C}}\text{-}OH$$

Acid Strength →

41. A student added NaCl to ethanol in the polar aprotic solvent DMF, and no reaction took place. To the same solution, he then added HCl. A reaction took place resulting in chloroethane. Which of the following best explains the student's results?

  A. The addition of HCl increased the chloride ion concentration which increased the rate of the reaction and pushed the equilibrium to the right.
  B. The chloride ion is a better nucleophile in a polar protic solvent and the HCl protonated the solvent.
  C. The HCl protonated the hydroxyl group on the alcohol making it a better leaving group.
  D. The HCl destabilized the chloride ion complex between the chloride ion and the solvent.

42. All of the following will increase the rate of the reaction shown below EXCEPT:

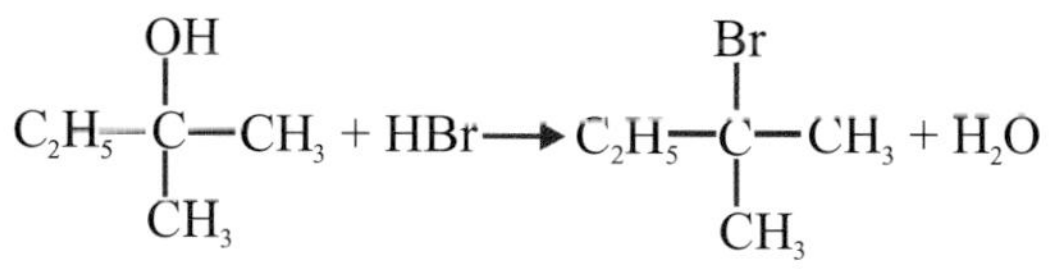

$$\underset{\underset{CH_3}{|}}{\overset{\overset{OH}{|}}{C_2H_5-C-CH_3}} + HBr \longrightarrow \underset{\underset{CH_3}{|}}{\overset{\overset{Br}{|}}{C_2H_5-C-CH_3}} + H_2O$$

  I. increasing the concentration of tertbutyl alcohol
  II. increasing the concentration of hydrobromic acid
  III. increasing the temperature

  A. I only
  B. II only
  C. III only
  D. II and III only

43. The following reaction is one of many steps in the laboratory synthesis of cholesterol. What type of reaction is it?

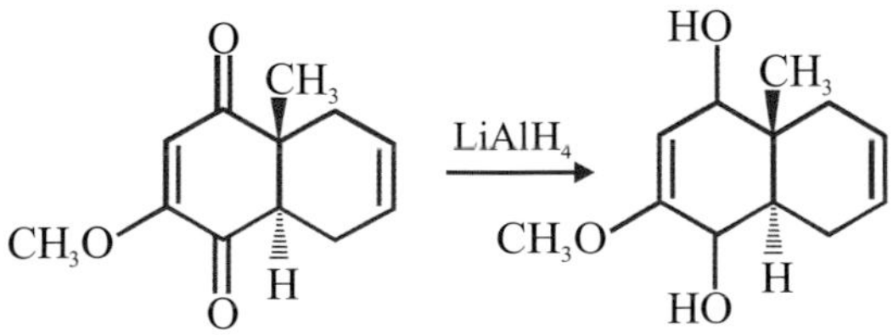

  A. reduction reaction
  B. oxidation reaction
  C. catalytic hydrogenation
  D. electrophilic substitution

44. Labetalol is a β-adrenergic antagonist which reduces blood pressure by blocking reflex sympathetic stimulation of the heart.

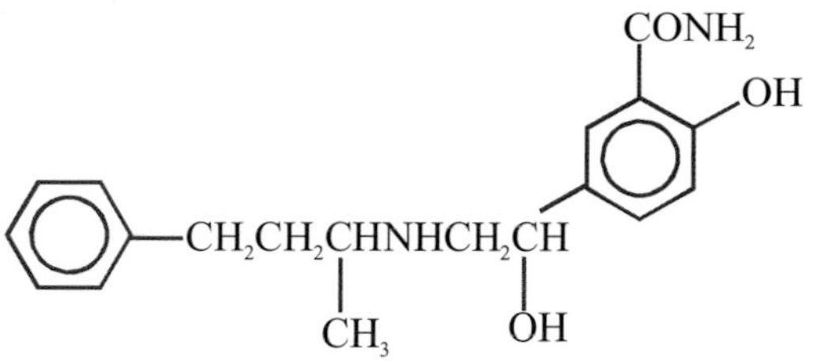

labetalol

Which of the following intermolecular bonds contributes least to the water solubility of labetalol?

A.

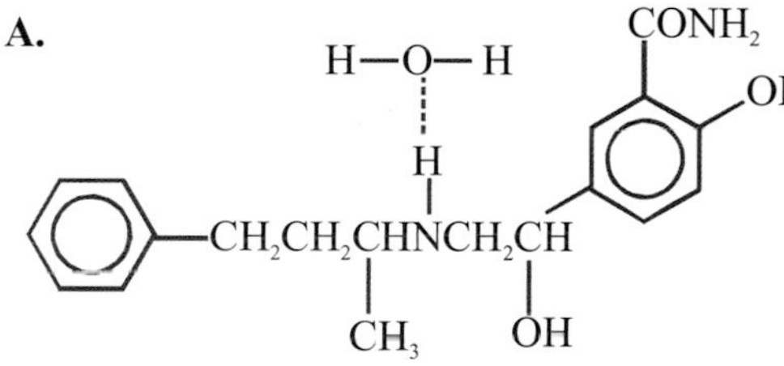

B.

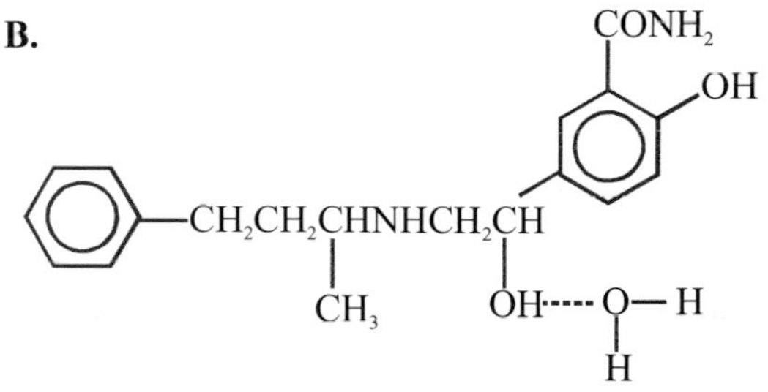

C.

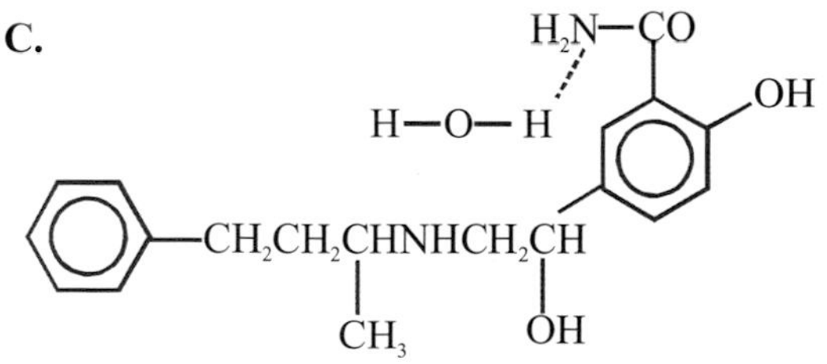

D.

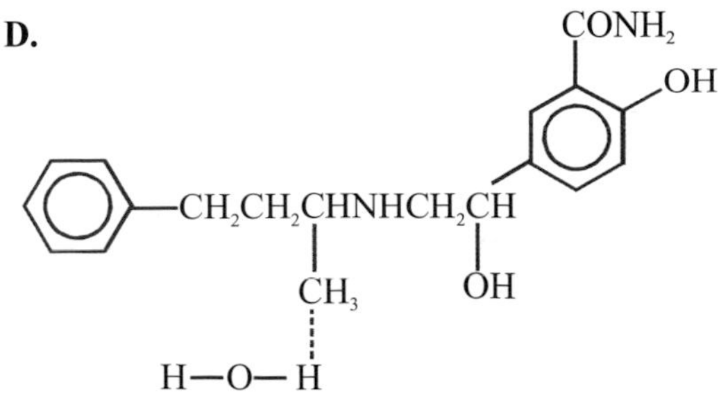

45. The Lucas test distinguishes between the presence of primary, secondary, and tertiary alcohols based upon reactivity with a hydrogen halide. The corresponding alkyl chlorides are insoluble in Lucas reagent and turn the solution cloudy at the same rate that they react with the reagent. The alcohols, A, B, and C, are solvated separately in Lucas reagent made of hydrochloric acid and zinc chloride. If the alcohols are primary, secondary, and tertiary respectively, what is the order of their rates of reaction from fastest to slowest?

    A.   A, B, C
    B.   B, A, C
    C.   C, B, A
    D.   B, C, A

46. Reactions 1 and 2 were carried out in the presence of peroxides. Which of the following is the most likely explanation for why Product B fails to form?

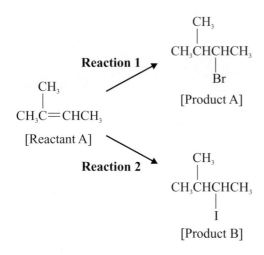

[Product A]

[Reactant A]

[Product B]

    A.   Hydrogen halides always yield products of Markovnikov's addition.
    B.   Reactions 1 and 2 show Markovnikov and anti-Markovnikov addition, respectively.
    C.   Peroxide dependent anti-Markovnikov addition succeeds only with bromine.
    D.   Markovnikov addition reactions 1 and 2 are driven by reagent concentrations.

47. The most common reaction of alcohols is nucleophilic substitution. All of the following correctly describe S_N2 reactions, EXCEPT:

    I.   reaction rate = k [S][Nucleophile]
    II. racemic mixture of products results
    III. inversion of configuration occurs

    A.   I and II only
    B.   II only
    C.   III only
    D.   I, II and III

48. Which statement is the most likely explanation for why 1-chloro-1, 2-diphenylethane proceeds via S_N1 at a constant rate independent of nucleophilic quality or concentration?

    A.   1-chloro-1, 2-diphenylethane prefers S_N2 mechanism for rapid substitution
    B. S_N1 rate-limiting step determines the overall reaction rate
    C.   1-chloro-1, 2-diphenylethane concentration increase will not cause an increase in product synthesis
    D.   reaction product accumulation has a direct effect on the rate-limiting step

STOP.

Carbonyls and Amines

A **carbonyl** is a carbon double bonded to an oxygen. The double bond is shorter and stronger than the double bond of an alkene. Aldehydes, ketones, carboxylic acids, amides, and esters all contain carbonyls. Whenever you see a carbonyl on the MCAT think about two things: 1) **planar stereochemistry** and; 2) partial negative charge on the oxygen, **partial positive charge on the carbon**. The planar stereochemistry of a carbonyl leaves open space above and below, making it susceptible to chemical attack. The partial positive charge on the carbon means that any attack on the carbonyl carbon will be from a nucleophile. Aldehydes and ketones typically undergo nucleophilic addition, while other carbonyl compounds prefer nucleophilic substitution. The partial negative charge on the oxygen means that it is easily protonated.

3-1
The Carbonyl

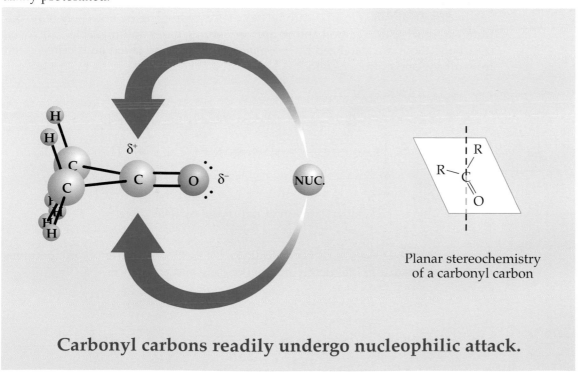

Planar stereochemistry
of a carbonyl carbon

Carbonyl carbons readily undergo nucleophilic attack.

3-2
Aldehydes and Ketones

You should be able to recognize and give the common name for the simple **alde-hydes and ketones** shown below.

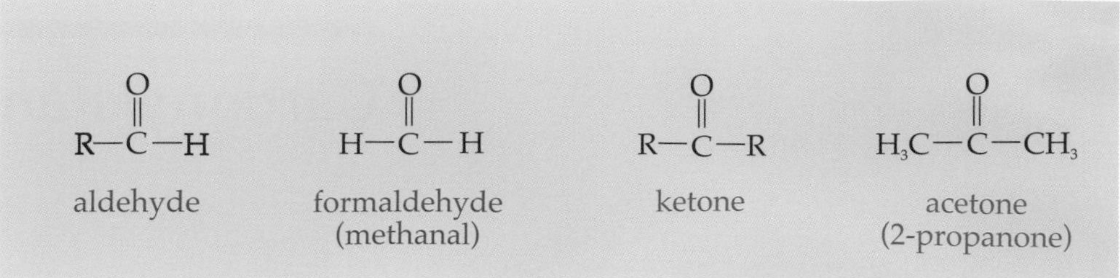

| aldehyde | formaldehyde (methanal) | ketone | acetone (2-propanone) |

3-3
Physical Properties

Aldehydes and ketones are more polar and have higher boiling points than alkanes and alkenes of similar molecular weight. However, they cannot hydrogen bond with each other, so they have lower boiling points than corresponding alcohols. Aldehydes and ketones do accept hydrogen bonds with water and other compounds that can hydrogen bond. This makes them excellent solvents for these substances. Aldehydes and ketones with up to four carbons are soluble in water.

3-4
Chemical Properties

Most of the time on the MCAT an **aldehyde** or ketone will be acting either as the **substrate in nucleophilic addition** or as a Bronsted-Lowry acid by donating one of its **α-hydrogens** (alpha-hydrogens). A carbon that is attached to a carbonyl carbon is in the **alpha position** and is called an **α-carbon**. The next carbon is called a *β-carbon*; the next is the *γ-carbon* and so on down the Greek alphabet. An α-hydrogen is any hydrogen attached to an α-carbon. Normally hydrogens are not easily removed from carbons because carbon anions are very strong bases and unstable. However, α-carbon anions are stabilized by resonance. This anion is called an *enolate ion* (*en* from alkene and *ol* from alcohol).

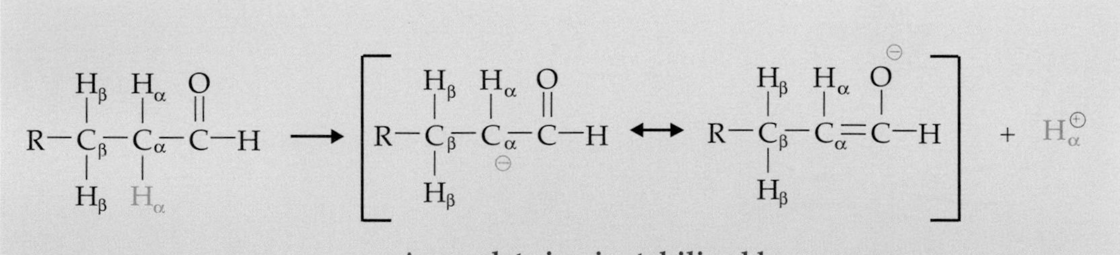

An enolate ion is stabilized by resonance.

When the β-carbon is also a carbonyl (called a β-dicarbonyl), the enol form becomes far more stable due to internal hydrogen bonding and resonance.

The dicarbonyl increases the acidity of the alpha hydrogen between the carbonyls, making it more acidic than water or alcohol.

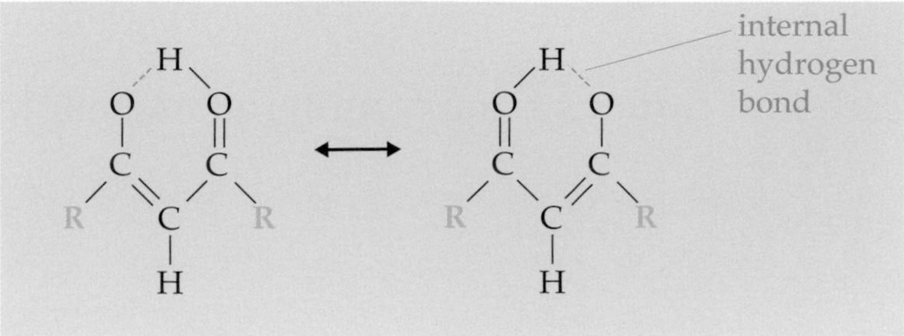

Enol stabilization of β-dicarbonyl

Because alkyl groups are electron donating and a ketone has two alkyl groups attached to the carbonyl, the carbonyl carbon of the conjugate base of the ketone is less able to distribute negative charge and is slightly less stable than that of an aldehyde. Thus aldehydes are slightly more acidic than ketones. This same property makes aldehydes more reactive than ketones. Both aldehydes and ketones are less acidic than alcohols. Any electron withdrawing groups attached to the α-carbon or the carbonyl tend to stabilize the conjugate base and thus increase acidity.

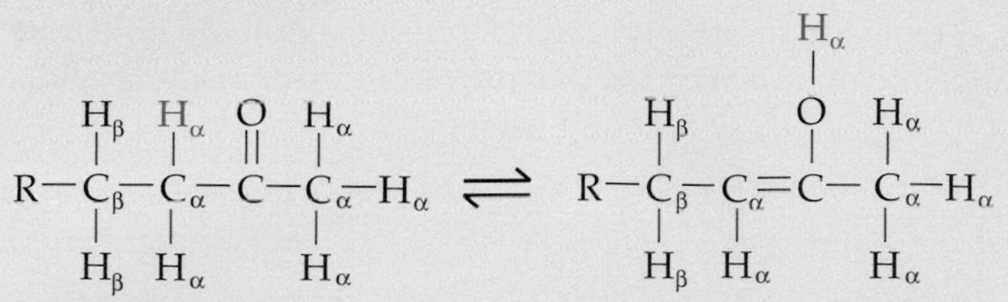

**Keto-enol tautomerization
is a reaction at equilibrium
and NOT a resonance.**

Due to the properties of the α-hydrogen and carbonyl, ketones and aldehydes exist at room temperature as enol **tautomers**. Tautomerization involves a proton shift, in this case from the α-carbon position to the carbonyl oxygen position. Both tautomers exist at room temperature, but the ketone or aldehyde tautomer is usually favored. Tautomerization is a reaction at equilibrium, not a resonance. (Remember, in resonance structures atoms don't move and neither resonance structure actually exists.)

There are other forms of tautomerization but keto-enol tautomerization is the most likely form to be tested on the MCAT. In order to recognize other forms, simply watch for the proton shift in equilibrium.

Aldehydes and ketones react with alcohols to form *hemiacetals* and *hemiketals*, respectively. In this reaction the alcohols react in typical fashion as the nucleophile. When aldehydes and ketones are attacked by a nucleophile, they undergo addition. Aldehydes and hemiacetals, and ketones and hemiketals, exist in equilibrium when an aldehyde or ketone is dissolved in an alcohol; however, usually the hemiacetal or hemiketal is too unstable to isolate unless it exists as a ring structure. If a second molar equivalent of alcohol is added, an *acetal* is formed from a hemiacetal, or a *ketal* is formed from a hemiketal.

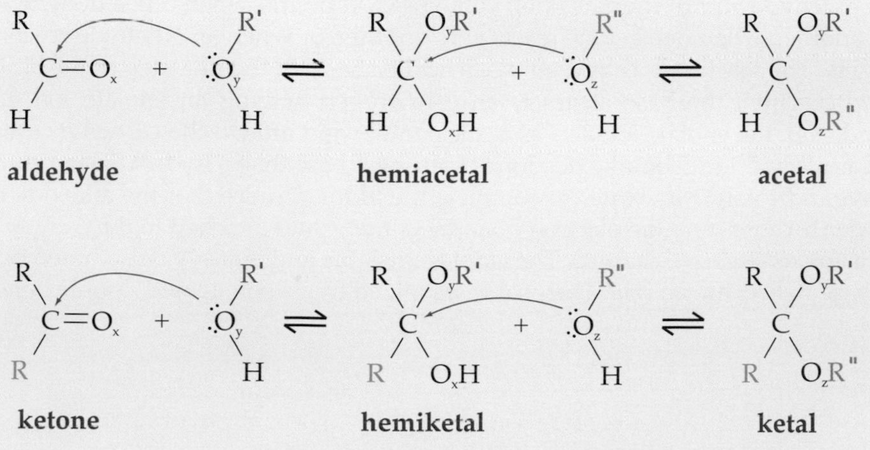

3-5
Formation of Acetals

aldehyde   hemiacetal   acetal

ketone   hemiketal   ketal

The aldehyde products can be easily distinguished from the ketone products by the lone hydrogen. The hemi products can be distinguished from the acetals and ketals because the hemi products both have alcohols while the full acetals and ketals don't. Hemi formation is catalyzed by acid or base. In formation of acetal and ketal from the hemi forms the hydroxyl group must be protonated to make a good leaving group, thus this part of the reaction is catalyzed by acid only.

Because acetals and ketals are unreactive toward bases, they are often used as *blocking groups*. In other words, a base would typically act as a nucleophile to attack an aldehyde or ketone at the carbonyl carbon, but the aldehyde or ketone can be temporarily changed to an acetal or ketal to prevent it from reacting with a base.

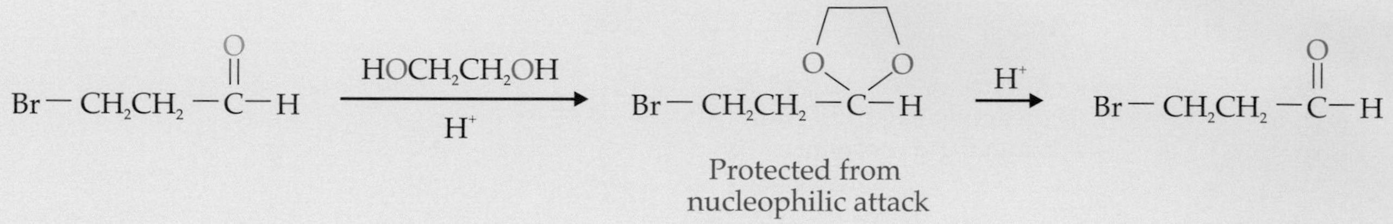

Protected from
nucleophilic attack

In a similar reaction, when aldehydes or ketones are dissolved in aqueous solution, they establish an equilibrium with their hydrate, a geminal diol.

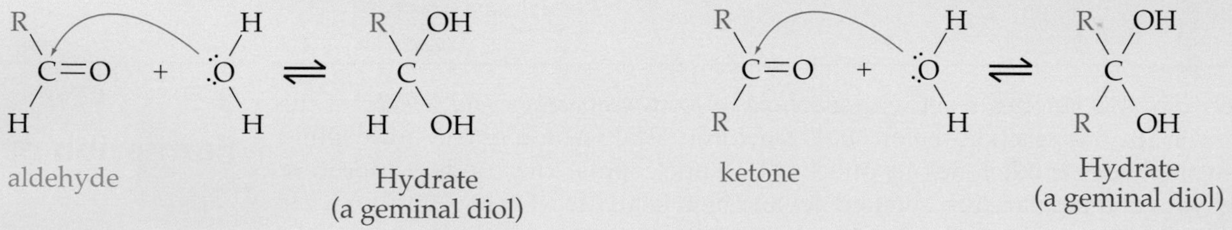

| aldehyde | | Hydrate (a geminal diol) | ketone | | Hydrate (a geminal diol) |

3-6
Aldol Condensation

Aldol condensation is a favorite on the MCAT because it demonstrates both α-hydrogen activity and the susceptibility of carbonyl carbons to a nucleophile. *Aldol* (ald from aldehyde and ol from alcohol) condensation occurs when one aldehyde reacts with another, when one ketone reacts with another, or when an aldehyde reacts with a ketone. The reaction is catalyzed by an acid or base. In the first step of the base-catalyzed reaction, the base abstracts an α-hydrogen leaving an enolate ion. In the second step, the enolate ion acts as a nucleophile and attacks the carbonyl carbon to form an *alkoxide* ion. The alkoxide ion is a stronger base than a hydroxide ion and thus removes a proton from water to complete the aldol. (Notice that the alkoxide ion is stronger because it has an electron donating alkyl group attached to the oxygen, thus increasing its negative charge.) The aldol is unstable and is easily dehydrated by heat or a base to become an *enal*. The enal is stabilized by its conjugated double bonds.

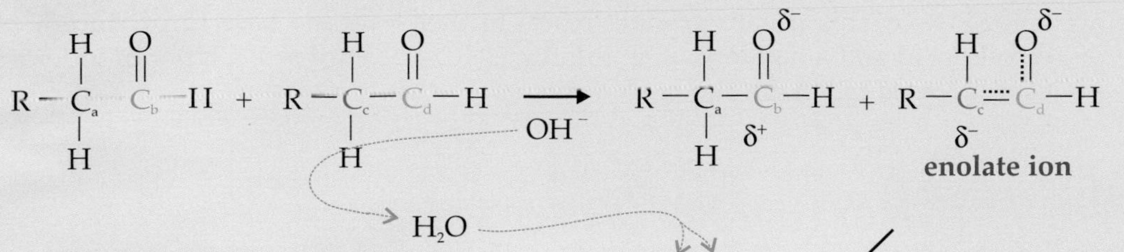

The first part of this reaction is technically called aldol addition but is sometimes referred to as aldol condensation. The aldol to enal step is actually the condensation part of the reaction and almost always accompanies aldol addition. Although complicated, this reaction is easy to remember if you keep in mind the acidity of the a-hydrogens and the planar configuration of the carbonyl, which makes it susceptible to nucleophilic attack. You must know this reaction for the MCAT.

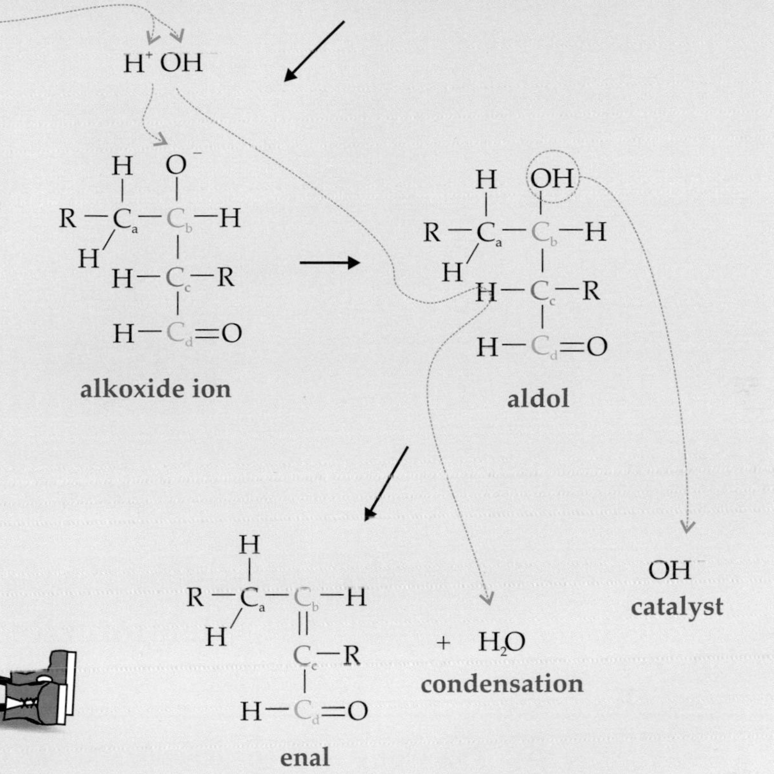

Halogens add to ketones at the alpha carbon in the presence of a base or an acid. When a base is used, it is dfficult to prevent halogenation at more than one of the alpha positions. The base is also consumed by the reaction with water as a by-product, whereas the acid acts as a true catalyst and is not consumed.

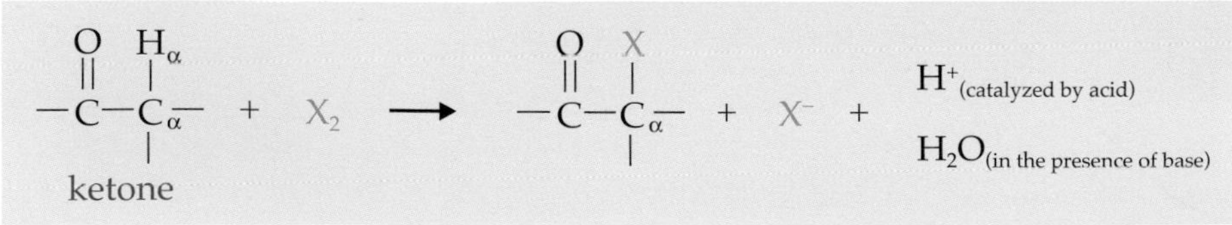

3-7
Halogenation and the Haloform Reaction

When a base is used with a methyl ketone, the alpha carbon will become completely halogenated. This trihalo product reacts further with the base to produce a carboxylic acid and a haloform (chloroform, $CHCl_3$; bromoform, $CHBr_3$; or iodoform, CHI_3). This is called the Haloform Reaction.

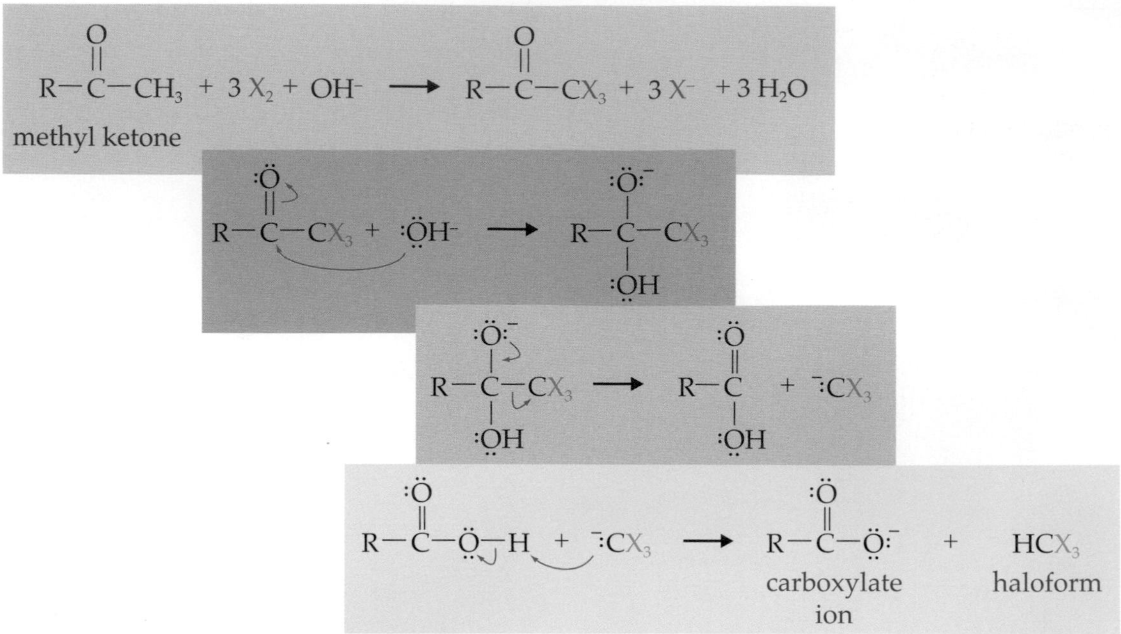

Haloform Reaction

3-8
The Wittig Reaction

The Wittig reaction converts a ketone to an alkene. A phosphorous ylide (pronounced "ill' -id") is used. An ylide is a neutral molecule with a negatively charged carbanion.

The ketone behaves in its normal fashion, first undergoing nucleophilic addition from the ylide to form a betaine (pronounced "bay' -tuh-ene"). However, the betaine is unstable and quickly breaks down to a triphenylphosphine oxide and the alkene. When possible, a mixture of both cis and trans isomers are formed by the Wittig reaction.

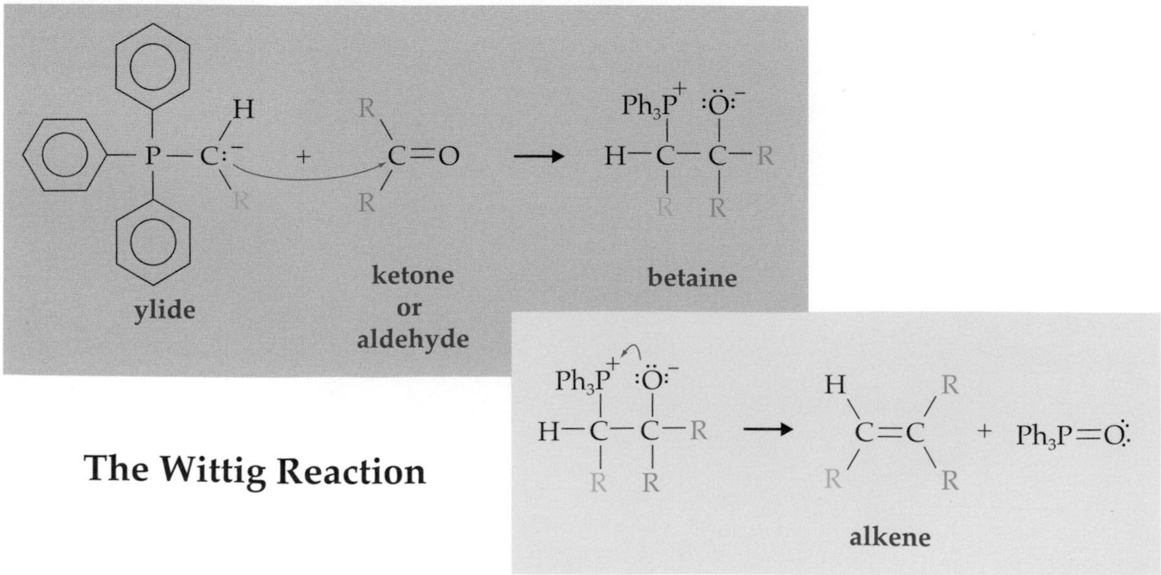

The Wittig Reaction

A carbonyl compound with a double bond between the α and β carbon has some special properties. As mentioned above, its carbocation is stabilized by resonance. The electron withdrawing carbonyl pulls electrons from the double bond and makes it less susceptible to electrophilic addition. Thus, rather than the electrophile adding to the double bonded carbon, it may sometimes add to the oxygen, forming the enol-keto tautomers.

Even more strange is the ability of the β-carbon to undergo nucleophilic addition directly. This is sometimes called *conjugate addition*.

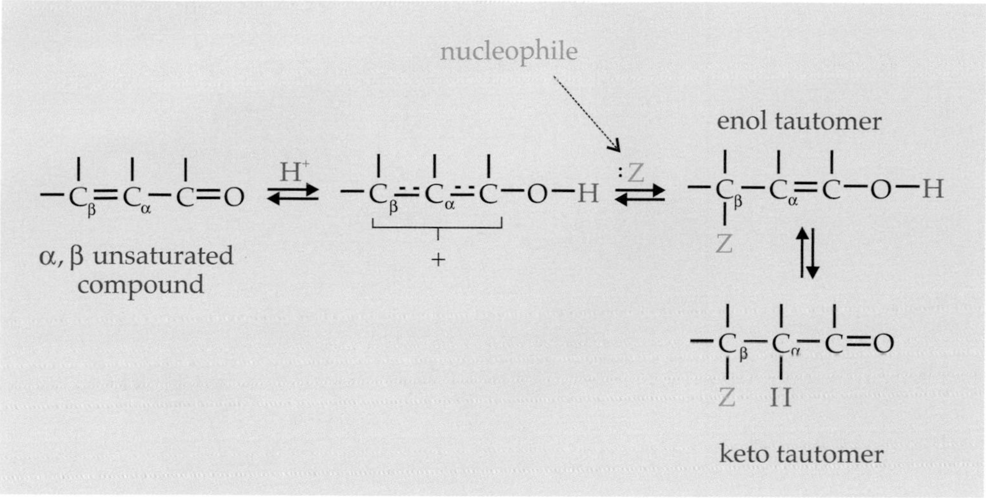

3-9
α–β Unsaturated Carbonyls

Of course, we know that aldehydes and ketones undergo nucleophilic addition at the carbonyl, and for many nucleophiles this carbonyl addition is still the major product in the above reaction.

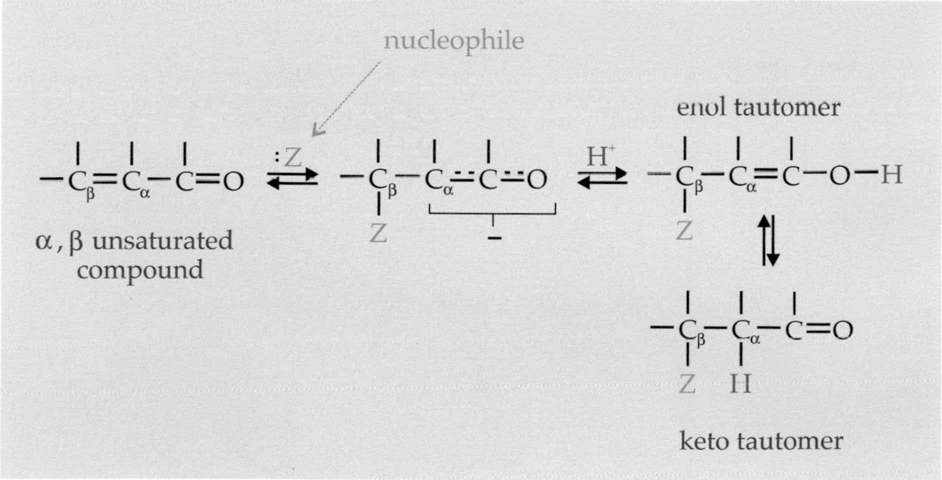

49. What is the major product of the crossed aldol reaction shown below?

$$C_6H_5\overset{O}{\overset{\|}{C}}H \ + \ CH_3CH_2\overset{O}{\overset{\|}{C}}H \xrightarrow[10\,°C]{OH^-}$$

A.

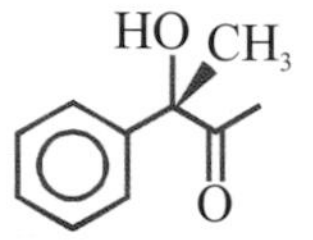

C.

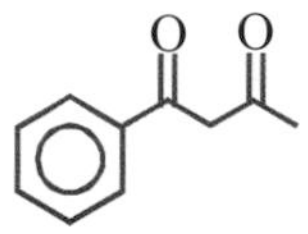

B.

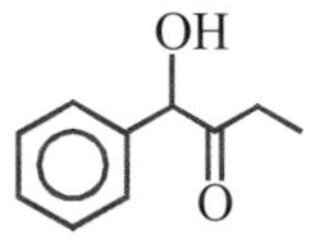

D.

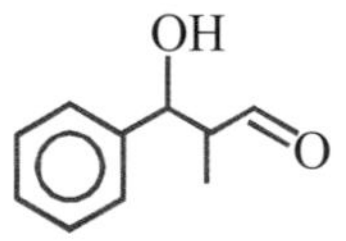

50. Which of the following statements are true concerning the molecule shown below?

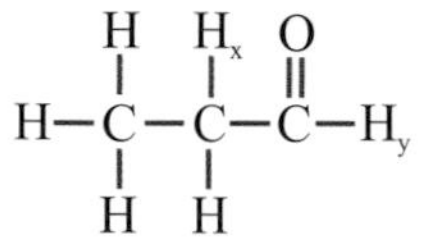

$$H-\underset{\underset{H}{|}}{\overset{\overset{H}{|}}{C}}-\underset{\underset{H}{|}}{\overset{\overset{H_x}{|}}{C}}-\overset{\overset{O}{\|}}{C}-H_y$$

   I. H_x is more acidic than H_y.
   II. H_y is more acidic than H_x.
   III. This molecule typically undergoes nucleophilic substitution.

   A. I only
   B. II only
   C. I and III only
   D. II and III only

51. Which of the following is the product of an aldehyde reduction reaction?

A.

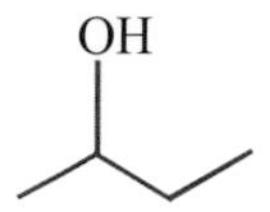

C.

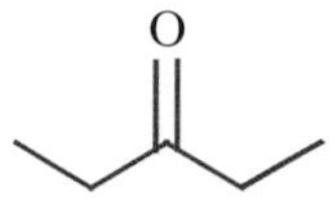

B.

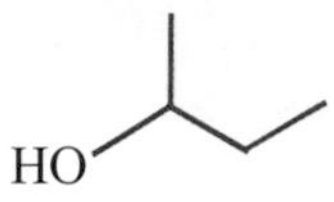

D.

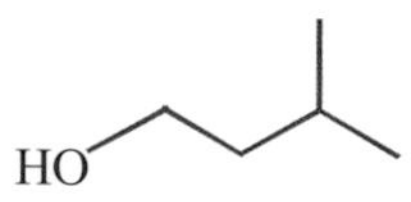

52. If the first step were omitted in the following set of reactions, what would be the final product?

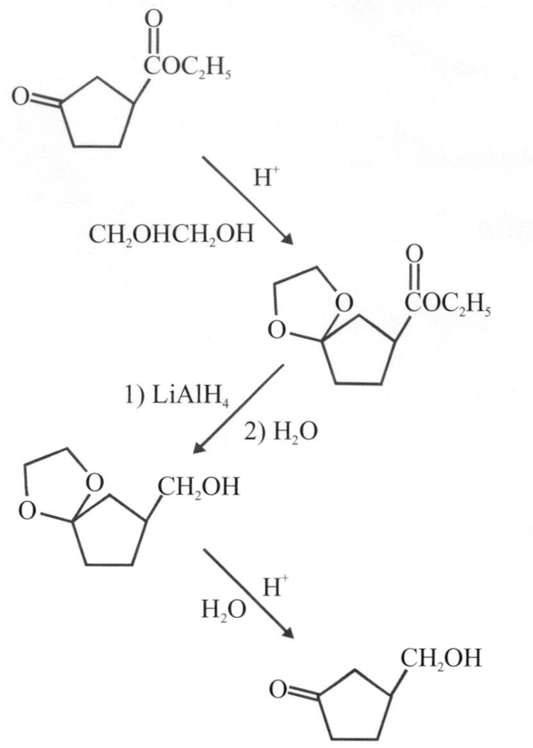

A.

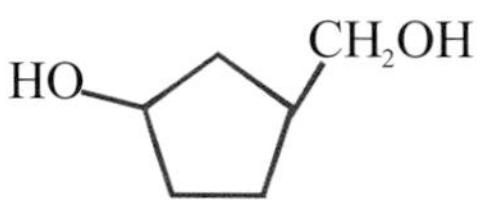

C.

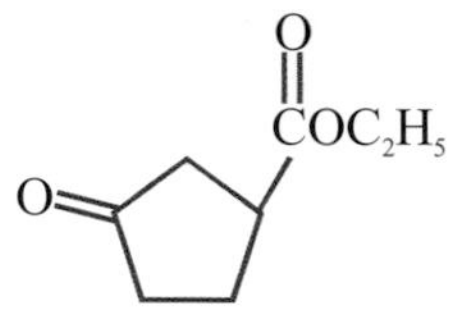

B.

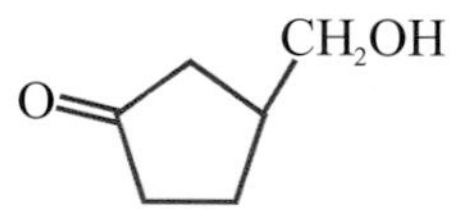

D.

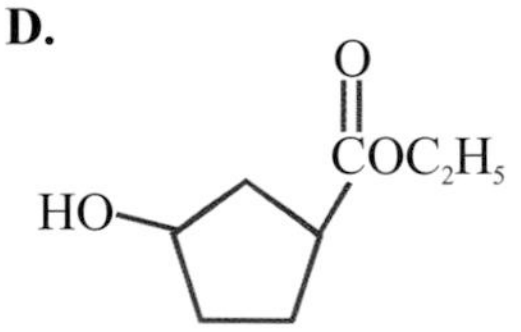

53. Which of the following is the strongest acid?

A.

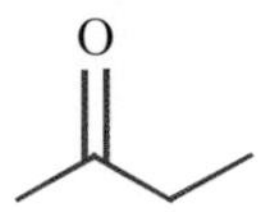

C.

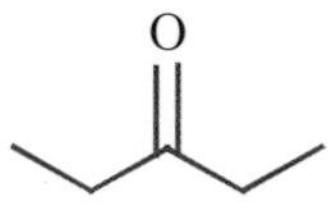

B.

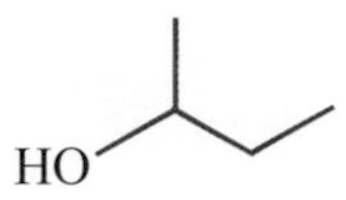

D.

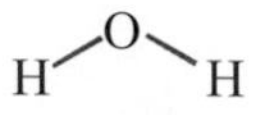

54. Aldehydes are readily oxidized to yield carboxylic acids, but ketones are inert to oxidation. Which is the most likely explanation regarding this difference in reactivity?

   A.   Aldehydes have a proton attached to the carbonyl that is abstracted during oxidation. Ketones lack this proton and so cannot be oxidized.

   B.   Reducing agents like HNO_3 are sterically hindered by ketone's carbonyl carbon.

   C.   Aldehydes and ketones are of similar hybridization.

   D.   The rate of the forward oxidation reaction is equal to the rate of the reverse reduction reaction in ketones.

55. 1,3-cyclohexane dione is shown below.

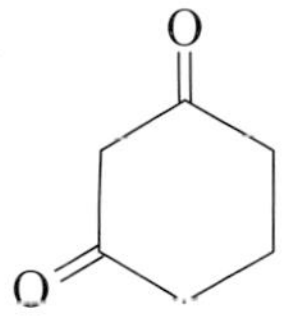

[1,3 cyclohexane dione]

Which of the following is not a tautomer of 1,3-cyclohexane dione?

   A.   **C.**

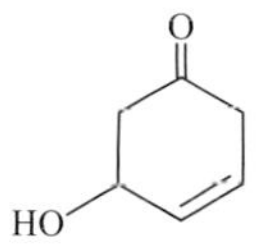

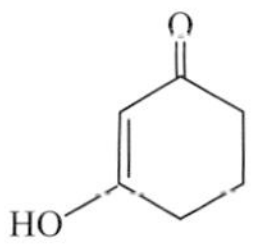

   B. 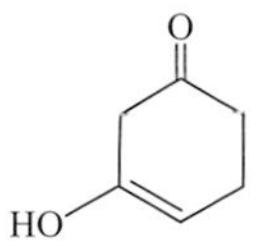   **D.**

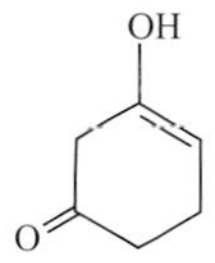

56. Glucose reduces Tollens reagent to give an aldonic acid, ammonia, water, and a silver mirror. Methyl β-glucoside does not reduce Tollens reagent. Based on the structures shown below, which of the following best explains why methyl β-glucoside gives a negative Tollens test?

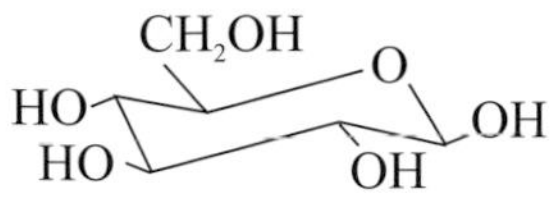

Glucose 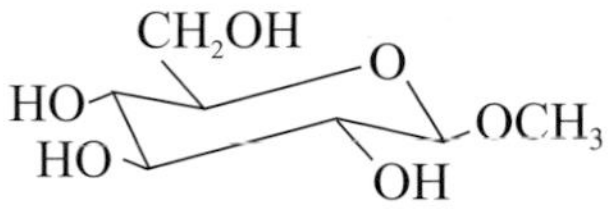   methyl β-glucoside

   A.   Aldehydes are not oxidized by Tollens reagent.

   B.   Ketones are not oxidized by Tollens reagent.

   C.   Hemiacetal rings are stable and do not easily open to form straight chain aldehydes.

   D.   Acetal rings are stable and do not easily open to form straight chain aldehydes.

STOP.

3-10
Carboxylic Acids

You should be able to recognize and give the common name for the two simplest **carboxylic acids** shown below.

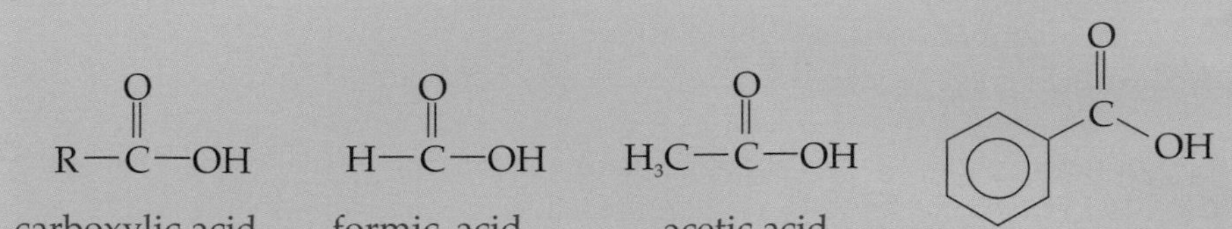

carboxylic acid   formic acid   acetic acid
                       (methanoic acid)   (ethanoic acid)   benzoic acid

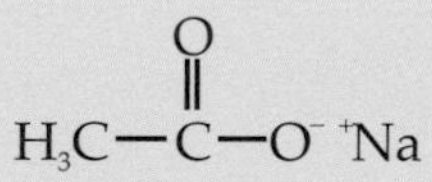

Carboxylic acids where the R group is an alkyl group are called *aliphatic acids*. The salts of carboxylic acids are named with the suffix *-ate*. The *-ate* replaces the *-ic* (or *-oic* in IUPAC names), so that "acetic" becomes "acetate". (Acetate is sometimes abbreviated –OAc.) In IUPAC rules, the carbonyl carbon of a carboxylic acid takes priority over all groups discussed so far.

Sodium acetate
(sodium ethanoate)
A salt of acetic acid.

On the MCAT, look for carboxylic acid to behave as an acid or as the substrate in a **nucleophilic substitution reaction**. Like any carbonyl compound, its stereochemistry makes it susceptible to nucleophiles. When the hydroxyl group is protonated, the good leaving group, water, is formed and substitution results.

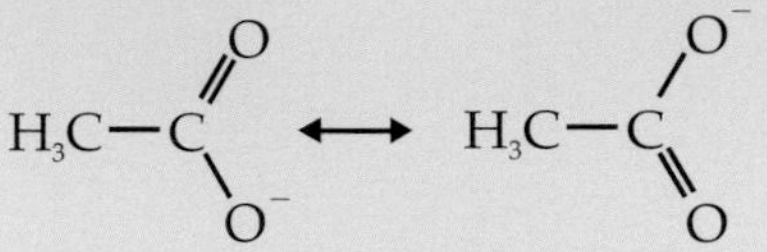

Resonance stabilization
of a carboxylate ion

As far as organic acids go, carboxylic acids are very strong. When the proton is removed, the conjugate base is stabilized by resonance.

Electron withdrawing groups on the α-carbon help to further stabilize the conjugate base and thus increase the acidity of the corresponding carboxylic acid.

3-11
Physical Properties

Carboxylic acids are able to make strong double **hydrogen bonds** to form a dimer. The dimer significantly increases the boiling point of carboxylic acids by effectively doubling the molecular weight of the molecules leaving the liquid phase. Saturated carboxylic acids with more than 8 carbons are generally solids. The double bonds in unsaturated carboxylic acids impede the crystal lattice and lower melting point.

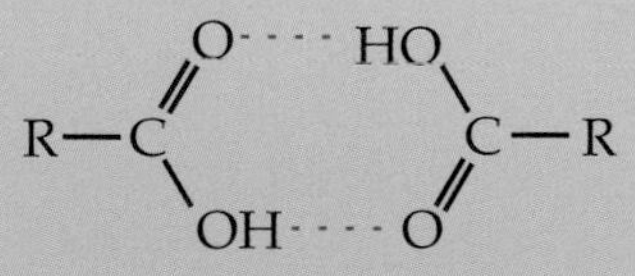

Hydrogen bonded dimer

Carboxylic acids with four carbons or less are water soluble. Carboxylic acids with more than 10 carbons are not. Carboxylic acids are soluble in most nonpolar solvents because the dimer form allows the carboxylic acid to solvate without disrupting the hydrogen bonds of the dimer.

When a carboxylic acid loses CO_2 the reaction is called **decarboxylation**. Although the reaction is usually exothermic, the energy of activation is usually high, making the reaction difficult to carry out. The energy of activation is lowered when the β-carbon is a carbonyl because either the anion intermediate is stabilized by resonance or the acid forms a more stable cyclic intermediate. (A carboxylic acid with a carbonyl β-carbon is called a *β-keto acid*.)

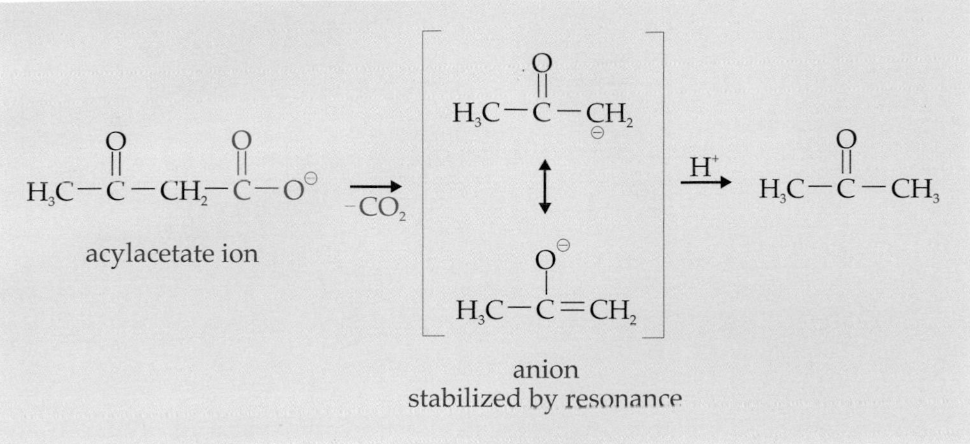

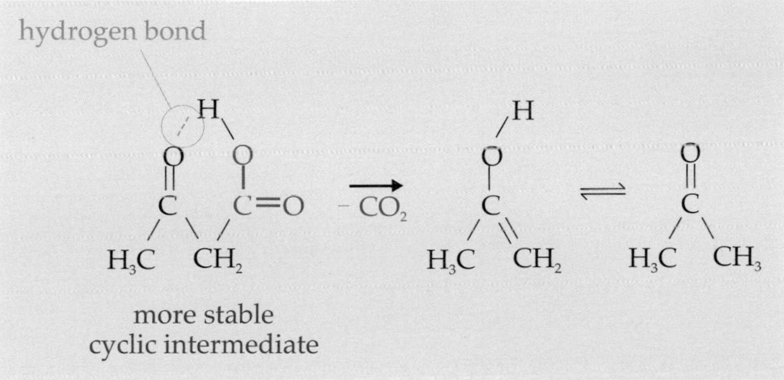

3-12
Decarboxylation

acylacetate ion

anion
stabilized by resonance

hydrogen bond

more stable
cyclic intermediate

Notice that the first reaction starts with the anion and the second reaction starts with the acid. Notice also that the final products of both reactions are tautomers.

Derivatives of carboxylic acids contain the *acyl* group.

Inorganic acid chlorides like $SOCl_2$, PCl_3, and PCl_5 each react with carboxylic acids by nucleophilic substitution to form *acyl chlorides* (also called acid chlorides).

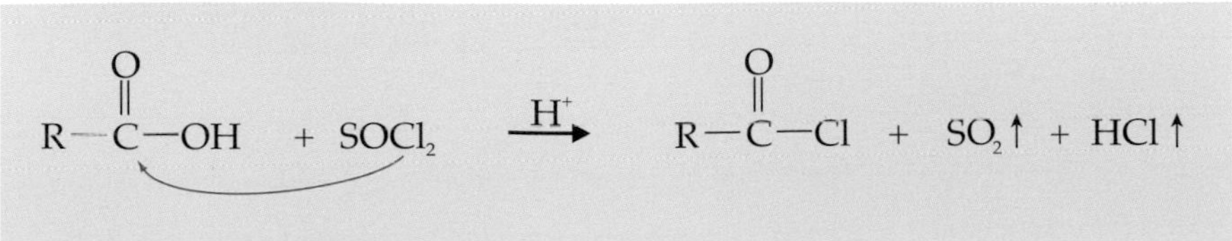

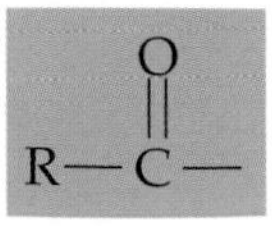

3-13
Carboxylic Acid Derivatives

$$R-\overset{\overset{O}{\parallel}}{C}-OH \ + \ SOCl_2 \ \xrightarrow{H^+} \ R-\overset{\overset{O}{\parallel}}{C}-Cl \ + \ SO_2\uparrow \ + \ HCl\uparrow$$

acyl group

Acyl chlorides are Bronsted-Lowry acids, and, just like aldehydes, they donate an α-hydrogen. The electron withdrawing chlorine stabilizes the conjugate base more than the lone hydrogen of an aldehyde, making acyl chlorides significantly stronger acids than aldehydes.

Acid chlorides are the most reactive of the carboxylic acid derivatives because of the stability of the Cl^- leaving group.

Acid chlorides are the most reactive of the carboxylic acid derivatives. Acid chlorides love nucleophiles.

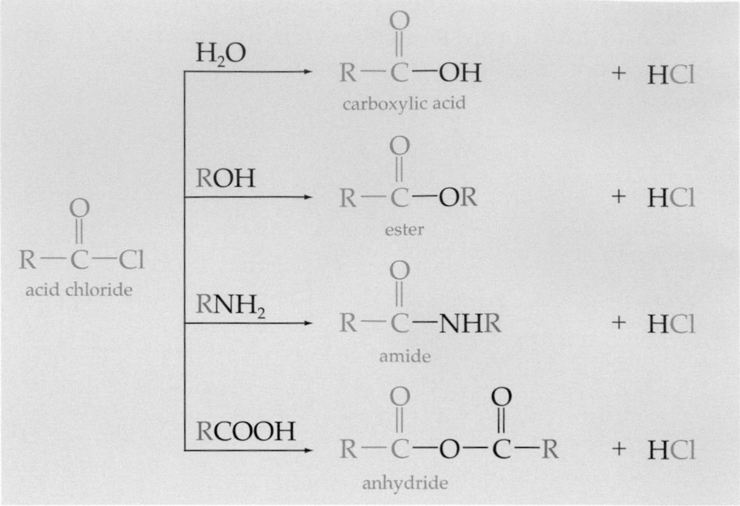

All carboxylic acid derivatives hydrolyze to give the carboxylic acid. Typically, hydrolysis can occur under either acidic or basic conditions.

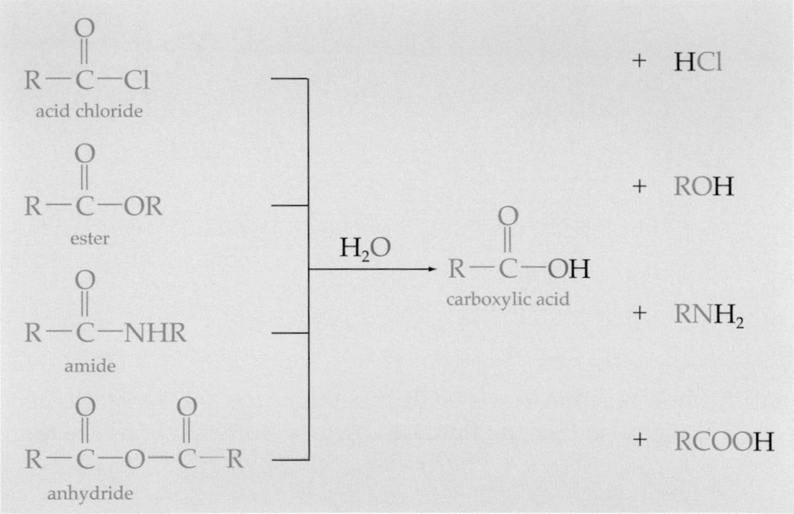

Alcohols react with carboxylic acids through nucleophilic substitution to form **esters**. A strong acid catalyzes the reaction by protonating the hydroxyl group on the carboxylic acid.

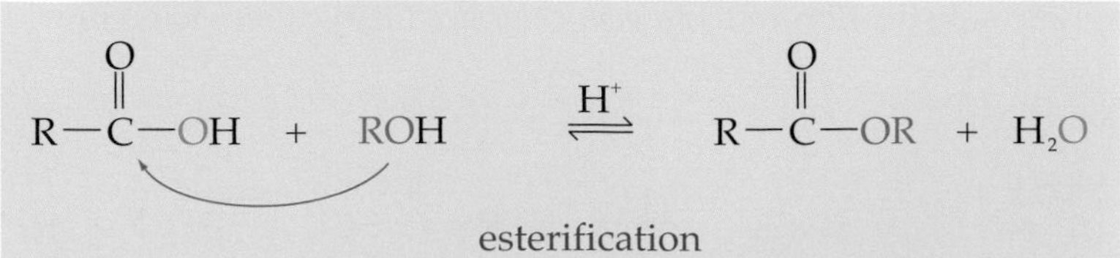

esterification

The yield in this reaction can be adjusted in accordance with LeChatlier's principle by adding water or alcohol. A more effective method for preparing esters is to use an anhydride instead of a carboxylic acid in the above reaction.

Alcohols react in a similar way with esters in a reaction called **transesterification**, where one alkoxy group is substituted for another. An equilibrium results in this reaction as well, where the result can be controlled by adding an excess of the alcohol in the product or the reactant.

Transesterification is just trading alkoxy groups on an ester.

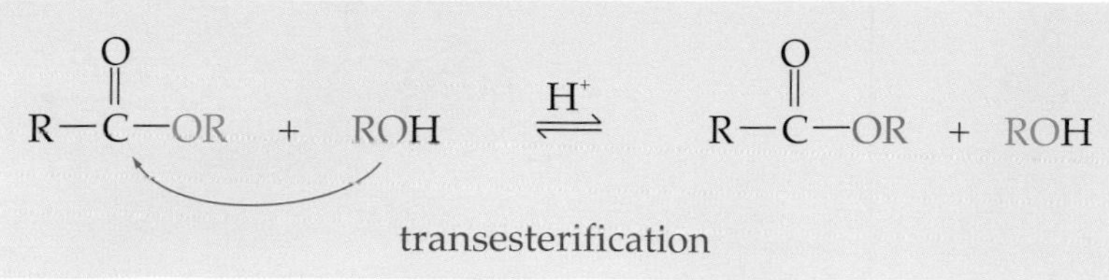

transesterification

Once again, you should watch for the β-dicarbonyl compounds, which increase the acidity of the alpha hydrogens between the carbonyls. Specifically, with esters you have acetoacetic ester. **Acetoacetic ester synthesis** is the production of a ketone from acetoacetic ester due to the strongly acidic properties of the alpha hydrogen. A base is added to remove the alpha hydrogens. The resulting enolate ion is alkylated by an alkyl halide or tosylate leaving the alkylacetoacetic ester. Alkyacetoacetic ester is a β-keto ester that can be decarboxylated by the addition of acid. The acetoacetic ester synthesis is finished with the decarboxylation leaving the ketone.

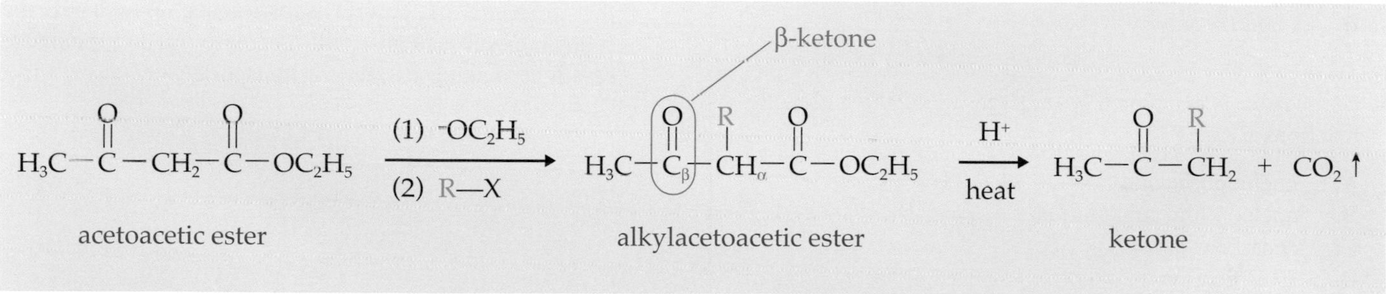

Acetoacetic ester synthesis

Amides are formed when an **amine**, acting as a nucleophile, substitutes at the carbonyl of a carboxylic acid or one of its derivatives. (Amines are discussed in the next section of this lecture.)

In all of the reactions with carboxylic acid derivatives, the carbonyl carbon is acting as the substrate in nucleophilic substitution. Rather than memorize all these reactions, you should remember that carboxylic acids

Many of these reactions are reversible, but equilibrium will prefer the more stable products. In other words, since a strong base makes a poor leaving group, the equilibrium will favor the formation of the compound whose leaving group is a stronger base. This explains the order of reactivity of carboxylic acid derivatives.

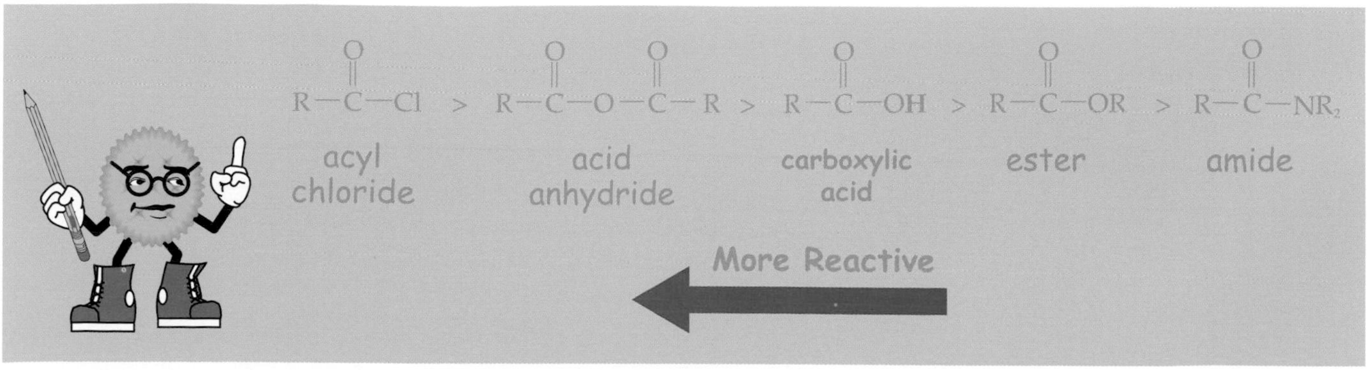

More Reactive

57. All of the following can form hydrogen bonds with water EXCEPT:

    A. aldehydes
    B. carboxylic acids
    C. ethers
    D. alkenes

58. Which of the following are products when an alcohol is added to a carboxylic acid in the presence of a strong acid?

    I. water
    II. ester
    III. aldehyde

    A. I only
    B. II only
    C. I and II only
    D. I and III only

59. Carboxylic acids typically undergo all of the following reactions EXCEPT:

    A. nucleophilic addition
    B. nucleophilic substitution
    C. decarboxylation
    D. esterification

60. Which of the following will most easily react with an amine to form an amide?

    A. acyl chloride
    B. ester
    C. carboxylic acid
    D. acid anhydride

61. Which of the following compounds will result in a positive haloform reaction, which only occurs with methyl ketones?

    A. $CH_3C\equiv N$
    B. $C_6H_5COCH_3$
    C. CH_3CH_2CHO
    D. CH_3CH_2COOH

62. Phthalic anhydride reacts with two equivalents of ammonia to form ammonium phthalamate. One equivalent is washed away in an acid bath to form phthalamic acid.

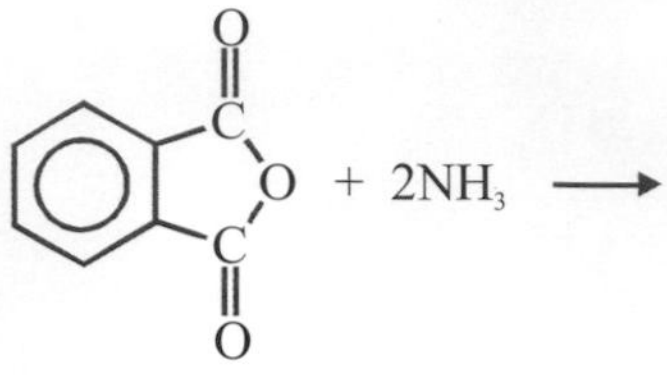

Phthalic anhydride

What two functional groups are created in phthalamic acid?

    A. a carboxylic acid and an amide
    B. a carboxylic acid and a ketone
    C. a carboxylic acid and an aldehyde
    D. an aldehyde and an amide

63. The normal reactivity of methyl benzoate is affected by the presence of certain substituents. Which of the following substituents will decrease methyl benzoate reactivity making it safer for transport?

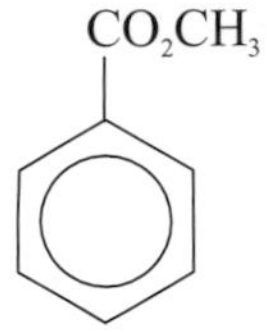

CO_2CH_3

[Methyl benzoate]

    A. NO_2
    B. hydrogen
    C. Br
    D. CH_3

64. When mildly heated with aqueous base or acid, nitriles are hydrolyzed to amides. What may be the product of hydrolysis under stronger conditions?

    A. aldehyde
    B. ketone
    C. ester
    D. carboxylic acid

Amines are derivatives of **ammonia**. You should be able to identify ammonia and all types of amines.

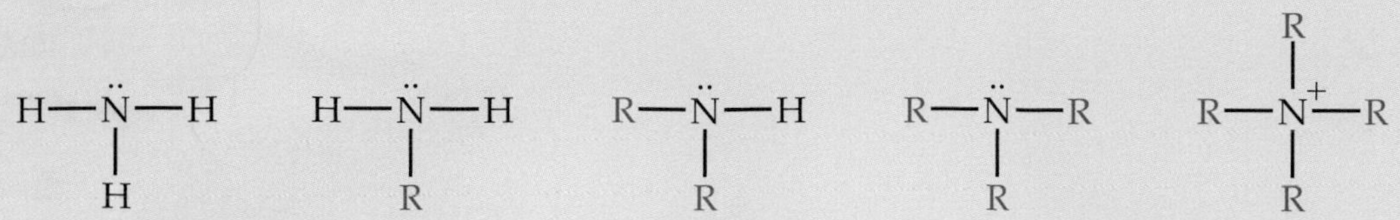

3-14

Amines

$$
\text{H}\overset{\overset{\displaystyle ..}{}}{\underset{\underset{\displaystyle \text{H}}{|}}{\text{N}}}\text{H} \qquad \text{H}\overset{\overset{\displaystyle ..}{}}{\underset{\underset{\displaystyle \text{R}}{|}}{\text{N}}}\text{H} \qquad \text{R}\overset{\overset{\displaystyle ..}{}}{\underset{\underset{\displaystyle \text{R}}{|}}{\text{N}}}\text{H} \qquad \text{R}\overset{\overset{\displaystyle ..}{}}{\underset{\underset{\displaystyle \text{R}}{|}}{\text{N}}}\text{R} \qquad \text{R}\overset{\overset{\displaystyle \text{R}}{|}}{\underset{\underset{\displaystyle \text{R}}{|}}{\overset{+}{\text{N}}}}\text{R}
$$

ammonia primary amine secondary amine tertiary amine quaternary amine

Notice that **nitrogen can take three or four bonds**. When nitrogen takes four bonds it has a positive charge. Also notice the lone pair of electrons on nitrogen. When you see nitrogen on the MCAT and it has only three bonds, you should draw in the lone pair of electrons immediately. On the MCAT, there are three important considerations when dealing with nitrogen containing compounds:

1. they may act as a Lewis base donating their lone pair of electrons;

2. they may act as a nucleophile where the lone pair of electrons attacks a positive charge; and

3. nitrogen can take on a fourth bond.

Ammonia and **amines act as weak bases** by donating their lone pair of electrons. Electron withdrawing substituents decrease the basicity of an amine whereas electron donating substituents increase the basicity of an amine. However, steric hindrance created by bulky functional groups tends to hinder the ability of an amine to donate its lone pair, thus decreasing its basicity. For the MCAT you should know this general trend of amine basicity from highest to lowest when the functional groups are electron donating: 2°, 1°, ammonia.

Aromatic amines (amines attached directly to a benzene ring) are much weaker bases than nonaromatic amines because the electron pair can delocalize around the benzene ring. Substituents that withdraw electrons from the benzene ring will further weaken the aromatic amine.

Since amines like to donate their negative electrons, they tend to stabilize carbocations when they are part of the same molecule.

3-15

Physical Properties

Given the shape of amines we might expect some secondary and tertiary amines to be optically active. However, at room temperature the lone pair of electrons moves very rapidly (as many as 2×10^{11} times per second in ammonia) from one side of the molecule to the other, inverting the configuration. Thus each chiral molecule spends equal time as both its enantiomers. If we imagine that the tertiary amine drawn above is rapidly inverting, it becomes easier to appreciate the manner in which large substituents sterically hinder the electrons.

Ammonia, primary amines, and secondary amines can **hydrogen bond** with each other. All amines can hydrogen bond with water. This makes the lower molecular weight amines very soluble in water. Amines with comparable molecular weights have higher boiling points than alkanes but lower boiling points than alcohols.

Don't become confused by memorizing too much detail about the physical properties of ammonia and amines. For the MCAT, just keep in mind that ammonia and amines hydrogen bond, which raises boiling point and increases solubility.

3-16
Condensation with Ketones

Amines react with aldehydes and ketones losing water to produce **imines** and **enamines**. (Substituted imines are sometimes called *Schiff bases*.) In this reaction the amine acts as a nucleophile, attacking the electron deficient carbonyl carbon of the ketones. As expected, the ketone undergoes nucleophilic addition. An acid catalyst protonates the product to form an unstable intermediate. The intermediate loses water and a proton to produce either an enamine or an imine. If the original amine is secondary (2°), it has no proton to give up, so the ketone must give up its alpha proton. As a result, an enamine is produced. If the original amine is primary (1°), it gives up its proton to form an imine.

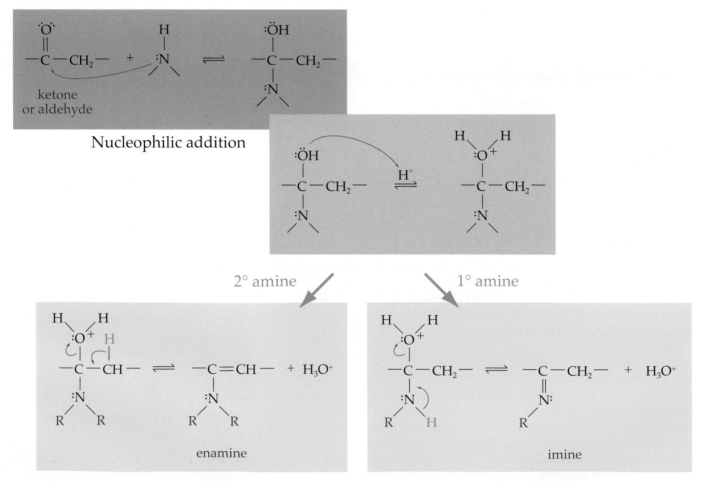

Nucleophilic addition

2° amine   1° amine

enamine   imine

Dehydration   Dehydration

Note that if too much acid is used in this reaction, the amine will become protonated before the first step. The protonated amine will have a positive charge and become a poor nucleophile, preventing the first step of the reaction from going forward.

The imine product shown exists as a tautomer with its corresponding enamine.

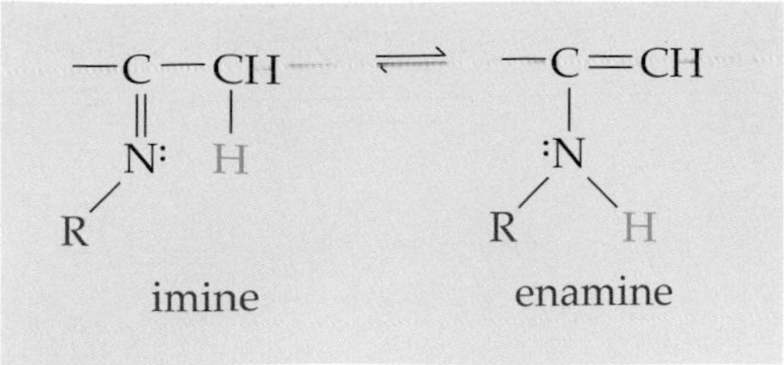

Tautomerization

It is possible to replace the oxygen of a ketone or aldehyde with two hydrogens by adding hot acid in the presence of amalgamated zinc (zinc treated with mercury); however, some ketones and aldehydes may not be able to survive such a treatment. For these ketones and aldehydes, the **Wolff-Kishner Reduction** may be used. The first step of the Wolff-Kishner Reduction follows the same mechanism as imine formation shown on the previous page only a hydrazine is used rather than an amine. The addition of hydrazine to the ketone or aldehyde produces a hydrozone by nucleophilic addition. A hot strong base is added to the hydrazone to deprotanate the nitrogen and produce the desired product with water and nitrogen gas as by products. A high-boiling solvent is usually used to facilitate the high temperature.

3-17 Wolff-Kishner Reduction

The Wolff-Kishner Reduction does nothing more than reduce a ketone or aldehyde by removing the oxygen and replacing it with two hydrogens. You can do the same thing by adding hot acid to a ketone or aldehyde, but some ketones and aldehydes can't survive the hot acid. That's where the Wolff-Kishner Reduction comes in.

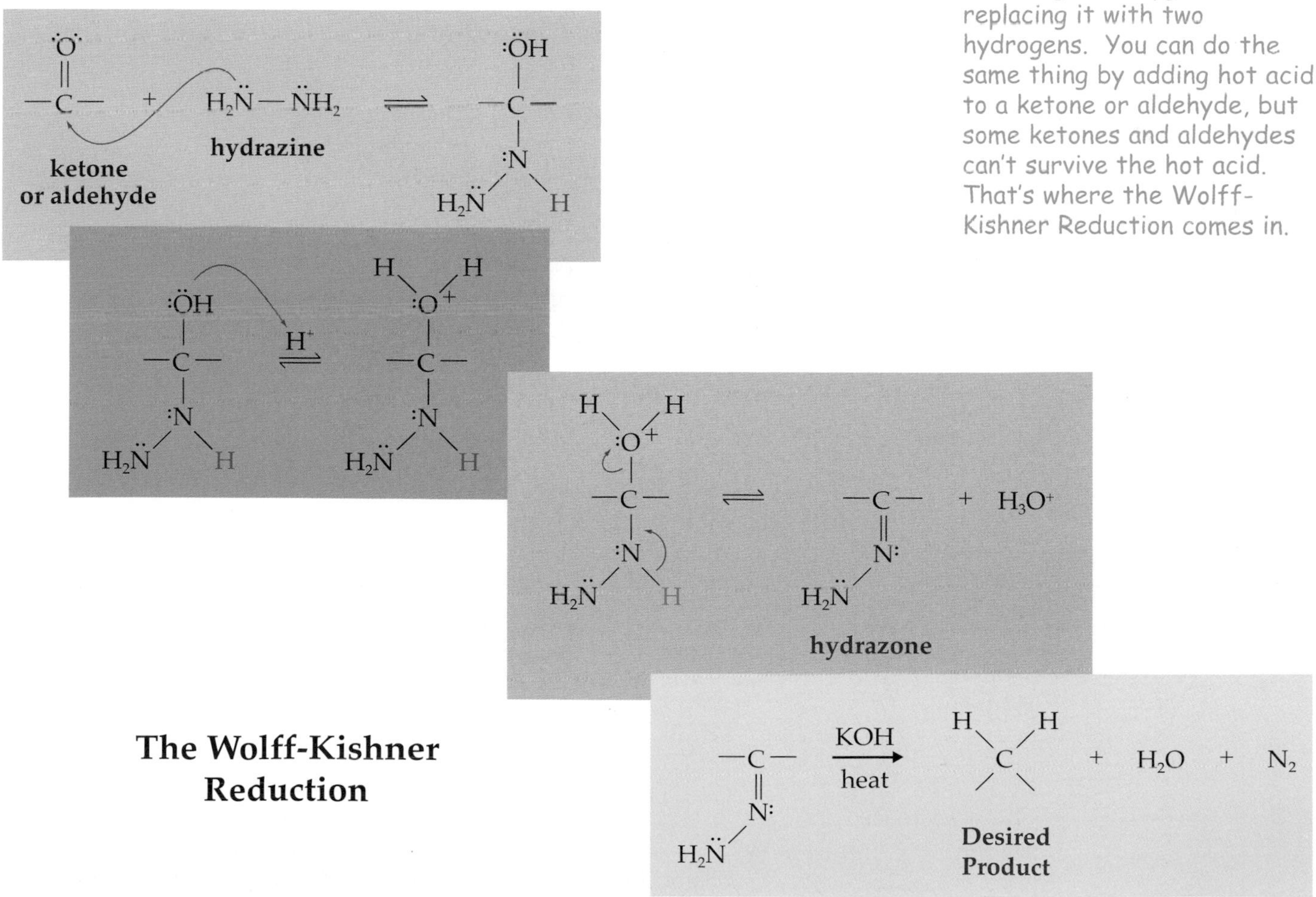

The Wolff-Kishner Reduction

3-18
Alkylation and the Hofmann Elimination

Amines can be alkylated with alkylhalides.

$$NH_3 \quad + \quad R-X \quad \longrightarrow \quad RNH_2 \quad + \quad HX$$

$$NRH_2 \quad + \quad R-X \quad \longrightarrow \quad R_2NH \quad + \quad HX$$

$$NR_2H \quad + \quad R-X \quad \longrightarrow \quad R_3N \quad + \quad HX$$

$$NR_3 \quad + \quad R-X \quad \longrightarrow \quad R_4N^+ \quad + \quad X^-$$

This is a nucleophilic substitution reaction with the amine acting as a nucleophile.

As a leaving group, an amino group would be $^-NH_2$, so amino groups are very poor leaving groups. However, an amino group can be converted to a quaternary ammonium salt by repeated alkylations. The quaternary ammonium salt is an excellent leaving group.

The elimination of a quarternary ammonium salt usually follows an E2 mechanism requiring a strong base. The quarternary alkyl halide, typically an ammonium iodide, is converted to a quarternary ammonium hydroxide using silver oxide.

$$R-\overset{+}{N}(CH_3)_3{}^-I \quad + \quad \tfrac{1}{2}Ag_2O \quad + \quad H_2O \quad \longrightarrow \quad R-\overset{+}{N}(CH_3)_3{}^-OH \quad + \quad AgI\downarrow$$

Heating the quarternary ammonium hydroxide results in the **Hofmann elimination** to form an alkene.

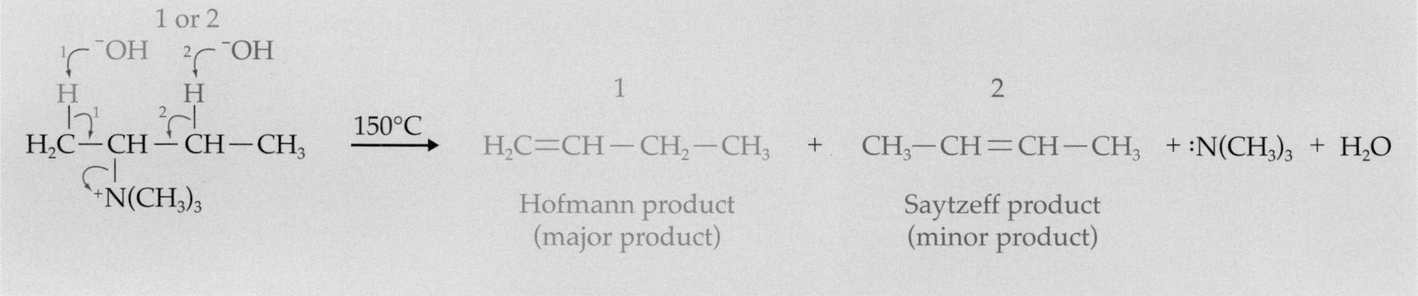

The Hofmann Elimination

Notice that the LEAST stable alkene is the major product in the Hofmann elimination, called the Hofmann product.

3-19
Amines and Nitrous Acid

Nitrous acid is a weak acid. A strong acid can dehydrate nitrous acid to produce nitrosonium ion and water.

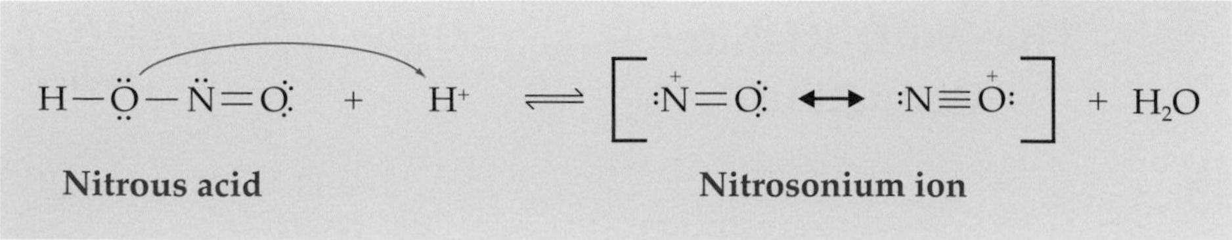

Nitrous acid   **Nitrosonium ion**

Most reactions with amines and nitrous acid involve the nitrosonium ion.

Primary amines react with nitrous acid to form *diazonium salts*. Aliphatic (nonaromatic) amines form extremely unstable salts that decompose spontaneously to form nitrogen gas. Aromatic amines also form unstable diazonium salts, but at temperatures below 5°C they decompose very slowly.

The reaction, called **diazotization of an amine** goes as follows. Nitrous acid is protonated by a strong acid to form the nitrosonium ion. Nitrosonium ion reacts with the primary amine to form *N*-nitrosoammonium, an unstable compound. *N*-nitrosoammonium deprotonates to form *N*-nitrosoamine. *N*-nitrosoamine tautomerizes to diazenol. In the presence of acid, diazenol dehydrates to diazonium ion.

This reaction is pretty long. When thinking about nitrous acid and primary amines, just think diazonium ion, and remember that only aromatic amines work.

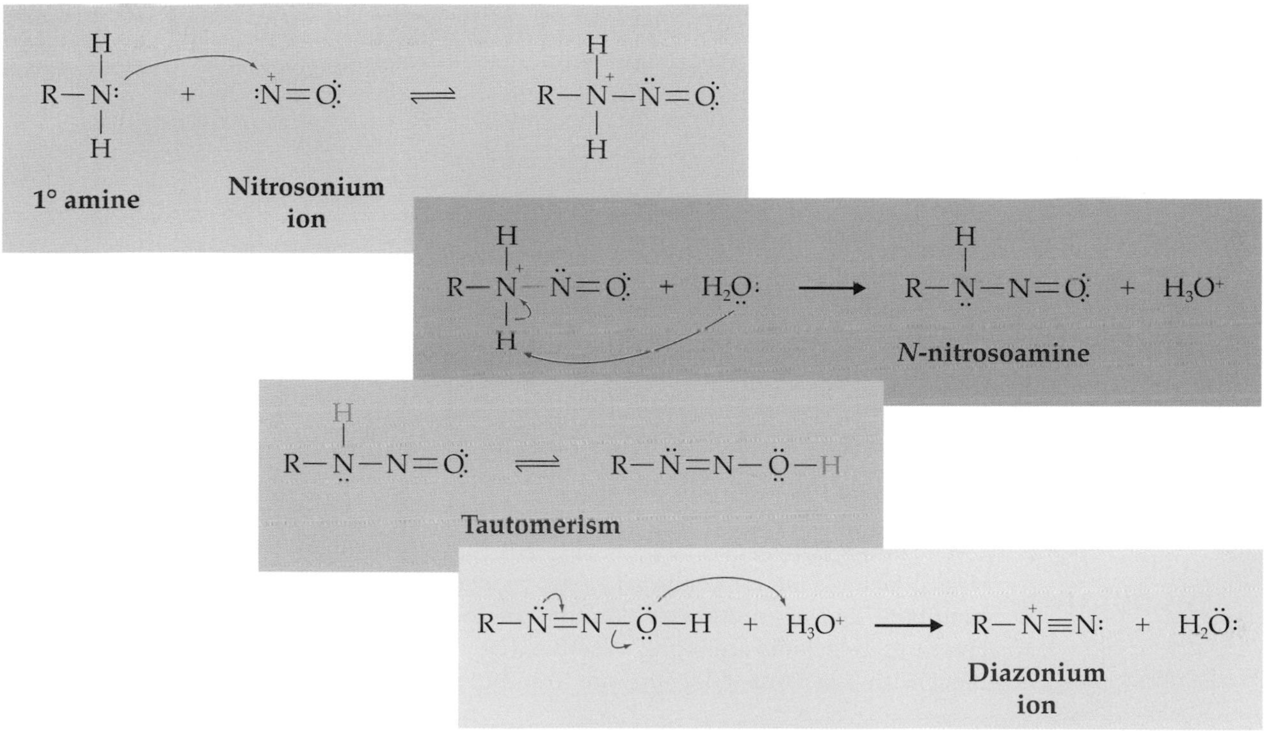

Diazotization of an Amine

The diazonium group can be easily replaced by a variety of other groups, making the diazotization of an amine a useful reaction.

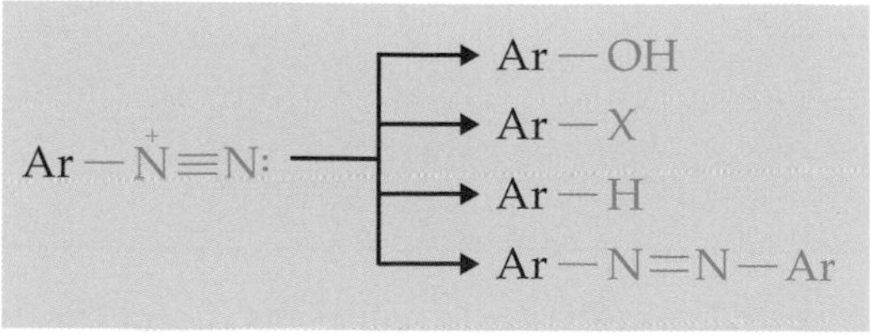

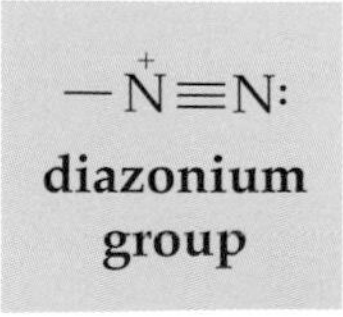

$$-\overset{+}{N}\equiv N\text{:}$$

diazonium group

Unlike primary amines, secondary amines have an extra R group instead of the tautomeric proton. No tautomer can form. Notice from the diazotization reaction above that, if the *N*-nitrosoamine can't make a tautomer, the reaction will be stopped at the *N*-nitrosoamine. When nitrous acid is added to a secondary amine, the product is an *N*-nitrosoamine.

3-20
Amides

Amides that have no substituent on the nitrogen are called primary amides. Primary amides are named by replacing the -ic in the corresponding acid with -amide. For instance, acetamide is formed when the –OH group of acetic acid is replaced by –NH$_2$. Substituents on the nitrogen are prefaced by N-. For instance, if one hydrogen on acetamide is replaced by an ethyl group, the result is N-ethylacetamide.

Amides can behave as a weak acid or a weak base. They are less basic than amines due to the electron withdrawing properties of the carbonyl. Amides are hydrolyzed by either strong acids or strong bases.

Amides with a hydrogen attached to the nitrogen are able to hydrogen bond to each other.

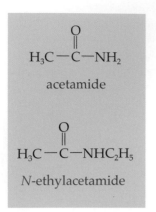

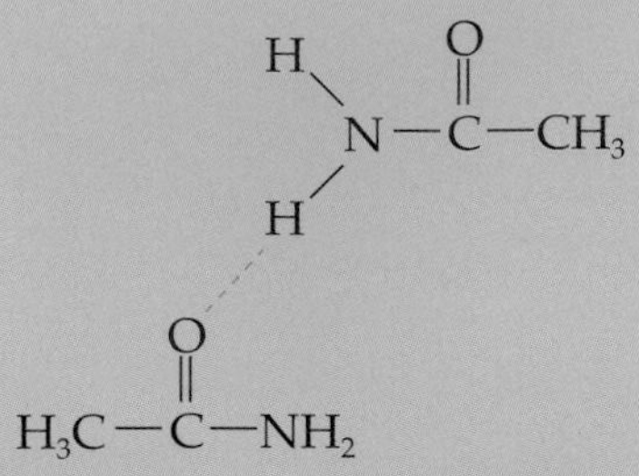

acetamide

N-ethylacetamide

Hydrogen bonding

3-21
β-Lactams

Cyclic amides are called lactams. A Greek letter is assigned to the lactam to denote size. β-lactams are 4-membered rings, γ-lactams have 5 members, δ-lactams have 6 members, and so on. Although amides are the most stable of the carboxylic acid derivatives, β-lactams are highly reactive due to large ring strain. Nucleophiles easily react with β-lactams. β-lactams are found in several types of antibiotics.

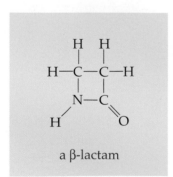

a β-lactam

3-22
The Hofmann Degradation

Primary amides react with strongly basic solutions of chlorine or bromine to form primary amines with carbon dioxide as a by-product. This reaction is called the **Hofmann degradation**. The amide is deprotoned by the strong base. The deprotonated amide picks up a halogen atom leaving a halide ion. The product is an N-haloamide. The N-haloamide is more acidic than the original primary amide and is deprotonated as well. Now a tricky rearrangement occurs. The R group of the amide migrates to the nitrogen to form an isocyanate. Isocyanate reacts with water to form a carbamic acid. The carbamic acid is decarboxylated, giving off carbon-dioxide and leaving the amine.

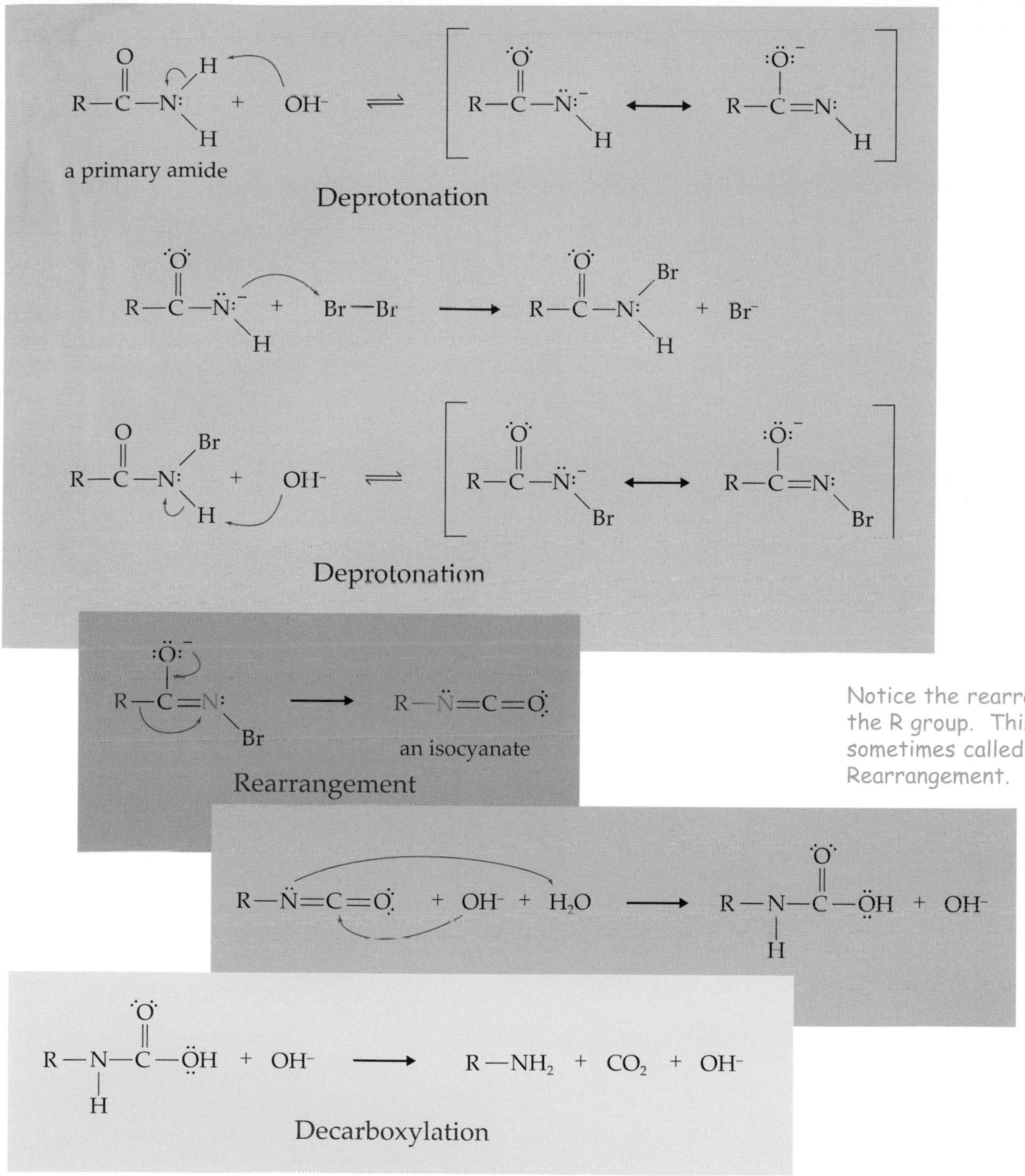

a primary amide

Deprotonation

Deprotonation

Rearrangement

an isocyanate

Notice the rearrangement of the R group. This reaction is sometimes called the Hofmann Rearrangement.

Decarboxylation

The Hofmann Degradation

The advantage of the Hofmann degradation over other methods of producing amines is that other methods rely upon an S_N2 mechanism. This prevents the production of amines on a tertiary carbon. The Hofmann degradation can produce amines with a primary, secondary, or tertiary alkyl position.

3-23
Phosphoric Acid

You need to know the structure of **phosphoric acids** for the MCAT. When heated, phosphoric acid forms **phosphoric anhydrides**. Phosphoric acids react with alcohols to form esters.

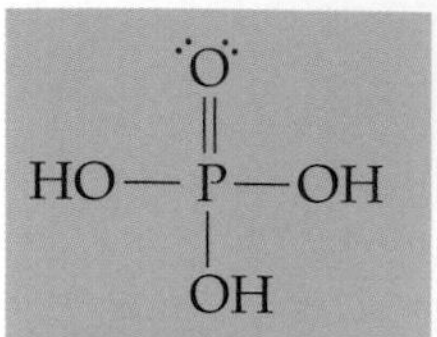

$$\overset{\displaystyle \overset{..}{\underset{..}{O}}}{\underset{\displaystyle OH}{\underset{\|}{HO-P-OH}}}$$

Phosphoric
acid

Ester linkage

$$RO-\overset{..O..}{\underset{OH}{\overset{\|}{P}}}-O-\overset{..O..}{\underset{OH}{\overset{\|}{P}}}-O-\overset{..O..}{\underset{OH}{\overset{\|}{P}}}-OH$$

Anhydride
linkage

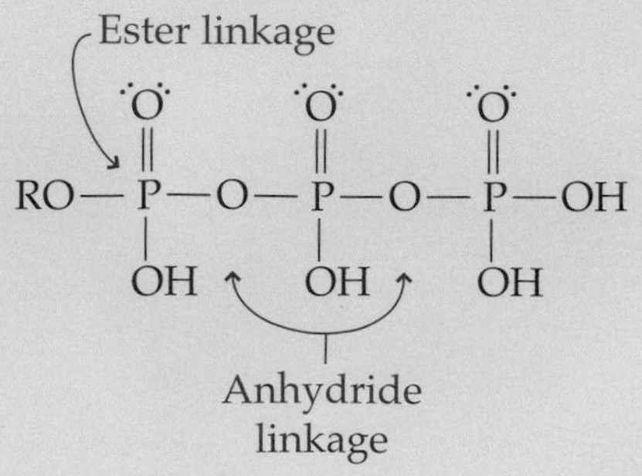

In a living cell at a pH of about 7, triphosphates exist as negatively charged ions, making them less susceptible to nucleophilic attack and relatively stable. ATP is an example of an important triphosphate.

65. If all substituents are alkyl groups, which of the following is the least basic amine?

A. primary
B. secondary
C. tertiary
D. quaternary

66. Ammonia is best described as:

A. a Lewis acid
B. a Lewis base
C. an electrophile
D. an aromatic compound

67. Which of the following would have the lowest solubility in water?

A.

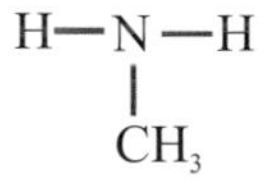

$$H-N-H$$
$$|$$
$$CH_3$$

C.

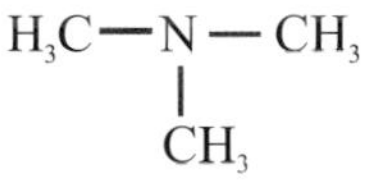

$$H_3C-N-CH_3$$
$$|$$
$$CH_3$$

B.

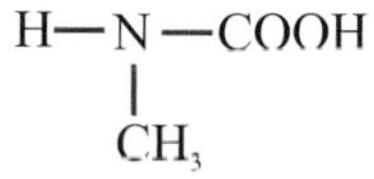

$$H-N-COOH$$
$$|$$
$$CH_3$$

D.

$$H_3C-N-COOH$$
$$|$$
$$CH_3$$

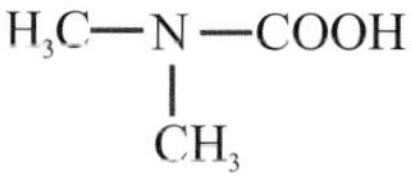

68. Which of the following is a possible product of the reaction shown below?

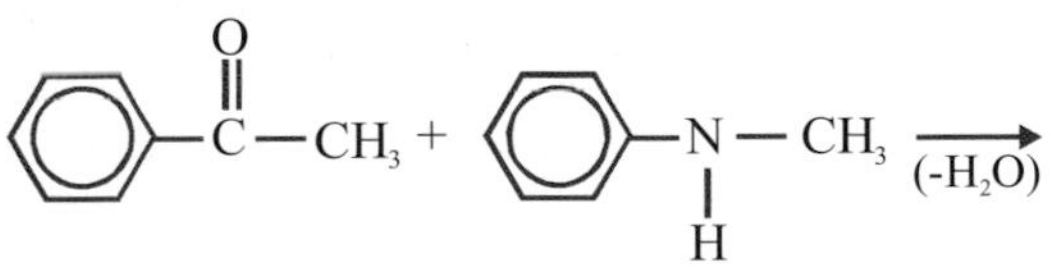

A.

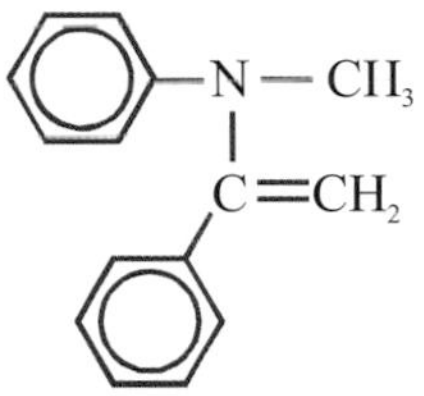

C.

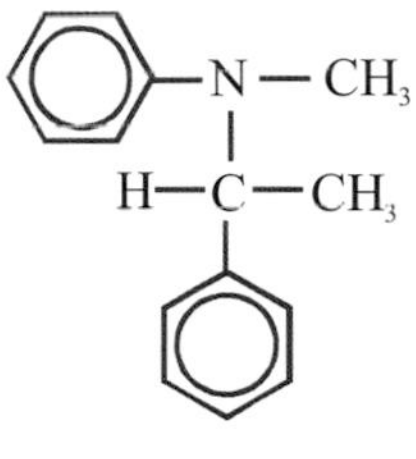

B.

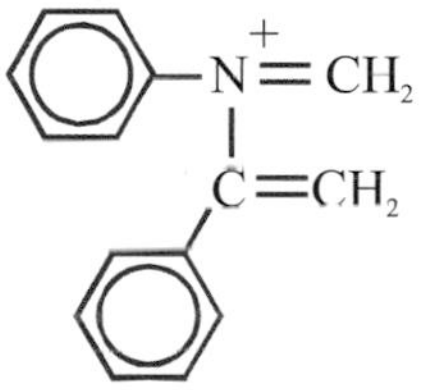

D.

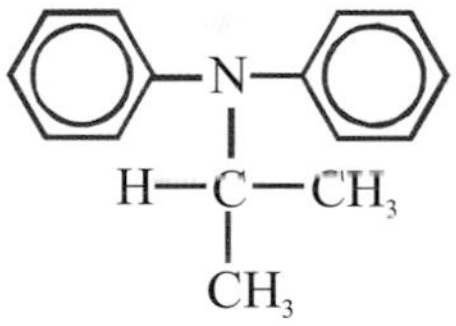

69. Ethylamine can be alkylated with iodomethane in the presence of a strong base. The strong base is needed:

A. to neutralize the strong acid ethyl-methylamine that is formed during the reaction.
B. to neutralize the strong acid HI that is formed during the reaction.
C. to protonate the methyl group.
D. to deprotonate the methyl group.

70. In the prepolymer shown below, which of the following moities contains the most reactive bond?

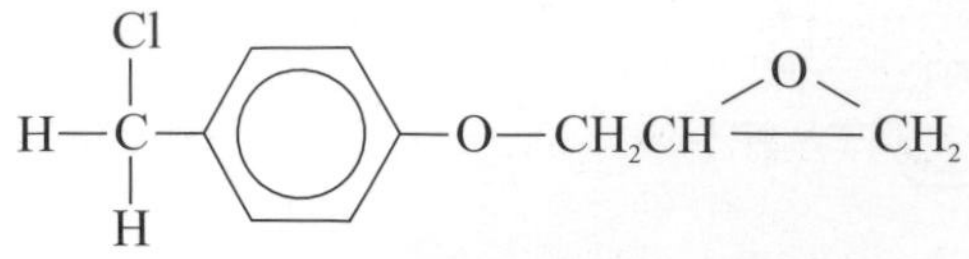

Prepolymer

A.

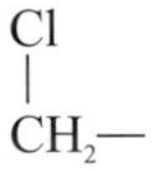

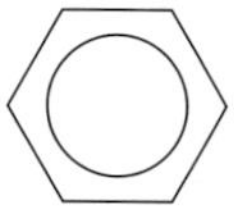

C.

$-O-CH_2-$

B.

D.

Cl
|
CH_2-

$-CH \overset{O}{\diagdown} CH_2$

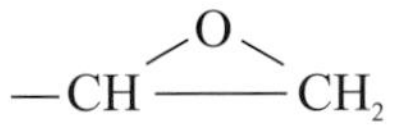

71. In a coordinate covalent bond, the shared electrons are furnished by only one species. Which of the following molecules is LEAST likely to be involved in a coordinate covalent bond?

A. sodium chloride (NaCl)
B. chlorate ion (ClO_3^-)
C. ammonia (NH_3)
D. water (H_2O)

72. When D_2O is added to cyclohexanone, all acidic hydrogens (atomic weight = 1) are replaced with deuterons (atomic weight = 2). What is the new atomic weight of cyclohexanone following D_2O treatment?

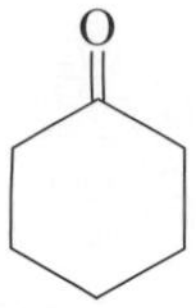

Cyclohexanone
(Atomic weight = 98)

A. 98
B. 100
C. 102
D. 108

STOP.

Biochemistry and Lab Techniques

Fatty acids are long carbon chains with a carboxylic acid end. They serve three basic functions in the human body: 1. they serve as hormones and intracellular messengers (i.e. *eicosanoids* such as *prostaglandins*); 2. they are components of the phospholipids and glycolipids of cell membranes; 3. they act as fuel for the body. The first of these functions will not be tested on the MCAT unless it is explained in a passage. For the second function of fatty acids you should be able to recognize the structure of a phospholipid as shown in Lecture 3 of the biology manual.

4-1

Fatty Acids

As fuel for the body, fatty acids are stored in the form of *triacylglycerols*. Triacylglycerols can be hydrolyzed to form glycerol and the corresponding fatty acids in a process called **lipolysis**. Notice that this process is simply the reverse of esterification. In the lab triacylglycerols can be cleaved by the addition of NaOH, a process called **saponification**. Saponification is the production of soap.

For nomenclature purposes, the carbonyl carbon of a fatty acid is assigned the number 1. The carbon next to the carbonyl is called the α-carbon (alpha carbon) and the carbon at the opposite end of the chain is called the Ω-carbon (omega carbon). The pK_a of most fatty acids is around 4.5, so most fatty acids exist in their anion form in the cellular environment.

The carbon chains on fatty acids may be **saturated or unsaturated**. Fatty acids are **amphipathic**, meaning they contain a hydrophobic and a hydrophilic end. Since the hydrophobic carbon chain predominates, fatty acids are **nonpolar**.

$$
\begin{array}{ccc}
\begin{array}{c}
\text{H}\;\;\;\;\;\;\text{O} \\
|\;\;\;\;\;\;\;\;\| \\
\text{H}-\text{C}-\text{O}-\text{C}-(\text{CH}_2)_n-\text{CH}_3 \\
|\;\;\;\;\;\;\;\;\text{O} \\
\|\\
\text{H}-\text{C}-\text{O}-\text{C}-(\text{CH}_2)_n-\text{CH}_3 \\
|\;\;\;\;\;\;\;\;\text{O} \\
\|\\
\text{H}-\text{C}-\text{O}-\text{C}-(\text{CH}_2)_n-\text{CH}_3 \\
| \\
\text{H}
\end{array}
&
\xrightarrow[\text{+H}_2\text{O}]{\text{lipases}}
&
\begin{array}{c}
\text{H} \\
| \\
\text{H}-\text{C}-\text{OH} \\
| \\
\text{H}-\text{C}-\text{OH} \\
| \\
\text{H}-\text{C}-\text{OH} \\
| \\
\text{H}
\end{array}
\;+\;
\begin{array}{c}
\text{O} \\
\| \\
\text{HO}-\text{C}-(\text{CH}_2)_n-\text{CH}_3 \\
\text{O} \\
\| \\
\text{HO}-\text{C}-(\text{CH}_2)_n-\text{CH}_3 \\
\text{O} \\
\| \\
\text{HO}-\text{C}-(\text{CH}_2)_n-\text{CH}_3
\end{array}
\end{array}
$$

| **triacylglyceride** | **glycerol** | **fatty acids** |

The important things to remember about fatty acids are molecular structure, lipolysis, energy storage, and that they enter into the Krebs cycle two carbons at a time.

Fatty acids are highly reduced, which allows them to store more than twice the energy (about 9 kcal/gram) of carbohydrates or proteins (about 4 kcal/gram). Fatty acids are stored as **triacylglycerols** in **adipose cells**. Lipolysis of triacylglycerols takes place inside the adipose cells when blood levels of epinephrine, norepinephrine, glucagon, or ACTH are elevated. The resulting fatty acid products are then exported to different cells for the utilization of their energy. Once inside a cell, the fatty acid is linked to Coenzyme A and carried into the mitochondrial matrix by the γ-amino acid L-carnitine. The fatty acid is then oxidized two carbons at a time with each oxidation yielding an NADH, FADH$_2$, and an acetyl CoA. Each acetyl CoA enters a cycle of degradation closely resembling the Krebs cycle.

4-2
Amino Acids

Amino acids are the building blocks of proteins. A single protein consists of one or more chains of amino acids strung end to end by **peptide bonds.** Hence the name **polypeptide**. You must be able recognize the structure of an amino acid and a polypeptide. A peptide bond creates the functional group known as an **amide** (an amine connected to a carbonyl carbon). It is formed via condensation of two amino acids. The reverse reaction is the hydrolysis of a peptide bond.

dipeptide

amino acids

Amino acids used by the human body are α-amino acids. They are called alpha-amino acids because the amine group is attached to the carbon which is alpha to the carbonyl carbon, similar to α-hydrogens of ketones and aldehydes.

Since nitrogen is comfortable taking on four bonds and oxygen is comfortable with a partial negative charge, the peptide bond takes on a partial double bond character. The double bond character prevents the bond from rotating freely and affects the secondary and to some extent the tertiary structure of the polypeptide.

Notice the R group on each amino acid. The R group is called the **side chain** of the amino acid. Nearly all organisms use the same **20 α-amino acids** to synthesize proteins. Two more amino acids, *hydroxyproline* and *cystine*, are produced after the polypeptide is formed. **Ten** amino acids are **essential**. ("Essential" means that they cannot be synthesized by the body, so they must be ingested. Some books list 8 or 9 amino acids as essential. The discrepancy involves whether or not to list as essential those amino acids that are derivatives of other essential amino acids.) Each amino acid differs only in its R group. The R groups have different chemical properties. These properties are divided into four categories: 1. acidic; 2. basic; 3. polar; and 4. nonpolar. All acidic and basic R groups are also polar. Generally, if the side chain contains carboxylic acids, then it is acidic; if it contains amines, then it is basic. Only the three basic amino acids have an **isoelectric point** (discussed below) above a pH of 7; all other amino acids have an isoelectric point below 7.

nonpolar	polar	acidic	basic
valine	serine	aspartic acid	histidine
isoleucine	threonine	glutamic acid	arginine
proline	cysteine		lysine
methionine	tyrosine		
alanine	glutamine		
leucine	asparagine		
tryptophan			
phenylalanine			
glycine			

It is unlikely that the MCAT would require you to know into which chemical category that an amino acid will fall; however, here are the amino acids listed under their specific categories, just in case.

Polar side groups are **hydrophilic** and will turn to face an aqueous solution such as cytosol. Nonpolar side groups are **hydrophobic** and will turn away from an aqueous solution. These characteristics affect a protein's tertiary structure.

Although we often draw an amino acid as:

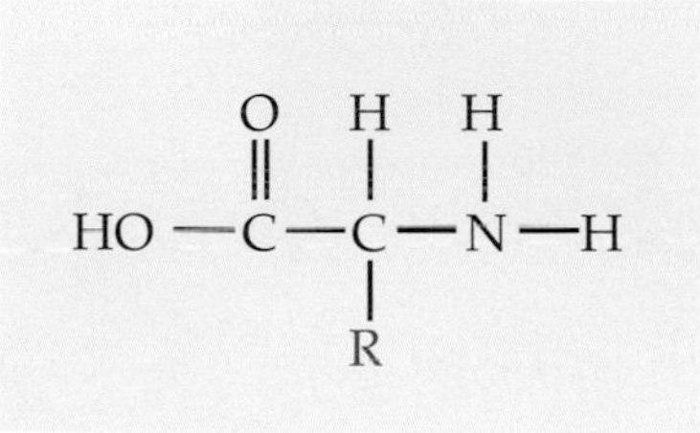

it actually never exists as such. In the cytosol, amino acids exist in one of the three forms drawn below:

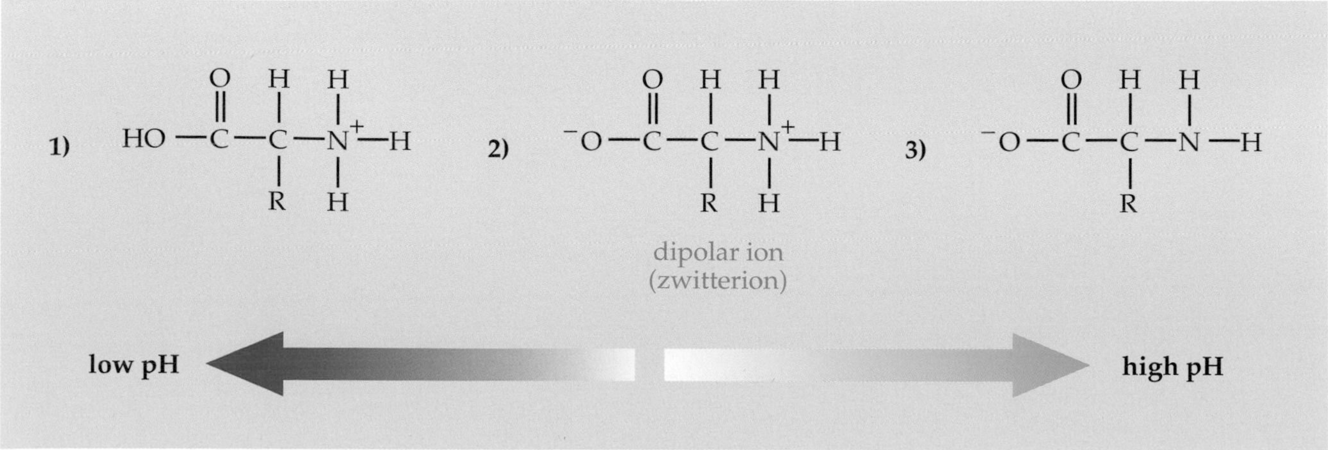

dipolar ion (zwitterion)

low pH ⟵⟶ high pH

Close examination of species 1 reveals it to be a diprotic acid. If we choose an amino acid with no ionizable substituents on its R group, and we titrate it with a strong base, we observe the following: As the pH increases, the stronger acid, the carboxylic acid, is first to lose its proton, creating species 2, its conjugate base. When species 1 and 2 exist in equal proportions, we have reached the half-equivalence point. As we continue the titration, we remove the proton from all of the carboxylic acids until we have 100% of species 2. The pH at this point is called the **isoelectric point, p*I*.** (Technically, the p*I* for any amino acid is the pH where the maximum number of species are zwitterions.) Continuing the titration, the base begins to remove a proton from the amine. When we have equal amounts of 2 and 3, we are at the second half-equivalence point of our titration. Once we have removed the acidic proton from each amine group leaving 100% of species 3, we have reached the second equivalence point. The isoelectric point is dictated by the side group of an amino acid. The more acidic the side group, the lower the p*I*; the more basic the side group, the greater the p*I*.

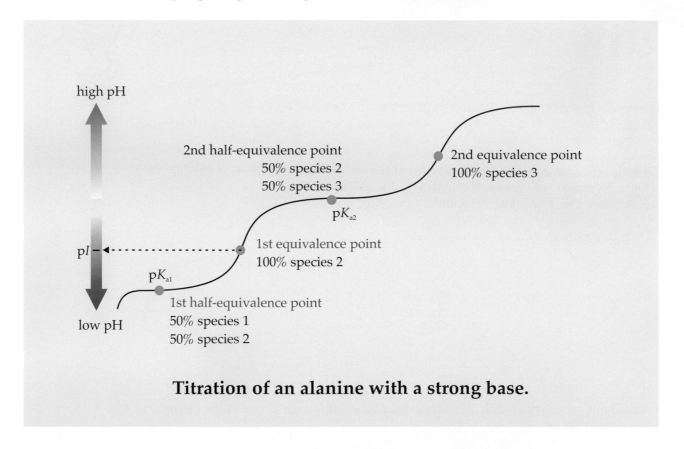

Titration of an alanine with a strong base.

> Questions 73 through 80 are **NOT** based on a descriptive passage.

73. Electrophoresis can separate amino acids by subjecting them to an electric field. The electric field applies a force whose strength and direction is dependent upon the net charge of the amino acid. If a solution of amino acids at a pH of 8 underwent electrophoresis, which of the following would most likely move the furthest toward the anode?

A. lysine
B. arginine
C. glutamate
D. histidine

74. Fatty acids and glycerol react within the body to form triacylglycerides. Which of the following functional groups are contained in any triacylglyceride?

A. aldehyde
B. carboxylic acid
C. ester
D. amine

75. The partial double bond character of a peptide bond has its greatest effect in which structure of an enzyme?

A. primary
B. secondary
C. tertiary
D. quaternary

76. Which of the following nutrients has the greatest heat of combustion?

A. carbohydrate
B. protein
C. saturated fat
D. unsaturated fat

77. A student conducted the titration of an amino acid with a strong base. The point in the titration when 50% of the amino acid exists as a zwitterion is called:

A. the isoelectric point.
B. the equivalence point.
C. the half-equivalence point.
D. the end point.

78. Which of the following amino acids has the lowest solubility in aqueous solution?

A.

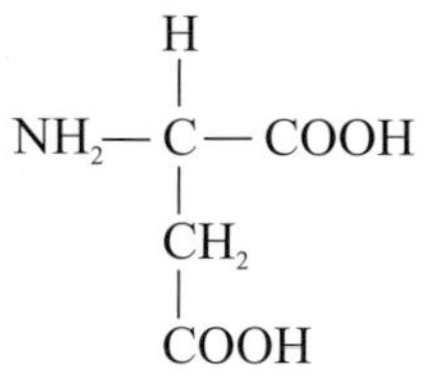

(Asp)

B.

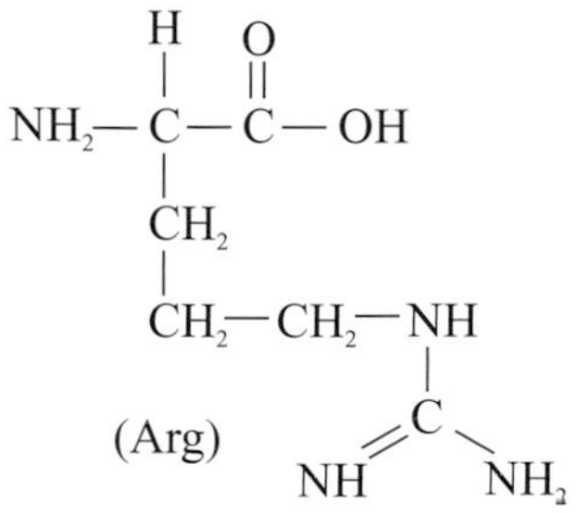

(Arg)

C.

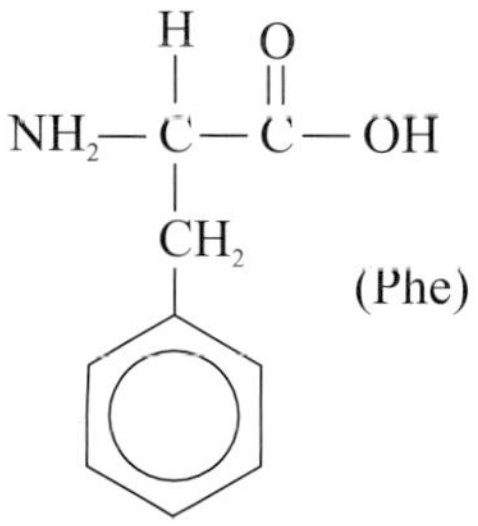

(Phe)

D.

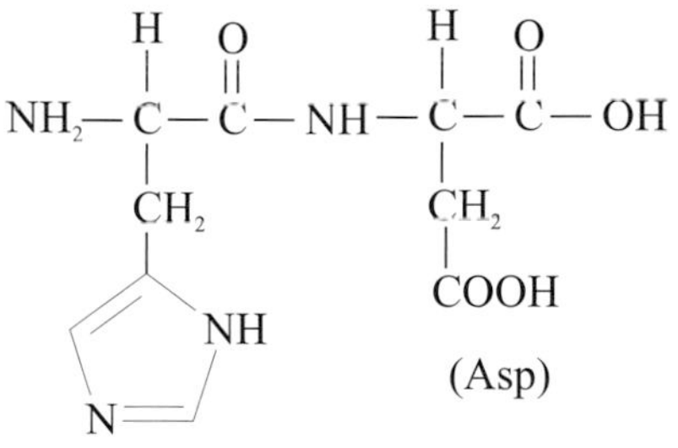

(His) (Asp)

79. How many complete monomers can be extracted from the compound below and utilized for analysis?

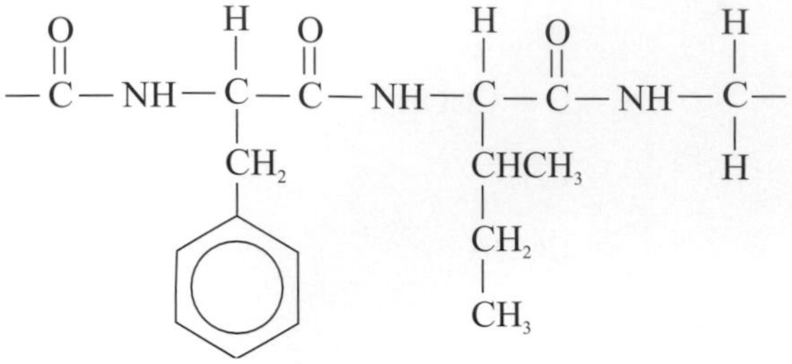

A. 2
B. 3
C. 4
D. 8

80. Based on structural properties alone, which of the following compounds is most likely to interrupt alpha-helix structures found in myoglobin?

A.

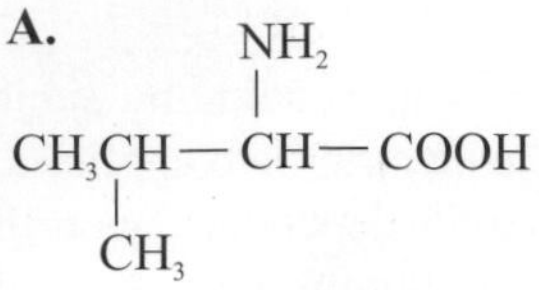

B.

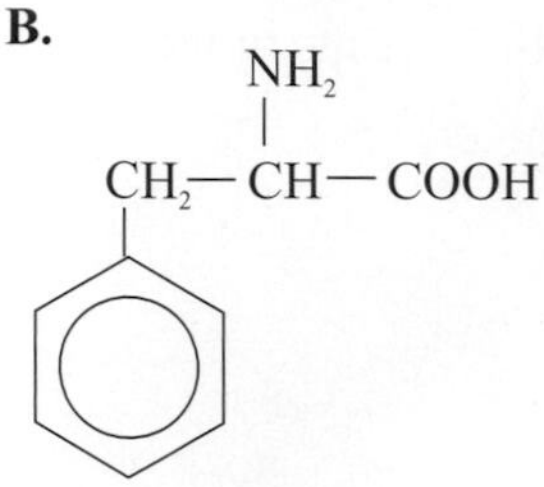

C.

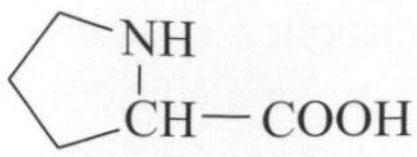

D.

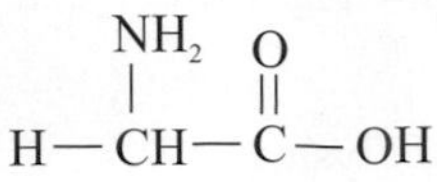

STOP.

4-3

Carbohydrates

Carbohydrates can be thought of as carbon and water. For each carbon atom there exists one oxygen and two hydrogens. The formula for any carbohydrate is:

$$C_n(H_2O)_n$$

The carbohydrate most likely to appear on the MCAT is fructose or glucose. Both are six carbon carbohydrates called **hexoses**. These may appear as Fischer projections or ring structures. The Fischer projections are shown below:

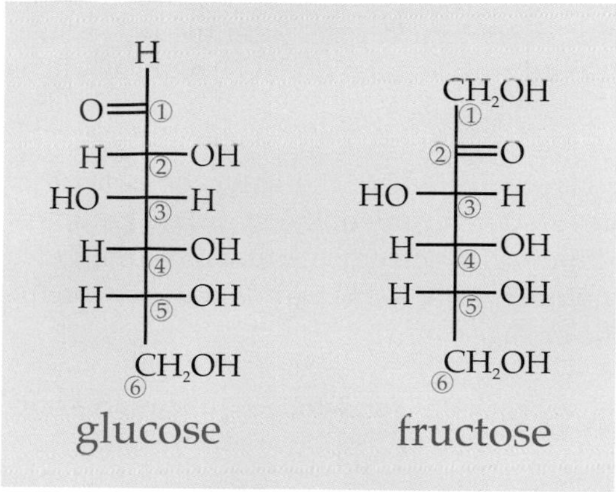

glucose

fructose

Notice that glucose is an aldehyde and fructose is a ketone. Polyhydroxyaldehydes like glucose are called **aldoses**. Polyhydroxyketones like fructose are called **ketoses**. Carbohydrates are also named for the number of carbons they possess: triose, tetrose, pentose, hexose, heptose, and so on. The names are commonly combined making glucose an **aldohexose**.

Notice also that several of the carbons are chiral. Carbohydrates are labeled D or L as follows: When in a Fischer projection as shown, if the hydroxyl group on the highest numbered chiral carbon points to the right, the carbohydrate is labeled D; if to the left, then L.

In a carbohydrate the alcohol group on the chiral carbon farthest from the carbonyl may act as a nucleophile and attack the carbonyl. When this happens, nucleophilic addition to an aldehyde or ketone results and the corresponding hemiacetal is formed, creating a ring structure. Carbon 1 in the diagram below is now called the anomeric carbon. The **anomeric carbon** can be identified as the only carbon attached to two oxygens because its alcohol group may point upwards or downwards on the ring structure resulting in either the α or β anomer. The anomer shown in the diagram below is the α anomer.

The cyclic structures are named according to the number of ring members (including oxygen): a five-membered ring is called a **furanose**; a six-membered ring is called a **pyranose**. So the glucose ring becomes **glucopyranose**.

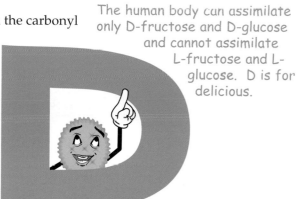

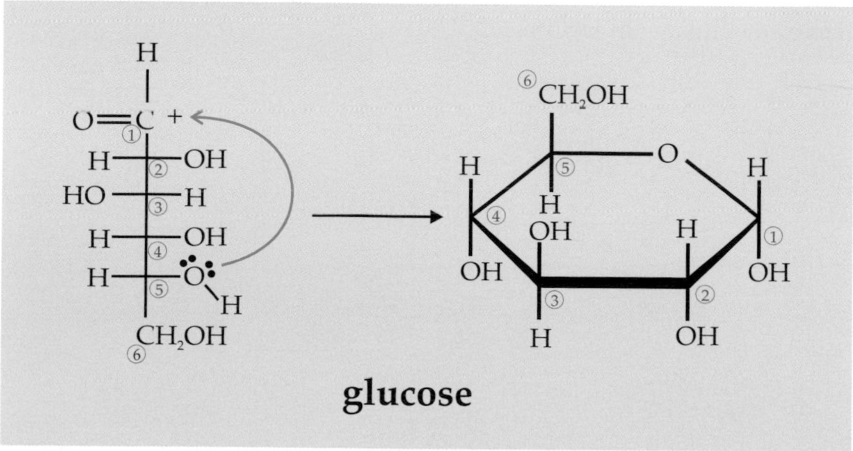

The human body can assimilate only D-fructose and D-glucose and cannot assimilate L-fructose and L-glucose. D is for delicious.

glucose

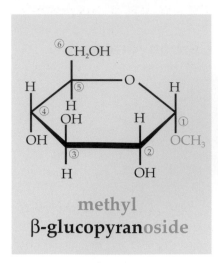

**methyl
β-glucopyran**oside

Names of reducing sugars end in -ose; names of nonreducing sugars end in -oside. This detailed nomenclature of carbohydrates is unlikely to be tested directly on the MCAT, but it doesn't hurt to know it.

Sugars that are acetals (not hemiacetals) are called glycosides. The names of such sugars end in -oside. For instance, if the hydroxyl group on the anomeric carbon of glucose were replaced with an O-methyl group, it would form methyl glucopyranoside. The group attached to the anomeric carbon of a glycoside is called an *aglycone*.

Tollens reagent is a basic reagent that detects aldehydes. Aldoses have an aldehyde on their open-chain form and reduce Tollens reagent. Tollens reagent promotes enediol rearrangement of ketoses so that ketoses also reduce Tollens reagent. Recall from Lecture 3 that acetals are used as blocking groups because they do not react with basic reducing agents. Since Tollens reagent must react with the open-chain form of a sugar, glycosides (which are closed ring acetals) do NOT reduce Tollens reagent, while nonglycosides do.

Disaccharides and polysaccharides are glycosides where the aglycone is another sugar. The anomeric carbon of a sugar can react with any of the hydroxyl groups of another sugar, but there are only three bonding arrangements that are common: a 1,4' link; a 1,6' link; and a 1,1' link. The numbers refer to the carbon numbers on the sugars. The linkages are called glycosidic linkages.

There are several disaccharides and polysaccharides for which you should know the common name.

Sucrose: 1,1' glycosidic linkage: glucose and fructose (This linkage is alpha with respect to glucose and beta with respect to fructose. It is more accurately called a 1,2' linkage because the anomeric carbon on fructose is numbered 2, not 1 like glucose.)

Maltose: α-1,4' glucosidic linkage: two glucose molecules

Lactose: β-1,4' galactosidic linkage: galactose and glucose

Cellulose: β-1,4' glucosidic linkage: a chain of glucose molecules

Amylose: α-1,4' glucosidic linkage: a chain of glucose molecules

Amylopectin: α-1,4' glucosidic linkage: a branched chain of glucose molecules with α-1,6' glucosidic linkages forming the branches

Glycogen: α-1,4' glucosidic linkage: a branched chain of glucose molecules with α-1,6' glucosidic linkages forming the branches

Glycosidic linkages are broken via hydrolysis. Without an enzyme, they are broken down only slowly by water. Animals do not possess the enzyme to break the β-1,4' glucosidic linkage in cellulose. Some adult humans lack the enzyme to break the β-1,4' galactosidic linkage in lactose.

81. How many stereoisomers exist of D-altrose, shown below?

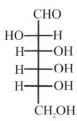

D-altrose

A. 2
B. 8
C. 16
D. 32

82. Which of the following types of reactions describes ring formation in glucose when the alcohol group collides with the carbonyl?

A. hemiacetal formation
B. hemiketal formation
C. acctal formation
D. ketal formation

83. Which of the following is the ketose most abundant in fruits?

A. fructose
B. glucose
C. proline
D. glycerol

84. From only the drawing shown below, which of the following statements can be discerned as true?

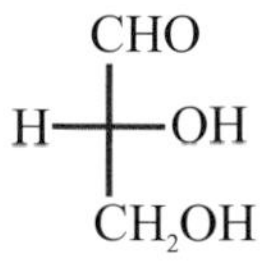

CHO
H——OH
CH₂OH

I. The molecule is a carbohydrate.
II. The stereochemical designation of the molecule is D.
III. The molecule rotates polarized light clockwise.

A. I only
B. II only
C. I and II only
D. I, II, and III

85. Which of the following statements are true concerning carbohydrates?

I. Carbohydrates can exist as meso compounds.
II. The human body is capable of digesting all isomers of glucose.
III. Glucose is an aldehyde.

A. III only
B. I and II only
C. I and III only
D. I, II, and III

86. Aspartame, saccharine and sodium cyclamate are all synthetic sweeteners used to replace glucose.

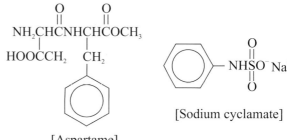

[Aspartame]

[Sodium cyclamate]

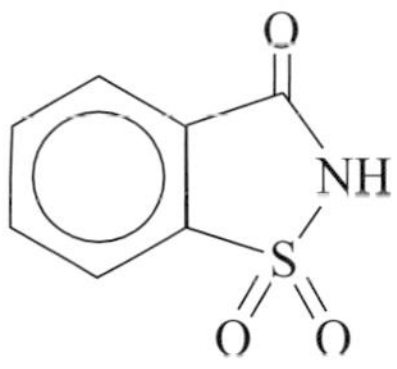

[Saccharin]

Which of the following properties are shared by both glucose and the synthetic sweeteners?

I. All activate gustatory receptors at the tip of the human tongue.
II. All can hydrogen bond.
III. All are carbohydrates.

A. I only
B. III only
C. I and II only
D. I, II, and III

87. Fructose can cyclize into a five-membered ring known as a furanose. The hydroxyl group on which carbon of fructose behaves as a nucleophile during the formation of a furan?

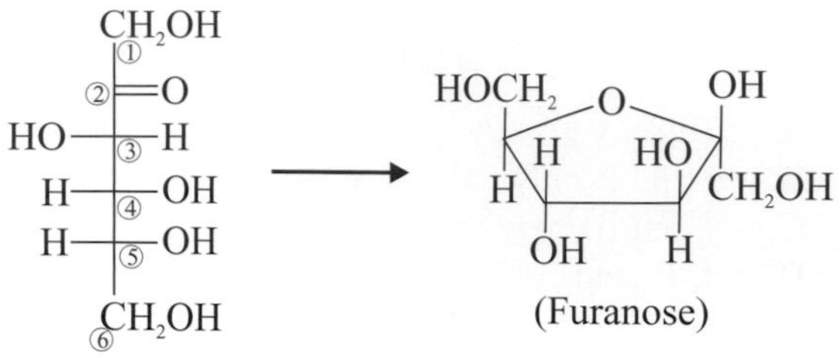

(Furanose)

A. carbon 1
B. carbon 3
C. carbon 5
D. carbon 6

88. Sugar A and B are what type of carbohydrates, respectively?

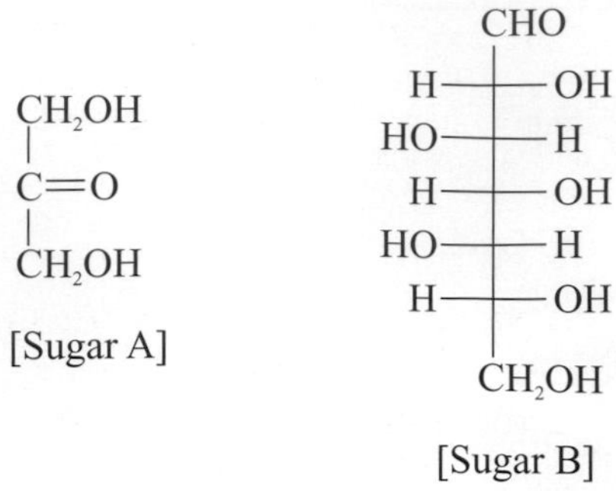

[Sugar A]

[Sugar B]

A. ketotriose and ketohexose
B. aldotriose and aldohexose
C. aldotriose and ketoheptose
D. ketotriose and aldoheptose

STOP.

There are three types of lab techniques that you must know for the MCAT: spectroscopy, spectrometry, and separations. Spectroscopy will be either **nuclear magnetic resonance (nmr)**, **infrared spectroscopy (IR)**, or **ultraviolet spectroscopy (UV)**. You will need to understand how **mass spectrometry** works. Separation techniques will include **chromatography, distillation, crystallization**, and **extraction**.

4-4
Lab Techniques

NMR refers to **nuclear magnetic resonance** spectroscopy. The nucleus most commonly studied with nmr is the hydrogen nucleus, but it is possible to study the nucleus of carbon-13 and other atoms as well.

4-5
NMR

Nuclei with an odd atomic number or odd mass number exhibit *nuclear spin* that can be observed by an nmr spectrometer. The spin creates a magnetic field around the nucleus similar to the field created by a small magnet. When placed in an external magnetic field, the nucleus aligns its own field with or against the external field. Nuclei aligned with the magnetic field have a lower energy state than those aligned against the field. The stronger the magnetic field, the greater the difference between these energy states.

When photons (electromagnetic radiation) of just the right frequency (energy state) are shone on the nuclei, those nuclei whose magnetic fields are oriented with the external magnetic field can absorb the energy of the photon and flip to face against the external field. A nucleus that is subjected to this perfect combination of magnetic field strength and electromagnetic radiation frequency is said to be in resonance. An nmr spectrometer can detect the energy absorption of a nucleus in resonance.

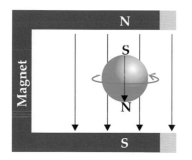 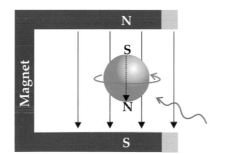

low energy state   high energy state

In nmr, the frequency of the electromagnetic radiation is held constant while the magnetic field strength is varied.

Absent any electrons, all protons absorb electromagnetic energy from a constant-strength magnetic field at the same frequency (about 60 MHz in a magnetic field of 14,092 gauss). However, hydrogen atoms within different compounds experience unique surrounding-electron densities and are also uniquely affected by the magnetic fields of other nearby protons. The electrons *shield* the protons from the magnetic field. As a result, the external field must be strengthened for a shielded proton to achieve resonance. Thus protons within a compound absorb electromagnetic energy of the *same frequency* at *different magnetic field strengths*.

An nmr spectrum (shown on the next page) is a graph of the magnetic field strengths absorbed by the hydrogens of a specific compound at a single frequency. The field strength is measured in *parts per million, ppm*, and, despite the *decreasing* numbers, *increases* from left to right. The leftward direction is called *downfield* and the rightward is called *upfield*. All the way to the right is a peak at 0 ppm. This peak

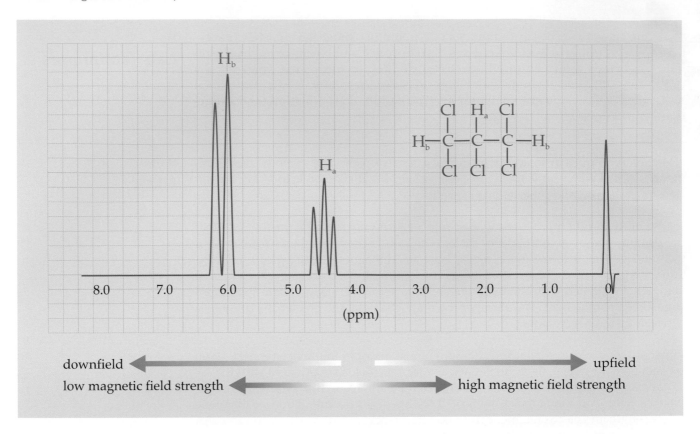

downfield

low magnetic field strength

upfield

high magnetic field strength

is due to a reference compound (tetramethylsilane, discussed below) used to calibrate the instrument.

Although nmr is based on quantum mechanics and can be a very complex subject, there is actually very little to understand about nmr for the MCAT. First and most importantly, remember that, **unless otherwise indicated, nmr is concerned with hydrogens**. Given an nmr spectrum, you should be able to identify which peaks belong to which hydrogens on a given compound, or which of four compounds might create the given spectrum. To do this you must understand the following:

- **Each peak** represents **chemically equivalent hydrogens**;
- **Splitting** of peaks is created by "neighboring hydrogens".

$$CH_3-\underset{\underset{CH_3}{|}}{\overset{\overset{CH_3}{|}}{Si}}-CH_3$$

Tetramethylsilane

Each peak indicates one or a group of chemically equivalent hydrogens (in other words, hydrogens indistinguishable from each other by way of their positions on the compound). Such hydrogens are said to be *enantiotropic*. Enantiotropic hydrogens are represented by the same peak in an nmr spectrum. They have the same **chemical shift**. Chemical shift is the difference between the resonance frequency of the chemically shifted hydrogens and the resonance frequency of hydrogens on a reference compound such as tetramethylsilane. Tetramethylsilane (shown above) is the most common nmr reference compound because it contains many hydrogens that are all enantiotropic and are very well shielded. In the graph above, although not all of the H_b are attached to the same carbon, they are stereochemically similar, and thus represented by the same group of peaks. Their chemical shift is approximately 6.0 ppm.

The area under a peak is proportional to the number of hydrogens represented by that peak. The more chemically equivalent hydrogens, the greater the area. The tallest peak does not necessarily correspond to the greatest area. The **integral trace** is a line drawn above the peaks that rises each time it goes over a peak. The rise of the integral trace is in proportion to the number of chemically equivalent hydrogens in the peak beneath it. A newer instrument, called a *digital trace*, records numbers which correspond to the rise in the line. The exact number of hydrogens cannot be determined from the integral trace or the digital trace; only the ratio of hydrogens from one peak to another can be determined.

Lateral position on a spectrum is dictated by *electron shielding*, thus limited predictions can be made based upon electron-withdrawing and electron-donating groups. Electron-withdrawing groups tend to lower shielding and thus decrease the magnetic field strength at which resonance takes place. This means that hydrogens with less shielding tend to have peaks downfield or to the left. Likewise, electron-donating groups tend to increase shielding and increase the required field strength for resonance.

Splitting (called **spin-spin splitting**) results from neighboring hydrogens that are not chemically equivalent. (*Spin-spin coupling* is the same thing except that it also includes hydrogens that are chemically equivalent. The MCAT will not test this distinction.) The number of peaks due to splitting for a group of chemically equivalent hydrogens is given by the simple formula, **$n + 1$**, where *n* is the number of **neighboring hydrogens** that are not chemically equivalent. A neighboring hydrogen is one that is on an atom adjacent to the atom to which the hydrogen is connected.

For proton nmr spectroscopy, follow these steps:

- Identify chemically equivalent hydrogens.

- Identify and count neighboring hydrogens that are not chemically equivalent. Use n + 1 to figure the number of peaks created by splitting for the chemically equivalent hydrogens.

- If necessary, identify electron withdrawing/donating groups near the chemically equivalent hydrogens. Withdrawing groups will move their signal to the left.

Something else you should know: Aldehyde protons have a very distinctive shift at 9.5 ppm. Watch for it.

In a rare situation, carbon nmr may also appear on the MCAT. Remember, the nucleus must have an odd atomic or mass number to register on nmr, so carbon-13 is the only carbon isotope to register. Treat carbon nmr the same way as proton nmr, except ignore splitting.

Of course, nmr can be more complicated than is described here. However, like everything else on the MCAT, any complications tested will be explained and answerable from this small body of knowledge just presented. We have provided one more spectrum on the next page in order for you to test your understanding. Before reading further, turn the page and see if you can predict which hydrogens belong to which groups of peaks.

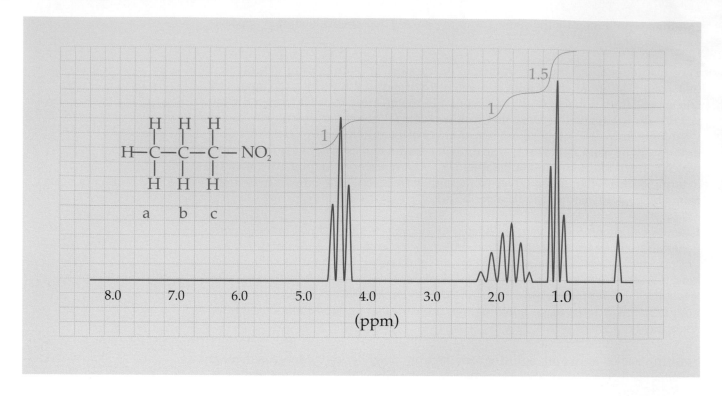

ANSWER: Each letter, *a*, *b*, and *c*, represents a group of chemically equivalent hydrogens. The groups of peaks from left to right correspond to the *c*, *b*, and *a* hydrogens respectively. Since NO_2 is electron-withdrawing, the *c* hydrogens are further downfield. The *b* hydrogens have 5 neighbors, so their peak has 6 peaks. The digital trace shows the peak furthest upfield as having 1.5 times as many hydrogens as the other peaks. The ratio of *a* hydrogens to *b* or *c* hydrogens is 3 to 2, so this must be the peak representing the *a* hydrogens.

4-6
IR Spectroscopy

A dipole exists when the centers of positive and negative charge do not coincide. When exposed to an electric field, these oppositely charged centers will move in opposite directions; either toward each other or away from each other. In infrared radiation, the direction of the electric field oscillates, causing causing the positive and negative centers within polar bonds to move toward each other and then away from each other. Thus, when exposed to **infrared radiation**, the polar bonds within a compound stretch and contract in a vibrating motion.

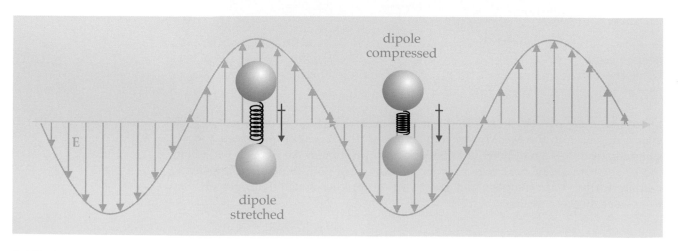

Different bonds vibrate at different frequencies. When the resonance frequency of the oscillating bond is matched by the frequency of infrared radiation, the IR energy is absorbed. In **IR Spectroscopy**, an infrared spectrometer slowly changes the frequency of infrared light shining upon a compound and records the frequencies of absorption in reciprocal centimeters, cm⁻¹ (number of cycles per cm).

If a bond has no dipole moment, then the infrared radiation does not cause it to vibrate and no energy is absorbed. However, energy can also be absorbed due to other types of stretching and scissoring motions of the molecules in a compound.

The most predictable section of the IR spectrum is in the 1600 to 3500 cm⁻¹ region. Below are some distinguishing characteristics of this range of the IR spectrum for the functional groups MCAT may test. You should be familiar with these shapes and frequencies.

IR questions on the MCAT used to be as easy as reading a chart. Now, the MCAT is sometimes requiring limited memorization of the IR spectra of certain functional groups. The most likely spectra that would be asked by MCAT are the $C=O$, a sharp dip around 1700 cm⁻¹; and the O-H, a broad dip around 3200-3600.

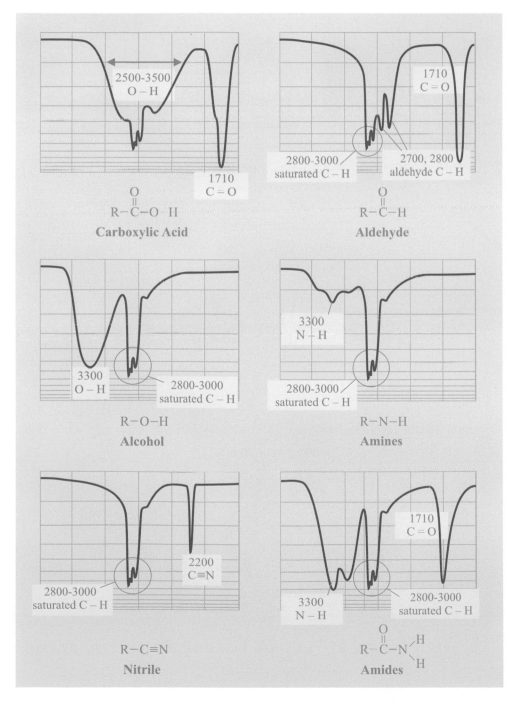

Limited predictions about vibration can be made based upon the *mass of the atoms involved* and the *stiffness of the bond* between them. Atoms with greater mass resonate at lower frequencies; stiffer bonds, such as double and triple bonds, resonate at higher frequencies. Bond strength and bond stiffness follow the same order: $sp > sp^2 > sp^3$.

An IR spectrum can help identify which functional groups are in a compound, but it does not readily reveal the shape or size of the carbon skeleton. However, two compounds are very unlikely to have exactly the same IR spectrum. This makes an IR spectrum like a fingerprint for each compound. Many of the complex vibrations that distinguish one compound from a similar compound are found in the 600 to 1400 cm⁻¹ region, called the **fingerprint region**. Below are three sample spectra that include the fingerprint region. Know where the fingerprint region is, and know why it is called the fingerprint region, but use the higher frequency range to identify functional groups.

The fingerprint region of the IR spectrum is unique to nearly all compounds, but it is very difficult to read it. You should know about the fingerprint region, but you should use IR to identify functional groups based upon the region from 1600 to 3500 cm⁻¹.

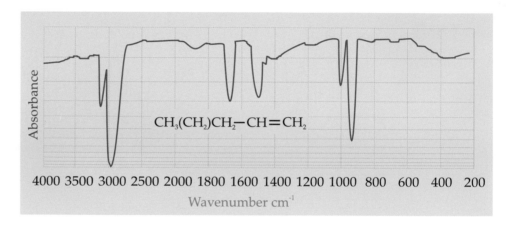

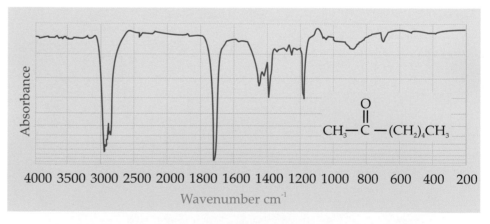

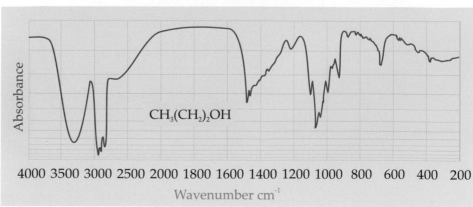

The wavelength of ultraviolet light is between 200 and 400 nm, much shorter than infrared light and at a much higher energy level. Ultraviolet (UV) spectroscopy detects conjugated double bonds (double bonds separated by one single bond) by comparing the intensities of two beams of light from the same monochromatic light source. One beam is shone through a sample cell and the other is shone through a reference cell. The sample cell contains the sample compound to be analyzed dissolved in a solvent. The reference cell contains only the solvent. The sample cell will absorb more energy from the light beam than the reference cell. The difference in the radiant energy is recorded as a UV spectrum of the sample compound.

The UV spectrum provides limited information about the length and structure of the conjugated portion of the molecule. When a photon collides with an electron in a molecule in the sample, the electron may be bumped up to a vacant molecular orbital and the photon absorbed. These are typically π-electron movements from bonding to nonbonding orbitals ($\pi \rightarrow \pi^*$). Electrons in σ-bonds usually require more energy to reach the next highest orbital, and thus they are typically unaffected by wavelengths of greater than 200 nm. Conjugated systems with π-bonds, on the other hand, have vacant orbitals at energy levels close to their highest occupied molecular orbital (HOMO) energy levels. The vacant orbitals are called LUMO (lowest unoccupied molecular orbital). UV photons are able to momentarily displace electrons to the LUMO, and the energy is absorbed. If a conjugated system is present in the sample, the sample beam intensity I_s will be lower than the reference beam intensity I_r. The absorbance A is given by $A_\lambda = \log(I_s/I_r)$. The absorbance is plotted on the UV spectra. Absorbance also equals the product of concentration of the sample (c), the length of the path of light through the cell (l), and the *molar absorptivity* (ε)(or *molar extinction coefficient*).

$$A = \varepsilon cl$$

The molar absorptivity is a measure of how strongly the sample absorbs light at a particular wavelength. It is probably easiest to think of it mathematically as $\varepsilon = A/cl$.

Ethylene, though not conjugated, absorbs wavelengths at 171 nm. Absorption at this wavelength is obscured by oxygen in the air. Butadiene has a higher HOMO and lower LUMO than ethylene, allowing for an absorption at 217 nm. Conjugated trienes absorb at even longer wavelengths. The longer the chain of conjugated double bonds, the greater the wavelength of absorption. The rule of thumb is that each additional **conjugated** double bond increases the wavelength by about 30 to 40 nm. An additional alkyl group attached to any one of the atoms involved in the conjugated system increases the spectrum wavelength by about 5 nm. **Isolated** double bonds do not increase the absorption wavelength.

UV spectra lack detail. Samples must be extremely pure or the spectrum is obscured. To the right is a UV spectrum of 2-methyl-1,3-butadiene dissolved in methanol. The methyl group increases the absorption wavelength slightly. The methanol solvent makes no contribution to the spectrum. Spectra are typically not printed, but instead given as lists. The spectrum to the right would be listed as:

λ_{max} = 222 nm ε = 20,000

4-7
Ultraviolet Spectroscopy

UV starts at around 217 nm with butadiene.

The rule of thumb for UV is 30 to 40 nm increase for each additional conjugated double bond, and a 5 nm increase for each additional alkyl group.

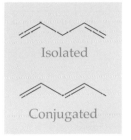

Isolated

Conjugated

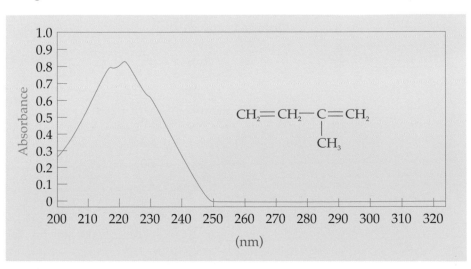

Carbonyls, compounds with carbon-oxygen double bonds, also absorb light in the UV region. For instance, acetone has a broad absorption peak at 280 nm. In this example, the electron can be excited from an unshared pair into a nonbonding π-orbital. ($n \to \pi^*$)

4-8
Visible Spectrum

If a compound has eight or more double bonds, its absorbance moves into the visible spectrum. **β-carotene**, a precursor of vitamin A, has 11 conjugated double bonds. β-carotene has a maximum absorbance at 497 nm. Electromagnetic radiaton of 497 nm has a blue-green color. Carrots, having β-carotene, absorb blue-green light, giving them the **complementary color** of red-orange.

4-9
Mass Spectrometry

Mass spectrometry gives the molecular weight, and, in the case of high resolution mass spectrometry, the molecular formula. In mass spectrometry, the molecules of a sample are bombarded with electrons, causing them to break apart and to ionize. The largest ion is the size of the original molecule but short one electron. This cation is called the *molecular ion*. For instance, if methane were the sample, the molecular ion would be CH_4^+. The ions are accelerated through a magnetic field. The resulting force deflects the ions around a curved path. The radius of curvature of their path depends upon the **mass to charge ratio** of the ion (m/z). Most of the ions have a charge of 1+. The magnetic field strength is altered to allow the passage of different size ions through the flight tube (shown in the diagram). A computer records the amount of ions at different magnetic field strengths as peaks on a chart. The largest peak is called the base peak. The peak made by the molecular ions is called the **parent peak**. Notice that the parent peak is made by molecules that did not fragment.

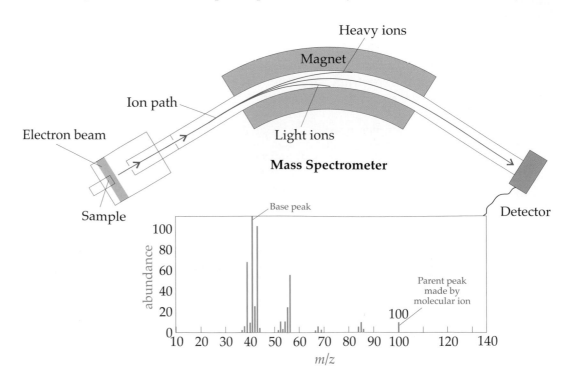

Look for the parent peak all the way to the right of the spectrum. Only heavy isotopes will be further right. All peaks are assigned *abundances* as percentages of the base peak. In the diagram on the previous page, the parent peak has an abundance of 10 because it is 10% as high as the base peak.

4-10
Chromatography

<u>Chromatography</u> is the resolution of a mixture by passing it over a surface that adsorbs the compounds within the mixture at different rates. The mixture is usually dissolved into a solution, establishing the moving phase. The surface adsorbs compounds from the mixture, establishing the stationary phase. The compounds in the mixture that have a greater affinity for the surface move more slowly. Typically, the more polar compounds elute more slowly because they have a greater affinity for the stationary phase. The result of chromatography is the establishment of separate and distinct layers, one pertaining to each component of the mixture. Different types of chromatography include:

Solid to Liquid

Column chromatography is where a solution containing the mixture is dripped down a column containing the solid phase (usually glass beads). The more polar compounds in the mixture travel more slowly down the column, creating separate layers for each compound. Each compound can subsequently be collected as it elutes into the solvent and drips out of the bottom of the column.

In *paper chromatography* (shown on the right) a small portion of the sample to be separated is spotted onto paper. One end of the paper is then placed into a solvent. The solvent moves up the paper via capillary action and dissolves the sample as it passes over it. As the solvent continues to move up the paper, the more polar portions of the sample move more slowly because they are attracted to the polar paper. The less polar portions are not attracted to the paper and move more quickly. The result is a series of colored dots representing the different sections of the sample with the

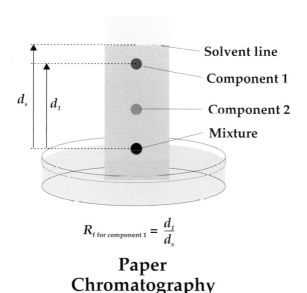

$$R_{\text{f for component 1}} = \frac{d_1}{d_s}$$

Paper Chromatography

most polar near the bottom and the least polar near the top. An R_f *factor* can be determined for each component of the separation by dividing the distance traveled by the component by the distance traveled by the solvent. Nonpolar components have an R_f factor close to one; polar components have a lower R_f factor. The R_f factor is always between 0 and 1.

Thin layer chromatography is similar to paper chromatography except that a coated glass or plastic plate is used instead of paper, and the results are visualized via an iodine vapor chamber.

Gas to Liquid

In *gas chromatography* the liquid phase is the stationary phase. The mixture is dissolved into a heated carrier gas (usually helium or nitrogen) and passed over a liquid phase bound to a column. Compounds in the mixture equilibrate with the liquid phase at different rates and elute as individual components at an exit port.

4-11
Distillation

<u>Distillation</u> is separation based upon vapor pressure. A solution of two volatile liquids with boiling point differences of approximately 20°C or more may be separated by slow boiling. The **<u>compound with the lower boiling point (higher vapor pressure) will boil off and can be captured</u>** and condensed in a cool tube. Be careful. If a solution of two volatile liquids exhibits a positive deviation to Rault's law, the solution will boil at a lower temperature than either pure compound. The result will be a solution with an exact ratio of the two liquids called an *azeotrope*. An azeotrope cannot be separated by distillation. 5% water and 95% ethanol make an azeotrope that has a lower boiling point than pure water or pure ethanol. An azeotrope can also form when the solution has a higher boiling point than either pure substance. *Fractional distillation* is simply a more precise method of distillation. In fractional distillation, the vapor is run through glass beads allowing the compound with the higher boiling point to condense and fall back into the solution.

4-12
Crystallization

Crystallization is based upon the principle that **<u>pure substances form crystals</u>** more easily than impure substances. The classic example is an iceberg. An iceberg is formed from the ocean but is made of pure water, not salt water. This is because pure water forms crystals more easily. You should know that crystallization is a very inefficient method of separation; it is very difficult to arrive at a pure substance through crystallization. Crystallization of most salts is an exothermic process.

Extraction is based upon **solubility due to similar polarities**. Like dissolves like. We start with an organic mixture on top of an aqueous layer. They have different polarities and don't mix. There are three steps:

4-13

Extraction

1. add a strong acid and shake. The acid protonates bases like amines in the organic layer, making them polar. The polar amines dissolve in the aqueous layer and are drained off.

2. add a weak base. The base deprotonates only the strong acids like carboxylic acids, making them more polar. The polar carboxylic acids dissolve in the aqueous layer and are drained off.

3. add a strong base. The strong base reacts with the rest of the acids (hopefully all weak acids like phenol). These acids dissolve in the aqueous layer and are drained off.

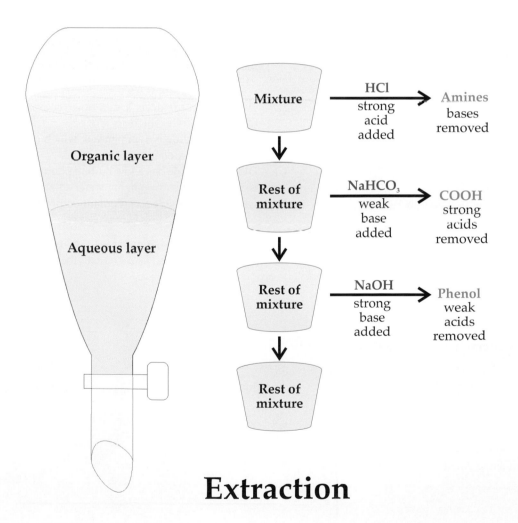

Extraction

89. All of the following are true concerning nmr spectroscopy EXCEPT:

   A. Protons are distinguished when they absorb magnetic energy at different field strengths.
   B. Downfield is to the left on an nmr spectrum.
   C. Functional groups are distinguished when they absorb magnetic energy at different field strengths.
   D. Delocalized electrons generate magnetic fields that can either shield or deshield nearby protons.

90. Extraction is an effective method for separating compounds which can be treated with an acid or base and made to differ in:

   A. boiling point.
   B. molecular weight.
   C. water solubility.
   D. optical activity.

91. A carbonyl will absorb infrared radiation at a frequency of approximately:

   A. 700 – 900 Hz
   B. 1630 – 1700 Hz
   C. 2220 – 2260 Hz
   D. 3300 – 3500 Hz

92. In thin layer chromatography polar compounds will:

   A. rise more slowly through the silica gel than nonpolar compounds.
   B. rise more quickly through the silica gel than nonpolar compounds.
   C. move to the left through the silica gel.
   D. move to the right through the silica gel.

93. Which of the following statements are true concerning separations?

   I. Any two compounds with sufficiently different boiling points can be separated completely by distillation.
   II. Crystallization is an efficient method of compound purification for most compounds.
   III. Distillation is more effective when done slowly.

   A. I only
   B. III only
   C. I and III only
   D. II and III only

94. *Refining* is the separation of crude oil into four primary products:

Petroleum Product	Boiling Point (°C)
Straight-run gasoline	30-180
Kerosene	175-300
Gas oil	295-400
Lubricating wax	425-700

Petroleum product refining can also be described as:

   A. high pressure distillation
   B. nuclear magnetic resonance separation
   C. liquid chromatography extraction
   D. organic phase purification

95. Which statement accounts for the fact that dimethyl sulfoxide is miscible in water, whereas dimethyl sulfide is not?

$$CH_3-\overset{\overset{\displaystyle O}{\|}}{S}-CH_3 \qquad CH_3-S-CH_3$$

Dimethyl sulfoxide (bp 187°C)   Dimethyl sulfide (bp 37°C)

   A. Dimethyl sulfoxide is a non-polar compound that rapidly penetrates the skin.
   B. Dimethyl sulfide is symmetrical, which causes it to develop a dipole moment.
   C. Dimethyl sulfide has a low boiling point and density issues prevent it from being water soluble.
   D. Dimethyl sulfoxide is a dipolar compound.

96. What is the predicted number of ^{13}C nmr peaks for methylcyclopentane and 1,2-Dimethylbenzene, respectively?

Methylcyclopentane   1,2-Dimethylbenzene

   A. 2,3
   B. 3,4
   C. 4,4
   D. 5,3

100

STOP.

STOP!

DO NOT LOOK AT THESE EXAMS UNTIL CLASS.

30-MINUTE
IN-CLASS EXAM
FOR LECTURE 1

Passage I (Questions 1-6)

With few exceptions, enantiomers cannot be separated through physical means. When in racemic mixtures, they have the same physical properties. Enantiomers have similar chemical properties as well. The only chemical difference between a pair of enantiomers occurs in reactions with other chiral compounds. Thus resolution of a racemic mixture typically takes place through a reaction with another optically active reagent. Since living organisms usually produce only one of two possible enantiomers, many optically active reagents can be obtained from natural sources. For instance: (S)-(+)-lactic acid can be obtained from animal muscle tissue; and (S)-(-)-2-methyl-1-butanol, from yeast fermentation.

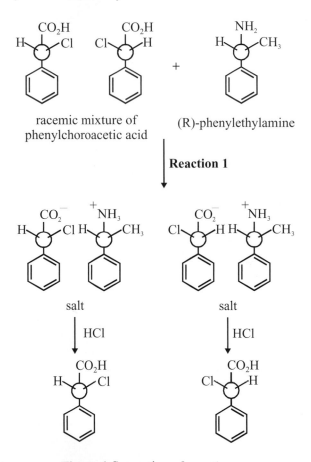

Figure 1 Separation of enantiomers

In the resolution of a racemic acid, a solution of (R)-phenylethylamine is reacted with a racemic mixture of phenylchloroacetic acid to form the corresponding salts. The salts are then separated by careful fractional crystallization. Hydrochloric acid is added to the separated salts, and the respective acids are precipitated from their solutions.

Resolution of a racemic base can be accomplished in the same manner with tartaric acid.

1. Quinine, a natural anti-malarial, is commonly used as an optically active reagent to resolve acidic enantiomers. How many chiral carbons exist in the quinine molecule drawn below?

OCH₃

Quinine

A. 1
B. 2
C. 3
D. 4

2. Which of the following alcohols is a natural product of anaerobic respiration?

A.

C.

B.

D.

3. The salts created in Reaction 1 are:

A. diastereomers
B. enantiomers
C. structural isomers
D. meso compounds

GO ON TO THE NEXT PAGE.

4. The following reaction proceeds with retention of configuration:

$$CH_2BrCHOHCO_2H \xrightarrow{\text{Zn, H}^+} CH_3CHOHCO_2H$$

If the product is the naturally occurring lactic acid, which of the compounds below could be a reactant?

A.

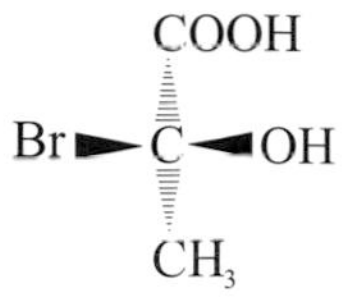

COOH
Br—C—OH
CH₃

C.

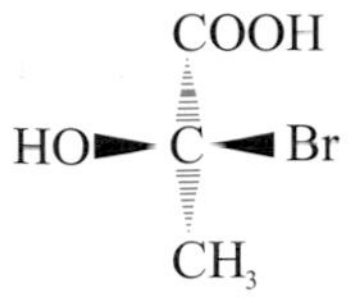

COOH
HO—C—Br
CH₃

B.

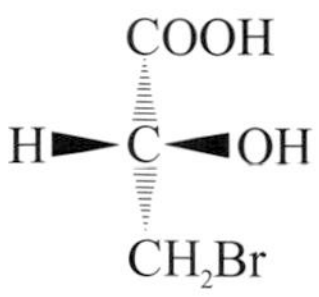

COOH
H—C—OH
CH₂Br

D.

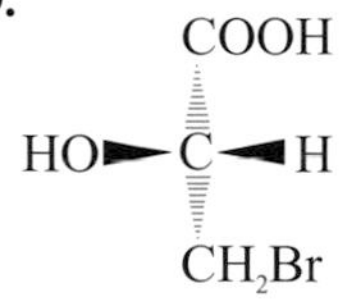

COOH
HO—C—H
CH₂Br

5. D-(+)-glyceraldehyde undergoes the series of reactions below to yield two isomers of tartaric acid. What type of isomers are they?

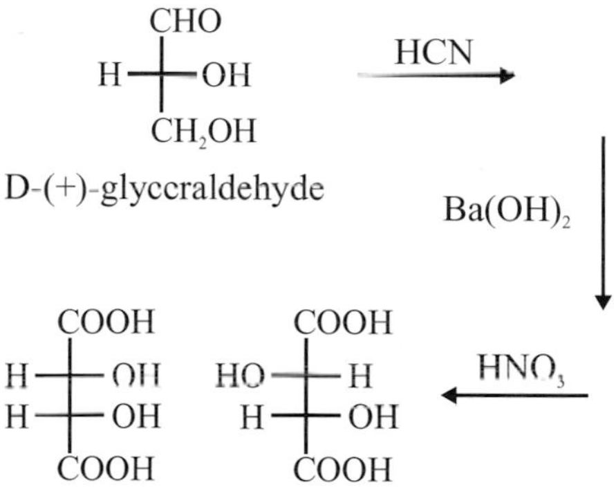

CHO
H——OH
CH₂OH

D-(+)-glyceraldehyde

$\xrightarrow{\text{HCN}}$

$\downarrow \text{Ba(OH)}_2$

COOH   COOH
H——OH   HO——H
H——OH   H——OH
COOH   COOH

$\xleftarrow{\text{HNO}_3}$

tartaric acid
isomers

A. enantiomers
B. diastereomers
C. structural isomers
D. conformational isomers

6. Which of the following compounds might be used to resolve a racemic mixture of acidic enantiomers?

A.

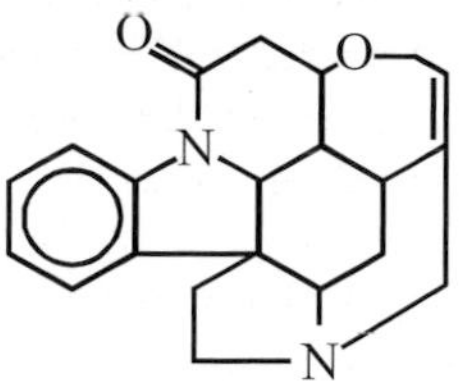

strychnine

B.

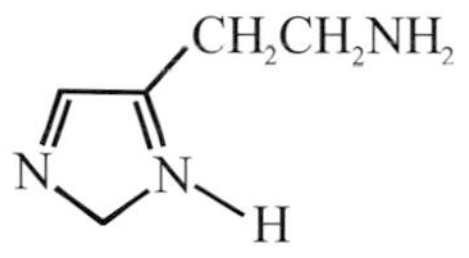

CH₂CH₂NH₂ (on imidazole ring)

histamine

C.

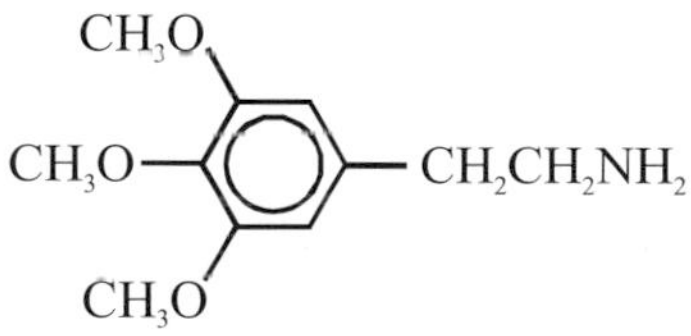

CH₃O, CH₃O—, CH₃O (on benzene ring) — CH₂CH₂NH₂

mescaline

D.

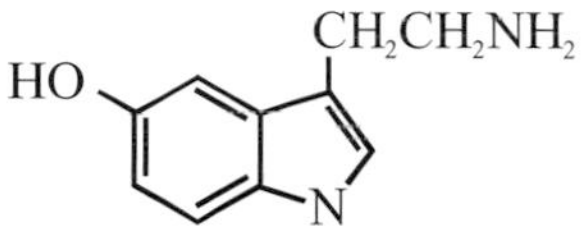

HO— (on indole ring) CH₂CH₂NH₂

serotonin

GO ON TO THE NEXT PAGE.

Passage II (Questions 7-13)

A chemical reaction is *stereoselective* when a certain stereoisomer or set of stereoisomers predominate as products. A reaction is *stereospecific* if different isomers lead to isomerically opposite products.

Bromine adds to 2-butene to form the *vic*-dihalide, 2,3-dibromobutane. A student proposed the following two mechanisms for the addition of bromine to alkenes.

In order to test each mechanism the student designed two experiments.

Mechanism A

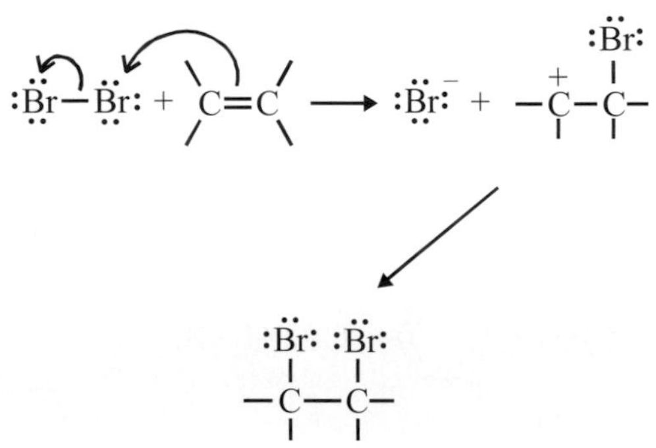

vic-dihalide

Mechanism B

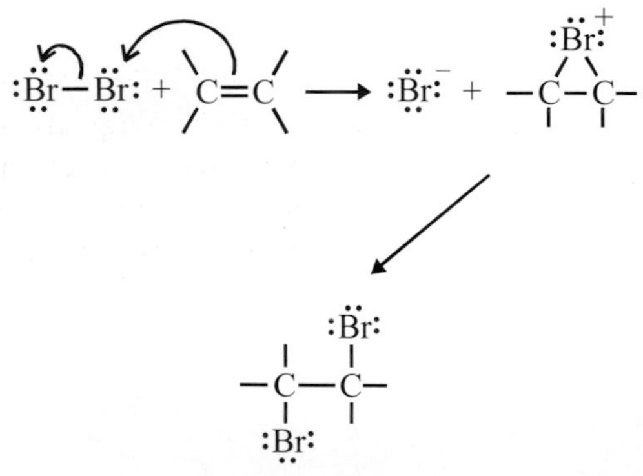

vic-dihalide

Experiment 1

Cyclopentene was dissolved in CCl_4. Bromine was added to the solution at low temperatures and low light. The product tested negative for optical activity. An optically active reagent was then added and, upon fractional distillation, two fractions were obtained. Each fraction was then precipitated and rinsed in an acid bath. The final products were found to have opposite observed rotations.

Experiment 2

The same procedure as in Experiment 1 was followed for both the *cis* and *trans* isomers of 2-butene. The results depended upon which isomer was used.

7. In the second step of *Mechanism B*, the bromine ion acts as:

A. a halophile.
B. a catalyst.
C. an electrophile.
D. a nucleophile.

8. If *Mechanism B* is correct, how many fractions should the student obtain from the distillation in Experiment 2 when the trans isomer is used?

A. 1
B. 2
C. 3
D. 4

9. What is the expected angle between the bonds of the carbocation in *Mechanism A?*

A. 90°
B. 109°
C. 120°
D. 180°

10. The results of the experiments demonstrate that *Mechanism B* is correct. The addition of bromine to alkenes is:

A. stereoselective but not stereospecific.
B. stereospecific but not stereoselective.
C. both stereoselective and stereospecific.
D. neither stereoselective nor stereospecific.

GO ON TO THE NEXT PAGE.

11. If, instead of CCl_4, water is used as the solvent in a halogen addition reaction, a halohydrin is formed. The student proposed that such a reaction would follow *Mechanism A* with water replacing bromine as the nucleophile. If this hypothesis is correct, which of the following is the most likely product for the addition of bromine to propene in water?

 A. 1,2-dibromopropane
 B. 1,3-dibromo-2-propanol
 C. 1-bromo-2-propanol
 D. 2-bromo-1-propanol

12. If *Mechanism B* is correct, the trans isomer in Experiment 2 will produce:

 A. a meso compound.
 B. a pair of enantiomers.
 C. only one optically active compound.
 D. a pair of structural isomers.

13. In *Experiment 1*, why did the student use low light and low temperature?

 A. to decrease the rate of the reaction
 B. to prevent combustion of the alkene
 C. to avoid contamination of the product via a radical reaction
 D. to increase the yield of the endothermic reaction

Passage III (Questions 14-19)

It is possible for asymmetrical molecules to distinguish between identical substituents on some symmetrical molecules. Such symmetrical molecules are called *prochiral*.

The molecule in Figure 1 is an example of a prochiral molecule. The asymmetrical enzyme attaches only to hydrogen 'a' and not to hydrogen 'b'. All known dehydrogenases are stereospecific in this manner.

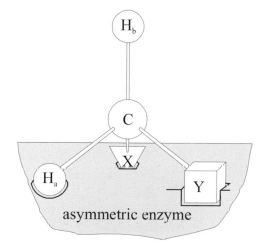

Figure 1 An asymmetrical enzyme distinguishing between identical substituents on a symmetrical molecule.

Experiment 1

An experimenter labeled oxaloacetate with ^{14}C at the carboxyl carbon farthest from the keto group. The oxaloacetate was allowed to undergo the portion of the Kreb's cycle depicted in Figure 2. The acetyl group donated by acetyl CoA is not removed during the Kreb's cycle. The experimenter found that all of the label emerged in the CO_2 of the second decarboxylation.

GO ON TO THE NEXT PAGE.

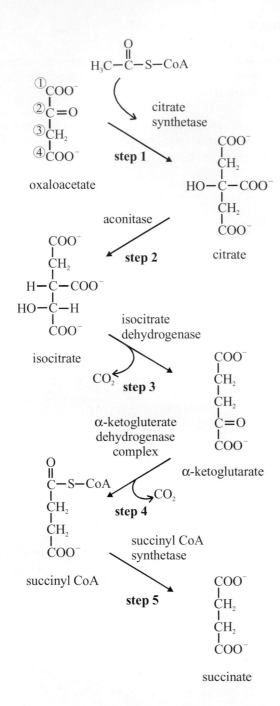

Figure 2 A portion of the Kreb's cycle

14. Which of the following reactants in step 1 of Figure 2 contains a water soluble vitamin as a component part?

A. citrate
B. oxaloacetate
C. acetyl CoA
D. citrate synthetase

15. All of the following molecules are prochiral at the third carbon EXCEPT:

A. succinate
B. citrate
C. α-ketoglutarate
D. isocitrate

16. Which one of the carbons numbered in oxaloacetate is removed from isocitrate by the decarboxylation in step 3 of Figure 2?

A. 1
B. 2
C. 3
D. 4

17. The hybridization of the labeled carbon in oxaloacetate, citrate, and α-ketogluterate, respectively, is:

A. sp^2; sp^2; sp^2
B. sp^2; sp^2; sp^3
C. sp^2; sp^3; sp^2
D. sp^3; sp^3; sp^3

18. Which of the following structures is the enol form of α-ketogluteric acid?

A.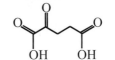
C.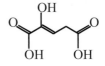

B.

D.

19. What are the products when deuterium labeled alcohol is reacted with NAD^+ in the presence of alcohol dehydrogenase as shown below?

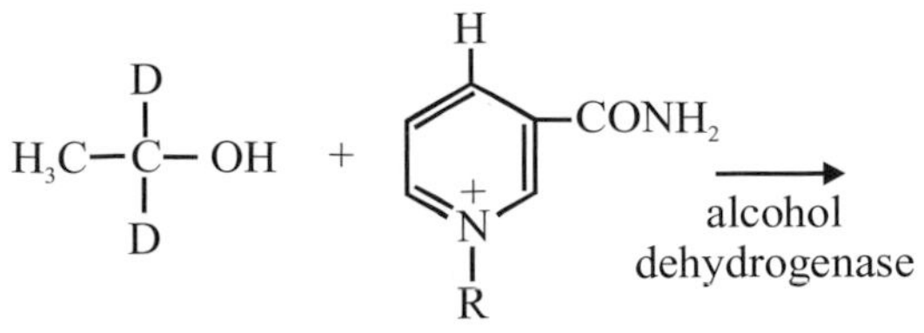

A.

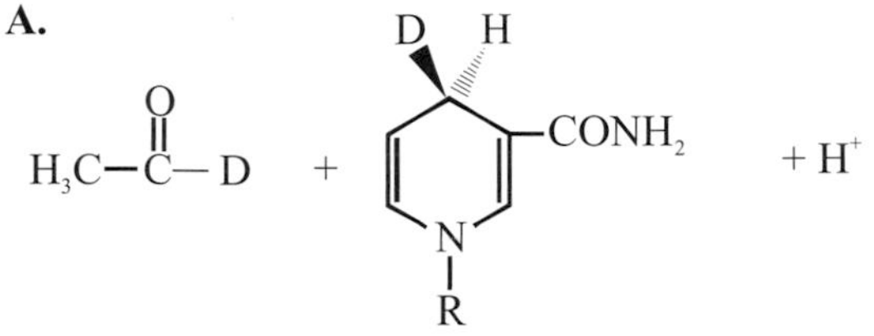

B.

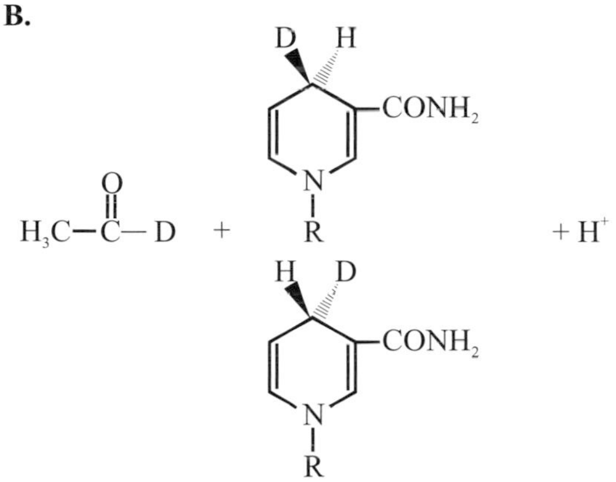

C.

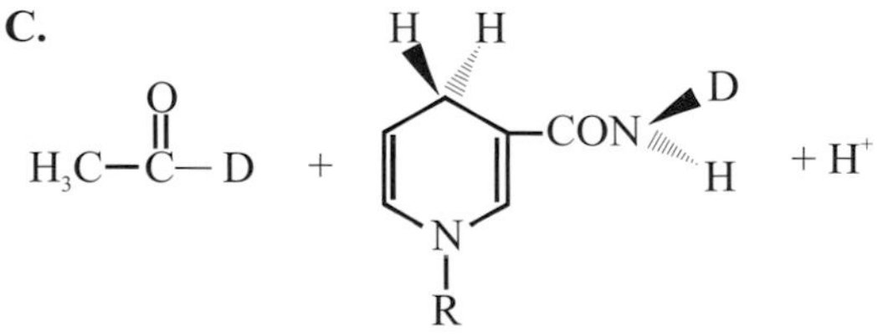

D.

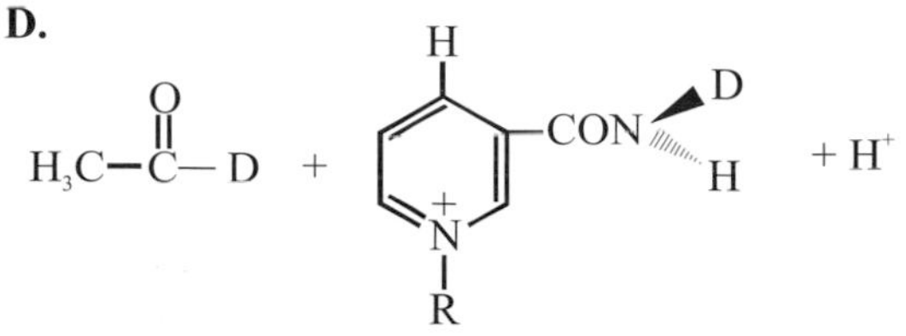

Questions 20 through 23 are **NOT** based on a descriptive passage.

20. Which of the following is true concerning meso compounds?

   I. They are achiral.
  II. They rotate the plane of polarized light.
 III. They contain a chiral carbon.

  A. I only
  B. I and II only
  C. I and III only
  D. II and III only

21. Which of the following is true concerning chirality?

   I. Chiral molecules are never the same as their mirror images.
  II. All chiral molecules have a mirror image which is their enantiomer.
 III. If a molecule is not the same as its mirror image, then it is chiral.

  A. I only
  B. II only
  C. III only
  D. I, II, and III

22. The name of the compound shown below is:

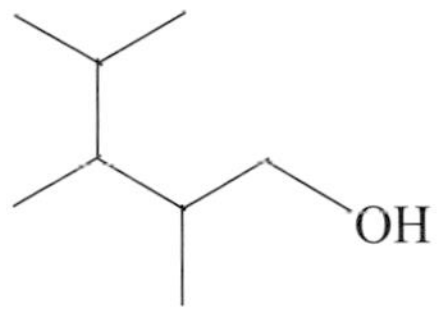

  A. 2-isopropyl-3-methyl-5-pentanol
  B. 3-isopropyl-2-methyl-1-butanol
  C. 2,3,4-trimethyl-1-pentanol
  D. 3,4,5-trimethyl-1-hexanol

23. Which of the following is true concerning conformational isomers?

  A. No conformer can be isolated.
  B. They only exist at high energy levels.
  C. The anti-conformation has the highest energy level.
  D. At low temperatures the anti-conformation is the most common.

STOP. IF YOU FINISH BEFORE TIME IS CALLED, CHECK YOUR WORK. YOU MAY GO BACK TO ANY QUESTION IN THIS TEST BOOKLET.

STOP.

30-MINUTE
IN-CLASS EXAM
FOR LECTURE 2

A chemist performs the following experiment.

Step 1

Chlorine is added to (*S*)-*sec*-butyl chloride at 300°C. The reaction proceeds with retention of configuration. The products are carefully separated by fractional distillation. The chemist identifies five fractions as isomers of dichlorobutane and labels them: Compounds A, B, C, D, and E. Compounds C and D are formed in a 7 to 3 ratio. The boiling points of all five compounds are listed in Table 1.

Compound	Boiling Point
A	134°C
B	124°C
C	118°C
D	115°C
E	104°C

Table 1 Boiling points of selected fractions from Step 1

Step 2

The labeled compounds are each checked with a polarimeter for the rotation of plane-polarized light. Only Compounds A, B, and C are optically active.

Step 3

Upon nmr spectroscopy, Compounds C and D were revealed to be stereoisomers.

24. After the distillation in Step 1, which of the following properties, if known for each fraction, would identify a fraction as a dichlorobutane?

 A. boiling point
 B. melting point
 C. molecular weight
 D. observed rotation

25. Compounds A and E are:

 A. diastereomers.
 B. enantiomers.
 C. conformational isomers.
 D. constitutional isomers.

26. If (*R,R*)-2,3-dichlorobutane is found to have a specific rotation of $[\alpha]_D^{20}$ -25.66, then which compound has a specific rotation of $[\alpha]_D^{20}$ +25.66?

 A. Compound A
 B. Compound B
 C. Compound C
 D. Compound D

27. Which of the following is NOT true concerning the compounds listed in Table 1?

 A. Although the relative configuration about the original chiral center is retained, the absolute configuration may have changed.
 B. Both configurations about any new chiral center appeared in equal proportions.
 C. One of the compounds is a meso compound.
 D. Although the relative configuration about the original chiral center is retained, the direction of observed rotation may change.

28. Compound E is most likely which of the following?

 A.   C.

 B.   D.

29. If NaOH is added to (*S*)-sec-butyl chloride, what is the most likely product?

 A. (*R*)-sec-butyl alcohol
 B. (*S*)-sec-butyl alcohol
 C. (*S*)-2-chloro-2-butanol
 D. (*R*)- 2-chloro-2-butanol

GO ON TO THE NEXT PAGE.

Passage II (Questions 30-36)

The *neighboring mechanism* occurs when a neighboring atom or functional group otherwise not involved in a reaction, affects the reaction by carrying electrons close to the reacting group. If the neighboring group helps to expel the leaving group, it is said to give *anchimeric assistance.*

The halohydrin 3-bromo-2-butanol undergoes the following reactions with hydrobromic acid.

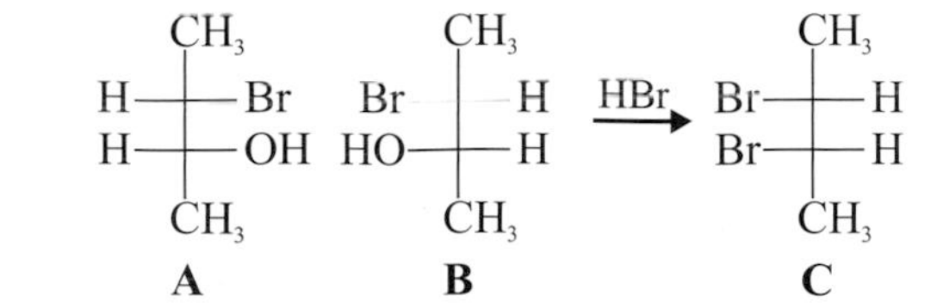

Reaction 1

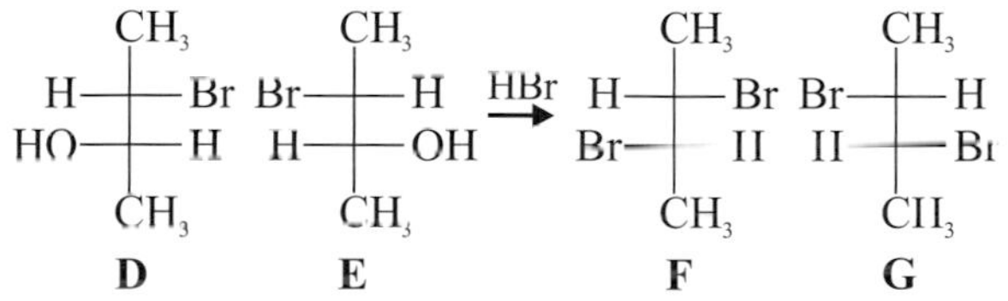

Reaction 2

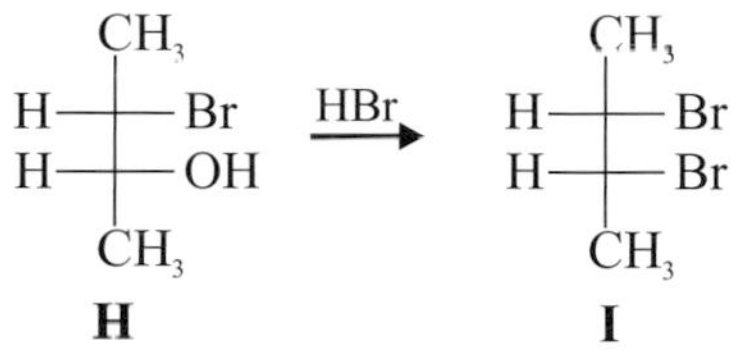

Reaction 3

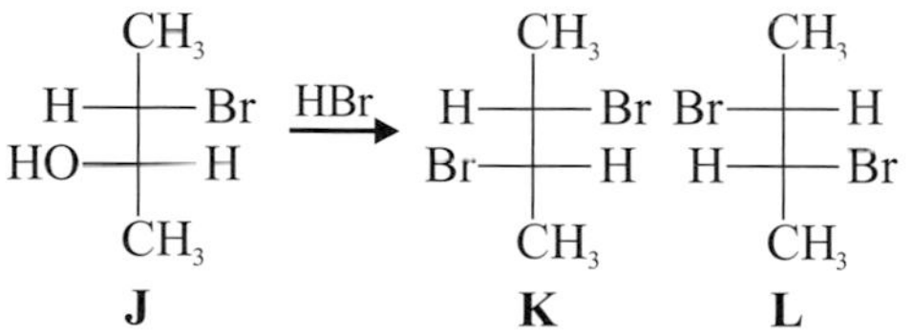

Reaction 4

A chemist proposed the following *neighboring mechanism* to explain the results of the above reactions:

Mechanism I

When the alcohol is protonated by the hydrobromic acid, the attached bromine attacks the adjacent carbon, ejecting the leaving group to form a bromonium ion. The bromine ion is then equally likely to attach via pathway a or b in Figure 1. Both the formation of the bromonium ion and attachment of the bromine ion are similar to an S_N2 mechanism where attachment of the nucleophile and detachment of the leaving group occur in a single step.

The process of bromonium ion formation is related to rearrangement of the carbon skeleton of carbocations. A nearby atom or group may relieve the electron deficiency of another atom through induction, resonance, or, as in bromonium ion formation, by actually carrying the electrons to where they are needed.

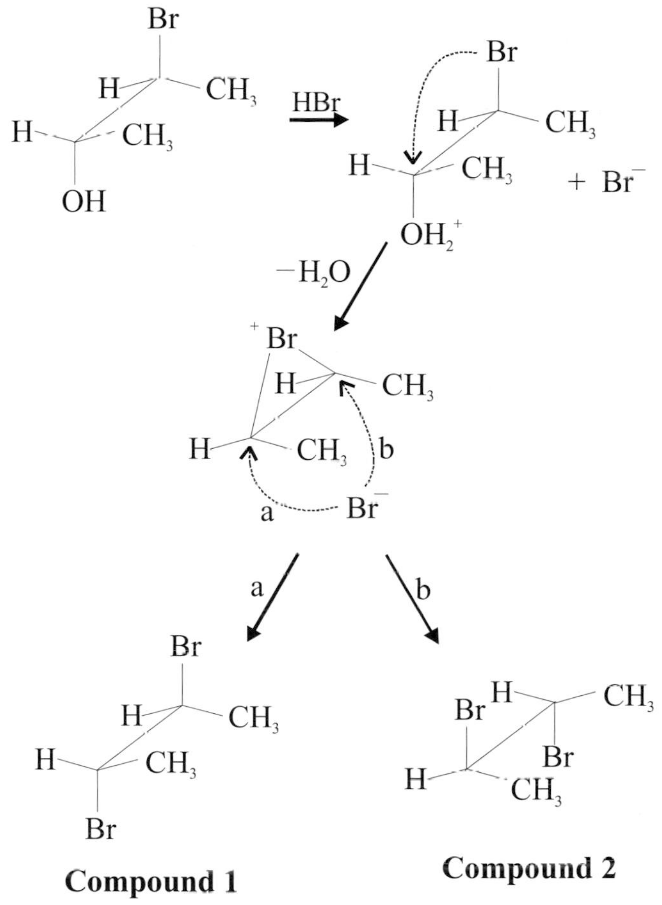

Figure 1 Diagram of Mechanism 1

30. How many stereoisomers exist of 2,3-dibromobutane?

A. 1
B. 2
C. 3
D. 4

GO ON TO THE NEXT PAGE.

31. Which of the following statements is true concerning Reaction 4?

A. Product K shows retention of configuration at both chiral centers and product L shows inversion of configuration at both chiral centers.

B. Both products K and L show inversion of configuration at one chiral center and retention of configuration at the other chiral center.

C. Only product K shows retention of configuration at one chiral center and inversion of configuration at the other chiral center.

D. Only product L shows retention of configuration at one chiral center and inversion of configuration at the other chiral center.

32. An even mixture of which of the following compounds from the reactions in the passage will rotate plane-polarized light?

I. A and B
II. C and I
III. H and J

A. I only
B. II only
C. III only
D. I and II only

33. Which of the following techniques could be used to distinguish the products of Reaction 1 from the mixture of products of Reaction 2?

A. mass spectroscopy
B. distillation
C. rotation of polarized light
D. infrared spectroscopy

34. If no neighboring mechanism occurred in Reaction 4, the expected products would be:

A. compounds K and L only.
B. compound K only.
C. compound L only.
D. compound C only.

35. Assuming HCl reacts similarly to HBr. which of the following would be the expected product of pathway 'b' of Mechanism 1 for the reaction given below?

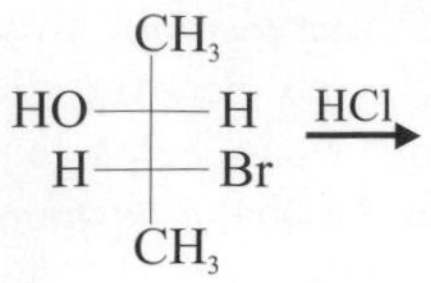

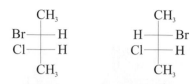

A.

CH₃
Br——H
Cl——H
CH₃

C.

CH₃
H——Br
Cl——H
CH₃

B.

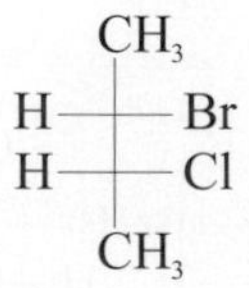

CH₃
H——Br
H——Cl
CH₃

D.

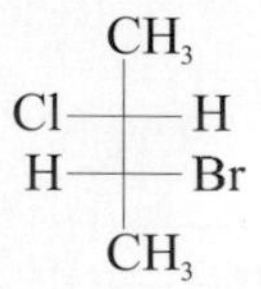

CH₃
Cl——H
H——Br
CH₃

36. According to Mechanism 1, which of the following most likely affects the initial rate of Reaction 3?

I. the concentration of reactant H
II. the concentration of HBr
III. the concentration of product I

A. I only
B. II only
C. I and II only
D. I, II, and III

GO ON TO THE NEXT PAGE.

Passage III (Questions 37-42)

Complicated alcohols that cannot be obtained on the market are often synthesized in the lab with a Grignard reagent. The Grignard reagent is made by reacting metallic magnesium with an organic halide. Many types of organic halides may be used, including primary, secondary. and tertiary alkylhalides and aromatic halides. However, the reagent is a very powerful base and it is impossible to prepare it from a compound having a hydrogen more acidic than an alkene. The halide may be a chloride, bromide, or iodide but chlorine based reagents require a special solvent.

The basic formula of a Grignard reagent is RMgX. The magnesium-carbon bond is covalent but extremely polar making the Grignard reagent a strong nucleophile. It is this characteristic of the reagent that is used in the synthesis of alcohols.

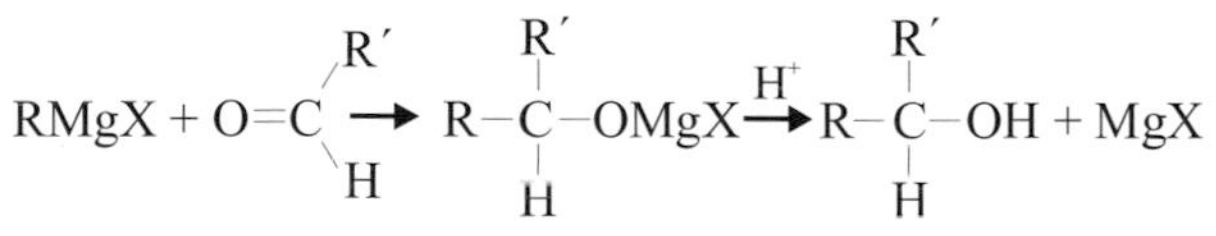

$$RMgX + O{=}C{\overset{R'}{\underset{H}{\diagdown}}} \rightarrow R{-}\underset{H}{\overset{R'}{\underset{|}{\overset{|}{C}}}}{-}OMgX \xrightarrow{H^+} R{-}\underset{H}{\overset{R'}{\underset{|}{\overset{|}{C}}}}{-}OH + MgX$$

Reaction 1 Alcohol synthesis from a Grignard reagent

In alcohol synthesis, the reagent reacts with a carbonyl compound to make the magnesium salt of the corresponding alcohol. The product is then bathed in dilute mineral acid forming an alcohol and a water soluble magnesiumhalide salt.

37. Which of the following compounds would make the best solvent in a Grignard synthesis with an alkylbromide?

   A. H_2O
   B. $(C_2H_5)_2O$
   C. $C_2H_3O_2Na$
   D. C_2H_5OH

38. What type of reaction takes place between the Grignard reagent and the carbonyl compound?

   A. S_N1
   B. S_N2
   C. nucleophilic addition
   D. bimolecular elimination

39. Which of the following alcohols would react the most strongly with a Grignard reagent?

   A. CH_3OH
   B. $(CH_3)_3OH$
   C. $CH_3CHOHCH_3$
   D. $CH_3(CH_2)_{11}CH_2OH$

40. Which of the following compounds could be reacted with the Grignard reagent shown below to create a tertiary alcohol?

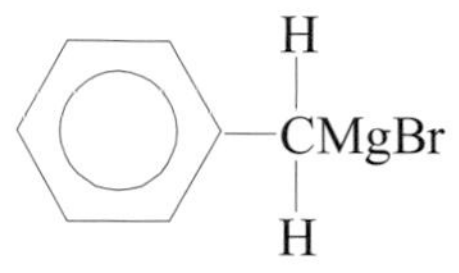

   A.   **C.**

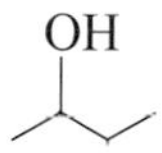

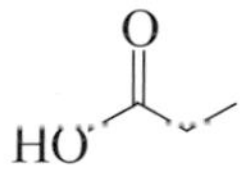

   B.   **D.**

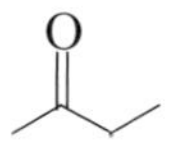

41. Which of the following most accurately represents the charge distribution in the magnesium-carbon bond of the Grignard reagent?

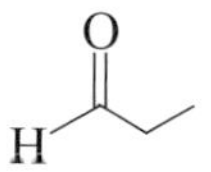

   A. $^{\delta+}CMg^{\delta-}$
   B. $^{\delta-}CMg^{\delta+}$
   C. $^{\delta+}CMg^{\delta+}$
   D. $^{\delta-}CMg^{\delta-}$

42. If the alcoholic product of Reaction 1 were oxidized by H_2CrO_4 and acid, what would be the major product?

   A. an aldehyde
   B. a carboxylic acid
   C. a ketone
   D. an alkene

GO ON TO THE NEXT PAGE.

Questions 43 through 46 are **NOT** based on a descriptive passage.

43. The dehydration of 2-pentanol in the presence of a strong acid and heat results in a(n):

A. alkane
B. alkene
C. aldehyde
D. carboxylic acid

44. Which of the following has the greatest boiling point?

A. methane
B. methanol
C. chloromethane
D. ammonia

45. NaCl will not react with ethanol via an S_N2 reaction because:

A. an hydroxide ion is less stable than the chlorine ion.
B. an hydroxide ion is more stable than the chlorine ion.
C. steric hindrance prevents the reaction.
D. the chloride ion is a better nucleophile than the hydroxyl group.

46. Which of the following is the most soluble in water?

A. 1-butanol
B. butane
C. 1-butene
D. propane

STOP. IF YOU FINISH BEFORE TIME IS CALLED, CHECK YOUR WORK. YOU MAY GO BACK TO ANY QUESTION IN THIS TEST BOOKLET.

30-MINUTE
IN-CLASS EXAM
FOR LECTURE 3

Passage I (Questions 47-52)

In 1877 two chemists working together developed a new method for the preparation of alkylbenzenes and acylbenzenes. In the Friedel-Crafts acylation, named after these two chemists, an acyl group is added to benzene in the presence of a Lewis acid. The Lewis acid usually reacts with the acyl group to form an acylium ion. The acylium ion is stabilized by resonance. Next, the acylium ion acts as an electrophile attacking the benzene ring to form an arenium ion. The arenium ion then loses a proton to generate the final product. Powerful electron-withdrawing groups on the benzene ring such as another acyl group will block this reaction.

Naphthalene is the simplest and most important of the fused ring hydrocarbons. Five percent of all constituents of coal tar are naphthalene. Naphthalene can be manufactured using the Friedel-Crafts reaction via the reaction pathway shown in Scheme 1.

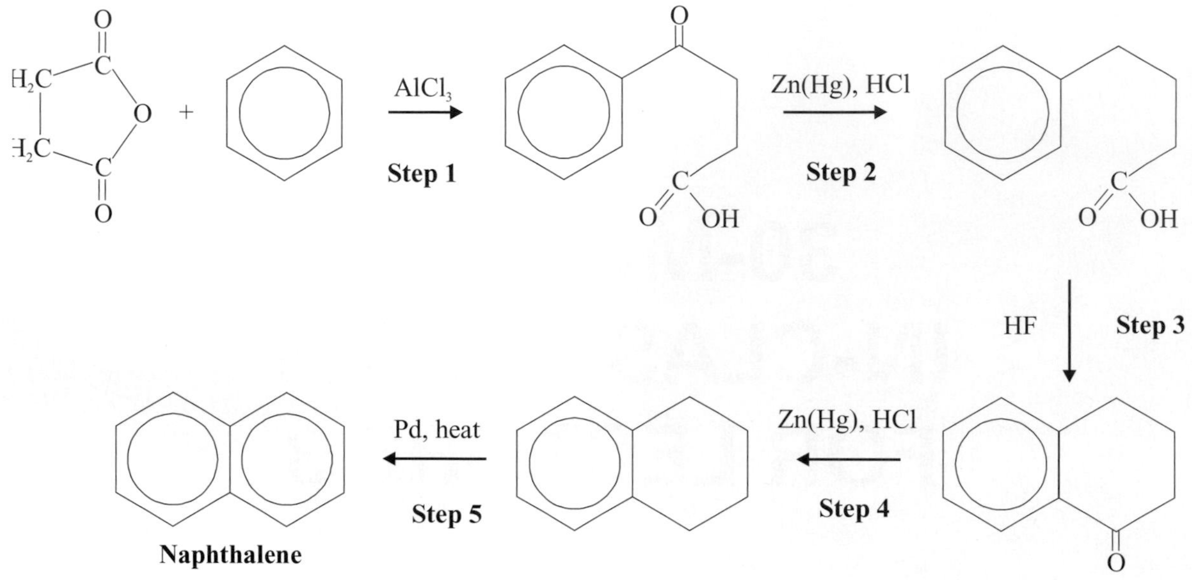

Scheme 1

47. The Friedel-Crafts reaction occurs twice in Scheme 1. Which two steps represent Friedel-Crafts reactions?

- **A.** steps 1 and 3
- **B.** steps 1 and 5
- **C.** steps 2 and 4
- **D.** steps 3 and 5

48. Step 2 is which of the following types of reactions?

- **A.** an oxidation reaction
- **B.** a reduction reaction
- **C.** an elimination reaction
- **D.** a Friedel-Crafts reaction

49. Why is step 2 necessary in order for ring closure to take place in step 3?

- **A.** Step 2 activates the ring by changing the electron releasing alkyl group to an elcctron withdrawing acyl group.
- **B.** Step 2 deactivates the ring by changing the electron releasing acyl group to an electron withdrawing alkyl group.
- **C.** Step 2 activates the ring by changing the electron withdrawing acyl group to an electron releasing alkyl group.
- **D.** Step 2 deactivates the ring by changing the electron withdrawing alkyl group to an electron releasing acyl group.

GO ON TO THE NEXT PAGE.

50. What are the most likely products of the following reaction?

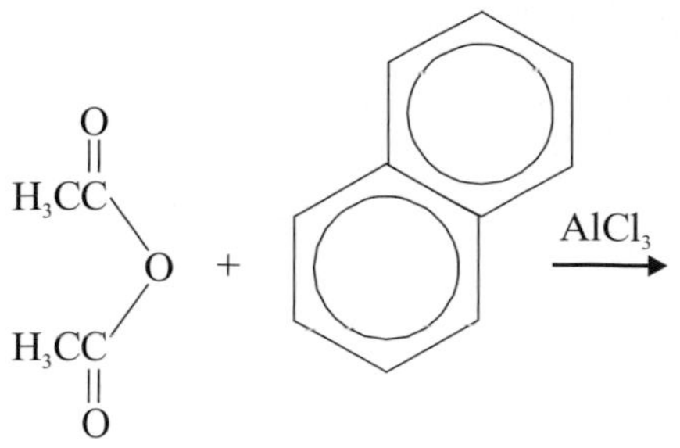

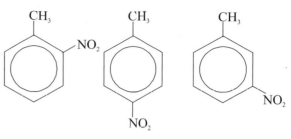

A.

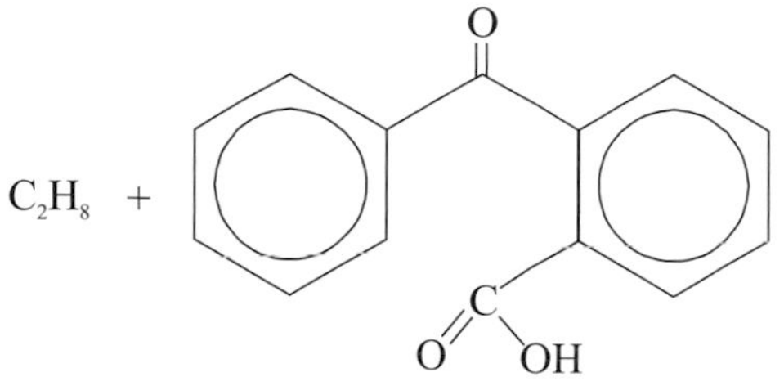

C_2H_8 +

B.

CH_3COH +

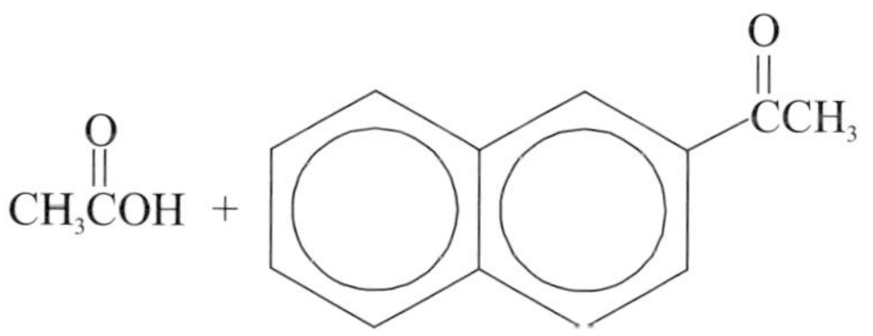

C.

CH_3CH +

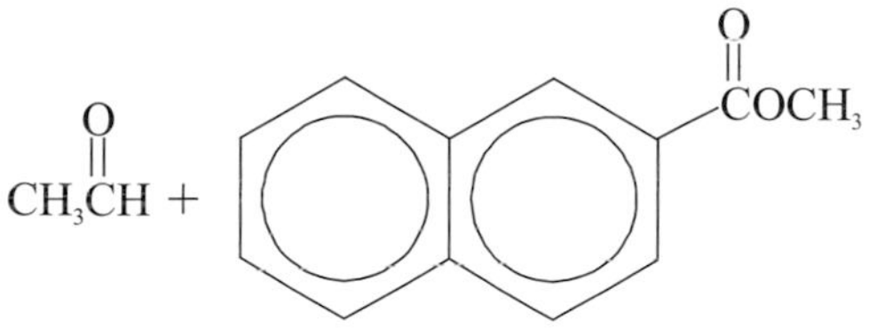

D.

CH_3CH +

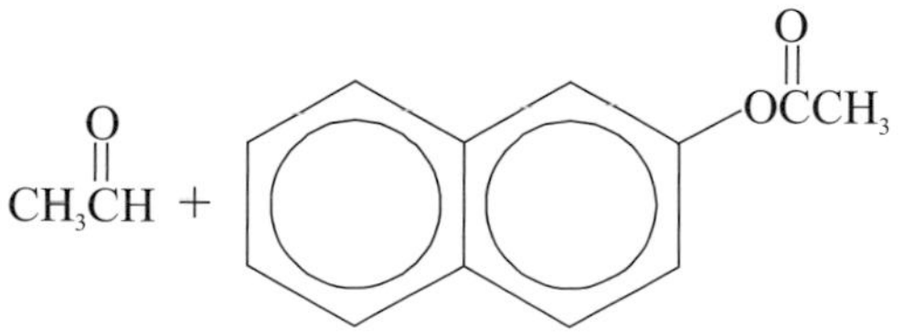

51. Toluene reacts with nitric acid to form the following products:

o-Nitrotoluene (59%) p-Nitrotoluene (37%) m-Nitrotoluene (4%)

If the position of substitution were chosen at random, what would be the expected percentage of m-nitrotoluene from the reaction?

A. 0%
B. 4%
C. 33%
D. 40%

52. Which of the following is an acylium ion?

A.

$AlCl_4$

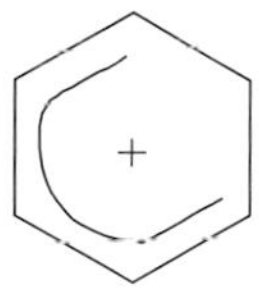

C.

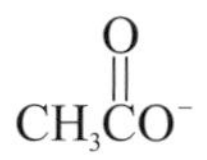

CH_3CO^-

B.

D.

CH_3C^+

117

GO ON TO THE NEXT PAGE.

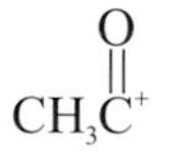

When unknown compounds are identified without the aid of spectroscopy, classification tests are used. Reacting the carbonyl in a ketone or aldehyde with an amine (2,4 dinitrophenylhydrazine) to form an imine is the easiest way to detect a ketone or aldehyde (Reaction 1). The imine that forms is a highly colored solid. The color of the solid also helps to indicate structural characteristics. Ketones and aldehydes with no conjugation tend to form imines with yellow to orange colors, while highly conjugated ketones or aldehydes form imines with red color.

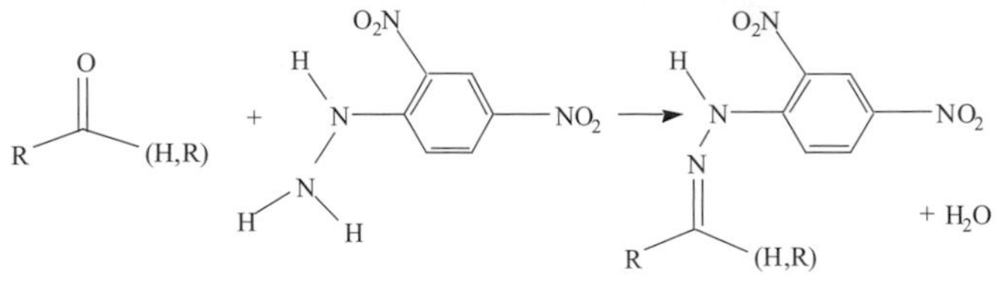

2, 4-nitrophenylhydrazine   dinitrophenylhydrazone

Reaction 1

The presence of a colored solid confirms the presence of a ketone or aldehyde, but the imine formation does not indicate whether the unknown is a ketone or aldehyde. A second classification test is used to distinguish the two functionalities. This test is called the Tollens' test, and the significant reaction is shown in Reaction 2.

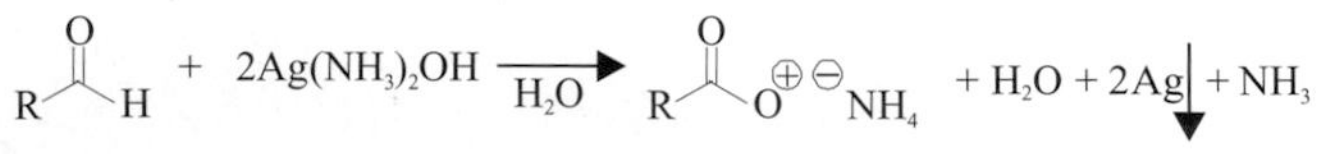

Reaction 2

Aldehydes will form a silver mirror or a black precipitate if the test tube is dirty, while ketones will not.

Once the unknown is determined to be a ketone or an aldehyde, the melting point of the imine derivative is determined. The melting point and other physical characteristics (i.e., solubility of unknown and boiling point or melting point of the unknown) are used to determine the unknown's identity. The information is compared to tables in books which contain the melting points of derivatives and other physical data for organic compounds.

53. Why does the Tollens' test produce solid silver with aldehydes and not with ketones?

    A.   Ketones are more sterically hindered than aldehydes.
    B.   Aldehydes can be oxidized to the carboxylic acid, while ketone cannot.
    C.   Ketones do not have an acidic proton while aldehydes do have one.
    D.   Aldehydes are more sterically hindered than ketones.

54. A red 2,4 dinitrophenylhydrazone is obtained from the reaction of an unknown with an amine. Of the following four structures, which ketone or aldehyde could have formed this imine?

    A.

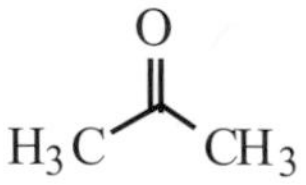

    B.

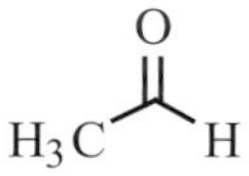

    C.

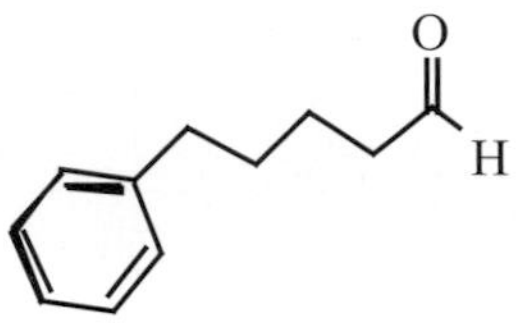

    D.

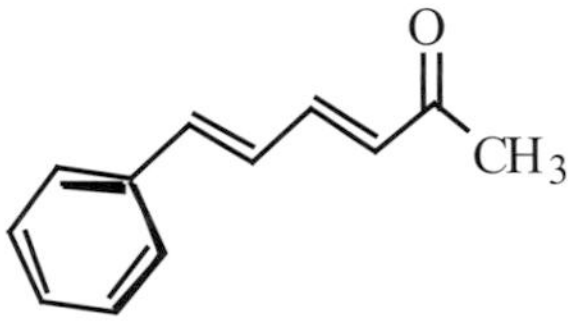

55. What type of reaction is Reaction 1?

    A.   bimolecular elimination
    B.   dehydration
    C.   hydrolysis
    D.   saponification

56. In Reaction 1, the nitrogen of the amine is

    A.   a nucleophile
    B.   an electrophile
    C.   an acid
    D.   an oxidant

57. The structures shown below are:

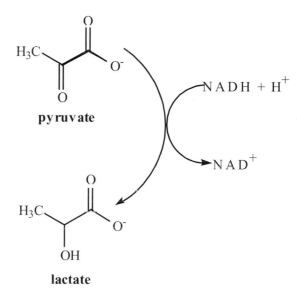

and

A. enantiomers
B. diastereomers
C. epimers
D. tautomers

58. The hemiketal of acetone can be formed by adding:

A. HCl
B. CH$_3$OH
C. NaOH
D. formaldehyde

59. Instead of using the Tollens' test, a student uses nmr spectroscopy to distinguish an aldehyde from a ketone. What should the student expect to find?

A. More splitting in the nmr peaks of ketones than of aldehydes.
B. Less splitting in the nmr peaks of ketones than of aldehydes.
C. One peak downfield in the aldehyde but not in the ketone.
D. Two peaks upfield in the aldehyde but not the ketone.

Passage III (Questions 60-66)

During high-frequency stimulation of muscles, an anaerobic condition is created. As a result, the pyruvate produced from glycolsis (the breakdown of glucose to produce ATP) is converted to lactate by single enzyme mediation (Figure 1) rather than the pyruvate entering the Krebs cycle. The lactate formation maintains NAD$^+$ for glycolsis, but produces less ATP than the completion of the Krebs cycle.

Figure 1 Conversion of pyruvate to lactate

The lactate produced by this cycle is passed into the blood and is transported to the liver. In the liver, the lactate is converted back to glucose. This cycle is called the Cori cycle.

The increase in the lactic acid produced from glycolysis causes metabolic acidosis and muscle fatigue.

60. Which of the following is true concerning the acidity of pyruvic acid and lactic acid?

A. Pyruvic acid is more acidic.
B. Lactic acid is more acidic.
C. Both acids have the same acidity.
D. Relative acidity cannot be determined based on structures alone.

61. The transformation of pyruvate to lactate is:

A. a decarboxylation
B. an oxidation
C. a reduction
D. hydration

GO ON TO THE NEXT PAGE..

62. The product of the reaction below is:

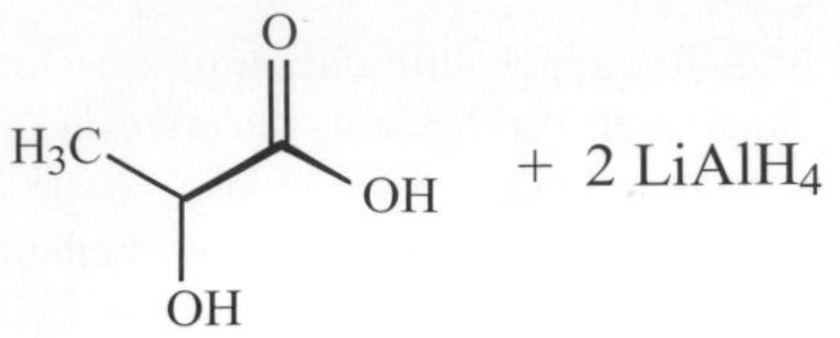

lactic acid

$+ 2 \text{ LiAlH}_4$

A.

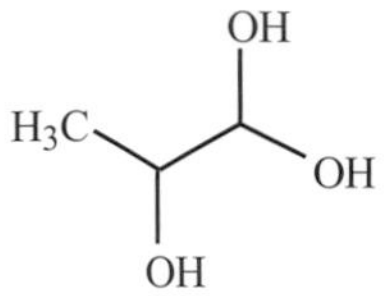

B.

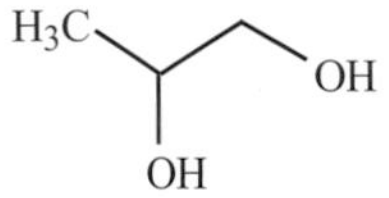

C.

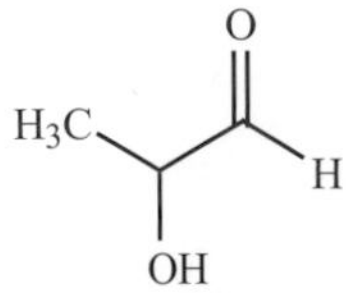

D.

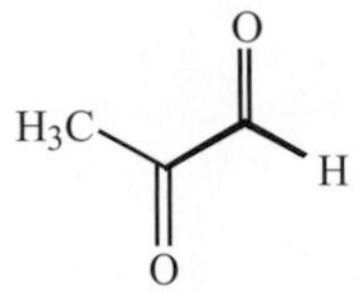

63. Why does weightlifting produce lactic acid buildup in muscle tissue?

A. Some highly active muscle tissue uses ATP faster than can be supplied by aerobic respiration.
B. Some highly active muscle tissue uses ATP faster than can be supplied by anaerobic respiration.
C. Lactic acid is always a byproduct of ATP production.
D. The Krebs cycle produces lactic acid.

64. Under aerobic conditions additional ATP is produced, following glycolysis, when:

A. pyruvate enters the Krebs cycle.
B. pyruvate is converted to lactate.
C. lactate is converted back to glucose in the liver completing the Cori cycle.
D. muscles become fatigued.

65. What is the product of the following reaction:

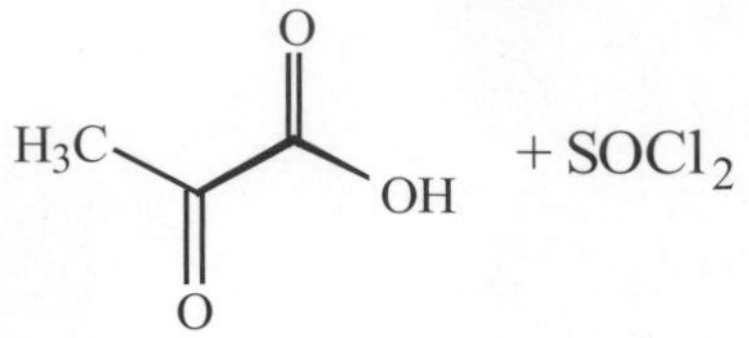

$+ \text{SOCl}_2$

A.

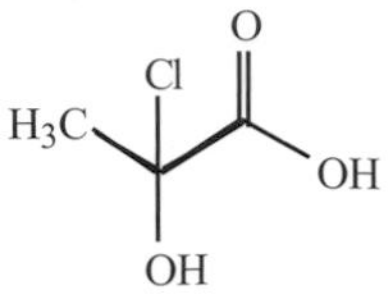

B.

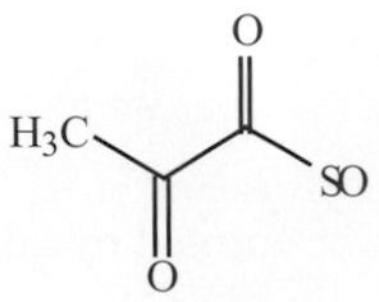

C.

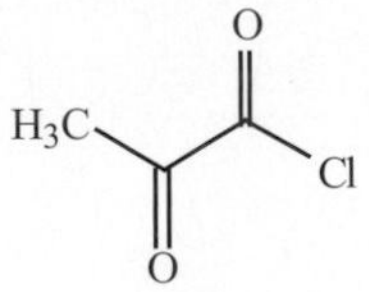

D.

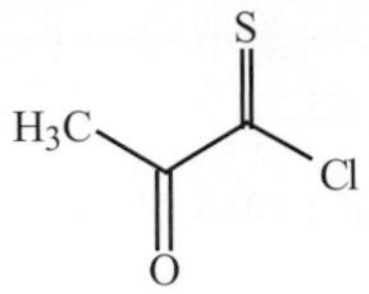

66. How do the water solubility and boiling point of pyruvic acid and lactic acid compare?

A. Pyruvic acid has a higher boiling point and is more water soluble.
B. Lactic acid has a higher boiling point and is more water soluble.
C. Pyruvic acid has a higher boiling point but lactate is more water soluble.
D. Lactic acid has a higher boiling point but pyruvate is more water soluble.

Questions 67 through 69 are **NOT** based on a descriptive passage.

67. When nucleophilic substitution occurs at a carbonyl, the weakest base is usually the best leaving group. What is the order of reactivity in a nucleophilic substitution reaction from most reactive to least reactive for the following compounds?

   I.   acid chloride
   II.   ester
   III.   amide

   A.   I, II, III
   B.   I, III, II
   C.   III, I, II
   D.   III, II, I

68. All of the following reactions may result in a ketone EXCEPT:

   A.   ozonolysis of an alkene.
   B.   aldol condensation.
   C.   oxidation of a primary alcohol
   D.   Friedel-Crafts acylation

69. All of the following qualities of a carbonyl carbon make it a good electrophile EXCEPT:

   A.   its stereochemistry
   B.   its partial positive charge
   C.   its planar shape
   D.   its lone pair of electrons

STOP. IF YOU FINISH BEFORE TIME IS CALLED, CHECK YOUR WORK. YOU MAY GO BACK TO ANY QUESTION IN THIS TEST BOOKLET.

STOP.

30-MINUTE
IN-CLASS EXAM
FOR LECTURE 4

In 1888 Emil Fishcer set out to discover the structure of (+)-glucose. Methods for determining absolute configuration had not yet been developed so Fischer arbitrarily limited his atten-tion to the eight D configurations shown in Figure 1. Starting with a sample of glucose and these eight possible structures, Fischer deduced the correct structure of glucose by following a process of elimination similar to the four steps described below.

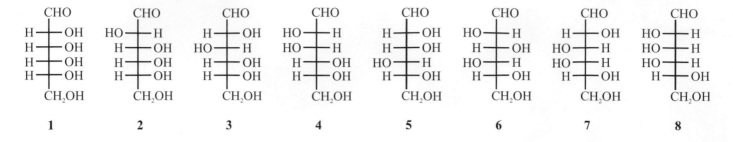

Figure 1

Steps used by Fischer to determine the structure of glucose:

1. Aldoses react with dilute nitric acid at both the CHO group and the terminal CH_2OH group to produce a CO_2H group at either end. Glucose produces an optically active compound in this reaction.

2. Aldoses can be degraded by the following two reactions. First the aldehyde is oxidized with bromine water to form a carboxylic acid. Next the carboxylic acid is decarboxy-lated with hydrogen peroxide and ferric sulfate leaving an aldehyde. The new aldose is one carbon shorter. When glucose is degraded in this manner, and the product is oxidized by dilute nitric acid, an optically active com-pound is formed.

3. The Kiliani-Fischer synthesis lengthens the carbon chain of an aldose by one carbon at the aldehyde end and forms a new aldose with its corresponding epimers. When glucose and its epimer are produced from the correspon-ding pentose via the Kiliani-Fischer synthesis, and then both epimers are reacted with dilute nitric acid, both form optically active compounds.

4. The two remaining possible structures for glucose were now examined. The end groups (CHO and CH_2OH) were exchanged on each. When the end groups were exchanged on one of the sugars it remained as the same compound. However, when the end groups of glucose were exchanged, a new sugar was created.

70. How many stereoisomers are possible for glucose?

    A. 2
    B. 8
    C. 16
    D. 32

71. The reactions between an aldose and dilute nitric acid as described in step 1 are which of the following types of reactions?

    A.   reduction
    B.   oxidation
    C.   hydrolysis
    D.   elimination

72. If only step 2 is performed, which of the structures in Figure 1 are eliminated as possible structures of glucose?

    A.   1 and 2 only
    B.   1, 4, and 7 only
    C.   1, 2, 5, and 6 only
    D.   3, 4, 7, and 8 only

GO ON TO THE NEXT PAGE.

73. Which of the following pentoses, when undergoing the Kiliani-Fischer synthesis, will yield D-glucose and D-mannose?

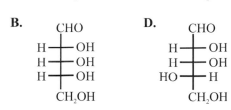

74. D-(+)-glyceraldehyde was allowed to undergo the Kiliani-Fischer synthesis, and the reaction ran to completion. After separation of any isomers, how many optically active products were formed?

$$
\begin{array}{c}
\text{CHO} \\
\text{H}\!-\!\!\!-\!\text{OH} \\
\text{CH}_2\text{OH}
\end{array}
$$

D-(+)-glyceraldehyde

- **A.** 0
- **B.** 1
- **C.** 2
- **D.** 4

75. Which structures can be eliminated by step 1?

- **A.** 1 and 7 only
- **B.** 4 and 6 only
- **C.** 1, 4, 6, and 7 only
- **D.** 2, 3, 5, and 8 only

76. Before carrying out step 4, Fischer had eliminated all but two possible structures for glucose. Which of the following was the structure that step 4 proved NOT to be glucose?

- **A.** 2
- **B.** 4
- **C.** 5
- **D.** 8

Passage II (Questions 77-82)

In 1951 a chemist made $C_{10}H_{10}Fe$ by reacting two moles of cyclopentadienylmagnesium bromide (a Grignard reagent) with anhydrous ferrous chloride. The structure of the resulting stable solid was uncertain and became an area of great interest in the following years. The structure proposed by the original chemist is shown in Figure 1.

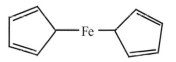

Figure 1. Proposed structure 1

Chemists later proposed a new structure called a "sandwich" complex which is shown in Figure 2.

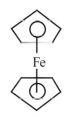

Figure 2. Proposed structure 2

The spectroscopy for $C_{10}H_{10}Fe$ is shown in Tables 1 and 2.

Chemical Shift	Coupling Pattern	Integral Value
4.12 ppm	singlet	10

Table 1 Proton NMR data

Frequency	Description of Peak
2900 cm^{-1}	very strong

Table 2 IR peaks
at frequencies greater than 1500 cm^{-1}

When $C_{10}H_{10}Fe$ is reacted with acetic anhydride in the presence of an acid as shown in Reaction 1, a dark orange solid is formed with the molecular formula $C_{12}H_{12}OFe$. The reaction of $C_{10}H_{10}Fe$ with the anhydride helped scientists to confirm which structure was valid.

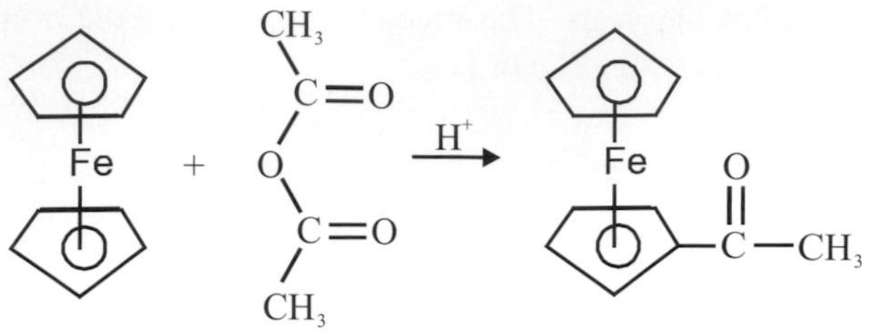

Reaction 1

A summary of the spectroscopy for the product shown in Reaction 1 is given in Tables 3 and 4.

Chemical Shift	Coupling Pattern	Integral Value
2.30 ppm	singlet	3
4.20 ppm	singlet	5
4.50 ppm	doublet	2
4.80 ppm	doublet	2

Table 3 Proton NMR data

Frequency	Description of Peak
2900 cm^{-1}	very strong
1700 cm^{-1}	very strong

Table 4 IR peaks at frequencies
greater than 1500 cm^{-1}

77. What is the other product that is produced in Reaction 1 but not shown?

   A.   a carboxylic acid
   B.   a ketone
   C.   an aldehyde
   D.   an ester

78. The source of the new peak in the IR data after the reaction with acetic anhydride comes from:

   A.   a carbonyl stretch.
   B.   a C-H stretch.
   C.   the coupling of two protons.
   D.   a C-C-H bend.

79. The NMR peak at 2.30 ppm in Table 3 is from protons:

   A.   on the carbon of the double bonds in the cyclopentadiene ring.
   B.   on the carbon of the methyl group attached to the cyclopentadiene ring.
   C.   on the carbon of the methyl group attached to a carbonyl carbon.
   D.   on the carbon of the cyclopentadiene ring, not in a double bond.

80. Why is it important that the ferrous chloride be anhydrous in the reaction to form $C_{10}H_{10}Fe$?

   A.   The cyclopentadienylmagnesium bromide will react with water.
   B.   The ferrous chloride will turn to ferric chloride.
   C.   Ferrous chloride will not dissolve in water.
   D.   The water would catalyze the reaction and it would erupt.

81. In Figure 2, the five-membered rings are:

   A.   aromatic
   B.   antiaromatic
   C.   nonaromatic
   D.   aromaticity can not be determined for any structures that do not contain benzene

82. How does the spectroscopy done before the reaction indicate that structure 1 is not the true structure?

   A.   If structure 1 were the true structure, there would be 3 chemical shifts in Table 1.
   B.   If structure 1 were the true structure, there would be 4 chemical shifts in Table 1.
   C.   If structure 1 were the true structure, there would be a frequency of 1700 cm^{-1} and not a frequency at 2900 cm^{-1} in Table 2.
   D.   If structure 1 were the true structure, there would be a frequency of 1700 cm^{-1} as well as the frequency at 2900 cm^{-1} in Table 2.

In a student experiment designed to demonstrate microscale extraction techniques, the three compounds shown in Figure 1 are dissolved in diethyl ether and separated. Their physical properties are shown in Table 1.

9-Fluorenone   Ethyl 4-aminobenzoate   Benzoic Acid

Figure 1 Compounds to be separated by extraction

The mixture is created by dissolving 50 mg of each compound in 4 mL of diethyl ether. 2 mL of 3 M HCl is added creating a two phase system. The system is mixed thoroughly and then allowed to separate. The aqueous layer is removed and the step is repeated with the remainder of the mixture.

6 M NaOH is added to the extracted aqueous solution. The solution is cooled in an ice bath and precipitate is collected and washed with distilled water. The precipitate is then weighed and the melting point is determined.

The remaining mixture is now separated by extraction with two 2 mL portions of 3 M NaOH. 6 M HCl is added to the alkaline solution, which is then cooled to form a precipitate. The precipitate is then weighed and the melting point is determined.

The remaining component is washed with distilled water. Next, 250 mg of Na_2SO_4 are added. The Na_2SO_4 is then filtered off using a filter pipet and the remaining solution is transferred to an Erlenmeyer flask. The Erlenmeyer flask is placed in a warm sand bath. A precipitate forms and is weighed and the melting point determined.

Compound	mp(°C)	bp(°C)	specific gravity
9-Fluorenone	122		
Ethyl 4-aminobenzoate	89		
Benzoic acid	154		
Diethyl ether		40	1.33

Table 1 Physical properties

83. What is the function of the Na_2SO_4 when added to the ether solution?

    A. Na_2SO_4 catalyzes the separation of the 9-fluorenone and ether.

    B. Na_2SO_4 catalyzes the separation of the benzoic acid and ether.

    C. Na_2SO_4 removes the remaining impurities of the solution.

    D. Na_2SO_4 acts as a drying agent.

84. Which of the following comes out in the aqueous layer of the first extraction with 3 M HCl?

    A.   9-fluorenone
    B.   ethyl 4-aminobenzoate
    C.   Benzoic acid
    D.   diethyl ether

85. What is the expected molecular weight of the compound extracted by NaOH?

    A.   46
    B.   122
    C.   165
    D.   180

86. In the first extraction, the aqueous layer will be:

    A.   below the organic layer because it has a lower density than the organic layer.

    B.   below the organic layer because it has a greater density than the organic layer.

    C.   above the organic layer because it has a lower density than the organic layer.

    D.   above the organic layer because it has a greater density than the organic layer.

87. What is the purpose of the warm sand bath?

    A.   Heat evaporates the ether concentrating the 9-fluorenone.

    B.   Heat evaporates the ether concentrating benzoic acid.

    C.   Heat accelerates the endothermic precipitation reaction.

    D.   Heat accelerates the exothermic precipitation reaction.

GO ON TO THE NEXT PAGE.

Questions 88 through 92 are **NOT** based on a descriptive passage.

88. IR spectroscopy is normally used to distinguish between:

    A. neighboring protons on different compounds.
    B. neighboring protons on the same compound.
    C. different functional groups on the same compound.
    D. acids and bases.

89. Which of the following is true concerning amino acids?

    A. Amino acids are monoprotic.
    B. Amino acids have peptide bonds.
    C. The side chain on an α-amino acid determines its acidity relative to other α-amino acids.
    D. All amino acids have water soluble side groups.

90. Peptide bond formation is an example of:

    A. saponification.
    B. electrophilic addition.
    C. bimolecular elimination.
    D. dehydration.

91. Triglycerides are composed from which of the following?

    A. esters, alcohols, and phospholipids
    B. fatty acids, alcohol, and esters
    C. fatty acids and glycerol
    D. glycerol and fatty esters

92. Which of the following is water soluble?

    A. a saturated fatty acid
    B. an unsaturated fatty acid
    C. the side chain on valine
    D. glucose

STOP. IF YOU FINISH BEFORE TIME IS CALLED, CHECK YOUR WORK. YOU MAY GO BACK TO ANY QUESTION IN THIS TEST BOOKLET.

STOP.

ANSWERS &
EXPLANATIONS
FOR
30-MINUTE IN-CLASS
EXAMS

ANSWERS FOR THE 30-MINUTE IN-CLASS EXAMS

Lecture 1	Lecture 2	Lecture 3	Lecture 4
1. D	24. C	47. A	70. C
2. B	25. D	48. B	71. B
3. A	26. C	49. C	72. C
4. D	27. B	50. B	73. A
5. B	28. C	51. D	74. C
6. A	29. A	52. D	75. A
7. D	30. C	53. B	76. B
8. A	31. A	54. D	77. A
9. C	32. C	55. B	78. A
10. C	33. B	56. A	79. C
11. C	34. D	57. D	80. A
12. A	35. C	58. B	81. A
13. C	36. C	59. C	82. A
14. C	37. B	60. A	83. D
15. D	38. C	61. C	84. B
16. A	39. A	62. B	85. B
17. A	40. D	63. A	86. C
18. C	41. B	64. A	87. A
19. A	42. C	65. C	88. C
20. C	43. B	66. B	89. C
21. D	44. B	67. A	90. D
22. C	45. A	68. C	91. C
23. D	46. A	69. D	92. D

MCAT ORGANIC CHEMISTRY	
Raw Score	**Estimated Scaled Score**
23	15
22	14
21	13
19–20	12
18	11
17	10
15-16	9
14	8
12-13	7
11	6
10	5
8-9	4

EXPLANATIONS TO IN-CLASS EXAM FOR LECTURE 1

Passage I

1. **D is correct.**

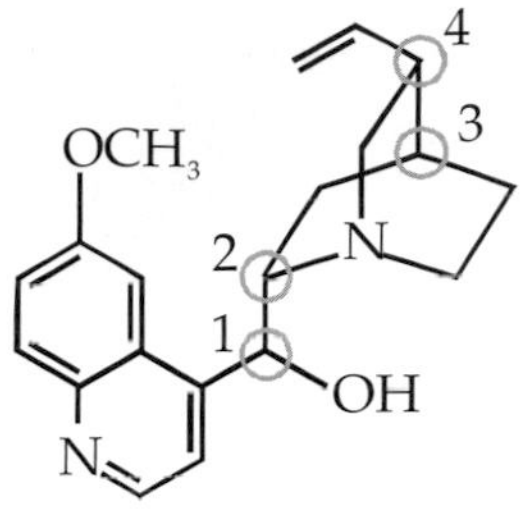

Quinine

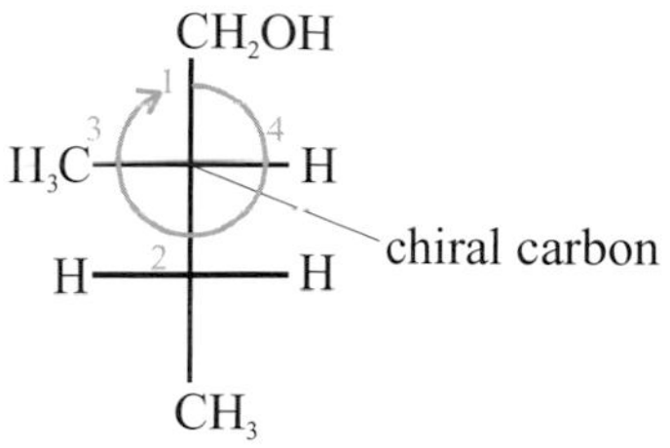

2. **B is correct.** Fermentation is anaerobic respiration. The passage states that (S)-2-methyl-1-butanol is the product of the fermentation of yeast. Looking at this molecule (above right), we prioritize the groups around the chiral carbon. Since the lowest priority group (the proton) is projected sideways, we must reverse the direction of our prioritization circle. This gives us the S configuration.

3. **A is correct.** The salts are stereoisomers because they have the same bond-to-bond connectivity, and they must be diastereomers because they can be separated by physical means (crystallization).

4. **D is correct.** Both A and C are wrong because they have the bromine attached to the wrong carbon to be the reactant. Since we know that configuration is retained, we simply substitute a hydrogen atom for the bromine and look for the molecule with the S configuration. (Remember, we are looking for the configuration of the product, not the reactant, so we must substitute the hydrogen for the bromine.) Retention of configuration does not mean that absolute configuration is retained; it means that there is no inversion. Because the lowest priority group is to the side in a Fischer projection, we reverse the direction of the circle shown below.

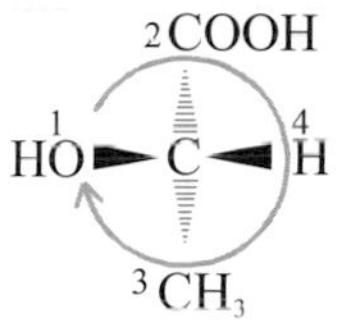

5. **B is correct.** The isomer on the left is a meso compound and has no enantiomer. Both isomers have the same bond-to-bond connectivity and are therefore diastereomers.

6. **A is correct.** Strychnine is the only chiral molecule and thus the only possibility. The passage states that the only chemical difference between enantiomers is their reactions with chiral compounds. Strychnine is often employed as a resolving agent for racemic acids.

Passage II

7. **D is correct.** The bromine ion is a negatively charged intermediate looking for a positive charge. Question: What's a halophile? Answer: Who cares? No one taking the MCAT. Answer choice A is a trap.

8. **A is correct.** The trans isomer will produce only a meso compound. If you're confused by this question, see the explanation to question 12 below.

9. **C is correct.** The carbocation carbon should be planar with bond angles of 120°.

10. **C is correct.** The reaction produces only certain stereoisomeric products so it is stereoselective. Experiment 2 says that the products depend upon the isomeric formation of the reactants, so it is stereospecific. Any reaction that is stereospecific is also stereoselective, but the converse is not true.

11. **C is correct.** The key is that the secondary carbocation is more stable than the primary (and most likely to form). You don't need to know what a halohydrin is to answer this question. Just look at Mechanism A, and substitute water for bromine as the nucleophile (the negatively charged species).

12. **A is correct.** Since the addition is always anti (attachment on opposite sides), only the meso compound will be formed. This is a very difficult question to visualize. Draw it out.

These are the same compound.
It is a meso compound

13. **C is correct.** Bromine will add to the alkane section of the ring when exposed to light via a radical reaction.

Passage III

14. **C is correct.** Acetyl CoA is a coenzyme. Vitamins are components of coenzymes.

15. **D is correct.** Isocitrate's third carbon is chiral. All of the other compounds' third carbons are attached to two distinct substituents and two identical substituents.

16. **A is correct.** The removal of either carbon 2 or 3 would break the chain, so the answer must be either carbon 1 or 4. The radio labeled carbon is carbon 4. Since this is removed in step 4 (as per the passage), the answer must be carbon 1.

17. **A is correct.** The labeled carbon is carbon 4, a carbonyl carbon throughout.

18. **C is correct.** An enol is both an alkene and an alcohol at the same carbon. The question refers to the tautomeric pairing of an alkene and enol. In that pairing, a proton shifts to the carbonyl oxygen and the oxygens' electrons form a carbon-carbon double bond. D is wrong because it does not have a carboxyl at both ends. A is wrong because it is a ketone – not an enol (A is α-ketogluterate). The carbon attached to the alcohol in B does not have a double bond, so it is wrong.

19. **A is correct.** The passage states that all known dehydrogenases are stereospecific in reactions with prochiral molecules. NADH is prochiral at the deuterium labeled carbon in answer choice A. B does not show a stereospecific reaction. In answer choice C a substitution reaction occurred at the amine, and an addition reaction occurred on the ring. This can't be correct. More importantly, in answer choice C the deuterium is not distinguishable from the hydrogen. This is not stereospecific. Answer choice D has too few hydrogens.

Stand Alones

20. **C is correct.** Meso compounds are (by definition) achiral although they do contain chiral carbons. They are not optically active (do not rotate plane-polarized light).

21. **D is correct.** All are true.

22. **C is correct.** If you missed this, then go back and study nomenclature.

23. **D is correct.** D and C are opposites, so one is likely to be true. At low temperatures, some conformers can be isolated.

EXPLANATIONS TO IN-CLASS EXAM FOR LECTURE 2

Passage I

Step one produces five dichlorobutanes among other products. These are separated by distillation to give:

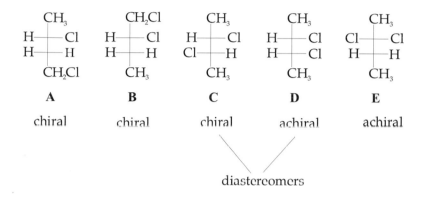

(*S*)-sec-butylchloride

24. **C is correct.** The molecular weight of all the dichloro products would be 127 and differ from all other possible products in this regard.

25. **D is correct.** As per the passage, only compounds C and D are stereoisomers (thus answers A and B are wrong). But all the compounds are dichlorobutane, so any two must be structural isomers. Structural isomerism is the same as constitutional isomerism.

26. **C is correct.** This question simply asks, "Which compound is the enantiomer to (*R,R*)-2,3-dichlorobutane?" Since we have retention of configuration, only one enantiomer of 2,3-dichlorobutane is made. The one that is made will be a stereoisomer to the meso compound and will rotate plane-polarized light in the opposite direction of (*R,R*) enantiomer. Enantiomers rotate polarized light, so compound A, B, or C must be this enantiomer. And since C and D are stereoisomers, one must be the meso compound of 2,3-dichlorobutane and one must be the (*SS*) enantiomer of (*R,R*)-2,3-dichlorobutane.

27. **B is correct.** From the passage, the configurations of C and D appeared in a 7:3 ratio. As per question 26, C and D are the SS and SR configurations of 2,3-dichlorobutane.

28. **C is correct.** Compound E is achiral, and is not the meso compound because D is (see question 26). Answer A is meso. Answer choice B could not have been formed because there is a change in relative configuration about the original chiral compound. Answer D is chiral. Only answer choice C is left.

29. **A is correct.** A reaction will most likely occur via an S_N2 mechanism with Cl⁻ as the leaving group. The reaction would then proceed with inversion of configuration (and stereochemistry). Since the priority of OH and Cl are both first, the configuration of the product is R.

Passage II

30. **C is correct.** 2,3-dibromobutane has two enantiomers and a meso compound. Four stereoisomers are possible according to the 2^n formula, but since there is a meso, only 3 exist.

31. **A is correct.** In product K the relative configurations are the same as the reactant. In product L, the relative configurations are reversed.

32. **C is correct.** A & B is a racemic mixture. C & I are the same meso compound. H & J are diastereomers, which rotate plane-polarized light to different degrees.

33. **B is correct.** The compounds are diastereomers, so they have different physical properties (like boiling points) and could thus be separated by distillation. A and D are wrong because both compounds have the same mass and the same functional groups. Neither group rotates polarized light, since Reaction 1 produces a meso compound and Reaction 2 produces a racemic mixture.

34. **D is correct.** The reaction would be a simple S_N2 reaction at the hydroxyl carbon proceeding with inversion of configuration to produce the meso compound.

35. **C is correct.** In pathway b, both configurations are inverted, and the halogen already attached to the molecule replaces the OH group.

36. **C is correct.** Although there are two steps, both reactants are required for the first step. The acid is needed to protonate the hydroxyl group. Products do not affect the initial rate.

Passage III

37. **B is correct.** Ether is the best choice for any solvent question on the MCAT. The passage states that the reagent will react with any hydrogen more acidic than an alkene hydrogen. A and D are more acidic than an alkene. C is a salt, not a solvent. In most cases, but not all, a solvent should not react with the reactants.

38. **C is correct.** The partially negative charged carbon on the Grignard reagent acts as a nucleophile and adds to the carbonyl carbon.

39. **A is correct.** Methyl alcohol is the strongest acid and will thus react the most vigorously with a Grignard reagent. The strongest acid is the primary alcohol with the shortest carbon chain.

40. **D is correct.** From the passage we know that the carbon attached to the Mg will act as a nucleophile on the carbonyl carbon. Only D will result in a tertiary alcohol.

41. **B is correct.** The passage states that the bond is covalent and polar and that the carbon is a good nucleophile. Thus the carbon would have a partial negative charge.

42. **C is correct.** Oxidation of a secondary alcohol always produces a ketone.

Stand Alones

43. **B is correct.** The dehydration of an alcohol forms a double bond.

44. **B is correct.** In this case, the differences in molecular weights (methane: 16; methanol: 32; chloromethane: 50.5; ammonia: 17) is outweighed by the extreme bond strength differences. Stronger intermolecular bonds increase boiling point. Hydrogen bonds are the strongest intermolecular bonds. Oxygen is more electronegative than nitrogen and so makes stronger hydrogen bonds. The boiling points are methane: -164; methanol: 65; chloromethane: -24.2; ammonia: -33. Notice that, although ammonia is one-third the weight of chloromethane, its hydrogen bonding gives it a boiling point nearly as high. By comparing the boiling points of ammonia and methanol (or even water), you should notice also how much stronger the hydrogen bonds of oxygen are than those of nitrogen.

45. **A is correct.** The hydroxyl group must be protonated in order to react with the chloride ion in an S_N2 reaction.

46. **A is correct.** The alcohol can form hydrogen bonds with water.

EXPLANATIONS TO IN-CLASS EXAM FOR LECTURE 3

Passage I

47. **A is correct.** According to the passage, a Friedel-Crafts reaction substitutes *something* (an acyl group) onto a benzene ring in the presence of an acid. Steps 1 and 3 are the only steps that involve substituting onto a benzene ring.

48. **B is correct.** Step 2 must be a reduction reaction because we lose oxygen and gain two hydrogens.

49. **C is correct.** Benzene rings are activated by electron releasing groups and deactivated by electron withdrawing groups, so A and D must be wrong. The passage states that acyl groups are electron withdrawing, so B must be wrong. The passage also states that acyl groups block the Friedel-Crafts reaction. Step 2 removes the ketone, which is an acyl group.

50. **B is correct.** Scheme 1, step 1 shows an anhydride reacting with an aromatic ring in the presence of $AlCl_3$ to form a carboxylic acid and a ketone. This reaction has the same form. This is a Friedel-Crafts reaction.

51. **D is correct.** There are two meta positions out of five possible positions. $2/5 = 0.4$ or 40%.

52. **D is correct.** According to the passage, the acylium ion must be positively charged because it acts as an electrophile, so A and C are out. B is no good because the acylium ion attacks the benzene ring so it must be producible from the anhydride in step 1. That leaves only D.

Passage II

53. **B is correct.** Reaction 2 shows an aldehyde being oxidized to a carboxylate ion to form the precipitate. Answer A is true, but does not answer the question. C and D are false.

54. **D is correct.** According to the passage, red coloring indicates a highly conjugated product. Only choice D has alternating double and single bonds.

55. **B is correct.** Water is lost.

56. **A is correct.** Nitrogen often acts as a nucleophile.

57. **D is correct.** Memorize this.

58. **B is correct.** You should recognize this reaction.

59. **C is correct.** You should know that an aldehyde will demonstrate a peak (downfield) when compared to a ketone.

Passage III

60. **A is correct.** The carbonyl group withdraws negative charge, stabilizing the conjugate base of pyruvate.

61. **C is correct.** Ketones can be reduced to yield secondary alcohols.

62. **B is correct.** Double reduction of a carboxylic acid. The secondary alcohol is already fully reduced.

63. **A is correct.** Lactic acid is a by-product of anaerobic respiration. Under active use conditions, some muscle tissues switch completely to anaerobic respiration.

64. **A is correct.** Aerobic means O_2 is present.

65. **C is correct.** Memorize this reaction.

66. **B is correct.** Lactate can form hydrogen bonds, which increase its water solubility and boiling point.

Stand Alones

67. **A is correct.** The chlorine ion is the weakest base, then the alkoxide ion, then the NH_2^-. Note that you don't need to know what an acid chloride is to answer the question.

Exam Explanations

68. **C is correct.** Note that you don't need to know the Friedel-Crafts reaction to answer this question.

69. **D is correct.** Carbonyl carbons don't have a lone pair of electrons.

EXPLANATIONS TO IN-CLASS EXAM FOR LECTURE 4

Passage I

See page 132 for a complete diagram of Passage I. Structure 1 is eliminated by steps 1, 2, and 3; structure 2 is eliminated by steps 2 and 3; structure 4 is not eliminated except by step 4; structures 5 and 6 are eliminated by step 2; structure 7 is eliminated by steps 1 and 3; and structure 8 is eliminated by step 3.

70. **C is correct.** Glucose has four chiral carbons so there are 2^4 possible stereoisomers for glucose. The passage shows half of them.

71. **B is correct.** Converting an aldehyde or a primary alcohol into a carboxylic acid is done via oxidation. If you didn't remember this, you are reminded in step 2 of the passage.

72. **C is correct.** Step 2 removes the top carbon from each structure and places a CH_2OH group at both ends of the new structure. Structures resulting from 1, 2, 5, and 6 would each have a plane of symmetry and would be (optically inactive) meso compounds.

73. **A is correct.** C and D are wrong because for a D-isomer, the hydroxyl group on the second carbon from the bottom must be on the right. Furthermore, if the hexoses that are created by the Kiliani-Fischer synthesis from B, C, and D were degraded and oxidized by nitric acid, all would result in meso compounds (optically inactive). To see this, add one chiral carbon just below the aldehyde (making both epimers). Now replace the end groups with carboxylic acids. All now form (at least one) meso compound. You don't need to know the structure of mannose for the MCAT and it is not given in the passage, so you know that this is extra information. Ignore it. As for answer A, the passage explains that the Kiliani-Fischer synthesis adds one more chiral carbon above the other chiral carbons of an aldose as viewed in a Fischer projection. Answer A must be correct because structure 3 in Figure 1 is glucose. If you recognized the structure of glucose, you could have made this question easier, but the passage also states (in step 2) that, when degraded and oxidized by nitric acid, glucose leaves an optically active compound.

74. **C is correct.** A pair of enantiomers would be formed by the addition of one chiral carbon. Only one configuration of glyceraldehyde is used, so that chiral carbon does not increase the number of enantiomers.

75. **A is correct.** 1 and 7 produce meso compounds, which are optically inactive.

76. **B is correct.** This question is answerable from the information in step 4 alone. If you do step 4 on all the answer choices, only structure 4 produces the same sugar.

Passage II

77. **A is correct.** Just count the atoms and see what you get.

78. **A is correct.** You should probably memorize that a carbonyl stretch is 1700. Remember that IR measures the existence of functional groups.

79. **C is correct.** The integral value is three. This is the only place where there are three protons.

80. **A is correct.** A Grignard is a strong base and will react with water.

81. **A is correct.** This should be an easy question. Each ring actually has a negative charge giving it 6 pi electrons, which equals $4n + 2$ where $n = 1$.

82. **A is correct.** The protons close to the iron would have a different chemical shift than the protons farther from the iron. There are three different carbons with hydrogens attached: the ones attached to the iron, the ones attached to those, and the ones attached to those.

Passage III

83. **D is correct.** Water has some slight solubility in organic extracts. Inorganic anhydrous salts such as magnesium, sodium, and calcium sulfate readily form insoluble hydrates, removing the water from wet organic phases. Answers A and B must be wrong because the ether is distilled from the last fraction in the sand bath. There is no basis for thinking sodium sulfate could remove impurities.

84. **B is correct.** The acid protonates the basic amino group on ethyl 4-aminobenzoate, making it soluble in the aqueous solution. The other compounds are not basic and would not be made soluble by the acid.

85. **B is correct.** The benzoic acid will be deprotonated by NaOH, making it soluble in the aqueous layer. The MW of benzoic = 122.

86. **C is correct.** From the table, we see that diethyl ether has a greater density than water, which will make it sink. However, this is NOT always true for extractions; sometimes the aqueous layer is heavier.

87. **A is correct.** From Table 1 we see that ether has a low boiling point. As the ether evaporates, the neutral compound, 9-fluorenone, is concentrated.

Stand Alones

88. **C is correct.** IR distinguishes functional groups.

89. **C is correct.** Proteins have peptide bonds, not amino acids, so B is wrong.

90. **D is correct.** Water is removed to form peptide bonds.

91. **C is correct.** Fatty acids and the three-carbon backbone of glycerol form triglycerides.

92. **D is correct.** Valine's side chain is hydrophobic. Fats are hydrophobic, and glucose is soluble in water.

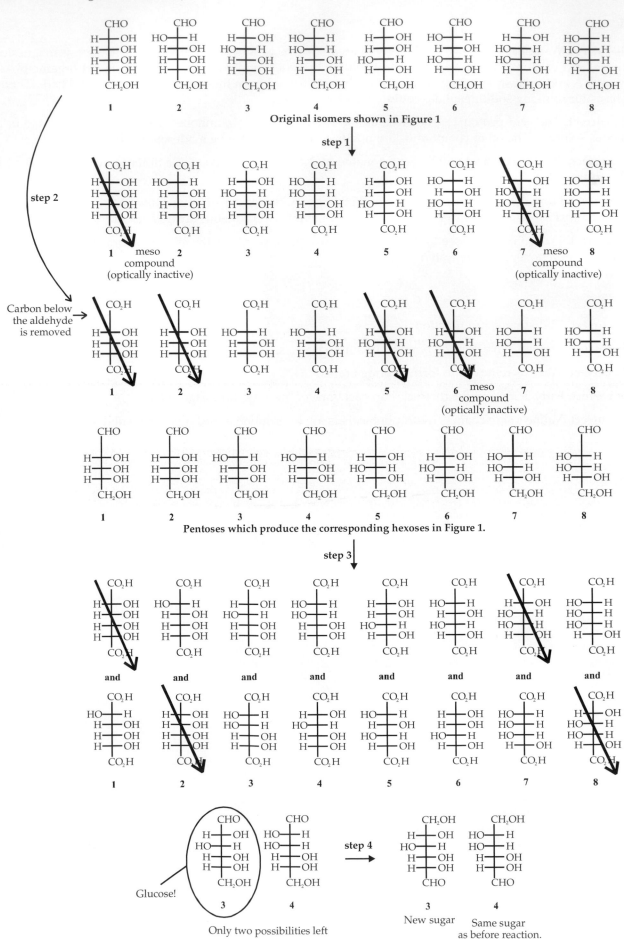

Original isomers shown in Figure 1

step 1

step 2

Carbon below the aldehyde is removed

meso compound (optically inactive)

meso compound (optically inactive)

meso compound (optically inactive)

Pentoses which produce the corresponding hexoses in Figure 1.

step 3

and

Glucose!

step 4

Only two possibilities left

New sugar

Same sugar as before reaction.

Steps used by Fischer to determine glucose

ANSWERS & EXPLANATIONS

FOR

LECTURE QUESTIONS

8. **B is correct.** The following IUPAC rules of nomenclature must be used to name an alkane:

    - Find the longest continuous carbon chain to serve as parent name – in this case, nonane.

    - Number the carbons of the parent chain, beginning at the end nearest to the most branch points.

    - Identify and number the parent chain substituents – in this case, two methyl (on carbons 4,7) and one ethyl (on carbon 3) groups.

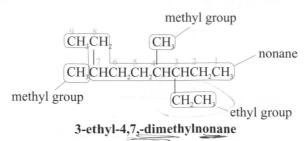

3-ethyl-4,7,-dimethylnonane

9. **A is correct.** B is missing a hydrogen. C has the charges reversed. In D, nitrogen has five bonds.

10. **C is correct.** The number of σ-bonds on the three species respectively is 3, 4, 3.

11. **B is correct.** The bonds are stabilized by resonance and are shorter and stronger than carbon-carbon alkane bonds but longer and weaker than carbon-carbon alkene bonds.

12. **D is correct.** A π-bond has 100% p character and is at a higher energy level than a σ-bond.

13. **D is correct.** Moving atoms is a violation of the rules of resonance. The actual molecule is always at a lower energy level than any of its resonance structures. Although A and B are true, they don't answer the question. Notice that A and B say the same thing. This is a good indicator that they are both wrong.

14. **C is correct.** sp hybridization allows the formation of a triple bond, which consists of one σ-bond and two π-bonds. Triple bonds display 180° bond angle linear geometry and are stronger than double or single bonds. Double bonds are sp^2 hybridized with 120° trigonal planar geometry. sp^3 hybridization, such as seen in the single bonds of tetrahedral compounds (i.e., methane), have 109.5° angles.

15. **C is correct.** NaCl and CCl_4 are provided as reference compounds.

Compound	Dipole moment (D)
NaCl	8.75
CH_3Cl	1.95
H_2O	1.85
$H_2C=N=N$	1.50
Benzene	0
CCl_4	0

16. **B is correct.** The rule of thumb is that any carbon chain with four or fewer carbons is usually a gas. 2-methylbutane is a five-carbon compound and is therefore a liquid. A skeletal backbone of 16 carbons or more is usually seen in lipids and waxes.

17. **A is correct.** At least one of the double-bonded carbons in every other answer choice has two substituents exactly the same.

18. **C is correct.** C is the only carbon attached to four different substituents so is therefore the only chiral carbon.

19. **B is correct.** B is a meso compound with a plane of symmetry through the middle of the oxygen atom and the third carbon. All three other molecules are chiral.

20. **D is correct.** A has no chiral carbon. B is named improperly. It is a trichloro compound. C is a meso compound. In D, the number 4 carbon is chiral. Any chiral molecule has an enantiomer.

21. **B is correct.** Both carbons are chiral in each compound, but B is a meso compound.

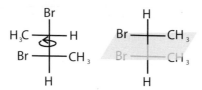

22. **D is correct.** All isomers are made up of the same set of elements and have identical molecular weights. Structural isomers are further subdivided by carbon chain differences, functional group position, and type variations. For instance, ethyl alcohol and dimethyl ether are structural isomers.

$$CH_3CH_2OH \qquad CH_3OCH_3$$

Ethyl alcohol   Dimethyl ether

23. **B is correct.** Absolute configuration describes the R or S configuration around a chiral atom. Observed rotation describes the direction of rotation of plane-polarized light. The direction of rotation cannot be predicted by the absolute configuration alone.

24. **C is correct.** Diastereomers – epimers, anomers, and geometric isomers – are stereoisomers that are not mirror images of each other. A meso compound is an achiral molecule, which is identical to its mirror image.

EXPLANATIONS TO THE QUESTIONS IN LECTURE 2

25. **A is correct.** A contains no tertiary carbons.

26. **C is correct.** Bromine is the most selective.

27. **D is correct.** Cycloheptane has the most ring strain and is at the greatest energy level. It will produce more heat per mole than methane or ethane because it is a larger molecule.

28. **D is correct.** *Cis* groups on cyclohexane will never be both equatorial or both axial while in the chair configuration.

29. **D is correct.** Only termination does not produce a radical. Conjugation is not a step in halogenation.

30. **C is correct.** Alkanes (i.e., *n*-butane) are a class of saturated hydrocarbons containing only carbon-carbon single bonds. They are unreactive and are either straight-chained or branched. Cycloalkanes (i.e., cyclobutane), on the other hand, contain rings of carbon atoms. Although free rotation is possible around carbon-carbon single bonds in alkanes, geometric hindrance greatly reduces the possibility of rotation in cycloalkanes. For this reason, cycloalkanes are "stuck" as cis or trans isomers. The cis isomer has both substituents on the same side of the ring, while the trans form has substituents on opposite sides of the cycloalkane ring.

31. **B is correct.** Primary hydrogen atoms are attached to primary carbons. Primary carbons are bound to only one other carbon. This parent compound houses five primary carbons with three hydrogens on each one.

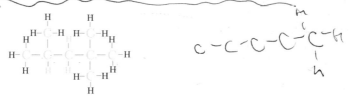

32. **C is correct.** There are four main reaction types seen in organic chemistry: addition, elimination, substitution and rearrangement. In an *addition reaction* (A + B → C), two reactants add together to form a single product. One reactant splitting into two products is known as an *elimination reaction* (A → B + C). *Substitutions*

(A—B + C—D → A—C + B—D) occur when two reactants exchange parts to yield two new products. *Rearrangement reaction* (A → B) is defined by a reactant undergoing bond reorganization to give an entirely new product.

---

33. **C is correct.** The most stable alkene is the most substituted. *Trans* is more stable than *cis*.

34. **D is correct.** The most reactive will be the one with the lowest energy of activation. Since D makes the most stable carbocation (a tertiary carbocation), it is the most reactive in an electrophilic addition reaction.

35. **A is correct.** Don't let the ring structure intimidate you. Look for the functional groups and ask yourself "How do they react?" The only functional group that we know here is alkene. It's not electrophilic addition; it must be ozonolysis of an alkene. Ozone is a radical and highly reactive. It rips right through the double bond of an alkene. The result is a cleavage of the alkene at the double bond to form two aldehydes.

36. **D is correct.** This reaction is dehydration of an alcohol and proceeds with rearrangement of the carbocation intermediate from secondary to tertiary. (See page 35.)

37. **B is correct.** This is hydration of an alkene and follows Markovnikov's rule.

38. **D is correct.** Anthracene is a larger version of benzene, a prototypic aromatic compound. It satisfies Huckel's rule, which states that if a compound has *planar, monocyclic rings with 4n + 2 π electrons* (n being any integer, including zero), it is by definition an aromatic compound. Benzene houses six π electrons, a pair for each double bond (while anthracene has 14 π electrons).

39. **B is correct.** The question stem presents a mechanism for an elimination reaction (the product gains a double bond) that relies on a rapid C—H bond dissociation as the rate-limiting step. When the heavier deuterium (D) is used instead of a pure hydrogen atom, the reaction rate decreases because of a stronger carbon—deuterium bond.

40. **B is correct.** Isoprene is a diene (alkene), which occupies an irregular shape as a result of all those double bonds. When stretched, disorganized chains straighten out but can always revert back to their original random state. Isoprene *vulcanization* (cross-link induction) serves to prevent stretching.

---

41. **C is correct.** The hydroxide ion is more basic than the chloride ion and substitution will not result unless the hydroxide is protonated to make water, which is less basic than the chloride ion. The answer choices requiring knowledge of solvents should be immediately dismissed as being too difficult for the MCAT.

43. **B is correct.** This is an S_N1 reaction and increasing the concentration of the nucleophile will not affect the rate of the reaction because the slow step is the formation of a carbocation. Adding heat always increases the rate of the reaction.

43. **A is correct.** Reduction of a ketone produces a secondary alcohol. In this case two ketones were reduced. You might recognize $LiAlH_4$ as a reducing agent but you don't need to.

44. **D is correct.** D is not a hydrogen bond.

45. **C is correct.** Regardless of whether or not the mechanism is S_N1 or S_N2, the hydroxyl group will not leave until it has been protonated. For S_N1, the formation of the cation, although rate determining, is very fast after protonation. For S_N2, the chloride ion must collide with the opposite side of a protonated molecule, so many collisions do not result in a reaction. Thus, S_N1 is faster. Tertiaries are the fastest to react in S_N1, then secondaries. Primaries react only through S_N2. Tertiaries react in less than a minute; secondaries in 1 to 5 minutes; while primaries may take days. This is a very tough MCAT question. You may have two of these per MCAT at the most. The important thing on a question like this is not to spend too much time. Narrow it down to A or C and take your best guess.

46. **C is correct.** Anti-Markovnikov alkene free radical addition is demonstrated by reaction mechanisms 1 and 2, both of which rely on peroxides as reagents. Based on the experimental results provided by the question stem, anti-Markovnikov addition only succeeds using HBr.

47. **B is correct.** *S$_N$1 substitution reaction:*
  - two-step reaction
  - follows first order reaction kinetics (rate = $k[S]$)
  - proceeds through a carbocation intermediate
  - prefers tertiary carbons to increase carbocation stability
  - prefers protic solvent
  - produces a racemic mixture of products

  S$_N$2 substitution reaction:
  - one-step reaction
  - follows second-order reaction kinetics (rate = $k[S][Nucleophile]$)
  - proceeds through a transition state
  - prefers primary carbons
  - prefers aprotic solvent
  - produces optically active product
  - causes an inversion of stereochemistry

48. **B is correct.** S$_N$1 mechanism depends on the rate-limiting step, which is the carbocation formation and is nucleophile independent; all subsequent steps occur at a much faster rate and do not affect the rate of the reaction.

EXPLANATIONS TO THE QUESTIONS IN LECTURE 3

49. **D is correct.** Even if you don't recognize the reaction, the name aldol means that the product must be an alcohol. This eliminates C. You should recognize that the alpha hydrogen is the most reactive hydrogen on an aldehyde or ketone. For A or B to be correct, the carbonyl hydrogen must be removed while the alpha hydrogen remains intact. Not likely. Notice also that since in an aldol reaction between two aldehydes the product must be an aldehyde, A, B, and C are eliminated; they are ketones.

50. **A is correct.** Only H$_x$ is an alpha hydrogen. Aldehydes and ketones typically undergo nucleophilic addition, not substitution.

51. **D is correct.** The reduction of an aldehyde results in a primary alcohol. A and B are the same molecule; both secondary alcohols.

52. **A is correct.** Ketones reduce more easily than esters. The first step is ketal formation to form blocking groups so that the ketone is not reduced. If the first step were omitted, the ketone would be reduced to a secondary alcohol.

53. **D is correct.** Water is a stronger acid than alcohol, which is stronger than aldehyde, which is stronger than ketone.

54. **A is correct.** When aldehydes are oxidized, they lose the hydrogen attached to the carbonyl carbon. Ketones have no such hydrogen to lose.

55. **C is correct.** Tautomerization is an equilibrium represented by a proton shift. Ketones tautomerize to form enols where the carbonyl carbon from the ketone becoms part of an alkene by forming a double bond with a neighboring carbon. In choice C, the carbonyl carbon does not form part of the alkene.

56. **D is correct.** The Tollens test gives a silver mirror for reducing sugars. Reducing sugars are hemiacetals in their ring form and either aldehydes or ketones in their straight-chain form. Acetals do not open easily because they contain the blocking groups discussed under "Formation of Acetals". However, to answer this question you just need to see that methyl β-glucoside is an acetal. Choice A is incorrect because glucose is an aldehyde and reduces Tollens reagent. Choice B is irrelevant because neither sugar is a ketone. Additionally, Tollens reagent promotes enediol rearrangement of ketones to aldehydes. Choice C is incorrect because glucose is a hemiacetal that opens to an aldehyde and reacts with Tollens reagent.

57. **D is correct.** Alkenes have no N, O, or F with which to hydrogen bond.

58. **C is correct.** This is an esterification reaction. (See page 66.)

59. **A is correct.** Carboxylic acids typically undergo nucleophilic substitution, not addition.

60. **A is correct.** This question may require a little too much knowledge for the MCAT. It is more likely that a question like this will be associated with a passage that explains reactivity of carboxylic acid derivatives. To find the answer, we look at the strengths of the leaving groups:

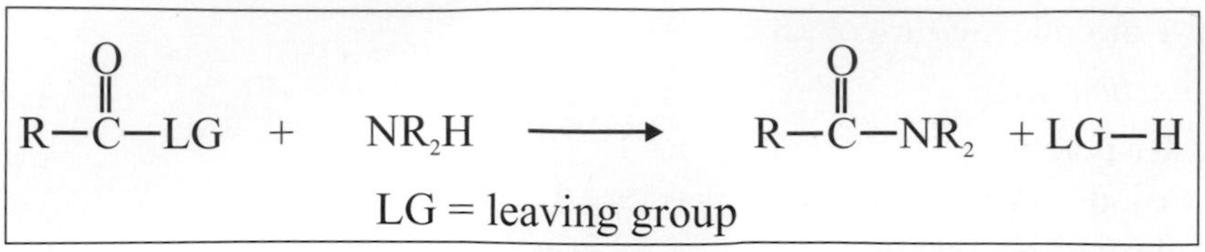

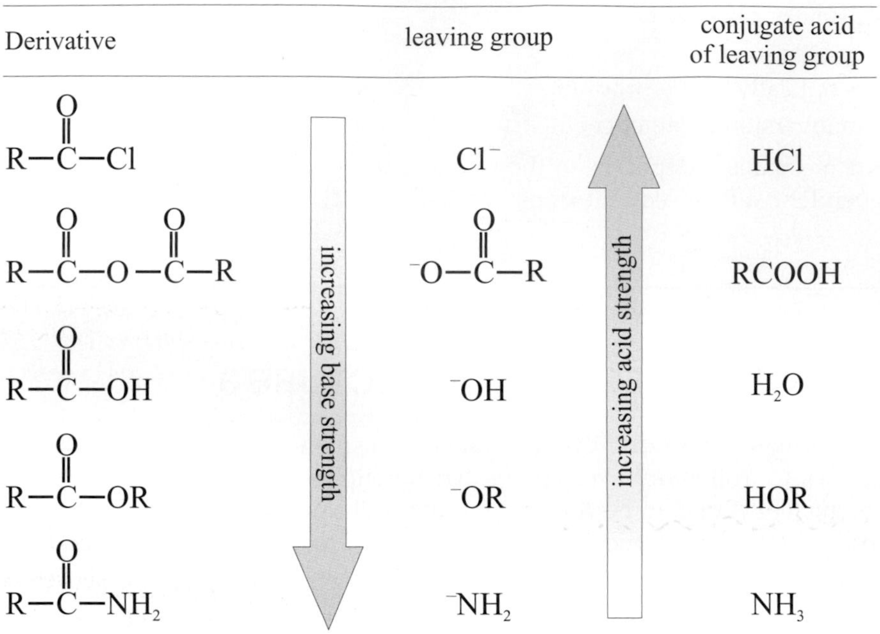

The weakest leaving group is the most stable and the most likely to be formed.

61. **B is correct.** This is the only methyl ketone listed.

62. **A is correct.** The anhydride reacts with ammonia to form an amide and a carboxylate ion. The addition of acid to the carboxylate creates carboxylic acid.

63. **A is correct.** NO_2 is an electron withdrawing substituent (deactivating) that stabilizes the methyl benzoate, decreasing reactivity. This will make the compound safer for transport and storage.

64. **D is correct.** Stronger conditions take the reaction further. Under acidic and basic conditions, an amide hydrolyzes to a carboxylic acid.

---

65. **D is correct.** The quaternary amine with all alkyl groups is not basic at all since its electrons have already been donated.

66. **B is correct.** Ammonia can donate a pair of electrons to act as a Lewis base.

67. **C is correct.** This molecule cannot hydrogen bond as easily as the others.

68. **A is correct.** The amine acts as a nucleophile and adds to the ketone. You should be able to predict this based upon your knowledge of amines and/or ketones.

69. **B is correct.** This is a simple alkylation of an amine. You should have this reaction memorized. Even if you don't, only B and D are possibilities for a base. Ethyl-methylamine is not an acid.

70. **D is correct.** Epoxides, oxygen-containing cyclic compounds, have much higher reactivity levels than other

ethers. This is due to a highly strained three-member ring that can be opened by nucleophilic attack. Benzene is stabilized by electron delocalization, which is possible in aromatic compounds.

71. **A is correct.** Sodium chloride is a prototypic example of an ionic bond. In a coordinate covalent bond, both shared electrons come from the same atom; for instance, a Lewis base (i.e., ammonia) or oxygen-containing compound (i.e., water). Although both shared electrons come from the same atom, a coordinate covalent bond is a single bond similar in chemical properties to a covalent bond.

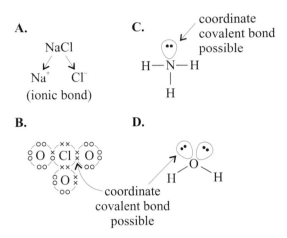

72. **C is correct.** Cyclohexanone ketone is flanked by four acidic alpha hydrogens, which will be replaced by deuterium. Since each deuterium is twice as heavy as hydrogen, the atomic weight is expected to increase by four (from 98 to 102).

EXPLANATIONS TO THE QUESTIONS IN LECTURE 4

73. **C is correct.** By definition, in electrophoresis negatively charged amino acids will move toward the anode. Only amino acids with an acidic isoelectric point will be negatively charged at a pH of 8. All amino acids except histidine, arginine, and lysine have acidic isoelectric points. Most likely on the MCAT, a question like this one would be accompanied with isoelectric points given in a passage. However, it is possible that a rare question would require you to memorize the three basic amino acids: histidine, arginine, and lysine.

74. **C is correct.** This reaction is between a carboxylic acid and an alcohol to form an ester. See page 66.

75. **B is correct.** The pleated sheet and the α-helix are explained by the rigid structure of the peptide bond, whose double bond character prevents rotation.

76. **C is correct.** Saturated fats have the greatest energy storage potential, about twice that of carbohydrates and proteins.

77. **C is correct.** The isoelectric point is where 100% of the amino acid exists as a zwitterion. The isoelectric point occurs at the first equivalence point.

78. **C is correct.** The solubilities of amino acids differ based upon the R group. Phenylalanine has a benzene R group and is the least polar amino acid listed. The carboxylic acids and amines on the other R groups increase solubility. You may have also memorized the four groups of amino acid side chains as either nonpolar, polar, acidic, or basic. Acidic, basic, and polar amino acids have greater water solubility than nonpolar amino acids.

Lecture Question Expls.

79. **A is correct.** You may read this question and be uncertain of what it means by "monomer". Such an experience is not uncommon on the MCAT. The minimum that you need to understand for this question is that a monomer is some type of "equivalent unit". Since it is an MCAT question, you should assume that monomer refers to something that you already know. You make his assumption because MCAT doesn't test science that is not covered in these books. Next you need to recognize the chemical shown as a polypeptide. You need to know that polypeptides are divided into amino acid residues, and you must be able to recognize where these residues begin and end.

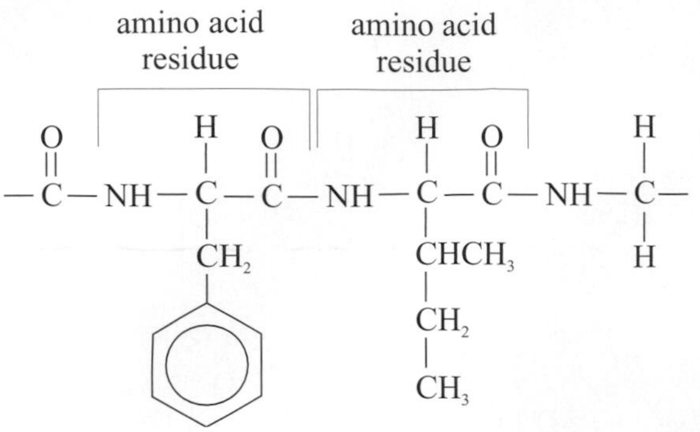

80. **C is correct.** A proline residue interrupts alpha-helix formation because the amide nitrogen has no hydrogen to contribute to the alpha-helix structure.

---

81. **C is correct.** The formula for the number of isomers of a carbohydrate is 2^n, where n is the number of chiral carbons.

82. **A is correct.** In this question you must know that glucose is an aldehyde and that an aldehyde and alcohol react to form, first, a hemiacetal. If a second equivalent of alcohol is added, an acetal will form.

83. **A is correct.** Of the choices, only fructose is a ketose. Notice that you did not have to know anything about fruit in this question. This question could have been rephrased as, "Which of the following is a ketose?"

84. **C is correct.** The general formula for a carbohydrate is $C_n(H_2O)_n$. Since this carbohydrate is in the Fischer projection with the aldehyde or ketone at the top, and the bottom chiral carbon is positioned to the right, it is of the D configuration. The only way to know about polarized light is to use a polarimeter.

85. **A is correct.** Carbohydrates have different functional groups on either end and cannot exist as a meso compound. Humans cannot digest all isomers of carbohydrates. Humans cannot digest L-glucose for example. You must know that glucose is an aldehyde.

86. **C is correct.** You may not remember that the gustatory receptors at the tip of the tongue stimulate a sweet taste. You don't need to because you should recognize that glucose and the artificial sweeteners can all hydrogen bond. You should also know that glucose ($C_{12}O_6H_{12}$) is a carbohydrate (is made from carbon and water alone), but the synthetic sweeteners are not. They contain nitrogen and other elements not contained in carbohydrates.

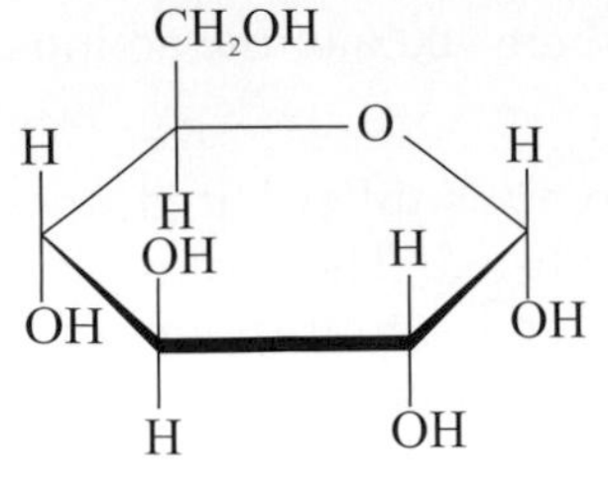

[Glucose]

87. **C is correct.** Carbon 5 hydroxyl group acts as a nucleophile by attacking the number 2 carbonyl carbon, leading to α or β furanose ring formation.

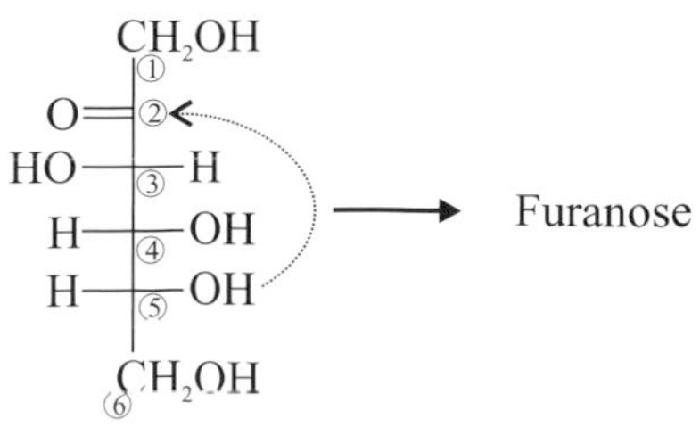

88. **D is correct.** Sugar A is a ketotriose and Sugar B is an aldoheptose.

---

89. **C is correct.** nmr deals with protons, not functional groups. D is true but is far more information about nmr than you are required to know.

90. **C is correct.** Extraction is based upon solubilities.

91. **B is correct.** It is possible that one question on the MCAT may require specific knowledge of the IR table of frequencies for groups as basic as the carbonyl.

92. **A is correct.** The silica gel in TLC is polar and bonds more strongly to the more polar molecules, causing them to rise more slowly.

93. **B is correct.** Distillation will not completely separate two compounds which form an azeotrope. Crystallization is a very inefficient method of purification. Distillation is more effective when done slowly.

94. **A is correct.** The *distillation process*, a workhorse of the chemical industry, relies on extreme varying of boiling points to separate complex chemical mixtures like petroleum. The tall towers seen at oil refineries are in fact distillation columns. *Liquid chromatography* is column chromatography, which separates compounds based on polarity, size, charge, and/or liquid or gas phase differences. *Nuclear magnetic resonance* (nmr) spectroscopy induces energy absorption to determine different types of carbon and/or hydrogen present in a compound.

95. **D is correct.** Dimethyl sulfoxide is a dipolar compound with a high boiling point as a result. It is miscible in water because it can hydrogen bond.

96. **C is correct.**

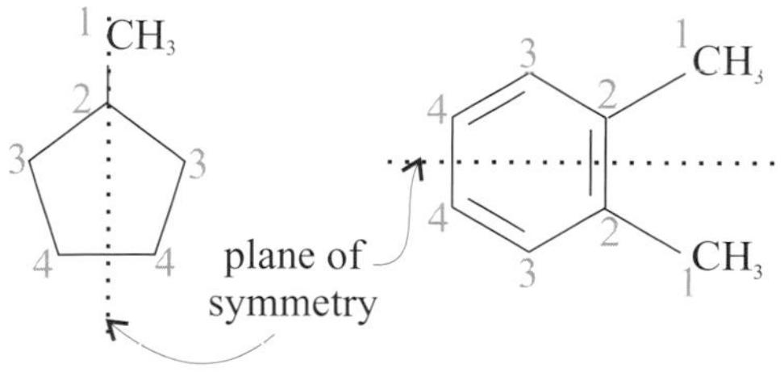

4 peaks on C^{13} nmr

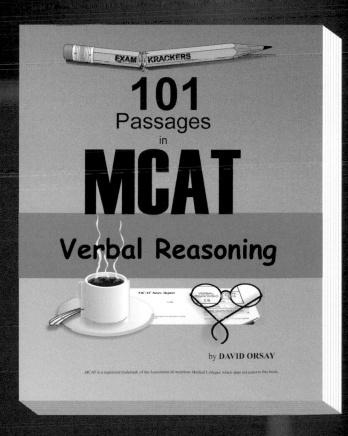

About the Author

Jonathan Orsay is uniquely qualified to write an MCAT preparation book. He graduated on the Dean's list with a B.A. in History from Columbia University. While considering medical school, he sat for the real MCAT three times from 1989 to 1996. He scored in the 90 percentiles on all sections before becoming an MCAT instructor. He has lectured in MCAT test preparation for thousands of hours and across the country for every MCAT administration since August 1994. He has taught premeds from such prestigious Universities as Harvard and Columbia. He was the editor of one of the best selling MCAT prep books in 1996 and again in 1997. Orsay is currently the Director of MCAT for Examkrackers. He has written and published the following books and audio products in MCAT preparation: "Examkrackers MCAT Physics"; "Examkrackers MCAT Chemistry"; "Examkrackers MCAT Organic Chemistry"; "Examkrackers MCAT Biology"; "Examkrackers MCAT Verbal Reasoning & Math"; "Examkrackers 1001 questions in MCAT Physics", "Examkrackers MCAT Audio Osmosis with Jordan and Jon".

www.examkrackers.com

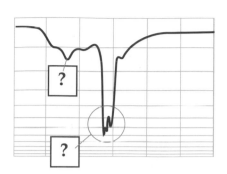

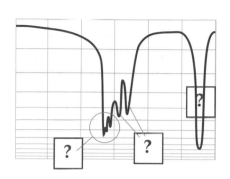

www.examkrackers.com

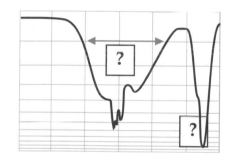

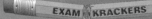

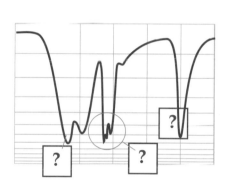

www.examkrackers.com

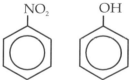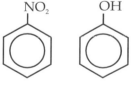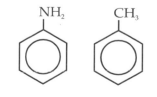

Name the Derivatives

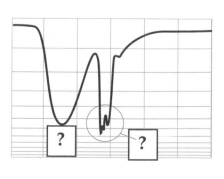

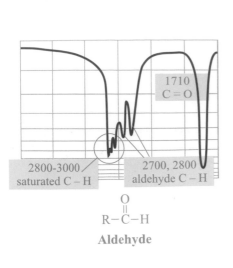

2800-3000
saturated C – H

1710
C = O

2700, 2800
aldehyde C – H

$$\underset{\mathbf{Aldehyde}}{R-\overset{\overset{\displaystyle O}{\|}}{C}-H}$$

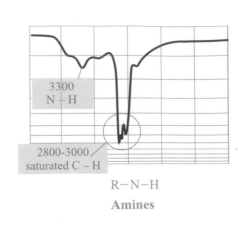

3300
N – H

2800-3000
saturated C – H

R–N–H

Amines

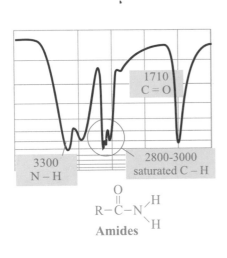

1710
C = O

3300
N – H

2800-3000
saturated C – H

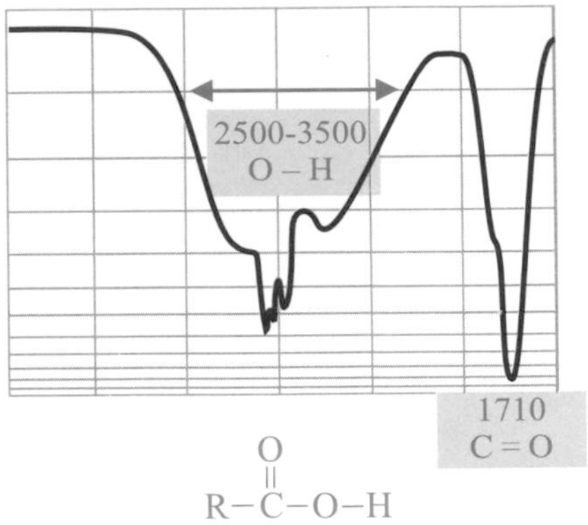

$$\underset{\mathbf{Amides}}{R-\overset{\overset{\displaystyle O}{\|}}{C}-\overset{\overset{\displaystyle H}{|}}{\underset{\displaystyle H}{N}}}$$

2500-3500
O – H

1710
C = O

$$\underset{\mathbf{Carboxylic\ Acid}}{R-\overset{\overset{\displaystyle O}{\|}}{C}-O-H}$$

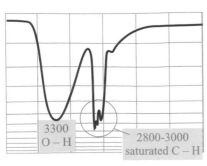

3300
O – H

2800-3000
saturated C – H

R–O–H

Alcohol

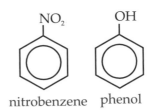

nitrobenzene   phenol

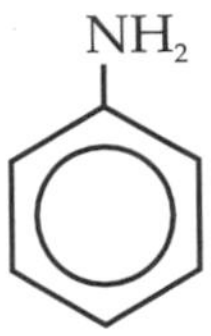

aniline   toluene   benzoic acid

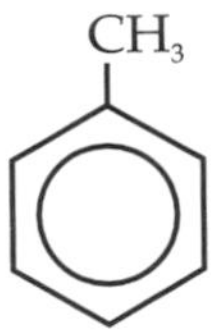

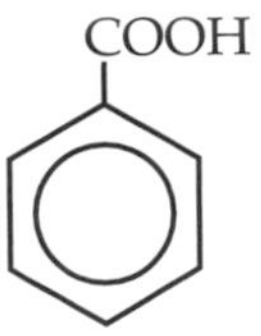

Page 41

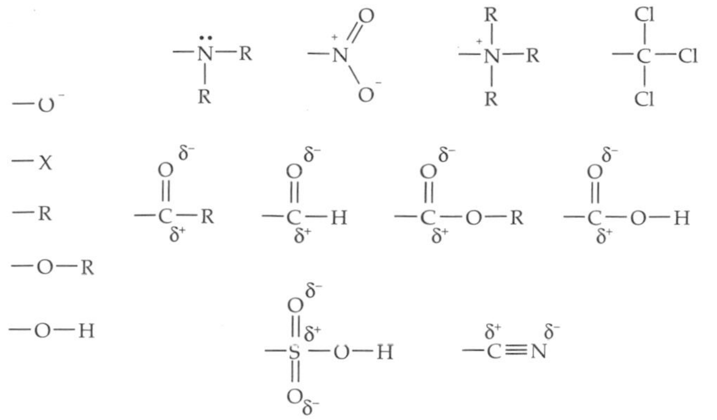

Find the Electron Donating Groups

What are the six ways that S_N1 differs from S_N2?

$$Cl_2 \ + \ CH_4 \xrightarrow{\text{light}}$$

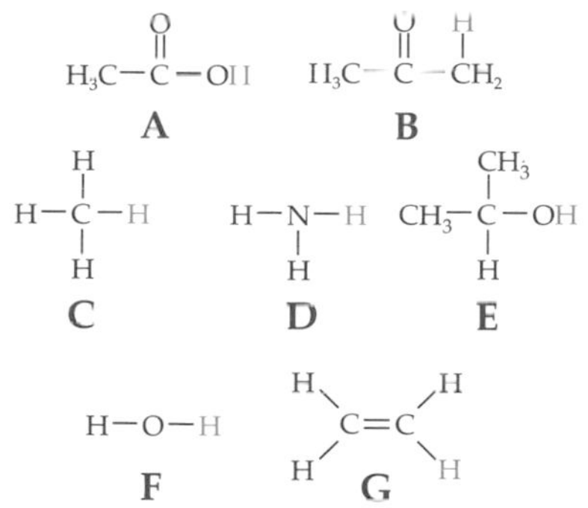

Arrange Green Protons in order of acid strength

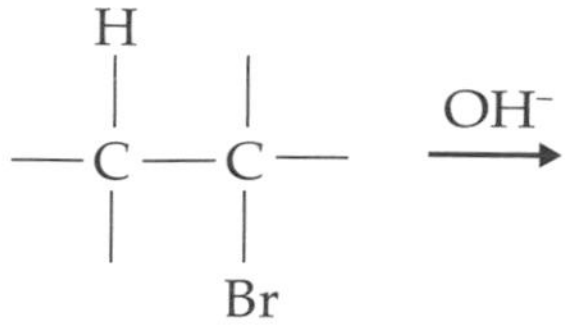

$$CH_4 \ + \ 2O_2 \xrightarrow{\text{flame}}$$

The nucleophile: S_N2 requires a strong nucleophile, while nucleophilic strength doesn't affect S_N1.

1st S: S_N2 reactions don't occur with a sterically hindered **Substrate**. S_N2 requires a methyl, primary, or secondary substrate, while S_N1 requires a secondary or tertiary substrate.

2nd S: A highly polar **Solvent** slows down S_N2 reactions by stabilizing the nucleophile.

3rd S: The **Speed** of an S_N2 reaction depends upon the concentration of the substrate and the nucleophile, while the speed of an S_N1 depends only on the substrate.

4th S: S_N2 inverts **Stereochemistry** about the chiral center, while S_N1 creates a racemic mixture.

5th S: S_N1 may be accompanied by carbon **Skeleton** rearrangement, but S_N2 never rearranges the carbon skeleton.

Page 46

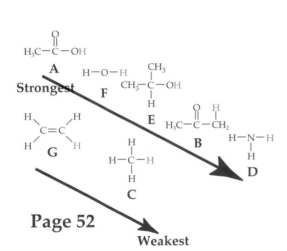

$-O^-$ $-O-H$ $-\overset{\displaystyle ..}{N}-R$
                          $|$
                          R

$-R$ $-O-R$

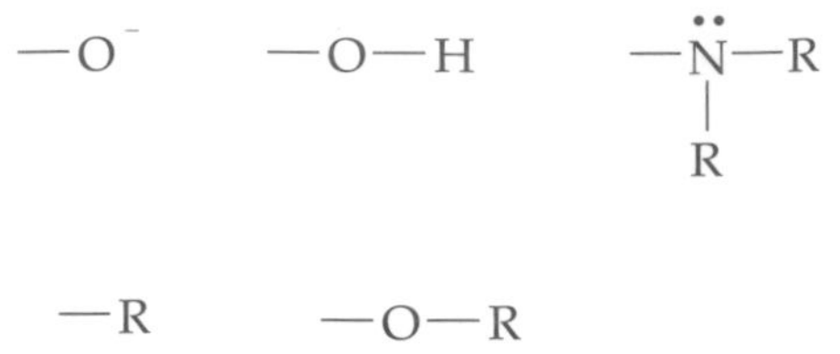

**Electron Donating Groups
Page 40**

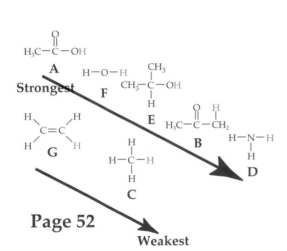

Page 52

$\longrightarrow$ $Cl\cdot\ +\ CH_3Cl$

**Halogenation
Page 31**

$\longrightarrow$ $CO_2\ +\ 2H_2O\ +\ Heat$

**Combustion
Page 30**

$\longrightarrow$ $\displaystyle C=C\ +\ H_2O\ +\ Br^-$

**Dehydrohalogenation
Page 35**

$$CH_2{=}CH_2 + H_2 \xrightarrow{\text{Ni, Pd, or Pt}}$$

$$\underset{\displaystyle \text{R}}{\overset{\displaystyle \text{R}}{\text{R}-\text{C}}}-\underset{\displaystyle \text{H}}{\overset{\displaystyle \text{OH}}{\text{C}}}-\text{CH}_3 \xrightarrow{\text{H}^+}$$

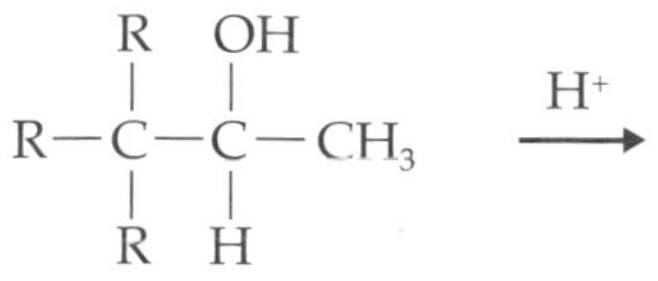

$$\text{C}{=}\text{C} \xrightarrow[\text{2) Zn, H}_2\text{O}]{\text{1) O}_3}$$

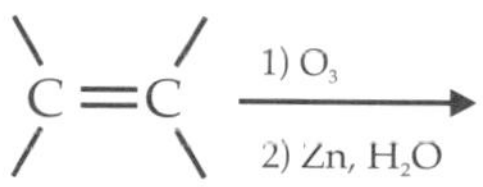

$$\underset{\displaystyle \text{H}}{\overset{\displaystyle \text{H}_3\text{C}}{\text{C}}}{=}\underset{\displaystyle \text{H}}{\overset{\displaystyle \text{H}}{\text{C}}} + \text{HBr} \longrightarrow$$

$$\text{C}{=}\text{C} + \text{BH}_3 \longrightarrow \xrightarrow{\text{H}_2\text{O}_2, \ \text{OH}^-}$$

$$\text{C}{=}\text{C} + \text{Br}-\text{Br} \longrightarrow$$

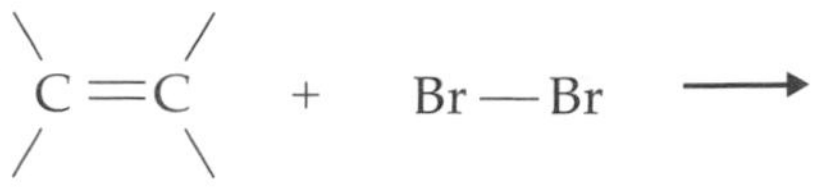

$$\longrightarrow \quad \underset{R}{\overset{R}{C}} = \underset{R}{\overset{R}{C}} \underset{\underset{H}{\overset{H}{C}}}{\overset{H}{C}} \quad + \quad \underset{R}{\overset{R}{C}} \underset{H}{\overset{H}{C}} = \underset{H}{\overset{H}{C}} \quad + \ H_2O$$

major product   minor product

Dehydration of an Alcohol
Page 35

$$\longrightarrow \quad CH_3CH_3$$

Hydrogenation
with a Heterogeneous Catalyst
Page 36

Electrophilic Addition
Page 37

$$\longrightarrow \quad \overset{}{C} = O \ + \ O = \overset{}{C}$$

Ozonolysis
Page 36

Halogenation of an Alkene
Page 38

$$\longrightarrow \quad -\underset{H}{\overset{|}{C}} - \underset{OH}{\overset{|}{C}} -$$

Hydroboration
Page 38

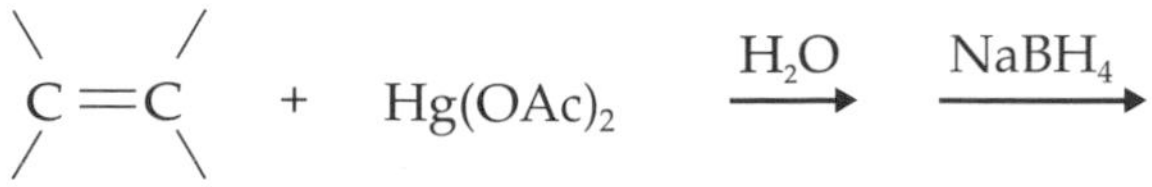

$$C=C \quad + \quad Hg(OAc)_2 \quad \xrightarrow{H_2O} \quad \xrightarrow{NaBH_4}$$

$$RMgX \quad + \quad \underset{R}{\overset{R}{C}}=O \quad \xrightarrow{H_3O^+}$$

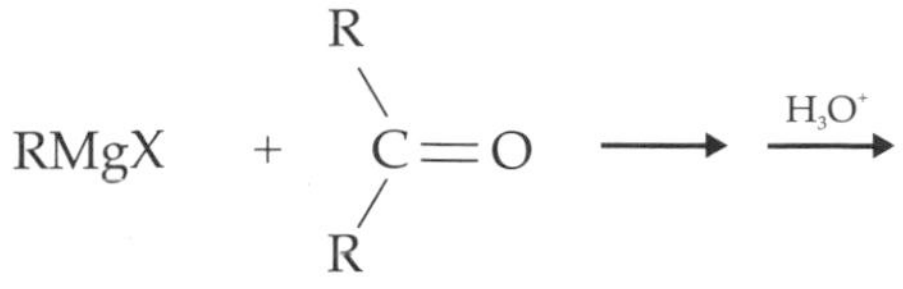

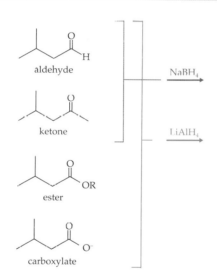

aldehyde

ketone

ester

carboxylate

$\xrightarrow{NaBH_4}$

$\xrightarrow{LiAlH_4}$

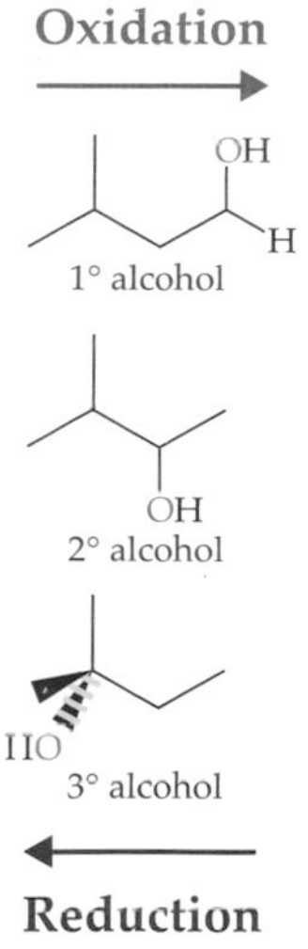

Oxidation
$\longrightarrow$

OH

H

1° alcohol

OH

2° alcohol

HO

3° alcohol

$\longleftarrow$
Reduction

$$CH_3CH_2OH \quad + \quad HCl \quad \longrightarrow$$

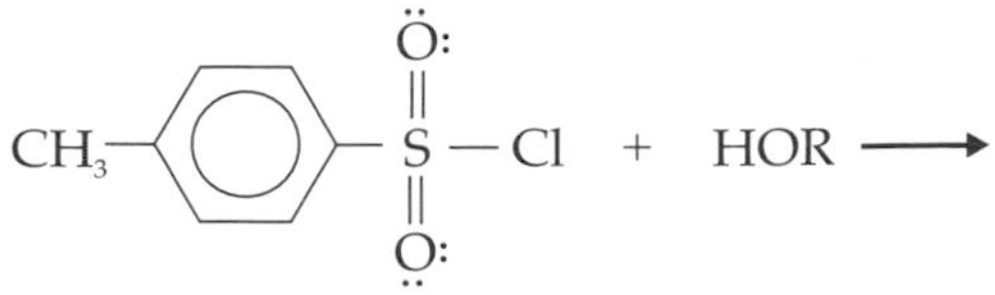

$$CH_3-\underset{\overset{\ddot{O}:}{\underset{\ddot{O}:}{\|}}}{S}-Cl \quad + \quad HOR \quad \longrightarrow$$

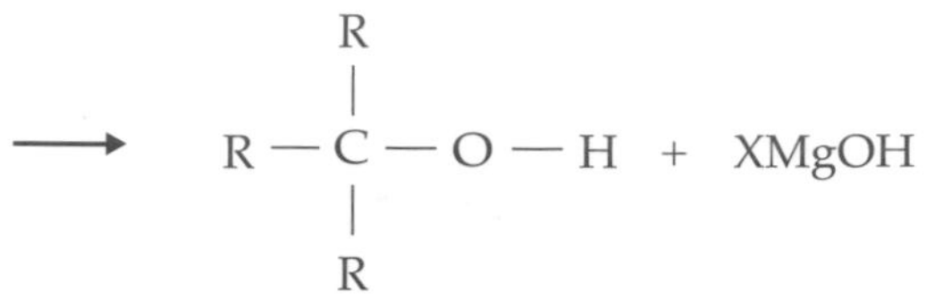

Grignard Synthesis of an Alcohol
Page 47

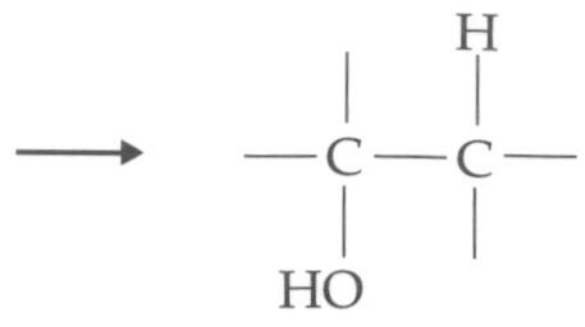

Oxymercuration/Demercuration
Page 38

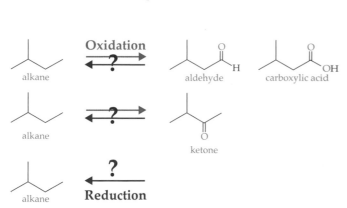

Oxidation and Reduction of Alcohols
Page 49

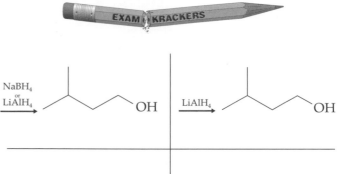

Reduction
Page 48

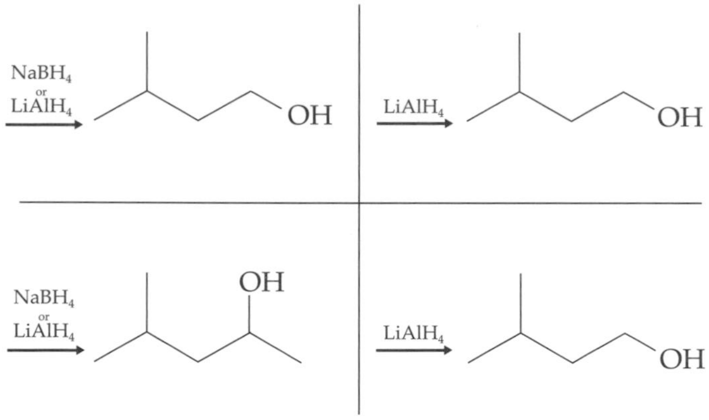

An alkyl tosylate

Formation of a Sulfonate
Page 50

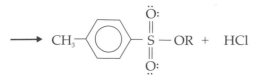

CH₃CH₂Cl + H₂O

Substitution
Page 50

ROR + HBr $\longrightarrow$

$$\underset{\text{vic diol}}{\overset{\overset{\text{HO}\quad\text{OH}}{|\quad\quad|}}{\underset{\underset{\text{H}_3\text{C}\quad\text{CH}_3}{|\quad\quad|}}{\text{CH}_3-\text{C}-\text{C}-\text{CH}_3}}} \quad\xrightarrow[\text{heat}]{\text{H}^+}$$

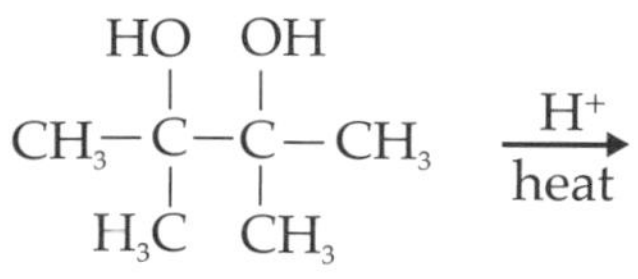

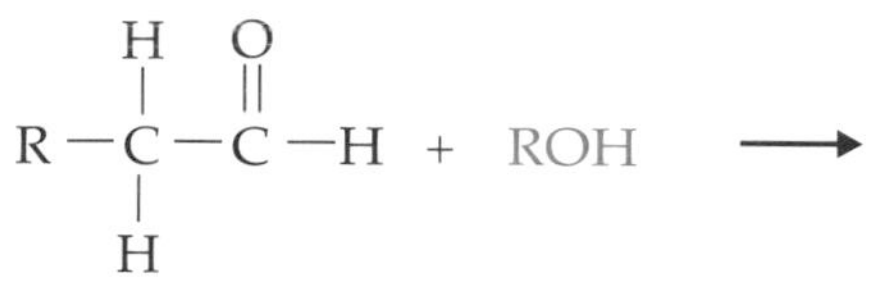

$$\underset{}{\overset{\overset{\text{H}\quad\text{O}}{|\quad\quad\|}}{\underset{\overset{|}{\text{H}}}{\text{R}-\text{C}-\text{C}-\text{H}}}} + \text{ROH} \quad\longrightarrow$$

$$\underset{\text{epoxide}}{\overset{\overset{\text{O}}{\diagup\,\diagdown}}{-\text{C}-\text{C}-}}$$

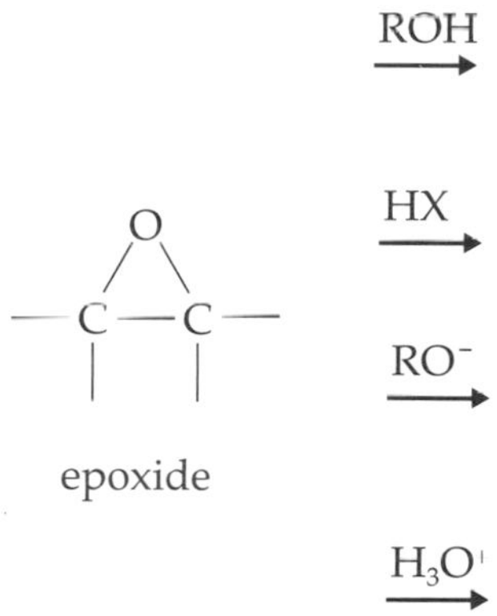

$\xrightarrow{\text{ROH}}$

$\xrightarrow{\text{HX}}$

$\xrightarrow{\text{RO}^-}$

$\xrightarrow{\text{H}_3\text{O}^+}$

$$\underset{}{\overset{\overset{\text{O}}{\|}}{\text{R}-\text{C}-\text{H}}} \quad\xrightarrow[\text{H}^+]{\text{HOCH}_2\text{CH}_2\text{OH}}$$

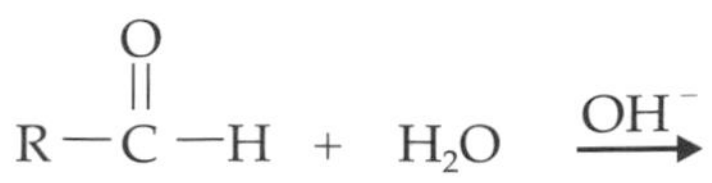

$$\underset{\text{aldehyde}}{\overset{\overset{\text{O}}{\|}}{\text{R}-\text{C}-\text{H}}} + \text{H}_2\text{O} \quad\xrightarrow{\text{OH}^-}$$

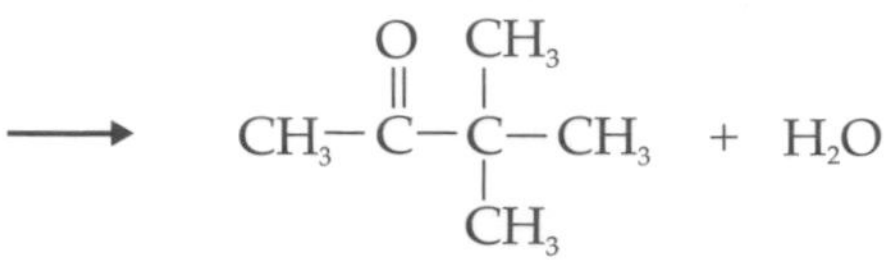

$$\longrightarrow \quad CH_3-\overset{\overset{\displaystyle O}{\|}}{C}-\overset{\overset{\displaystyle CH_3}{|}}{\underset{\underset{\displaystyle CH_3}{|}}{C}}-CH_3 \quad + \quad H_2O$$

Pinacol Rearrangement
Page 51

www.examkrackers.com
www.examkrackers.com

$$\longrightarrow \quad ROH \quad + \quad RBr$$

Acid Cleavage
Page 52

$$\xrightarrow{ROH} \quad -\overset{\overset{\displaystyle OH}{|}}{C}-\overset{\overset{\displaystyle |}{|}}{\underset{\underset{\displaystyle OR}{|}}{C}}- \qquad \xrightarrow{RO^-} \quad -\overset{\overset{\displaystyle O^-}{|}}{C}-\overset{\overset{\displaystyle |}{|}}{\underset{\underset{\displaystyle OR}{|}}{C}}-$$

$$\xrightarrow{HX} \quad -\overset{\overset{\displaystyle OH}{|}}{C}-\overset{\overset{\displaystyle |}{|}}{\underset{\underset{\displaystyle X}{|}}{C}}- \qquad \xrightarrow{H_3O^+} \quad -\overset{\overset{\displaystyle OH}{|}}{C}-\overset{\overset{\displaystyle OH}{|}}{\underset{\underset{\displaystyle OH}{|}}{C}}-$$

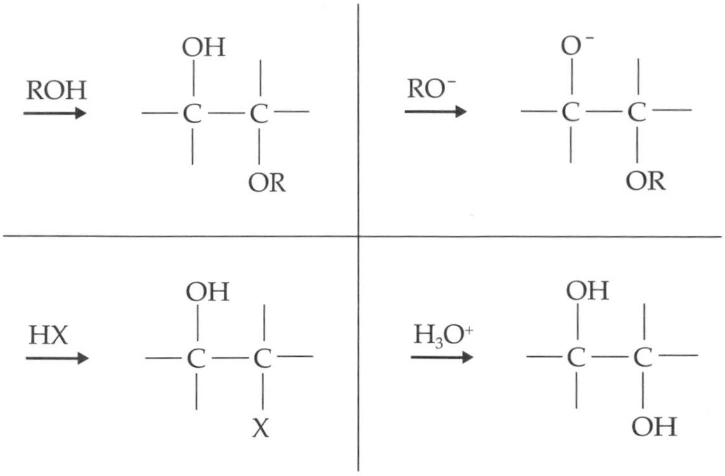

From the Same Reactant
Page 52

www.examkrackers.com
www.examkrackers.com

$$\longrightarrow \quad R-\overset{\overset{\displaystyle H}{|}}{C}-\overset{\overset{\displaystyle OH}{|}}{\underset{\underset{\displaystyle OR}{|}}{C}}-H$$

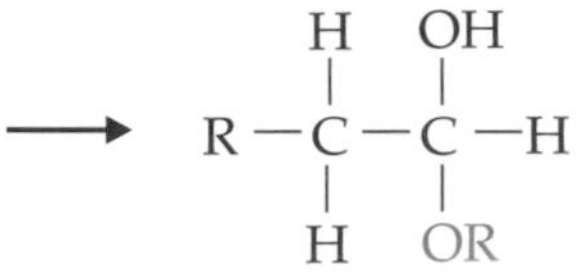

Hemiacetal Formation
Page 57

$$\longrightarrow \quad R-\overset{\overset{\displaystyle OH}{|}}{\underset{\underset{\displaystyle H}{|}}{C}}-OH$$

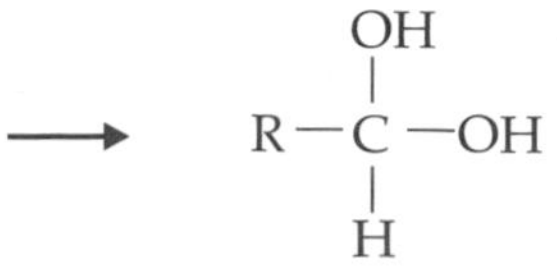

hydrate

Gem Diol Formation
Page 58

www.examkrackers.com
www.examkrackers.com

$$\longrightarrow \quad \underset{R-\overset{}{C}-H}{O\diagdown\diagup O}$$

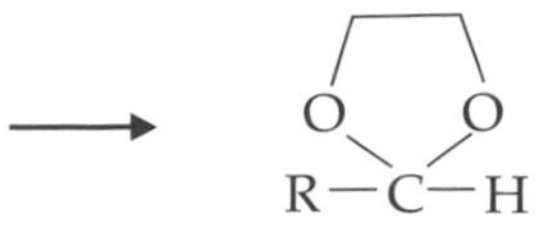

Acetal formation
Blocking Groups
Page 58

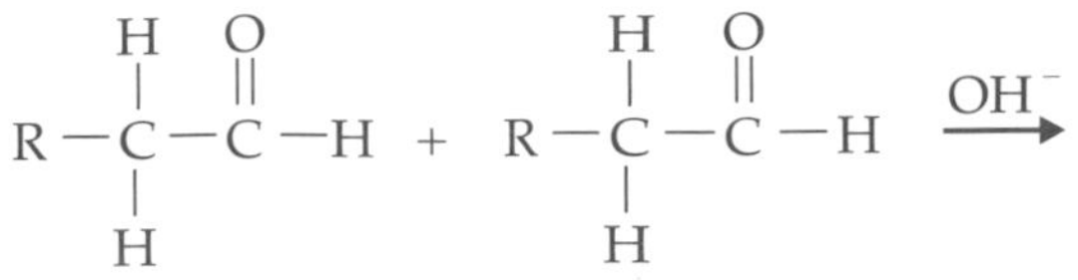

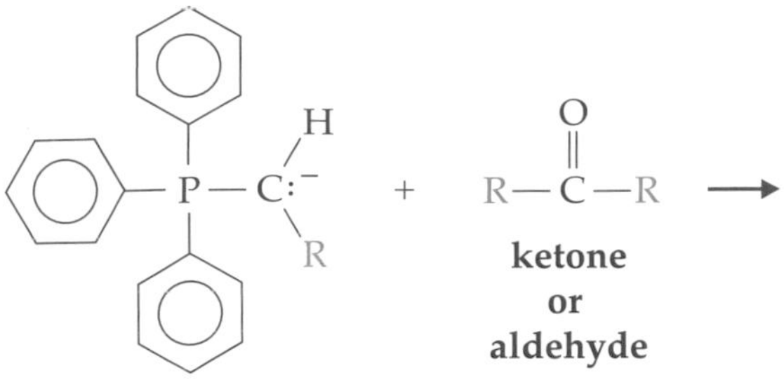

ylide

ketone
or
aldehyde

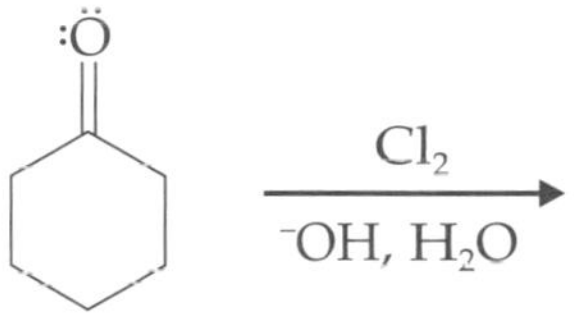

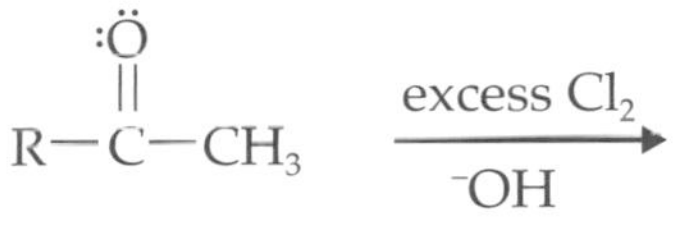

methyl ketone

thionyl
chloride

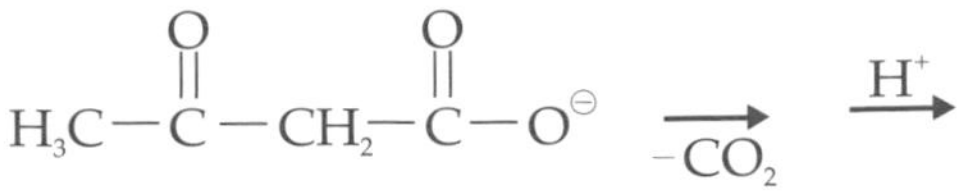

acylacetate ion

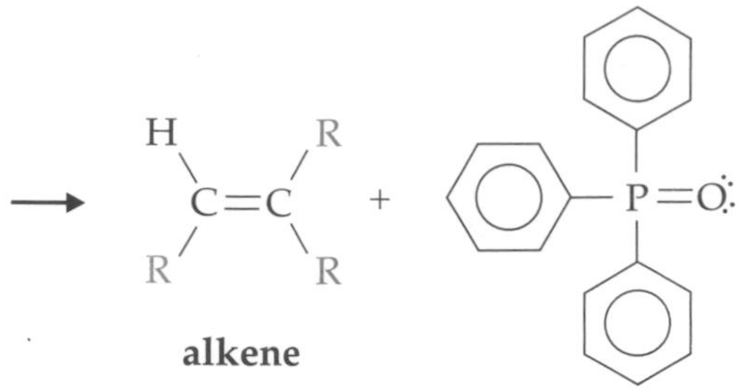

alkene

The Wittig Reaction
Page 60

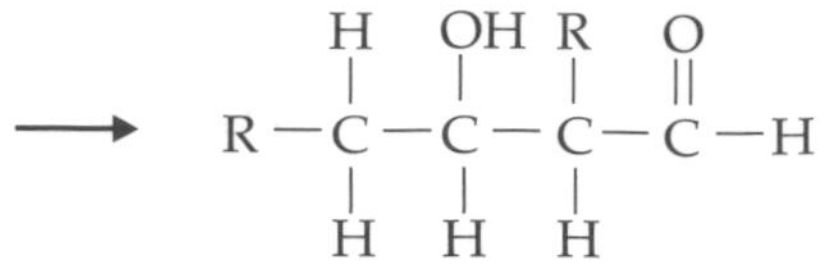

Aldol Addition
Page 59

$R-\overset{:O}{\underset{}{C}}-\overset{..}{\underset{}{O}}:^-$ + $HCCl_3$

carboxylate   chloroform
ion

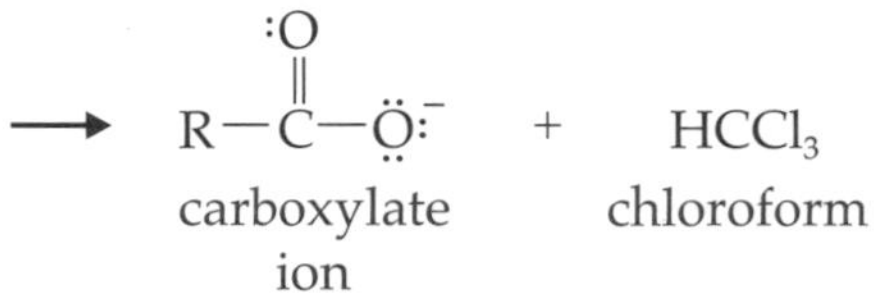

Haloform Reaction
Page 60

+ Cl^- + H_2O

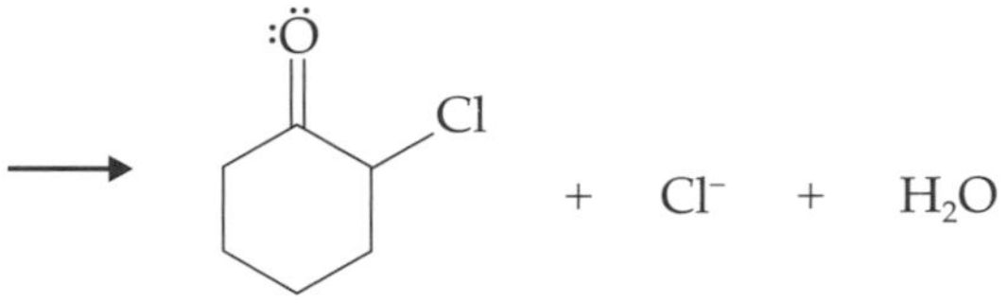

Base Promoted Halogenation
Page 59

$H_3C-\overset{O}{\underset{}{C}}-CH_3$

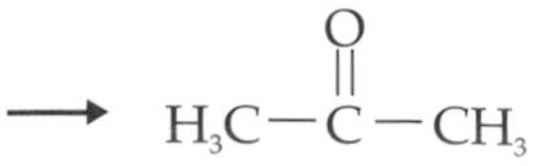

Decarboxylation
Page 65

$R-\overset{O}{\underset{}{C}}-Cl$ + $SO_2\uparrow$ + $HCl\uparrow$

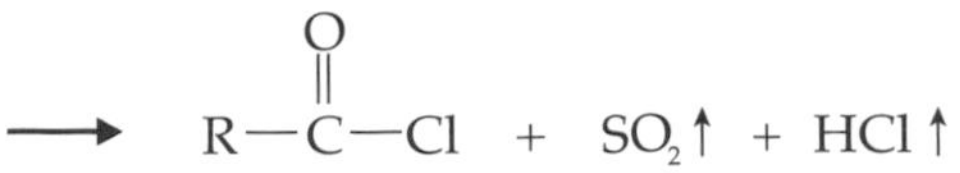

Acid Chloride Synthesis
Page 65

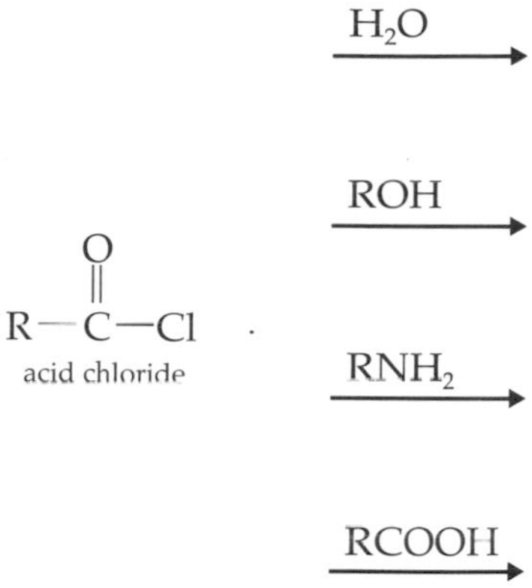

$$\text{R}-\overset{\overset{\displaystyle O}{\|}}{\text{C}}-\text{Cl}$$
acid chloride

$$\xrightarrow{\text{H}_2\text{O}}$$

$$\xrightarrow{\text{ROH}}$$

$$\xrightarrow{\text{RNH}_2}$$

$$\xrightarrow{\text{RCOOH}}$$

1-888-KRACKEM

$$\text{R}-\overset{\overset{\displaystyle O}{\|}}{\text{C}}-\text{Cl} \qquad \xrightarrow{\text{H}_2\text{O}}$$
acid chloride

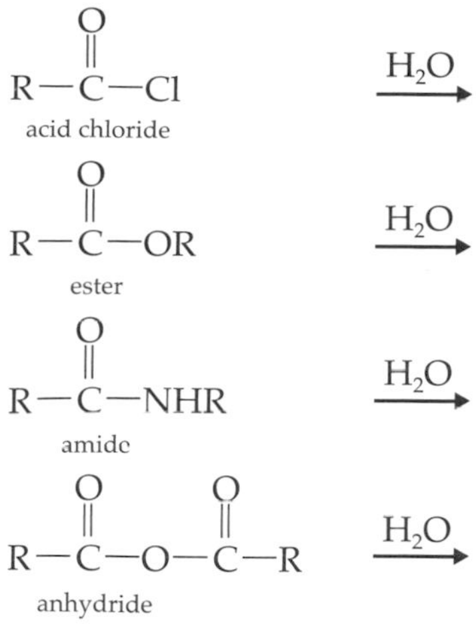

$$\text{R}-\overset{\overset{\displaystyle O}{\|}}{\text{C}}-\text{OR} \qquad \xrightarrow{\text{H}_2\text{O}}$$
ester

$$\text{R}-\overset{\overset{\displaystyle O}{\|}}{\text{C}}-\text{NHR} \qquad \xrightarrow{\text{H}_2\text{O}}$$
amide

$$\text{R}-\overset{\overset{\displaystyle O}{\|}}{\text{C}}-\text{O}-\overset{\overset{\displaystyle O}{\|}}{\text{C}}-\text{R} \qquad \xrightarrow{\text{H}_2\text{O}}$$
anhydride

1-888-KRACKEM

$$\text{R}-\overset{\overset{\displaystyle O}{\|}}{\text{C}}-\text{OH} \;+\; \text{ROH} \qquad \xrightarrow{\text{H}^+}$$

1-888-KRACKEM

$$\text{R}-\overset{\overset{\displaystyle O}{\|}}{\text{C}}-\text{OR} \;+\; \text{ROH} \qquad \xrightarrow{\text{H}^+}$$

1-888-KRACKEM

$$\text{H}_3\text{C}-\overset{\overset{\displaystyle O}{\|}}{\text{C}}-\text{CH}_2-\overset{\overset{\displaystyle O}{\|}}{\text{C}}-\text{OC}_2\text{H}_5 \qquad \xrightarrow[\text{(2) R}-\text{X}]{\text{(1) }^-\text{OC}_2\text{H}_5} \qquad \xrightarrow[\text{heat}]{\text{H}^+}$$
acetoacetic ester

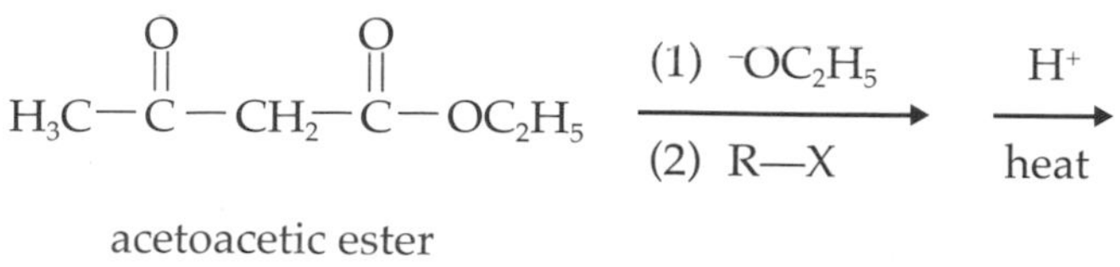

1-888-KRACKEM

$$-\overset{\overset{\displaystyle \cdot\overset{\cdot\cdot}{\text{O}}\cdot}{\|}}{\text{C}}-\text{CH}_2- \;+\; \overset{\text{H}}{\underset{\text{R}\;\;\;\;\text{R}}{\overset{|}{\text{N}}}} \qquad \xrightarrow{\text{H}_3\text{O}^+}$$
ketone
or aldehyde

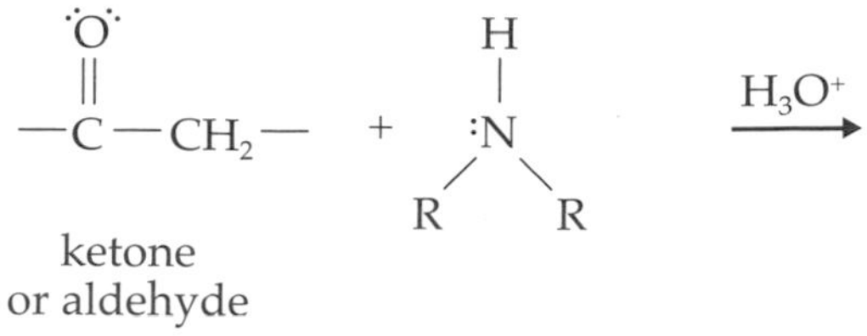

1-888-KRACKEM

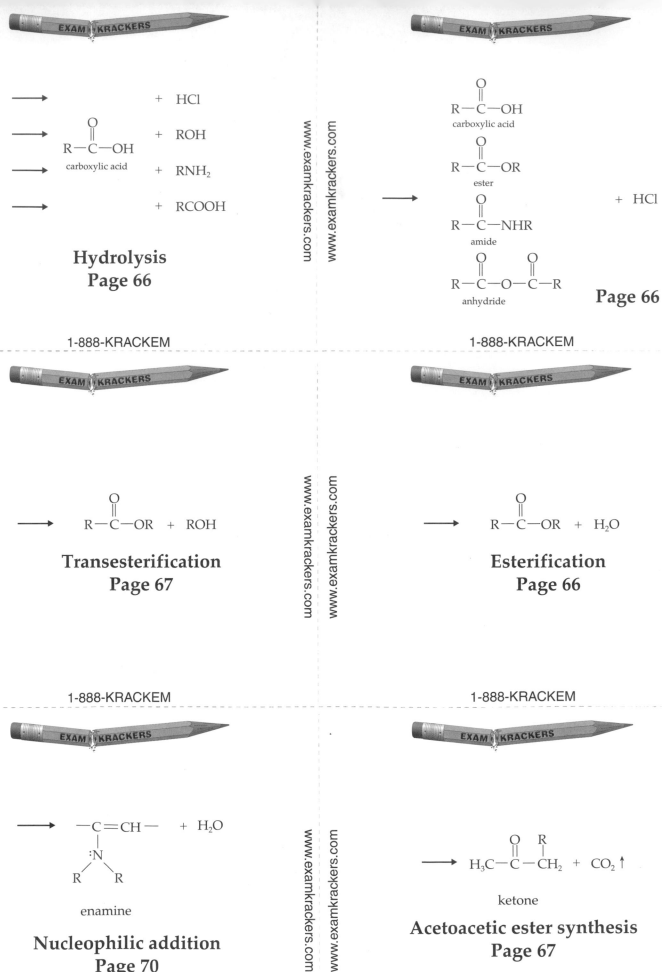

→   + HCl

→   R—C(=O)—OH   + ROH
        carboxylic acid

→   + RNH₂

→   + RCOOH

**Hydrolysis
Page 66**

R—C(=O)—OH
carboxylic acid

R—C(=O)—OR
ester

R—C(=O)—NHR
amide

R—C(=O)—O—C(=O)—R
anhydride

→   + HCl

Page 66

→   R—C(=O)—OR   + ROH

**Transesterification
Page 67**

→   R—C(=O)—OR   + H₂O

**Esterification
Page 66**

→   —C=CH—   + H₂O
      |
     :N
    R   R

enamine

**Nucleophilic addition
Page 70**

→   H₃C—C(=O)—CH₂—R   + CO₂↑

ketone

**Acetoacetic ester synthesis
Page 67**

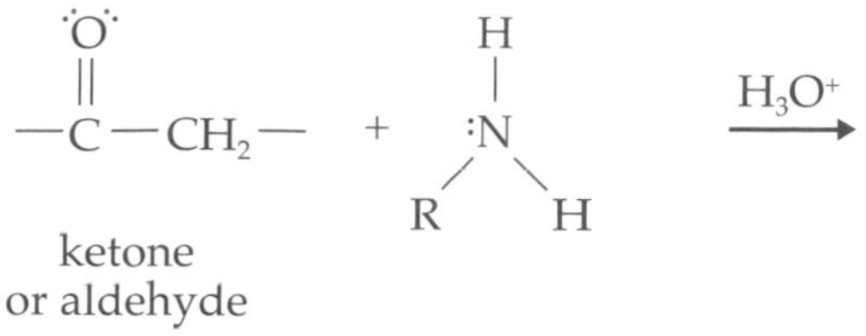

$$\underset{\substack{\text{ketone} \\ \text{or aldehyde}}}{-\overset{\overset{\ddot{O}}{\|}}{C}-CH_2-} \quad + \quad \underset{\substack{R}}{\overset{H}{\underset{H}{:N}}} \quad \xrightarrow{H_3O^+}$$

ketone
or aldehyde

$$\underset{\substack{\text{ketone} \\ \text{or aldehyde}}}{-\overset{\overset{\ddot{O}}{\|}}{C}-} \quad + \quad \underset{\substack{\text{hydrazine}}}{H_2\ddot{N}-\ddot{N}H_2} \quad \xrightarrow{H^+} \quad \xrightarrow[\text{heat}]{KOH}$$

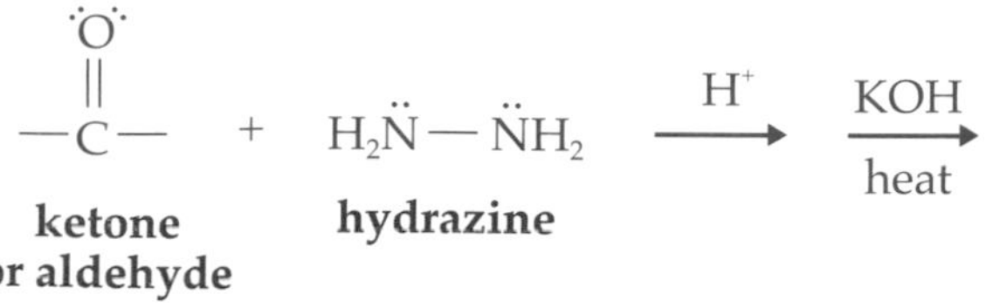

$$NH_3 \quad + \quad R-X \quad \longrightarrow$$

$$\underset{\substack{\\ ^+N(CH_3)_3}}{H_3C-\overset{\overset{}{|}}{CH}-CH_2-CH_3} \quad \xrightarrow[150^\circ C]{\text{base}}$$

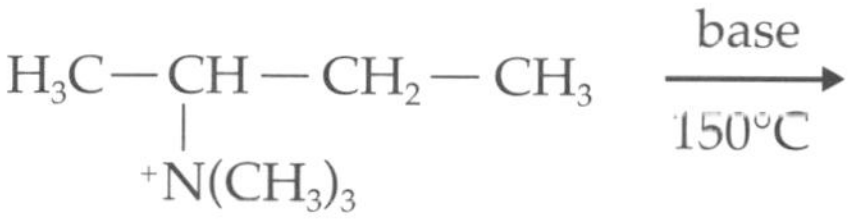

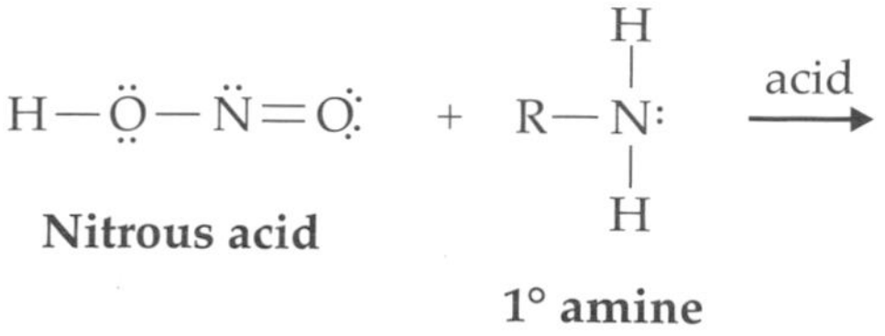

$$\underset{\textbf{Nitrous acid}}{H-\ddot{O}-\ddot{N}=\ddot{O}:} \quad + \quad \underset{\substack{\\ \textbf{1° amine}}}{R-\overset{H}{\underset{H}{N:}}} \quad \xrightarrow{\text{acid}}$$

$$\underset{\substack{\text{a primary amide}}}{R-\overset{\overset{O}{\|}}{C}-\overset{H}{\underset{H}{N:}}} \quad + \text{ Base} + Br_2 \quad \longrightarrow$$

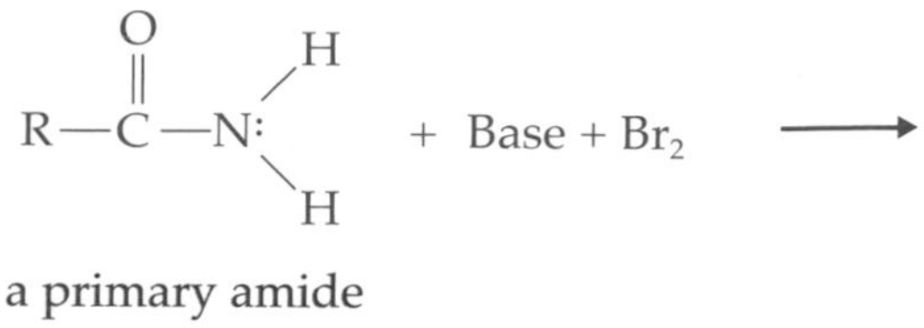

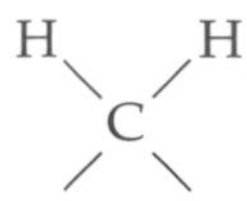

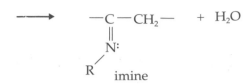

$$\longrightarrow \underset{\substack{| \\ \text{C} \\ \diagup \diagdown}}{\overset{\text{H} \quad \text{H}}{}} + H_2O + N_2$$

**Desired
Product**

The Wolff-Kishner
Reduction
Page 71

$$\longrightarrow \underset{\underset{R}{\overset{||}{\text{N:}}}}{-\text{C}-\text{CH}_2-} + H_2O$$

imine

Nucleophilic addition
Page 70

$$H_2C{=}CH-CH_2-CH_3$$

Hofmann product
(major product)

$$\xrightarrow[150°C]{\text{base}} \quad + \quad CH_3-CH{=}CH-CH_3$$

Saytzeff product
(minor product)

$$+ :N(CH_3)_3 + H_2O$$

The Hofmann Elimination
Page 72

$$\longrightarrow \quad RNH_2 + HX$$

Alkylation of an amine
Page 72

$$\longrightarrow R-NH_2 + CO_2 + OH^-$$

a primary amine

The Hofmann Degradation
Page 74

$$\longrightarrow R-\overset{+}{N}{\equiv}N: + H_2\overset{..}{O}:$$

**Diazonium
ion**

Diazotization of an Amine
Page 73